CW00743299

THE JOSEF SLONSKÝ SERIES

Books 1-3

Graham Brack

SAPERE
BOOKS

THE JOSEF SLONSKÝ SERIES

Published by Sapere Books.

20 Windermere Drive, Leeds, England, LS17 7UZ,
United Kingdom

saperebooks.com

Copyright © Graham Brack, 2019

Graham Brack has asserted his right to be identified as the author of this
work.

All rights reserved.

No part of this publication may be reproduced, stored in any retrieval
system, or transmitted, in any form, or by any means, electronic,
mechanical, photocopying, recording, or otherwise, without the prior
written permission of the publishers.

This book is a work of fiction. Names, characters, businesses, organisations,
places and events, other than those clearly in the public domain, are either
the product of the author's imagination, or are used fictitiously.

Any resemblances to actual persons, living or dead, events or locales are
purely coincidental.

BOOK ONE: LYING AND DYING

Chapter 1

There are some beautiful parts of Prague, thought Bear, but Holešovice is not one of them.

He plodded on through the cold morning air, hands thrust deep into his jacket pockets and shoes crunching on the ice that was scattered in lumps on the pavement. Few tourists came to this part of town, though Bear conceded to himself that the Letná was a nice park, somewhere to take the children on a Sunday and unwind a bit. The looming bulk of the Arena reminded him that there was always the hockey to come here for, the regular winter entertainment that he enjoyed when he could afford it, which was not too often, and when he was off shift, which seemed to happen even less.

He glanced at his watch. 04:24. Whoever heard of a shift starting at a quarter to five? When the latest agreement had been reached with the railway management, the hours to be worked had turned out not to be easily divisible by the number of days to be worked, with the result that one of the team had to come in a quarter of an hour early each morning by rotation. Since they could do nothing useful until the others turned up fifteen minutes later, Bear failed to see any point in this arrangement, but rules are rules, so here he was, tramping in to work on a frosty February morning in Holešovice.

He carried on down Za Elektrárnou and rounded the corner into Partyzánská. Even the *bufet* was still shut. They had the good sense not to open until six, so he never managed to get any breakfast there. He could see the metro station ahead of him, and just below it the service road he followed to enter the mainline station where he worked. There was someone sleeping on the concreted area where a couple of cars could park. Poor so and so — it had been a cold night, hardly fit for sleeping rough, even if they were well bundled up.

As he drew closer, he wondered if he should wake the sleeper up and urge him to move before the police drove past and ran him in. It might be kinder to let him spend a couple of nights in a nice warm cell. Illogically, Bear decided that he would look at the sleeper's face. If he looked young and innocent, he would wake him. If, on the other hand, he was a wino, Bear would leave him alone.

Thus it was that Bear passed by around three metres from the sleeper's feet, only to see that the person was not sleeping. The staring eyes told him that. She also had a protruding tongue and what looked like a livid scratch on her neck. Bear had seen a few dead bodies during his military service, so he did not panic, but looked around for help. There was a man coming over the brow heading towards the tram stop, whom Bear hailed. It so happened that the newcomer had a cellphone, which they used to summon the police, but then he said he had seen nothing that the police could possibly want to know and he dared not be late for work, so he headed for the tram. As for Bear, he had no great love of work, and this offered a perfect reason to delay going there, so he sat patiently waiting for the police to arrive.

The uniformed police were first, but within moments they had summoned the detectives on duty and retreated to the warmth of their car. They allowed Bear to sit in the back, but kept the window wound down so that they could order people to keep well away from the body. After about twenty minutes a battered old police car pulled up behind them, and a battered old policeman climbed out, stretched himself, and turned his collar up against the sharp wind.

Josef Slonský had been a policeman in Prague for nearly forty years, working his way up from the lowest of the low to a position of almost no influence whatsoever. Although he was a lieutenant, he never expected to make captain, and did not care one bit. His remaining ambition in the police force was to make it to retirement age without any young yob bashing his skull in with a lump of wood, and needling his superiors just enough to satisfy his sense of insubordination without leaving him vulnerable to reprisals. In this he had done extremely well, and Captain Lukas regularly read the police handbook to see if there were grounds to let Slonský go early.

The old detective scratched his thigh thoughtfully and surveyed the crime scene.

'Navrátil?'

'Sir?'

'Had breakfast?'

'No, sir.'

'Me neither. Damn. Have a word with the troglodytes in the squad car while I go and see what's what.'

Navrátil was uncertain exactly what sort of word was needed, but after two days with Slonský he was beginning to understand his new boss. Slonský did not really want someone from the academy to care for, but he did want someone to be a gofer for him. In return for small domestic services like making coffee, he was prepared to dispense occasional pearls of wisdom that might benefit Navrátil's career. Lots of people told Navrátil that Slonský was a good cop. None of them actually wanted to work with him, but they were all agreed that he was a good cop.

Navrátil hovered by the window, hoping to be invited into the warm car, but there was no sign of such a courtesy from his uniformed colleagues. They explained that the guy in the back seat was the one who had called them, and they had then called the detectives' office. No, they had not called a pathologist, because that was a decision for the detective when he arrived on the scene.

Navrátil walked over to Slonský.

'Should I call a pathologist?'

'Bit late for a bloody dentist,' Slonský replied, and walked off to inspect the head from another angle.

Chapter 2

Dr Novák knew Slonský of old. Each had a healthy public contempt for the other's profession tempered by the knowledge that the other was a good exponent of it. The detectives let Novák do his work for a few minutes before curiosity got the better of them.

'Any idea who we're looking for?' asked Slonský.

'You're after a left-handed dwarf, red hair, slight stoop, smokes French cigarettes.'

Navrátil flipped open his notebook.

'Don't bother,' Slonský told him. 'Dr Novák always blames things on left-handed dwarves. If we ran them all in this would be a crime-free paradise.'

Novák smiled. Behind his thick glasses his luminous blue eyes glinted with pleasure.

'It's hard to get a good time of death because she wasn't killed here. There's no blood and the livid patch isn't the lowest point, so the body has been moved. I'll do the usual back at the mortuary, but for now I'm satisfied that she was strangled somewhere else and brought here. I know the temperature here, and I know her temperature now, but I don't know what it was when she was left here or where she was before that. My guess — but don't hold me to it — is that she was killed around midnight and brought here about two to three o'clock.'

Slonský nodded. 'There are people coming and going up until midnight, so the murderer would risk being seen. On the other hand, you don't want to be stopped driving around Prague with a stiff in the passenger seat.'

'How do you know she wasn't in the boot?' asked Navrátil.

Novák grinned. 'Tell him!'

Slonský put a fatherly arm around Navrátil's shoulder.

'You see, son, women are a lot heavier than you'd think when they're dead. Try lifting a dead one out of a car boot, even assuming you've been able to fold her into it, and you'll do yourself a mischief. Look at how she's lying. She was sitting in the passenger seat, probably with a seat-belt holding her upright. In the dark she would just look like she was having a nap to anyone who spotted her. Then when they arrived here the murderer reversed into the space, opened the door, and just gave her a nudge. Then he pulled the feet free of the car, checked no-one was looking, and took off.'

'How do you know he reversed?'

'Because you have to do any criminal the courtesy of assuming he isn't a complete idiot. First, he would want to tip the body out on the side away from the main road in case anyone passed by. Second, the front seat is marked by where she fell on the ground. If he drove in forwards, she would be almost on the grassy bank and nearer the end of the concrete. Unless, of course, she drove herself here after she was strangled, in which event we're looking at the wrong side of the car. But all in all, I think you'll find my hypothesis is more likely.'

Novák was directing the photographer's attention to the key points he wanted recording.

'He's a bright lad, is old Slonský. Listen to him, son, and one day you might make it to the dizzy heights of lieutenant.'

Slonský took it in good part. 'Haven't you got an anus to swab somewhere?'

'All in good time. Don't mind me. I'll carry on here while you go and talk to that nice man who found the body.'

Slonský could see no reason to put it off any longer and ambled across to the car. The policemen swiftly urged Bear to get out to speak to the lieutenant.

'Tell me what you saw.'

Bear told him.

'There wasn't anyone taking a length of rope off the neck of the woman when you got here?'

'Course not.'

'I know. Just hoping. One day, by the law of averages…'

Slonský turned back to look at Novák busily gesticulating to the photographer, the paramedics with their body bag, and a passer-by who was passing by too close.

'Thanks for calling us, Mr … Bear. Why do they call you Bear?'

Bear opened the top two buttons on his shirt to reveal a mat of black hair.

'Fair enough,' said Slonský. 'If we've got your address you can go.'

'Gave it to these boys,' Bear replied, and began to walk along the side road, keeping well away from the body on the other side.

Slonský called after him. 'Bear! One last question.'

Bear turned round and stopped.

'Where's the best place around here to get a sausage?'

Navrátil cradled the hot coffee.

'Not hungry?' asked Slonský.

'Had one.'

'I know. I saw you. But you're a growing lad.'

'I'm full.'

Slonský shrugged. Young men today! He took another slug of coffee, a bite of his *párek* and sighed with satisfaction.

'Not a bad sausage, this. For fifty crowns, that is.'

'Sir,' began Navrátil, 'shouldn't we be out … doing something?'

'We are doing something, Navrátil. We're preparing ourselves for a long day with a decent breakfast.'

'But the murderer —'

'Keep your voice down! He could be here, for all we know.'

Navrátil gulped. 'He could be getting away.'

'He could,' conceded Slonský. 'But since we don't know who he is and we can't arrest all one million, two hundred thousand inhabitants and hold them for questioning, it's not clear to me why we need to skip breakfast. Carry on like that, lad, and you'll fade away to nothing long before you make captain.'

This was not something likely to happen to Slonský, who was rather generously proportioned. There were three reasons for this. First, he had a genetic disposition to the fuller figure (he claimed), a propensity evidenced by his aunt whose backside he alleged had been the model for the plinth of the Stalin statue overlooking the river. Second, Slonský had a prodigious appetite and rarely missed a meal. He claimed that this did not affect him because the furious workings of his brain consumed any number of calories and kept him slim and trim. Third, he was without any doubt the laziest policeman in Prague, and probably in Central Europe. Slonský rarely saw the need to rush, and was frequently to be found conserving his energy with his feet on his desk. When Captain Lukas queried this, Slonský told him that complete physical immobility was a prerequisite if the mental processes were not to be interfered with by extraneous nervous signals from moving muscles. Since he solved the case he was working on within a couple of hours — a denouement made more likely by the fact (that he omitted to tell Lukas) that he already had a signed confession — Slonský had been left to do his own thing thereafter. However, this was the first time that he had been trusted with an academy graduate of his own to corrupt.

Slonský finished his *párek* and grabbed his hat and gloves.

'Come on, Navrátil. We haven't got time to waste sitting here in the warm.'

Navrátil opened his eyes wide. He hoped he had not dropped off in the warm interior of the café, where the fire reminded him of his grandmother's house with its sweet smell of gas.

'Sorry, sir. Where are we going now?'

'Back to headquarters. We don't have any forensics to go on, we don't have a suspect and we don't have a motive, so I reckon our best bet is trying to find out who the victim is. She didn't have a handbag with her so we'd best see what missing persons reports have come in.'

They arrived at the car and Slonský opened the passenger side door.

'You can drive.'

'Forgive my asking, sir, but *do* you drive?'

'I've got a licence. Army gave it to me when I did my national service. They wanted me to drive a tank, Navrátil, so I took it for a spin round Hungary when we were on manoeuvres. Good place to learn to drive, Hungary is; big, flat, open plain and very few buildings.' He paused for effect. 'One less now. Those things turn on a fly's armpit, Navrátil. You should have seen the fraternal greetings I got from the Hungarian sitting on the outside privy.'

'You ran over a privy?'

'Of course not. No, I demolished his house while he was in the privy. If I'd run over the privy he'd have been salami and he wouldn't have been so upset. Still, he got some compensation and a new house somewhere, I shouldn't wonder. Navrátil, that light was red. I know we're the police but it looks bad if you jump lights, son.'

'Sorry, sir. I must have been distracted.'

'Anyway, in answer to your question, I can drive, but I don't. What's the point of a car in Prague? The roads are choked, there's no parking anywhere and the metro is cheap and quick. Of course, I get a car, but then I can do my charitable bit by letting you drive, Navrátil, because you wouldn't qualify for a car, so I let you drive mine. Say "Thank you, Lieutenant".'

'Thank you, Lieutenant.'

'Think nothing of it, Navrátil. I certainly do. Hang on, I just want to get a couple of rolls at the bakery. Pull up on the crossing, I won't be long.'

The note of Novák's telephone message was succinct. "There is something here you will want to see", it said.

'We'll take him at his word,' said Slonský. 'Get the car started, lad, and I'll be down in a minute.'

Navrátil put his coat back on, grabbed his notebook and looked for a spare pen. When he reached the front door Slonský was already in the passenger seat.

'Sorry, sir. Thought you had something to do.'

'I did. And I did it. First rule of police work, Navrátil: never miss a chance to splash your boots. Who knows when it'll come round again?'

They drove to the pathology department where Dr Novák was in mid-autopsy, but they were ushered in.

'Is this one mine?' asked Slonský.

'She is. Mid to late twenties, a bit of cosmetic dentistry, probably locally done, no distinguishing marks.'

'No tattoos? I thought all young women got themselves tattooed now.'

'Not this one.'

'Inconsiderate bitch. Anything else?'

Novák paused for dramatic effect.

'Yes, there's something very interesting under her knickers.'

12

'You'll excite the boy. Navrátil, pay no attention to this sad old man. Every woman has something interesting under her knickers, so I'm told.'

'Not like this one, Slonský. This one is without parallel in my experience.'

Novák walked round the table to their side and prepared to re-enact the first part of the post mortem examination.

'We removed her clothing and laid her here —'

'Can't you get arrested for that?'

'You're the policeman, you tell me. It didn't take us long to notice that there was something very unusual in her vagina.'

Novák held out a tray, in which there was a small plastic bag containing a roll of coloured paper.

'You can handle it. I've finished with it now.'

Slonský donned some gloves.

'Have you counted it?'

'Counted and recorded,' Novák replied. 'Two hundred and forty-nine thousand, two hundred and fifty crowns.'

'My piggy bank had a slit in its back,' Slonský said, 'but I suppose this works just as well. That's a decent amount of money, but a hell of an awkward place to keep it if you need to pay off a taxi.'

'It would have been,' agreed Novák, 'but I don't think she put it there. It had urine on the outside.'

'Now you tell me,' Slonský complained, his face crumpled with distaste.

'I've washed it. And a bit of pee never hurt anyone. My point is that the likeliest reason for that is that her bladder emptied when she died and the urine got on the bag as someone inserted it.'

Slonský slowly walked around the table to inspect the body from all sides.

'I wonder why they didn't make it a round two hundred and fifty thousand? It would have been a smaller bundle of notes for a start.'

'Maybe that number means something, sir. Like the price of something, or a loan repaid.'

'Nice idea, Navrátil. Of course, it may just have been her life savings, but she isn't much older than you. Have you got two hundred thousand in the bank?'

'No, sir! Nowhere near. I'd have to work for over a year to earn that, and by the time I'd paid my rent —'

'Yes, I've got the point. I've worked a lot longer than you and that would be a very welcome sum for my savings. Novák, on the other hand, probably makes that each month.'

'I wish,' the pathologist muttered.

'So, we've got a young lady who has somehow managed to put together a nice little nest egg which she keeps safe by shoving it up her whatsit.'

13

'No, someone else shoved it up her whatsit. She was already dead. And you haven't given me a handbag, so I'm assuming there wasn't one there.'

'You assume correctly. While you're deducing you wouldn't like to tell me who she is and who did it?'

'No, that's your job. But I may have a little extra help for you. When we extracted the money I was able to do the usual little extras, and one of those tells me that there had been recent sexual activity.'

'How recent?'

'Very. Last night, I'd say. And my trusty little swab has collected a nice sample of semen, so I can do a DNA test. If you ever catch a suspect, I should be able to tell you if you've got a match.'

'She didn't use a condom, then.'

'No. But she seems free of germs, so I don't think she was a prostitute. You can't be certain, but there's no sign of a lot of use down there.'

Slonský's flippancy evaporated as he knelt at the victim's head.

'Navrátil, would you do me a favour? Nip out into the corridor and find me a good-looking woman in her twenties or thirties.'

'Sir?'

'I take it you've got one or two in this God-forsaken place, Novák?'

'Depends what you want them for. But yes, there are a few.'

Navrátil realised that he was not going to receive an explanation, and did as he was asked. In the reception area he found the receptionist and her supervisor, and asked the supervisor to mind the desk while he borrowed the receptionist. He had to offer his police identity card for close inspection before they agreed and he was able to conduct her to the mortuary.

Navrátil held the door open and followed her in, which put him in the perfect place to impede her running away when she saw the body on the slab.

'Don't mind her, she won't bite,' said Slonský. 'You've seen a naked woman before, I'm sure.'

'Is she … dead?'

Slonský considered his answer carefully.

'She's certainly a bit under the weather. But I'm no doctor, you'll have to ask Novák.'

Novák tutted.

'What I'd like you to do, miss, is come round here next to me and look carefully at this woman's hair. Now, I know very little about hair, but I reckon that's a pretty expensive hairdo. She's got those little red stripey bits hidden in the middle —'

'Highlights,' offered the receptionist.

'Exactly. And I've seen a few of those, and there's not many people tone them in as well as this lot. Am I right?'

14

The receptionist looked closely. As she bent over she inhaled sharply.

'French perfume,' she said. 'I'm not exactly sure which one but it's not cheap.'

'Excellent! Keep going!'

'Well, her nails are well kept, except for that broken one.'

Novák held up the hand.

'Broken in a struggle. She had tiny chips of leather under the nails, as if she had clawed the back of a pair of gloves.'

'Not unreasonable if you're being strangled. Carry on.'

'I don't think she does much in the way of housework. No wedding ring, see?'

Novák held up another bag.

'This gold cross and chain were in her clothes. I think they were probably wrenched off as she was attacked.'

The woman looked closely at the jewellery.

'Again, that's not cheap. It's real gold, not plated. Nice stuff! I've never had anything like this. In fact, I don't think I've seen one like it in the shops in Prague.'

'We can tout it round a few jewellers, Navrátil,' Slonský said. 'See if anyone knows where she could have got it.'

'The same goes for her earrings,' declared the receptionist. 'Not garnet or opal like most of us. Hoops with two real diamonds. She must have had a well-paid job.'

'You don't think she's a whore?' asked Slonský conversationally.

The young woman recoiled from the body.

'Is she? No, she can't be. I mean, I know she's got a few nice things, but she doesn't look … easy.'

'Dead people rarely do. And even a tart is somebody's daughter.'

'But if she was … like that, wouldn't her boss have taken the good jewellery off her?'

'They're called pimps and you're absolutely right. That stuff wouldn't have lasted five minutes in the lap-dancing places. I suppose she could be a hotel escort, in which event we're stuffed because no hotel is going to admit that she ever set foot in the place.'

'We could ask for the security videos,' Navrátil suggested, pleased that a sensible idea had come to him.

'We could,' agreed Slonský, 'and you can spend many a happy afternoon watching hours of people going in and out of doors. The thing is, Navrátil, that it takes the best part of twenty-four hours to watch twenty-four hours of live action video. We can do that if we can find a hotel that looks a likely prospect.'

The receptionist was inspecting the victim's toes.

'Nasty corn there. Badly fitting shoes, I suppose.'

Novák reached behind himself to retrieve a plastic crate.

'The very shoes.'

The receptionist cooed.

'They're nice! I wouldn't mind some like that. Italian leather slingbacks.'

Slonský beamed.

'Pay attention, Navrátil. You're going to have to put all this technical stuff in your report. That's a good expert you've found us.'

The receptionist smiled at Navrátil, who blushed slightly.

'They're not new,' she said. 'The heel is worn down. I couldn't walk in these without a bit of practice. They're quite high.'

'Can you tell the size?' asked Slonský.

'Thirty-eight,' said Novák. 'Did it with callipers. You can't read it on the inside.'

'What about the brand?'

'It's not easy to read, but it looks like something or other Gozzi.'

'Alberto Gozzi?' asked the receptionist. 'You wouldn't get them for under five thousand. There aren't many places in Prague you can get those.' She pondered for a moment. 'I've seen them in a place in the New Town, somewhere along Na Příkopě.'

'Write that down, Navrátil! It'll save you a lot of walking later.'

Within a few minutes Navrátil's notebook was filled with addresses of hairdressers, jewellers and shoeshops that might possibly have equipped the young lady, and the receptionist, suitably flattered by Slonský's encomiums on her intelligence and powers of observation, returned to her post to discuss her half-hour with anyone who would listen.

'Get on to headquarters, Navrátil. They've got a tame artist they use. Ask him to draw the girl with her eyes open. We can't put her picture in the paper looking like this. No rush, so long as he gets it done by tonight.'

Slonský swept out of the room without any acknowledgement of Novák.

'Is he always like this?' asked Navrátil.

'No,' conceded Novák. 'Sometimes he can be quite brusque.'

Navrátil expected to go straight out on his tour of the shops, but Slonský restrained him.

'Waste of effort until you get a photo, lad. Unless, of course, they've only ever sold one pair of shoes or done one hairdo. This is going to be a long day, so we'd best fortify ourselves with a bit of lunch. I'm off out for a sausage and a beer. Coming?'

'I'm not hungry yet, sir.'

'Suit yourself, but don't come running to me if you die of starvation. If anything urgent comes up, I'm at the café on the corner.'

He remained at the café on the corner for nearly two hours, and had not returned when Captain Lukas wandered into the office.

16

'On your own, Navrátil? Where's Slonský?'

'Gone to lunch, sir, but he suggested one of us ought to stay by a phone in case the artist had finished his picture.'

'Really? Well, I hope Slonský remembers you need a lunch break too. I don't want my trainees fainting in the street. Tell the lieutenant I'd like a verbal report when he returns.'

Slonský appeared behind Lukas in the doorway.

'No need, sir. I can do it now.'

'Ah, good! Well, how is it going?'

'The dead person is a woman, sir, with a quarter of a million crowns in a plastic bag up her private parts.'

Lukas' mouth opened and closed several times.

'That is extraordinary!'

'I'm not sure, sir. For all we know there may be women all over Prague with their life savings between their legs.'

Lukas frowned.

'Your flippancy is misplaced, as always, Slonský. This is a very serious affair.'

'Murder always is, sir. She was strangled somewhere else, taken to Holešovice by car and dumped near the mainline station. We don't have an identification yet but young Navrátil here showed great initiative by asking a receptionist at the hospital where the victim could have bought her clothes, and as soon as he has a likeness to work with, he'll be trawling indefatigably round town.'

Lukas beamed at the young policeman, who was blushing at the unexpected and unwarranted praise.

'Well done, Navrátil. I can see I was right to pair you with this old warhorse. Keep me posted, Slonský!'

He swept out of the door with the grace of a poorly hitched caravan.

'Why did you tell him it was my idea, sir?'

'Because I don't need the praise and you do. Captain Lukas is an honest man and a fair cop, but he's a shallow as a dried-up puddle. Never embarrass him, never let him down and try as hard as you can never to tell him anything you don't want the world to know. Now, any word from Novák?'

'Not yet, sir.'

'Damn! We don't need a work of art, just a good likeness. Hand me the phone, lad.'

Slonský dialled Novák's number and chatted briefly with the pathologist.

'He says the artist is there but it'll be another hour or two yet, Navrátil. Come on, we're off to the metro station at Holešovice.'

'Can I ask why, sir?'

'We're going to speak to the rough sleepers there.'

'There weren't any, sir, or we'd have talked to them this morning.'

Slonský stopped in his tracks, turned and sighed deeply.

'Now, Navrátil, I've built you up as a bright lad and you do this to me. Of course there weren't any rough sleepers there this morning. Who turned up first?'

'The squad car, sir.'

'Exactly. So when a car turns up with "Police" written on its side, what are rough sleepers going to do? Scarper! Only a dimwit would hang around to be arrested.'

'But if they'd seen anything, wouldn't they have reported it?'

'They might. But they're not supposed to be there, they may not have the money for a phone call, and they might be worried that the killer would turn on them. Having said all that, it was a cold night and I guess they squeezed under the canopy at the bus station side to keep out of the wind, so they wouldn't be able to see the parking area fifty metres down the hill. But if we're lucky one of them might have seen a car, and it's the only lead we've got, so get your skates on.'

The homeless men seemed to know Slonský and were relaxed when he approached, though a little suspicious of Navrátil.

'Good afternoon, gentlemen,' Slonský announced. 'I'm not interested in giving you any trouble. I need some help.' He waved his badge at nobody in particular. 'A young woman was found strangled down the hill there early this morning, and don't tell me you didn't know that.'

'We didn't,' one protested, 'but we knew it was something important when the uniformed guys didn't chase us off. Even so, best not be around. Police and homeless don't mix.'

'I couldn't give a toss about that. More important things than moving you on.' He counted heads, turned to Navrátil and shoved a banknote in his hand. 'Navrátil, get some coffee for us all, will you? There's a place in the station.'

The men nodded their appreciation.

'What I need to know is when the body was dumped and if anyone saw a car that might have done it.'

The small group stamped their feet to keep warm and shrugged their shoulders. Nobody had seen the body dumped, and cars had run past all night, so that was no help at all. Slonský was not surprised, but he had hoped that there might be some chance of a step forward in the investigation.

Navrátil handed out the coffees, and the men grabbed them in their frozen hands, wrapping long, blue fingers around them. The braver ones took a sip of the scalding, tarry liquid.

'I don't know…' began a young one with a tattoo of a snake wrapped round his neck.

'Yes?' asked Slonský.

'Well, it might have nothing to do with it, but there was a big German car that came by around two or half past two.'

'German?'

'BMW or Merc. Didn't really look too closely. I think it was beige or some similar colour. Anyway, I saw it come over the bridge and towards us here, then as it went past us it seemed to be slowing down. I didn't watch where it went, but I thought from the engine noise that it must have parked somewhere nearby.'

'What did you think they stopped for?'

'I guessed they were … courting.'

'You mean shagging?'

'Maybe. Anyway, there was no point in spying on them, because after a minute or so the car drove off again. But I didn't hear any other car slow down near us.'

The others furrowed their brows as if weighing his story against their own experience. One lifted his cap and scratched his head as if thinking was an unnatural act.

'There was a truck around one o'clock.'

'Closed truck or pick-up?' asked Slonský.

'Pick-up. Something written on the side but I couldn't read it from here. But I think the driver was on his own. He stopped at the bend down the hill but he didn't turn his engine off.'

Slonský smiled broadly.

'Thanks, fellas. I knew I could count on you.'

He waved goodbye and led Navrátil back to the metro.

'Shouldn't we take statements, sir?'

'They won't give them, Navrátil, and if we'd asked we'd have got nowhere. What would we use them for? If we find our killer, identifying his car isn't going to be the key to nailing him. But at least we've got a plausible time and a possible car.'

'Shall I ask the motor licensing authorities to give us lists of owners of beige BMWs and Mercedes?'

'Navrátil, do you like watching paint dry? There'll be thousands, and we can't say for sure it was beige. Let's find our man, then corroborate our suspicions with these snippets.'

The officer at the main desk had an envelope for Slonský when they returned to the station.

'What do you think, lad? Good likeness?'

'I'd recognise her in the street.'

'Doubt you'll see her there now, but it'll do us nicely. Be a little angel and run it over to the publicity department so they can get it in the papers for the morning. They'll want some flannel so tell them where she was found but leave it at that.

What we want is big headlines saying "Did you know this woman?". Then go home — we've done enough for today and we're going to need all the rest we can get. See you here at seven tomorrow.'

Navrátil nodded and disappeared through the double doors, leaving Slonský leaning against the front desk.

'How's he doing?' asked Sergeant Mucha.

'Navrátil? He's all right. Got to learn to pace himself though. You get nowhere rushing.'

Slonský dumped his battered hat on his head, shrugged the coat back onto his shoulders, and turned towards the door.

'Fortunately he has the great advantage of having me to show him the ropes.'

The portrait duly appeared in the Prague newspapers, though it achieved less prominence in some than Slonský would have liked, prompting him to remark that a photograph of the naked corpse would certainly have made the front page in that kind of rag.

Navrátil occupied himself in a tour of the shops, clutching a single shoe in a plastic evidence bag and the jewellery in another. He found a jeweller who recognised the cross and chain, but admitted that he had sold a few recently and could not remember to whom. However, he had only had them in stock within the last year. Another thought it possible that he might have sold the earrings but was unable to say when or to whom, and it was with a sense of disappointment and failure that Navrátil reported back to Slonský in the evening.

'Can't say, or won't say?' Slonský demanded.

'He said he couldn't,' replied Navrátil.

'That's what his mouth said,' Slonský muttered. 'What did his eyes say?'

'Sir?'

'You'll have to learn to watch the eyes, Navrátil. You see, lad, villains lie. I've complained about it to Captain Lukas, but that's just the way it is. It's not like detective novels when you accuse a man and he stretches his arms out all ready for the cuffs and tells you it's a fair cop.'

'I understand that, sir, but I'm not sure I can tell if someone's lying as easily as that.'

'Navrátil, would it surprise you to learn that I was Bohemian downhill skiing champion in 1973?'

Navrátil's jaw dropped open. 'Yes, it would, sir.'

'So it should, Navrátil, because it's a complete lie. See, you're getting the hang of it already. Let's go and see the chap with the earrings and I'll give you a master class.'

As they left the shop, Navrátil hung expectantly on Slonský's verdict.

'Well, sir, was he telling the truth?'

Slonský bustled impatiently away.

'You never told me he had a squint, Navrátil.'

'But he hasn't…' Navrátil began, before realising he was talking to thin air, for Slonský was already sitting in the passenger seat.

Chapter 3

Slonský was, it seemed, a poor sleeper, which accounted for his early arrival — and dishevelled appearance — at the station on the following day. He was standing at a table which he had covered with pieces of paper stuck together with sticky tape to form a single large sheet on which some sweeping black lines had been drawn with marker pen.

'Holešovice, Navrátil. A bit of artistic licence, but it'll do for our purposes. Station here, metro here, bus station here, body here. Now, the first tram past arrives at this stop at 04:50. The metro starts a few minutes later. If our killer knows the area he probably knows the tram times.'

'How do we know he knows the area?'

'We don't, but it's unlikely he'd drive around town with a stiff in the front seat looking for a good site. Even if he didn't know this exact spot, he knew that Holešovice was the sort of place he'd find somewhere to dump her.'

'It's very public, though.'

Slonský paused, tapping the marker pen against his teeth.

'Yes, it is. So we deduce …?'

'He knows nobody will be around when he drops the body off. Or he doesn't care.'

'Or he wants the body found quite quickly. He could have driven on for a few minutes and hidden her in a quiet area of the park. Maybe he wanted her found, because he'd have realised that she would be seen within a couple of hours of being left there.'

'Why would he want her to be found? Don't criminals normally hide their crimes?'

A grave shadow passed over Slonský's face.

'Psychopaths don't.'

'You think it could be a serial killer?'

'No.'

'Why not, sir?'

'Grammar, Navrátil. To be a serial killer you have to have killed at least twice, and so far as we know, he hasn't, so he can't be a serial killer.'

Slonský picked up his coat and headed for the door.

'Where are we going, sir?'

'A matter of the utmost importance, Navrátil. Breakfast.'

The portrait was on the front page of most of the papers, but the Prague public were hardly running apace to the nearest police station to identify her. This seemed not to worry Slonský, who merely observed that if she was an "evening worker", her friends or customers were probably still fast asleep, as he wished he was himself. To Navrátil's immense frustration, they busied themselves all morning with other tasks, one of which was to console an elderly lady in Karlín who was convinced that someone had stolen her porch light although there was no sign that one had been over her door for several years. Navrátil tried to explain that since the paint on the building covered the area under the site of the alleged lamp, it was likely that the lady was mistaken, but she abused him, his mother and the Prague police in general. Navrátil returned to the car rather crestfallen.

'It's no good, she won't believe me.'

Slonský folded his newspaper meticulously and pondered for a few moments before easing himself out of the car.

'That's better,' smirked the old dear. 'You look like a proper policeman.'

'See?' Slonský commented to Navrátil. 'Not stupid at all. Now then, grandma, explain to me why you put the light up.'

Navrátil opened his mouth to protest, but Slonský silenced him with a fierce look.

'When they took the old one away after the war. I tried to tell him —' she jerked her head towards Navrátil — 'but these youngsters know nothing. He probably doesn't remember the war, not like you and me.'

'So the old light went and you sorted your own one out? Very resourceful of you.'

The old lady preened herself.

'You have to take care of things yourself. Can't expect the district council to do everything.'

Slonský pointed to the upper window.

'Navrátil, in that bedroom you'll find an electric cable that's been chopped off. It used to have a bulb on the end and someone's run off with it. Hooligans, I expect. Have you got your landlord's phone number? I'll ring him and get him to put a proper light up.'

The woman found a scrap of card and Slonský copied it into his notebook. Navrátil appeared with a length of frayed flex in his hands.

'How did you know?'

'Because, Navrátil, you looked for a light and couldn't see one, whereas I looked for a power lead and saw the chopped end dangling over the windowsill up there, a metre higher.'

'But she said the light was missing, not a power lead.'

'Exactly, Navrátil. It was missing. No point in looking for it, then, was there?'

Slonský smiled angelically and lowered his bulky frame into the car.

'My brain's slowing down. It could do with a pastry or two. Come on, lad, put your foot down.'

'Is detective work always like this?' Navrátil asked.

'No,' Slonský replied, 'sometimes it's even more boring.'

They were sitting in an unmarked car watching a building. Since it was in a rundown area of the city, they had left their normal car behind and had been allocated a ramshackle old Škoda with around two hundred thousand kilometres on the clock, a top speed that would have disgraced many a cyclist, and a patch of corroded doorsill that whistled as they drove along.

'Try to look less official, lad,' Slonský counselled. 'Take your tie off if you want.'

'Are you going to take yours off?'

'No point. Everybody knows me. Disguise is a waste of time when you've got a face like this.'

'But if they know you're a policeman, won't they know I'm one too?'

'Ah, spot the logical flaw in that argument, Navrátil! I said they know me. I didn't say they knew what I am. I've cultivated anonymity for many a year. Everybody knows me but they don't know my business. They've met me in a bar or having a sausage somewhere, but so far as anyone knows I'm just someone who works in some office or other. You don't get to be as nondescript as I am by accident, Navrátil. You have to work at it. I wasn't born grey, you know. I'm a self-unmade man.'

Slonský smiled, happy with the epithet he had just bestowed upon himself, and stored it away to use spontaneously later.

'I know I'm going to regret asking this, sir —'

'Then don't. Not worth putting yourself through any more humiliation than life is planning to send your way anyway.'

'… but why are we watching a pole-dancing club at four in the afternoon? It's shut.'

'Exactly. So if anyone goes in, we're more likely to get a good view of him, since it's daylight and the place is deserted. At one in the morning with a crowd of punters hanging around it'd be a lot more difficult.'

'But why should anyone turn up?'

'Because if our information is correct — which I increasingly doubt — a delivery of stolen pilsner is likely to be made, and I don't expect they'll leave it outside the door. They'll want cash, and a bit of help unloading the truck I shouldn't wonder.'

Navrátil drummed the steering wheel.

'They could come any day.'

'They could,' conceded Slonský, 'but today is favourite. If it was stolen last night, the chances are they'll want rid of it pronto. Ever tried to hide a letter from your mother, Navrátil?'

'A school report, once.'

'Then you'll know how difficult it is. So just think how hard it is to hide a truckload of beer in Prague, where every other male inhabitant can sniff out a bottle of beer at fifty metres through two locked doors. No, they'll get it moved on as fast as they can.'

There was a rumble as a lorry pulled into the street.

'Ah!' Slonský beamed. 'A beer delivery.'

'Yes, but this one's legit. A company lorry.'

Slonský stared at him.

'You poor devil. We're going to have to work hard on that innocent veneer of trust, Navrátil. If you were going to deliver beer without drawing attention to yourself, what sort of vehicle would be best for the job?'

'A beer lorry, I suppose.'

'Oh, look, that's what we have here! An odd coincidence, wouldn't you say?'

Slonský read the licence plate over his radio. A few moments later the disembodied voice told them what they needed to know.

'Should be a red Škoda Fabia, Lieutenant.'

Slonský climbed out of the car, and waited for Navrátil to join him.

'Come on, son, let's go and arrest the driver of that red Škoda Fabia full of lager.'

To Slonský's surprise, the afternoon and evening brought no identification of the body.

'She's a striking girl, well groomed. Somebody must be missing her, Navrátil.'

'Perhaps she lived alone.'

'Maybe, but we know she wasn't on her own last night. Somebody had her, and somebody killed her.'

'But the murderer isn't going to contact us, sir.'

Slonský sighed deeply.

'I suppose not. But you'd think they'd do it once in a while just out of cockiness. Make yourself useful, lad — fetch your notebook and start making a list of people who might be missing her. For a start, she had a decent amount of money and some expensive tastes, but Novák doesn't think she's a prostitute.'

'A mistress, then?'

'Could be. Or a young wife of a middle-aged man who has made his pile. If she had a regular job her employer ought to have missed her by now.'

'If only we had her handbag, sir.'

'Never mind that. If only her mother had sewn her name in her knickers like my mum did.'

'I don't suppose it's worth checking —'

'No. Novák isn't so dim that he'd miss a surname in someone's pants. We have to assume it wasn't there.'

'Maybe she's just one of those people that don't have anyone to miss her.'

Slonský's face clouded over. When he spoke, his voice was quieter than usual, colder and firmer.

'I've known some real villains in my time, Navrátil. Human filth of the worst kind. And they all had someone to miss them. I remember a party secretary who had a local rival fed into a furnace a few centimetres at a time; his mother was heartbroken when he was shot. Until someone proves otherwise to me, I'll go on believing that every human being matters to someone.'

He picked up his hat and moved decisively for the door.

'There's only one thing to do, Navrátil. Let's get a beer.'

Two hours later, they were surrounded by wet beer mats and Navrátil was beginning to think that he would go home — the moment he remembered where home was. Being slightly built, he could hardly match Slonský, who appeared to be a practised drinker.

'Another one over here,' Slonský called to the waiter.

'I don't think I can manage another one,' Navrátil protested.

'Nonsense.'

'Why are we drinking anyway? We don't have anything to celebrate.'

'That's not the only reason for a drink, Navrátil. If you only drank to celebrate the Czech Republic wouldn't have much of a brewing industry.'

'To forget, then?'

'On the contrary, Navrátil, I drink for a religious reason. I'm a beer Buddhist.'

'I didn't think Buddhists drank beer.'

'Don't they? Poor devils. No, I drink to achieve enlightenment, which is a religious state much desired by Buddhists.'

'Enlightenment?'

'Exactly. There is a point, Navrátil, at which the brain ceases to maintain its tenuous hold on reality and allows itself to be carried along in the flood of ideas. It casts itself free of all earthly shackles and enters a meta-existence of cause and effect beyond reasoning.'

Navrátil frowned and composed the next sentence as carefully as his brain would allow after eight beers.

'You what?'

'In the normal run of things, Navrátil, the brain proceeds like a train, along predetermined tracks. It can't free itself of these ideas and preconceptions because a lifetime of training and constraint stops it doing so. But consider for a moment the average two-year-old. If you tell him you have an elephant in a matchbox, he doesn't doubt you. He wants to know how you got it in there. His mind is free, Navrátil, to roam as widely as it wishes, like a soaring swallow. Nothing is impossible to such a mind, and that's precisely the state I aim to achieve.'

'And you think beer will help?'

'It always has in the past. You order another while I go and add to the Vltava.'

Chapter 4

The following morning was bright, warm and sunny. Outside the surviving birdlife of Prague was singing fortissimo, or so it seemed to Navrátil. A prolonged shower did little to help the sensation of devils prodding the backs of his eyeballs with their tridents, and nothing in his pantry did anything to make him believe that there was the remotest chance that it would stay down if he could once swallow it.

He was therefore more than a little surprised to arrive at work to find Slonský with his feet on his desk while he attacked a *párek* and a takeaway coffee.

'How can you eat that? Or anything else, for that matter?'

'I have a constitution moulded by the Communist years. If you'd been picky about your food then you'd have starved.'

'Don't you feel even a bit queasy?'

'Should I?' Slonský asked innocently, as if the idea that a heavy drinking bout might affect your appetite the next day had never occurred to him.

'Never mind. I'd better find some water.'

Navrátil was halfway down the corridor when he heard Slonský call after him.

'If you can't find water, try some Hungarian beer. It's the next best thing.'

When Navrátil returned, Slonský was looking thoughtful.

'It was something you said last night that inspired me,' he explained.

'I said? What did I say?'

'You said it was a shame she didn't have her name sewn into her knickers.'

'You said that, sir!'

'Did I? Then I'm brighter than I thought. Anyway, how did the murderer know that she didn't have her name sewn into her knickers?'

'Maybe he didn't care.'

'He took the handbag.'

'Well, since he made love to her, he probably got to see her underwear.'

'Do you look, Navrátil?'

'Eh?'

'When you're with a woman, do you check her pants out?'

'Well, I … I haven't … but if I did …'

'Exactly. It's an unnatural act. But whether he did or didn't, he might have handled her clothes. That's what I asked Novák.'

'And?'

'Nothing. Now, she may have taken off her own clothes and put them back on herself. And perhaps he wore gloves to dispose of the body. But I can't picture anyone going to bed with a girl and wearing gloves while he did it.'

'Which rules out a crime of passion?'

'Well, he was farsighted enough to have gloves there. It was a cold night so he may have just had them with him, but this begins to look premeditated. Which is good, Navrátil. Where there's a plan, we can discover it. It's the sudden, irrational killing that is hardest to detect.'

'So we have a man who takes a woman out, buys her dinner, takes her back to his flat or hers, makes love to her, kills her then dumps her body where it will be found quickly.'

'Where did you get the bit about dinner?'

'The stomach contents. Novák's report doesn't sound like the kind of meal someone would cook for themselves. Asparagus, for example.'

'We could waste a lot of time tracking down shops that have asparagus in February, but let's run with your idea for a minute. If that's the case, they must have eaten in a restaurant somewhere that has asparagus on the menu.'

Navrátil's face sank.

'I can see you're one step ahead of me, lad. But it'll take a lifetime to visit all Prague's restaurants. We'll do it if we have to, but for the moment let's try the wholesale greengrocers. See how easy it is to get asparagus and if anyone can tell us who has been buying it. Might narrow things down a bit.'

When Navrátil returned, Slonský had his feet on his desk, a coffee in his hand, and a broad smile on his face.

'Almost all the big hotels, sir. Not too many restaurants have bought asparagus lately, but it still gives us a lot to do.'

'Not necessarily, my boy,' Slonský replied. 'The great Czech public has come to our aid.'

He slid a brown paper envelope across the desk. Navrátil opened it cautiously to find a single photograph within.

'No note?'

'No note. Recognise the girl?'

'It's her! It's the victim.'

'And who is she having dinner with?'

Navrátil scrutinised the picture closely before his jaw dropped.

'Isn't that —'

'It is. Now isn't that a turn-up for the book?'

Slonský was promenading around the office, or as much of it as was accessible to him given his physique and the small gaps between desks.

'Now, the first question is when this picture was taken. I have an idea about that and with a bit of luck we'll have that confirmed fairly soon. I'm assuming that the Minister didn't send me the photograph himself. I like to think that if our public figures are knocking off women other than their wives they'll be decent enough to exercise a bit of discretion.'

'But he's having dinner with her in a public place.'

'Indeed he is, but men can have dinner with women for innocent reasons.'

'He's holding her hand across the table.'

'Ah, that's the way it looks. I'll grant that there's a degree of intimacy here.'

'There's also a near-empty bottle of white wine. But he's drinking mineral water. She must have drunk that bottle by herself.'

'And Novák found evidence of wine in the victim's stomach.'

Navrátil's mouth unaccountably ran dry.

'You think this was taken on the night she died?'

'Not necessarily. Perhaps our informant just wanted us to know how we'd identify her. But then he could have put the name on a bit of paper himself, so I jump to the conclusion that it's the link with our much beloved boss, the Minister of the Interior, that our informant wanted to emphasise. If, of course, this proves to have been taken on that evening then we can ask the Minister some pointed questions.'

'The clock in the corner of the picture shows twenty to nine.'

'And the clock in the corridor outside shows ten to six, but that doesn't mean everything in this station happens then. You see, Navrátil, your generation labours under the disadvantage of not having grown up under Communism. For people of my age, rampant cynicism comes naturally. We always disregard the obvious and assume that things are not what they seem.'

'That's fair enough,' conceded Navrátil, 'but I can't interpret that picture any other way than that the Minister was having dinner with our murder victim in compromising circumstances.'

'It certainly looks that way,' agreed Slonský. 'I suppose she could be his sister or niece.'

'Well, there are nieces and "nieces", but I wouldn't hold my sister's hand like that.'

'No, neither would I. You've got younger eyes than me, lad. Can you see what's on her plate?'

Slonský handed Navrátil a large, brass-handled magnifying glass.

'I didn't think detectives really used these!'

'Essential piece of equipment, Navrátil. Though I use it mainly for getting splinters out of my thumb. Still, it's not only Novák who relies on technology.'

'I can't see much — the angle across the plate isn't right.'

'Neither could I.'

'We might be able to recognise the restaurant, though.'

'Don't spend too long on it. Right, that's long enough. If you haven't got it by now, we'll fall back on the old-timer's technique of asking the suspect.'

'You think the Minister is a suspect?'

'No, Navrátil, not *a* suspect. *The* suspect. We haven't got another one.'

'But he's a Minister.'

'If you'd known some of the Ministers we've had in the past, strangling a woman and ramming a bag of money up her doodah would seem small beer, believe me. Status and position are no guide to honesty. You'd think a priest would be as law-abiding as they come, but we had one in Žižkov who was one of the great cat-murderers of our time. Used to take them out with a handgun from his back door. Good shot, too — there aren't many people who could get a running tabby right up the fundament from thirty metres.'

'There's a world of difference between killing a woman and shooting a cat.'

'Of course there is, but you might think differently if you were a cat. And who do cats have to protect them against lawlessness if not the Prague police department? Granted, cats aren't voters, or we might have a better government than we've got, but they're still entitled to our protection. And who's to say that the man shooting a cat today isn't practising to wipe out his wife tomorrow?'

'Well, the priest wouldn't be. He wouldn't have a wife.'

'And a good thing too, if he's going to go round shooting them up the backside. I rest my case. Hand me the internal phone directory, would you?'

Slonský thumbed through it and dialled a number.

'Technician First Class Spehar.'

'Lieutenant Underclass Slonský. I've got a photo sent in anonymously that needs your expert attention.'

'In an envelope?'

'Of course. My assistant and I have pawed it mercilessly but you may still get something off it.'

'Are your fingerprints on file?'

'Mine are. Don't know about Navrátil's.'

Navrátil shook his head vigorously.

'He tells me he hasn't given his dabs in. If I send him across with the evidence you can do the necessary at the same time.'

'How long have I got?' asked Spehar, suspecting that he knew the answer.

'Don't ask me, I'm not your doctor. But if you don't drink industrial spirits, it'll be longer.'

Slonský replaced the handset and thrust the photograph and envelope into Navrátil's hand.

'Copy the photo first, then run this over to the lab. Spehar will be waiting for it. Tell him that you have to swear him to secrecy about the contents and that he is the only person other than us to have seen it. That way he'll get the thing off his desk and back to us as fast as his little legs will carry him. In the meantime, I will go to the café and invest in some coffee and breakfast for us both.'

'Coffee sounds good,' Navrátil allowed, 'but you can hold the breakfast for me.'

'I'll get you one anyway,' beamed Slonský. 'If you don't want it I'm sure I'll find room for it.'

Technician First Class Spehar proved to be a slightly built man with a balding head, half-moon glasses and a neat grey beard. His name badge described him as "Technician First Class Spehar", leading Navrátil to wonder if that was what his parents had named him. It was quite possible that nobody knew his first name. I wonder what his wife calls him, pondered Navrátil, as he waited patiently for Spehar to complete the evidence receipt and attach a docket to the plastic sleeve.

Deftly, the technician flipped the envelope open and extracted the photograph with his gloved hand.

'Now, what have we … My God! Isn't that …?'

'Yes. That's why we'd like it back quickly, please.'

'And is that the girl in the newspaper?'

'I can't discuss that. Operational reasons.'

'No, of course. Silly of me. Right, I'll get straight onto it. We'll give it the works.'

Navrátil had no idea what 'the works' might be, but it sounded like a superior quality of forensic service so he thanked Spehar and left him to get on with 'the works' with all speed.

When he returned to the office Slonský was sitting with his feet on the desk and a broad smile on his face.

'Your coffee is on the radiator. I hope you haven't changed your mind about breakfast, because it's a bit late. I've almost finished yours.'

'What's that, then?' asked Navrátil, pointing at a cardboard parcel.

'That's mine. I thought I'd better eat yours first, while it was hot. Now, exciting things have been happening while you've been swanning around the forensics lab. The boys in the press office have come up trumps.'

'Why do these things always happen when I'm out?'

Slonský shrugged. 'Why do footballers always score when I'm in the toilet? One of the great mysteries of life, lad, and one that has taxed greater minds than ours. Now, where did you put that copy?'

Navrátil produced the copy of the photograph. Slonský placed it on the left side of his desk before opening a second envelope and spreading its contents across the right side.

'Photographs of the Minister provided by the government press office, showing him going about his various duties on the day before the body was found. Fortunately he likes having photographers around, so we've got a pretty good record of his day. Notice anything, Navrátil?'

'Same shirt, same tie.'

'Precisely. Now, we can assume, I think, that a ministerial salary will run to more than one shirt and tie. That being so, we have to compute the odds that these photographs were all taken on the same day.'

'Maybe he always wears that tie with that shirt.'

'A plausible assumption, but the suit is the same too. And notice that the gap from the underside of the tie knot to the top of the first stripe looks very similar, so his habits extend to always tying his tie in the same way. Possible, but surely the likeliest conclusion is that these were all taken on one day. And since we know when the press photos were taken, that enables us to date the dinner date.'

'The cautious side of me still thinks we shouldn't jump to conclusions.'

'And you should certainly listen to it, Navrátil. But as a working hypothesis we're entitled to think the two go together, and no doubt if we're wrong about that the Minister will tell us so when we go to see him.'

'We're going to see the Minister?'

'We can't ignore the evidence, Navrátil. Someone is dead, and the Minister was with her shortly before she died. We have to ask him about it. At the very least he can explain why he hasn't contacted us to identify her. After all, you would expect the man in charge of policing in this country to help the police do their job, wouldn't you?'

'He may be too busy to see us.'

'Standard rules apply, Navrátil. He can co-operate at his office, or we can bring him down here for questioning if he prefers.'

'Sir, aren't you a bit … wary of accusing a minister?'

'No, and if you think that way you'd better pack your things now. A criminal is a criminal, whatever else he may be, and he gets nailed whoever he is. And while there may be some question about what constitutes a crime as regimes change, strangling a woman is on everyone's list of bad things you shouldn't do. But we'll do things by the book. Let's go and see Lukas.'

Slonský may not have been wary of accusing a minister, but Lukas certainly was. Several careful examinations of the photographs persuaded him at last that there was a need to ask some questions of the Minister, but he insisted that he should make the appointment and accompany Slonský to the Minister's office.

'I want to hear what goes on for myself,' he said, omitting to add 'and intervene if necessary', though they both knew that was what he meant.

'Of course, sir,' replied Slonský. 'I shall be the epitome of respect and discretion.'

'No, you won't,' answered Lukas. 'You don't know how. You'll be a bull in a china shop as usual. But I can't deny that the Minister has some explaining to do.'

The Minister's secretary had booked them an appointment shortly before noon, so Slonský and Lukas were conducted into the Minister's presence precisely on time, while Navrátil waited in the anteroom.

The Minister was a small man, but he had a huge desk. Slonský computed its dimensions and concluded that if the Minister laid his head on the desk he would not be able to reach to the two ends. He also thought that the Minister might be sitting on a cushion to raise him up a little.

The desk's surface was highly polished and free from clutter. A blotter occupied the centre, with a telephone and a computer monitor to the Minister's left. He was wiggling a mouse around as they entered, and completed whatever he was doing on his computer before inviting them to sit in a pair of chairs a couple of metres from the far side of his desk.

'I understand you need my help with a delicate matter,' the Minister oozed. He stopped short of making a steeple with his hands but the motion was clearly in his mind before being dismissed as a cliché.

'Just so, Minister,' Lukas began. 'We are investigating the murder of a young woman and we have come across some material that requires some … interpretation.'

He rose and slid the dinner photograph across the desk. The Minister picked it up and examined it closely without any comment or change in his facial expression.

'I see. Is this the murder victim?'

'We believe so.'

'Then of course you must ask for an explanation. But I'm afraid my help will be limited. I barely know the woman.'

'You seem to be on quite close terms in the photo,' Slonský interjected before Lukas could frame a response.

'A dinner companion,' announced the Minister. 'Not someone I knew well.'

'But you didn't respond to our public appeals to identify the victim,' Slonský continued. 'Why was that?'

The Minister threw his head back to unleash a rolling chuckle.

34

'I don't read the news, Lieutenant. I make it. I don't need to look at newspapers because I already know the interesting stuff.'

'I'd have thought the murder of someone you had dinner with was of passing interest, sir. But no matter. We still need her identified.'

'Irina. One moment.' He reached into an inside pocket and extracted a slim pocket diary. 'Gruberová. Irina Gruberová.'

'And can you date this dinner, Minister?'

The Minister picked up the photograph again and frowned.

'I don't think so.'

'There were a number of such dinners, then?'

'A small number.'

'A small number like three, or a slightly larger number — ten, say?'

'Three or four.'

'Does the restaurant give it away?'

'Not really. It's a favourite place of mine.'

'If you'd give us the address the reservations book might help us.'

The Minister scribbled an address on a leaf from his jotter pad and passed it to Lukas.

'I don't usually make a reservation. I find I don't need to.'

'We understand,' Lukas assured him.

'Does your appointment diary give us a date, Minister?' asked Slonský, a little more deliberately than was strictly necessary.

'It's not the kind of appointment I would put in my diary, Lieutenant.'

'I understand. Perhaps I could help with a suggestion. It seems to us that it may have been taken on Tuesday evening, because the government press office has supplied us with these pictures taken on Tuesday afternoon. You'll see you appear to be wearing the same clothes.'

'It could have been Tuesday,' the Minister admitted. 'Irina and I had a working dinner then.'

Slonský opened his mouth to speak but Lukas had anticipated the next question.

'May we ask why you use the word "working", Minister?'

'Miss Gruberová was helping me to organise my wife's birthday party.'

'And her particular expertise was in …?' asked Slonský with the air of a man who did not believe there could be a satisfactory answer to his question.

'She wasn't formally trained,' explained the Minister cautiously. 'It was more in the nature of a natural gift.'

'And I suppose that, since this would be a surprise party, your wife would not be in a position to support your alibi because you wouldn't have told her about the meeting.'

'Why should I need an alibi?' asked the Minister.

'Because you seem to have been the last person to see Miss Gruberová alive, Minister. And it's normal practice to begin with the assumption that the last known contact is the likeliest murderer.'

If this perturbed the Minister, he hid it well.

'Of course. That is how things are done. I understand that. But I need hardly explain that I did not, in fact, kill her.'

'And I need hardly explain that almost every murderer I have ever known has said the same thing.'

The Minister frowned and ostentatiously pulled back his sleeve to check his watch.

'Do you remember what you both ate, Minister?'

'I'm sorry?'

'On Tuesday, at your working dinner. Did you keep the receipt for your expenses claim?'

'I don't think the powers that be would let me claim for a dinner on a family matter, Lieutenant,' the Minister chortled. Lukas joined in the laughter, as if to emphasise that he would not allow Slonský to put such a dinner on his expenses either.

'I don't have a family to discuss at dinner,' replied Slonský. 'The menu?'

'I'm not sure. I usually have soup and then something traditional. I think I had a pork steak.'

'And your companion?'

'She had melon, I think, and a schnitzel.'

'With asparagus?'

'Yes, I believe it was. We just ordered some assorted vegetables and shared them. I don't particularly like asparagus, so I didn't bother with it.'

An attendant entered with a tray of coffee, poured for the Minister, and then for Lukas and Slonský, in that order, despite having to walk past Slonský to serve Lukas.

'And after dinner, Minister?'

'I drove Miss Gruberová to her flat and then went home.'

'Perhaps you had some outstanding business to complete in Miss Gruberová's flat.'

'No, I walked her upstairs to her door and left her there.'

'I see. What time was this?'

'About ten, I think.'

'And was there anyone in Miss Gruberová's flat when you got there?'

'I don't think so. The lights weren't on inside, and so far as I know she lived alone.'

'Could you let us have her address?'

'I don't think I know it precisely. She gave me directions.'

'Her phone number then.'

'I'm not sure I have it.'

'You must have had it at some time, Minister, in order to arrange the dinner.'

'I suppose I must. Let me see.' After some leafing through his diary he recited a number.

'Thank you. We may be able to track her address from this.'

'I hope so. It wasn't far from the restaurant, somewhere near the Slavia stadium in Strahov.'

Slonský drained his cup.

'I'm sorry, I'm stopping you finishing your coffee, Minister. We may have to ask your wife to verify the time you arrived home.'

'Of course. I'm not sure she'll be able to help you — she was already in bed when I got in.'

'Yes, that's what she told me,' Slonský said, causing Lukas' eyebrows to jerk violently upwards. 'You see, Minister, we've been keeping something from you. Before she died, Miss Gruberová made love to a gentleman friend. Naturally, if there had been someone in the flat, we would have assumed that he was responsible. But since you say there wasn't, that poses a difficulty.'

'I said I didn't see any lights, Lieutenant. That doesn't mean there wasn't an intruder in the dark.'

'Understood. And of course we'll check out that line of enquiry once we know where the flat is.'

'Excellent. I'm sure we all want you to redouble your efforts to catch the man responsible for this outrage. Captain, I expect you to put all the resources you can into the investigation. If I can help in any way, please let me know.'

'That's very good of you, Minister,' Lukas answered, inclining his head in acknowledgement.

The Minister drained the last of his coffee from his cup. Slonský jumped to his feet, produced a plastic envelope from his pocket, and dropped the cup into it.

'I'm sorry, Minister. I was taking your consent for granted,' he announced guilelessly.

There was a long silence.

'Of course. Now, if there's nothing else …'

'That's very good of you, Minister!' Slonský mimicked Lukas' comment as they walked through the polished corridors back to their car.

'It would do you no harm to learn some manners, Slonský. Fancy snatching the Minister's cup like that.'

'It's evidence. His DNA will be on it.'

37

'You could have asked him to give a swab.'

'Men like him don't give swabs. He'd probably get an underling to do it for him.'

'Do you seriously expect to get a match with the swab from that young lady?'

'No. He's probably got an underling who does that for him too.'

'Slonský!'

'Well, his type makes me sick.'

'He is our superior, Slonský.'

'That's why he makes me sick. How can you look up to someone who cheats on his wife so flagrantly?'

'I remind you, Slonský, that he denied having intercourse with Miss Gruberová.'

'And that's another reason why he makes me sick. He's a liar.'

'Innocent until proven guilty.'

'Guilty as hell in my eyes. Does he take us for idiots? The girl is holding his hand in that picture. You only have to see the look in her eyes to know that she isn't going to be bonking someone else a couple of hours later. Even if he took her home at ten, which I acccpt, is it likely that he left her there and within a couple of hours someone had arrived, had persuaded her into bed, had her and strangled her? I don't think so.'

'I grant appearances are against him. What do we do now?'

'I drop this cup in to Novák. It might be good if you signed the evidence bag too. Then we wait for the DNA match. And if, as I expect, it matches the swab, we turn up at the Minister's office with a bunch of squad cars, throw a blanket over his head and march him outside while the press photographers click away merrily.'

'No, Slonský, you'll do no such thing. The arrest of a minister is a very serious business and must be handled properly. I must inform my superiors who will in turn report to the Prime Minister so that he can make arrangements for the continuity of government.'

'We mustn't give him the chance to destroy evidence, sir. He mustn't know we're coming. Please emphasise that to the Prime Minister.'

'I don't think I'll … do you think so? The Prime Minister?'

'Well, you're the senior officer. And your bosses are too spineless to want to tell the PM one of his ministers has murdered a young woman.'

'Yes, I see what you mean. But I can't ask the Director of the Police Service to act with discretion and tact. He won't listen to me. Perhaps the best bet is if the Director and I go to see the Prime Minister while you get your men into position at the Ministry ready for our signal.'

'My men? I don't have men. I have a man.'

'Yes, where is Navrátil? He was outside the Minister's office.'

'He's been doing a little job for me, sir.'

Lukas stopped dead, goggling at Slonský's back as the detective strode away.

'Slonský! Tell me there has been no impropriety here!'

Slonský carried on walking.

'All right, sir. There has been no impropriety here.'

'Slonský! Do I see your fingers crossed behind your back?'

Navrátil was in the back seat when they got in.

'Been waiting long?' asked Slonský.

'Long enough,' Navrátil replied.

'Well, we're here now. What did you find out?'

'His typist didn't know her. The doormen were sure she had never been inside the building, and she hadn't signed in.'

'False name?'

'You need formal identification to get in, sir. Unless she had something that persuaded the security men she was someone else, she hasn't been in.'

'She could have pestered him by phone.'

Lukas felt the need to interrupt. 'Look, what is this? Are you suggesting that she came to the ministry to make a scene?'

'Well, if she had we'd have a motive for killing her. A public figure can't have women turning up at his office alleging intimacy.'

'You've got her phone number. You can check the calls she made.'

'It's a landline. She must have had a mobile phone.'

'How can you know that?'

'She was the mistress of a busy man. There are bound to be last minute changes to plans and she can't sit by the phone waiting for instructions on the off chance. He must have been able to keep in touch with her. Besides, how many women of her age don't have mobile phones these days?'

'So we must see whether her address was used for billing a mobile phone.'

'And his. He may have given her a phone. She won't have called his office or home, so the chances are that she called a mobile phone he had. Which is probably now at the bottom of the Vltava. If you'll drop us off here, sir, Navrátil and I have some business in this area.'

The captain obliged, and Slonský watched him drive around the corner and disappear from sight.

'Nice uniform. Shiny buttons.'

'What urgent business do we have here, sir?'

'The Minister told us to redouble our efforts, Navrátil. So we're going for *two* beers and *two* sausages.'

The desk sergeant leaned over the counter in a conspiratorial fashion. 'Do I detect that substances are about to hit the fan?'

'You do, old friend. I am taking aim at this very moment. But how did you know?'

The lean figure reached under the counter. 'Technician First Class Spehar left this for you.'

'Good old Technician First Class Spehar! The title suits him.'

'He's always first class?'

'No, he's always a technician. Now, Navrátil, let's hide ourselves in some discreet place and see what Spehar has to tell us.'

Slonský opened the door to the main corridor and held it open while he bellowed. 'I hope this report explains why the Minister of the Interior denied shagging that woman who was found dead a couple of hours after he left her.' He winked at the desk sergeant. 'Uninformed gossip is a terrible thing, eh? Better to have facts to work on.'

'The right and proper order of things, Navrátil,' Slonský explained, 'is that I sit with my feet up scanning the report while you make coffee. Instant will do. Top drawer of the filing cabinet.'

'There are no files in this drawer, sir.'

'That's because it's marked "Unsolved Crimes", so I don't need a cabinet as big as that. Plenty of space for coffee and other essentials.'

Navrátil took the kettle to fill it, while Slonský read Spehar's report.

'Does it get us anywhere, sir?'

'A load of technical stuff about the paper used, but it's widely available. There are no fingerprints on the photograph except ours, but there are quite a lot on the envelope, presumably including the postman, someone at the sorting office, and so on. But it's not unknown for blackmailers to forget they've handled an envelope when they bought it, so we live in hope.'

'You think it's blackmail?'

'No, or our informant would have sent the picture to the Minister, since no doubt he would pay better than we do. I thought of blackmail because it involves stuffing pictures in envelopes. Anyway, if we get a suspect it may be that his prints will match.'

Slonský frowned. 'Sadly it's a self-seal envelope.'

'Sir?'

'He didn't need to lick it to seal it. Spehar has sent off a swab for DNA testing but he doesn't expect it to be very useful. Now, he says the address is more promising.'

'Address?'

'Navrátil, can you stop answering everything I say with a question? Yes, the address. My address. Somehow the sender knew that I was working on the case.'

'It was in the newspapers.'

'It was in one newspaper, Navrátil. The others that named me didn't come out until after this was posted. Incidentally, it was posted in the Ninth district. It shows no sign of being folded so it may have been posted at a post office rather than in a street postbox. Spehar says the address has been computer-generated using a laser printer.'

'Meaning?'

'There you go again, another question! Meaning that it's more likely to have been done at work than at home. Not conclusive, of course — there must be plenty of people with a laser printer at home — but most people with home computers will have inkjet printers. And Spehar, clever chap that he is, notes that if we find the computer his whizzkid colleagues may be able to prove that my address was in its memory.'

'It doesn't advance us too much, then.'

'Oh, I don't know. But then I've read the last paragraph. Of course, I already knew it, but it's good to know that Spehar comes to the same conclusion as me. Did you look at the envelope?'

'Of course. Plain brown, a bit bigger than A4.'

'The stamp?'

'Of course — he'll have licked the stamp!'

'No, he dipped it in a bit of water. No saliva on it at all, I reckon, but Spehar is checking that. Look at the address.'

Navrátil held the plastic evidence envelope at arm's length and tilted it to catch the maximum amount of light.

'He knows you're in the Criminal Detection department, and your rank.'

'It would be odd if it wasn't being investigated by the Criminal Detection department, wouldn't it? And my rank was in the newspaper. Look at the address, Navrátil!"

Navrátil shook his head. 'No, nothing. It's spelled wrongly, of course, but —'

'At last! It's spelled wrongly. He's missed the háček on the 'š' of Holešovice. Now, that suggests two things. First, he probably doesn't live in the district, or he'd have written it so many times it would be second nature. But the more important point is that it doesn't matter to him. He doesn't see any meaningful difference between an 's' and an 'š'. He's a foreigner, Navrátil.'

'Maybe his printer just doesn't print háčeks properly.'

'Ah, but Technician First Class Spehar has thought of that. "There is no sign that any attempt has been made to deposit laser toner in the háček field," he writes.'

'Okay, but maybe he deliberately spelled it wrongly to put us off the scent so we would think he wasn't a Czech.'

Slonský's face fell. 'You're not as green as you are cabbage-looking, Navrátil. He may indeed. But he knows who the Minister of the Interior is by sight, and not many Czechs would pass that one.'

'He's one of the more recognisable ministers, sir.'

'He's certainly one of the shortest, Navrátil. What do you think — one metre fifty-five? And did you notice his desk layout?'

'I was outside, sir.'

'So you were. Well, Navrátil, you'll have to rely on my powers of observation. The Minister used his mouse with his left hand.'

'So?'

'So maybe this time Novák has hit the nail on the head. Our Minister is a left-handed dwarf.'

Chapter 5

Sergeant Adamec was a lugubrious, slow-moving walrus of a policeman who had been detailed by the Strahov station hierarchy to help Slonský find Gruberová's apartment. The details given by the Minister were no use at all. He described a couple of landmarks and a very general description of the building that seemed to be applicable to most of the houses in the area. As for the telephone number, it proved to be an internet café and nobody there knew where she lived. Adamec had checked the station records but nothing had come to their attention, and the district council did not have a record of her either.

'Not surprising if she was renting, though,' Adamec muttered. 'It would be the landlord who appeared there.'

Slonský sighed. He had met some miserable swines in his time but it was depressing him just to be on the same planet as Adamec.

'It can't be every day that the Minister of the Interior comes to Strahov. Somebody must have recognised him.'

'Maybe it's because nobody recognised him that he came here,' said Adamec. 'Bit of peace and quiet. I could do with that myself.' He sat on a windowsill and mopped his brow. It was a cold day, but Adamec was struggling after this unaccustomed effort. 'It's all go, this serious crime lark. I don't know how you stick it.'

'Trying to find the killer of a fellow citizen helps to keep me going,' barked Slonský, who realised immediately how pompous it sounded. 'Let's apply a bit of lateral thinking. If you had a bit on the side and wanted to get a flat for her round here, where would you look?'

'I don't know.'

'But it's your area!' Slonský snarled.

'I know,' Adamec explained in his most reasonable tone, as if addressing a particularly dim five-year-old. 'But I don't have a mistress, so I don't know how a man who has one would think.'

'Humour me,' whined Slonský. 'Let's pretend.'

'I don't know if I can. It's so far out of my experience.'

Slonský removed his battered grey fedora to let the steam escape from his head, pinched the crown into shape, and replaced it carefully.

'Are you married?'

'Yes,' said Adamec, fishing in his pocket to produce an elderly black and white mugshot. 'Maria. Twenty-eight years together. She's a gem.'

'Yes,' said Slonský. 'She must be. Children?'

43

'Little Petr and Little Maria. That's them there. Of course, that was ten years ago. They're bigger now.'

'They would be,' agreed Slonský. 'Your name wouldn't be Petr, would it?'

'Yes!' Adamec cried. 'How did you know?'

'Lucky guess. Or detective's intuition. Well, suppose young Maria came to you and said "Dad, I want a flat of my own here, respectable area, somewhere I can keep nice", what would you say?'

'I'd say "You stay at home with your old dad until you're ready to get married, young miss".'

'And suppose she was ready to get married?'

'Then I'd keep out of it. She's her husband's responsibility then. Take my word for it, coming between a girl and her intended is a bad move, Lieutenant. You can't win. Anyway, why all these questions? Is your daughter moving out?'

Slonský was beginning to feel that murderers may not all be bad people. Some might just have spent an hour with someone like Sergeant Adamec.

'I don't have a daughter. I was trying to imagine how the murder victim would choose an apartment.'

'But didn't you say she was someone's mistress?'

'Yes. The Minister's.'

'Well, she wouldn't have chosen, would she? He would.'

'I thought that, but he says he doesn't know where it is.'

'So how could she afford this unless he was paying for it? Did she have another job somewhere?'

'If she did, they haven't missed her.'

'Maybe she did work that you don't have to clock in for. On the game, for instance.'

'Too clean.'

'Lap-dancing?'

'Possible. But then, how did the Minister meet her?'

'Maybe he goes lap-dancing.'

'That is too disgusting a picture for words, Adamec.'

'I meant as a customer, not a performer.'

'Thank goodness for small mercies. She must have had friends, though. Young women are sociable, aren't they? They all have friends. How come none of them has tried to contact us?'

'Perhaps they don't read newspapers. Watch a lot of television, though. Here, are you going to do one of those reconstructions on the television?'

'That depends.'

'On what?'

'On whether Tom Cruise is free to play you. Come on, Adamec, you and I are old-timers. We don't understand this modern world. If she doesn't have a tax number, and she doesn't seem to be on the game, how does she afford a flat?'

'Easy. Lover boy pays for it.'

'Then he must be paying in cash, because he knows we can get his bank records and then he'd be exposed as a liar if we find he's been paying her rent.'

Adamec chewed on a toothpick he had found in a pocket. 'Do you remember a case up here about five years back? Man who sawed his wife's head off so her body would fit in a trunk?'

Slonský pushed his hat higher on his forehead. What was the man rambling about? 'Yes. Little weedy fellow who got fed up with her talking while he was trying to read.'

'That's the one. We nailed him because he bought the saw at a hardware store and the shopkeeper remembered him. Then we proved the saw was used to lop her head off.'

'Yes, but we couldn't prove he'd killed her. He admitted it was his saw, but said he had nothing to do with the killing or the decapitation.'

'Where we went wrong,' mused Adamec, 'was that we tried to prove he had bought the saw in order to cut her head off. We were trying to prove he'd planned the whole thing. Whereas, as he subsequently admitted when he was locked in the loony-bin, there was no planning at all. He just flipped and grabbed the nearest thing to hand, which happened to be a distinctive saw.'

Slonský sighed deeply. 'If there was a point to this walk through history it has escaped me, Adamec.'

'Just that the lover might have hidden the payments if he planned the murder, but if it was an impulse he may not have realised that he left a smoking gun.'

Slonský showed an unexpected burst of energy in bounding to his feet.

'Adamec, if it wasn't one of the most disgusting ideas I've ever had, I'd kiss you! I'll get Navrátil onto it right now.' He took out his telephone and searched for Navrátil's number. 'Damn! I don't have his number. Never mind, I'll call the office and get someone to tell him. While I'm doing that, think harder! We have to find that girl's flat.'

Lukas listened carefully to Navrátil before shaking his head solemnly. 'It's out of the question. How could I possibly get permission to examine a Minister's bank account?'

'You could ask him, sir. After all, he voluntarily gave us his DNA sample.'

'Ah. Not quite. But I take the point. After all, if he is innocent, why would he object? And as our Minister he has to set an example, after all. But I'd better have a word with my superiors, Navrátil. Tell Slonský I'll speak to the Director of the Criminal Police about it.'

Navrátil coughed gently.

'Was there something else, Navrátil?'

'Lieutenant Slonský is concerned that if the Minister is alerted to our interest in him, he may destroy vital evidence.'

'Surely not! He is, after all, the Minister of the Interior, Navrátil. His job is to ensure the efficiency of the police, and destroying evidence would hardly achieve that.'

'No, sir. But he may be more worried about going to jail for the rest of his life.'

Lukas gaped as if the possibility of the Minister's guilt had just occurred to him.

'I can't imagine a minister in our government killing a young woman in such a vile manner. What is the world coming to?'

'Surely in the old days ministers did far worse, sir.'

'But that was under the old regime — ill-educated men who had no moral fibre, not elected politicians. The Minister is a university graduate, Navrátil. He holds a doctorate.'

'If there is the least chance that he may be guilty, sir, we can't be seen to be going easy on him just because he is our boss.'

'Of course not. Quite improper. Must be seen to be … without fear or favour.'

'So I can ask for a disclosure warrant, sir?'

'Can we do it discreetly?'

'Any judge will do, sir. I'll find one who'll keep it to himself. If you'll just sign the application here, sir.'

Lukas held the paper for some time with all the trepidation of a constitutional monarch asked to sign a death warrant.

'I'll take it with me, Navrátil, and get the Director to sign it.'

Navrátil knew Slonský had returned by the colourful language emanating from the office. 'They should pension off some of these old sergeants. Adamec must be eighty if he's a day.'

'He isn't retired yet, sir.'

'Mentally, I mean. Not a clue about his own patch. No idea where her flat could be. And the man is a walking photograph album. If I see another picture of his nauseatingly cherub-cheeked offspring —'

'Captain Lukas wants you, sir.'

'Me? Why?'

'He wants you to go with him to see the Director to get a warrant to examine the Minister's bank account.'

'Do we know who the Minister banks with?'

'No, sir.'

'Then getting a warrant may be a bit problematic, lad. We won't know what to do with it if we get one.'

'Isn't that always true?'

'Normally, Navrátil, we just ring round asking if the banks know Mr X of such and such an address. Sooner or later we strike lucky. It's a bit more difficult asking banks if a minister is a client.'

Slonský examined the floor in thought before marching out of the room.

'Come, Navrátil! We're going to see if we can find Klinger.'

Klinger was a slick-haired man in a dark suit and crisp white shirt who inhabited a nondescript office on the floor above.

'Why is it that visits from you always involve skulduggery, Slonský?'

'It's a gift. Can you do it or not?'

'I'm not sure. I'll have to make a couple of calls.'

'Fine. We'll wait.'

'The kind of calls I don't want people listening in on.'

'Fine. We'll wait outside.'

Slonský and Navrátil closed the door behind them. It soon opened again, as Klinger poked his head out. 'Outside and far away, where you can't listen in,' he insisted.

'You know your trouble, Klinger. A lack of trust.'

'Maybe that's why I'm a fraud officer,' Klinger replied, and watched as they made their way to the next doorway.

'Another couple of doors, please,' said Klinger.

'It's rubbing off on you, Klinger. You're developing an untrusting mentality. I could be very hurt.'

'Do you want the details or don't you?'

Slonský pushed Navrátil ahead of him. 'Don't dawdle, Navrátil. Do as the nice man says.'

Klinger emerged a few minutes later with a scrap of paper. 'I can't say it's his only bank account, but it's the one his salary gets paid into.'

'How did you get this?'

'Never mind.'

'No, I'm impressed! It can't be easy to get details off a government payroll department.'

'It is if you tell them you think he's been underpaid. Now hop off before someone sees you talking to me.'

'I owe you one, Klinger.'

'You owe me about eighteen, actually. But who's counting?'

'I was beginning to think you weren't coming, Slonský,' said Lukas.

'Tied up looking for the girl's flat, sir.'

'The Director is waiting for us.'

'Very good of him to work late for us, I'm sure.'

'Slonský, it's only four o'clock. He's hardly working late.'

'If you say so, sir.'

They were greeted by the Director's secretary and invited to sit down while she told him they were there.

'You could have smartened yourself up a bit, Slonský. It is the Director we're seeing.'

Slonský inspected himself carefully. 'I did. I never claimed to be a male model.'

'When did you last polish those shoes?'

Slonský furrowed his brow. 'When did the Berlin Wall come down?'

Lukas was deeply shocked. You could tell because his mouth fell open and he moved it like a landed catfish gasping for air.

'Joke, sir.'

'No laughing matter, Slonský.'

'No, sir. Anyway, I must have cleaned them at least twice since then.'

The secretary reappeared and held the door open. They entered, Lukas leading the way, and found the Director advancing towards them with his hand extended in greeting.

'Lukas. Slonský, isn't it? Sit, please.'

'Thank you, sir. You know why I asked to see you?'

'Yes, Lukas. Bad business. But if there are suspicions they must be investigated. Explain to me why you think a discovery warrant is needed.'

'The murder victim was last seen in the company of the Minister, sir.'

'And he admits they met?'

'Yes, sir. He left her at ten o'clock, he says, and forensic evidence suggests she died within two hours.'

'During which time someone had her,' interjected Slonský.

Lukas cringed with embarrassment.

'That's suggestive,' agreed the Director.

'That's what I thought,' said Slonský, 'but Captain Lukas is a stickler for doing things by the book and quite rightly said we needed more. The question is, who paid the rent on her flat in Strahov?'

'Nice area?'

'We haven't found it yet. But since nobody has missed her, we assume she didn't share.'

'Or he killed the flatmate too,' suggested the Director.

Lukas looked from one to the other as if watching a tennis rally.

'I hadn't thought of that,' admitted Slonský. 'That'll be why you're a Director and I'm just a humble footsoldier.'

'Anyway, sir,' Lukas continued, 'we want to know if he has been paying for the flat, since he says he doesn't know where she lived. If we find he has, then it casts doubt on his story.'

'DNA,' the Director muttered. 'If they made love, can we match the DNA?'

'We've got a sample from the girl, and the Minister gave us a sample of his.'

'Very public-spirited of him. Presumably he didn't know he was under suspicion. Did he waive his right to have a lawyer present?'

'Not exactly,' Lukas stammered.

'He didn't need one,' Slonský explained. 'He's a lawyer himself. He can be his own lawyer.'

'I'm not sure the court will go along with that when the time comes, Lieutenant.'

'He didn't object, sir. In fact, when I asked he said "Of course", didn't he, Captain?'

'Yes, I believe he did.'

'You were present?' the Director asked. 'That's all right, then.'

Lukas was unsure why his presence made it all right, and equally unsure whether he wanted to admit to having been there, but the Director's mind had raced ahead.

'The DNA will take a day or two. So we need to see the Minister's bank account to see if he has been paying for the flat?'

'That's it, sir,' agreed Slonský.

'Have you got the bank's details?'

Slonský offered Klinger's piece of paper.

'This looks a bit clandestine,' said the Director.

'Properly obtained, I'm sure,' Lukas interjected in a tone that indicated that he was actually very unsure of it.

'From the Minister's office, sir. His staff were sure he would want to assist us in every way.'

The Director smiled slightly.

'Very commendable. It makes things much easier for us, doesn't it? Nice when suspects co-operate.'

'Isn't it?' agreed Slonský, now certain that he had been rumbled.

The Director took the application and signed it with a flourish.

'I've amended it slightly. It now covers that bank account and any others the Minister may happen to have with the same bank, Captain.'

'Thank you, sir,' chorused Slonský and Lukas.

'You don't need a judge's countersignature. I've certified that for reasons of operational urgency we need to move quickly. I'll notify the appropriate people that it's been done.'

'What a nice man!' Slonský said. 'Very helpful. Easy to see how he got where he is.'

'Quite. Slonský, where did you really get that account number?'

'We already had it, sir.'

'Really?'

'Of course, it would be quite improper of me to divulge if any enquiry of a financial nature were under way elsewhere in the police, sir.'

'Of course. And I wouldn't need to know that.'

'Nor should you, sir. It might colour your thinking about him if you thought he might not have paid all his taxes.'

'Slonský! Don't tell me any more! I insist you keep the details to yourself and don't talk about it to me again.'

'As you wish, sir,' said Slonský, and allowed himself a roguish smirk.

Navrátil was feeling very proud of himself. He had a map of Prague on the desk and was busy putting pins into it.

'Amusing yourself, Navrátil?'

'I may be on to something, sir.'

'Say on, young prince. I am all ears.'

'Well, sir, they didn't recognise her at the internet café, but there must be a reason why she gave that number.'

'Except she didn't. I bet the Minister gave us that one to lead us into a dead end. He rang her mobile. If she'd gone to the café often enough to pick up casual messages, they'd have known her there.'

Navrátil was slightly upset that Slonský had already travelled along this line of thought, which he had believed was entirely original.

'Cheer up, lad. That's a map of Strahov and those pins aren't internet places, so give me the rest.'

'They're places where you can buy milk, sir.'

'Milk?'

'Everyone needs milk, sir. Almost everyone, to be more exact. But if you live on your own you just pick it up when you need it. So I thought Miss Gruberová must buy milk somewhere near her flat. And after a few tries, I struck lucky.'

'Well done, lad!'

'This one here, sir. The old woman recognised the photo.'

Slonský blanched.

'You didn't show her the picture with the Minister?'

'Not all of it, sir. I made a copy of half of it. She only saw the victim.'

'Thank heavens for that. And?'

'She said she didn't recognise the drawing in the newspapers because the eyes were wrong.'

'Wrong? You mean she had three or something?'

'No, sir. You can see what she meant from the photo. Miss Gruberová had hooded eyelids. The woman says she always looked half asleep.'

'If she was up all night getting bonked by the Minister she probably was. But pray continue.'

'She doesn't know exactly where the victim lived, but she says it can't be far away because she sometimes came to the shop without a coat.'

Slonský beamed with delight.

'You are destined for high things, son. When you are Director of Police, remember old Slonský gave you your first break and see if you can't bump the pensions up a bit. But why the other pins?'

'I wanted to see where she would have to live if that shop was the nearest to her flat. There are shops here and here, so the best bet looks like somewhere in these four streets.'

'Right. Ring Strahov and get Adamec to meet us. I don't care if he's finished his shift. Tell him we're going to do door-to-door along those streets and we could do with any spare men he can find. It's going to be a long evening, so I'm off to the canteen to get us some sausages and coffee. And because you've been good, you get a pastry too, young man.'

Chapter 6

Adamec had found three young policemen who stood in the cold night air blowing on their hands.

'Are they old enough to be out at this hour?' Slonský asked.

Adamec looked them over carefully. 'It's us,' he concluded. 'We're getting older. They say you know you're getting old when the policemen look young.'

'Fair enough. Gather round, lads! Now, Navrátil has a photo and a drawing for each of you. I want you to share these streets here and knock on everyone's door. We're trying to find the murder victim's flat.'

A hand was raised tentatively.

'Yes?'

'Sir, if she's the victim she won't answer.'

Slonský resisted the very real temptation to kick a police officer.

'Quite right, lad, she won't. So make a note in your little black book that there was no-one in. If someone answers, ask them if they know the woman in the pictures and where she lived. If you get an address, call your loving Sergeant, and he'll tell me.'

Navrátil and the three policemen trudged off through the snow, leaving Adamec and Slonský on the main road.

'What do we do now?' asked Adamec.

'No point standing out here,' replied Slonský. 'Let's find a nice warm bar and wait for a call.'

It was not too long in coming. A woman identified the victim as her upstairs neighbour, and correctly named her as Irina Something-or-other.

'Good enough for me, Navrátil,' announced Slonský. 'Anyone have a key?'

'She gave me the landlord's number, but there's no reply.'

'Adamec?'

'I'll get a locksmith. There's one we use.'

'There, that's what comes of keeping your brain warm. You lads go and warm up. Not you, Navrátil. I need you here with me. You should have thought of that before you made yourself indispensable.'

'Am I indispensable, then?'

'For the moment. But don't puff yourself up. I'm fickle like that. We're going to talk to the near neighbours. I want to know if any of them saw anything on Monday night, especially a car arriving around ten or leaving a bit later.'

'We didn't ask the Minister what kind of car he has, sir.'

'I asked his secretary. He has a beige Mercedes.'

When the locksmith arrived it took him only a few minutes to dismantle the lock and allow entry. The Scene of Crime team were quickly in action, dusting and measuring, while Slonský stood in each doorway in turn, silently inspecting the room and committing the layout to memory.

'Tidy place,' he pronounced. 'Some nice stuff.'

'No coffee cups waiting to be washed,' Navrátil noted.

'Interesting bedroom, wouldn't you say?'

'A bit girly for my taste, sir.'

'Undoubtedly. But I bet you have sheets on your bed.'

'I bet she did too, sir.'

'So our murderer took them with him, thereby removing a source of forensic evidence. I hope that doesn't catch on or our lives will get a lot harder.'

One of the Scenes of Crime team glanced over at them.

'No prints on the bedside furniture. But there are two nice thumbprints on the bed-head.'

'Really? How careless. You might want to check them against the cup I dropped in the other day.'

Navrátil appeared to be enacting some strange ritual.

'What are you doing, Navrátil?'

'I'm trying to think how the thumbs would be if he gripped the headboard while he was … occupied, sir.'

'I'm sure he gripped it nice and hard, son, so they'll be good prints. Well, I think we've done all we can here. Nobody saw anything, not even the murderer staggering downstairs with a dead woman wrapped in a sheet over his shoulder. Whatever happened to old women, Navrátil? When I was a lad all the women in our street knew everything I'd been up to and shopped me to my mother without a moment's thought. Now they don't even see a neighbour being murdered and carted off. Come on, let's get some sleep. It'll be a long day tomorrow.'

'It's been a long day today, sir.'

Slonský smiled faintly.

'I suppose it has, hasn't it? But it's what makes the blood rush in your veins, all this sort of thing. We're on the move, lad, and someone is going to be behind bars soon.'

Chapter 7

Slonský gazed out of the window as the rising sun reflected from the windows of the buildings across the street.

'I've got the report, sir. The Scenes of Crime team must have worked through the night.'

'That's because I told them to. What have we got?'

Navrátil scanned the cover sheet rapidly.

'The prints on the bed-head match those on the cup, sir.'

'Well, the Minister can hardly deny being in the bed, then. He lied to us, Navrátil. I can't wait to tell Captain Lukas. He'll be so shocked.'

Slonský picked a folder from his desk and handed it to Navrátil.

'Have a look at that, lad. The DNA on the cup matches the swab from the victim.'

'It's looking pretty bleak for the Minister, then, sir.'

'Look a little further, Navrátil. There are two sheets in that folder.'

'The Minister's bank statement?'

'Yes. And look at last Tuesday.'

Navrátil gulped.

'A cash withdrawal. Two hundred and forty-nine thousand, two hundred and fifty crowns.'

Lukas read and re-read the notes. 'I don't mind admitting I'm shocked, Slonský. Absolutely shocked. To think that a minister of the state could have a mistress, kill her and lie to us about it. Does he think we're fools? The very man who should know better than any other minister what we can do. It's … it's …'

'Shocking?'

'Exactly! I'm shocked. Well, our duty is clear. I must take this to the Director and arrange for the Minister's arrest. It's your case, Slonský. I'm sure the Director will agree to your being present to get the credit for the arrest.'

'That's not necessary, sir.'

'Nonsense. It's a job well done for the whole department. We have to be seen to have done our duty.'

'Will you be telling the Prime Minister we're about to bang one of his ministers up for murder, sir?'

Lukas performed his goldfish impersonation one more time.

'I think someone should, sir. It would be a shame if he read it in the papers first.'

'Well, it's hardly my place … surely the Director —'

'I'm sure the Prime Minister will want to be convinced of the strength of the evidence, sir, so he'll want to speak to the senior officer in charge.'

'It's your case, Slonský.'

'But you're my superior, sir. I must defer to you.'

'Slonský, why do I think that there is something you aren't telling me? Is this arrest unsafe?'

'You've seen the evidence, sir.'

'Indeed. It's clear we must arrest him. But it's going to cause a bit of a hoo-ha.'

'Well, it isn't every policeman that gets to arrest his own boss, I grant you.'

'So what will you be doing while I go up to see the Prime Minister, Slonský?'

Slonský grimaced. 'Navrátil is at her flat looking for an address for a next of kin, sir. Somebody ought to be told that she has died.'

Lukas dropped his head onto his chest. That was another job he would prefer not to have to do. All things considered, going to the PM's office with the Director would be more comfortable.

'Very well. You and Navrátil examine the flat and inform the next of kin while I tidy things up here. But come and see me as soon as you've finished. And don't speak to the press under any circumstances, Slonský.'

Slonský agreed readily. He hated speaking to the press at any time, a natural consequence of his belief that journalists were, in many cases, more morally repugnant than murderers. When he condescended to share a few words it was either to ask them to help him or to spread misinformation about a case. In any event, it was unlikely to be Slonský that journalists wanted to speak to, especially after he told them in strict confidence that Lukas had been the one who arrested the Minister.

The Director was a fast reader. Before Lukas had managed to arrange his uniform so he could sit without creasing the tail of his jacket, the Director was on his feet and reaching for his uniform hat.

'Clear enough, Lukas. It's not conclusive but the forensics prove he was there, the money is strongly circumstantial and his alibi stinks. I have a telephone call to make, then we'll take this dossier to the Prime Minister and ask him to help us arrest the Minister discreetly.'

'I'm sure he will appreciate that, sir. The Prime Minister, I mean.'

'I'm told there's no love lost between them, Lukas. Would you mind stepping outside and asking my secretary to order my driver round to the front? We'd best go by car.'

Slonský pushed the door open with his foot and slipped crab-wise into the flat, each hand holding a cup of coffee with a pastry balanced on top.

'Keep your strength up, lad,' he explained to Navrátil, who was sitting at a small dining table on which he had arranged some small piles of papers.

'Nothing to connect her directly to the Minister, sir. No love letters, birthday cards, thank you notes.'

'There wouldn't be. He'd give her a few coins and tell her to buy her own. Family?'

Navrátil silently handed him a couple of sheets of cheap notepaper.

'Must be her mother. Not very educated spelling and a shaky hand equals an old lady who doesn't write much. Anything before this?'

'No, sir. It looks as if she had only been in Prague a year or so. Do you know the village, sir?'

'It's out towards Kladno, I think. Perhaps thirty kilometres away. We can radio in and check before we set out. God, it's depressing. Her own mother doesn't seem to know she's dead yet. Any signs of a father?'

'He's mentioned in the second letter, sir. "Dad sends his best." But no other family.'

Slonský scanned the room once more. He had already imprinted it in his memory the night before, but in daylight it looked a little shabbier. The furniture was neat, but not expensive.

'She had a bit of taste, bless her. Cheap sofa but some nice cushions on it. She's worked hard at polishing out the scratch on that table. Just missed a bit where it chipped the edge, look. How old was she?'

'I haven't found anything like that, sir. All her official stuff must have been in a handbag we haven't got. There are a few bags in the wardrobe but they're all empty.'

Slonský slurped his coffee and took a large bite from the pastry, chewing slowly and without enjoyment.

'Phone bills?'

'There's one for her mobile phone. We can get call records from that. I've started the ball rolling with the phone company.'

'Good lad. Well, best drink up, son. We can't put off going to see the mother.'

Lukas was sitting to attention. The Director seemed relaxed enough, but this was the Prime Minister they were talking to, and Lukas felt uneasy at proximity to the powerful. He had been offered a coffee and was paralysed with the fear that he might spill it on the carpet, as a result of which he was sitting bolt upright with the saucer wedged in his lap and had not tasted a drop.

'Never liked the shifty little devil. Doesn't surprise me if he topped his mistress. Let's get him over here and you can slap the cuffs on him.'

'I'd hoped to avoid that, sir,' the Director replied.

'Really? Shame. I'd have enjoyed that. Well, you know best. But if he falls down the stairs a few times during questioning, I won't take it amiss. I never wanted him but there was pressure from coalition colleagues to give him a top job. At least now I can put my own man in.'

The office door opened and a middle-aged man with an immaculate dark suit and white shirt slithered into the room noiselessly.

'Komárek, please telephone the Interior Ministry and ask the Minister to come here at once. No excuses. And don't tell him who is here.'

'Very good, Prime Minister.'

When he had gone, the three men sat in silence, the Director relaxed in his seat, Lukas rigid and watchful, and the Prime Minister doodling on a notepad.

'I don't suppose you'd reconsider the handcuff thing?' he asked hopefully.

Navrátil slowed as they approached the exit slip road, and was relieved to see the promised police car waiting there. He pulled in to the side of the road about thirty metres further on, and stepped out of the car to greet the local officers.

'Sergeant Tomáš,' announced a barrel-shaped officer who emerged from the driver's seat and flapped a hand like a seal's flipper in the general direction of his colleague. 'And that's Officer Peiperová.'

Slonský completed the introductions.

'Bad business,' said the sergeant.

'Do you know the family?' asked Slonský.

'I don't,' admitted the sergeant, 'or, at least, not particularly well. But Peiperová was at school with Gruberová.'

'She was a year or two ahead of me,' explained the young officer, who was a tall woman with thick, yellow-blonde hair which she had somehow managed to pile inside her uniform cap.

'Brothers or sisters?'

'There's a brother, but he's been away from home for a few years now,' Peiperová explained. 'I can't say I knew Irina well, but it's a shock to me so I can imagine what it will be like for her poor mother.'

'Father not around?'

'In body, if not entirely in spirit,' Tomáš interjected. 'He's well known to us. Likes a drink, then gets pulled in for some sort of hooliganism. Usually public nuisance, like urinating in someone's shop doorway. But he's quietened down a lot lately. Poor devil is a bit damaged now. Brain running on empty.'

'Let that be a warning to you, Navrátil,' Slonský snapped.

'Me? Why me?'

'I'm responsible for you, lad. We don't want that fine brain of yours turning to mush. Well, we'd best get it over and done with. Shall we follow you?'

They returned to their respective cars and smoothly pulled into the traffic. The squad car turned left and after two or three minutes took another left before following the road to the end of the metalled surface. A glutinous muddy track lay before them, but they continued barely fifty metres before the police car signalled right and they turned into a small yard. To the left of them was a fairly substantial old house, though in need of some redecoration and a bit of repair to the rendering at head level. In front there was a chicken shed and a fenced compound where the shed's inhabitants scratched and pecked their way through their days. On the right-hand side there was a barn of sorts, relatively derelict but still housing some old tools and a quantity of hay.

'Seen better days,' Slonský concluded.

'Haven't we all,' the sergeant replied.

The house's back door opened and a dumpy, grey-haired woman was framed in the doorway. She rubbed her hands on her apron and squinted into the low sun.

'Mrs Gruberová?' Slonský asked.

The woman nodded.

'I'm Lieutenant Slonský of the Criminal Police in Prague. This is Officer Navrátil, who works with me. And Sergeant Tomáš and Officer Peiperová are from the local police.'

'Is something wrong? Is it Irina?'

Chapter 8

If the Minister was surprised to see Lukas again, he hid it well. He stood in front of the Prime Minister's desk for a moment, then looked around for a vacant seat.

'No point in getting ourselves comfortable,' the Prime Minister barked. 'Unpleasant business, best done quickly.'

'Unpleasant business, Prime Minister? What unpleasant business?'

The Director stepped forward and formally cautioned the Minister before telling him he was being arrested for the murder of Irina Gruberová.

'But this is preposterous!' the Minister squealed. 'She was alive and well when I left her.'

'I would strongly advise you to say no more without your lawyer present,' said the Prime Minister. 'Needless to say, I shall have to relieve you of your office. I'll go to see the President later. Perhaps you'd leave any official keys on my desk before they cart you off to pokey.'

The Prime Minister turned his back and returned to work, leaving a bewildered Minister to walk to the car in the company of Lukas and the Director. As they reached the office door, the two policemen turned and saluted smartly.

'Shame about the handcuffs,' muttered the Prime Minister.

Mrs Gruberová cried silently as Peiperová sat beside her and patted the back of her hand.

'I know this is distressing,' Slonský began, 'but we need to ask you some questions to help us find the person who did this. I'm sure you'd want to help us if you can.'

The old woman nodded mutely.

'How long had your daughter been in Prague?'

'A bit less than two years.'

'Do you know what she did for a living?'

Mrs Gruberová looked away for a brief moment, sufficient to tell Slonský that she was unhappy with the answer she had to give.

'She got a job as a dancer in a club. A man saw her in Kladno and offered her a job. It was better paid than anything she could get around here.'

'But, if you'll forgive me, it sounds as if you weren't happy with the arrangement.'

'What mother could be happy with her daughter working in such a place? Irina always said nothing nasty happened to her, but if you go around showing yourself to men like that they're bound to get ideas about the sort of girl you are.'

'You don't happen to know the name of the club?'

She shook her head. 'No. But she stopped working there after a while. She told us last September that she had a boyfriend and he didn't like her working there, so he made her give it up and gave her money instead.'

'How did you feel about that?'

'I thought he would marry her, but I got to thinking that he must already be married and that keeping her like this wasn't proper. Irina never mentioned marriage and when I raised it with her she said I was silly and marriage was old-fashioned. Well, maybe I am old-fashioned, but who'll want to marry her after she's been living with a man?' There was a pause before Mrs Gruberová choked back a sob and corrected herself. 'Who would have wanted to marry her, I mean.'

Slonský let her cry for a while in the silence. When he finally spoke, his voice was unusually soft, and there was just a hint of pain in it. 'I'll find him, Mrs Gruberová. Someone will pay for what has happened to your daughter.'

The first interview with the ex-Minister was short and entirely unproductive. It was conducted by Lukas and the Director and was punctuated by demands for lawyers to be present.

'Of course,' said the Director. 'We just wanted to give you the opportunity to avoid the wasting of police time.'

'I'm innocent!' Dr Banda insisted. 'I have told you exactly what happened.'

'Unfortunately,' the Director responded, 'that is what you have not done. You have attempted to mislead us. You said you left Miss Gruberová at her door and drove home.'

'I think I said that, yes.'

'But you know that in fact you accompanied her into her flat and made love to her there.'

Banda lowered his head. 'I admit I did that.'

'So your first statement to the police was untrue?'

'Yes.'

'A deliberate lie?'

'Yes.'

'That presents us with some difficulty, Dr Banda. You were, after all, the Minister in charge of policing. It would be reasonable, I suggest, to expect a man in such a position to offer the police every assistance when investigating a crime.'

'I didn't want it known that I was consorting with a whore.'

Lukas' face reddened. Before he knew it, he had spoken. 'Nothing we have found supports that suggestion!'

Banda raised his head slowly and fixed Lukas with an intense gaze.

'Then look harder.'

Navrátil, Slonský and Tomáš were standing outside the door, getting some fresh air while Peiperová helped Irina's mother look for any useful documents and letters.

'Sir, why do you keep saying you'll find the man who did this when we already have?'

'Because, Navrátil, I don't yet have the evidence to convict him. It's all circumstantial and a good lawyer will get him off. I need more, and the best way of getting it is to let people think I'm still looking.'

Tomáš pricked his ears up.

'You've arrested someone? Is that the boyfriend?'

'Yes,' said Slonský, 'but don't talk about it yet. I'm not confident we'll be able to keep him in custody. He can afford a good lawyer and I wouldn't be surprised if the slimy creep was at the front desk now.'

'The boyfriend?'

'No, his lawyer. Although "slimy creep" fits both of them.'

Sergeant Mucha enjoyed this part of his work. The lugubrious desk sergeant had few pleasures in his working day, and aggravating an expensive Prague lawyer came high on his list.

'Come along, Sergeant! You can't mean to tell me you're expecting to keep my client locked up like a common criminal.'

'Well, from where I'm standing a common criminal is exactly what he is, sir.'

'Do you have any evidence for that assertion?'

'Not assertion, sir; personal opinion. As for evidence, that will be disclosed to the defence in the usual way at the usual time.'

The lawyer changed tack. If the sergeant could not be browbeaten, perhaps the unctuous approach would work.

'Perhaps if you gave us an idea of the evidence you have, we might be able to explain away any little … misunderstanding there might be and save you a lot of time.'

'Your client could have saved us a lot of time by telling the truth in the first place, sir. And you'll know that I am a mere desk sergeant, so I'm hardly likely to give out information on a case the Director has taken a personal interest in.'

'Perhaps I could see the Director and explain my client's position.'

'I don't keep the Director's diary, sir. You'd have to contact his office for an appointment.'

'Very well. I can see I'm getting nowhere here. You are being extremely obstructive, Sergeant.'

'Thank you very much, sir. One does one's best.'

Mrs Gruberová had little more to tell them. She had last seen her daughter at the New Year when Irina came home for a short visit.

'Did she seem happy?'

'Yes, very happy. She said she had been taking driving lessons and was going to order a new car, so she would be able to drive down to see us more often.'

'A new car? Did she mean brand new?'

'Yes. She said she would have to wait for the dealer to get the one she wanted.'

Slonský mimed to Navrátil to make a note of that.

'Do you know the make of car?'

'A little Škoda. I don't know all the types. Just a small one, she said.'

'Did she mention the colour?'

'She liked bright colours. She wanted a red one but she wasn't sure that they did them in red.'

'Well, perhaps we can find the dealer she went to. Did she tell you about any friends in Prague?'

'Just her boyfriend.'

'Did she give him a name?'

'Not that I remember. She said he was quite famous so she never talked about him because she didn't want the press sniffing round. I said it was coming to something when a girl wouldn't tell her own mother her boyfriend's name, but she wouldn't budge. She could be very stubborn sometimes. Do you think he really is famous?'

'If he is who we think he is, then you would know of him,' Slonský replied.

'Don't you know who I am?' shouted Banda.

'Yes,' said Sergeant Mucha, 'you're the noisy little sod in cell five. Now keep it down or we'll have to get the police doctor to give you a sedative.'

'I'm your direct superior! I'm responsible for the police in this country.'

'Then you've got a lot to answer for,' said Mucha. 'They're a complete shambles. Anyway, you're nobody's superior now. You're the prisoner in cell five in a borrowed jumpsuit. Still, you've made the evening paper.'

'What does it say?' asked Banda anxiously.

'I can't remember,' sniffed Mucha. 'I only read the sports pages.'

Chapter 9

The radio news announced the removal of Dr Banda as Minister of the Interior and introduced his replacement.

'Didn't take long to sort that out,' announced Slonský. 'I bet the Prime Minister had that up his sleeve all along.'

'But now everyone knows that we've arrested Banda,' protested Navrátil. 'Every step we take will be watched.'

'Probably. But we'll just keep saying we're not talking about it. After all, it's an active crime investigation. We can't go telling the press every little thing.'

'We usually do,' said Tomáš.

'I know,' replied Slonský, 'but that's when we want to. Now we'll keep our counsel and let him sweat a bit. If we put a bit of pressure on, he'll crack. Speaking of which, Navrátil, let's drop Sergeant Tomáš off at the police station and get back to Prague. We've got some questioning to do.'

'He's very stubborn,' said Captain Lukas, 'not to mention uncooperative.'

'Yes, sir.'

'The Director got nowhere with him.'

'I dare say the Director was constrained by the burden of his position, sir.'

'What?'

'He didn't feel he could give the suspect a slap, sir. Being the Director of the Criminal Police, sir.'

'None of us can "give the suspect a slap", Slonský. Is that clear?'

'I wasn't proposing to, sir. But it won't be long before that lawyer of his springs him from custody if we don't get some more evidence.'

'Yes, he's been ringing HQ all afternoon asking to see the Director. Fortunately the Director wasn't available.'

'No, sir, he wouldn't be. He's a clever man, sir; he wouldn't make himself available with this lot going on.'

'And the lawyer is complaining about the way Sergeant Mucha spoke to him. He says Mucha was uncommonly rude.'

'I doubt that, sir. Mucha is rude to everyone. I don't think he singled out Dr Banda's lawyer.'

'Well, the Director says it's our case, so I suppose there's no harm in your questioning the suspect. But nothing untoward, Slonský! I don't want this enquiry threatened by an excess of zeal on your part.'

'Thank you very much, sir. I've never been accused of an excess of zeal before.'

Navrátil had already conducted the same dialogue eight times when he struck lucky.

'I'm looking for a car dealership that may have ordered a car for a young woman, possibly in the name of Gruberová. The chances are that the car hasn't been collected.'

'Yes, that's us. A Fabia, I think, with a nippy little engine. Hang on — yes, she ordered one about three weeks ago. It came in on Tuesday but she hasn't collected it yet.'

'I'm afraid she won't. The lady has been murdered.'

There was a little torrent of street Czech down the line.

'Had she paid a deposit?' asked Navrátil.

'A small cash deposit, but not the usual.'

'How much was left to pay?'

'Forty-nine thousand, two hundred and fifty crowns.'

Armed with this information, Navrátil set off in search of Slonský, but there was no sign of him in his office. On the basis that if he had left the building he would have passed the front desk, Navrátil went down to the lobby and interrogated Sergeant Mucha.

'Has Lieutenant Slonský gone out?'

'No, he's behind me.'

Navrátil looked closely, but there was no sign of Slonský there. Anyone is entitled to a hallucination, he thought, but an imaginary Slonský was a real lulu of a vision. It was hard to imagine any street drug that could induce such a sight.

Mucha observed the puzzled look on the young policeman's face.

'Behind the wall. He's questioning a suspect in the cells.'

'On his own? Doesn't he have to have a witness?'

'Yes and no. Yes, if he were undertaking conventional questioning he would need a witness. But he's Slonský. He has his own methods.'

Mucha turned away with a grin and shook his head in admiration for the low cunning of the old detective.

Intrigued and not a little concerned, Navrátil pushed the swing door open and looked down the spartan corridor. It was bare, except for a power lead plugged into the wall by the third cell on the left, which then snaked into cell six.

Navrátil began to walk down the corridor, vaguely aware that he could hear music and that he recognised the piece. He could also hear the unmistakable sounds of a prisoner being assaulted. Dull thuds were followed by groans, expulsions of air, and an occasional slap on skin. Fearing the worst, he quickened his pace.

Cell five was across the corridor from cell six, and as he drew level with the doors he realised that his suspicions were unfounded. The ex-Minister was in cell five, and the top of his head could be seen at intervals as he jumped to look through the door grille. Cell six certainly offered a disturbing sight, but not the one that Navrátil had expected.

Slonský was sitting on the cot, clutching a pillow to his stomach. At intervals he punched it hard, followed by a cry of pain. When he spoke it was in a higher-pitched voice than he normally used.

'No more! I'll tell you everything if you just leave me alone!'

Navrátil opened his mouth to speak but was silenced by a signal from Slonský, who held a finger across his lips before continuing, in his own voice: 'You said that before. Why should I believe you this time?' He then hit the pillow again. 'Either you co-operate or you get another one!'

Navrátil now realised that the power lead was connected to a compact disc player that was belting out Frank and Nancy Sinatra singing *Something Stupid*. Slonský turned up the volume and then emitted a completely unprovoked howl of pain.

'Not the face, Navrátil! Never hit the face!'

'What's happening in there?' yelled Banda from cell five. 'Who are you beating?'

'Mind your own business!' Slonský responded. 'We'll talk to you later.'

The track ended, but now Navrátil discovered that Slonský had set it to repeat. He was about to protest when Slonský wrapped an arm round his shoulder and steered him down the corridor to the desk. Only once the door was closed behind them did Slonský speak.

'You nearly fouled that up, lad. Still, I think it went well.'

'He'll think I've beaten a prisoner!' howled Navrátil.

'I hope so,' said Slonský. 'That was the whole point.'

'I don't understand, sir.'

'I want him to be pliable when we interview him. I need something to break that arrogant shell of his, and the prospect that we might reach across the desk and give him a biff should do nicely.'

'But he's Minister of the Interior! He'll know it's illegal for police to hit suspects.'

'Oh, Navrátil, Navrátil! What do they teach you at the academy these days?'

'So young, and so innocent!' agreed Mucha.

'You two are winding me up,' Navrátil complained. 'All right, so I don't understand. Explain it to me.'

Mucha rested his elbows on the desk and leaned forward conspiratorially.

'It's because he was Minister for the Interior that this will work.'

'Exactly,' agreed Slonský. 'It's a dead cert winner with him.'

'As you rightly point out,' Mucha began, 'a police officer mustn't lay hands on a suspect. And, as you again are correct to remind us, the Minister would know that. But if police regularly slapped suspects, would they tell the Minister?'

'Of course not! He'd be the last …'

'Enlightenment dawns!' announced Slonský. 'Exactly, my lad. He'd be the last person to know. In fact, he wouldn't want to know, because he wants the police to be effective and clear up unsolved crimes, and if a sly poke in the ribs now and then helps them to do that, he's not going to cramp our style. So naturally our dear ex-Minister takes it for granted that prisoners get clobbered, but that he doesn't hear about it.'

'It stands to reason,' Mucha chimed in. 'Entirely logical.'

'So since he is expecting a bit of police brutality, it's helpful to fall in with his wishes. If he complains, Sergeant Mucha here will show the register that proves that there was no prisoner in cell six this afternoon, so one can't have been beaten up. The poor ex-Minister must be deluded. It happens to the finest of minds when they're in solitary confinement all day.'

'He's entitled to an exercise period though, isn't he?'

'Sadly, staff cuts mean that no-one can be spared to accompany him, so on grounds of security we are unable to let him out,' Mucha declared.

'Nice touch that,' said Slonský, 'on account of it was this Minister who said that if efficiency savings meant prisoners didn't get all their exercise breaks, who cares?'

'Well, *he* does — now,' said Mucha.

'It's been an educational experience for him, then,' agreed Slonský.

'But what about the Sinatra music?' enquired Navrátil.

'I like Sinatra,' Slonský replied.

'Me too,' said Mucha.

'And I don't have a CD player at home. If I didn't play it here I'd never get to hear it.'

Mucha began to sing.

'And then I go and spoil it all by saying something stupid, like —'

'— *I love you,*' chorused the two older men.

'You're barking mad, the pair of you!' Navrátil announced. 'You pretend to beat up a prisoner and you play music at the same time so you can sing along.'

'Ah, no,' Slonský interrupted, 'allow me to correct you there. I don't sing while I'm thumping suspects. As you've just discovered, my singing voice definitely constitutes cruel and unusual punishment.'

'You're not kidding there,' said Mucha.

'No,' continued Slonský, 'Sinatra has to manage without me. But he does a good job of masking the noises, which means that our diminutive friend in cell five only catches snatches of what is going on, which makes him doubly suspicious. His imagination will come up with things we couldn't begin to stage.'

Mucha chuckled. 'Remember that hoodlum who convinced himself that his mate was being anally gang-banged by the Prague police?'

'Yes,' said Slonský. 'I never knew how he arrived at that conclusion. But he confessed double quick when we opened his cell door.'

'But when they discover they've been conned, won't they tell the court we've obtained a confession under duress?'

'No, Navrátil, because they know by then that there was no duress and that they'll look like grade A idiots if they claim that there was. Who wants to stand up in court and say that they only confessed because they thought that the sound of Sergeant Mucha pumping up his bicycle tyres was actually due to their colleague being gang-banged by a bunch of shirt-lifters?'

'Lucky he's so short,' opined Mucha. 'It enhances the effect.'

'Too right,' agreed Slonský. 'There must be a lot of things in life he doesn't quite see. Fortunately he's too short to see that there was nobody in cell six. Leave him to stew a few minutes, then go and retrieve the CD player.'

'Will do. I might give the floor a quick mop too.'

'That'd be good. There's a theatrical side to you I hadn't anticipated, Mucha.'

'That's me,' agreed Mucha. 'Give me an audience of one and watch me perform.'

Navrátil had collected the car dealer's statement, which Slonský was reading through.

'That's clear enough. So that explains the forty-nine thousand two hundred and fifty crowns. But what about the other two hundred thousand? If Banda withdrew the smaller sum to pay for the car, what was the two hundred thousand for?'

'Rent? Deposit on a flat?'

'Who knows? And why insert it in Irina's whatsit? Why not take it back again if it links him to her?'

'Forgot it?'

'No, he can't have done. Any way you look at it he inserted it after he strangled her. Why give away the money?'

'Maybe it was an impulse.'

'But he came equipped with a plastic bank bag. They won't have given it to him like that. He put it in there. Do we know for sure that it was the Minister that withdrew the money?'

Navrátil waved a videocassette.

'Bank security footage from the branch by the castle. You can see the Minister making the withdrawal, and the time and date stamp on the tape matches the date on the bank statement.'

Slonský laid the cassette next to the bank statement and the car dealer's statement and scrutinised each in turn.

'What's wrong, sir? It all fits.'

'Yes,' said Slonský, 'it all fits. Except for one thing. Banda isn't an idiot. And we still don't know why he killed Irina.'

'He doesn't seem to be heartbroken. Maybe he fell out of love with her and was worried she would spill the beans.'

'She knew the score. There would be nothing traceable. If it got out it would hardly damage him terminally. One day he would dump her and she'd just have to dust herself off and get on with her life. And why draw out the money if he was about to strangle her anyway?'

'To lull her into a false sense of security? Put her off her guard? If he gave her the cash for the car she'd think he still loved her. Perhaps he'd promised the money — after all, the car was due in that weekend. You can imagine her telling him she needed the money that night to get the car a day or two later.'

'But if he was having second thoughts, why didn't he tell her to take a running jump before he gave her the money?'

'A pay-off? Sort of "Leave me in peace and I'll buy you a car".'

'Possibly. But why take her out to dinner, then?'

'So he could tell her in public and she couldn't make a scene.'

'But then he drove her home and they made love. I haven't had much to do with women for many a long day, lad, but I can't see a girl you've just dumped inviting you into her bed.'

'I suppose not. Not that I would know,' Navrátil added hurriedly.

'Well, there's only one way to find out. Let's go and interview him.'

'When you say "Interview him"…'

'Cassette recorder, no violence, all above board, Navrátil. What do you take me for?'

Mucha and a junior officer were standing guard over Banda, who sat at the interview table, a hunched figure in a jumpsuit that was at least one size too big for him. The ends of the legs flopped over his shoes and he had turned the cuffs back to allow his hands some freedom.

'Official interview,' announced Slonský. 'The caution still stands.'

'I don't want him near me,' squealed Banda.

'Navrátil? Why not?'

'He hits people! I heard you tell him off for doing it.'

'I don't think so. Navrátil, have I ever told you off for hitting a suspect?'

'No, sir.'

'That would be a very serious disciplinary offence indeed. But since Dr Banda has concerns, why don't you sit by the door over there, out of arm's reach. I mean, out of harm's way.'

'What did you do to that unfortunate in the cell opposite?'

'What unfortunate? What cell? Mucha, do you know anything about this?'

'No, Lieutenant. That cell isn't occupied and hasn't been since Sunday night.'

'You were in there earlier,' Banda screamed. 'I saw you go in. And there were those horrible noises.'

'I don't think Mr Sinatra would be pleased to hear you describe his singing as horrible noises. You want to watch that — he had some bad friends, you know.'

'Good thing he's dead,' Mucha added, 'or he might have been upset by that.'

'I think you must be over-excited,' said Slonský in his most soothing voice. 'Shall we get on with the interview?'

He recorded the date and time, and listed those present. On hearing his name, Mucha pointed to the door and slipped out.

'Sergeant Mucha has just left the room,' Slonský said. 'Why he couldn't do that before I recorded his name, I have no idea.'

'I'm saying nothing without my lawyer present,' declared Banda.

'Very wise, sir. But of course your co-operation or lack of it may be a factor in court.'

'I used to tell my clients not to talk until I got there.'

'Well, you are here,' Slonský pointed out, 'so we can begin. The account you gave of your evening with Miss Gruberová contained, as you have admitted, some inaccuracies. Would you now like to tell us what really happened?'

Banda sat with his arms folded.

'The accused declines to answer. Then I'll tell you what I think happened. You rang up and arranged to meet. At the end of your working day, around eight o'clock, you met up for dinner at the restaurant you named. The waiting staff confirm that you were both there that evening. During the evening you presented Miss Gruberová with the money for a car that you had promised. She was very grateful. She invited you in when you drove her home, and the pair of you made love. At some time after you climaxed you strangled her, inserted the car money in her vagina, dressed her again and drove her to Holešovice, where you dumped her body by the main railway station.'

'Fiction. Pure fiction,' said Banda.

'It can't all be fiction,' Slonský retorted, 'because some of it is lifted directly from your statements. And when I dropped in on the restaurant last night they agreed that the two of you had dinner there.'

'It's accurate enough until we get to the climax. Then I dressed and left.'

'Did she dress?'

'I think she said she was going to take a shower. She wasn't dressed when I left.'

'Did you see anyone else on your way out?'

'No, but there must have been, I suppose, given that someone killed her soon after I went.'

'Or you did it yourself, of course. So where could this invisible man have been hiding, do you think?'

'I don't know. Since I didn't see him, how could I know where he was?'

'Let's return to the matter of the car money. Do you admit going to a bank near your office on the morning of the killing and withdrawing the money for the car?'

'Yes.'

'Why?'

'I'd promised it. I like to keep my promises.'

'There's a bit of a fine distinction between refusing the money, and giving it but then murdering the recipient, wouldn't you say?'

'This is preposterous!'

'So you wouldn't agree with me?'

'No!'

'So the accused sees no distinction at all between refusing to keep his promise and keeping it but snatching the money back.'

Banda's hand snaked out and switched off the cassette. Slonský stared him down for a few seconds, then he turned the recorder back on.

'The recorder was turned off by the accused and was off for less than twenty seconds,' Slonský recorded. 'Isn't that the case, Dr Banda?'

'Yes.'

'I don't think we heard you.'

'Yes! Yes, I turned the tape off. No, it wasn't off for long.'

'Temper, temper!' cooed Slonský. 'Would you like us to give you a moment to collect your thoughts?'

'There's no need. I'm perfectly collected, thank you.'

'Would you like a glass of water?'

'No, thank you.'

'Perhaps a biscuit?'

'No, thank you.'

'Do you have an anger management problem? I only ask because you're clenching your fists.'

'That's because I find you intensely annoying.'

'Just doing my job, sir. Trying to find the murderer of a young Czech girl whom you admit to having screwed just minutes before she was strangled.'

'We don't know it was only minutes before.'

'*You* don't know that,' agreed Slonský.

'That's it,' Banda announced. 'I'm not saying any more until my lawyer is here.'

'Fair enough,' said Slonský. 'Navrátil, call Sergeant Mucha and have the accused returned to his cell.'

Mucha and the young uniformed policeman escorted Banda to the cells. Slonský waited until they had gone, then turned to Navrátil with a broad smile on his face.

'That went very well, I think. Beer and a sausage, Navrátil?'

The bottle smashed against the brick wall, and the thrower sank back onto a bench in the square. A stout figure in a dark coat slipped onto the bench beside him.

'They killed my girl. Where were you when they killed my girl?'

'I know,' said Tomáš. 'Come on, I'll give you a lift home.'

'Aren't you going to arrest me like normal?'

'Not tonight, Václav. You're entitled to throw a bottle or two tonight.'

Chapter 10

The morning newspapers made interesting reading, thought Slonský. The sacking of the Minister and his arrest by the police were given due prominence on the front pages of all the papers, except one tabloid that chose to lead with a story about a television personality who had denied having cosmetic surgery. The press release announcing the arrest had come, by agreement, from the Prime Minister's office; the police had declined to give any details of the charge, nor to reveal where the ex-Minister was being held, though every resident of Prague knew where that would be. And the majority of them were wrong. If everyone arrested finished up at Pankrác, it would need a capacity bigger than the Sparta football stadium.

It was the best time of the day, thought Slonský, the half hour or so before everyone began arriving. Time when he could do his best thinking. Today his best thinking was devoted to one subject: why would an intelligent man like Banda, who had been the personification of caution all his adult life, do something as profoundly stupid as inserting nearly a quarter of a million crowns in his girlfriend's vagina? Was he two-faced enough to make love to her one minute, and despise her enough to humiliate her corpse like that a few minutes later? Well, he was a politician. Being two-faced probably came naturally to him. But even so …

Captain Lukas entered the room.

'Is it going to stick?' he asked.

'I'm not sure, sir,' Slonský replied. 'We'd best be cautious about what we say.'

'Thank you,' said Lukas. 'I'll make sure we are. What worries you?'

'I don't believe a man like Banda does silly things. And this was a profoundly silly thing to do. If Banda turned murderer he'd be better at it than this.'

Lukas pulled up a chair and sat down heavily.

'Josef, we've both known intelligent men do really stupid things.'

'Yes, I suppose we have. But this man does nothing by impulse. He's a cold, unemotional piece of flint. If he put the money inside her he did it for a reason. And I can't think what that reason could be. Until I can, I can't be sure he's our man.'

'The evidence tells its own story.'

They sat in silence for a few moments as Slonský revisited the evidence trail in his head.

'He seems guilty. I can't explain how he could be innocent in the face of the evidence.'

Lukas lifted himself out of the chair with a degree of effort.

'Well, we all know things aren't always what they seem.'

As the Captain headed for his office, Slonský repeated his words to himself. 'Things aren't always what they seem. No, they aren't. Why aren't they?'

When Navrátil arrived about a quarter of an hour later he found Slonský in a state not far off a trance. He was gazing fixedly at a blank wall and mumbling as if reciting his catechism.

'Are you all right, sir?'

'Never better. Lukas is a genius, you know that?'

'Captain Lukas? Our Captain Lukas?'

'Things are not always what they seem. That's what he said. And he's right.'

'Sir?'

'Navrátil, what do we know? We know that the Minister made love to Miss Gruberová, and that she was strangled very soon afterwards; so soon, in fact, that we can probably pin it on him. But we've been assuming he was alone.'

'He was, sir. He drove her back from the restaurant. And she'd hardly do … what she did … in front of an audience.'

'But suppose he'd arranged for an accomplice to be there. She was a fit young woman and he isn't exactly Samson, is he? How did a little runt like him pin down a girl like that? If he'd knocked her out I could understand it, but she was strangled. She fought — remember the leather under her nails? — so how did he subdue her? But if he had an accomplice, it's easy. He makes love to her, leaves the door open when he leaves; the accomplice comes in, strangles the girl, and there's no sign of forced entry. If the Minister is quick enough he can even get home to establish an alibi. Maybe his wife isn't lying; maybe he really was home when Irina was killed.'

'But if a third party did it, why insert the money? Wouldn't a hired criminal just pocket it? There's no hint that he was disturbed, and he disposed of the body as and when he wanted.'

Slonský mulled this argument over for a while to the accompaniment of mumbling and staring as before.

'Who wanted her dead, Navrátil? Who is most likely to want a mistress out of the way?'

'A wife, I suppose.'

'Exactly. A wife who gives her husband an alibi.'

'It's a pretty feeble, inexact alibi, sir.'

'Yes, but we can't prove it isn't true. We've been looking at the alibi as Banda's alibi provided by his wife. Actually, they're guaranteeing each other. And if they're in it together, it could be false as a ninety-crown note.'

'You've lost me, sir.'

'Mrs Bandová finds out about the girlfriend. She makes a scene. The girlfriend can't harm Banda's career — he'd shrug it off, like so many do — but if his wife divorces him and sells the story to the press, he's in trouble. He agrees to get rid of Irina, but Mrs Bandová knows of only one way to guarantee that he doesn't go on seeing his mistress behind her back. So they cook up a plan. He'll be the usual loving friend, take her to dinner, take her home, make sure he leaves DNA traces on her, make sure there is evidence tying him to the crime. Then he leaves and establishes an alibi while the murderer kills her. It might be Mrs Bandová herself or, more likely, someone she recruited. Now, here's the cunning bit. If we don't charge Banda, suspicion could fall on the real murderer, so Mrs Bandová's security depends on Banda being charged. The best guarantee of non-prosecution she can have is if we think he's guilty but got away with it. We'll devote all our efforts to nailing him and forget to look for anyone else.'

'But he might get convicted. How does that look so cunning?'

'Because he won't. We can't quite prove it was him. His lawyer will ask whether he is so stupid as to leave his sperm inside the victim, or to put money we can easily trace to him inside her vagina. He'll create just enough doubt to get his man off. Banda will threaten to sue the rear end off anyone who accuses him of having done it, and he's protected from a life in jail because he has already been acquitted and he can't be charged with the same crime again.'

Navrátil was unconvinced, but could not disprove the argument.

'So how do we test this theory, sir?'

'Cherchez la femme, Navrátil.'

'Sir?'

'The woman, lad. Let's go and talk to the Minister's wife. If she genuinely didn't know about the mistress, my theory falls to bits. But if she did know, we have to put the frighteners on them by hinting that we're after her rather than him. If she is in the dock, the sperm evidence and the money don't help her. Far from making her look too stupid to be guilty, they make her look like a jealous wife who gave a whore her earnings after she killed her.'

'I'll get the car, sir.'

'You do that, Navrátil. Meanwhile I'll go and get some essential detective equipment.'

'Sir?'

'A flask of coffee and some pastries, my boy. I can't think on an empty stomach.'

Chapter 11

Banda's wife opened the door herself. She was a tall, attractive woman, with chestnut brown hair that just brushed her shoulders, and some expensive-looking pearl stud earrings. Her eyes, though green in colour, flashed red with annoyance when she discovered who they were.

'Should I call my lawyer?'

'If you wish, but we don't intend this as a formal interview.'

'You say that now, but if I say something that helps your case against my poor husband, you'll use it, caution or no caution.'

'There are rules about that, madam. And I don't need to bolster the case against your husband. I want to hear your side of it all.'

'Mine? I have nothing to do with it.'

'Your loyalty to your husband does you credit, Mrs Bandová, particularly since he has admitted that he betrayed you with a younger woman.'

'Not to me, he hasn't.'

'Perhaps not. But you're an educated woman, and the Minister isn't the sort of man to spend his life with someone who isn't an intellectual match. You've got brains; you must have known something was going on.'

'Brains, yes, but not experience. I don't know what a man does when he has a mistress. He didn't buy her jewellery and leave it lying around, if that's what you're getting at.'

'What about your intuition? Didn't that tell you something? Aren't women supposed to know these things?'

She chewed her knuckle for a moment in deep thought, as if the action would help her keep something to herself. It failed.

'He had been a little distant.'

'Distant?'

'Undemonstrative.'

'You mean he slept in the spare room?'

'No! But it's certainly true that he showed less interest in me.'

'But you didn't know Miss Gruberová?'

'Certainly not. She wasn't the sort of woman I would meet socially, Lieutenant.'

'Your husband tells us she was helping him to plan your birthday party.'

'Does he? Far-sighted of him. It isn't for another eight months yet.'

Slonský smiled gently.

'Looks like he's slipped us both a pack of lies, then.'

'He's not a bad man, Lieutenant. He's been incredibly stupid, but he's not wicked.'

'I wouldn't argue with that assessment, madam, and coming from his wife it carries some weight. But was he stupid enough to kill?'

'Maybe. But he couldn't swat a fly. He hasn't the stomach to be a killer. If he was going to turn to crime it would be something like fraud, something where he could pit his wits against yours. Killing someone he didn't give a toss about isn't his style.'

'Didn't he love her?'

'Albert doesn't love anyone except himself, Lieutenant. He's fond of me and the children, but he's not a loving person.'

'So why have a mistress, if not for love?'

'I don't know. Because he can, because he likes the thrill of his little secret, because his friends have all got one. I don't know.'

'Forgive me, but I have to ask. Could it be just for sex?'

She gave a small, but mirthless laugh.

'His appetite did not exceed mine. If quantity was all he wanted, he could have topped up here. But he is a busy man and he was often "tired" at the end of the day.'

'So he'd rather have burger out than steak at home.'

'Indelicate but accurate. Steak was waiting for him.'

'Did you have Irina Gruberová killed, madam?'

'Irina? Is that her name? No, I didn't. I wouldn't have known where to find her.'

'You don't seem to bear her as much animosity as I'd have expected.'

'In what way?'

'You don't call her a whore or bitch.'

'If she'd been either of those things Albert wouldn't have touched her. He was fastidious, you know. Very fussy about things like clean white sheets.'

Slonský returned his hat to his head. His voice carried a definite tone of sadness as he told her what she already feared.

'Your husband could spend a long time in prison, Mrs Bandová. Maybe he didn't personally strangle Miss Gruberová, but it could well be that he ordered it to be done.'

'Both those thoughts had occurred to me, Lieutenant. Neither is pleasant.'

'What will you do?'

'I have no idea. He's my husband. I took a vow and I always intended to keep it. I can't give up at the first little difficulty.'

Slonský raised his hat, bade her a good evening, and walked back to the car with a heavy tread. After he took his seat, he remained for a few moments staring into the darkness in silence before motioning to Navrátil to start the engine.

'A remarkable woman, that. He doesn't deserve her.'

'You've given up on the idea that she might have organised it, then?'

'I never really thought it, but we had to take it into account. Did you see the family photographs on the side table?'

'No, sir. You were in the way.'

'Nice kids. Two of them. Unfortunately the boy looks like his father, but we all have our cross to bear. Put your foot down, lad, I could do with a beer or two.'

'Were you ever married, sir?'

Slonský turned in his seat to inspect Navrátil closely.

'Now what made you ask that?'

'Sorry, sir. Just curiosity. I've never heard anyone mention a wife but you talked to Mrs Bandová as if you knew a bit about marriage.'

'I talk to Novák about steeplechasing but I'm not a horse, Navrátil.'

'No, sir. Sorry, sir.'

'Yes, as it happens I was married, Navrátil. In my salad days, when I was green. Not long after I joined the police, I married a girl called Věra. Tall, blonde, bit of a catch if I do say so myself. We met at some Party function or other.'

'Love at first sight?'

'No, I don't really know what brought us together. Probably the local Party Secretary telling us both we should be thinking about getting married, so doing it with each other seemed the most labour-saving arrangement. He believed it was every Czech's duty to produce two little Czechs to keep the country populated.'

'Children?'

'No, puppies. Of course, children! We didn't get that far, though. A combination of shift work for me, a bit of grief about the Prague Spring and the fact that she found some leather-jacketed poet who persuaded her that getting shafted on a rug was an authentic piece of romance. She packed her bags and I was left on my own.'

'The Prague Spring, sir?'

'Surely you've heard of it, Navrátil. Or don't they teach you about our nation's history at school these days?'

'Yes, I've heard of it, sir. But I didn't understand why it interfered in your marriage.'

Slonský sighed.

'Pull in over there, lad, and let's have a sausage at that bar.'

Slonský took a large bite and chewed rhythmically.

'I wonder what domestic animal this is made from? Hand me the pickles, son.'

Navrátil sipped his beer, feeling a little shamefaced that he had asked the question in the first place. It was really none of his business, and he had no idea whether there was still an open wound in Slonský's heart, though it was very hard to think of Slonský as a man with tender feelings. It was rather like considering that a hippopotamus might enjoy ballet.

'How old were you when the Communists were turfed out, Navrátil?'

'Five or six, sir.'

'I thought so. It was grim, Navrátil. Grim, joyless, frightening, stifling, monochrome, all the things you'll have heard and more. I joined the police in 1967 as a young man. They didn't have the academy in those days, so I went in as a humble cadet. I must have been a bit younger than you are now. They gave me a uniform, proper boots for the first time in my life, a gun — and a fairly healthy wage by the standards of the day — in exchange for which I was expected to defend the motherland against capitalist aggressors, Yankee imperialism and old women crossing the road in the wrong place. Aren't you thirsty?'

'Just taking my time, sir. Don't let me stop you.'

'Don't worry, you won't.'

He waved to attract the waiter.

'Give the cat another diuretic and fill this up. So, Navrátil, our great nation was choking itself slowly, and then along came Dubček.'

'I remember him.'

'You remember him as an old man. He was impressive then, but as a party leader he was electrifying. For the first time we had someone who seemed to understand what a damn awful life lots of us led, and we believed he could change it. We had newspapers that told the truth. Some of them even contained some news other than tractor output figures and the various meetings of the bigwigs. We heard that not everything in our Socialist utopia was going exactly to plan. People managed to get on the television to say that the roads were full of potholes and they'd been waiting five years for a motorbike. It may not seem much to you, Navrátil, but it was a big deal to us. It was during the Prague Spring that I got married. It seemed like a time for new starts. Then we discovered the Russians were cheesed off about it all.'

'They invaded, didn't they?'

'No, lad, they were invited in to restore law and order and provide fraternal support to the Czech workers. Or some such claptrap. Yes, they invaded. Dubček was carted off and we got Husák. Two Slovaks, note, but one of them wasn't bad despite that. Husák didn't hold with all this freedom. Steadily he wound the clock back and repression was restored, and who do you think got the job of doing the repressing?'

'The Army?'

'Husák wasn't sure that they could be trusted, at least not alone. And he wasn't sure we could be either. But by getting the police and army to do it together and report on each other's performance, he kept us both in check. And that's when

Věra started giving me a hard time. She said I was betraying the Spring movement and I ought to resign. I didn't think resignation was an option, unless you enjoy a stay in Pankrác. It seemed that everything that happened was a direct consequence of my inadequacies. When Jan Palach burned himself to death at the top of Wenceslas Square, I got the blame. She said it was people like me who drove him to it. As it happened, I was over the river and didn't even hear about it until she told me. I sometimes used to wonder if I had been there, would I have put the flames out to save his life, or let him burn so he could complete his sacrifice?'

'Would you?'

'I still don't know, and if I don't know now, I never will. It's been nearly forty years, and it seems like only weeks ago. When I finished work the next day I walked up to the top of the square. There were workmen scrubbing the ground to remove the charring. He hadn't died yet, but the doctors couldn't save him. I don't know how hard they tried. Alive, he was just a student, but dead, he spoke for all of us. I stood where he had burned and then — I don't know what came over me — I saluted.'

Slonský swilled his glass around and inspected the eddies in his drink.

'Policemen weren't too popular in Prague just then. You'd get barged in the trams and people would accidentally stamp on your feet. Someone spat on my back when I was on the beat. But when I brought my arm down to my side one of the workmen clapped his hand on my shoulder and muttered "You're all right, son". No praise I've ever had has meant as much to me as that.'

They sat for a while in silence. Navrátil felt that he should let the other man speak first.

'I think I've had enough, Navrátil. Let's go home.'

Chapter 12

Slonský was sitting at his desk in the morning, shuffling sheets of paper and drawing lines connecting phrases on them, when Navrátil approached him with an outstretched hand containing a paper towel.

'What's that?'

'I had a parcel when I got home. My mum's been baking. Try one.'

Slonský peered into the towel. There was a small strudel.

'I can't take your last pastry.'

'I've got a tinful.'

'Oh, well, in that case, thank you very much!'

Slonský took a bite and rolled it over his tongue.

'Your mum's not a bad pastrycook, Navrátil. You'll have a hard time finding a girl who can cook like that.'

'They're out there, sir. My generation's not that different to yours.'

'No, I don't suppose it is. We all think the younger generation is going to hell in a handcart. You will when you're my age. Listen to me, I sound like my dad.'

'Was he like you, then?'

'Depends what you mean by "like me". He had a heartbeat and testicles, but that's about it for resemblance, so far as I can remember. Now, to work, son! Last night I had a brainwave. Perhaps the Minister's car would have some traces of Irina's dead body in it, so I got forensics onto it first thing.'

'And?'

'I don't know yet. They don't seem to start till eight. The snag is, we know the live Irina was in the car, so I'm not sure if they're clever enough to distinguish material from the dead Irina. It may just prove what we already know, but it's worth a try. Now, what are you going to do today?'

'Whatever you tell me to, sir.'

'No, lad, no clues! I want you to tell me what you think you should be doing.'

Navrátil had not expected an initiative test, and was momentarily nonplussed.

'Well, if the Minister did it, or caused it to be done, then he might have been spotted leaving.'

'Nobody owned up to that the other night. Waste of time doing more of the same.'

'Then we need to shake his alibi. See if we can get him rattled by making him repeat his story over and over to see if he forgets something.'

80

'Worth a try. But he's a politician, Navrátil. Telling the same lie repeatedly is something he can do with his eyes shut. We need to up the stress levels a bit. Why don't you ask Mucha for his mobile phone, then meet me in cell eight.'

'Eight? Who's in eight?'

'No-one yet. But there will be.'

'You can use my phone if you want, sir.'

'Thanks, Navrátil, but yours is a bit modern for me. Mucha has a particularly fine old phone.'

Navrátil was getting used to some unusual requests, but this one was a little more than normally abnormal.

Nevertheless, he did as he was asked and around half an hour later he bore a satchel into the corridor leading to the cells, and found cell eight at the far end on the left.

Slonský was washing some towels in a large bucket.

'Ah, there you are. Plonk it by the table there.'

Slonský spread a wet towel on the floor and stood an old metal-framed chair on it. Taking his handcuffs from his pocket, he attached one end to the chair and left the other dangling.

'Now, lad, be a little angel and tell Mucha we're ready.'

Ready for what, thought Navrátil as he walked back to the desk. The mind boggled.

'The Lieutenant says he's ready,' Navrátil announced. 'What for?'

Mucha shook his head and smiled.

'He's a naughty boy sometimes. You've got to hand it to him, life around Slonský is never dull.'

Navrátil returned to the cell and waited. Plainly nobody was going to tell him anything.

After a few minutes the door was pushed open and Banda walked in. He was naked apart from a large red towel.

As soon as he saw Slonský he turned on his heel and tried to leave, but Mucha blocked the doorway and pushed the ex-Minister into the room.

'Take a seat,' said Slonský. 'Cuff him to the chair, Sergeant — right hand only, he'll need his left hand. He's left-handed, you see.'

'What are you doing?' squealed Banda. 'What's going on? You said I was going to take a shower.'

Slonský reached into his trouser pocket and unfolded a piece of paper.

'Brno, last March. Remember?'

He began reading from the press cutting.

'"We must not forget the rights of victims. We cannot allow excessively liberal ideas of human rights to prevent our bringing criminals to justice. I will expect the police to be vigorous in pursuing, arresting and questioning suspects." I found that very inspiring. It sets a tone, doesn't it? One of your best speeches, if I may say so.'

'You didn't bring me here to ask for my autograph.'

'Only on a statement. Anyway, you and I are going to have a little chat.'

Slonský opened the satchel and extracted a brown bakelite box which he flipped open. He lifted out a telephone handset and put it on the table.

'We won't be needing that,' he said.

There was a roll of flex in the box, consisting of red and black wires twisted together. He unwound a few inches and attached the ends to the terminals on the hand-cranked generator of the field telephone.

'I'll do the business end, Navrátil. All I need you to do is to crank that handle a couple of times. It doesn't need much.'

Navrátil looked doubtful but did as he was asked. Slonský held the tips of the wires a couple of centimetres apart and appeared satisfied as a spark leaped between them.

'You just can't beat old-time Czech engineering, Navrátil. Can't have been used for twenty years and still starts on the button. Watch and learn, lad. It's very important to earth the wires before the next bit, or someone could get a nasty shock.'

He wrapped one wire round the metal handcuff and stood poised with the other.

'Now, where does this go?'

Banda tried to pull his arm out of the handcuffs.

'This is outrageous. I am not going to confess under duress. You know it won't be admitted in court.'

'I just want the truth,' said Slonský. 'Court can wait. Once we know what happened, we can find the evidence. Of course, back in the good old days, we'd just manufacture evidence if it helped us get a conviction. This takes you back, doesn't it, Mucha? I didn't think we'd see our old friend again. Think of all the sterling service this little chap has done over the years.'

He smiled at Banda.

'If this terminal could talk he could reel off a list of celebrity genitals you wouldn't believe.'

Banda tried to get to his feet but the handcuffs hindered him and his bare feet slipped as the wet towel slithered beneath him. Mucha grasped him firmly round the shoulders and pushed him down onto the chair.

'No, don't!'

The ex-Minister was wild-eyed with fear. Navrátil stepped forward to intervene but as he moved he saw Slonský frowning at him.

'Did you arrange to have Irina Gruberová killed?'

'No! Why would I? We were having fun together.'

'So why pay her off? A parting gift?'

'I promised her a car. I kept my promise. I never intended her any harm.'

'So if you didn't kill her, who did?'

'How should I know? It wasn't me! You have to believe me.'

Slonský grasped Banda's chin and forced him to look into his eyes.

'You're wrong there. I don't have to believe you. I can believe what I want.'

Banda struggled but Mucha had him in a tight grip.

Despite squirming and throwing his upper body from side to side, Banda could not escape, and presently began to weep.

'Don't do this! I behaved badly, but I'm not a murderer. I ought to have cared more when she died, but I couldn't let you see how I felt. She was a sweet girl, and I would never have harmed her, I swear.'

Slonský nodded, and Mucha took a step back.

The prisoner continued to sob, and wiped his nose and eyes on a dry towel that Mucha gave him.

'Take him to the showers, Sergeant, and let him tidy himself up.'

Mucha steered Banda through the door, while Slonský picked up the wet towel and the field telephone and walked off down the corridor, Navrátil chasing him as he went.

'What were you doing there, sir? You can't do that to a suspect!'

'I just have. Worked, didn't it? Just like it always did in the past. If that wasn't the truth, I don't know what is.'

'He could report you.'

'What for? Helping him prove his innocence? I don't think so.'

'You threatened and humiliated him.'

'I don't know if he would have got that much of a shock, because I've never actually needed to do that. Just showing them the kit is enough. In medieval times the day before you tortured somebody you showed him the tools of the trade, then you left him to think. I wouldn't have given him a shock. But he had to believe I might do it. I was taking a chance because he might be stubborn enough to call my bluff, but you have to give it a try, don't you?'

'I don't believe what I've just seen,' Navrátil muttered. 'You terrorised him.'

'Don't come over all bleeding heart with me, lad,' snarled Slonský. 'I've got one aim, to find Irina Gruberová's killer, and that's what I'll do, whatever it takes. She deserves that. And, by the way, I wasn't the one who was turning the crank handle.'

He shoved the swing doors open and disappeared from view, leaving Navrátil standing in the corridor, confused and just a little bit frightened himself.

Slonský and Navrátil waited patiently as Lukas digested the information they had just imparted.

'You think he's innocent after all? I can't see the Prime Minister being too happy that he sacked a minister who turns out not to be guilty.'

'Everyone is guilty, sir,' offered Slonský. 'They may not be guilty of what they're charged with, but everyone has done something.'

'Cynical, and hardly reassuring,' Lukas observed.

'But true, sir.'

'You may be right, but I'm not sure that it will comfort the Prime Minister.'

'If we're asked, sir, the reason for the Minister's dismissal is surely that he failed to co-operate with our enquiries, thereby failing to meet the ethical requirements of his office.'

'That's very literate of you, Slonský. I'll just make a note for future reference.'

'On top of that, he's a lying little adulterer who didn't give a fig for his adoring girlfriend.'

'I won't make a note of that, Slonský.'

'Very good, sir.'

'So when are we going to release him?'

'Do we have to? He's stopped demanding his freedom. And he might not want to face the press. Besides which, the public may want us to arrest someone else if we let him go. All in all, it's probably better if we keep him banged up for a while.'

'There are limits, Slonský. If his lawyer kicks up it'll probably be only a day before he has to be set free.'

'I think we could probably still get a conviction with the evidence we have, sir. The fact that my private intuition tells me he probably didn't do it is irrelevant.'

Lukas cleared his throat noisily.

'Was that a meaningful harrumph, sir?'

'I think,' Lukas mused, 'that we might not yet discover the Minister's innocence and we could reasonably continue to think of him as the prime suspect.'

'Definitely, sir. He must be our prime suspect, because he's our only suspect.'

Slonský beamed benignly.

'There are times,' Lukas opined, 'when I think you may be the nearest thing we have to a Good Policeman Švejk, Slonský. Insubordinate, in an innocent, non-threatening sort of way.'

'Thank you, sir.'

'But where do we go now? If not Banda, then who?'

'I honestly don't know, sir.'

Navrátil was surprised to find that Slonský stopped only briefly at the office to collect his hat and coat before marching purposefully out into the street.

'Where are we going, sir?'

'To do some research, Navrátil. We need an environment suitable for deep thinking and reflection, free from distractions. And here it is.'

'A bar?'

'Beer, sausages, comfortable chairs — what more could we want? I need to think hard. Be a good lad and amuse yourself while I get my brain oiled.'

'There must be something more useful I can do.'

'No doubt. And when you think of it, do it. Just don't ask me for suggestions.'

With which, Slonský pushed the door open and was swallowed into the darkness, leaving Navrátil standing with his hands in his pockets and his mouth half open.

Navrátil had an idea. It was a peculiar idea, and he could not quite see where it would lead, but he had nothing else to offer, so he grabbed his file and marched upstairs to see if Klinger was free.

Klinger listened carefully to Navrátil's questions. They showed an uncommon degree of shrewdness, he thought. Someday Navrátil may have a future in the fraud department, provided Slonský did not ruin him with his addiction to beer, sausages and untidy mental habits.

As for Navrátil, he returned to the office with a sense that he had an expert's backing for the bizarre theory that he was beginning to form. He was no wiser about where it was leading, but in a landscape with no signposts, the smallest marker is a handy thing to have.

As it happened, Navrátil was crestfallen to discover that Slonský had independently arrived at the same odd notion.

'You think someone is out to frame Banda?'

'I can't see how else to explain it all,' Navrátil replied.

Slonský perched his feet on the desk.

'You're probably right, but it leaves us having to think of a perpetrator and a motive. I agree that he is being framed, but I can't think who would do it and why.'

'Someone who wants his job?'

'Another corrupt minister? Two, in the same government? Surely not! Navrátil, you'll get a reputation for cynicism. Still, it would be good fun to tell the Prime Minister he's got to sack another minister. Wouldn't do much for team spirit, banging one minister up for trying to frame another one.'

'But you understand the point I was making, sir?'

'Oh, yes, Navrátil. You did well. The Minister said what he said about the cash withdrawal, and it's a key bit of evidence. I just can't see who it points at.'

There was a critical story in the evening newspaper, claiming that Banda was unlikely to be charged and that the police were no nearer finding an alternative suspect.

'This is appalling!' Lukas protested. 'It undermines all we're trying to do.'

'Yes, sir,' agreed Slonský. 'It's true, too.'

'That is quite beside the point! This is speculation of the worst kind. We must answer it with action, Slonský. We must ram these words down the journalist's throat. I cannot imagine what he thought he was doing.'

Navrátil had not had the opportunity to read the article, but studied it as they walked back to their office.

'Doesn't this make your blood boil, sir?'

'You get used to it, Navrátil.'

'But where did they get this from? There's only you, me and maybe Mucha who could have known this.'

'As Captain Lukas said, it's speculation of the worst kind. Pure guesswork.'

'Who is this journalist anyway? Valentin?'

'Come along, lad. I've got to meet someone in the Old Town. You can come too.'

The meeting was, predictably, in a bar. The bar was, equally predictably, not particularly select in either its setting or its clientele. A scruffy middle-aged man sat in a corner trying to complete a puzzle in a scrunched-up newspaper, inexpertly folded. To Navrátil's surprise, Slonský bought three beers and placed one of them in front of the man.

'This, Navrátil, is Mr Valentin.'

Valentin nodded a greeting.

'Job suit you?' he asked.

'Very good. I especially liked the bit about muddled leadership of the investigation and whether the involvement of a minister had led to higher ranks becoming involved who no longer had day-to-day experience of murder inquiries.'

'That's word for word. You must actually have read it.'

'You mean in the paper, or when I helped you write it?'

'You disparage my talents, sir. I demand satisfaction! I have a reputation as a sozzled hack to maintain.'

'And you're doing it very well.'

Valentin pointed at Navrátil.

'Is he all there?'

'You mean that vacant expression? Yes, the brain works very well. He's a good lad, is Navrátil. One day I shall hang up my handcuffs and he'll slide effortlessly into my place, you mark my words. Navrátil, cultivate this old hack and you'll have a valuable ally. I take it that gormless look indicates that you're surprised by this turn of events?'

'You could say that, sir, yes.'

'Then let me admit you to my innermost thought processes while I can still remember what they are. How did we first link the murder to the Minister?'

'Someone sent us a photograph.'

'Exactly. Someone out there wanted us to know what was going on, and gave us the evidence to pin the crime on Dr Banda. Now, it seems to me to be a reasonable supposition that our penfriend wanted Banda fingered for the crime. It seemed plausible that if we let him or her know that Banda wasn't going to be fingered, he might send us a bit more evidence.'

'So this is a trick to get the original source to get back in touch with us?'

'A long shot, I admit, but maybe the best we have at present. And to give the story credibility, it couldn't come from us. If it came from someone unconnected with the police, it would carry more weight. Enter Mr Valentin here, who, for a modest amount of beer and first chance at the big story when we get it, was prepared to blacken our names in the gutter press.'

'To be honest,' said Valentin, 'for the chance to blacken your name I'd work for nothing.'

'Spoken like a true member of the fourth estate. Navrátil, Mr Valentin's glass is empty. Be a good lad and fill it for him, would you?'

'Can you manage another too?' asked Navrátil.

Slonský gave him a disapproving look and drained his glass.

Chapter 13

The following day, Slonský gave Navrátil the day off, once it became clear that there had been no response to the newspaper story. In the afternoon, Irina Gruberová was laid to rest in her home village, and the mourners might have noticed a slightly portly man in a crumpled overcoat standing in the churchyard, who appeared to be on speaking terms with Sergeant Tomáš.

'How's it going?' the sergeant enquired.

'Not well. The prime suspect is still the prime suspect; there's no good evidence to exonerate him, but I just can't picture him being so stupid. We're working on the principle that someone framed him.'

Tomáš nodded.

'Understandable. If I'd had something on him, I'd have framed the little sod myself.'

'But why would you do it? He loses his job, but how do you win?'

'It's just the pleasure of seeing another human being suffer, I suppose,' Tomáš shrugged. 'What is it the Germans call it? Schadenfreude? Joy at another's misfortunes.'

'Okay, I can understand that. But it takes some planning. And it costs an innocent girl her life. Why not accuse him of a tax fiddle, or corruption? Why harm someone else? Why not just kill the Minister?'

'Well, I guess whoever it was knew about the mistress and realised it could hurt Banda. He didn't have to create anything, because Banda did that himself.'

Slonský perked up at once.

'Tomáš, you're a genius! If I ever have a vacancy for a driver, I'll give you a call.'

'No thanks, I like it here. But what have I said?'

'You said "whoever it was knew about the mistress". That's right. And he knew he could go to that restaurant and have a good chance of getting a photo. How did he know that?'

Novák sipped his pear brandy.

'This is either brilliant or completely hare-brained, and I can't decide which.'

They were in the restaurant and Slonský had a tape measure in his hand.

'You understand this better than me. Where was this photograph taken from?'

Novák measured the height of a wineglass in the photograph, then a matching wineglass on the table. He scribbled some sums on a paper napkin, took the tape measure from Slonský, and started to walk backwards from the table where Banda and Gruberová had been sitting.

'That table there,' he announced, pointing at a table for two against the wall.

Slonský raised his eyebrows at the restaurant manager, who flicked through the reservations book.

'Table for one at 7.45, name of Lukas.'

'Did he pay by credit card?'

The restaurant manager clicked a few keys on a computer terminal.

'No, cash.'

'Remember him?'

'Afraid not. He can't have been here long, because we gave his table to a couple at nine o'clock.'

Novák drained his glass.

'Presumably, Banda didn't recognise him, or he wouldn't have let himself be photographed.'

'He'd have the cameraman slightly behind him. Probably didn't even notice he was there. In Banda's eyes, he was being very discreet. No hanky-panky at the table. Just a pair of business colleagues having a meal together.'

'They were lovers, Slonský! You can't disguise that.'

'Can't you? I remember a police captain who thought nobody knew he was shafting his driver. They kept a respectable distance in public and genuinely thought nobody had any reason for suspicion.'

'Nice girl?'

'Who said it was a girl? I can see Banda being just as arrogant. If he was trying to keep it secret, he'd believe he'd succeeded.'

'Okay, but humour me a minute. We're arguing that the man who took the photo knew enough to know Banda would be here with Irina. That argues for someone familiar with Banda and something Banda wanted to be discreet about. So surely if Banda saw someone he knew here, he'd know he'd been rumbled.'

'Then our source must have sent someone else to take the photograph. But how he used a camera in here without being noticed is a mystery to me.'

'But not to me,' Novák smirked, raising his mobile phone so that Slonský could see a photograph of himself waiting impatiently while the restaurant manager checked if "Lukas" had paid by credit card. 'You didn't know I'd taken that, did you?'

Slonský checked his own mobile phone.

'Can they all do that?'

'Your antique model is probably the only cellphone in Prague that can't.'

'Well, phones are for phoning. Who needs a camera in a phone anyway?'

'Our blackmailer does,' responded Novák. 'As you said, he couldn't do this without one.'

'It isn't blackmail,' Slonský muttered. 'The photo was sent to us a day or so after it was taken. That isn't time for them to call Banda and get him to pay them off. There's nothing he could do to stop this getting out. It wasn't a question of money. Someone wanted to bring him down.'

'Not necessarily. They may have been planning to blackmail him, then read that Irina had been murdered and realised they knew who the prime suspect was. Even if they aren't public-spirited citizens who want to help the police in every way, they'd know the chances that Banda would be able to pay up, even if he wanted to, wouldn't be good.'

'It's possible. The trouble is, too many things are possible.'

'Any significance in the name Lukas?'

'You mean he was expecting Lukas to get the case? Maybe.'

'Your Captain isn't that well known. Could the informant be a policeman?'

'That's possible too. But then why not claim the credit for nailing Banda himself? Why send it to me?'

'Maybe he's too far down the food chain.'

Slonský sat at the table opposite Novák and rubbed his eyes.

'I don't know. We're not getting anywhere.'

Novák held out his glass for another brandy. The restaurant manager obliged.

'He'll pay.'

Slonský sighed. It was not worth arguing about that either.

'Just a thought,' mused Novák. 'Have you shown the photograph to Banda?'

'Yes, to prove he must have known Gruberová.'

'And does he know when it was taken?'

'Yes, he volunteered that from his diary.'

'Then does he know who took the photo? You're assuming he didn't know someone was here, but that doesn't necessarily follow. He may have recognised someone here but not been worried about it, if it was a friendly face. But now he may know who set him up.'

Slonský's brain was racing.

'If he does, then no doubt he'll be in touch the first chance he gets. We could let him have a private phone call — all suitably tapped, of course.'

'Surely he's not so dim as to fall for that?'

'No, I suppose not. But then if the photographer knows that Banda recognised him and is about to be released, maybe he will give us something else to stave off Banda's revenge. I feel another little chat with Valentin coming on.'

The restaurant manager coughed politely.

'If you don't mind,' he said, 'I'd like to earn a living by letting some customers in. Paying ones,' he added pointedly.

'Novák, sort the man out,' Slonský snapped as he marched to the door.

An advantage of dealing with the gentlemen of the gutter press is that they are regular in their habits. They can usually be found in a particular chair in a particular bar at unvarying times of day, so finding Valentin would not have taxed even Captain Lukas on one of his bad days, Slonský reflected.

'I was just about to go home to bed,' claimed Valentin.

'At eight o'clock? I doubt that very much. Unless you're in a nursing home and they insist on it, of course.'

'My funds are exhausted. What is the point of staying?'

'Is this a hint that you'd like me to buy you a drink?'

'I wouldn't insult you by refusing your act of charity. In fact, I'm prepared to give you repeated opportunities to be charitable.'

Slonský ordered a couple of beers and explained what he wanted.

'If I do this, can I have a head start if your informant gets in touch again?'

'I won't lie to you, old friend. If I can do it, I will. But there's a chance I won't be able to release any information if it proves to be useful to the investigation.'

'I know that. And I trust you to tell me as much as you can, and perhaps a bit more if I'm a really good boy. Now, let's compose our little tale. Front page headline?'

'Let's be a bit more subtle. Late breaking stuff jammed in at the foot of the front page?'

Valentin sucked the end of his pencil in thought.

'That would imply we'd heard about it late at night, and I'm not clear how we could do that. Who's his lawyer?'

'Koller.'

'Old Koller or Young Koller?'

'Ye gods, there are two of them?'

'Son qualified last year.'

'It's the old man. The one who runs the tennis club.'

'Does he play in Armani, I wonder? Never mind, innocent musing that will enliven a tedious midnight hour sometime. So, that publicity-loving hound is unlikely to object if we run a story saying that he is vigorously defending his client and is confident he will soon be released due to lack of evidence.'

'Especially since he has actually done damn all for his client, so far as I can tell.'

'Ah, that's because he doesn't like being associated with clients who might actually go to jail. If it looks like going belly up it won't be very long before he discovers a conflict of interest that means he can't act on Banda's behalf — unless, of course, the fees are spectacular.'

'Banda can pay. I've seen his bank account.'

'No chance of a photocopy some time, I suppose?'

'That would be highly improper!' Slonský replied in an outraged tone. 'I'll see what I can do when this has died down a bit.'

'Fair enough. Refill those glasses with brain fuel and let's start writing.'

Chapter 14

Banda had not seen a newspaper for several days, but he was allowed to see Valentin's handiwork. He smirked at the thought that he might soon be released.

'I wouldn't read too much into that,' Slonský announced. 'I'm a notorious liar.'

'You don't have the evidence to hold me,' declared Banda. 'You can't have, because I'm innocent.'

'There's a non sequitur there, or do I mean a metaphor?' mused Slonský.

'I think it's a non sequitur,' replied Mucha, 'if I remember my Latin from school.'

'Something that doesn't follow? You mean, he may be innocent, but that doesn't mean we haven't got evidence that proves he isn't.'

'Nailed it in one, Lieutenant. It must be true, because our prisons are full but nobody who gets jailed is ever guilty, or so they say.'

Slonský shook his head.

'No, everyone is guilty of something. Not necessarily what we bang them up for, but everyone has some little secret they'd rather keep to themselves. Isn't that right, Dr Banda?'

'I've already admitted I could have behaved better, but that's a far cry from being a murderer.'

Slonský turned a chair round and straddled it while he rested his chin on the back.

'You may be right. But if you'll permit me to put a contrary opinion, here we have a young lady found murdered with your seminal fluid running down her leg, dumped from a car that is the same make and colour as yours, after having dinner and sex with you and after you failed to remember a flat you'd been to — unless the bedhead was outside when you were making love, which I find unlikely — and after you failed to report that you knew a young woman we were trying to identify and whose face was all over the newspapers. Not only that, but a quantity of money you withdrew from your bank, in full view of security cameras, was found in her vagina. A vagina to which, I remind you, you had recently had abundant access, and how many people can we say that about?'

'It only needed one other,' Banda remarked with a heavy sigh.

'So you're saying the murderer waited politely till you'd finished, then he ran in, strangled Miss Gruberová, found a large sum of money and, rather than pocket it, amused himself by shoving it up her before putting her clothes back on her and driving her five kilometres across town in a car just like yours to dump her by a busy railway station?'

Banda jutted his chin forward defiantly.

'Yes,' he growled.

'Fair enough,' said Slonský as he headed for the door. 'It's good to know what we're up against. If you happen to think of a name for this murderer, you might want to give me a shout.'

Navrátil heard Slonský's footsteps approaching and tried hard to look industrious, a task made appreciably more difficult by not having anything in particular to do.

'Ah, there you are, lad! Some of us have done a day's work by now.'

'Sorry, sir. I slept in.'

'Well, you've had a few hard days.'

'It won't happen again, sir.'

'Don't be daft. Of course it will. We all crash out from time to time. Occupational hazard of being a policeman. Just don't let me catch you making a habit of it.'

'Yes, sir. I mean no, sir.'

'We'll say no more about it, unless of course I want something off you. What did you get up to on your day off, then?'

'Saw my mum.'

'Jolly good.'

Slonský riffled through a few papers, had a good scratch while gazing at the large map on the wall, then sat in his chair with a loud sigh.

'Been baking again, has she?'

Mid-morning, Captain Lukas sauntered into the room.

'I've had a telephone call from Mr Koller,' he announced. 'He is concerned that his client has not yet been released.'

'What did you say, sir?' Slonský enquired.

'I said that I have a number of cases currently occupying me and I would make the necessary enquiries, which is what I'm doing now. We can't hold him much longer, Slonský.'

Slonský worried at his thumb with his front teeth.

'I know. I'm just hoping something will turn up.'

'If I remember this morning's newspaper, you were quoted as saying that you had no reason to hold Banda anyway. It's just as well Mr Koller hasn't seen that. Why do you so regularly put your foot in it?'

'I was hoping that the real murderer would give me something more to keep Banda under lock and key, sir. I know we can't wait long, but sometime today something may happen. If the real killer thinks Banda is getting off, he may help us a bit. In any event, he won't kill again if it means letting Banda off the hook because he is in custody.'

Lukas turned a sickly shade of white.

'You think this could be a serial killer?'

'I hope not, sir, but we can never be sure until he's locked up. Of course, Dr Banda is at risk himself with the killer still at large. Our cell is the safest place for him.'

Lukas recovered his composure.

'I may make that suggestion to Mr Koller. I'm sure he wouldn't want to insist on his client's release if there's a homicidal maniac out there waiting for him.'

'No sane person would, sir. But he is a lawyer.'

A little after two o'clock Sergeant Mucha called.

'Someone just delivered a package addressed to you.'

'It's not my birthday. Was it a tall, leggy blonde in a short skirt?'

'No, it was a motorcycle courier with greasy hair and a star tattooed on his neck.'

'So what did he leave?'

'It's addressed to you! How would I know?' Mucha sounded outraged.

'You didn't open it?'

'Certainly not. But I did ask who sent him. He says he was told by phone to go to a block of flats and look in a particular person's mail box. There would be an envelope there and if he opened it there would be something to deliver and a handsome fee for doing so.'

'And was there?'

'A padded envelope and a thousand crowns. Not bad for ten minutes' work.'

'We'll be right down. Or at least Navrátil will.'

Slonský put the phone down and smiled at his assistant.

'Better go by way of the canteen, lad, and bring some coffee and a sausage or two. I think somebody up there likes us.'

Banda's cell was looking rather more lived-in now. He had been allowed a table at which to write, and low piles of paper, meticulously sorted, covered half its surface. He was writing vigorously. Unfortunately he no longer had the gold fountain pen with the mother of pearl inserts in the barrel that he used at his desk at the ministry. It was now in a cardboard box that Mrs Bandová had been invited to collect so that his personal effects did not go missing before he was released. The Prime Minister's abominable secretary sniffily conveyed the message with an undertone that implied that the release could well be sometime around 2050. All Banda was allowed was a wooden pencil bearing someone else's teethmarks. Since he was not allowed an eraser, presumably in case he committed suicide by breaking it in half and ramming a piece up each nostril, he was obliged to consider his words carefully before committing them to paper, but Banda would have done that anyway. He finished the letter he was writing and called Sergeant Mucha.

'I'd be obliged if you would arrange for this to be posted,' he said. 'I assume I haven't been given an envelope so that you can read it before it is sent.'

'You assume correctly,' replied Mucha. 'There's nothing questionable in it that might offend my delicate sensibilities, I hope?'

'Of course not,' Banda growled. The man was insufferable. If he ever got his old ministry back there would be a few policemen put out to grass before you could say 'Welcome back, Minister.'

Mucha scanned the letter.

'I'm not posting that!' he announced. 'What kind of language is that to use about a Prime Minister?'

'Where?'

'There.'

'It says "Philistine".'

'Does it?' asked Mucha doubtfully. 'You want to work on your handwriting, mate.'

'It does. And don't call me mate. I'm not your mate.'

'Dead right,' said Mucha. 'I'm too fussy for that.'

Navrátil was pressed against the far wall as Slonský contemplated the envelope on his desk.

'Are you sure it's not a bomb, sir?'

'Why should it be a bomb?'

'It's in a padded envelope. And if he thinks you're getting close to him it's the kind of thing a murderer might do.'

'Navrátil, it takes a certain set of skills to make a letter bomb. Someone who strangles women is not a prime candidate for a cold-hearted bomb-maker. Besides, Mucha almost certainly steamed it open before he rang upstairs, and since there wasn't a hell of a bang from the front desk I feel fairly confident about opening it. But if you want to cower any further away, Lukas isn't in his office at the moment.'

Navrátil was barely reassured, but he did not wish to be thought craven, so he advanced three or four paces towards the desk as Slonský peeled the envelope open.

'I was wrong, lad,' he announced, causing Navrátil to flinch in anticipation of an explosion that failed to come. 'No, Navrátil, I was wrong about Mucha steaming it open. The seal was intact. Now, what have we here?' Reaching into the envelope, he slid out a large colour photograph and examined it closely. 'Weird. Why send this to me?'

Navrátil inched closer and accepted the photograph that Slonský proffered him. It took him a moment or two to understand what he was looking at.

'I know that man, don't I? The one in the pool.'

'Not in the biblical sense, I hope. It's the opposition's spokesman on finance, Daniel Soucha.'

'Who's the other man?'

'Don't know.'

'What's Soucha doing?'

'Well, I doubt he's checking if it's a whistle.'

Navrátil blushed.

'I mean, why is he letting people take pictures of him doing that sort of thing? There are still plenty of people who wouldn't vote for a gay man.'

Slonský stood up and arched his back to relieve the stiffness he felt more with each day that passed. The sun was setting behind the rooftops in a dramatic peach-coloured sky. There was a sharp chill in the air, but Slonský opened the window and leaned out. There was the profound quiet of a city muffled in snow, broken by chugging buses and the occasional whine of a spinning car wheel as it slipped on the icy road.

'It's not a new photo, Navrátil. Look at the garden through the windows — roses in full bloom, which is unusual in Prague come February. So why hang on to it that long? Why send it to a homicide detective? What they're doing is not a crime, assuming the dark-haired man is as old as he looks.'

Suddenly Slonský snapped his fingers.

'Right, lad, we'll get nowhere setting each other puzzles like that. Let's get some answers. Run it across to Spehar and let's see if it came from the same source as the first photo. Then we need to find out where it was taken. Judging by the angle I'd guess it's a still from a security camera in the roof over the pool. It's a pool in a private house, and I'll lay odds it's not Soucha's own or he'd have known the camera was there. So the first thing to do is to find out where it was taken.'

'I thought you said the first thing to do was to take it to Spehar, sir.'

'Yes. And this is the next first thing. Off you go, youngster. I'm going to find Valentin.'

Slonský returned within the hour.

'Didn't you find him, sir?'

'Of course I found him, Navrátil. I'd be a pretty poor detective if I couldn't find a toper who spends all his days in one of three or four bars within a few streets in town.'

'Could he help us?'

'I didn't ask. I just wanted him to find an expert for us. It's going to take a couple of hours so we've just got time to line our stomachs. I have a feeling it could be a heavy session tonight, so get some sustenance inside you.'

Valentin was sitting in a booth rather than his usual stool near the door.

'The chief problem with this seat is that you have a devil of a job catching the waiter's eye. My glass has been empty for nearly ten minutes,' he muttered.

'Let me fill it for you, old friend. No, I insist.'

'I wasn't arguing.'

'I know, but if people hear me say that they'll think it can't be you in this booth.'

Slonský smirked as he barged to the bar, returning with four large glasses of beer. He set one before each of them and put the fourth on a coaster in front of the seat opposite Valentin.

'You and I are having the outside seats, Navrátil. It's best if people don't get a good look at our guests.'

'Guests? Who's the other guest?'

A young bearded man in the next booth stood up and tapped Navrátil on the shoulder.

'I am. Shift over so I can get in.'

He extended a large hand and greeted each in turn. He plainly knew Valentin, who introduced him to Slonský and Navrátil.

'This is Martin,' announced Valentin. 'Be content with his first name.'

'Of course. Pleased to meet you, Martin.'

'I hear you have something I'd very much like.'

'I think so. But I can't give it to you. At least, not yet. It's evidence. But I'll see to it you get first option on it — assuming, that is, that whoever sent it to me doesn't publish it himself first.'

Slonský reached inside his coat and slid a folder across the table. Martin arched his eyebrows with curiosity before raising the flap and carefully examining the contents.

He let slip a low whistle.

'Do you know who this is?'

'I think it's Soucha.'

'So do I. That's dynamite.'

'You didn't know?'

Valentin waved a hand between them.

'Hello? I'm here. May I see, so I know what you're talking about?'

Slonský nodded, and Martin passed the folder across the table to Valentin.

'Well, I never knew that!' the old journalist exclaimed.

'Neither did I,' said Martin, 'and it's my job to know. If he's managed to keep this quiet for so long, and I haven't heard so much as a whisper, he must be very discreet.'

Navrátil could contain his curiosity no longer.

'What exactly is your job, Martin?'

'I trade scurrilous stories to the press. I used to edit an underground magazine, but when it didn't need to be underground anymore it switched to running exposés of corruption. Really big ones get sold on, like this one will when I can use it.'

'Is it a big story? There must be plenty of gay politicians.'

'Yes, but not in top jobs. This will finish Soucha's career. I can't believe he's been that stupid. And I can't believe I didn't know.'

Slonský drained his glass.

'I didn't know either. That's why I needed to check it with you. And if you didn't know, that suggests that only a very small number of people did. Since Spehar tells me the label on the envelope came from the same printer as the first envelope, it means we can narrow down our possible suspects. It's got to be someone who knew the Minister was having an affair and also knew that Soucha was gay. Not only that, he knew where he could collect photographic proof of both facts. He's an insider.'

'But there's one thing I don't understand …' Navrátil began.

'No, there are lots of things you don't understand. This is just the latest.'

'Point taken. But if these connections narrow down our possible killers, why draw our attention to himself by sending us the pictures? Does he want to be caught?'

Slonský stared at the ceiling in deep thought.

'That's a very good question, lad, and I shall ponder it carefully while you get us another round of drinks.'

'I'll help you carry them,' volunteered Valentin, and showed a surprising agility in sliding from his seat without disturbing Slonský.

Slonský rubbed his chin in thought while Martin examined the photograph again.

'Any idea where it was taken?'

'That's what I'm pondering. Nowhere I've been. It must be a big house to have a pool that size. But Soucha has a lot of powerful friends — bankers, industrialists and so on — so it wouldn't surprise me if he was a guest there.'

'But if he's discreet, as you seem to be telling me, then he can't risk someone just walking in on that. They must be alone in the house.'

'Or the other man owns it. But I have no idea who he is, and anyone who owns a house this size near Prague I would know.'

'Could it be taken abroad?'

Martin nodded slowly.

'Soucha travels quite a bit. There's only one way to find out. You'll have to ask him. If you need a shorthand writer, I'll make myself available any hour of the day or night just to see his face when you show him this.'

Slonský smiled.

'I think I'll have to manage with Navrátil, but thanks for the offer.'

Chapter 15

The next morning Slonský made an appointment to see Soucha, then told Navrátil they were going to make a detour.

'You won't need your coat. It's a detour inside this building.'

At the foot of the stairs they turned towards the cells.

'I just want to run something past Banda. Watch his reaction for me.'

Mucha opened the door and they entered. Banda glanced at them with an irritated expression.

'Have you come to molest me again?'

'No. I wondered if you felt like giving me some help.'

Banda put his pencil down carefully.

'Why should I want to help you?'

'So I can help you.'

'And how would that be, precisely?'

'Do you know Daniel Soucha?'

Banda pursed his lips.

'I know of him. He's by no means a friend.'

'I see.'

Slonský turned to leave.

'Why do you ask?'

'Oh, nothing really. It's just that he's having the same trouble with his relationships that you are.'

'Someone murdered his girlfriend? I can empathise. Are you going to lock him up too?'

'Not yet. We're going to have a coffee with him first.'

Mucha closed the door behind them.

'Well, Navrátil?'

'Nothing. But what was I supposed to be looking for?'

'He didn't doubt that Soucha would have a girlfriend. So he didn't know either. And if he didn't know, he couldn't have arranged to have the picture sent. And therefore, in my humble but conclusive opinion, he isn't the murderer. Quod erat demonstrandum.'

'Quod what?' asked Mucha.

'Erat demonstrandum. "Which was to be proved." It was a test, Mucha.'

'Oh. Did I pass?'

Soucha was a tall, slim man with a floppy shock of blond hair that repeatedly fell over his right eye when he moved his head. Cartoonists concentrated on that piece of hair which, in their representations, became bigger and more unmanageable as the years passed. In some versions now it jutted from his head like a cantilever, extending well beyond the tip of his nose and flopping across his right shoulder when it collapsed. He showed Slonský and Navrátil to seats around a low glass table and brushed his hair back as he unbuttoned his jacket and sat in a single fluid motion.

'I'll come straight to the point, sir. I'm afraid this isn't going to be pleasant.'

Soucha looked at each of them quizzically.

'Bad news? Someone in the family died?'

'No, sir. It's about you. Someone has sent me a document that I need to ask you about.'

If Soucha was concerned, he hid it very well indeed. He looked just like a man who had no idea what Slonský was talking about.

'Fire away, then.'

Slonský passed him the envelope. Soucha hesitated, as if unsure whether he was meant to look inside, then peeled back the flap and pulled out the photograph. As he realised its content his face passed from Mediterranean tan to Nordic white.

'Good God. I ... Where...?'

'It was posted to me, sir. No covering letter. I take it that you recognise yourself as the gentleman on the right.'

Soucha swallowed hard.

'Yes. That is me.'

'And the other gentleman?'

'Look, we're not doing anything illegal. Why are you asking me about it?'

'We're investigating a serious crime, sir, and the circumstances in which this was received suggest to me that there is a connection. I just don't know what it is. I hoped you would.'

'Does this have to get out? I mean, you'll exercise discretion about who gets to see —'

'Oh, yes, sir. If my questions are answered satisfactorily no-one else need see it. Though, of course, the sender may have made other copies.'

If Soucha was pale before, he became rather grey now.

'Let's get it over with. What do you want to know?'

Slonský motioned to Navrátil to make notes.

'The other gentleman, sir?'

'I don't know him.'

'You seem to know him rather well in the photograph, if I may say so, sir.'

'I only met him a few days before at a party. He's called Mario.'

'Mario?'

'Presumably a nickname.'

'You don't say, sir? Mario. Write that down, Navrátil.'

'I think he's foreign. Austrian, maybe. He spoke Czech with an accent.'

'And you haven't seen him again?'

'Lunch a few days later. Then we lost touch.'

'Do you have a phone number for him?'

'He stopped answering.'

Soucha took out his cellphone and found the number, which he showed to Navrátil.

'Dial it, Navrátil.'

Soucha rubbed his hands together in a compulsive washing motion as they waited.

'Number unobtainable, sir,' Navrátil reported.

'Shame. Where did you meet?'

'It was a party at the National Theatre. I went to see a play and was invited to join the host for some wine and nibbles.'

'"Nibbles", sir?'

'You know, canapés. That sort of thing.'

'We're not big on canapés in the police, sir. They're rarely offered. But your host introduced you to Mario.'

'No, he was just there. I'm not sure who brought him. He didn't seem to be with anyone in particular.'

Slonský shifted uncomfortably in his seat.

'I don't mean to offend, sir, but I don't know anything about … that sort of lifestyle, and I need to understand how this happened. If nobody knew that you were that way inclined, how did you and Mario recognise that you were kindred spirits?'

'You just know, Inspector. When you're "that way inclined" you get a sense for who else feels the same way. Presumably Mario sensed it about me.'

'So he approached you?'

'Yes, I suppose he did. I was chatting to a few friends when I noticed him looking at me intently. It was a bit unnerving, to be honest. Then he smiled and when I detached myself he walked over to say hello.'

'And one thing led to another.'

'Not immediately. We agreed to meet at the weekend.'

'Where, sir?'

'Our original plan was to meet at a restaurant and see what progressed. But on the Friday I was talking to a friend who offered me the use of his summer house if I ever wanted it.'

'That's very generous, sir.'

'Yes. I said I'd like to do that one day, and he said he wasn't using it at the weekend, and perhaps I'd like to look it over. I would be doing him a favour because he hadn't had time to go out there for a few weeks and he'd like to know it was in good repair.'

'Was this recently, sir?'

'Last summer, I think.'

'So you agreed to go out there. Very helpful of you, I'm sure. Weren't there any staff in a place this size?'

'He said nobody lived in. There were a few people in the village who came up when he needed a cook or a gardener, for example, but it would be empty. He suggested I might like to take some company.'

'I imagine he didn't know about Mario, then.'

'No, he offered to fix me up with a girl if I wanted, but I said it would be good to get away to do a bit of writing.'

'Who was this kindly benefactor, sir?'

'Dr Sammler. Theodor Sammler.'

'And how do you know him?'

'He was quite a big donor to the party.'

'Was?'

'Could still be. But I met him first after he provided a lot of IT equipment for our central office. I gather he's some sort of wheeler-dealer.'

'Where would I find Dr Sammler?'

'I don't know. Central Office could probably tell you.'

Slonský mulled this information for a few moments, then picked up his hat and held out a hand.

'Goodbye, sir. Thanks for seeing us. Navrátil, pick up the photo, please. We'll see ourselves out, sir.'

As they strode to the car, Navrátil shook his head wonderingly.

'He just lent a stranger his house! Who goes around doing that?'

'Very kindly people, Navrátil. Trusting, gentle kindly souls. People like you, in fact. And, of course, the occasional complete villain. Let's see what we can find out about Dr Sammler.'

Chapter 16

Klinger's eyes narrowed and flicked from Slonský to Navrátil and back to Slonský again.

'Why do you want to know about Theodor Sammler?'

'Idle curiosity.'

'I believe the idle bit. I suppose you aren't going to tell me.'

'You know I'd like to,' Slonský said soothingly, 'but my lips must remain clamped together like a nun's knees.'

Klinger held his steepled fingers to his lips while he thought.

'At least answer me this. Do you have any evidence that Sammler has done anything that my department ought to know about?'

'No. But the fact that you ask suggests you have.'

Klinger got up and went to the filing cabinet, drawing out a slim folder with a number of coloured sticky notes protruding at the edge. Slonský noted with delight that a green sticker was out of alignment with the others, and watched silently as Klinger opened the file and carefully repositioned it, before closing the folder again and holding it up to check that the edges of the stickers formed a straight line.

'If I had, life would be easier. Sammler is a German businessman. He's lived here in Prague for about twenty years on and off. Daddy was a rich industrialist somewhere in West Germany, and we assume he bankrolled young Theodor, because the youngster first seems to have come here around 1986. He got a job with an Austrian bank and came back a couple of times over the next year or so. But he really comes to official notice after the Velvet Revolution when we privatised a lot of our businesses. Do you remember the coupons?'

Navrátil shook his head.

'Vaguely,' said Slonský.

Klinger smiled in anticipation of the opportunity to give these neophytes a lesson in financial matters.

'Briefly, any adult Czech could buy a book of vouchers for thirty-five crowns. They could then register it for another thousand crowns, in exchange for which they got points. The points were used to bid for shares in companies that the government was selling off. Most Czechs didn't understand the system and, frankly, couldn't be bothered, but a few banks hit on a way round this. They would manage your points for you, and even pay you a fee. You gave them your vouchers, and they did all the rest. Of course, quite often the return for the banks was huge, but all you'd got was whatever you sold the vouchers for. Sammler cooked up one of the first of those schemes, but it was actually rather clever. He borrowed money on the strength of the shares he had just bought, which enabled him to buy more shares, which pushed the price up, so he could then redeem his loan more cheaply. If he was slick it was money for nothing. Ownership of some large Czech assets passed to foreigners, and while we enjoyed the money coming in, there was an inevitable backlash.'

He paused to sip his coffee and invite questions, of which there were none. Navrátil had not understood and Slonský just wanted to get to the end of the story.

'Friend Sammler was clever enough to get out of voucher trading and offer his services to the government to get some of those assets back. He didn't have a lot of successes, but he didn't need many. A select few gave him a big return. He found foreign owners who needed cash, and he would buy a stake in something they owned. But the deal would include a clause allowing him first option on the rest of that asset if they ever sold it. Then, as sure as night follows day, there would be a collapse of the company's share price, and the asset would be quietly sold to Sammler's bank to get some cash in quickly and discreetly. It's estimated he may have paid only sixty per cent of the true value of what he bought. Sammler's bank became very rich, and he did quite well out of it too. What none of us knew then was that Sammler had owned the Austrian bank all along, or at least he controlled it.'

Navrátil wanted to ask a question, and was sorely tempted to raise a hand as if in class.

'Was any of this illegal?'

'Probably not. And I don't hear of anything now that is definitely illegal. I just wonder why he stays here instead of using his undoubted financial skills in Germany where he could make a real killing.'

'Maybe he likes Prague,' suggested Slonský.

'He doesn't seem to like much at all. He does the Prague Castle circuit, knows all the top people, but hates publicity, doesn't have expensive hobbies — not one for fast cars or flashy holidays.'

'He has a country house though.'

'Yes, he does. You heard that? Not exactly a cottage, is it? But there are bigger ones, and he doesn't spend a lot of time there, I understand. If I didn't know better I'd say he only keeps it so he can lend it out to people who might thereby feel they owe him a favour.'

'There you are!' exclaimed Slonský. 'I knew we'd agree on something if I came here often enough.'

Klinger leaned forward abruptly.

'You know something, don't you? You've heard a whisper. Come on, Slonský, out with it.'

Slonský sighed.

'Between us?'

'Between us,' Klinger confirmed.

'You know this murder we're investigating. It turns out that Sammler lent his house to one of the suspects. I just couldn't see why he would do that.'

'Is the suspect a politician?'

'Yes.'

'Well, there you are then. Why does Sammler do anything? Definitely not for charitable reasons. He's an arch-capitalist, Slonský. He believes everything has its price — and everyone.'

'Why did you lie to Klinger just then?' asked Navrátil as they trotted down the stairs.

'He brings out the worst in me. I can't resist telling him a little story.'

'But Soucha isn't a suspect for the Gruberová murder, sir.'

'No, but Banda is.'

'Has he visited the country house too, sir?'

'I don't know,' said Slonský. 'But it's worth asking, don't you think?'

Banda's scribbling was his sole amusement. Mucha had given up rationing his paper and had left him a ream of flimsy copy paper, which Banda had turned into some letters, a few complaints, and several chapters of autobiography. If he had hopes that the latter would prove a bestseller, they were sabotaged by his exclusion of any matters of general public interest, such as how he had murdered his girlfriend.

He glanced up briefly as Slonský entered the cell.

'Have you come to torment me again?'

'Only if absolutely necessary. Though I can't guarantee I won't hum a Sinatra tune or two.'

Banda laid his pencil down parallel to the top of his page and turned to Slonský to indicate that he was prepared to give him his full attention.

'How can I help?'

'I wondered if you knew a Dr Theodor Sammler.'

'Of course I do. Who doesn't?'

'I don't.'

Banda shrugged to convey that anyone who was anyone would know Sammler, but that Slonský might not fall into this group.

'Perhaps you would write me a letter of introduction.'

'If it helps me get out of this place, bring me a better pencil and I'll get onto it straight away.'

'I wouldn't be in too much of a hurry to get out if I were you. If you didn't kill Irina, whoever did might be upset if you aren't blamed for it, since he must have gone to such trouble to frame you.'

'I didn't kill her, and that's a chance I have to take. Though I hope that the police will ensure my safety by catching the real killer.'

It was Slonský's turn to shrug.

'We might, if we've got nothing better to do.'

Banda closed his hand tightly around his pencil and breathed deeply to dissipate his anger.

'I'm not sure I like you,' he hissed.

Slonský leaned forward until their noses were almost touching.

'I'm not sure I give a toss,' he replied.

The two men held their stares like boxers at a championship weigh-in, until Banda threw his pencil aside in annoyance.

'This is ridiculous. Ask me what you want, then leave me in peace.'

'Tell me about Dr Sammler.'

'I know very little about him personally. We met regularly, as you would expect given that he is a leading financier in the Czech Republic and has been very helpful to this and previous governments.'

'How regularly?'

'Perhaps once or twice a month. Rarely one to one, but we move in the same circles in the Castle district. However, if Sammler wanted to speak to me he had only to ring my office and I would make time for a man of his importance.'

'Have you ever been to his country house?'

'No. I don't even know where it is. I'm not sure he does either. He's not a country lover, Slonský. Dr Sammler is thoroughly urban.'

'Any family?'

'No, I don't believe so. Certainly I've never heard mention of any. I think he lives alone near his office, perhaps with a housekeeper.'

'Is he a socialite?'

Banda laughed.

'Sammler? A playboy? No, he's a German. He doesn't believe in fun. In a previous age he'd have been a Puritan.'

'So he didn't approve of your relationship with Miss Gruberová, then?'

'He neither approved nor disapproved, at least not to my face. He's a cultured man who is better bred than to comment on another man's private affairs.'

'Any idea how he feels about homosexuality?'

'No, nor do I know what football team he supports, his shoe size or his favourite wine. If you're asking me if he is one, the answer is no. If he needs a female escort, he has no trouble finding one. But he is a very self-contained man, Lieutenant. He seems not to crave human relationships very much, other than those devoted to business.'

'Money is his passion, then.'

'He's not a man to have passions. He likes an ordered life and hobbies and interests would just get in the way. Oh, he enjoys good food or a night at the opera, but he's just as happy with a plate of stew and reading a book. Now, will you tell me why you're asking me all this?'

Slonský opened the cell door.

'No,' he replied, and closed it behind him.

To Slonský's great surprise, Valentin was wearing a tie. It was greasy, stained and abominably knotted, but it was undoubtedly a tie.

'Are you meeting someone?' Slonský enquired.

'No,' replied Valentin, 'so if you're buying drinks I can accept without feeling I'm taking advantage.'

'Navrátil will see to it. He knows the drill by now. So, why have you got a dog's leash hanging round your neck?'

'You're the detective. Detect.'

Slonský rubbed his chin in a pantomime of deep thought.

'Well, it can't be a woman.'

'I'm hurt by the suggestion that it can't be a woman. It happens that it isn't, but I can still pull a woman if I choose to. I just don't choose to, that's all.'

Slonský looked more closely. Finding that this did not help, he stood, grabbed a hanging light and pointed it directly at Valentin.

'You've shaved. Recently. Certainly today, and probably early afternoon — or as you journalists call it, breakfast time.'

'Getting warmer.'

'You wouldn't shave because you wanted to, so it was expected by the person you were interviewing. And since nobody's opinion has the slightest effect on you except one man, I deduce that you were seeing your editor.'

'Bravo. And that's why a brandy wouldn't come amiss.'

'Not a happy man?'

'He wasn't, and I'm not. I need a big story, Slonský. Something for the front page. And I need it quickly. He's given me a week to find him something or he stops the salary and I have to go freelance. So, old chap, have you got a titbit for me?'

'I wish I had.'

'No chance this juicy murder of yours is going to be tidied up in a week?'

'Don't know. Not much sign of it.'

'And you're adamant I can't use the picture of Soucha and his little friend?'

'No! Definitely not. You know I'd give you something if I could. I will just as soon as I can, but at the moment I'm stuck. Maybe I'm losing my magic touch.'

'Yes,' agreed Valentin sourly.

They sat in silence until Navrátil joined them.

'Took me an age to find a waiter. He's on his way.'

'That's because you don't look like a drinker. They gravitate to the likes of me,' growled Valentin. 'Better pickings. With luck I may keel over and forget my wallet, then they'll help themselves to a big tip.'

The waiter arrived with the beers and was promptly sent to fetch a large brandy for Valentin.

'Tell you what,' said Slonský. 'I'm so sympathetic to your misfortune I'm even going to pay for this one myself.'

'If only I had a camera,' Valentin retorted. 'No-one will believe this without photographic proof. I might even have been able to get it on the front page.'

'Between bouts of sarcasm,' Slonský said, 'tell me what you know about Theodor Sammler.'

'German.'

'Knew that.'

'Banker.'

'Knew that too.'

'That's me done.'

'You? The greatest investigative journalist Prague has ever seen?'

'You're only saying that because it's true.'

'No, I'm laying the flattery on with a trowel to get you to try harder.'

'Not much point. Sammler is a grey man. He doesn't party much, he doesn't court publicity, he doesn't flash his cash around. He just knows a lot of people and makes a lot of money.'

'Legally?'

'A banker making money legally in Prague? Are you taking the —'

'No. I just meant is he the sort of person to get involved with shady stuff?'

'Not that I've heard. Crafty but legit, so far as I know.'

'So there's no scandal?'

'I don't think so.'

Slonský took a large slurp from his beer and fell silent for a few moments.

'If he's such a good money-maker, why stay here? He could be coining it in Frankfurt among his own kind.'

'His contacts are here, I suppose. It's taken him years to build up his address book. And I bet those Germans have got Frankfurt sewn up. He wouldn't get a look in.'

Navrátil was feeling as dispirited as the others.

'Looks like this line of enquiry is going nowhere then.'

'No,' agreed Slonský. 'The deadest of dead ends.'

Valentin leaned forward and dropped his voice.

'Look, I'll see if my paper's man in Vienna knows anything. That's where Sammler was between Germany and here. I'll need a few crowns for the phone call, though.'

Slonský handed him a note.

'That's my own money. Don't waste it.'

Mucha looked disgruntled.

'I was beginning to wonder if you were ever coming back,' he moaned.

'How nice of you to pine,' replied Slonský, 'like a faithful lap-dog.'

'You don't need a lap-dog,' Mucha mumbled. 'You need a guard dog.'

'If you'd said I needed a guide dog I wouldn't have argued right now,' Slonský sighed. 'We're getting nowhere fast.'

Mucha leant across the desk and whispered something to Slonský.

'Just what we needed. Okay, I'll deal with it. Give me a few minutes to think.'

'Well, don't take too long. I was off duty an hour and a half ago.'

'Off duty? You? I thought you slept here.'

'If I did I'd probably get more sex.'

'And on that happy observation I'll bid you good night,' Slonský said. 'I'll call you later.'

Navrátil was waiting in the corridor by the swing door.

'What was that about?'

'Never you mind. Just another complication visited on us from above. If you haven't already discovered it you'll soon learn that we solve crime despite the support of our superiors, not because of it.'

'Do you need me for anything more?'

'No, lad, off you go. I'll see you at seven tomorrow morning.'

He walked on a few steps, then turned and called along the corridor.

'Not here, though. I'll meet you at the Florenc metro station.'

Chapter 17

They sat in the car with their gaze fixed on an alleyway between two buildings.

'More coffee?' asked Slonský.

'I'd better not. I'll have to break cover and find a toilet if I do.'

'There's one in that café. And while you're there you can get me another coffee.'

'Why are we here, sir?'

'Because we had a tip-off, Navrátil. There's every chance someone will be selling some guns here. Can't ignore a hint like that.'

Navrátil squirmed in his seat, trying to allow some air to reach his back.

'Is the source reliable?'

'One of the best. Mucha's brother.'

Navrátil's alertness level rose sharply, propelling him forward in his seat.

'Mucha's brother? Is he mixed up in that sort of thing?'

'Of course not. But he's extraordinarily well-informed. He has some great contacts.'

'Such as?'

'You wouldn't expect me to reveal his sources, Navrátil.'

'I suppose not. But they're good?'

'Always have been in the past.'

'So has he been responsible for putting lots of criminals away, then?'

Slonský turned to face Navrátil. His deep frown disclosed some puzzlement at the question.

'None, so far as I know.'

'I don't understand. How can he be a great source if nobody gets nailed on his evidence?'

'The fact that we never catch anyone doesn't mean it's not Grade A intelligence, Navrátil. It must be — I've graded it that way. He has wonderful contacts and no doubt one day cultivating him will pay off. This could be the day.'

Navrátil scanned the alleyway while trying to assimilate the information he had just received.

'So are we spending a lot on him?'

'Not much. Today's snippet, for example, is costing us two tickets to the Sparta game on Sunday.'

Navrátil shrugged.

'Cheap enough, if it pays off.'

'It already has.'

'How do you mean?'

'I think it's time I initiated you into one or two secrets of the art, Navrátil. But first I must swear you to secrecy. Do you promise you won't reveal anything I'm about to tell you, even if Lukas threatens to pull out your toenails?'

'Of course not. The first sign of pliers and I'll squeal like a piglet.'

'Any sane man would. But the need for secrecy will be very clear, even to you. I have great respect for your trusting and honest nature, lad. It does you great credit. But it's a damn nuisance when it comes to fighting crime.'

Slonský took a sip from the cold coffee and winced as he realised that the last warmth it retained came from his hand grasping the cardboard cup.

'Mucha's brother told us that there is a good chance that guns, possibly including some used in unsolved crimes, would be traded here this morning.'

'Is that what Mucha whispered to you last night?'

'Not exactly. But if you inspect Mucha's log you'll see that his brother phoned to tip us off.'

Navrátil blinked furiously. This did not make sense.

'When? Mucha didn't mention it.'

'Indeed he didn't. But his log book does. And I'm entirely confident that you'll find an entry in there about a message from Little Sparrow.'

'Okay, so how did "Little Sparrow" know this was going on?'

'Because I told him. Close your mouth, lad, you look simple.'

'You made up an informer?'

'Of course not. Mucha's brother is real enough. He's a plumber in Vysočany, I think. Though whenever I want one I doubt whether plumbers really exist.'

'So how did you hear about the arms deal?'

'Ah, I made that bit up.'

'Why? We're wasting time when we've got a killer to chase.'

'Because what Mucha whispered to me was that a bunch of goons from the Director's Office were going to be paying us a visit this morning to go through the team's cases and audit their methods. That includes us. I don't want to sit there while some acne-ridden youth questions what we've been doing. I don't mind explaining myself to you — we're colleagues, and I'm meant to be teaching you — but I can do without that lot pulling all our files to bits. So the best way of avoiding that was to find something that got us out of the office and couldn't be put off. An arms deal fits the bill, wouldn't you say?'

'So you rang Mucha's brother…?'

'No, I rang Mucha and Mucha told his brother what he'd already written in the log book. Young Mucha doesn't mind — he gets two tickets for the Sparta game and if it doesn't work out he just says it's what he overheard in a bar and he never swore to its accuracy.'

'But hasn't anyone noticed that he has never provided a useful lead?'

'He did once, come to think of it. He reported a motorist for driving with defective headlights.'

'But nothing came of it, you said.'

'Of course not. Colonel Tripka is a very senior police officer. Nobody is going to arrest him for that. But it was a good laugh when the car ownership record was faxed through and pinned on the canteen noticeboard.'

Navrátil felt that his head was reeling yet again.

'But the bottom line is that we're sitting doing nothing useful when we could be chasing a murderer.'

'True. But the choice is that we either sit here doing nothing useful, or we sit in our office doing nothing useful and getting hassled by the Director's hit squad. So are you going to get that coffee or not?'

Slonský pushed the door open, walked through, then turned round and came straight back out again.

'They're still there. Let's go for a sausage somewhere.'

'How do you know?'

'Mucha's jacket is hanging behind the desk. That's the signal.'

Navrátil searched his memory.

'I've never seen Mucha's jacket hanging up.'

'That's what makes it such a good signal. Keep to this side of the road, lad, so they can't see us from the windows.'

There was a shrill ring as Slonský's mobile phone jumped into life.

'Don't recognise the number. It's probably the goon squad wanting to know when we'll be back.'

The phone stopped ringing, only to be replaced in seconds by the marimba that Navrátil used as his ring tone.

'Don't answer…' snapped Slonský, but Navrátil was too quick.

'Navrátil,' he said.

Mucha's voice snarled at him.

'Tell Slonský to answer his bloody phone.'

Navrátil looked at his phone in surprise as Mucha rang off abruptly.

'It's Mucha. He says I've got to tell you to answer your phone.'

Within moments, Slonský's phone rang again.

'National Theatre Box Office,' said Slonský.

'Good try,' said Mucha. 'Got a pencil? I've got a phone number for you.'

Slonský relayed the number to Navrátil who copied it into his notebook.

'Who is it?' asked Slonský.

'Someone called Peiperová.'

'Don't know her.'

'Yes, you do. You met her when you went out to Gruberová's parents' place.'

'Tall blonde with a ponytail?'

'How would I know?' Mucha spat. 'Just call her before the Spotty Ones realise I'm talking to you.'

'Good point,' allowed Slonský. 'Get off the line and stop holding me up.'

'Whose is the number?' enquired Navrátil.

'Officer Peiperová.'

'Oh, the tall blonde —'

'…with the ponytail, yes. Not that I noticed. But I bet you did. Watch yourself, Navrátil, hormones have been the ruin of many a promising young policeman. Now, read that number back to me so I can call her.'

Peiperová answered quickly, and explained that she had been trying to find out more about the murdered girl.

'I got the class list from school and managed to find about eight of the girls.'

'About eight? Either it was eight or it wasn't.'

'Sorry, sir. Eight.'

'Good work, Officer. Do you have a list?'

'Yes, sir.'

There was a hesitation in her voice.

'What are you not telling me, Peiperová?'

'I hope you don't mind, sir, but I spoke to them to see if they could help.'

'That depends on what you asked them. And whether any of them is the murderer, of course.'

If you can hear a blush, Slonský heard it in Peiperová's voice.

'Sorry, sir. I didn't think of that.'

'Never mind. It's done now. What did they have to say?'

'Four or five of them … four of them say they haven't spoken to her since they left school. One hadn't seen or spoken to her since she went to Prague. The sixth one used to go out with Gruberová's brother when she was about fifteen so she still drops by from time to time to visit the mother, and she says Irina was there when she last went about two months ago.'

'Did they talk?'

'Mostly family talk, but Irina let out that she had a boyfriend in Prague. Markéta pressed her to say who he was, but all she could get was that everyone would be surprised when it got out.'

'She said "When it got out"?'

'Yes, sir. Markéta was very clear about that. Irina was expecting it to come out at some time, not soon, but definitely at some point.'

'That's interesting. Very good —'

'There's more, sir. The other two knew a bit more. Maria said that Irina told her that her boyfriend was a married man in his late thirties. He had rented her flat for her. Irina wouldn't give her the address because she said she couldn't risk anyone turning up while her boyfriend was there, but she let slip that it was in Strahov. She didn't know how much the rent was because her boyfriend paid it directly to the owner every six months.'

'Good work —'

'So I rang a letting agent in Prague and pretended I wanted a flat in Strahov like she had, and he asked me how much I wanted to pay, so I asked what the going rate was and he reckoned I'd be lucky to get anything below eleven thousand a month.'

'You've been a busy young officer, Peiperová.'

'But the really interesting one was Julia, sir.'

'Julia?'

'Julia went to school with Irina, but she works in Prague, sir. She went with Irina when she got the job as a dancer, but Julia still does it. She didn't know who the boyfriend was, but she was worried that Irina might have hooked up with a gangster. She says you get some rough types in those clubs, sir.'

'You don't say, Officer.'

'So when she saw Irina out shopping, she tried to catch up with her for a chat. She was wearing heels so she couldn't run, and she saw Irina go into a small restaurant, and that was when she found out who her lover was, sir. Not a gangster at all — quite the opposite, in fact. It was —'

'I know who it was, Peiperová. Have you told anyone?'

'No, sir. Just you.'

'Good. Keep it that way. You've done well, Peiperová. Are you there for a while?'

'Shift finishes at six, sir.'

'Well, Officer Navrátil and I are going to come to see you and get all this on paper.'

'I've written it all out, sir.'

'Good. Then Navrátil won't have so much writing to do. But we'll come anyway. There's a limited amount we can do in Prague at the moment. We'll see you in an hour or so.'

Slonský snapped the phone shut.

'Now why haven't you done all that?' he barked at Navrátil.

Peiperová had gone to make coffee.

'Navrátil, could you try not to look quite so much like a puppy when she talks to you?'

'Sir?'

'She's a good-looking girl who also seems to have a brain, but you're not selling yourself too well sitting there with a mouth as wide as a waste bin and dribble running down your chin.'

'I'm not dribbling,' Navrátil protested, but ran his hand over his chin just in case. 'Anyway, we're here on business.'

'Good of you to remember that, Navrátil. This is no time for lovey-dovey stuff.'

Peiperová pushed the door open and backed into the room bearing a tray.

'If you weren't dribbling before…' muttered Slonský, earning himself a glower from a reddening Navrátil.

'Is Sergeant Tomáš around?' asked Slonský.

'In the other room, sir.'

'Then I'll just go and have a word. It's only polite. You two chat about something, but not the case. I don't want to miss anything important.'

Before Navrátil could think of anything to say, Slonský had left the room and was stomping along the corridor.

'Well, that went well,' Slonský announced as they drove back to Prague.

'Yes, sir. But couldn't Officer Peiperová have simply faxed her report to us as she suggested?'

'You astonish me, Navrátil. One minute you're complaining we're not working on the case, so I arrange a nice trip out for you, and you carp about it.'

'I just thought we might have been able to use the time more productively.'

'I could. But could you?'

'Sir?'

Slonský sighed deeply and pushed his hat to the back of his head in exasperation.

'Don't tell me you wasted that golden opportunity I set up for you.'

'Sir?'

'You don't think I actually wanted to talk to Tomáš?'

'Sir?'

'Will you stop saying Sir in that half-witted tone of voice? I was hoping you would use the opportunity to get to know Officer Peiperová better.'

'She is nice, sir.'

'I know, Navrátil. I know exactly how nice you thought she was, and if she'd been sitting on my side of the desk she'd have seen for herself how taken you were with her. You'll have to learn some more self-control, Navrátil.'

'Sir!'

'You're lucky you didn't tip the desk over. Never mind that, lad, did you get her phone number?'

'I already had it, sir. You gave it to me.'

'That's the station number, Navrátil. I asked about her phone number.'

'I may have done, sir. On a completely different matter, do you think you'll need me on Saturday? I thought I might take a bus out to Kladno and see the countryside a bit.'

'I hope you've arranged a local guide, young man.'

'Yes, sir.'

Spehar's report confirmed that the photograph of Soucha had been addressed using the same printer as that of Banda and Gruberová. The surprise in Spehar's folder was that he had shown some initiative. Realising that the picture had been grabbed from a security camera, he had asked Navrátil where the house was so that he could get copies of the videotapes. Navrátil had forgotten to mention this, largely because he thought Spehar was only asking so that he could complete his paperwork accurately.

The owner had been out, explained Spehar, but there had been a security firm's plate on the gate, so he had telephoned them and a guard met him at the house. He had been careful not to disclose the reason for asking, but said that one of the house guests wanted to prove he had been there on a particular day. The guard showed him where the recording equipment was, and Spehar had used one of his clever little gadgets to transfer the files to a portable hard disk. The videos were therefore still at the house, but Spehar had copies. He thought Slonský might find the enclosed DVD of great interest.

His curiosity piqued, Slonský went straight to the canteen, with two objects in mind. First, he needed something to eat. Once that was secured, he would look for someone who could work a DVD player.

Chapter 18

Navrátil slept as well as any man could whose dreams featured a police uniform being removed, fortunately not his own. If he felt that his life may be about to change dramatically, that was as nothing compared with the shock awaiting him when he arrived at work.

Slonský was wearing a suit. That is to say, he was wearing a suit that did not look as if he had been sleeping in it for several years. He also sported a new tie. Navrátil knew it was a new tie because Slonský had omitted to remove the price label that dangled behind it.

'Are you going somewhere, sir?'

'We both are, Navrátil. It's time we had a few words with Dr Sammler, I've got an appointment with him at ten o'clock. We're getting a full ten minutes, Navrátil. I hope you're impressed.'

'I wish I'd known, sir. I'd have worn something more respectable.'

'You're perfectly respectable, lad.'

Navrátil combed his hair carefully and decided that he had better mention the price label to Slonský.

'Damn. Got any scissors, Navrátil?'

'No, sir.'

'Then go and ask Klinger. Klinger will have scissors. Klinger has everything.'

Klinger had scissors. Not only did he have small curved nail scissors, office scissors, first aid scissors and large wallpaper scissors, he also had a small pair of scissors built into his Swiss army knife, and he was prepared to let Navrátil borrow one of his pairs, provided he received a full briefing first in case there was something about Dr Sammler the fraud department ought to know.

Navrátil decided that 'ought to know' could not possibly encompass the forthcoming interview, since the relevance of that could only be assessed after it had taken place. He also reminded himself that Klinger had assumed that Banda had been in Sammler's house, which was the connection that Slonský must be investigating, so he explained that Slonský believed that Sammler may have possessed information about Banda of which he could not have realised the importance. They were going to have a brief word with him this morning to clarify exactly what the relationship between Sammler and Banda was.

'There! That didn't hurt, did it? But if Sammler mentions the word "Switzerland" at any point during this morning's little chat, no doubt you'll tell me about it when you bring the scissors back later,' said Klinger, giving what he believed was a cheery smile. Navrátil found it acutely unnerving.

'What did you tell him?' asked Slonský.

'Sir?'

'I warned you about that yesterday, son. Try to sound intelligent if you can. What did you tell Klinger?'

'He wanted to know what was going on in the investigation, sir.'

'Of course he did. And you wanted his scissors, so he finally had a bargaining tool. So what did you tell him? Before you answer, bear in mind that I've got the scissors and I could ruin your fun with Peiperová with one little snip.'

'I told him we were going to talk to Dr Sammler this morning to find out what relationship he had with Dr Banda.'

'You make it sound like they were a pair of shirt-lifters, Navrátil, but that should keep Klinger happy.'

'You might choose your words more carefully, Slonský,' Captain Lukas announced from the open doorway. 'Has somebody died?'

'Sir?'

'The suit, man. For once you look as if you've made an effort.'

'We're going to see Dr Sammler, sir.'

'Ah. Good. First-class. Be careful, Slonský. Don't want to upset him.'

'Unless he's the killer, sir. Can I upset him then?'

Sammler strode from his desk, hand extended in welcome, and showed them to some fine antique chairs in front of his desk.

'No computer, sir?'

'Over there. I'll let you into a secret. I can't work at this desk. It's completely impractical. But it is handsome, isn't it?'

'Yes, sir.'

Sammler spoke Czech rapidly and without hesitation, though with a trace of a German accent. He was sloppy about the difference between voiced and unvoiced consonants, particularly "s" and "z", but he exuded confidence. To Slonský's surprise, he smiled readily and spoke quite softly.

He was a well-built man, conservatively dressed with a stiff white collar on his striped shirt and starched white cuffs that protruded from his jacket and revealed elegant oval gold cufflinks. If you had never met him before you would know he was a banker.

'I'm grateful to you for giving us some of your valuable time, Dr Sammler.'

'Not at all. If I can assist your enquiries it is plainly my duty to do so.'

119

'Thank you. I must ask you to regard this conversation as confidential. Do you know Daniel Soucha?'

'Yes, of course. Although he is currently an opposition politician, those of us in the financial world try to maintain courteous relations with all sides.'

'May I ask, sir, whether you have lent him your country house?'

'Yes, I did. I think it was last summer. He needed a break, poor man, and I offered him the house for the weekend. To be perfectly frank, it suited me too. I probably ought not to say this, but the staff get sloppy when I don't use it for a while. I thought it would sharpen them up before I had guests there.'

Slonský produced the photograph of the swimming pool.

'Someone has sent us this, sir. Is that your pool?'

Sammler studied the photograph carefully. His mouth twisted in a grimace.

'Yes, it is. And that is Daniel Soucha. Though I have no idea who the other gentleman may be.'

'He wasn't invited by you, sir?'

'No. Though I ought to say that I placed no restrictions on Mr Soucha inviting any guests he wished. I might have hoped he would have shown better manners than to use my home for this … sordid connection.'

'Mr Soucha told us that you offered to send a girl to the house for him.'

'Yes, I did.'

'Would that be a prostitute, sir?'

'An escort, certainly. I had in mind someone who would offer a bit more than mere sex. But it wasn't my business where they finished up. I just wanted to give the man some relaxation.'

'Very friendly of you, sir. Have you ever done the same for Dr Banda?'

'I saw he'd landed himself in a spot of bother. No, I've never lent him my house. Of course, we know each other well, and in this business if someone influential asks you for a favour, you do what you can.'

'What kind of favours would those be, sir?'

Sammler hesitated.

'I hope I can rely on your discretion, Lieutenant. The lifestyle Dr Banda is obliged to lead is an expensive one. Before he joined the government he had a healthy income. Ministers of his level of experience and competence usually take a pay cut when they take office. They need an understanding bank manager.'

'So Dr Banda is a customer here, sir?'

Sammler smiled.

'I believe you already know that, Lieutenant. Didn't your Mr Klinger tell you?'

Slonský smiled back.

'There's a difference between gossip and fact, sir. Thank you for your help.'

'Not at all. It rather looks as if I've backed two poor horses, doesn't it?'

'Never mind, sir. There'll be other horses, no doubt.'

'No doubt,' agreed Sammler, as he held the door open for them.

'Well?' enquired Slonský.

'Well what, sir?'

'What did you make of him?'

'He seemed very German, sir. Not a bundle of fun.'

'He looked genuinely shocked by the photo. And he happily agreed that he offered the escort, so he obviously wasn't embarrassed by that.'

'So if he offered to arrange an escort, he plainly didn't know about Soucha's tastes.'

Slonský stopped walking and looked quizzically at Navrátil, who pulled up abruptly.

'What a quaint way of expressing it, Navrátil. His "tastes". I like that.'

'But if he wants to influence Soucha he'd want to give him something he values, and Soucha doesn't value a girl.'

'Yes, but Soucha doesn't want anyone to know about his "tastes", so he has to act as if he has been influenced, or he looks ungrateful. Even if he doesn't want the girl, he has to behave as if he does. So Sammler has no way of knowing that his bribe isn't the right thing to give, because Soucha will tell him it is.'

Navrátil punched the button at the pedestrian crossing.

'The girl would tell him, wouldn't she?'

'Would she? If you gave her five thousand crowns to have dinner with Soucha and spend the night there, and Soucha doesn't want you to do that, are you going to tell? Of course not, in case Sammler wants his money back. You'll join in the lie and tell anyone who asks that Soucha is a superstud who kept you up all night. You'll want people to think you really earned that cash.'

The traffic paused for a moment, and they crossed the road. Navrátil had to wait for a few moments for Slonský to catch up.

'We should have taken the car, son. I don't know why I let you talk me out of it.'

'I didn't say —'

'Now, the girl has a good reason to keep it to herself. But on the other hand, if she has discovered Soucha's secret, she can make a lot of money out of that knowledge.'

'Blackmail?'

'I think they call it "knowledge management" these days. But it's all academic, because there wasn't any such girl.'

'So that got us nowhere.'

'I wouldn't say that. We know that Banda banks with Sammler.'

'We already did. Klinger found out and we got a bank statement.'

'Yes, but how did Sammler know that Klinger had been asking about Banda's account? Klinger told us he'd called in a favour to get it, and he asked Banda's office. He didn't ask the bank.'

'I'd better check that with Klinger when we get back.'

'You do that, lad. I'll be across the street doing some quality control on their beer. Join me when you finish.'

'Klinger says he didn't contact the bank.'

'So who did he ask at Banda's office?'

'The Minister's private secretary. Presumably she told Banda about the so-called underpayment and he rang the bank.'

'Meaning he rang Sammler personally. And Sammler would wonder why Klinger wanted to know about Banda's account.'

'But when Banda was arrested, Sammler would know why we were looking at him.'

Slonský slurped up a mouthful of beer.

'That's yours.'

'Thanks.'

'Don't thank me. I told them you'd be paying.'

Chapter 19

There are some sights so startling that the human brain immediately refuses to believe them. Disregarding the evidence that it is receiving, it prefers to conclude that it is gripped by an hallucination. This explains why Slonský did not respond promptly when Klinger spoke to him.

'I said, I've been speaking to Technician Spehar,' Klinger repeated.

'What are you doing here?' Slonský responded. 'Has the garlic fallen off our doorpost?'

'Very risible. Now, is there somewhere in this filthy hole that I could sit down?'

Navrátil offered a chair, which Klinger swept with a few strokes of his handkerchief before sitting. There was then a brief pause while the fraud officer carefully refolded the handkerchief and returned it to his pocket.

'I have received an envelope through the post,' Klinger began.

'You too, eh? The Post Office is breaking all records for successful deliveries.'

'Please concentrate on the matter in hand.'

'Is this going to take long? Only I'll send Navrátil for some coffee if it is. I don't function too well first thing and the truth is, I've had a bit of a shock. I've never seen you on this floor before. I always assumed you came in through the front door and somehow rematerialised one floor above us.'

'It's a measure of the seriousness of the position that I have changed my habits, Slonský,' Klinger replied. 'Make the most of it — it may never happen again.'

'Do you want coffee or not?'

'If it's station coffee, then no, thank you. But don't let me stop you.'

'Navrátil — just two coffees then. And get one for yourself if you want. Pray continue, Brother Klinger.'

Navrátil was reluctant to leave, since it seemed likely that something earth-shattering was about to be revealed, and hovered just outside the door where he could hear Klinger's revelations.

'I have received a letter —'

'You said that.'

'A letter that contained some information of a most interesting nature, at least to me. Of course, I sent the envelope to the laboratories for examination, and Technician First Class Spehar has just telephoned to tell me that the envelope in question is identical to two that have been sent to you. He has suggested that we should meet to discuss this turn of events. That is what I am doing now.'

Slonský remained resolutely unexcited.

'It's true that I've had two envelopes. Didn't I mention that?'

'No, you did not.'

'Then I'll tell you the whole story. Navrátil, stop hanging around in the corridor and get yourself back in here. The coffee can wait.'

It was Klinger's turn to be surprised. For Slonský to defer refreshment of any kind was a rare occurrence.

Slonský produced a large folder and offered it to Klinger.

'You know that we are investigating the death of one Irina Gruberová, who was the mistress of Dr Albert Banda, of whom you may have heard.'

'And whose bank account details I furnished for you, at your request.'

'Yes, thank you. Or are you expecting hidden microphones to capture the fact that it wasn't your initiative?'

Klinger flapped his hand impatiently.

'The involvement of Dr Banda came to our notice because someone sent us a photograph of him having dinner with the victim on the evening of her death. That photograph came in an envelope that we passed to Technician First Class Spehar for examination.'

'Did the examination provide any useful information?'

'It was posted in the Ninth district, probably at a post office, and was addressed using a laser printer. Some time later, I received an identical envelope, this time containing a photograph of another prominent politician, Daniel Soucha.'

'Soucha! I know him.'

'Then you may not want to see the photograph. But it's in evidence envelope B2 if you do.'

Klinger riffled through the stack before him, extracted the envelope and examined the contents.

'I'm surprised. Financial circles gossip like any other, but I'd never heard any suggestion that Soucha went in for that kind of thing.'

'That seems to be the general reaction. Soucha was a bit surprised himself.'

'You showed him the photograph?'

'It seemed more tactful than putting it on the internet and inviting him to download it. The interesting thing about this photo is where it was taken.'

'The country house of Theodor Sammler.'

'You know it?'

'No, but I recall you asked me about it, and now I know why. And Sammler, as we know, knows Banda.'

'He's his bank manager, if that's the right word for someone who sits on the top floor making millions.'

Klinger drummed his fingers on the edge of the desk as he thought.

'There have been rumours for some time that Banda was under financial pressure. He was a very wealthy man before he joined the government, but his investments have not done well lately. With a reduced salary, and no change to his outgoings, it wouldn't surprise me if he had needed the help of someone like Sammler.'

'Yes, we know all that,' Slonský confirmed, causing Klinger to raise an eyebrow.

'You knew all this and you didn't tell me?'

'I thought someone with contacts like yours was sure to know it already.'

'Flattery will not divert my wrath, Slonský. I expressly asked young Navrátil to share anything relevant to my department.'

'Which he would have done, had we found any evidence of naughtiness. But being skint is not a crime yet, thank God. And of course poverty is relative. The Banda children are not exactly going round with their backsides hanging out of their trousers.'

'No,' conceded Klinger, 'but the holiday in the Mediterranean will probably have to be scaled down, which will hurt him just as much.'

'It will have to be scaled down,' agreed Slonský, 'because he's in cell five downstairs and we don't normally let remand prisoners hop off to the Med for a bit of R&R.'

Klinger indicated agreement with a sharp nod of his head.

'Do you think Banda killed her?'

'We haven't got a better candidate yet.'

'He doesn't strike me as the murdering kind.'

'Neither did Kvapil, who ran amok in the Roma camp a couple of years ago. One of the nicest chaps you could hope to meet, if you didn't have any gipsy blood in you. Which he, of course, corrected by letting it all drain out of you through your neck.'

'Kvapil and Banda are very different animals. Banda is a more cerebral type.'

'If you're going to follow the Lukas line that it's unthinkable that he is a murderer because he has a university doctorate, I beg to differ, and be warned that I'm prepared to use reasonable force to defend my position.'

Klinger held his hands up in a gesture of surrender.

'It's your case; not my business. My interest is in the little bundle I've had through the post.'

'Say more, gentle sage.'

'The envelope contains a set of documents showing large transfers of currency to a bank account in Liechtenstein. Ordinarily I would have no access to the details of that account, but our informant has helpfully provided a certificate of ownership.'

Slonský whistled.

'How did he get that?'

'I have no idea. Liechtenstein banking security is legendary. Only the bank where it's held would have that information and they wouldn't release it short of an Interpol warrant. Even then, they'd argue first.'

'And who is the lucky account holder?'

'One Leoš Holec.'

'Never heard of him.'

'You haven't. I have. Holec is a senior adviser to the Finance Ministry and the National Bank.'

'Does that mean that sneaking large sums of money out of the country is okay?'

'It means it definitely is not okay, especially if they're sums of money far in excess of anything that has been declared to the tax authorities. Holec has been banking more money in Liechtenstein than he has been earning in this country, yet he appears not to have any other income. Conclusion?'

'Some kind person has been sending him the occasional postal order.'

'For several million crowns at a time. And presumably Holec has been doing something to earn this largesse. And we further presume that whatever he has been doing, he won't want us to look into it. But we will.'

Navrátil interrupted to ask the obvious question. 'Could Sammler have known about these payments?'

'They weren't made by his bank — at least, not by the Czech part of it. And I can't imagine that bankers talk about this kind of arrangement openly. But if anyone could know, Sammler is the kind of person who might.'

Slonský rolled his pencil back and forth across his desk, an action that he expected would irritate Klinger intensely.

'Do you have to do that?'

'Sorry. It helps me think. So you'll call in Holec and try to find out who arranged this, but if it wasn't Sammler then tying Sammler to it is likely to be very difficult. We'd have to show that he definitely knew about it. It's the same problem we face with Soucha and Banda. Sammler doesn't seem to have known that Soucha was gay, and Banda says he showed no interest in his private affairs and therefore probably didn't know about Gruberová.'

'But if Sammler is the only link between them, he has to be involved,' offered Navrátil.

'Obvious, but false logic,' Klinger replied. 'He may be the only link we know about, but as soon as the defence find one other that's our case in ruins. And the connections between Sammler and any one of them are tenuous.'

'I hate to say it,' said Slonský, 'but Klinger is right. We'd never get a conviction based on our guess that Sammler knows three important people. And even if Sammler has this information, it only has value if he keeps it to himself. How can he profit by it getting out? If he knows about Gruberová or Mario —'

126

'Mario?' asked Klinger.

'The other man in the photo. To repeat, if he knows about Gruberová or Mario he has a hold over Banda and Soucha, but only so long as nobody else knows. Once the cat is out of the bag, his grip is broken, so he is the last person to want to let it out. There has to be someone else that we don't know about.'

'Agreed,' said Klinger. 'But who?'

'Difficult to say,' Slonský pronounced, 'since we don't know about them. But let's think about a strategy to plug some of the gaps in our knowledge. How quickly can you pull in Holec?'

'Given the sums involved, it could be sometime today.'

'Then you'll be able to ask him how these transfers were arranged. There can only be a small number of people who would know about this set-up. Then we take your list and cross-check it against Soucha and Banda to look for the links.'

'And if there are none?'

'Then Banda goes down for a very long time because there's probably enough to implicate him. Besides, I don't like the little greaseball.'

'Hardly adequate reason for imprisoning him, Slonský,' Klinger said.

'I don't know; it's pretty convincing from where I'm sitting.'

Navrátil felt moved to interject.

'But sir, if we've agreed he's being framed, and we put him away, doesn't that mean the real criminal has got away with it?'

'Don't be a nit-picker, Navrátil. We want a criminal, and we'll have found a criminal. There may not be a perfect match between what he has done and what he goes down for, but that's a small administrative detail. However, I take the point that in an ideal world we should only jail men for their own crimes and not other people's, so I promise I'll really try to find someone else.'

When Klinger had gone, Slonský decided that he had better brief Lukas on the latest developments. Navrátil was despatched to the canteen with instructions to wait ten minutes before he bought the coffee so it would still be hot when Slonský returned.

'I'm perturbed,' Lukas declared. 'This murder is becoming a complicated web of crime.'

'Exactly, sir.'

'It takes a lot to get Klinger to come down to this floor. He keeps muttering about dirty doorknobs.'

'I believe it's a recognised medical condition, sir.'

'Having dirty doorknobs?'

'No, being worried about them. But there's no doubt that Technician Spehar has done us a great service. If he hadn't been alert we might never have put these envelopes together.'

Lukas sucked the leg of his spectacles pensively.

'It's leaving things a bit to chance, don't you think?'

'Sir?'

'Well, I mean, if one chap is sending all these envelopes, and he wants us to realise that this is all part of one big plan, sending them to two policemen who might never speak to each other is a fairly inefficient way of getting that across.'

Slonský jerked upright in his chair.

'I didn't think of it as one plan, sir. I thought it was just information that came to hand being sent to whomever was best placed to pick it up and deal with it.'

'So murder stuff would come to you, and fraud stuff to Klinger, just because that's the natural way of things?'

'Yes. No point sending fraud papers to me — I don't know the first thing about financial crime, except that they keep putting the price of German beer up.'

'Hardly criminal, Slonský.'

'Matter of opinion, sir.'

'But — to return to my point — why send the picture of Soucha to you? If it's criminal, it should go to the vice squad.'

'I thought we agreed it wasn't criminal, sir.'

'Then why send it to us at all? If he wants a fuss, he should send it to the gutter press. He can't know that we're going to take a blind bit of notice of it.'

Slonský stood and thrust his hands deep into his pockets. He thought better when he walked, so he started pacing the length of Lukas' rug, back and forth, all the while thinking hard.

'So you're arguing that the key to this is the photo of Soucha, because it has no value on its own. Sent to us, we would ignore it. If it went anywhere else, it would provoke a reaction, but not the reaction the sender wants. The sender sent it to us because he wanted us to act upon it, but because it wasn't criminal there must be another reason why he thought we might follow it up. There's some link in his mind that we haven't worked out yet.'

'That's about the sum of it,' said Lukas, who was actually quite uncertain that Slonský's summary represented his own thoughts at all.

'Is he telling us Soucha killed Irina?'

'That's a bit far-fetched, Slonský. Why would Soucha do that?'

'But the sender forwarded both pictures to me. He sees a connection where I don't. Soucha and Banda have something in common.'

Lukas' eyes opened wide as a thought flitted through his head.

'Could it be that he has murdered Mario? Both men's lovers have been killed.'

'But then he would have sent the picture after one crime but probably before the other. We know he didn't send the first picture until Irina's discovery was in the newspapers, but there haven't been any gay Austrians killed in Prague for a while.'

'Get onto the report system, Slonský. See if there are any murder victims anywhere in the Czech Republic who could possibly be Mario. It's a slim chance, but it's all we have at the moment.'

'Get onto the report system, Navrátil. See if there are any murder victims anywhere in the Czech Republic who could possibly be Mario. It's a slim chance, but it's all we have at the moment.'

Navrátil scribbled a note to himself.

'Do you really think that's the link, sir?'

'I don't know, Navrátil. But neither do you, and we won't until you do the search, so shift yourself. I'll be down in the cells when you finish.'

Slonský flicked the door open with his foot and entered with a cheery 'Room service!'

'Very droll,' said Banda. 'Have you come to threaten me in some new way?'

'No,' said Slonský. 'I come bearing gifts.'

He handed Banda a 25cl bottle of red wine and a plastic beaker.

'I can't give you glass, I'm afraid, in case you smash it and slice your jugular with the shards.'

'I wouldn't give you the satisfaction,' Banda replied. 'But I should thank you for this s*mall* token.'

'Not at all. It's all part of our new justice system. Since the new Interior Minister arrived there have been some changes.'

'Don't rub it in. And, as one who knows the new minister personally, enjoy the honeymoon. It won't last.'

'Got any dirt on him we could save for a rainy day?'

Banda considered.

'It would be disloyal to share discreditable information about a coalition colleague. But if you have an idle moment you might want to consider how his son got a scholarship to a large American university.'

Slonský smiled broadly.

'I can see this heralds a whole new era of co-operation between the accused and forces of law and order. Mind if I sit?'

'It's your house. I'm a guest here.'

Slonský perched himself on the end of the bed. It was a tricky operation, since the cot was rather lower than Slonský had expected.

'I'd like to talk about your relationship with Daniel Soucha.'

'I don't have a relationship with Daniel Soucha.'

'I mean a professional relationship.'

'I don't have a professional relationship with him.'

'What's he like?'

Banda sipped his wine, not without an involuntary grimace.

'A populist of the worst kind. His grasp of economics is feeble, his approach to law and order is slack and his ethics are questionable.'

'In the interests of balance,' Slonský enquired, 'what are his bad points?'

'He is the darling of the chattering classes. Looks good on television. But there's no substance to him.'

'What could he have against you?'

Banda's beaker paused abruptly in its upward course.

'Against me? Why would he have anything against me?'

'You're a political rival.'

'Of course. I thought you were hinting at something personal.'

'I might have been.'

Banda sit in silence for a few moments, thinking deeply.

'You're suggesting that he might be behind the framing of me?'

'It doesn't sound likely, unless he then decided to do the same to himself in a sudden fit of even-handedness. But evidence has come to hand that suggests that there is a link between you. I can't begin to imagine what that could be, but the obvious answer was to ask you.'

'I wish I could help, but I can't think of any possible link between me and that serpent.'

'Apart from the fact that you're both in the manure in a big way.'

'If you say so. But I'm getting quite a lot of writing done here. If I could have some new curtains, perhaps a room with a view…'

'I'll have a word with the hotel manager.'

'That neanderthal on the front desk?'

'Sergeant Mucha? He's good at what he does. I've known him for years. Just remember that there are nasty people out there gunning for you, but so long as Mucha is between you and the outside world, you're safe in here.'

'Forgive me if I refuse to be comforted by that thought.'

'Do me a favour. Keep thinking about my question. The bottom line is that you don't get out until we bring someone else in.' Slonský rose from the bed. 'I have to take the bottle, I'm afraid. It's glass. Just promise me you won't do anything silly with the beaker and you can keep the wine.'

Banda raised his right hand.

'I do so swear.'

'Thank you. Now I must go and visit my other guests. We must do this again sometime.'

Holec looked unwell. He was perspiring, his colour was poor and his hands trembled as he mopped his brow with a large white handkerchief.

'I'm waiting, Mr Holec,' Klinger intoned, evenly but with a hint of menace.

'I don't know anything. I didn't open this account. I haven't made any payments into it.'

'Come now, Mr Holec. To open such an account, one needs a passport. Here is a copy of your passport attached to the application form. Do you seriously expect me to believe that you lent your passport to someone who looks enough like you to open an account in your name? And you didn't notice your passport had gone missing?'

'It's not my money,' Holec whined.

'It won't be now,' conceded Klinger. 'We'll repatriate it. And since you say it isn't yours I'm sure you'll willingly sign some paperwork allowing us to reclaim the cash and examine all the transactions connected with it.'

Holec bowed his head and began to wring his hands. Klinger sat patiently, something that he had perfected over a few years. Sit still, keep quiet, let them speak when they want to fill the silence.

'I didn't realise it was so much. I only did one thing for them.'

'Who are "they"?'

'It's an investment fund in Austria. They contacted me because I was organising the sale of a company here and their bid had been ruled out of time. They wanted to argue about the timetable and I said that it couldn't be changed but in any event there was a better deal about to come up, and told them about another sale. It wasn't illegal! I just gave them advance notice.'

'And?'

'They bought the company before it went on the market, and next thing I knew a bankers' draft for a hundred thousand euros was sitting on my desk. I obviously couldn't bank it here, so I asked around for ways of disposing of it.'

'You mean hiding it.'

'Yes, I suppose I do. If I'd known then what I know now, I obviously should have shredded it or sent it back. But it was a bit like a finder's fee. I didn't see anything wrong in it.'

'However, Mr Holec, that does not explain these other sixteen transactions, some for much larger sums.'

'I don't remember them all. The same firm used to ring and ask about investments in the old Eastern bloc.'

'I can't help noticing that one of these payments is for rather more than fifteen million euros. That must have been quite a profitable deal for them if they could afford to pay you that much commission.'

'That was a Romanian cement works. I didn't realise that their properties were sitting on top of an oilfield. They'd kept it quiet but the Austrians must have assumed I'd known.'

'And they were very grateful, it seems.'

'Yes. So it seems.'

'And it never crossed your mind to give this money back.'

'I didn't think I'd done anything illegal.'

'Well, you didn't pay tax on it. And there is an interesting debate to be had as to whether a government adviser should profit personally from the sale of assets. But in any event you know as well as I do that sending such large sums abroad without declaring them is an offence.'

'I'll willingly pay the tax,' Holec squealed.

'With what? The assets will be confiscated and, so far as I can see, your other accounts don't contain enough to pay this amount of tax. Oh, dear, Mr Holec, prepare yourself for a few years in jail.'

Holec began to sob.

'My wife!' he cried. 'The shame will kill her. She's not strong.'

Klinger pushed his chair back and gathered his papers together.

'You've got time to divorce her before the trial begins. Then she can tell her friends that she knew you were a devious little criminal and they'll congratulate her for finding you out before we did.'

Mucha entered bearing a cardboard box. Slonský glanced up from his paperwork and greeted him.

'Wife finally slung you out, eh? Well, you can't sleep here.'

'Ha-de-ha-ha. These are not my possessions. My life runs to more than a videotape and a couple of badly typed statements. Where's Navrátil?'

'Lying in a meadow somewhere plaiting wild flowers for his true love's hair. I couldn't stand the big sad eyes any longer so I sent him to Kladno to check something in one of the statements from Gruberová's friends. He's turned into a fearsome mythical beast, half man, half puppy.'

'Navrátil the were-puppy.'

'That's about the size of it. We'd better requisition some silver bullets in case he turns on us at the new moon.'

'I'll check the stores.'

'So what's in the box?'

'I thought it would be a nice simple case for him to cut his teeth on. Old dear at Smíchov burgled by three lads. One of them works for a television installation company. He had been there a day or two ago and rigged a window so it wouldn't close properly. He denies it, of course, but one of the boys is busy spilling all the beans he can.'

'How sweet. I love it when kids play nicely together.'

'The problem was that due to some illegal parking they couldn't get their truck down her street, so they parked it on an office forecourt and ran backwards and forwards loading it up. Unfortunately, they didn't spot the security cameras on the office building, so we have a nice clear videotape and a couple of confessions. One of them is holding out but I thought Navrátil would enjoy wrapping it up.'

'Will it keep till tomorrow?'

'I'll charge them all anyway.'

'Just leave the box on his desk and I'll get him on it as soon as he comes back. *If* he comes back, that is. Since he fell for Officer Peiperová his brain has gone to mush. What is it with women, old pal? I'm no expert, but you've managed it. How many years have you been married?'

'Twenty-eight, and around half of them have been happy. I find it helps if I have as little as possible to do with her family. Her dad was a good type, but then he went and died on me.'

'Selfish so-and-so.'

'That's what I thought, leaving me alone with his wife and his other daughters. My wife's not a bad sort, but her sisters are harpies.'

'If it makes you feel happy I'll ticket their broomsticks if I see them parked around town.'

'You do that. Just watch for them turning you into a frog.'

When Mucha had left Slonský remembered another piece of security footage that he had watched several times without really understanding what he was watching. However, it spurred him to pick up the phone to Spehar.

'That clever gadget of yours — did it pick up any other days apart from the weekend that Soucha stayed at the house?'

'I copied the entire hard disk. However far it goes back, we've got it.'

Slonský flicked through his files and gave Spehar a date to check. He grabbed his coat and decided to take a walk, possibly taking in a sausage stall on the way.

Slonský ambled down the ramp to the underground garage, ducking under the black and yellow barrier that filled the whole of the opening. There was a small cabin at the back of the car park by the elevators from which a figure clad all in maroon emerged.

'This is a private car park, sir. If you're visiting anyone here I must ask you to go to the front door.'

'I don't do front doors,' replied Slonský, waving his badge at nobody in particular. 'Can we have a little chat in that palatial sentry-post of yours?'

The guard waved him ahead and offered Slonský a cup of instant coffee, which was accepted with alacrity.

'Quite a swish set-up you have here,' the detective said.

'State of the art, they tell me.'

'Do you open the barrier from here?'

'I can, but most of the time the number-plate recognition system does it automatically.'

'So it knows all the regulars?'

'Yes.'

'We're investigating a break-in earlier this year. It seems that the villains couldn't park outside so they must have hidden their vehicle off the street somewhere.'

'Won't be here, unless it was a skateboard. Nobody gets in or out without being checked.'

'Is there a log?'

'There will be. The boss is a stickler for that. The system itself logs all the entries by the cars it knows. We keep a separate sheet for visitors.'

He reached above him to produce a black folder which he offered to Slonský. Slonský fished in his pocket for a little slip of paper on which he had written a registration number that he carefully avoided letting the security guard see.

'How do I get to see the residents' log?'

'Surely none of them can be involved. They're all respectable people.'

'No doubt they are, but they may have disreputable friends who borrow their cars. I'd like to be able to exclude your tenants from my enquiries, but without the log…' He shrugged expressively.

The security man clicked a couple of buttons on his keyboard.

'What date?'

'Tuesday, 7th February.'

A few more clicks called up a list of entries and exits for the date in question. Slonský read it attentively.

'Can we go over to the next day?'

'There you go. Anything useful?'

'Oh yes,' said Slonský, then, seeing the guard's surprise he added, 'it's always helpful to be able to exclude someone from your enquiries. Could I make a copy of this just to prove the point?'

The guard printed off a couple of pages at Slonský's direction.

'Thanks. And thanks for the coffee. I'll see myself out.'

Slonský allowed himself a broad smile as he climbed the ramp to the outside world. This called for a celebration pastry. Shame Navrátil was not there to share in it, but Slonský could have one for him too.

*

Chapter 20

Slonský was no chess player, but he played a mean hand of *sedma* when his head was clear, and he knew the importance of not rushing the last few tricks just because you had made a breakthrough. It was simply too easy to mess up when it all seemed to be going well. Before making any further moves he decided to write out what he had discovered and run it past Navrátil, inviting him to look for holes in the argument. If it passed that test, the next step was to take it to Lukas, who would doubtless prove a less demanding hurdle.

The less demanding hurdle chose that moment to make an impromptu visit to Slonský's office.

'Ah, Slonský, a word if you please.'

Slonský tried to close the folder both hurriedly and nonchalantly at the same time, and was acutely aware that he must have looked every bit as guilty as he appeared to his grandmother at the age of eight when she was investigating a case of gingerbread theft and unexpectedly climbed up to his tree house.

'Of course, sir.'

'The Prosecutor's office has been in contact with me. The Prosecutor has been reading the newspapers, Slonský.'

'I've warned him about that, sir. They're a tissue of lies and ill-informed speculation. I believe you said so yourself.'

'Be that as it may, Slonský, he doesn't like what he is reading.'

'Has he tried changing his newspaper, sir?'

'It is what he isn't reading that disquiets him, Slonský. He isn't reading about an arrest, and he isn't reading about a charge.'

'It's his job to decide on a charge, sir, not mine.'

'Don't be obtuse, Slonský. His point is that the question is not even being asked of him, and he would like me to explain why.'

Slonský let out a deep exhalation of relief.

'That's all right then. For a moment I thought I was going to have to come up with something.'

'You do, Slonský, because I can't answer him unless you answer me.'

Slonský was not a small man, and when he decided to stand to attention in the centre of the office floor Lukas found the experience rather intimidating.

'Beg to report, sir, that I am keeping the Prosecutor uninformed as a mark of respect to his integrity, sir.'

Slonský could have sworn that Lukas mouthed the words silently as he mulled them over.

'A mark of respect to his integrity? What the devil does that mean?'

Slonský stood at ease.

'Who appointed the Prosecutor, sir? Dr Banda did. It could therefore be argued that the Prosecutor may be beholden to Dr Banda and any decision other than charging the ex-Minister would look to some eyes like a cover-up.'

'Ye-es…' began Lukas, rather uncertainly.

'But at the same time charging him may look like political opportunism of the worst kind — kicking a man when he is down.' Slonský bent close to Lukas so that he could drop his voice in revealing the full cunning of the plan he had just concocted on the hoof. 'By not giving the Prosecutor a decision to make until I have incontrovertible proof of either guilt or innocence, sir, I am protecting him from ill-informed public criticism and possible interference from higher circles.'

'Yes, yes, I can see that,' agreed Lukas. 'I'll put those points to the Prosecutor and see what he says.' In the doorway he paused. 'You, er, might just give me a written note of your argument — just so I don't forget to mention something important.'

'Certainly, sir. Within the hour.'

Slonský watched the door close and breathed another large sigh of relief.

'God,' he muttered, 'I hope he never gets promoted. I could never strike that lucky again.'

The unsuspecting prey was grazing contentedly, chewing slowly and silently, as the great predator sighted him and carefully weighed up the right moment to strike. With a coffee in one hand and the least disgusting of the available sandwiches in the other, Slonský dropped into the seat opposite Němec, who reacted instinctively by wrapping his hairy forearms around his bowl to protect his soup.

Slonský was generally given to formality, but Němec had always rated the familiar greeting.

'Ahoj, Josef.'

'You're looking a bit peaky. Everything all right?'

Němec was fairly sure that he looked in the best of health. Of course, he could do with losing a kilo or two — who couldn't? — but for his age he was doing pretty well, he thought.

'Yes, fine, thanks. Why the sudden concern for my health?'

'It would be such a shame if anything happened to spoil your retirement when you're so close to it.'

Němec tore off a mouthful of bread, sprinkled a little salt on it, and chewed it thoughtfully.

'Slonský, how long have we known each other?'

'Thirty-eight years, old pal.'

'That's right. We know each other better than any other pair in the whole police force, I reckon. So when I detect some kind of scheming going on, you'd better believe I know what I'm talking about. I know you dread retiring, so why should you think I'd be any different?'

'Because you have a family, and grandchildren to play with, and lots of things you've told me you want to do. You said you wanted to go skiing in the Alps, for example.'

'Slonský, I said that in 1976. We weren't going anywhere then. My skiing days are behind me.'

'Lots of breweries you haven't visited. That vegetable plot of yours — you work miracles on it in your time off, so think what you could do if you could work on it full time.'

'I don't like the heavy emphasis on "full time" in that last comment of yours. Why don't you just tell me what you're after? Then I can tell you to stick it up your backside and we can part the best of friends.'

Slonský took a mouthful of roll. To his horror, it proved to contain salad.

'Hell, that's like eating a hedge. Give me a napkin so I can spit it out.'

'You should have had the soup. I was enjoying that till you came.'

'The fact is, you have it in your power to do me a great favour at little or no cost to yourself. Have they given you a finishing date yet?'

'Last day of April. Why?'

'Advert out to replace you?'

'Internal selection.'

'Have you got your eye on anyone?'

'No. I haven't promised it. I don't see how I could, since it won't be my decision.'

'That's fine. Just wanted to know my plan wasn't a waste of time.'

'You have a plan?'

'Yes.'

Němec eyed Slonský with great suspicion.

'I'm just trying to remember any plan of yours that ever worked out well for anyone but you. No, I can't think of one.'

'There was the trip to go climbing in the Tatras with those young policewomen.'

'I broke my wrist, remember. Someone sitting not too far from me yanked on the rope when I hadn't fixed it to the pin and I slid down the rockface. Not your finest hour.'

'You persist in looking on the black side, Josef. Those girls were so impressed with the stoic way you bore the pain. If you'd played your cards right you could have got off with any of them.'

'I could, if I hadn't been in a hospital in Poprad getting my arm put back together without adequate painkillers while you lot were having a high old time in the mountains.'

'Point taken. But this plan will be for the good of the force, trust me.'

Němec slurped another spoonful of soup.

'No more broken bones?'

'Guaranteed.'

'I won't be retired in disgrace?'

'Not unless you've done something I haven't heard about. You haven't, have you?'

'You sound like a gossip columnist. No, I haven't. And I'm going to keep it that way, so if it involves bending the law, count me out.'

'Not in the least, old friend. What do you take me for?'

'Out of respect for our friendship, Slonský, I won't answer that.'

Navrátil had run off to play with the contents of Mucha's cardboard box, so Slonský was left to his own devices for a few hours. There were two things he had to do, so he tossed a coin to decide which to do first. It came down heads, so he tossed it twice more until it came down tails, then went off to see Captain Lukas.

Lukas read Slonský's memorandum carefully, then returned to the top and read it again.

'I see Captain Němec has put his name to this.'

'Yes, sir. It's typical of the selfless generosity of the man.'

'Indeed. A first class officer. We shall miss him. When does he retire?'

Slonský replied a little too quickly. 'Thirtieth of April, sir.' He added, as an afterthought, 'I think.'

'Well, I'm bound to say I'm rather surprised, Slonský. I had you marked down as a confirmed misogynist.'

'No, lapsed Catholic, sir.'

'It's certainly a novel idea. And it meets several of the Director's requirements for force development.'

That's not a coincidence, thought Slonský, who had spent his evening reading the damn things over and over until he could recite them in his sleep.

Lukas had suddenly grown suspicious.

'You don't have any plans to get rid of Navrátil, do you?'

'Certainly not, sir. The boy is a future star and I intend to mould him in my own image to further his prospects.'

Lukas clearly did not believe that modelling oneself on Slonský would further anyone's career, but he let the point go. The old detective obviously meant well, and there was no denying that Slonský and Navrátil were becoming a very effective team.

'I think,' said Lukas, 'that I shall add my name to this proposal and we shall see what our superiors make of it. If we're successful, have you anyone in mind for the job?'

'Oh, yes,' said Slonský, but then held his peace.

Navrátil was in the interview room, writing out some of the notes that he had scrawled.

'How did it go, son?' asked Slonský.

'Šmíd and Dort are singing a sweet tune, but I can't get anywhere with Jiskra,' Navrátil replied.

'Where's Jiskra now?'

'Next door, looking very smug. The other two won't implicate him directly.'

'Why not?'

'I think they're frightened of him.'

'Are you frightened of him?' Slonský's concern was obvious.

'No. He thinks he's hard but he hasn't met any of the real hard nuts.'

'Thought not. I'll be back in two minutes and then we'll sort this out together.'

Slonský paid a quick visit to the washroom and rejoined Navrátil. They pushed the door open and greeted Jiskra, who was slouching in a chair looking exaggeratedly cool.

'When do I get out?' he asked.

'Let's say around three years from now and counting,' said Slonský.

'You can't pin anything on me,' said Jiskra. 'I'm out of here.'

'No,' said Slonský, 'you're inside for three years heading towards four and if you give me grief I can make sure it's nudging five.'

'Yeah, well, I ain't getting convicted so it don't matter what the sentence might have been.'

Slonský growled.

'If I had my way we'd add eighteen months for grievous bodily harm to the Czech language. However, I don't get to decide on the length of your sentence.'

Jiskra grinned.

'But,' Slonský continued, 'I can recommend where you serve it. Present for you.'

He suddenly tossed a small bar of wet soap he had picked up in the restroom against Jiskra's knee. It dropped to the floor, and Jiskra leaned forward to pick it up.

'What's that?' he asked.

'That,' said Slonský, 'is the last time you'll dare to pick up a bar of soap you've dropped for the next four years.'

Jiskra's gaze flicked nervously between them.

'You're joking, right?'

'I'm joking, wrong,' said Slonský. 'Remember some of your cellmates won't have seen a woman since bubble perms were in fashion and everyone was going round in shell suits.'

'I'll ask for solitary.'

'You can't ask for solitary!' Slonský's scornful voice boomed across the chamber. 'They don't do single occupancy rates at Pankrác. You're damn lucky if you get a whole bed to yourself.'

'Don't matter. You can't get me put away without evidence.'

Slonský grabbed the arms of the chair and glowered into Jiskra's eyes.

'Even if you could enjoy the showers in Pankrác, what do you think it's going to do to Šmíd and Dort when I tell them about it in a few minutes? Do you think they'll be as fearless as you are? Or do you think they'll whimper like babes and sign anything that gets them a nice quiet prison in the country somewhere? Your call. You've got as long as it takes Navrátil and me to grab a quick coffee.'

Slonský steered Navrátil outside and they headed for the canteen.

'Do you really think he'll co-operate ten minutes from now?' asked Navrátil.

'I don't know. We never will, because you're not going back in ten minutes. We'll leave him alone for a good long time to work up a sweat. By the time you go back he'll have decided you've abandoned him to be the plaything of a bunch of hairy lifers and he'll be so pleased to see you he'll sign a blank confession. Now, where are we going for coffee?'

They left the building and were immediately accosted by Valentin, who looked anxious.

'I was trying to think how I could get you to meet me,' he admitted.

'We were just going out for morning coffee,' beamed Slonský. 'Care to join us?'

'Maybe something a bit stronger than coffee. There's a café on the corner.'

'I know,' said Slonský. 'Ghastly place, always full of policemen. Come on, this way.'

He strode across the road and soon had the three of them arranged around a small table with a coffee before each and a small brandy keeping Valentin's cup company.

'What's the big story?'

'I was hoping you'd have one for me. Remember my deadline? I don't want to go back to the days when I had to work for my living, Slonský. I need that retainer. And when I tell you what I've got for you, I think you'll agree I deserve a helping hand from the forces of law and order.'

141

Valentin savoured the first brandy of the day, oblivious to the tension he was generating in his audience.

'Well?' asked Slonský. 'We haven't come here to watch you drink.'

'You asked me what I knew about Sammler, and I admitted I knew very little, but I thought my colleague in Vienna would know more. So I rang him.'

'I know,' said Slonský. 'I paid for the call.'

'And you got your money's worth. The chap in Vienna had a strange, incomplete sort of story to tell, but it hinges on a photograph. Apologies for the quality — he faxed it to me — though truth to tell the original isn't much better.'

Valentin offered a black and white photograph. It showed four young people apparently sharing a picnic. To the right, a woman was resting her head on a man's shoulder. They were listening to a girl playing the guitar. In the foreground a young man had a notebook open and was writing something.

The woman cuddling the man had blonde hair reaching below her shoulders. He was the owner of a curly beard and a pair of rimless spectacles. Both of them wore a standard intellectual's outfit of roll neck sweater and jeans. The guitarist was wearing something lighter in colour. Her face could not be seen clearly because the picture showed only a profile. The writer had thick, dark hair and was wearing a corduroy or velvet jacket and jeans.

'Recognise him? That's Theodor Sammler, according to our man in Vienna.'

'Date of the picture?'

'I'll come to that, but probably around 1971 or 1972. Sammler had not long started as a student at Tübingen.'

Valentin took a further sip of his brandy, then noticed that it was empty. This discovery threw him into such confusion that he stopped talking until Slonský took command of the crisis and ordered another.

'The reason for dating it 1971-2 is the woman on the rug with the bearded guy. She is Gudrun Ensslin.'

The theatrical pause for a reaction produced absolutely nothing.

'We're obviously meant to know who Gudrun Ensslin is, but I don't. And Navrátil won't have any chance.'

'Gudrun Ensslin was one of the leaders of the German Rote Armee Fraktion. You know, the Baader-Meinhof mob.'

'Terrorists,' said Slonský. 'Sammler was hanging out with left-wing terrorists?'

'So it seems. It can't be before 1970 because he was still at home then, and in June 1972 Ensslin was arrested and never got out before she committed suicide in prison in 1977.'

'Date?' snapped Slonský.

'18th October. You'll remember that the Red Army Faction tried to engineer an exchange of prisoners by kidnapping an industrialist and then hijacking a Lufthansa airliner. When this failed to work, the leaders committed suicide in prison. Now, plainly the involvement of a leading establishment banker in terrorism would be big news, but there is absolutely nothing around to indicate that. He doesn't seem to have been at the kidnapping or the hijacking, and none of those who continued the Red Army struggle name him or even seem to know of him.'

'Interesting, but how does it help us?'

'First, because the story doesn't end there. It was whispered that Sammler was using daddy's money to bankroll some of the RAF's work. His father's reaction was to prevent young Theodor having access to any bank accounts except his own little allowance, but also to decide that he must be removed from Germany to break links with his former friends and get the West German police off the Sammlers' backs. Theodor had finished his doctorate by 1977 so he was sent off to Austria to work for a small bank there. He proved to be the cuckoo in the nest. Within five years he had more or less taken full control.'

'I can imagine that,' said Slonský. 'He wouldn't like being number two to anyone.'

'That brings me to the second interesting fact our man had for us. You were speculating the other day as to why Sammler doesn't go back to Germany to make his fortune on the bigger stage in Frankfurt. The simple answer is that he can't. The German police never formally closed their enquiry into his links with terrorism and he is worried he could still be arrested.'

'It's a long time ago,' said Slonský. 'Who would remember all that now?'

Valentin drew a long, satisfying slurp and smiled broadly.

'His father would.'

'Sammler's father is still alive?'

'Alive and in the pink. He lives in a retirement home in the Black Forest. He is ninety-three but still in full possession of his marbles, they say. And he hasn't spoken to Sammler since that day in 1977 when he put him on the train to Austria.'

Navrátil shook his head.

'I can't imagine your own dad not speaking to you for thirty years.'

Valentin ignored the comment.

'I got on to our man in Frankfurt, who gave me a few more details. By the way, you owe me for the phone call. I've got old Sammler's address in case you want a word. It seems that his prime concern was that his son was turning into a Communist fellow traveller, so the father's idea was to take him away from his circle of bad influences, and give him a healthy pile of cash to make his fortune. Old Sammler reasoned that when the money started coming in, Theodor would be hooked on capitalism, and so it proved.'

'So does this exonerate Sammler, or point the finger at him?' asked Slonský.

Valentin appeared shocked at the mere suggestion that he might know the answer to this.

'You're the cops,' he said. 'You work it out.'

'It's a tenuous link in the chain of evidence,' Slonský decided. 'A photograph showing someone who might be Sammler having a picnic with someone who might be a famous terrorist without anything to suggest that Sammler was ever a fellow traveller.'

'Except his dad's belief,' Navrátil added. 'Presumably his dad had his reasons.'

Slonský finished his beer with one long glug.

'Well, there's only one way to find out,' he told them. 'We'll have to ask him.'

'You want to go where?' gasped Lukas.

'The Black Forest, sir. It's in Germany,' Slonský added helpfully.

'I know where it is, Slonský. I also know how far away it is. It must be six hundred kilometres or more.'

'I've done some research, sir. That's the price of two flights, and that's the corresponding rail fare. But then we have to get to the nursing home, which is a fairly long taxi ride. Whereas if we take a police car, I reckon the fuel will come to that figure at the bottom. So all in all we'll be saving you around two thousand crowns by driving.'

'Very considerate of you.'

'So even with an overnight stay somewhere —'

'No! Six hours each way doesn't warrant a hotel.'

'But with an interview between the journeys, sir, and a lot of ground to cover —' Lukas scrawled across the paper.

'Very well! One night, in a guest house, with a simple dinner and breakfast. And this had better be worthwhile, Slonský.'

'All approved,' Slonský announced. 'Now, key tasks before we go. Navrátil, you're in charge of the commissary.'

'I thought that was a big bird that couldn't fly.'

'That's a cassowary, Navrátil. A commissary is what you're in charge of — a big picnic hamper with ample bread and sausages to see us through our epic journey. We'll each take one small bag. I'll go down to the motor pool and see what kind of car they'll let us have. Anything I've forgotten?'

'Do you speak German, sir?'

'Only "Don't shoot, I'm a friend". You?'

'Not a word, sir. And I'd guess that our chances of finding a German policeman who speaks Czech must be slim, so shouldn't we take an interpreter with us?'

'Good idea, Navrátil. Organise it. We can't pay them, but there may be someone who'd like a free day trip to the Black Forest. And I suppose I'd better tell the German police what we're up to, in case they discover we're there.'

Navrátil decided the best prospect of finding a German speaker was to ask Sergeant Mucha, who seemed to know everything that went on in the building.

'A fluent Kraut-speaker? I don't think so.' He scanned the duty roster in the hope that a possibility would leap out at him. 'Isn't Klinger a German name?' he wondered.

Navrátil tapped on the door, and waited for the crisp 'Come!' from within.

'Ah, Navrátil, isn't it? Have you come to seek a transfer? We're always on the lookout for likely lads in the fraud squad.'

'Not just at the moment, sir. I'm trying to find a fluent German speaker and someone suggested that you might be one.'

'Did "someone"? Well, you may tell Sergeant Mucha that I do indeed speak German tolerably well. What do you want one for?'

Navrátil summed up the discussion with Valentin.

'Well, isn't that fascinating? I can see why Slonský wants to speak to Sammler's father. Although what this has to do with the murder he's supposed to be investigating isn't at all clear to me, unless it's his contention that Sammler murdered someone in Germany before his father kicked him out.'

'I don't think so, sir.'

'When do you leave?'

'Tomorrow morning, sir. Seven o'clock sharp.'

Klinger sprang to his feet and marched briskly to the door, holding it open for Navrátil.

'I shall be ready at 06:50. And I hope that Slonský will have obtained a suitable vehicle instead of that battered insurance write-off he normally makes you drive.'

Chapter 21

Thursday dawned, and Navrátil and Klinger were waiting in the entry hall of the police headquarters when a slick white Volkswagen Passat glided to a halt on the yellow lines outside.

'Will this do?' asked Slonský through the open window.

'I'm impressed,' said Klinger. 'A 3.6-litre engine, I believe. How did you manage to get the use of this?'

'By swapping the keys for those of the eight-year-old Škoda Octavia they were going to give us.'

'You mean you haven't booked this out?' gasped Klinger.

'Of course I have,' said Slonský. 'Old Dlouhý asked me to read out the registration, so I read this one to him, and he wrote out the paperwork. Then we both signed it. When he discovers it he's hardly likely to tell everyone he's so short-sighted he can't actually do his job properly, is he?'

Klinger pursed his lips in a moue of disapproval.

'That seems to me perilously close to taking advantage of the lame and halt,' he said.

'Fair enough,' said Slonský. 'Shall I take it back and get the Octavia?'

'It's a matter for your conscience rather than mine. But the seats are rather nice, aren't they?'

'Right, in you get. Klinger, do you want to sit in the front with me, or have the whole back seat to yourself?'

'I'll be happy to spread myself out in the back, if that's agreeable to all,' Klinger responded, and climbed in before anyone had time to object. Navrátil put the bags in the boot and walked back to address Slonský through the driver's window.

'Have you forgotten your bag, sir?'

Slonský reached into the footwell beneath him and held up a small snap-top freezer bag.

'Pants, socks, toothbrush, razor. It's only one night, Navrátil, not an Arctic expedition. Now, get in before some overzealous traffic cop books us.'

Klinger had brought a book. He was the sort of person who always had a book on the go, usually of the kind that he would describe as "improving". In this particular case, he was reading an economics text by Hayek and not, as Slonský affected to believe, one by Hašek.

'Though I don't doubt for a minute that Hašek would have written an economics textbook if he had thought there was money to be made from it,' Klinger commented acidly.

'Ah, a true Czech,' said Slonský. 'Not one to let mere profound ignorance prevent him from expressing an opinion.'

'Or, indeed, teaching others,' Klinger added.

'Well, so long as you keep one step ahead — Jesus Maria! — Navrátil, take that car's number. Did you see that? Nearly had my wing mirror off. We'll ring it through to traffic when we get back.'

'Let it go, sir. I'm sure we'll see more bad driving as we go.'

Klinger muttered something about motes and beams, but since Slonský did not know what a mote was, and had not heard clearly anyway, he let it pass.

'I'll drive for the first two hours or so, then you can take over, Navrátil. Klinger, do you want a drive?'

'I'm enjoying being chauffeured around, thank you, but if you wish I'll take a turn. It will be interesting to experience a really powerful engine.'

'What do you normally drive, sir?' asked Navrátil.

'I don't. A car is such a millstone in Prague.'

'You don't drive,' said Slonský, 'but you're planning to take the two of us on a death spin along the highway?'

'I *don't* drive, but I *can* drive,' Klinger corrected him. 'The jury is still out on some others.'

The journey was relatively uneventful. Navrátil took over after a couple of hours, and was able to calculate that Slonský's average speed exceeded the speed limit at any given point in the journey so far. Rolling along at a more sedate pace, they reached the halfway point around ten o'clock, which prompted Slonský to suggest that a refreshment break was in order.

'We can spare ten minutes for a coffee,' he told them.

Half an hour, a coffee, a sandwich and a pastry later, they were back on the road. Klinger had purchased some tissues and was washing his hands with a gel from a small squeezy bottle he kept in his briefcase. Navrátil was wishing he had not been talked into having both a sandwich and a pastry. Slonský was regretting not having taken a few extra minutes to top up with a second coffee and perhaps a pancake.

'Did you see the state of those washrooms?' asked Klinger. 'Not a good advertisement for the country.'

'We've crossed the border,' said Slonský. 'They're German washrooms.'

'I know that,' Klinger replied. 'And they reflect badly upon German standards.'

'Tut, tut,' Slonský answered. 'The Sudetenland, the Holocaust and they've got a dirty toilet.'

'You may mock,' Klinger sniped, 'but standards are standards. It's in the attention to detail that we learn so much about the real priorities of a people.'

Slonský closed his eyes as if to take a nap, but suddenly turned to look fiercely at Klinger.

'What did you just say?'

Klinger carefully placed his bookmark between the pages, closed the book gracefully, and addressed Slonský slowly as if speaking to the local village idiot.

'I said that it is in their attention to detail that people give their priorities away.'

Slonský's face lit up.

'Nobody speak to me for a while. I have an idea, and I need to think deeply about it. To the untrained eye it will look as if I am asleep, but actually my brain will be running like a hamster in a wheel.'

As a result of Slonský's nap, and Klinger's total immersion in his book, Navrátil was still driving two hours later as they approached the turn to Stuttgart.

'Excuse me,' Navrátil said, 'but is anyone going to give me directions?'

'I don't have the address,' Klinger responded. 'You'll have to wake Slonský.'

'That's rather difficult when I'm driving,' Navrátil answered.

'Of course,' said Klinger. 'But you could pull up at the side of the road, wake him, then start driving again.'

'No need,' came a sonorous voice from the body beside him. Slonský's eyes were still shut, but he handed Navrátil a sheet of paper from his top pocket.

'That's the address. I got directions off the internet. They're on the back. Brilliant thing, the internet. I even got an aerial photograph of the nursing home.'

'That will be very useful,' said Klinger, 'if we fly over it. But since Navrátil is driving I expect us to continue at road level the rest of the way. Are they expecting us?'

'I didn't want anyone coaching him, so I haven't told them,' Slonský explained.

'You did what?' gasped Klinger.

'No, I didn't what,' Slonský said. 'And I accept that he may not be there when we arrive, though where else would he go?'

'Heaven,' snapped Klinger. 'Old people do that with the minimum of notice.'

'No consideration, some people,' agreed Slonský. 'But if he's popped it, we'll just turn back and enjoy the trip.'

'And how will you explain that to Captain Lukas, sir?' Navrátil enquired.

'I'll probably just leave a note on his desk saying it was a wasted journey because you forgot to ring ahead to check Old Sammler was still alive, Navrátil.'

'That's not fair, sir!'

'No, it isn't,' Slonský agreed. 'It's called life, Navrátil, and you're suffering from it. Though I suspect life isn't so bad when you consider the alternative.'

'I'll stick up for you, Navrátil,' Klinger interjected, though without looking up from his book. 'You need never fear this behemoth while I'm around to offer you a bolthole in the fraud squad.'

'Fraud squad?' spluttered Slonský. 'When did you become a squad? There's only two of you. How can two people be a squad?'

'There are only two of us *at present*,' Klinger conceded, 'but that is because we haven't replaced Kobr.'

'Ah, yes, Kobr,' said Slonský. 'When does he get out?'

'About two years, I think.'

'Bit long to hold his job open for him, then.'

Klinger looked at Slonský over the top of his spectacles.

'I fear Kobr's chances of reinstatement with the fraud department are not likely to be good. Other departments may be less picky. Criminal investigation, for example.'

'No, I think we'd go along with your judgement there, Klinger. After all, you know him best, having been colleagues and all that.'

'Colleague is, perhaps, a little strong,' said Klinger. 'We were not on terms of great fellowship.'

'Do you ever visit?'

'I think to do so might be … tactless,' Klinger answered. 'And difficult.'

'Yes, I can see that,' said Slonský. 'Must be an awkward conversation when one of you is a police officer and his former colleague is hanging from the wall in chains.'

'How very medieval of you, Slonský,' Klinger smoothly replied. 'Kobr is in an open prison where he runs the library, I believe.'

'Just so long as they don't let him run the prison amenities fund.'

Navrátil's curiosity was given full rein.

'What did this Kobr person do?' he asked.

'He overlooked a couple of bank accounts belonging to black marketeers, one of which had his name on it. Allegedly. And he delayed passing valuable information on to Klinger. Allegedly.'

'No, he definitely did that,' Klinger expostulated.

'And he allegedly did these things in exchange for allegedly having a wild night in a hotel with a couple of young dancers. Allegedly. Oh, hang on, that one was proved. Scrub the allegedlys.'

'In the interests of accuracy, it was four nights, Slonský, and seven dancers.'

'At the same time?'

'Working shifts, I believe.'

'Thank goodness for that. I was beginning to see Kobr in a whole new light. Navrátil, you see that big blue sign pointing towards Stuttgart? Well, that's the way to Stuttgart. You want to turn there.'

Two of the three had been expecting a Gothic pile, possibly a converted stately home, but the care home proved to be a very pleasant affair built on the side of a hill with a wonderful view across the forest.

'I wouldn't mind living here,' announced Slonský.

'I'll make enquiries about their waiting list,' Klinger offered, 'though I suspect the monthly rates may be beyond a police pension.'

The interior was a riot of carved wood. A few litres of petrol and a match and this could be the bonfire of a lifetime, thought Slonský. There were no nurses in uniform bobbing about, but a stoutly built lady in a grey business suit approached them wearing a name badge that suggested that she might be staff. Klinger dealt smoothly with the formalities, produced his badge, instructed the others to produce theirs, and they were all invited to sit on a large red leather sofa under the head of a confident-looking stag.

'I bet he didn't look that smug a few moments later,' whispered Slonský.

'That's the problem with being the alpha male,' declared Klinger. 'First go at all the women, but you're also the one the hunters want to take down.'

'Then I sympathise with you, Klinger, as the big alpha male of the fraud squad. Or was it department?'

'Tease me, and I shall deliberately mistranslate for you. I wonder how much help Mr Sammler will give you if he thinks you're from the Euthanasia Society.'

'Business before pleasure, Klinger. Then I'll use my police expenses to buy you a nice dinner. Or, given German prices, a tolerable starter and a glass of milk.'

The grey-suited matron was blocking out the light again.

'She says Mr Sammler will see us now,' Klinger said, and walked alongside the lady as she led them to Sammler's room.

'This isn't a room,' said Navrátil. 'It's a suite.'

'Very nice indeed,' agreed Slonský. 'The absence of a bed suggests this is just a sitting room.'

They introduced themselves to the old man who sat in a high-backed armchair, his legs swathed in a woollen rug. He was clearly very old, as shown by his sparse white hair, but his blue eyes, while slightly pale now, were keen and sharp, and his back was straight as he sat to attention in the chair. He did not appear to need anything that Klinger said repeated to him, and answered clearly and concisely.

'Please tell Herr Sammler that we are interested in the circumstances that led to his son's departure from Germany,' Slonský began.

The old man barked a few syllables back at Klinger.

'He wants to know why you want to know.'

Slonský handed Sammler the photograph of his son at the picnic. The old man held it tilted to the light, jutted his jaw out defiantly, and handed it back, before beginning to speak.

'That is my son Theodor. He is a man of not inconsiderable gifts. We were fortunate enough to be able to provide him with an excellent education, as a result of hard work and thrift. There seemed to be a danger that Theodor did not value this grounding that we had secured for him. He became wayward, and began mixing in undesirable circles.'

'Yet he completed his doctorate,' Slonský remarked. As Klinger translated the old boy eyed Slonský shrewdly.

'I can see you're not a bumpkin like most Czechs I've met. Yes, Theodor stayed at the university when many others fell by the wayside. That is a tribute to my dear late wife.'

He pointed to a photograph on the sideboard. Slonský stood to view it more closely.

'A fine-looking woman,' he pronounced.

'Not only fine looking, but intelligent,' said Sammler. 'Not a bubble-headed gossip like so many women. Theodora was in some ways the brains of the family. I had technical gifts, if I may say so. But Theodora was well read, and her German was so cultured. She taught Theodor to write well. She would tell him again and again that it does not matter how fine a man's ideas are, if he is unable to express them clearly. It made a great impression on the boy, and from a young age he wrote and spoke well.'

'He speaks good Czech too,' Slonský conceded.

'His mother was born in Bohemia,' Sammler replied.

'She was a Czech?'

'No, she was a German, born in Bohemia.'

Klinger glossed the translation.

'I think he means she was a Sudeten German.'

Catching the word 'Sudeten' Sammler quickly agreed.

'Yes, German by birth and heritage, though at that time her birthplace was in Czechoslovakia. She spoke some Czech, and I don't doubt Theodor heard her. Her own nanny was a Czech woman, so most of the lullabies she knew were in Czech.'

'May we return to the photograph, sir? Your wife was obviously instrumental in keeping Theodor at his studies.'

'Yes, she persuaded him that whatever his views, a completed education would be an asset to him and that his campaigning would have even more force if he were a known scholar.' He chuckled drily. 'She used to give him an odd example. How did Stalin come to the top of the pile in Russia? She said it was because, unlike his fellows, Stalin had grown up in a seminary and had been taught to speak well. After all, Russian was not his first language, yet he was able to defeat the others in debate. It made an impression on Theodor. His life might have been very different if she had lived — although, of course, the fact that she did not live was largely the result of his betrayal.'

'Betrayal, sir?'

'They were very close. He was an only child. Do you have children, Lieutenant? I thought not. I was fond of him, naturally, but there is a special bond between a mother and her son. I had grown up knowing that work would take me away from my parents, that separation was a part of independence. Having been uprooted at the end of the war, a secure home was very important to Theodora. She felt Theodor's departure very keenly, whilst, of course, absolutely agreeing with me that it was necessary.'

'May I ask what precipitated it, sir?'

Sammler did not answer for a moment, but reached for a large golden cord beside him and yanked on it. A distant bell rang, and within a few moments a young woman appeared at the door.

'Some tea, perhaps, for my guests, fräulein. And no doubt there will be some cake.'

The young woman nodded and left.

'They don't give me cake,' the old man grumbled. 'They say it's bad for me. As if I should worry about what's bad for me at ninety-three. Now, to continue, gentlemen. You have seen this photograph. You have some idea of the company that Theodor was keeping. I may say that I was a man of some substance even then, and perhaps that protected my son to some degree. If he was not fully involved in their atrocities that may have been because he was not entirely trusted. They were not convinced that he really shared their ambitions, given the future mapped out for him. As a result, it was not until that lot were jailed that Theodor was able to progress in their filthy organisation. I do not know precisely what part he played. He has given me his word that he was not directly involved in any violence towards others. He has refused to give his word that he obeyed the law at all times. I should like to be able to accept his word as that of a gentleman.'

'You have doubts, sir?'

'I do not have doubts as such. Only worries. The consequences of his actions did not weigh with him. If he were capable of some of these barbarities one read about, he was hardly likely to baulk at lying to his father, was he? How many of us have done that without being in any sense a criminal? If these years have taught me anything, it is to regret that I did not make the effort to understand my own father better. We had some fearful arguments, gentlemen, when I was a young man. I was twenty-six when the war broke out, and I soon found myself in the army. My father had served in his time, in the Kaiser's army in France. To my mind, we were doing the same thing. We were both serving Germany. But my father, while initially a supporter of Hitler, turned against him when he was sent to serve in a prison camp in Bavaria towards the end of the war. The younger men were all needed for the front, of course, so father was brought out of retirement and served as a Major. He would not tell me what he saw there, but said that if it came out, it would be an eternal shame for the Fatherland. I replied that I had every confidence in the nation's leadership. He became angry with me, and our relationship changed.'

The old man gazed out of the window for a moment, before clearing his throat gently and resuming his rigid position.

'Naturally, one can see now that my father was right. I was wrong, and I did not know what I was talking about. I should have admitted it and respected my father's view. When Theodor and I quarrelled, I said as much to him, but he laughed at me. He said that I ought not to be so quick to assume that I was wrong, that maybe youth sees more than experience, or some such tripe.'

The tea arrived, and was dispensed by the smiling young woman. She offered cake to each, and was about to leave when Sammler reminded her that she had inadvertently missed him out. She smiled weakly and gave him a plate and a slice of cake.

'It's a charade, of course,' said Sammler.

'Of course,' replied Slonský. 'If she really intended to miss you out she would not have brought a plate for you.'

Sammler laughed out loud, dabbing his eyes with a large handkerchief he produced from beneath the rug.

'Excellent! I think if you are intent on snaring Theodor he may have to be on his mettle to escape you.'

'May I ask about your own war service, sir?'

'Modest enough. I did very little fighting. That, you must understand, was not the result of any desire on my part. It was determined at an early stage that I had some administrative skills, and consequently I was sent for specialised training in logistics. I served out the war keeping the army supplied as best I could. When the war ended, I knew where some stores had been kept. It did not seem that the Americans had great need of them, whereas our people were suffering dreadfully.'

Slonský asked his next question after some deliberation.

'Forgive me if I have misunderstood. Do you mean that you were able to profit by selling the supplies?'

'You want to know if I made my money as a black marketeer? No, sir, I did not. I didn't need to. I took no money from Germans, though I was willing to accept American dollars from soldiers who wanted souvenirs to take home. I bartered some, and I gave some away, and in this way I gathered a large group of people who felt in some way beholden to me. When conditions improved, and I set up in business, this goodwill stood me in good stead. People trusted me where they did not trust others. When they had a little money, it was my little bank that they gave it to. So much of banking is about trust, gentlemen! They trusted me with their pfennigs, and were not concerned about the return so long as it was safe. I carried the risk and reaped the reward. As time went on, their many little nest-eggs grew, so they found more money to deposit. I began buying stakes in companies, and in twenty years or so I had become a regional force. This work involved sacrifice, of course. I could not allow myself to marry until I could keep a wife well, so I was thirty-four before I married Theodora. She had been kicked out of Bohemia with nothing. She had been well-to-do there, but she had only a donkey cart and the small amount that it could carry. I told her that I could not marry her until I could provide properly for her, and you know what she told me? That she placed no value on anything beyond my company and my love, and believed that if she hitched herself to me I would do more for her than any other man could. She had lost all, and did not expect ever to have that life again, but if it were possible, I would be the one who could make it happen. And I am proud to say that I did. I married her for better or for worse, and it was overwhelmingly for better, until Theodor spoiled it all.'

'You said that you quarrelled, sir, but that is not a reason to send your son into exile.'

'I believed that I was doing the right thing. I hoped that if he moved in other circles he would forget his infatuation with this left-wing tosh he had been imbibing. I thought that if he began to make his own money, his views would come more closely to approach mine. I told him straight that I would give him a fair share of my wealth so that he could follow his own path. If he chose to give it away to those hippies that was his affair, but he could set himself up well with it. However, I reminded him of the parable of the prodigal son, and told him that if he returned there would be no fatted calf.'

'You did not expect to see him again.'

'The police had begun to ask difficult questions. Naturally, one defends one's child, but I genuinely did not know if he had done any of these beastly things that were alleged of those people in the newspapers. But over the years I had made some good friends, one of whom was a very senior man in the police force. He telephoned one day and asked if we could meet in private. I kept a small flat in Frankfurt then, and we met there. My wife was at our main house. I explained to her that I would be late because I was meeting Max. That, perhaps, was a mistake. Would the young gentleman mind pouring me a little more tea, since he is nearest?'

Navrátil did so, feeling the need to bow slightly as he returned the cup to Sammler.

'A fine young man. They say the young are a waste of time, a disappointment to us, but they have always said that. My parents' generation said it of us, and look what we achieved in rebuilding Germany after the war! One day we have to get out of the way and let the young ones run things, and if they mess up then they will have their own youngsters to tell them so. Ach! It's unimportant. So much time wasted on stupid arguments. Now, back to business. As I told you, I met Max at my flat. He was serious, I would almost say pained. He told me that Theodor was under suspicion. He showed me the photograph that you have shown me today and that I hoped had been lost forever, along with some others. Theodor was too clever to do any of the dirty work himself. He followed his old man.'

Sammler gave a short, mirthless laugh and explained his last observation.

'He specialised in logistics. He obtained the things they needed. He could say that he did not know precisely what they were planning. That may or may not be true. But he made it possible. If they needed guns, he found them. Max produced a piece of paper that broke my world apart and killed my wife. He had an invoice for the delivery of some automatic weapons. Theodor had used my company's money to pay for these. To do this, he had not forged any signatures. He had signed the paperwork quite openly in his own name, but he had represented himself to the sellers as my agent. My name, my reputation, my entire business life was at stake. This could not be allowed to happen again. I assured Max that I had known nothing of this, and that eventually we would have discovered it, no doubt, during one of our audits and taken appropriate action. He said that any large ship houses a rat or two, and that he could probably ensure that this evidence was lost if I could guarantee that Germany would be rid of Theodor. He would, regrettably, have to keep it for a while to ensure that Theodor did not sneak back. He was apologetic, but I did not blame him. I would have done the same, and he was taking a considerable risk by speaking to me about this at all. And after it was done, he remained my friend, making no attempt to keep a distance from me. He knew how much it had cost me. A man needs friends like Max.'

Sammler paused for a moment. His eyes were damp with nascent tears which he dabbed away as he composed himself once more.

'When I arrived home Theodora asked me what Max had wanted. I told her exactly what I have told you. Of course, she was heartbroken, but she could see that there was no choice. Theodor must leave us. I told her that she could visit him, but he would not set foot in Germany again. To her credit, she sat beside me as I confronted Theodor a few days later. I told him to choose somewhere to go and offered to help. I thought he would throw it back in my face, but to my surprise he said he would be guided by me. I mentioned a small Austrian bank whose owner I knew quite well. Theodor thought that would be acceptable. I rang the man and told him that I wanted Theodor to get some experience outside the family firm so that he could prove that he had progressed on his own merits. I offered to pay his first year's salary if they would take him on. I said that they would be doing me a favour if they forgot that he was my son. Of course, they didn't understand what I meant, and thought I was just saying that I didn't want him given any special treatment.'

Sammler stopped speaking and licked his thin lips.

'I have regretted that conversation many times. I misled them. I had let a wolf into their sheep pen. Theodor took the bank off them. He proved to be incredibly ruthless in business. I hope that I had maintained proper standards in my own work. Certainly that was my aim. But Theodor had no such scruples. He has been successful, but at what a cost.'

'He has never married, sir.'

'So I understand. I am not surprised. Theodor does not seem to feel the need for relationships. He is not a clubbable man. He joins no societies, shares no interests. I once asked him why he did not have a girlfriend. His answer was deeply shocking to me. I will not repeat his exact words, but he said that every service that can be provided by a wife can be purchased from women more accomplished in those tasks, usually cheaper and without any continuing obligation. His language was extremely vulgar.'

'If I were to suggest that your son may have resumed his old ways, would it surprise you, sir?'

Klinger asked Slonský to repeat the question before he translated it.

'Are you sure you want to ask that?' he asked.

'Yes. I may be wrong, but I want to see his reaction.'

Klinger translated the question. The old man's eyes widened and he gripped the arms of his chair angrily.

'What my son does now, he answers for. I hoped he might have been cured, but is one ever cured of this infection? If it is as you say, it is all the more reason why he should not come back.'

Slonský leaned forward and spoke gently.

'I am sorry to have had to ask you that. It must have been distressing and I hope you will understand that I would have spared you that if I could.'

Klinger translated, while Sammler acknowledged the apology with a nod.

'A man must do his duty. I see that. This is yours. I see that too.'

'I hope that we will — that I will — prove to be mistaken. I have spoken to your son, and I shall have to interview him again. And now I think we should leave you to rest. I am grateful for your considerable assistance.'

Slonský stood, clicked his heels, and offered his hand. The old man shook it. Klinger followed suit, and then Navrátil shook hands too, speaking a few words of fractured German as he did so. Sammler smiled, patted the back of Navrátil's hand as he shook it, and his eyes filled with tears again.

Navrátil pushed past and left the room first, striding swiftly down the corridor.

'What did he say?' whispered Slonský.

Klinger looked puzzled.

'Something like "I'm pleased to have met your wife, sir".'

There was another rare event that evening. Slonský was not hungry.

They had left the nursing home in silence, and low in spirit. Slonský was not his usual ebullient self and climbed straight into the passenger seat without even asking who was going to drive. That'll be me then, thought Navrátil, whose emotions were confused and raw. He had genuinely liked the old man, who reminded him of the grandfather he would have liked to have had. His father's father had died when he was too young to remember, while his mother's father was a miserable old git. When the interview was over Navrátil could have cried, and hoped the others had not noticed. They had said nothing, of course, but that did not mean that his face had not betrayed him. He just wanted to go home now, but unfortunately he faced six hours in the car with Klinger and Slonský first, neither of whom was known for their delicacy when it came to other people's feelings. Being alone seemed so desirable, so Navrátil cut himself off and concentrated on his driving.

Klinger was angry. He believed that Slonský had had no business suggesting that Theodor Sammler had returned to left-wing terrorism without the slightest shred of evidence to back up such an assertion. If Old Sammler had asked Slonský for proof, what could he have said? And the allegation had come out of his mouth, albeit as an interpreter of Slonský's accusing words. He had given Slonský the opportunity to reconsider, but Slonský had blundered on regardless like the uncouth golem he sometimes seemed to be.

Slonský closed his eyes and rehearsed the interview. For some reason, while Slonský had difficulty with names, could not remember anyone's birthday other than his own and regularly forgot his PIN number when standing at a bank machine, he had a very good memory for conversations with witnesses. He could see now that his previous interpretations of the evidence were complete bunkum, and part of his brain was attempting to construct a verbal report for Lukas that would somehow explain that the new theory was actually just a subtle reworking of the old one, though differing in one or two minor details like having an alternative motive and killer. If he tried hard he could work through the events of that evening in early February and piece together a sequence that made sense. He could see where some of the evidence that filled the gaps would come from. But some of it would have to come from the murderer, and tricking them into letting it out was going to take a bit of nerve and a lot of low cunning. Fortunately, low cunning was

157

Slonský's strong point. He could limbo his way past most villains' defences if he could engineer the right opportunity, and he turned his mind to setting up that encounter.

'Where do you want to stop, sir?' Navrátil suddenly asked.

'Let's grab a bite anywhere you see,' said Slonský. 'I don't fancy a night away if you don't mind, Klinger.'

'I'm always happiest in my own bed,' came the reply. 'Let's stop for a little freshening up, then press on. Even with an hour's break, we should be home around midnight.'

They covered about half the distance home before Navrátil saw an inn just off the road. Klinger declared that anywhere must be better than that insanitary hole at which they had stopped in the morning, and Slonský had no opinion at all. They ordered their food and sat in a quiet corner, Slonský holding a beer, Klinger contemplating a dry white wine, and Navrátil trying to look enthusiastic about a mineral water when he really fancied a very large vodka. The sort of vodka that guaranteed that you would forget the last day and a half and wake up when it had all gone away.

Klinger straightened the beermat and positioned his wine glass precisely at its centre.

'So?' he said.

'So what?' asked Slonský.

'Exactly,' said Klinger.

Slonský delayed his answer by taking a large mouthful of beer, swallowing it, and licking his lips.

'Herr Sammler cannot know anything of the events we are investigating, but he believes that his son could be implicated.'

'He said no such thing,' said Klinger. 'He only took your rash statement at face value. He belongs to a generation that respects the police, so of course he didn't argue. How could he? He hasn't seen his son for thirty years.'

Slonský's eyes were diamond hard.

'He didn't know why we wanted to know, but he didn't ask. Doesn't that strike you as strange? Not once did he ask what we were investigating or why we wanted to speak to him. I think he knew that it must be serious, and it didn't surprise him. He said he would like to take his son's word for the claim that he had not been directly involved in any violence, but he plainly couldn't. He worded it exactly that way. Not "my son told me this and I believe him" but "I would have liked to have taken his word". He couldn't take that word because he didn't believe it. He knows his son is capable of violence.'

'You're reading too much into that,' said Klinger. 'First, because he was describing events that happened a long time ago, and those distant events become distorted in our memories. Second, because he knows his son bought weapons and maybe he thinks, as any right-minded person would, that there isn't any real moral difference between killing someone and making it possible for someone else to kill someone. Third, because what you heard was what I told you he said, and perhaps my German isn't up to such subtle differences.'

'Then write down the German and we'll ask another translator what they think. Do it now while it's fresh in your mind. As to the weapons, someone who buys guns for others to use might be just the sort of person who would pay someone else to strangle a young woman. Doesn't do his own dirty work, but is quite happy to have the dirty work done for him.'

Klinger could see no point in continuing the argument. He merely snorted to show that he disagreed, then decided to realign his glass on the mat to return some order to a chaotic world.

'Why strangled, sir?' asked Navrátil.

'Because it's a built-up area with lots of people around and a gun would attract attention, even in the Prague of today,' Slonský replied.

'But surely strangling a woman takes time. A knife would be quicker. Putting a pillow over her face when she's asleep would be easier.'

'Knives cause blood and blood is messy, Navrátil. Novák would have got us a lot more useful stuff if there'd been a puddle of blood. The murderer would have been spattered and might have been seen leaving, in which event being covered in blood could be a disadvantage.'

'He might have been seen leaving anyway,' said Navrátil. 'He couldn't know that he wouldn't meet someone on the landing or on the stairs. If he killed her when Novák says, then there could well have been people about.'

'He couldn't leave it any later, Navrátil, or she wouldn't have answered the door to let him in.'

'If you're casting Sammler as the murderer,' Klinger interrupted, 'then show us some evidence that she had ever met him, because without that your case falls down. Why would she let a complete stranger in at that time of night?'

Slonský picked up his beermat and tapped it rhythmically on the table top, not so much because it helped him think as because he was fairly confident that it would annoy the hell out of Klinger. He was right about that, even if he was wrong about everything else.

'Not hungry, Slonský?' Klinger enquired. 'The schnitzel is really rather good.'

'I've lost my appetite. Help yourself to anything you like the look of.'

'Thank you, but no, thank you. I've never been keen on second-hand vegetables, however careful their previous owner.'

Slonský picked up his fork again and speared a carrot.

'I hate waste,' he said as he chewed. 'I hate waste even more than I hate carrots.'

Klinger drained his glass and Slonský immediately sprang to his feet.

'Coming?' he asked Navrátil, and strode out to the car.

Navrátil guzzled the last of his water and hurried to catch his boss, whilst Klinger decided that one of them really ought to pay the bill.

When Navrátil arrived at the car, Slonský was in the driver's seat and the engine was running. Klinger took his time, but finally appeared and had to scuttle to shut the door as Slonský took off with Klinger only partly inside.

'I paid the bill,' said Klinger.

'Good,' replied Slonský. 'I'd hate to think of you washing up all night while we drove home.'

'I'll give you the receipt later, when you repay me.'

'You can sign it off yourself.'

'Ah, but this is a homicide investigation, nothing to do with the Fraud Squad.'

'Only a small fraction of the homicide team is in this car, whereas we've got half of the Fraud Squad here, which just shows the importance you attach to it.'

'What it shows,' said Klinger, 'is that I am not divisible into any meaningful smaller units. And don't even think of experimenting with your penknife in a lay-by.'

Chapter 22

The morning sun shone low on the Prague rooftops, but appeared to have elevated Slonský's mood. After a night's sleep he was obviously uplifted by something or other, because he was charging around the offices like a young pony exploring a new field.

Lukas was more than usually nonplussed.

'I just hope you know what you're doing, Slonský.'

'Maybe I do, and maybe I don't, sir, but it's time to rock the boat and see who falls out.'

'That isn't a reassuring metaphor, Slonský. Let me remind you that I am the captain of this ship, and if anyone goes overboard it isn't you who is going to be called to account. Well, not you alone, anyway.'

'Banda isn't in the danger I thought he was, because if I read this right, the perpetrator has already got what he wanted from him. He doesn't want Banda to escape the criticism he'll get for having an affair and he achieved all he needed when Banda was sacked. He didn't follow up on his original photo because he had got what he wanted, to wit, Banda's backside on the steps of the government buildings.'

'And suppose Banda sues us?'

'For protecting him? I'll sweet talk him, sir. I'll get him to agree to a statement that he was never a serious suspect but we needed to keep him in protective custody for his own safety. He'll be more than happy to get public confirmation from us that he was never really in the frame for Irina's murder.'

'But he was, Slonský. You put him there. You were convinced he had done it. And I understand that there was some monkey business involving a threat to his person that I wasn't told about.'

Slonský waved the argument away.

'A simple misunderstanding on the way to the showers, sir. Let me have a few words with him, and all will be well. I'll turn on the charm.'

Lukas threw his pen angrily onto his blotter.

'Damn it, Slonský, you don't have any charm! You're a public relations disaster area for this police force in general and my department in particular. I've protected you for a long time, but if this goes wrong on us I'll be very happy to sign your retirement papers.'

Slonský was taken aback. Lukas had never said that to him before. That hurt. It was a definite low blow. Slonský was not afraid of much but retirement frightened the hell out of him.

He rose slowly from his seat and picked up his folder.

'It won't go wrong on us, sir. I'll take full responsibility.'

'That goes without saying,' Lukas replied.

Banda was as surprised as Lukas had been.

'I can go? Just like that?'

'If you want. I don't think you're in any physical danger. The perpetrator wanted you humiliated, not dead.'

'Well, he certainly got that.'

'I'll be happy to issue a press release that your innocence was quickly established and that you remained here solely to give you protection.'

'And my wife?'

'She was never a suspect.'

'I mean, what will you say to her?'

'The same.'

'She's not a fool, Lieutenant. She knows you suspected me for some time. In fact, so far as I know she still thinks you do. Unless, of course, you've told her otherwise.'

'No,' admitted Slonský. 'But she never believed you'd done it anyway, so she doesn't need my word for it.'

Banda pursed his lips and thought deeply for a few moments.

'Very well. Give me a few minutes to get my papers together, bring me my own clothes, take me home and issue your statement and I'm happy to forget the whole thing.'

Slonský relaxed, until Banda continued.

'Provided, of course, that you tell the Prime Minister I'm innocent and I need a job.'

Lukas was apoplectic.

'Why should I go to tell the Prime Minister you've let Banda go?'

'Well, you arrested him, sir, not me.'

'On your recommendation!'

'But you insisted on reviewing the evidence yourself, sir. You said the evidence was sound. At the time, that is.'

'And I suppose you want me to make the Director go with me like last time?'

'I don't think he will, sir. But we could ask.'

'You let him go, you can tell the Prime Minister.'

'That would undermine your authority, sir.'

'Undermine … how?'

'Because if you arrest him and then I let him go, it looks like I'm criticising your decision, sir.'

Lukas stood so he could look Slonský squarely in the eye.

'If I go, then when I come back, I will take out your personnel file and drop a little note to those concerned to point out that you're ready to retire.'

Slonský could not avoid a small, but visible, shudder.

'Do you mean that, sir?'

'I certainly do.'

'Then I suppose I'd better go to see the Prime Minister, sir.'

Slonský managed to get a five-minute appointment within the hour, and was only two minutes late for it. He remained standing as he explained that Banda had been framed, and he hoped that the real culprit would soon be charged.

'So Banda didn't do it?'

'No, sir.'

'He'll want his job back, damn it.'

'But he did fail to co-operate with a police inquiry into a serious crime, sir. You were right to sack him for that.'

The Prime Minister doodled for a moment or two.

'You sound like Komárek,' he finally said. 'That's the sort of twaddle he talks when the opinion polls come out. You're absolutely sure Banda was framed?'

Slonský handed the Prime Minister the photograph of Soucha and Mario.

'The same person who sent us the photograph of Dr Banda with Miss Gruberová sent us this picture too, sir.'

'Good Lord! That's Thingummy, isn't it?'

'Daniel Soucha, sir.'

'God in Heaven! And I thought kissing babies for votes was bad.'

'I don't think he's electioneering, sir. The other gentleman doesn't have a vote here.'

'Soucha resigning?'

'I don't know, sir. He was very keen that this photograph should not get out.'

'I bet he was.'

The Prime Minister thought for a moment or two.

'Is Banda going to sue you for wrongful arrest?'

'He said he wouldn't if I told you he was innocent, sir.'

'What will he do now, I wonder?'

'I don't know, sir. It isn't going to be easy for him to carry on as if nothing had happened.'

'Leave him to me. There's a nice little job in Brussels I could offer him. The Deputy Director of the National Bank thinks he's going to get it, but I like him even less than I like Banda.'

'Thank you, sir.'

'Was there something else, Lieutenant?'

'May I ask a favour, sir?'

'Why should I do you a favour, Slonský?'

'Because you're a decent man, sir.'

'And in return?'

'I'll give you a weather forecast.'

'What is it you want?'

'I have a journalist friend who needs a scoop. If you were willing to give him the news of Banda's forthcoming appointment before anyone else gets it, he would be very grateful indeed.'

'A journalist?'

'Yes, sir.'

'Name?'

'Here's his card, sir. Telephone number on the back. Will it be this week, sir?'

'Yes, no point in dithering.'

'Thank you, sir. I'm very grateful.'

The Prime Minister cocked his head and raised an eyebrow.

'The weather forecast?'

'Very stormy, sir.'

'And why is that?'

Slonský told him what was to come. They parted cordially.

Navrátil was waiting for Slonský in the office.

'Sir, how would I go about getting a transfer to Kladno?'

'You come and ask me, and I tell you not to be so stupid and to get your brain back in gear.'

Navrátil held out an envelope.

'I just thought I'm not sure life in Prague —'

'Cobblers! You didn't think, your groin twitches every time Kladno is mentioned. Don't think I don't know what's behind this sudden interest in the Central Bohemian Police, Navrátil. It's tall and blonde and it has a backside like two coconuts in a sack.'

'Sir!'

Slonský took the envelope and threw it in the waste bin.

'Navrátil, you're a detective. Stick with me and you could become a really good one. But in this case your brain has gone soft, lad. Kladno doesn't have a detective department worth the name. It has a good dog-handling school, I grant you. If your idea of fun is running around in a padded jacket waiting for a German shepherd to sink its teeth into your arm, Kladno is the place for you. But if a crime is committed in Kladno, where is the regional police headquarters?'

'Zbraslav, sir.'

'And what is Zbraslav's address, Navrátil?'

'Prague 5, sir.'

'Prague 5, sir, yes, sir. It's just across town. So if you want to be a detective in Kladno, what the hell is the point of moving? This is the Kladno detective department.'

'Maybe I'm not cut out to be a detective, sir. Maybe I should try something else, you know, get a bit of wider experience.'

Slonský sighed and flopped heavily into his seat.

'I'd hoped I wasn't going to have to do this, Navrátil, but you leave me no choice. Sit down, lad.'

Navrátil obeyed, and Slonský picked up the telephone. He dialled a number that he had written in the back of his notebook and waited for it to be answered. When it was, he wasted no time on the customary civilities.

'I'll give you one thing,' he told the person on the other end, 'you can keep a secret. I've got Navrátil here. If I don't let him in on our little scheme he's going to blow the plan by moving to Kladno. Explain it to him.'

He handed the phone to Navrátil, who listened with increasingly wide eyes and an open mouth. At the end of the call Navrátil acknowledged that he had understood all that had been said. He had taken it all in, he claimed, and as he hung up he sat back in the chair and goggled.

'Well, don't sit there gawping, lad. Get us some coffee and get back to work. I take it you no longer want a transfer, now that Officer Peiperová has accepted a job here?'

The sausage tasted unusually good today, thought Slonský, and Navrátil's appetite appeared to have returned.

'But how did you work it, sir?' the younger man asked, his cheeks bulging with bread roll.

'Captain Němec is retiring. That left a vacancy, but in the current financial climate they couldn't afford another captain. They planned to do a bit of reorganising, bump someone up and do without a lieutenant. I argued that we needed another woman officer more than we needed a lieutenant, and I'm pleased to say the good captain agreed and persuaded Lukas. With two captains supporting the proposal and a bit of money saved to boot, it went through very quickly. And when I told Lukas of the good work Peiperová had done on her own initiative in interviewing those girls, he agreed that this was just the sort of young woman we needed. Brings the average age down, helps with the gender balance, all that sort of equality stuff. If she'd been a black lesbian it might have helped but you can't have everything.'

'Thank you, sir. We won't let you down.'

'Navrátil, during working hours there will be no "we". There will be you, and there will be her, but there will be no "we". Any of that sort of stuff and you'll both be out on your ears.'

'Understood, sir.'

'And try to cure yourself of the puppy look when she comes near you.'

'Yes, sir.'

'Ever heard of bromide, Navrátil?'

'No, sir.'

'They put it in soldiers' coffee, Navrátil, so they wouldn't have carnal thoughts. If you can't control them, get some.'

'Sir.'

'Navrátil, I'll say this just once. I'm not getting any younger, and Lukas is threatening to put me out to grass. If I don't bring this one in, it could be very soon, but I hope we'll get over this and I'll go on until they can't keep me any longer. When that happens, there'll be a vacancy for a lieutenant. Set your eyes on that, lad, and get yourself ready to make a real play for it when the time comes.'

'Yes, sir. Thank you, sir.'

'And if Klinger comes sniffing around offering you all the kingdoms of the world, tell him to get lost. You'd be wasted in the Fraud Squad.'

Navrátil nodded his agreement.

'Sir, did you say you'd let Banda go?'

'Yes, lad. He wasn't the killer.'

'When did you decide that, sir?'

'When I got Novák's post-mortem report.'

'That was ages ago, sir! It's at least three weeks.'

'I know, Navrátil.'

'So how did that clear Dr Banda?'

'Because Novák told us that the strangler was right-handed. Whereas we know that Banda is very much a left-hander.'

'So that's why you didn't want to be around when Internal Affairs came to read the files? You knew they'd ask why we were holding Banda if there was clear evidence to exonerate him. So why didn't they?'

'Firstly, because Novák kindly gave me a replacement report which I put into the file. And secondly...' Slonský produced a folded sheet from his inside breast pocket.

'What's that, sir?'

'Insurance, lad.'

'You didn't even show me this version. All that time you were putting the frighteners on Banda, you knew that he hadn't done it. Why, sir?'

'Oh, come on, Navrátil! How often do you get to arrest your own boss? I couldn't let a chance like that pass me by. Don't look so po-faced. I've never been as popular at the station as when we gave Banda a hard time. And don't forget it worked. He confessed to the affair, and before that he'd been a hard little nugget. And on top of that, it's true that Banda hadn't strangled her with his own hands, but he could have hired someone else.'

'So why have we let him go, sir, if he could have hired a killer?'

'That's your fault, Navrátil.'

'My fault, sir?'

'Yes. Or at least you and Klinger. But mainly you. You're too sharp for your own good, my boy. You gave me the security footage from the bank. Now, Dr Sammler is a technophile. He likes having all the best kit, and his bank has some of the finest security money can buy, including some high-definition video cameras. You and I watched that footage, and you concentrated on the time and date. But I watched his hands, Navrátil.'

'His hands, sir?'

'Navrátil, you'll have to curb this irritating habit of repeating what I've just said as a question. Yes, his hands. The picture doesn't let us see the notes, but we can see that the teller is counting them out. What's the biggest note in circulation, lad?'

'Five thousand crowns, sir.'

'That's right. So to make up two hundred and forty-nine thousand, two hundred and fifty crowns, what's the minimum number of notes you could use?'

'Well, I … five times ten is fifty … then you'd need … er.'

'I'll save you the trouble, son. You need forty-nine notes to make two hundred and forty-five thousand, then a pair of two thousand crown notes, a two hundred note, and a fifty. However you look at it, you can't do it in less than fifty-three notes. That's why it was such a fat bundle in the little plastic bag Novák showed us. But if you watch the cashier counting it out, there are nothing like fifty-three moves. I've counted them several times, and the best guess I have is that she gives him nineteen notes. That would be consistent with eight lots of five thousand, nine one thousand crown notes, a two hundred and a fifty. That's forty nine thousand, two hundred and fifty, exactly what Banda says he drew out. Why would he pick that particular number if he was lying? So far as I can tell, he really was giving her the money for the car, and no doubt she was grateful and that's why they finished up in bed. It makes no sense at all for him to kill her half an hour later. And if I teach you anything at all while you're with me, Navrátil, I'll settle for this. Criminals don't usually do things that make no sense. It may make no sense to you or me, granted, but they have their reasons for what they do, just like you and me. The big problem is that most of us have a crowd of people who have a reason to kill us. Looking for a person with a motive doesn't help in that sense. But if a suspect doesn't have a motive, they probably didn't do it.' Slonský chomped contentedly on his last mouthful. 'Unless they're a psychopath, of course,' he added. 'Then my theory is stuffed.'

Much to Slonský's surprise, there was a note waiting for him when they returned.

'I only wrote it down,' said Mucha. 'I'm not responsible if it makes no sense.'

'Oh, it makes perfect sense,' said Slonský. 'Who'd have thought Adamec would have had it in him? Mind you, it's taken him weeks to get round to it.'

Navrátil stretched his neck trying to read the note, but Slonský stuffed it in his pocket and charged up the stairs.

'Navrátil, go and see your friend Klinger and ask him if he knows who Gold Lion Property Investments are. If he doesn't, ask him to find out. If I'm not in the office, ring me when you get the answer. I'm going to make an appointment.'

Navrátil did as he was asked. Klinger called up an online database and clicked a few times.

'Why does Slonský want to know?' he asked.

'I don't know, sir. He had a message from the Strahov police station and immediately sent me to see you.'

'Strahov? Isn't that where the young woman lived?'

'Yes, sir.'

'Then I know why he wants to know. And so should you, Navrátil.'

Klinger wrote some names on a sheet of paper and passed them to Navrátil.

'Those are the directors of Gold Lion Property Investments. But I believe that only one of them will interest Slonský. And the other is just a stooge to keep the thing legal, I think.'

Slonský was invited to enter and led through to Sammler's inner office, a curious little cubicle behind his main office. There were no windows and the walls were painted black. Sammler sat in his shirtsleeves at a functional desk and invited Slonský to take the other chair. The personal assistant closed the door as he left.

'It's a bit claustrophobic, isn't it, sir?'

'I don't find it so, Lieutenant. I can do a lot of work here, generally free from interruptions. I'm sorry, that sounded ungracious. I know you have a job to do and you were good enough to make an appointment. What can I do for you?'

'I need to tidy up a few puzzling snippets of information, sir.'

'That sounds ominous,' Sammler smiled. 'Do I need my lawyer here?'

'Only if you have something to hide, sir.'

'Then fire away, Lieutenant.'

'I should begin by saying that everything I have with me is a copy, sir. I'm not allowed to bring the originals out of the evidence store.'

'Of course.'

'You see, sir, when we received a photograph of Dr Banda with Miss Gruberová, our scientific team told us that the envelope had been printed by someone who had not attempted to put the haček in our address. That led us to wonder if the sender was not a Czech.'

'There must be a lot of non-Czechs in Prague, Lieutenant. One sees them everywhere.'

'Indeed you do, sir. Not so many tourists in February, of course. Then we were able to narrow down the time of Miss Gruberová's death. Dr Banda told us that he had left her some time before that. He had an alibi provided by his wife.'

'Surely times of death are only approximate, Lieutenant. And don't wives often give their husbands alibis, wittingly or unwittingly?'

'No doubt, sir. But we were a little confused as to why Miss Gruberová let her murderer into her flat. If Dr Banda killed her, then he made love to her, waited an hour or so, then killed her, dumped her body and went home. His cellphone gives him a better alibi, because he used it at 22:48 that evening, and it was within fifty metres of his house when he did so. We can track that by some technical jiggery-pokery I don't begin to understand, sir.'

'I do, Lieutenant. You can tell which particular mast he was nearest to when he made the call. By triangulation you can work it very precisely. So that lets Dr Banda out. But what has that to do with me?'

'Well, no matter how friendly a young woman is, I doubt she'd answer her door at midnight. I was surprised that there were so few signs of a struggle. Just a few bits of leather under her nails where she had clawed at a pair of black gloves. It seems logical to suppose those were the murderer's gloves, don't you think, sir?'

'I suppose so. She'd wash her hands before bed, no doubt, so the leather must have got under her nails after that.'

'No doubt, sir. I'm glad you agree. To return to the question of why she let her murderer in, the answer, of course, is that she didn't. He didn't need her to, because he already had a key. Most landlords keep a spare key, don't they, sir?'

'Do they?'

'Miss Gruberová didn't pay any rent, so far as we could see. Dr Banda's bank accounts don't show any sign of any rent being paid. It looks as if the kindly landlord was letting the young lady live there rent-free. So I wondered who these paragons were, and we discovered that the flat is registered in the name of Gold Lion Property Investments.'

'And you will have discovered, I'm sure, that I am one of the directors of Gold Lion Property Investments.'

'Just so, sir. It's very good of you to help a young lady like this.'

'The young lady was incidental, Lieutenant. I was helping Dr Banda. He was very grateful. It does no harm to have a sympathetic hearing from a politician or two. And I may have a key, but I rather doubt it. I own quite a lot of property, and the keys are kept by a management agency who do all the spadework for me. Perhaps they could tell you who had it. I'm sure they keep records; I'd be very upset if they didn't. I'll give you their name.'

'Thank you, sir. Then Miss Gruberová's body was taken to the rear of the train station at Holešovice and dumped there. A beige German car was seen in the area at around the time the body was left.'

'Seen "around the time", Lieutenant? That's a bit vague, isn't it? And no doubt a German car led you to think there must be a German driver, so here you are. I'm sure there are quite a few German cars in Prague. And mine is registered here.'

'We didn't have a registration number with the sighting, sir. We don't know where the car was registered. Just that it was a German make. Let's move on a little. The body was left in the early hours of Wednesday, 8th February. This is a DVD taken from your country house's security system, sir. It shows you arriving there at 03:48 on that morning. Here's a still of you leaving your car. I note you're wearing black gloves, sir.'

'So I am. I own a lot of pairs of gloves, Lieutenant, but you're welcome to search the house for them.'

'I doubt we'll find them, sir. I'm sure whoever the murderer was, he'll have burned the gloves long ago.'

'And I wonder how you obtained this DVD, Lieutenant. Would it be admissible in court, do you think?'

'Your security company volunteered it, sir. May I compliment you on the clarity of the pictures, sir? It's a very good system.'

'German, of course. I own the company. If you ever want one, I could get you a special price.'

'Very kind, sir. I doubt the police would allow me to accept, unfortunately. And I don't have anything worth stealing.'

'Personal safety is important, Lieutenant. Allow me to point out that if Miss Gruberová had owned a security system you'd have had video of whoever it was entering her flat.'

'Yes, but allow me to point out that the murderer doesn't seem to have worried about that — as if he knew there wasn't one there, wouldn't you say?'

'Your words, not mine. Maybe he just wasn't of a suspicious nature.'

'Maybe. Oh, I almost forgot. Your city flat has a very good security system too, doesn't it? It recorded your car leaving the car park that night at 22.16. That's a little late to be going out, isn't it, sir?'

'Is it? I don't sleep very well. And it was a night like any other. I can't remember why I went out on that particular night at that particular time, before you ask.'

'Then we have the curious matter of Dr Banda's withdrawal from your bank. I'm obliged to my assistant for this part. You see, Navrátil doesn't know much about banks, so he asked our fraud expert to describe what happens once someone fills in a withdrawal slip. That slip, by the way, can't be found.'

'It happens. There are thousands of them. We lose the odd one here and there.'

'You see, Dr Banda's bank statement shows that he withdrew two hundred and forty-nine thousand, two hundred and fifty crowns. Exactly the same amount was found in Miss Gruberová's vagina. Leaving aside the question of why the murderer didn't steal it, unless he had plenty of money of his own, the coincidence is striking, isn't it? It clearly pointed at Dr Banda. Except that Dr Banda is adamant that he only withdrew forty-nine thousand, two hundred and fifty crowns, precisely the amount he had promised Miss Gruberová to buy her a car. Now, our expert says that if this was a mistake by the teller, it would have been discovered at the end-of-day reconciliation, whatever that is.'

'It's when we add up all the money that went in or out and check that it tallies with the amounts in hand at the end of the shift.'

'Thank you. I'm learning a lot today. So Klinger deduces that the alteration took place after the withdrawal slip went through to the back office. And to alter that someone would need some pretty serious authorisation rights on your computer system. I'm not clear why the alteration was made, unless it was to make it absolutely certain that we would link the withdrawal with the vaginal deposit. After all, Banda might have used a bit of it to get himself a bar of chocolate.'

'Naturally, the bank will be very keen to get to the bottom of this unauthorised withdrawal. I can guarantee our full co-operation with any inquiry.'

'I'll pass that on to Mr Klinger, sir. And Dr Banda will be keen to see his money returned.'

'If he can show that he only withdrew the smaller sum, that will follow as a matter of course.'

'I've spoken to the teller involved, sir. She supports his claim.'

'That's very helpful.'

'Then we come to the second photograph we received, which you may recall. It was taken at your country home.'

'How could I forget that?'

'It can't be easy, sir. A very limited number of people could have access to your security system to produce that photograph, wouldn't you say, sir?'

'Apparently not. You got one easily enough from the company. How do we know who else was able to do so?'

'Then there's the question of who knew there would be a picture there worth collecting. Mr Soucha told me he met Mario at a party. What he didn't tell me, but I have subsequently discovered, was that you were there too.'

'Was I? I don't particularly like parties, Lieutenant, but I have to go to a lot. It wouldn't surprise me if most of Prague had been at a party with me at some time.'

'But the thing that really puzzles me, sir, is why this photograph was sent to me? Homosexuality isn't illegal. And if the aim was to discredit Mr Soucha, surely the press would be more interested than the police. Then I thought it was a particularly crafty idea, because if I showed the picture to Soucha, as I was certain to do, he would know that this would hang over him all his days, so it would give a blackmailer real power. But the problem with that argument is that it works much better if he just sends the photograph to Soucha directly, because he avoids even the slight chance that I might put it in the bin. Not to mention that it's an unusual blackmailer who doesn't give the victim any way of getting in touch with him. Without a line of communication, how can there be blackmail?'

'It's a fascinating conundrum, Lieutenant. When you find the answer, perhaps you'll put me out of this suspense.'

'I think I've got the answer, sir. But bear with me a moment. I just want to have a little chat about the third envelope. This one contained some documents showing that Leoš Holec had been creaming off large sums into a foreign bank account. I'm sure you know Mr Holec, sir.'

'Certainly I do, and I must say I'm very surprised. He's a respected adviser to the government.'

'Yes, it does seem strange. What seems even stranger is that he keeps very detailed notes of his transactions, not being a practised criminal. It never occurred to him to hide the evidence. Thus he was able to tell us that these sums were payments from an Austrian investment trust called Salzburger Prudent Investment Trust. The curious thing is that the Austrian authorities say that this trust was closed some years ago. Its official address was at the head office of your bank, sir. Somehow it has continued to make payments when it no longer has any known bank accounts. How can that happen?'

'It's hard to see. Every transaction must have a counter-balancing transaction.'

'Yes. Of course, our Mr Klinger wondered if there is an alias account somewhere containing these balancing transactions that will never be claimed because actually nobody really owns it. It might be discovered one day on an audit, but that's a remote chance really. The samples are so small compared with the number of accounts you have. You could take samples for a generation and never hit on this one. And if you did, what would it prove? An oddity, certainly, but not definite illegality. I suppose it would have to be a fairly senior official in the bank who was able to keep issuing payments against an account that didn't really exist.'

'Someone like me, you mean.'

'I couldn't possibly say, sir. I'm completely untutored in the ways of banks.'

Sammler rocked back in his chair and gave a slight, tolerant smile.

'All right, let us suppose that I am some sort of criminal mastermind who kills a young woman and frames a friend for it. I admit none of this, it goes without saying, but let's play at pretending.'

Slonský smiled encouragingly.

'Yes, sir, that would be good.'

'The question you haven't answered is — why?

'You're absolutely right, sir. I haven't explained why. I was hoping you might do that, sir.'

'And how could I know why someone would do this?'

'I thought we were playing at pretending, sir. Make something up. You see, I can only see one plausible reason for it. But it sounded so bizarre that I needed someone to confirm that it could be correct. That's why I interviewed your father yesterday, sir.'

The effect of this statement on Sammler was very gratifying, thought Slonský. He looked shocked and concerned, however fleetingly, before recovering his composure.

'You will have heard that my father and I are estranged, Lieutenant. I'm not sure that he is an unbiased source where my shortcomings are under discussion.'

'No, sir. But he didn't argue about the underlying basis of what I think happened. You see, I think the key to understanding this chain of events is the picture of Soucha. Why would anyone send me that? The Vice Squad, possibly. The press, certainly. What can I do that the press can't do more efficiently to humiliate Soucha just as Banda was humiliated? The only possible answer is that I can put someone in court. If someone's plan was to get these three men into court, then there must be some illegality that I'm not spotting about Soucha and Mario. And the only idea that came to me is that Mario is younger than he looks. If our correspondent knew that Mario was under age, and could produce Mario after the story hit the press, that would really cause Soucha some problems, wouldn't it? First he is exposed as a gay man, then it turns out that Mario is under age, so the police's hand would be pretty well forced, wouldn't it? We'd have to prosecute or the tabloids would never give us a moment's rest. Then there's just too much evidence against Banda for us not to charge him too. It doesn't really matter whether we can make it stick or not, because the stench will follow even if a charge doesn't. And there's poor Holec.

Maybe what he did wasn't illegal, or not intentionally so, but it certainly looks bad, and our fraud colleagues can't ignore the sums involved. That's the link between them.'

'How inventive!' said Sammler. 'I'm finding this very entertaining. Do go on with this nonsense.'

'A government minister, a senior opposition politician, a civil servant, all in the dock. They're all as bad as each other. The whole system is rotten to the core. It all has to happen in a short time or the public might not jump to that conclusion. But if all three were on trial at the same time, that would really damage the system, wouldn't it? And that brings us to the little difficulty I had earlier. I knew who did it, but I couldn't work out why. And the why is now clear to me. Our murderer did it all to discredit the whole Czech political system. It took years of planning, slowly building up trust so that it could be betrayed, accumulating the cash for a very expensive series of pay-offs, giving free apartments to curry favour, but it would all be worthwhile if he could finally be proved right. If he could show that his former colleagues had been justified, if he could complete their work to deliver what he wanted, the millions of crowns would have been well spent. If people lost faith in their democratic institutions, then the ideological war that appeared lost for so long could be fired up again. The only question left is: who would do such a thing? An hour with your father, and I knew the answer to that. Am I right, sir?'

'I'm not a litigious man, Lieutenant, but you will realise that if you repeated this outside this room I would be entirely justified in suing you for defamation.'

'Yes, sir. Although, of course, it is a defence that I can show my claims to be substantially true and in the public interest.'

'Can you? Can you really, Lieutenant?'

Sammler's voice was louder, more forceful, slightly higher pitched as stress began to pull at his vocal cords.

'You've heard the evidence, sir.'

'Ah, yes, so I have. It boils down to a piece of video showing I went out late, but you don't know where. Another piece of video proving I went to my other house, and it was the early hours before I got there, but you don't know where I was between these times. You have no forensic results. You have a bank statement proving that a customer took money out of his account in my bank — so what? That's what it's there for. The withdrawal slip is missing, which could be suspicious, but since you don't have it, that's going to be fairly hard to establish, don't you think? You know that I rented the flat to Dr Banda's mistress and you don't know how she paid for it. It was a favour, Lieutenant. It makes me a good guy. I lent my home to another man who betrayed that trust by using my house for some tawdry coupling with an unknown person. And even if I pointed the finger at Holec, aren't I the sheriff in the white hat hunting down evil in its many forms?'

'I'm sure we'd all be very grateful for your public-spirited action, sir, if that was your motive. But I think your motive was very different. It's an elaborate plot requiring resources that hardly anyone else in Prague could bring to bear. To pull it off you'd have to be rich, well-connected and totally committed to the cause. And you're all those things.'

'I had a youthful flirtation with some excitable fringe groups. A lot of people did, but they didn't all become ideologically committed communists.'

Slonský nodded his agreement.

'That's what makes you special, sir. You did. You started as one, and unlike so many after the Wall came down, you remained one.'

'And your evidence for this is…?'

'Twenty years of working with people just like that. You get to know the type. Of course, a lot of our homegrown communists have either seen the light or gone to jail. There are still a few around, but they're losing hope, don't you think?'

Sammler's answer came back just a little too quickly.

'There are more about than you would think, Lieutenant. There's nothing to be ashamed of in wanting to bring about a more equitable distribution of wealth. If that's a crime, I'll gladly plead guilty.'

'Of course not, sir. I'd sign up for that myself, especially since a lot of people have more than me. But the Czech Republic has tried communism and decided it doesn't like it.'

'No, Slonský, it tried a watered-down imitation of communism. It tolerated a cadre of opportunists and incompetents. But when communism returns, this is exactly where it will start.'

Sammler spoke rapidly, occasionally mispronouncing the Czech words as he lectured his audience of one.

'The Czech Republic has a long tradition of social democracy and left-wing politics. Between the wars there was solid support for proletarian social justice. Remember that this was the only country where communism was voted in at a free election after the war. Look at the 1946 election. Over forty per cent of Czechs voted communist, and over thirty per cent of Slovaks. We didn't even have to cheat. The President nominated a communist Prime Minister. Around one in every four adult Czechs was a party member. Nobody made them do that! They believed in the cause. It's in their blood, Slonský. Give them leadership, and they'll be the first to return to the fold. One more push, a firm line from the top, serious socialist reform, and this will once again be the socialist nation it used to be. And once socialism has a beachhead in Europe, it can recapture the hearts and minds of the many who have become disillusioned with Western-style democracy. All those millions who struggle every day and watch the few amassing great fortunes and blowing them in a tasteless display of conspicuous consumption. And they will be grateful to the Czech people for leading them back to the road to socialist equality. The Czechs embraced communism, Lieutenant.'

'With respect, sir, that was before they'd tried something else. A generation has only known capitalism, and they seem to like it.'

'Like it? How can they like what their country has become?'

Sammler had jumped out of his chair and was animatedly addressing Slonský as if he were a large, sceptical crowd.

'Look at Prague! The big glitzy shops, the clubs, the bars. And, in front of them, the beggars kneeling for a crust. All those new cars, some built here, but Czech only in name, because everything that matters is in foreign hands. All those tourists coming here — is it for the culture, to admire the Czech contribution to civilisation? Of course not. They come for cheap beer and sex clubs. Is that what your bourgeois Czech Republic wants to be, Slonský? Are you proud that your young women are the easiest in Europe, that so many of them earn a living in this way? Have you seen that vile place in Smíchov, "Big Sister"? A brothel where everything is free because people pay to watch what you do live on the internet. A city with the history and culture that Prague has, and it's known to the world because you can watch tarts being screwed there from anywhere you like. Is that "success", Slonský? Is it "reform"? Is it what Havel and those other idiots fought for? In all those underground years were they itching to turn their country into a place where English yobs come to drink cheap beer and paw Czech women? Can you picture them plotting in their squalid little rooms to fill Prague with unemployment and all-night casinos? I didn't make those men behave badly. I didn't trick them. They did what they were going to do anyway. All I did was bring it into the light.'

'I'd have no quarrel with that if Irina Gruberová was still alive.'

'That stupid bitch! If she had co-operated and sold her story to the press she would still be alive now. She was willing to take Banda's money for the car, and let Banda pay for the flat. And when I pointed out that I paid for her flat and if I took it away Banda couldn't do a thing about it — and he wouldn't try anyway — she threatened to go to the police. With what, I asked? A complaint that I'd offered to make her rich by telling the truth? She said that Banda was a good man and she loved him, and he was going to leave his wife and marry her. As if! Then she said she would accuse me of breaking in and assaulting her. She began tearing her clothes and was going to scream. As if I'd be interested in molesting a dirty little cow like her. The only thing she loved was my money, so I helped her make love to my money.'

Sammler fell silent, and the awkwardness of the quiet in the room caused him to subside into the chair.

'Would you like to put that in a statement, sir?' asked Slonský.

'Of course not,' Sammler replied. 'I won't say any of that outside this room.'

'How do you know I didn't record it, sir?'

'You wouldn't have got into this room with a wire on your body. It's a special shielded chamber, and the small corridor behind my main office door contains all sorts of scanning equipment. As you enter, I know you're clean. You didn't record, and if you repeat it I'll just tell everyone you've made it up. As I proved to you before, you don't have a shred of evidence. You'll never prove it, and I'll never go to court. One day, this country will return to the true path, and I may be able to do you some good. Remember that, Slonský.'

Slonský picked up his hat and stood up.

'I'll be long since retired, sir. And I don't think I want someone like you to do me any good. I'll see myself out, sir.'

Slonský had not talked to himself since his childhood, but he drew some curious looks from passers-by as he stormed along the road towards the metro. People who swear and mumble often do. He was annoyed with himself for letting Sammler know that he had only circumstantial evidence against him, and although Sammler had lost his temper and said more than he might have planned, he could use none of it in court. Without Navrátil there, he had no witnesses either, but then if Navrátil had been there Sammler would have clammed up.

Maybe he didn't lose his temper, thought Slonský? He heated up and cooled down very quickly, yet he is supposed to be very self-contained and controlled. Maybe it was for show. Maybe he wanted me to understand the link between the cases because he was worried that no-one was getting it.

But if he couldn't nail Sammler, what then? That was the really uncomfortable part, because Slonský knew there was a bit of truth in Sammler's claim that the Czechs were egalitarian by nature. It was quite likely that if communism was going to make a comeback in Europe, Prague would have to be the starting point, because if you couldn't foment socialist revolution there, you would never do it anywhere else. And Sammler had started a snowball that might become an avalanche. If those three men appeared in court, the people might very well decide that the whole system was not worth preserving. Slonský closed his eyes to visualise where the future was taking him. How would Navrátil fare if he had to go through the years Slonský had himself faced? What would happen to all that Slonský had learned and worked for? Somehow he had to derail Sammler's plan. He had to stop the three stories hitting the press at the same time. As the escalator carried him up to street level, an idea came to him.

Slonský took out his cellphone and notebook. He had never liked keeping numbers on the phone in case it got lost, not to mention that he did not know how to enter them anyway, so he needed to riffle through the black book to find the number he wanted. To his relief, it was answered quickly. Time was of the essence, and there was not enough of it to allow him to think through his next steps. He had to work by instinct. But his instinct had rarely let him down before.

Chapter 23

The morning newspaper was a sensation. The photograph was reproduced in gorgeous colour right in the middle of the front page, though decency required that so much was blacked out that it could have shown almost anything.

Valentin was looking more than a little self-satisfied as he held court in his favourite chair, acknowledging the fellow journalists who came up to ask if there were any more revelations to come, particularly any more photographs of Soucha, and how he had ferreted this information out.

'Happy?' asked Slonský, as he slipped into a chair by Valentin's side.

'Contract should be in the bag, thanks. I knew I could count on you.'

'That's not what you said the other day.'

'I was under stress. I wasn't feeling myself. I had every confidence that my old mate wouldn't let me down. And that was a lulu. I wasn't expecting the go-ahead to print that.'

'Just remember you never spoke to me about it. Our copy is under lock and key at the office and no doubt the concerned citizen who sent it in sent you an entirely separate copy. I almost drew a moustache on him so people would know it wasn't our photo you'd got hold of.'

'Glad you didn't. It was fun trying to stick the black rectangles on so you couldn't see what he was doing but you knew who he was.'

'Have you heard from Soucha?'

'No. Surprising how quickly you can get a flight if you need to. We gave him an hour's start, unofficially. I think he may have gone to Turkey, but it doesn't matter. The key thing is that I got my scoop, and the editor is happy as a pig in poo.'

Slonský made to get up, but Valentin grabbed his arm.

'In view of the extreme joy of this occasion, I am prepared to buy you a large beer of your choice, with my own money. How about that, then?'

'Old friend, I would love to accept your kind offer, which I realise may never come my way again. I've waited thirty years for it, and I probably won't live another thirty. But your story should have started a tidal wave, and I need to be in the office to watch the ripples hit the beach.'

'There aren't any beaches in Prague. We're landlocked.'

'Then I'll have to look all the harder. But there will be ripples, Valentin. I don't know what will happen, but something will.'

Slonský sat patiently as Lukas read the morning paper.

'I'm appalled. Of course, the man will have to resign. As you say, this changes things.'

'If I'm right, sir, Dr Sammler must be very angry now. His plot needs all three stories in the news at once, and he held this one back from the press to maximise the impact. Now one story will be a nine days' wonder, over and done with before the other two get anywhere. He knows now that Banda won't be charged, and although Holec will be, a fraud trial takes months to set up.'

'Especially when Klinger is writing it up,' agreed Lukas. 'He'll want to cross-reference and index every item of evidence he has.'

'So the fact that this has unaccountably got into the press takes the timetable out of Sammler's hands, and I can't see how he can get control again.'

Lukas sucked the leg of his spectacles in deep thought.

'I'm not quite so sure that I would use the word "unaccountably", Slonský. I trust this department is not connected to that development?'

'Only Navrátil and I have access to the original, sir, and it's safely locked in my filing cabinet. Of course, copies may have been made in the lab. Who can tell where it came from? We'll probably never know.'

'So what does Sammler do now?'

'It's a little hard to say, sir. I've never been a fanatic or a murderer. But he can't influence the Gruberová or Holec cases, unless he decides to confess to killing Irina, which I think is unlikely. I think he has two alternatives. As I've told you, he knows I'm on his trail, so he may try to discredit me in some way to take his revenge, or he may realise that the game is up and that his plan failed.'

'Be careful, Josef. If you're right and he has already killed once, who knows how he will get his revenge on you? I think you should carry your gun, just in case.'

'I've got it on me, sir.'

'And have you remembered to put a magazine in it?'

'Brand new, never been used, sir.'

'Good man. Don't take this the wrong way, but you might want to think about checking it actually works. I doubt you'll have cleaned it for a while.'

Slonský took it from its holster and placed it on the desk for inspection. Lukas deftly checked it over.

'I'm very cautious about my own safety, sir,' explained Slonský.

'Good. Tell Navrátil to do the same. I wouldn't put it past Sammler to punish you by taking it out on Navrátil.'

Slonský's heart gave a little skip. That thought had not occurred to him. He could live with being dead, but having to carry the guilt of Navrátil's early demise would be a real burden.

'I will, sir. In fact, I'll do it now, sir.'

'You do that. I'm going to see the Director. If Sammler decides to try to frame you, it would be as well to launch a pre-emptive move by making sure the Director knows why that might be happening.'

'Thank you, sir. Sammler will be desperate. Who knows what he might do?'

'Who indeed? Anything is possible with a man like that.'

Navrátil was sucking the top of his pencil in rapt contemplation of a set of particulars supplied by letting agents.

'Didn't your mother tell you not to suck pencils, or the lead will go up your nose and enter your brain?' asked Slonský.

'She may have done,' agreed Navrátil. 'She warned me against all kinds of unlikely accidents. If I'm ever shot on duty I've got to get someone to check my underwear is clean before they take me to hospital.'

'Funny you should mention that,' commented Slonský. 'What's your shooting like?'

'I doubt I could match the Cat-Murdering Priest of Žižkov, sir, but if I'm ever attacked by a cardboard cut-out of a man, I'll be okay.'

'Good. Get your gun cleaned, oiled, loaded and on you. We don't know what Sammler will do next and whatever it is, I don't want him doing it to you.'

'Actually, sir, I think we do know. Valentin rang. He'd like you to call him back.'

'Call? Not meet? Where do I call him? He doesn't have a mobile.'

'He's at the newspaper, sir. The number is on your desk by the telephone.'

'Valentin? At the newspaper office? During daylight?'

Slonský dialled and asked to speak to the reporter, who sounded sober. In fact, he sounded scared and sober.

'Thank God you rang. Something very odd is happening here. I've had a phone call inviting me to follow up my story this morning. A young man called claiming to be Mario. He says he'll meet me at Kobylisy metro station if I come alone.'

'Did he have an accent?'

'Not really.'

'"Not really"? What kind of answer is that? Either he did or he didn't. Soucha said Mario was Austrian. Where did he get that from unless Mario had an accent?'

'I don't know. Look, all I want to know is whether it's safe to go.'

'I can't tell you that. We know Sammler must be rattled. I thought that if I couldn't stop his plan, I could mess it up by speeding one part along. Feeding you Mario now is probably a way of trying to regain the initiative. I'm just wary that it may be a stand-in, because we don't know where Mario has been. But you've got a photo of him, so you can check if he looks like the right young man.'

'Oh, great!' scoffed Valentin. 'I can hardly unfold that in the middle of the street to see if he looks right, can I?'

'Then scan it in, blow it up or do whatever you need to do to get a good image.'

'I can't improve a picture that actually doesn't show Mario's face clearly anyway. The attention is on Soucha — his face is plain as day. Mario's head is thrown back and to the side so you barely see it.'

'Then use your wits. Try asking a question or two, like proper journalists would. I can't see Sammler trying anything in a public place like a metro station. After all, if this is the real Mario he wants that story told. Just refuse to get into any cars. Stay in public. I'll get a few undercover police there. They won't be able to bring rifles, but they'll have handguns. We'll send them by metro rather than by car. When are you meeting?'

'Fifty minutes from now.'

Slonský growled down the line. 'Fifty minutes? Give us some notice, Valentin. It doesn't give me long to put this in place.'

'Hardly my fault. I rang half an hour ago but apparently you were kissing someone's backside.'

'Reporting to my chief and kissing his backside are two entirely separate things. Well, different, anyway. Just get there and we'll sort something out. Keep in touch.'

Slonský barked some orders at Navrátil and swept out of the room, flinging his coat over his shoulders as he went. Navrátil was a little put out, because he had no idea where he was going to find six guys with plain clothes and revolvers. However, the name Mucha came to mind.

Whatever happened at Kobylisy, Slonský had no intention of being there. If there is a trap, he thought, the one person they will be looking out for is me. The one person they might risk shooting in public is me. Not only that, the sausages are much better in town. If Slonský faced imminent death, he had no plans to die on an empty stomach. He was gnawing on a pork rib when his phone rang.

'Navrátil? You okay?'

'I'm fine. Nothing happened.'

'You mean he didn't turn up.'

'No, he showed as planned. And if it isn't Mario it's a very good lookalike.'

'So what's the story?'

Navrátil paused. His mouth sounded dry as if he did not want to tell the tale.

'Mario is a Roma boy.'

'You say "boy"? How old?'

'Nineteen.'

Slonský relaxed a little.

'But he's a ward of court. It seems he has personality problems so his parents couldn't cope with him and being on the move all the time meant he wasn't getting his treatment. He was in a home until he was seventeen, then he ran away. They caught him and put him under legal protection.'

'So how did Sammler find him?'

'Mario doesn't recognise the name Sammler. He says that his home found him a job but he doesn't like being indoors all day. Then someone said he would give him a job looking after horses. All he had to do was to say that his uncle was coming for him. One day he was called into the director's office and a man he had never seen before was waiting to take him to the horses.'

'And the home didn't check?'

'Doesn't sound like it. I've spoken to the woman in charge. She says she wasn't involved —'

'Funny how they never are.'

'— but the man seemed respectable, had some papers that seemed to show that he knew Mario, and Mario didn't say he didn't know him.'

'Because Mario was thinking about life with horses again. So does he know where he was taken?'

'Not a clue. He's actually not slow-witted. He just hasn't had much schooling and he gets angry because he can't express himself, says Valentin.'

'How did Mario get to the metro?'

'He says his uncle dropped him by car nearby and told him to wait there until he was collected at lunchtime.'

'And did we follow him when he left?'

'He got into a taxi that was already occupied. Olbracht tailed him on his bike but lost them. When he found the taxi again, it had a different fare. The driver told him he set them down at Florenc.'

'So they could have gone almost anywhere in Prague. Damn! What about Valentin?'

'He says he'll meet you in the cellar, and you would know where he meant.'

'Yes, I do. I only hope I get there in time.'

'You think he's in danger?'

'Yes, but I also think he's planning on getting very drunk.'

In fact, Valentin was relatively sober when Slonský arrived, having been collected by Navrátil on the way.

'Don't ever give me a scoop again,' he whined. 'My nerves won't stand it.'

'You wanted it,' said Slonský.

'That was before I knew I was going to get threatened over it.'

'Threatened? Who threatened you?'

'Mario said his uncle wanted me to tell his story, and I had to do that even if you tried to stop me, otherwise his uncle would be very angry with me.'

Slonský had a coffee, having once more refused a beer. Valentin wondered if he was sickening for something. Slonský stirred it slowly with his spoon, having dumped a ridiculous amount of sugar in it.

'You going to drink that or ice a cake with it?' Valentin asked.

'Hush, I'm thinking. Tell me what Mario said about himself.'

'He said he was nineteen, under the Court of Protection, has to see someone regularly, doesn't know where he lives. What else do you want to know?'

'When did he meet uncle?'

'End of last year. He says it was before the snow came.'

'That could be August in some places. He can't do better than that?'

'No. But he says it wasn't too far from here. Originally he came from somewhere to the east, because he remembers being taken to Frýdek-Místek as a boy. He thought it was a funny name.'

'Did you show him the photo?'

'I showed him the censored version from the newspaper. He thought it was funny.'

'Funny? Why funny?'

'Well, because they hadn't got any clothes on.'

'Did you ask him what happened in that swimming pool?'

'No, because it seemed unkind when someone had taken advantage of a young man to put him in that position.'

'You idiot! You empty-headed, balding drunken idiot!' snapped Slonský.

Valentin was more than a little hurt.

'I'm not balding,' he complained. 'Thinning a bit on top, maybe. But not balding.'

'That's not Mario! Damn! I should have seen this.'

'Seen what?' asked Navrátil.

'He'd probably told the real Mario to make himself scarce, so the chances are he couldn't find him again in a hurry. Even if he knows where he is, he's probably back in Austria waiting to be summoned when the occasion arose. There wasn't enough time between my seeing Sammler and your story appearing for him to get Mario back. But Sammler had a spare Mario up his sleeve. He probably spotted there's enough resemblance to pass a quick inspection, given that we don't have really detailed photographs of Mario. But he invited you, with no photographer. That's what he meant by alone. He wasn't warning off the police particularly — he wanted you to come without a photographer. No photos, no video, just your word for it that you'd met Mario.'

'Well, how was I to know? I never met the original Mario.'

'Exactly. But Sammler knew that if Mario 2 just told the truth about himself, that would be your story. And he frightened you into publishing it, because that generates the crime that hadn't been committed before.'

184

'Come again?'

'I told Sammler that the Soucha picture didn't show a crime. Sammler didn't know that the age of consent for these things is fifteen here. But if Mario is under the Court of Protection, Sammler doesn't need a crime. He just broadcasts what a scandal it is that the Czech Republic can't protect its mentally-deficient people from this kind of abuse. It becomes a story about Soucha taking advantage of a simpleton and the State not being sharp enough to prevent it. Damn!'

Navrátil was confused. 'How do you know it's not the same person, sir?'

'I know some youngsters with mental problems are uninhibited, but they know what they've done. Mario didn't react as if he knew what was happening in the photo. But more to the point, the photo was taken in the summer — remember the flowers? — whereas Mario says he met uncle before the snow came. If he's a Roma boy, he'll know the seasons. "Before the snow" is late autumn, not summer. Mario 2 was a late addition to the plan. More likely, he's Plan B, to be fished out if Plan A went tits up.'

'So what happens if I write that he was an impostor?' asked Valentin.

'Sammler gets angry. We need to keep you safe somewhere.'

'So what if I write that he wasn't an impostor?'

Slonský considered this option for a moment.

'You'd be an even worse journalist than I took you for. But I suppose Sammler would be happy, and it can't harm Soucha more than he's already hurt.'

'But it gives the initiative back to Sammler, sir,' protested Navrátil. 'How does that help us?'

'It gets him off Valentin's back. And Sammler might relax if he thinks the plan is back on track.'

'He can't relax, sir. He has to press it home while it's in people's minds.'

Slonský muttered a few words that he must have picked up in the street when he was younger.

'Okay, this is what we'll do. Valentin, get your editor to trail the story. Run something in tomorrow's edition saying you're going to have a really big story the day after. You can even say it's an astonishing development in the Soucha case. That should keep you safe, because Sammler won't polish you off when you've declared your intention of running the story he wants.'

'One extra day. Big deal. Pardon me if I don't turn cartwheels.'

'It's one extra day for you, but it's enough for us. Come on, we'll drop you by your office. Sleep there tonight.'

'Sleep in the office? How can you get any sleep in a newspaper office?'

'I'll buy you a nightcap.'

Slonský headed for the car while Navrátil and Valentin trotted along behind.

'Am I balding?' whispered Valentin. 'Would you call me balding?'

185

Chapter 24

Slonský rarely slept well, and his brain clicked over relentlessly as he rolled back and forth across his pillow. He recalled the first sight of Irina Gruberová's purple face, the grey snow beneath her, the policemen who refused to leave their warm car. Gruberová's eyes fixed on his, begging him to help her by catching her killer. He saw the body on the slab, the photograph of the intimate dinner, the look on Banda's face as he dropped his coffee cup into the evidence bag. Every moment of the enquiry was compressed into a single, short, restless night. Towards the end the visions started to cycle, always ending with a laughing Sammler walking free as Slonský found himself behind bars, looking out at a failure. He knew Sammler was guilty, but he could not prove it. And yet the evidence must be there somewhere. Whenever a crime was committed, evidence was left behind. All he had to do was find it. The proof is out there.

He turned his pillow over to find a cool side. Sammler is running this now. Sammler calls the tune, and we react to him; we have to wrest the initiative out of his hands and grab it for ourselves, Slonský told himself. But the Slonský in his dreams had no idea how that might be done. Putting the story in the newspaper bought them time, but it meant Sammler was still making the pace. Things were happening because he wanted them to. Slonský had to find something unexpected that threw Sammler's plan out of kilter. He pictured a smoothly running piece of black, antique machinery; pistons moved, cogs turned, steam hissed, and the machine pressed implacably on; Slonský had a large spanner and planned to push it into the gearing. He had no idea whether it would work or not, whether the engine might explode or even suck him in, but it was the only way of stopping the engine that he had. It had to be tried, because not to try was unimaginable. Slonský waved the spanner above his head like a banner, thrust it fearlessly into the slowest-moving gearwheels, and let go. That was when he woke up, and hence failed to discover what would happen if he did that.

Valentin's story ran as a lurid red splash across the corner of the front page. He had interviewed Mario, it said, and the exclusive interview would appear tomorrow, when they could devote enough space to do it justice. There would also be an exposé of the incompetent management of a certain young people's hostel, which one of Valentin's colleagues was working on.

Slonský was cleaning his gun once again. Parts littered the desk.

'Can you put that back together again?' Navrátil enquired.

'In my sleep,' said Slonský. 'It's pretty well all I did during my national service. Take them apart, put them together; take them apart, clean them, put them together.'

'Sir, I know it's not my place to question —'

'Then don't. Do I know what I'm doing? No. I'm flying by the seat of my pants. Last time he confessed, but there were no witnesses. This time there will be. He won't confess if he knows you're there, so I'll have to ensure that you aren't there. But you won't be far away. I'll be miked up and you'll be listening in.'

'Why don't we just bring him in, sir?'

'Because he'll shut up until his lawyer gets here, then they'll walk out of the door. Simple as that. If we want to nail him, he has to think it's an even game. He has to think he can taunt me with what he's done and get away with it.'

'Shouldn't you have a recorder, sir?'

'Too bulky. I couldn't use the recording anyway without a caution and all that jazz.'

'But you can't use my statement either.'

'I can if he doesn't object. And once he realises you've heard it, he'll know that the game is up. He can argue all he likes about circumstantial evidence, but if two policemen heard him confess, it's hard to claim he didn't.'

Navrátil nodded and got out of his seat.

'Can you give me ten minutes, sir?'

'Half an hour until we move off. Where are you going?'

Navrátil jerked his thumb.

'Church up the street, sir. Thought I might pop in and … collect my thoughts.'

Navrátil gently closed the door behind him.

'Say one for me while you're there,' mumbled Slonský.

Slonský telephoned Sammler's secretary to make an appointment. It was all terribly difficult, he was told. Unfortunately Dr Sammler had a string of very urgent appointments today. Slonský expressed the opinion that this might be a stalling tactic. How about 11:30? No, Sammler would be in a meeting with the Deputy Secretary at the Ministry of Finance. It started at 11:00 and was expect to last an hour. Then, after lunch, he had a meeting planned with some German businessmen who were funding a shopping mall. That couldn't possibly be postponed, because they were on their way there from Berlin. It would certainly take all afternoon until 16:30. Sadly, he would not be free then either, because he had to prepare for a speech he was giving at a dinner that evening for an Austro-Czech Society of some kind. Lunch? No, Prague Businessmen's Circle, meeting at 12:30 across the river. It would take time to get there and back given the traffic.

Slonský said that he understood, and that tomorrow would do. Half an hour should be more than sufficient. He had some new evidence that he needed to put to Dr Sammler that seemed to contradict the statement he gave the other day. A few moments later, Slonský had an appointment for 11:45 next morning. He allowed himself a small smile as he returned the handset to its cradle. The pressure on Sammler was building.

Navrátil was waiting by the car when Slonský emerged.

'Where to, sir?'

'City police office, District 1. It's on Letenská.'

'Why there, sir?'

'It's got a car park.'

Slonský climbed in, which seemed to leave little option for Navrátil but to do the same.

'Put your foot down, Navrátil. It would be good to be there by half past eleven.'

'Why, sir?'

'Navrátil, this investigation is henceforth being conducted on a need-to-know basis. And you don't need to know. At least, not yet. Patience, lad, patience.'

Navrátil pulled up by the police office and waited as he had been instructed. Slonský emerged after a few minutes with a uniformed city policeman and approached the car, motioning to Navrátil to wind the window down as he came closer.

'Right, Navrátil, listen carefully. I'll turn the mike on now. Can you hear it through your earpiece?'

'Yes, sir.'

'Good. I'm going to stand just past the bend there. This officer has his instructions. Your job is to follow me when I tell you. Is that clear?'

'You'll be in a car, then, sir?'

'That's the plan. Either that or I'll be running bloody fast to keep up with one.'

Slonský and the police officer marched up the street past the Ministry of Finance and disappeared from sight around a right-hand bend. Navrátil had very little idea what might be planned, and the small amount he understood did not appeal to him in the slightest.

The policeman busied himself ignoring the traffic chaos developing around him and keeping an eye peeled for the beige Mercedes. Slonský's instructions were unusual, but since they amounted to doing his job particularly well, he was happy to follow them. His boss seemed to know Slonský and had vouched for him, so that had to be all right.

The Mercedes had pulled out of the Ministry of Finance and was coming along the road towards them. The registration number was right, so the policeman stepped off the traffic island waving his arms to flag the Mercedes down. It came to a halt and the driver wound down the window.

'Is there a problem?' he asked.

'Yes. You pulled straight across that lane without signalling. Just because you're driving someone important doesn't mean you can ignore the rules of the road, you know.'

'I did not!' protested the driver.

'Right, out you get. Hands on the roof of the car.'

Sammler leaned across to speak through the window.

'Officer, I have an important meeting. Please send the fine to my office and we'll pay it.'

'It doesn't work like that, sir. Endangering other road-users can mean you lose your driver's licence.'

'I didn't endanger anyone,' the driver argued.

'I'm not arguing here,' the policeman replied. 'We can continue this at the station. It's just down the road there.'

'And how am I going to get to my meeting?' Sammler expostulated.

'I don't know, sir. But he isn't driving you. I suppose you'll have to drive yourself.'

Sammler snorted in annoyance, then opened the nearside rear door and walked round to the driver's side. He had to watch those other idiots who might have taken his door off, so it was a surprise to him when he sat down to find Slonský sitting beside him, who promptly clicked the central locking button.

'Good morning, sir,' said Slonský. 'Move off in your own time.'

'And why should I do that?' asked Sammler.

'Because I'm pointing this at you,' replied Slonský in his most guileless tone, holding his gun in his gloved hand.

'You wouldn't use it,' Sammler replied scornfully. 'It would be plain murder.'

'Not if you were armed too, sir. There's a gap in the traffic now.'

Sammler pulled out and began to follow the flow of cars.

'But I'm not armed, am I, Lieutenant?'

Slonský dug deep into his coat pocket.

'Fortunately I have a spare, sir. If I'm forced to shoot you, I'll casually drop this by your body as I perform the kiss of life very ineffectively.'

'That's not standard issue, is it?'

'No, it's a Makarov pistol. The East Germans had them. I got this one off an East German army officer I helped during an exercise.'

'Helped? How?'

'I stood him upright and took the weight of the heavy gun off his chest.'

'You stole it?'

'Technically, I took it off him because he was too drunk to use it safely. Call me old-fashioned if you like, but I have a thing about letting drunks get into fights when they have semi-automatic weapons on them. I just never got round to giving it back. It's their own fault. The Germans told us to make ourselves scarce before the military police got there. I thought being a patriotic gentleman you'd appreciate the attention to detail, sir, giving you a German gun.'

'I don't want a gun of any kind, Slonský, German or otherwise.'

Slonský could see that this was going to be difficult.

'You have to have a gun, or I can't shoot you. But you don't have to have it until after you're dead, otherwise you might use it.'

'This is preposterous,' Sammler growled. 'What's to stop me just running the car into a wall, or stopping to ask a policeman to arrest you?'

'The fact that you're an intelligent man, sir, so you'll see that anything other than falling in with my plans results in your lying dead somewhere. I may be under arrest, but that won't give you a lot of satisfaction. Dead men don't crow over their enemies.'

'Where are we going?'

'I thought somewhere quiet where we can talk. Somewhere in the countryside. Head westwards, please.'

'This is the end of your career, you know.'

'Yes, it could be,' agreed Slonský. 'Alternatively, it could be its finest moment, depending on whether I can get you to confess.'

'You know a confession obtained under duress isn't admissible in court.'

'Duress? What duress? You said yourself you didn't believe I'd shoot. So either you lied, and you think I really would shoot, or you aren't under duress. Can't have it both ways.'

Slonský glanced in the mirror. Navrátil was two cars back, keeping pace nicely.

'Right turn here, please. We'll go out on the highway. You can put your foot down if you like. But don't think of drawing attention to yourself by speeding. My fingers twitch when I'm driven too fast.'

Sammler's hands were glistening with sweat.

'I'm a personal friend of the Minister of Justice, you know.'

'No relevance to me, sir. Justice looks after courts; it's the Minister of the Interior that would impress me, if I hadn't already locked one up for a murder you committed. Incidentally, I think Dr Banda has a bone to pick with you. Don't expect a Christmas card this year.'

'It's a matter of indifference to me. He's one of yesterday's men now.'

'It takes one to know one, sir. You might want to start moving over to the right-hand lane, sir. We'll take Route 7 to Dejvice.'

'I'll have been missed by now, you realise. I have an appointment for lunch.'

'I shouldn't imagine you're too hungry just at the moment. I'll ring in a little while and ask them to keep it warm if you like. Turn right towards Jenerálka. Navrátil, go back to Prague and await further instructions.'

'Are you sure that's wise, sir?' Navrátil asked, before he remembered that it was futile because he did not have a microphone. He pulled off the road and feverishly considered his options. Should he obey his head, or his orders? He could not believe that Slonský seriously proposed to maltreat a suspect to get a confession, but on the other hand his boss had been perfectly happy to fake a beating and you could hardly overlook his treatment of Banda. Perhaps if Navrátil had not been so new and so junior, he might have decided differently, but he saw no alternative to doing what he was told, however much he felt that he ought to intervene. Then again, Slonský was hardly in a position to argue that an officer should always do what he was told. Several of their colleagues had described incidents when Slonský had ignored an order or "creatively interpreted" an instruction.

Navrátil sat at the side of the road and evaluated the alternatives as quickly as he could as he watched Sammler's car pull away from him.

Slonský glanced in the mirror again to confirm that Navrátil had pulled up.

'Ignore the village, sir. Follow the sign to Horoměřice.'

The road began to snake around between thick woods. Apart from the occasional house, there were trees on each side.

'This would be a good place to pull in, sir. Let's go for a walk in the trees.'

Sammler stopped the car, and Slonský immediately grabbed the keys.

'Just in case you were thinking of running back to the car and driving off, sir. Shall we go?'

'This is a nonsense,' protested Sammler. 'You plainly intend to shoot me in cold blood. Why should I co-operate?'

'Because if you co-operate I won't have to shoot you. I'd have thought that was clear. I'd much rather have you behind bars than in an urn on my mantelpiece. I want to have a little chat on neutral territory. We can debate the issues and perhaps come to an agreement. When you get out, twenty years or so from now, I'll probably be dead, but if I'm not you can come and hold me at gunpoint in return. Can't say fairer than that, can I? After you.'

Sammler trudged through the mud. The warmer weather had caused a thaw that turned the snow to water, and the frozen ground to black mud. Slonský indicated a drier patch alongside a rivulet. Sammler noticed that Slonský had stopped for a moment, and turned to see the old detective putting protective disposable overshoes on his feet.

'A little trick I learned off you, sir. You leave fewer footprints this way. That's what you did in the snow, wasn't it? Novák was stumped for a while till he did some experiments with rubber overshoes. Size 47 overshoes over size 44 shoes, he thought, reducing the definition at the edges. Was he right, sir?'

'Fantasy, pure fantasy.'

'I don't really need your confirmation, sir. Novák experimented until he could reproduce what he saw in the snow.'

'Then why waste your breath and try my patience?'

Slonský ignored the enquiry. He had never had much time for stupid questions.

'Then I puzzled over how you'd left no real tyre tracks in the snow, till I saw on the closed circuit cameras at your flat that you put a broom in the back of your car. A quick sweep would blur them quite nicely, wouldn't it? But why would you have a broom in your car? I notice you don't have one today.'

'There's no snow today, Lieutenant, or haven't you noticed? It's all circumstantial, and none of it convinces. How much further?'

'Tell you what, sir. Is the microphone putting you off? I wouldn't want you to feel inhibited about expressing yourself. I'll leave it here, shall I?'

Slonský placed the microphone on a tree stump, much to Navrátil's annoyance. Now he could not hear any of the dialogue between them. He hoped that Slonský was just trying to frighten Sammler into a confession, but he decided that he had better act quickly, just in case. He did not want Slonský's career to end like this.

'This is far enough. Let's talk.'

'Talk? About what?'

'About life, the universe, the price of fish, I don't know. Oh, and why a pretty young Czech girl is lying in a grave near Kladno fifty years too early. You know more about that than any man alive. Don't you feel any guilt?'

'No. Why should I?'

'Because you killed her. She was going to scream and you killed her, you said. But then I thought, no, that makes no sense. You couldn't let her live once you'd invited her to help with the plot, so whether she screamed or not, you were going to strangle her. You killed her and wrapped her in her own sheets to look like a laundry bundle. When you arrived at the back of the metro station you rolled her out like Cleopatra inside the carpet, and threw the sheets in the car, leaving her in the dressing gown and the first pair of shoes you could find for her. She must have put them out for the next morning, rather than having just taken them off, because they wouldn't have matched the outfit she was wearing in the photo. You knew there weren't traces of you on her clothes, but you couldn't be sure about the sheet because you'd knelt on it while you squeezed all the young life out of her.'

'A very colourful picture you paint. But you can't prove any of that.'

'Would you really sacrifice your life for communism?'

'Of course. A man needs something to believe in. What do you believe in, Lieutenant? The rule of law? Oh, I forgot, you interpret that as allowing you to shoot suspects. What happened to your oath, you hypocrite?'

'My oath, sir? My oath was to uphold justice, not the law. I spent twenty years of my life enforcing laws I didn't believe in. All those years of knocking on people's doors at three in the morning. They thought we did it to cause terror. Rubbish. We did it because people were less likely to be out then. We'd kick the door in then stand aside to let the security police do their dirty work. That was called upholding the law. I never believed there was any "justice" about it. My generation did that in every walk of our lives. We took bribes, but we were just as guilty if we gave them. There were just so many examples of the law turning a blind eye, not being applied fairly. Think of those show trials — Slánsky, Clementis, Margolius, Horaková. They didn't deserve to hang. The state has said so. Admittedly a bit late, but they've been formally exonerated, and much good did the pardon do them. They ended on the gallows, and the law of the day put them there. I upheld that law, but it wasn't justice. When the Wall came down and we made a new start, that was the most important thing for me. "No more upholding the law, Josef," I said to myself. "Your job is giving people justice." And I've tried to live by that. I've got a lot to make up for. No more than many and a lot less than some, but it's never going to be put right. All I can do is my best. And that's why you're here now. I want justice for Irina Gruberová, and you can give it to her by confessing.'

'Go to hell,' snarled Sammler. 'If the bitch is dead, so what? You can't make an omelette without breaking eggs. There are always collateral victims. Your precious capitalist west has littered Iraq with dead civilians who just happened to be next door to the wrong building. Was that justice? You make me sick. Such hypocrisy! We offer a new way, Slonský. No private property means no theft. International solidarity between workers means no war. There is another way, Slonský, and you and your kind are an obstacle to it. Mark my words, one day the red flag will fly again over Prague Castle. I hope you live to see it. It'll give you something to do while you twist in the wind dangling from a lamp-post.'

'If I thought that would stop you in your tracks, I'd settle for that. Here I am at nearly sixty, and I've finally found something worth dying for. I'd have willingly taken Irina's place to save her from the death you bestowed on her. I'd do anything to see you locked up.'

Sammler jabbed his finger violently at Slonský.

'That's it, isn't it? That's what you can't stand. It's not really about poor little Irina getting killed. It's the fact that I'll never face trial for it. It's the fact that you don't have any useful evidence — no forensics, no witnesses, no accusatory letters, not a thing. I could stand here and shout that I killed her, and you'd have to let me walk away. Free! And if you kill me, what does that make you? A common murderer. Is that what Czech law does for you? Is killing unarmed civilians okay with you? Is that what you want to be, Slonský? My murderer?'

Slonský stared into the spiteful eyes before him.

'I can live with that,' he said, taking a stride forward and firing left-handed into Sammler's right temple. Sammler looked uncomprehending for a moment before slumping back against the tree trunk and sliding down it. Moving quickly, Slonský peeled off his thin evidence glove, turned it inside out, placed it on Sammler's right hand and rubbed it vigorously to transfer any powder residue. Removing the glove again, he wrapped Sammler's fingers around the butt of the Makarov, pushed the car keys into Sammler's pocket, kicked some rotting leaves over any traces he may have left, and walked back to the main road, picking up the microphone as he went.

'You can come for me now, Navrátil,' he said, and began to walk along the road towards Jenerálka. A bus went past, but he ignored it. The only person he wanted to see was his young assistant, but Navrátil was not to be seen.

Slonský had been walking for about forty minutes when the car came towards him, and Navrátil stepped out. They stood facing each other in silence for a minute or so, then Navrátil held out a piece of paper.

'Receipt for the two coffees and pastries we had in Prague this afternoon,' he explained.

Slonský took it unsmilingly, and slipped it into his wallet before getting into the car.

Epilogue

In the wake of Sammler's death, Slonský had made a strange promise to himself. He would not lie about what had happened. If anyone realised that he had shot Sammler, he would admit it. It was not something that he was ashamed of. All he had done was rectify a failing in the law. Of course, he would go to jail for it, but the only person who knew, Navrátil, had kept his mouth tight shut. In fact, Navrátil had rationalised it away by telling himself that if he knew for certain that Slonský had killed Sammler he would have to report it, but by avoiding asking about it he could keep himself in ignorance and thus have nothing that he needed to report. It therefore suited both men not to mention the subject and they never had. From the moment that Navrátil picked Slonský up by the side of the road after the death they had said not a single word about that day.

Dr Novák's report had been unequivocal. The gun was in Sammler's hand, and had only Sammler's prints on it. There was some powder residue on Sammler's thumb and index finger. The bullet had undoubtedly come from the gun found at the scene. It was an open and shut case.

The body had been found after a bus driver reported that a car had been by the side of the road for several days. When Slonský had turned up at Sammler's office on the following morning for their pre-arranged interview, Sammler's secretary had been forced to confess that they did not know where he was. Slonský had duly reported as much to Captain Lukas, so Lukas had asked all police to look out for the car and its owner. Once the car was traced, a few policemen walked up into the nearby woods and found the body against a tree. Lukas was convinced that Sammler had realised that the game was up and had taken the easy way out rather than go to jail for a long time. The only slightly untidy part was that Sammler's secretary had deposed that Slonský had asked for the appointment, claiming to have important new evidence, but the old detective had admitted to Lukas that this had been a bluff. It had obviously frightened Sammler, and Lukas contented himself with the thought that this just proved the man's guilt, since he plainly believed that there could be important new evidence, whereas if he had been innocent he would have demanded to know what it was before agreeing to the interview.

The atmosphere in the office had been difficult for a while, but Navrátil was brightening considerably as the day approached when Officer Peiperová would be free to take up her new post in the detective division. Of course, she would not work directly for Slonský, but at least they were in the same building. Navrátil had not yet broached the question of sharing a flat with her, but the girl had to live somewhere and his own small flat was highly unsuitable. His mother would be shocked if Peiperová moved in, largely because she had never heard of her. He really must get around to mentioning it someday. Just not quite yet, he thought.

BOOK TWO: SLAUGHTER AND FORGETTING

Chapter 1

Holoubek was still sprightly for his age. He admired his physique in the shop window as he waited for the tram. Still slim, with barely a hint of a paunch. He looked after himself, and it showed in his appearance. His trousers had a crease, and he only needed his glasses for reading if the light was not too good, which it frequently was not in Prague at this time of year, as winter grudgingly gave way to what was laughingly called spring.

As with many men of his generation, he wore a hat, but then you would have to be silly not to do so with a wind like this one, whisking up any loose paper and driving it against the parked cars. He did not bother with gloves, though, and checked his hands for any sign of blueness. There were a few scattered liver spots, and the skin was rather papery in places, but he still had a firm grip and at least he did not shake like his old friend Miklín. Well, like Miklín used to shake, because he was long since dead. He had been quite lucky, because he had been worried about the progression of his Parkinson's disease and fortunately walked out in front of a bus while he was thinking about it. So every cloud has a silver lining, thought Holoubek, though admittedly Miklín probably would not have seen it that way.

Holoubek remembered Miklín lying there on the ground. Oddly, he had not looked frightened; just very surprised, as if a bus was the last thing he had expected to hit him as he jaywalked across the street. He had lived for a few minutes after the collision, but was unable to speak. Just as well, because his language was shocking when he was in his prime, so goodness knows what he would have said about being run over by a bus. And not even a Czech bus either; it was a German tour bus, all glass and swirling paint along the side. Miklín could see the dent in the front where his hip had made contact with the grille, and was satisfied to note that the headlight was broken. Funny how you remember those things, thought Holoubek. *I can't remember what I had for tea yesterday, and yet I can remember a road accident thirty years ago and the look on the victim's face.*

The tram was late. Only a minute or so, but what is the point of a timetable if the drivers do not keep to it? Things were slack nowadays, Holoubek told himself. People blamed the young, but Holoubek did not. It was the young who were going to have to tidy up the mess the world was in, and it was not their fault. He blamed their parents, his children's generation. Long sideburns, leather jackets, suede boots, ridiculous moustaches like Mexican bandits, and the women all flopping around with no proper underwear on and not a trace of make-up. Certainly there were some women who could do without make-up, but this lot were not among them. There was one across the street now. Must be fifty if she was a day, and she was wearing an orange tie-dye top and jeans. Jeans were all right if you had the figure for them, but her rear end looked like a badly packed rucksack.

The bell of the tram brought him back to this world. Holoubek climbed aboard and waved his pass in the air like they used to in the old days, when citizens were likely to report you if you travelled without a ticket. Not so public-spirited now, he thought. To his surprise, a young student offered him a seat, which Holoubek politely declined. Do I look that old, he wondered, looking around to see if anyone was inspecting him.

His son did not like him to travel around on his own, but Holoubek had lived in Prague all his life, and he knew every centimetre of it, except the new bits, of course. When he wanted to check his mind was still working properly, he would set himself the task of plotting a journey across town, recalling all the trams and buses and the best places to change. He had never really taken to the metro for some reason, unlike Cerha. Cerha was a companion he sometimes bumped into at the Red Apple, and they would compete to work out the routes. Holoubek was unsure whether Cerha was telling the truth when he said some of these journeys could be done by metro, or simply claiming to have won on the basis that Holoubek would not be able to disprove his route.

Today's journey was quite simple. Take the number 18 tram from Palouček to Národní třída, then switch to the number 17 for the rest of the journey, with a short walk at the end. Holoubek hoped that a ticket inspector might ask for proof that he was over seventy. It had happened to him once, and he had enjoyed being able to prove he was over age. He must look younger for that to happen, he thought. Admittedly it was about fifteen years ago, but it was the principle of the thing.

The principle of the thing. Exactly the reason that he was on the tram in the first place. His son had told him to let it drop, but Holoubek could not. It was the principle of the thing — but then he couldn't expect his son to understand that. He was one of the suede booted, leather jacketed, long haired near hippy generation. Authentic. That was the word he kept using. He said it was important to live an authentic life, whatever one of those was. So far as Holoubek was concerned, you were either alive or you weren't, and if you were alive, you had a life to lead, and you'd better get on with it and stop moaning. After all, there were plenty of people in the cemeteries who would tell you that you had nothing to complain about. One of them had been telling him that for a few months now. He had a complaint to make, and he needed Holoubek to make it because he could not do it himself, having been dead all these years.

Holoubek had searched a lot of rooms in his time, and there was not much you could tell him about hidey-holes. He was known for the rigour of his searches, and this despite having spent much of his career in the force at a time when every policeman had a lot of practice in searching. Barely a day went by when they were not turning someone's flat over looking for nothing in particular. As a result, Holoubek had learned a great deal about concealment. He could find a hollow wall, a concealed panel, a false skirting board, a package in a drain pipe or a recently moved floorboard that might be hiding something of importance.

However, in 1967, someone had almost got the better of him. They had been rummaging through a flat in the Old Town where they were absolutely certain there ought to be a roll of film, but despite a fairly thorough demolition of the place it had not come to light. Holoubek was dogged — some would say pathologically stubborn — so when the others had given up, he had indulged in his favourite technique of sitting in the middle of the floor, slowly scanning the room. In this way he had come to the conclusion that the film was not under or behind something, but inside it, and after some nifty work with his penknife he had found it inside the works of the record player.

He kept this information to himself, because he wanted to have somewhere private of his own in case the tables were ever turned, and over the intervening decades he had come up with a number of cunning places to keep items of various sizes and types.

The casual visitor to Holoubek's flat would have been impressed with its general tidiness, and perhaps felt a little sad that it was still mired in the seventies or eighties. There was, for example, an old-fashioned television in the corner. Holoubek could have afforded a flat screen model, but it would have had one major drawback. His confidential notes would not have snuggled inside the casing, taped to the underside of the top surface without causing a fire risk. Thus, before catching the tram, Holoubek had carefully unscrewed the back of the television, having disconnected it from the mains some time before, and had extracted a narrow manila envelope which was nestled in his inside jacket pocket. As he sat on the number 17 tram he rubbed his upper arm against the pocket to check the envelope was still there. Only a fool puts his hand in to check; you never know who might be watching. Satisfied that it was safe, he relaxed and enjoyed the journey.

Chapter 2

Captain Josef Lukas flicked through the folder one more time. Damn! There appeared to be only one way to do this. Damn! It was going to be an awkward interview, but that was what management was for. A man could not chicken out of his responsibilities.

Slonský knocked on the door, a redundant gesture since he had opened it first and begun to walk in.

'You wanted to see me, sir?'

'Yes, Slonský. You'd better sit down.'

Slonský obeyed, and adopted a facial expression of extreme innocence, as if he could not possibly have any inkling of what was coming.

'It's about retirement, Slonský.'

'I'm sorry to hear that, sir. We'll miss you.'

'Not my retirement, Slonský. Yours!'

When he had been small, Slonský had owned a dog of indeterminate breed whose response to the word 'bath' was one of profound anxiety morphing into abject terror. There was some irony in the fact that the word 'retirement' had the same effect on Slonský. He knew, of course, that it must come. He also knew that he was approaching the age when it would be laid before him, but he had hoped that if he kept solving crime they would let him stay on. He did not want to retire, because he had nothing else to do. He did not play dominoes and he had no interest in daytime television — or evening television, for that matter. He loathed gardening and his pension would not allow him to spend all day in a bar.

Lukas wore an expression of fatherly concern.

'Have you given any thought to retirement, Slonský?'

A small fire of rebellion kindled in Slonský's chest. If he was being put out to grass, he was damned if they were going to do that to him. He would preserve his self-respect by deciding that it was his choice.

'I can't deny it would be good to have some time to myself, sir.'

Lukas threw the folder on the desk. This was not going well.

'Look here, Josef. The thing is, with Němec retiring and the reorganisation going on, we can ill afford to lose you both in such a short time. I'm sorry, but I'm just not going to be able to let you go. You'll have to stay on a while longer.'

Slonský's heart turned a few flips of delight, though he tried to conceal his pleasure.

'As you wish, sir. I'm at the Department's disposal, as ever.'

He closed the door behind him and resisted the temptation to leap up and click his heels until he could not be seen through the frosted glass, behind which Lukas was grinning. He knew all along that Slonský was dreading retirement but it was so rare that he was able to get one over his lieutenant that he had been unable to resist. The puppet-master had had his own strings pulled.

'You're looking pleased,' said Officer Jan Navrátil, glancing up from a large printout of crime statistics.

'And I have reason to be, lad. I have been assured that I will be around to complete your education. The powers that be — or, more accurately, the power that is — has decided that I am indispensable to the smooth running of this department. This calls for a celebration. As soon as you've finished whatever it is you're doing, we'll decamp to a nearby hostelry and get our consciousness obliterated on Plzeň's finest product.'

'That'll be a while,' said Navrátil. 'I'm supposed to be compiling burglary statistics from the station returns for the whole of Prague.'

'Show me,' Slonský replied.

Navrátil handed over the binder of printout.

'Correct me if I'm wrong,' Slonský began, 'but this looks like a collation of burglary statistics to me. The very thing someone has asked you to put together. Allow me to point out that you already have one here.'

'Yes, but it's not right. Some of the stations misclassify crimes, and others don't use the online system properly. If you believed these figures you'd think that there was no burglary at all in Vysočany.'

'There probably isn't,' Slonský agreed. 'There'll be damn all worth nicking there.'

'I've been at it for two hours and it's no better.'

Slonský rested his hand on Navrátil's shoulder.

'Courage, lad! Fortitude! Nil desperandum but trust in Slonský. Who asked you to do this?'

'Captain Lukas.'

'And how does he know they're wrong?'

'Because they always are.'

'But does he know what the right number is? Of course not, or he wouldn't need you to work it out. Thus, it seems to me, whatever set of numbers you give him, he will accept as accurate so long as they're different to the ones he had before. Just make them up, lad.'

Navrátil was shocked. 'You can't just make up crime statistics.'

'Of course you can. We've done it for years. Not to mention economic statistics, voting figures, almost any set of numbers you care to name.'

'But we need accurate crime statistics.'

202

Slonský considered this novel argument for a few moments.

'Why?'

'Well, because … if we don't know where the crime is, how will we know where to concentrate our resources?'

'Crime is everywhere, therefore the police have to be everywhere. And we don't have any spare ones now so knowing we need more doesn't help us. Let me also draw your attention to the great flaw in that argument. Criminals tend to go where there aren't policemen. Thus, if we concentrate them in one area, the crime moves to a different one and we're worse off than if we'd left things alone. The only people who want to know where the crime is are the criminals. No point burgling an estate that has been cleaned out already. And accurate crime figures, which I remind you we now publish on the internet for any Tom, Dick or Harry to see, just make for economy of effort for the criminal. We're doing their research for them, Navrátil. At least, I'm not; you are.'

'That's so cynical. Our job is to prevent crime.'

'And how many crimes have you prevented sitting on your backside in this office all afternoon? Whereas if you and I had been tucking into a well-earned sausage down the road, we might have overheard criminals plotting a crime. They don't come into police stations to do it, Navrátil. Except the ones who are policemen themselves, of course.'

Navrátil chewed the end of his pencil while he tried to come to terms with the enormity of the course Slonský was setting before him.

'It's no good, sir. Making up figures is just plain wrong.'

Slonský leaned over Navrátil's shoulder.

'Not making them up is wasting time.'

A set of footsteps could be heard in the corridor. Slonský looked up in time to see a figure bearing a tray walking past the door.

'Hey, Matějka!' Slonský called.

The figure stopped walking and reversed one step. He did not attempt to turn, but nudged the door open with the back of his shoulder and turned his head to look through the resultant gap.

'What?'

'Will you answer a question for me?'

'Depends what it is.'

'Do you swear that the answer you are about to give is the truth, the whole truth and nothing but the truth?'

'Not till I know the question.'

'Fair enough. When did you last look at the crime statistics?'

'Why would I do that?' asked Matějka.

'Aha! I rest my case, Navrátil. It doesn't matter what the statistics say because nobody looks at them. Thanks, Matějka. By the way, Martinů just ran off with your ham sandwich.'

'How could ... Oi! Martinů! I want a word with you.'

Navrátil still looked uneasy.

'Go on, lad,' said Slonský in his most seductive voice. 'Make one up. You know you want to.'

'I don't! I can't!'

'Of course you can. All it takes is a small movement of that little pencil of yours with the soggy top. Forty-five is a nice number. Let's have forty-five of something. Forty-five housebreakings in Kbely — or perhaps forty-five car thefts in Libuš.'

'Why not forty-five garrottings in Kunratice?'

'Don't be ridiculous, boy. We'd have put a stop to that before now.'

Navrátil pounced. 'So if I made up a report of a garrotting in Kunratice, that would be shocking, but making up forty-five car thefts is acceptable?'

'I didn't say it was acceptable. I said it was accepted. You have a lot to learn about the traditional Czech approach to statistics, lad.' Slonský sat down and stretched his legs across his desk. 'Back in the old days — don't roll your eyes like that, Navrátil, people will think you're simple — we collected statistics on crime. Because we weren't very good at policing, a lot of crime went unpunished. This damaged confidence in the police force but, more importantly, the public felt unsafe. How can you sleep if you think you may be murdered in your bed? We had three alternatives, Navrátil. We could get better at detecting crime — obviously a non-starter. We could pin the blame on a scapegoat and tell the public it was all sorted out. Scapegoats were plentiful and the government wrote the court reports so that worked quite well, all things considered. Then someone came up with the masterstroke, Plan C. Stop collecting statistics. Once we had as many murders as we could handle, we stopped collecting the data. If the bigwigs said we would have no more than ten murders in Brno, then we stopped counting once we got to ten. This improved public confidence in the police, because each year the number went down a bit. People felt safer. They were just as likely to be bludgeoned to death as before, but the point is they didn't think they were.'

'That's scandalous,' Navrátil protested.

'No doubt. But it happened. You couldn't collect a statistic without knowing why it was wanted. Look, hand me down that big book off the top of the cabinet beside you and I'll show you what I mean.'

Navrátil collected the dusty volume and brought it to Slonský, who riffled through the pages until he came to a table.

'Ah, here we are, lad. This is a table showing the number of secret police informants in Czechoslovakia in 1950 and 1952. What's the population of Prague?'

'One and a quarter million.'

'Population of Plzeň?'

'I don't know. A hundred and fifty thousand, maybe?'

'We'll go along with that. Odd, then, that in 1950 there were seventy-five informants in Prague but 1,135 in Plzeň, wouldn't you say? Even odder, look at Ústí nad Labem. In 1950, there were forty-six informants, but just two years later there were over thirteen hundred. Now tell me, son, what do you think? Are those facts, or imaginative statistics?'

'Imaginative? Don't you mean imaginary?'

An indulgent smile flickered across Slonský's lips.

'No, I mean what I say. Imaginative in the sense of creative. Imaginary statistics are something completely different. Imaginary statistics are the ones we used to make us look good.'

Navrátil's head was spinning. He grabbed his temples with both hands in a pointless effort to make the world stop.

'Suppose your police district didn't have its ten murders. People would think they'd probably happened, but you were too useless to discover them. So if you didn't make your quota, you might invent an imaginary crime or two. This was a good thing, because our success rate on clearing up imaginary crime was nearly a hundred per cent. So, instead of reporting eight murders, of which we had cleared up two, we'd report ten murders of which we had solved four. See the power of statistics, Navrátil? With the stroke of a pen, we'd gone from a twenty-five per cent success rate to a forty per cent rate. The public were happy, we were happy, everyone was happy. They were simpler times then.' Slonský emitted a nostalgic sigh. 'I'm going to get us some coffee, Navrátil. By the time I come back I want that report finished so we can get on with some proper policing. How you do that is up to you.'

The tap on his shoulder made Slonský jump.

'Do you have to do that, Mucha? I nearly wet myself.'

'That's your age,' explained the desk sergeant. 'Sudden excitement and — whoosh!'

'There's no whoosh involved,' replied Slonský. 'I meant I almost spilled these coffees.'

'Whose are those?'

'One for me, one for Navrátil. His is the smaller one.'

'Which one is that?'

'I don't know until I get them upstairs, do I? Depends how much I spill. Anyway, what do you want?'

'There's an old man at the desk asking for you.'

'Why me? He doesn't have a black cloak and a large scythe, does he?'

'No, you're safe there. He's nearer to that than you are.'

'Thank goodness for that.'

Sergeant Pavel Mucha watched Slonský's face closely for a reaction as he explained who was waiting. 'It's Holoubek. Remember him?'

'Holoubek? Is he still alive?'

'Well, he was when I came looking for you, but given the time it's taken…'

'What does he want?'

'Don't ask me. You're the detective. I'm just a lowly desk sergeant.'

'Were you around when he was here?'

'Oh, yes,' said Mucha. 'Not at the desk then, but on the force.'

'Do me a favour, then. I'll fetch him upstairs if you get a third coffee and bring them up to my office.'

Slonský forced the cups into Mucha's hands and strode off along the corridor.

'I'll get one for myself, then, shall I?' asked Mucha in a resentful tone.

'If you like. You can pay for my two while you're at it. I left my money in my coat.'

Holoubek looked around as he sat in the chair Slonský offered him.

'Could do with a lick of paint,' he offered. He took a sip of coffee. 'That's no better either,' he decided.

'What can I do for you, Mr Holoubek?'

'Call me Edvard. I saw you mentioned a lot in the papers recently over that German chap who topped himself.'

'Dr Sammler.'

'That's the one. You did a good job running him down, I thought. Obviously took the easy way out rather than go to court and prison. Can't have been a simple case for you.'

'It wasn't,' agreed Slonský, glancing at Navrátil as he answered. His assistant appeared to be fascinated by an imaginary mark on his desk top.

'And I thought "Slonský: I remember a likely lad called Slonský from my time on the force. There can't be many of that name. I've never met another one."'

'My dad had it, but I agree it's uncommon. And I was on the force in your day.'

'So I thought to myself, that's the sort of man who can help me with my problem. Someone who remembers those days but wasn't high enough up to have been involved in it all.'

'Involved in what?'

Holoubek ignored the question as he expounded his thoughts. It was unclear whether he was deaf, single-minded or just plain rude.

'I saw young Tripka downstairs. What does he do now?'

'Colonel Tripka is in the National Anti-Drug Centre.'

'Young Tripka?' Navrátil blurted out.

'His father was a policeman before him. For a while they were both on the force at the same time, hence Old Tripka and Young Tripka,' explained Slonský.

'Old Tripka was an StB liaison officer,' Holoubek added.

'Responsible for keeping us out of the way when the Secret Police were running something. In which capacity,' Slonský added, 'I'm glad to say he was completely useless.'

'Total waste of space,' Holoubek agreed. 'Of course, they didn't trust him, so they didn't share their plans with him, so it was hardly his fault. Still, good to know his boy hasn't followed in his footsteps.'

'We don't have a secret police any more,' Slonský pointed out.

'Not that we admit to,' Holoubek said, 'but you and I know that can't be true, don't we? Where would our security be without a secret police, eh?'

Slonský saw no point in trying to answer a man who so clearly had a closed mind about the StB. Slonský's own recollection was that the secret police were a pretty ineffectual bunch much of the time, and that many of the "plots" they claimed to have foiled were actually little projects of their own that had gone off at half-cock. There was, to name just one, an entertaining confusion when an StB agent had borrowed some army explosives to equip a dissident cell to blow up a railway line on the outskirts of Prague, only to be arrested himself by the "dissidents" who turned out to be StB agents to a man. However, Slonský held the view that the Czech Republic was better off without these clowns, and he did not think Holoubek was likely to agree with him.

'You mentioned a problem,' said Slonský. 'What kind of problem?'

Holoubek paused and wiped his lips with a grubby handkerchief.

'I've got something on my conscience,' he began.

'Haven't we all?' agreed Slonský. 'You couldn't be a policeman then without your conscience having a rough ride now and again.'

'I know,' said Holoubek. 'But even so…'

'Why don't you just tell me the facts? I'm not going to judge you.'

Holoubek remained silent for a few seconds, made as if to speak, and stopped. After a moment or two, he seemed to have satisfied himself that he knew how to tell the story, and he began again.

'Cast your mind back to 1976.'

'I'll do that. Navrátil, don't even attempt it.'

'I'll tell you the story as I knew it. That doesn't mean that it's right, just that it's what I heard or saw. I was working the night shift when we got a call to a house in Ruzyně. That was when the airport wasn't so big. There were some nice villas out that way, and it turned out to be one of those we were called to. When we got there we found a young girl in a blood bath. She'd been stabbed multiple times and was lying in the bathroom where it looked as if someone had tried to make a tourniquet out of a towel to staunch the flow from an artery in her forearm. We couldn't get much information because there was no-one else there. The door was wide open, the lights were blazing, and there was evidence that at least three people had been drinking and eating, but no sign of them.'

'Did a male or female ring it in?'

'A male. Didn't give a name. Didn't sound drunk or stoned, though one of the other officers reckoned he could smell something in the room when he first arrived that might have been cannabis. But remember that this was 1976. We had no DNA testing then, and drugs weren't easily come by in Prague, so he may have been mistaken.'

Holoubek took a sip of coffee, though it must have been cold by now.

'We didn't know whose villa it was, but after a bit of hunting around we found some papers. It turned out to belong to a man called Válek, who was director of a factory making kitchen goods — you know, toasters, grills, that sort of thing. Válek was out at a function with his wife and the dead girl was his daughter Jana. He came home around two in the morning before we'd managed to trace him. Bloody mess. The idiots who were supposed to be guarding the front door let him wander in on the grounds that it was his house, so I soon had them shipped off to some God-forsaken hole in Slovakia where their lack of brains wouldn't be noticed.'

'Whose case was it?' asked Slonský.

'Well, mine at first, but it turned out that Válek had connections — his wife was sister to someone in high places — and after a day and a half I had Vaněček put in charge over me.'

'I didn't know him,' Slonský said.

'Not many more brains that those numbskulls I sent to Slovakia, but a few notches up the ladder. Knew which backsides to kiss. It didn't hurt that his brother was a film director who could get you tickets for things.'

'You're spared that now, Navrátil,' Slonský interrupted. 'The people who could lay their hands on things used to get on in life, whatever their talent or lack of it.'

'Vaněček looked good on May Day. He had a chest full of medals and nobody was very clear how he'd got them until we discovered that he sat on one of the committees that decided who got them. Vain man. Had a desk the size of Austria and nothing useful ever came off it,' Holoubek continued.

'What rank?'

'I'm not sure now. A long way above me, that's for sure. But he'd never been a policeman. He'd been in the army and transferred across via the People's Militia. He had no idea how to run an investigation. To his credit, he knew that. He took me aside on the first morning and told me that although he was nominally in charge, he was going to let me get on with it. I had to brief him twice a day so he could report up the line. It sounds like good delegation but actually it was work avoidance.'

Holoubek paused for a moment. He looked confused.

'Is there a toilet somewhere near? It's that damn coffee.'

'Navrátil, would you show Mr Holoubek to the toilet and escort him back?'

While they were gone, Slonský found a few biscuits in his desk to keep his brain energy stores fuelled. He had intended to share them, but they took too long to come back and missed out.

'Where was I?'

'You were telling us that you were left in charge when Vaněček took over.'

'For a while. But it wasn't an easy inquiry. We found the man who had called us. He lived a few doors away and had seen a car driving away at speed from the villa with its lights off. He insisted he had given his name to the officer who took the call, but it had not been recorded. Anyway, he had gone down to the house to complain about the noise and found the door open. He discovered the body and used the villa's telephone to call the police.'

'Did he have an alibi?'

'His wife said he had been muttering about the noise from around nine o'clock, so finally she had told him to either go and sort it out or stop moaning about it. Off he trotted down the road, and you know the rest. We couldn't find out who was there with her. None of her friends could give us a name for either of the lads we knew must have been there. She allegedly didn't have a boyfriend.'

'Any scientific evidence?'

'I'm just coming to that. Let me keep my thoughts in order. The pathologist told us we'd read it all wrongly. His view was that she hadn't been killed in a frenzied attack. She had been stabbed a lot of times, as if the murderer was trying to see how many different places he could stab her before she died. It was a bit like that game when you have to pull out sticks and see who makes the marble drop.'

'Two killers, then, competing?'

'It looked that way. The arm wound had been the one that killed her. It severed her artery. But the pathologist said she had been conscious throughout and the loud music was probably to drown out her screams. That, and a gag that had been in her mouth and split the junction of her lips on each side.'

'Had she been interfered with?'

'She certainly had. But the pathologist thought that only one boy had raped her. I didn't really understand the test but he reckoned there was only one lot of semen there.'

Holoubek began to look weary, and Slonský hoped that he would stay awake long enough to finish his story, or at least not lose his thread and start asking where he had got to.

'After a week or so Vaněček assigned me to another case for a few days, so I lost touch with what was happening, though colleagues told me the investigation was fairly aimless. You'll have had some of those, no doubt, when nothing seems to lead to anything worthwhile and you just find yourself doing something just so nobody can say you're doing nothing.'

'One or two,' Slonský agreed. 'Or a few hundred.'

'Well, you can imagine how surprised I was when I heard that Vaněček had made an arrest and that someone had been charged with the rape and murder. Things can happen quickly, as you know, but there hadn't been a sniff of the lead at the start of that week and I couldn't find anyone working on the case who knew where Vaněček had found the evidence. The man he had charged was called Ľubomír Bartoš. He was a Slovak, around thirty years old, with a list of convictions for cat burglary. First jailed when he was about seventeen. Now, I didn't know Bartoš from Adam, but the whole thing struck me as strange.'

'Earn your crust, then, Navrátil,' Slonský interrupted. 'Why would it strike Mr Holoubek as unusual?'

'Cat burglars aren't usually violent,' Navrátil suggested. 'They travel light, so they wouldn't carry a weapon.'

Holoubek nodded approvingly.

'Not bad, son. I checked the records for Bartoš's previous arrests. Not once had he been found with a weapon on him. Of course, you can do someone some damage with a jemmy or a screwdriver, but that's different to packing a weapon that could do the sort of injury done to that poor young girl.'

Navrátil was feeling a little smug, but that was soon put right by Slonský's next comment.

'Of course, you missed the key point, which is that cat burglars, by the very nature of their calling, are usually wiry little blokes because big men aren't that agile. And pinning down a woman who isn't drugged to rape her is easier for a big man than a skinny gymnast. How big was Bartoš, Edvard?'

'Around one metre sixty-five, perhaps sixty kilos. Not much bigger than the girl herself.'

'But he had an accomplice, didn't he?' Navrátil interjected. 'You told us there had been three people there.'

'Sharp lad, this one,' Holoubek told Slonský approvingly. 'Now there's another odd thing, because the scene of crime report that I saw now only mentioned one visitor. Vaněček didn't seem to be interested in finding the other man. He'd got one, and he constructed a series of events that only required one. According to this, the girl fainted from blood loss, then Bartoš raped her.'

'Couldn't it have been that way?' asked Navrátil.

'Now there you go again, lad,' Slonský growled. 'One thing right, then one thing wrong. You heard there were three there. But in any event I'll bet the pathologist knew she struggled during the rape.'

'Extensive bruising that wouldn't have been so marked if she hadn't been able to fight,' agreed Holoubek.

'So what did young Bartoš have to say about it all?'

'It's hard to say. At first, nothing. But he was hauled into court surprisingly quickly. I didn't know it was scheduled and I wasn't there, but one of his guards said he kicked up a hell of a racket when he discovered what he was charged with, and in the end the judges had him taken back to his cell and tried him in his absence. Tried in his absence and convicted in his absence.'

'But unfortunately not hanged in his absence.'

'No. But you're leaping ahead a bit. Between the trial and the execution I had a call from the remand prison in Olomouc. That's around two hundred and eighty kilometres from Prague, you know.'

'Yes, I know. Did you know that, Navrátil?'

'I do now.'

Holoubek leaned forward as if about to impart a great secret.

'The director wanted to know whether Bartoš was coming back. I said he wasn't, but asked why he was asking me. He said "Of course I'm asking you. You signed the transfer request." Of course I hadn't, so I asked if I could have a copy. He mumbled about the fact that he'd sent someone to be hanged on what turned out to be a forgery, and in those days you knew that the kind of people who could organise that would be the ones you didn't want to mess with, so he told me it wouldn't be "convenient" to make a copy, and his photocopier was broken, he claimed. But before he rang off I got one thing out of him. I don't remember the exact dates, but one thing was crystal clear. Bartoš couldn't have done it, because when the crime was committed he was already sitting in jail in Olomouc.'

'So what did you do?'

'I tackled Vaněček about it, but he just waved me off. Said the prison director was an idiot and had got the dates wrong. When I tried to ring the prison, the director had been reassigned and nobody was quite sure where he had gone. So I took a chance and went down to Pankrác Prison to talk to Bartoš. Unsurprisingly he wasn't keen to talk to me, because he thought I'd stitched him up. He said this fellow Holoubek had visited him in Olomouc and got him to sign something about a break-in in Prague. Bartoš couldn't actually read and write, but he didn't like to admit it. He was told if he admitted to this one he could forget the other eight

211

cases, so as he saw it he'd get a lighter sentence for one than he would for eight. I asked him who this other Holoubek was, but I didn't recognise the description and he couldn't tell me anything useful that would help me pin it down.'

'Could it have been Vaněček?'

'No, for two reasons. One, he was too bone idle to do that and two, he hadn't the brains to come up with it. I knew Vaněček hadn't left Prague. He might have known who went though, but I never got the chance to ask him. He wouldn't talk to me about it and then he was retired about three years later when he screwed up a case. Dead within nine months in a gardening accident. They reckon he had a heart attack and fell on a fence post. Stupid way an idiot like that would die.'

'So, if not Vaněček…?'

'Good question. I've often thought about it, and I don't know. But I've got one more clue. Bartoš was a Catholic and he asked for a priest before his execution. You didn't always get one, but he did, and the priest told me that as he was being dragged from his cell Bartoš shouted "Tell Holoubek he knows Mandy."'

'Mean anything to you?'

'No, not a thing. From the context it must have been either the murderer or the policeman who came to get him, and since I had no reason to think Bartoš knew the murderer, it must have been the policeman.'

'So we've got a miscarriage of justice and an unsolved murder. But they're nearly thirty years old.'

'I haven't finished,' Holoubek snapped. 'I got hold of Bartoš's things and drove to Slovakia to give them to his family. His mother wouldn't talk to me at first — she thought I'd been the one who'd stitched up her son — but I told her what I knew and said I'd try to clear her son's name. After a while I reached a dead end and I stopped, and there it stays to this day. But I'm not getting any younger, and it's weighing on my mind.' He fished in his pocket for the folder of papers. 'I've kept a few documents all these years. Some tell you what I've said, and some are copies of the original papers. Not many, but it's all I could get then. I don't know if the files are still around but if they are, you're the kind of man who could get them. Will you do this for me, Slonský? Will you help an old colleague's conscience?'

Slonský held his hand out for the folder.

'Out of respect for you, I'll read these. I'm not promising that we'll get anywhere. You've done this job, Edvard. You know what the chances are of picking up an inquiry successfully after thirty years.'

Holoubek nodded. 'Yes, it's a long shot. But at least I can say I've tried. And since it won't be long now before I'm going to meet up with Bartoš again, it would be good to be able to tell him I didn't forget him.' The old man picked up his coat and shook Slonský's hand. 'I'm grateful that you're even trying. Please keep me informed. I don't have a phone. Somehow when you've bugged dozens you don't want one yourself.'

'I'll get Navrátil to drop you off.'

'No point. I get free tram rides. We can't go wasting police fuel, can we?'

The faintest of smiles ran across his face fleetingly, then Holoubek turned away and tottered off along the corridor.

'Well, Navrátil, what do you think?'

'That's incredible. We hanged a man for a crime when we knew he couldn't have done it. Where was his lawyer when this was going on?'

'The chances are he got a court-appointed lawyer, who was probably told he'd confessed and who wouldn't want to oppose the State prosecutor anyway. The thought of pleading not guilty wouldn't occur to him. He'd see his job as finding some mitigating factors to reduce the sentence. Back then you didn't get too many people walking free once they were charged. It made the state look bad, you see. Can't have that.'

'But Bartoš died. It wasn't a case of eighteen months in jail then picking up where he left off. He went to the gallows.'

'He wasn't the first and he wasn't the last. Sit down and I'll tell you a bit of family history.'

Navrátil was concerned that he might be about to hear some shocking revelation, but took a seat where Holoubek had been sitting, across the desk from Slonský.

'How many Slonskýs do you know?'

'One. You.'

'Not a common name then. You heard me tell Holoubek that my dad had it. Not strictly true.'

'No?'

'No. Did you ever hear of Rudolf Slánský?'

'Yes, in history. Some kind of party bigwig just after the war.'

'Not just a bigwig. Slánský was general secretary of the Czechoslovak Communist Party. He was effectively number two in the country, second only to Gottwald. Then in 1951 Gottwald had him arrested and tried for treason, and he was hanged a year later. My dad was also called Slánský, and he decided that it wasn't a good name to have. Fortunately, his army discharge papers had been badly typed and the name was barely legible. Dad persuaded a clerk that the name was Slonský and managed to get a whole new set of papers in the Slonský name. That's why I'm a Slonský. But I was born a Slánský and that was my name until I was four or five.'

'Was it that bad?'

'It was worse than that bad. If people thought you were family of the accused, they'd shun you. You wouldn't get served in shops. A similar thing happened after the Russians came in 1968. If you'd been a progressive, some people idolised you, and others wouldn't pee on you if you were on fire. And the bit that got to me was that this wasn't foreigners doing this; this was Czechs doing this to Czechs. Or sometimes to Slovaks. Look at Holoubek. He's not a bad man at all, but you heard some of the things he had to do. And listen to the way he talks about Slovaks and Slovakia. He sent those guards there as if it was the end of the world. He said their lack of brains wouldn't be noticed there. I've met relatively educated Czechs who talk about Slovaks as if they were animals. I've never understood it. Okay, so they talk funny, but they're human beings. Most of them.'

Navrátil waited for Slonský to sit down again before speaking.

'Do you think you can help him? Won't all the files be gone by now?'

Slonský frowned in thought.

'Probably not. One thing we lead the world in is bureaucracy, and I can't imagine any clerk in the communist era deciding to throw any paperwork out unless he was specifically told to do so. In which event either the file was burned by 1977 or it'll be around now somewhere. I've no idea where, but the starting point is our own connoisseur of bureaucracy.'

'How long ago?' asked Mucha incredulously.

'Around thirty years. Nineteen seventy-six. Do you think those files will still be around?' asked Slonský.

'How should I know? And all this is to satisfy an old man's whim?'

'No, if the old man is right, it's to give a family justice. I'm up for that.'

Mucha shrugged his shoulders. 'Put that way, so am I. No point in being here if we aren't. Tell me some more, then. Where was it?'

'Ruzyně.'

'That would be here, then. Even through the reorganisations it's always been under the Prague office. Victim's name?'

'Jana Válková. Aged sixteen or so, I guess.'

'I remember that case. She was repeatedly stabbed, wasn't she? Who was the investigating officer?'

'Someone called Vaněček.'

Mucha chuckled. 'Vaněček? He was my boss for a while.'

Slonský became energised. 'What was he like?'

'Pretty useless. No, I take that back. He was completely useless. So far as I remember, he came to us from the army. He had been a staff officer responsible for planning. After the Russians came they didn't want anyone left in the Czechoslovak Army who might be able to plan a revolt, so he was moved out. If they'd had any sense they'd have left him in post, because any rebellion Vaněček organised would be doomed to failure.'

'He can't have been that bad. He got promoted several times.'

'Yes, he got promoted, but not for anything to do with military ability or policing skills. He was a grade A brown nose, always sniffing round the Presidium to see who could give him a leg up. But there was one thing he did well,' Mucha added grudgingly. 'He could certainly organise a parade.'

'A parade?'

'That was his main job. For years Vaněček organised the police element in the May Day parades. And if you wanted a bit of a show, Vaněček could lay it on for you. It didn't matter what it was, a band, a few police cars, if the price was right Vaněček could make it happen. He persuaded me to turn out as part of a guard of honour for a police officer's wedding once. We were introduced as "his men". None of us had ever clapped eyes on him before. Still, I bought my daughter her first bike on the proceeds of that.'

'Fascinating though this is, can we get back to the subject of the Válková file? How would we find out if it still exists?'

Mucha stroked his chin.

'We could look in the index. But to be honest, if there was anything controversial in the file, it wouldn't be in the general index. There is a private index but I don't have access to it. However, taking the whole thing into account, I think the best method of getting the file is just to ask for it.'

'Ask for it?'

'Yes. You know, just saying "Can I have it?"'

'Would that work?'

'Oh, yes! Gives it the appearance of normality. If you do it that way, the clerk who retrieves it probably won't even look at it, whereas if you make a big fuss about it they get very protective of their paperwork. If it doesn't exist any longer, they'll say so. Trust me, that's the way to do it.'

'I do trust you. Sort of. As much as I trust anyone.'

'That's your problem, old friend. You want to do everything yourself because you don't trust anyone else.'

Slonský waved a languid hand in the direction of a waiter, and was rewarded with a large glass of beer and a hunk of bread and cheese. He had taken a bite of it before he realised that he had actually ordered some sausage, but shrugged and carried on chewing. All around him there were the sounds of people enjoying themselves. It made you sick, he thought. All this frivolity and fun when so much is going wrong in the world.

The bar door opened and a small man with thinning hair and glasses came in. Although it was not a cold evening he was wearing a crimson scarf tied tightly at his neck, and a grey woollen overcoat. He removed both and laid them along a seat as he spotted Slonský's back.

'You look glum,' Valentin announced. 'Bad day?'

'Normal day,' replied Slonský. 'Bad is normal lately.'

'Come on,' said Valentin, 'I'll buy you a drink.'

'That's not normal,' Slonský noted. 'Are you sickening for something?'

'Fit as a fiddle, old pal. I never thought I would see having less drinking time as an improvement, but there you are. It just goes to show that you never can tell.'

Valentin was a journalist, or at least that was what he had managed to trick his editor into believing. Although quite well connected, his liking for a bottle or six had held him back. He and Slonský were long-time drinking companions, though they could go weeks without meeting up. At the moment, encounters were limited because Valentin was in demand.

At a time when Valentin's editor had been uttering dark threats about the removal of his retainer and a return to payment per story, Slonský had slipped Valentin two front page specials. The first had exposed a leading politician's liaison with a rent boy, while the second was an exclusive story that a recently dismissed government minister had been appointed to a plum job in Brussels. The fact that the minister had been sacked after Slonský wrongly arrested him for murder did not feature in Valentin's story. The result of these scoops was startling. Valentin was suddenly much in demand as a journalist and, although his retainer had been restored, he was having to work much harder because other magazines and media wanted him to work for them. This had severely restricted his drinking time, caused him to have a professional haircut rather than do it himself with a mirror and a pair of scissors, and had reacquainted him with the necktie as an everyday item of apparel. Admittedly "everyday" was a suitable description of the single tie he owned, but it was necessary if he wanted to appear on television. Valentin's television career had so far been limited to a short interview at 23:00 one Thursday evening and a recorded piece shown at breakfast time, but he lived in hope. Radio was rather kinder to him, and he had become a regular pundit on an afternoon phone-in where his characteristic blend of acerbic wit and complete failure to do any homework had won him something of a following amongst those who do not get out much.

'So what's the problem?' Valentin asked.

'Off the record?'

'Need you ask?'

'Yes. Just to be sure.'

'Then, for the avoidance of doubt, this is off the record.'

'I had a visit today from an old boy of around ninety who used to be a policeman.'

'You see, the good don't all die young.'

'No, I suppose not. His conscience is pricking him and he wants me to reopen a case from thirty years ago.'

'Don't touch it with a bargepole, that's my advice. If you fail everyone will say what a waste of time it was, and if you succeed the headlines will read "Police solve case after thirty-one years". It's not worth it.'

'Someone was hanged for something they didn't do, Valentin. That makes it worth it.'

Valentin inspected the bottom of his glass through the golden liquid for a few moments.

'Yes, I suppose it does. Who, when, why?'

'A fellow called Bartoš back in 1976. Accused of rape and murder of a girl called Jana Válková in Ruzyně. But he can't have done it because at the time the murder was committed, he was already in jail in Olomouc.'

'And his lawyer forgot to mention this in court?'

'Not a dickybird.'

'Who was his lawyer?'

'Good question. I'll have to find out.'

'It's not a unique event, Josef. A lot of people were banged up for things they didn't do, or there wouldn't be crimes today.'

'I know. But there's a difference between being banged up and strung up. I just can't see why someone would do that to a stranger.'

'Ah, the inexplicable crying out to be explained. I can sympathise with that.'

'But can we do it? How do we explain something that happened so long ago when a lot of those who were involved will be dead and gone?'

Valentin raised his glass to his lips and spoke cheerily.

'You don't know that. If you don't investigate, no-one will ever put this right. And if you can't succeed now, it isn't going to be any easier for anyone coming after you. You know you can count on my assistance.'

'Excellent,' said Slonský. 'You can have a read through the back issues from 1976 and see if there's anything in the papers I can use. Meantime, I'm going to have one more for the road. You've brightened me up, Valentin. I can see light at the end of the tunnel.'

'Careful,' Valentin replied. 'That light could be an approaching train.'

Chapter 3

Life with Slonský was full of non-sequiturs, thought Navrátil. Having been informed by his boss that they were going to do a little delving into Holoubek's case, just to see if there was enough in it to warrant asking Lukas if they could formally reopen the matter, Navrátil had quite properly asked where they were going to start.

'There's only one place to start with a case like this,' replied Slonský, before clamming up and saying no more on the subject. In the car his conversation was limited to deciding where they might grab a quick lunch and criticising Navrátil's use of the rear view mirror, though without his usual sharpness. It was as if the criticism were expected of him but his heart was not really in it.

'Pull in over there and we'll walk the rest of the way,' Slonský instructed.

The old detective flung open the car door and strode into the little cemetery, occasionally glancing at a small map he had drawn.

'She should be along this row somewhere,' he announced to nobody in particular, Navrátil having lagged a few metres behind as a result of having to lock the car up.

Navrátil felt unable to run given where they were, but was relieved when Slonský suddenly stopped and turned to face a black headstone on which some writing infilled with gold could be seen. It declared the occupant of the grave to be Jana Válková, born 23rd February 1959, died 16th July 1976, beloved daughter of Jan Válek and his wife Helena. For some minutes Slonský stood in silence as if paying his respects. He even removed his hat. Navrátil failed to see how this was advancing the inquiry but he knew better than to interrupt, so he waited patiently until Slonský squatted and picked a couple of weeds from the foot of the grave.

'What are we doing here, sir?'

'It helps. I don't know how, but being with the victim helps me. It makes me realise how important it is that we pin the blame on the person who put her there. Seventeen, Navrátil. A year older than I thought, but still it's no age. What would she be now — late forties? She should have a husband and maybe a couple of children, looking forward to being a granny. Instead of which she's been lying in this cold earth longer than you've been alive. I was twenty-eight when she was killed, lad. That's how long she's been waiting for someone to find her real murderer.'

'Bartoš is a victim too. Are we going to his grave?'

218

'He probably doesn't have one. More often than not they cremated criminals and scattered the ashes on the roads. If his family were lucky they may have been given an urn, but I wouldn't guarantee the right remains are in it.'

'Are her parents still alive, sir?'

'That's a good question, Navrátil. You can find me a good answer. If she's an only child born in 1959 the chances are her parents would be around seventy now, so they may still be about. The Social Security Administration in Křížová could tell you if they're drawing pensions. There can't be too many Váleks around and you've got their first names.'

'Will that be enough, sir?'

'What more do you want? Use your brain, son, if you have one. You know their surname, their first names, whom they were married to, the date of birth of their daughter — whom they will have registered — where they lived in 1976 and the fact that they were probably born between 1930 and 1935. If you can't find them with that little lot give up policing and try journalism.'

Slonský stomped off towards the car, and this time Navrátil deliberately gave him a ten metre start. As he climbed in the car he braced himself for a disagreeable journey if Slonský was in one of his moods, but the temper seemed to have dissipated in moments.

'Next stop the villa, Navrátil. Try using the mirror once or twice if you can, just for form's sake. And if you see a decent bakery, pull over. I'm peckish.'

There was not much of the villa still standing. It was surrounded with security fencing on which a large notice proclaimed that it was to be replaced by a prestige development of four shoeboxes created by a local developer. However, since the sign also proclaimed that they would be ready in autumn 2004, it looked likely that the developer had run out of cash.

Slonský fished in his pocket for a penknife.

'Anyone watching, Navrátil?'

'No, sir.'

'Good.'

Slonský busied himself in some secretive manoeuvre at the fence, until a loud click announced that a padlock had come undone and they were able to part the fence panels sufficiently to slip inside.

'Come on, Navrátil, don't dawdle.'

'I'm watching for the guard dogs, sir.'

'Navrátil, the sign is at least three years old. There probably never were guard dogs. I'd like to think if I employed dogs and someone rattled the padlock chain like I just did they would at least come over to see what was happening, if only out of curiosity. But I didn't hear a bark, so I think we can assume the dogs are long since gone.'

The front door was still present, though hanging slightly open. Slonský shoved it with his shoulder and they were able to stand in the entrance hall.

'That'll be the room where she was stabbed. She'd trailed blood from there to the bathroom. The pathologist thought the boys might have carried her there, because the blood droplets and spurts didn't make sense if she had been upright.'

Slonský turned down a side corridor and pushed a door open. He pointed to a pipe sticking out of the floor.

'Bath was there. So she was stabbed repeatedly to the left of the front door and then brought across the lobby and down here to be patched up. Why? They were never going to let her live once she'd seen them.'

Slonský flicked his diary open.

'Sunset in mid-July would be around nine o'clock. The man who found the body said the lights were blazing. We need to find out when he came over. Navrátil, are you making notes of this?'

'Yes, sir.'

'It can't have been that late because the man who found her hadn't gone to bed. And I don't suppose the murderers knew when Válek would return. But Holoubek said he was on night shift.'

Slonský ambled around the building for a few minutes, then stood in the doorway scanning the houses opposite.

'Nobody directly opposite, so they probably weren't going to be observed through the window.'

'There was probably a hedge too, sir. Look at the cuttings and the stumps by the fence.'

'Well spotted, lad. Which one of these is number twenty-six?'

They turned slightly right and walked up the road. Number twenty-six was the second house they passed.

'I wonder why the folks at the first house didn't seem bothered by the music. Anyway, Navrátil, this is where the man lived who found her.'

An elderly lady was putting a bag of rubbish in a bin at the back of the house. Slonský went forward to speak to her.

'Good morning, madam. You wouldn't be Mrs Kopecká, by any chance?'

'Who's asking?'

Slonský flashed his badge in mute response.

'There's no point showing me that, young man. I don't have my glasses.'

'Lieutenant Slonský, Criminal Police. And this is Officer Navrátil. We're here about the murder of Jana Válková.'

'You took your time getting here,' the lady replied. 'We rang in 1976.'

For once Slonský was lost for words, until an impish smile on her face told him she was teasing him.

'Would you like some coffee? I'm about to make some for my husband anyway.'

'Your husband? I didn't think he'd still … didn't think to ask about him.'

She led them into the back door.

'He's not been well,' she whispered. 'He can't walk much and it gets him down. And he forgets things. He says I didn't tell him, but I did. He just forgets things.'

The man in question was sitting in a winged armchair with his feet on a small stool. His ankles looked far too large for the rest of him, but Michal Kopecký had obviously been a lean, vigorous man. His hair still showed streaks of black within the silver, and he was neatly dressed in a checked shirt and navy trousers. He wore a padded waistcoat for warmth, beneath which his chest periodically heaved in an effort to fill his lungs.

'These gentlemen are from the police,' Mrs Kopecká explained.

'What have you done?' he asked. 'Have they come to arrest you?'

'Of course not,' she told him. 'They want to ask you about poor Jana Válková.'

Kopecký waved his hand dismissively.

'That was months ago,' he said. 'And I thought they hanged someone for it.'

'We did,' said Slonský, 'but I believe you said there were two of them. And we never found the other one.'

Kopecký's eyes glowed for a moment.

'That's right. There were three dirty beer glasses. I remember now.'

'Very good,' Slonský nodded encouragingly. 'Three beer glasses. Large ones, or small?'

'Half-litre glasses. One had a handle but two didn't. One had about two centimetres of beer left in the bottom.'

'And where were they?'

'In the kitchen.'

'That's the room straight in front of you when you come in the door.'

'Yes.'

'I know you've told us before, but I'd like to hear you tell the whole story if you can, Mr Kopecký. You were disturbed by the noise. When was this?'

'It went on all evening. Válek and his wife went out about seven, and the music started around eight or half past. At least, that's when we heard it, didn't we?'

His wife was not there to agree or argue.

'But your neighbour didn't complain, although he was nearer?'

'Old Hruška? He was deaf as a post. Of course, he was very old. Over eighty.'

'You're over eighty yourself, dear,' said Mrs Kopecká, who had returned with a tray of coffee and a plate of buns which she carefully placed in front of Navrátil.

'Am I? How old am I?'

'Eighty-two, dear.'

'Well I never.' Kopecký shook his head in astonishment, and showed no sign of continuing with his account.

'So you heard music about eight o'clock or shortly after. How long did you let it go on before you complained?' asked Slonský.

'Quite a while. You can't tell young people things. But I thought if I spoke to Jana she would understand. She was a sensible girl.'

'A very sensible girl,' agreed Mrs Kopecká. 'She used to come to me to practise her sewing. Her mother didn't sew, you see.'

'Not the sort of girl to keep bad company, then?'

'Oh, no!' said Mrs Kopecká. 'She was a good girl. Of course, she was at that age when they want to show a bit of independence, and she was very aware that Daddy was somebody. I mean, that he had a position.'

'We all did,' sniffed Kopecký. 'That's how we got these villas. You had to have a certain position.'

'What was your job, Mr Kopecký?'

'I made newsreels.'

'Don't be modest, dear,' said his wife. 'These gentlemen need to know a bit more than that. My husband was responsible for making government information films. Not the political ones, of course. But he made a lot of civil defence films. That's why he was such a good witness, that's what the policeman said.'

'I don't suppose you remember that policeman's name?'

'No, sorry. It's months ago now,' Kopecký apologised. 'Some kind of bird. Holoubek! That's it — though he was too dark to be a real dove, I remember my wife saying. We laughed about that when he'd gone.'

Slonský was intrigued.

'It's Mr Holoubek who asked me to come to see you. He's retired now, you see.'

'Nice man. But it was odd that he came, because they'd already arrested that cat robber.'

'Cat burglar, dear. They call them cat burglars,' his wife interjected.

'Do they? Well, that Slovak. But Holoubek kept saying to me "You're sure there were two men?" And he asked me if I knew how the men came or went. Well, I told him I'd seen a car driving off very quickly with no lights on. I'd mentioned that when I called.'

'I'm getting a bit confused, Mr Kopecký. On the night you called, Holoubek came to see you.'

'No, Holoubek was here. I remember seeing him. He was walking around in front of the villa shouting a lot. He woke us up at two o'clock shouting at the policemen by the gate. He told them they were going to be sent to the tiniest station he could find in the Tatra mountains to see if they could learn some common sense. I remember that.'

Slonský suppressed a chuckle. He could imagine Holoubek saying that to some poor, witless officers.

'But he didn't speak to you?'

'Not then. He sent some other officer to take a statement, then we heard nothing for a while. But about a week later another policeman turned up.'

'Can you describe him?'

'Middle-aged. Stocky. He kept his hat on so I didn't see his colouring.'

'In uniform?'

'No. Overcoat and dark hat.'

'He didn't give his name?'

'No. In those days the police didn't. But he must have been police because a police car brought him. I saw it parked outside and the driver waited.'

'So, when did you speak to Holoubek?'

'Like I said, when they were just about to hang that cat robber. He said he had to get to the bottom of it quickly because they were going to hang that man and then they would never find out who the other one had been. But he said he didn't think the Slovak had done the killing anyway, so there were two murderers out there still.'

Mrs Kopecká's hand flew to her mouth in shock.

'Michal! You never told me that.'

'I didn't want to worry you, dear. And I expect they're safely under lock and key now, because I haven't heard about any more killings around here since.'

If only that were true, thought Slonský. Maybe they just didn't register. Shame Lukas didn't have the same problems with his memory.

'Let's go back to that evening when you found the bodies. Friday, sixteenth of July, 1976. It was the Friday night?'

'Yes. Definitely Friday.'

'And you were disturbed around half past eight. Holoubek tells me you were grumbling about it to your wife and she told you to go and sort it out.'

'It wasn't quite like that. I didn't like to stop their fun, but it was getting on for bedtime, and you couldn't sleep with that racket.'

'So that was — what? Eleven-thirty? Midnight?'

'Good heavens, no,' said Mrs Kopecká. 'Ten o'clock.'

'Ten?' asked Slonský, who could not remember ever going to bed at ten.

'That's right,' said her husband. 'Early to bed, early to rise. Once the sun goes down, you go to bed. When it gets up, so do you. Always lived that way. I can't understand these people who lie in. They miss the best part of the day, don't you think?'

'Yes,' agreed Slonský quickly, marking Kopecký down as a grade A nutter.

223

'So a bit before ten I walked down the hill to their house to ask them to turn the music down. But as I got to the street I saw two lads run to a dark car and drive off at speed with no lights on.'

'No lights on — so it was after dark?'

'It hadn't been dark long, or we'd have been in bed. But they should have put their lights on. Nobody would see a dark car in that light.'

'So you carried on to the house?'

'Well, the music still needed turning down. I got to the gate and I could see the door open, and I suddenly thought "What if they've been robbed and all that music was to cover the noise?" So I pushed the door wide open, waited in case anyone else made a run for it, then I went in. The door to my left was open and that's where the music was coming from, but there was no-one in the room. The lights were on, and the furniture had been pushed back, I think, because there was a clear space in the middle of the floor. But what alarmed me was that the carpet was stained with fresh blood.'

'A lot of blood?'

'They say it always looks a lot, but I'd say there was at least a cupful, maybe more. The shape was like a crucifix. There were blotches of blood where her arms must have been, some more round her ankles, and some in the middle, by her … well, in the middle.'

'Like she'd been sexually assaulted?'

'I suppose so. I looked in the next doorway, which was the kitchen, but that looked in quite good order except for the three beer glasses. Then there was another door that turned out to be a closet, and the one beyond that was the bathroom. She was in there.'

'I don't want to distress you, but it would help if you could describe what you saw in detail.'

Kopecký closed his eyes and concentrated.

'Pale blue tiles to my left. A tub straight in front going across the room with the taps at the right hand end. Her left arm was draped over the side of the bath and blood was dripping down the white side. You couldn't see her, just the arm. I ran to see her. I don't think she was quite dead. She didn't respond, but she was very warm. I couldn't take her pulse because her arms were slimy with blood and I didn't know then that you could do it any other way. Her slacks and underwear had been pulled down and she was bleeding down there, and it looked like there were little punctures in her tummy and breast. One breast was exposed — her right one. There was a cross cut in her nipple. She was wearing a red and navy striped top and her hair was held together with a red band to make a ponytail. Her head was turned to her left and the right side of her face was bruised and covered with a smear of blood from just above her hairline, where there was a nasty bleeding gash. Her right arm had bled a lot and the curtain had been yanked down and wrapped around it. It was sodden with blood. There was a towel in her left armpit soaked with blood from a cut in her upper arm. Her feet were close together but you could see blood running down one foot from a cut over her ankle. And there was half a footprint.'

'Half a footprint?' Slonský did not recall that appearing anywhere in Holoubek's notes.

'The front part of a left boot. Some kind of shoe with a big tread pattern. Whoever wore it must have trodden in some blood and left the mark in the middle of the bathroom floor. There was a fainter mark by the door.'

'This is really good, Mr Kopecký. You obviously have a good memory.'

'Not now. I don't remember names. But scenes — that's what I did all my working life. It's a silly thought, I know, but I remember thinking that if I'd posed the scene I'd have put her in the bath the other way round. Who sits at the plug end?'

'Was there any water in the bath?'

'No, none.'

'And no knife?'

'There was a small blood-stained knife on the floor at the end of the bath where her feet were. Just an ordinary kitchen knife like my wife uses to peel potatoes.'

'But that can't have done the damage you saw. You didn't see another knife anywhere?'

'No, not a sign of one.'

'Let's go back to the two lads. You didn't see their faces?'

'No. They were quite a distance away. The one who got in the front was broader. Not fat, just muscular. The one who got in the back was much slighter.'

'Colouring?'

'I couldn't see in that light. And neither had much hair.'

'Skinheads, I expect,' Mrs Kopecká added.

'So the chunky one was the driver?'

Kopecký looked up, his face creased in a deep frown.

'No, they both got in the passenger side. I told the policeman that at the time. Someone else drove them.'

Slonský glanced at Navrátil, who looked as astonished as he was himself.

'A third man?' Slonský muttered.

Kopecký began humming. It took Slonský a little while to recognise the tune.

'One of my favourite films,' Kopecký explained. 'Orson Welles. Paul Hörbiger. Hedwig Bleibtreu.'

Slonský interrupted before Kopecký decided to give them the whole cast.

'So the car came to collect them, or it was there all the time?'

Kopecký stopped abruptly. 'What car?'

'The car the two men got into. Outside the Váleks' house.'

'When was this, old chap?'

'You were telling us about the day you found Jana Válková.'

'Ah, yes.' There was a pause before Kopecký continued. 'What was the question again?'

'Was the car they got into outside all night?'

'I can answer that,' said Mrs Kopecká. 'It can't have been, because I took old Mr Hruška a bit of strudel. He had a sweet tooth, but once his wife died … anyway, there wasn't a car outside then. That would be about eight o'clock.'

Slonský picked up his hat.

'Thank you both. You've been very helpful. And thank you for the coffee. Navrátil, any further questions?'

Navrátil's cheeks were puffed out with the last piece of bun he had hurriedly pushed into his mouth when he realised that they were leaving. He suspected that might have been why Slonský asked him the question, because he was rarely given any chance to ask a question of his own at interviews. He chewed fast and swallowed hard.

'Do you know what happened to Mr and Mrs Válek?'

Mrs Kopecká looked apologetic.

'I don't know exactly where and when they went, I'm afraid. They stayed here for a few months, but Mrs Válková couldn't face living in that house. They eventually managed to get a flat in Prague. Whether they're still there, I don't know. Of course, if he's still alive, Mr Válek would be retired by now. They didn't keep in touch.'

The detectives said goodbye and walked back to their car.

'Damn!' Slonský repeated several times.

'What's the matter, sir?'

'If it happened now, Navrátil, it would be an open and shut case. We'd get DNA off the beer glasses, we'd have forensics on the footprints, there'd probably have been video surveillance tapes on an estate like this.'

'Surely they could have done better with what they had, though, sir, even if it was thirty years ago?'

'That's what troubles me most, Navrátil. They could have done so much better. That's what you get for putting a jumped-up circus ringmaster in charge. I could do with something to take away the taste of that coffee, lad. Pull up at the first place you see.'

'There's a burger bar at the airport, sir.'

'Okay, Navrátil. Then pull up at the second place you see.'

Lukas quickly slipped on his best jacket and straightened his tie. It was important to set a good example to young officers. He could not recall meeting Peiperová before, and was therefore surprised when he discovered that she was quite a pretty girl, which Slonský had not mentioned, with long blonde hair bundled up into a knot of some kind at the back. She was also about as tall as Lukas, and she was in uniform.

Lukas stretched forward his hand in greeting, and was met with a formal salute, which he returned rather awkwardly and hurriedly.

'Ah, yes. Jolly good. Stand easy, Officer Peiperová.'

'Thank you, sir.'

'Look, we don't go in for all that formality here. Except on formal occasions, of course, when we tend to be more … formal. Please sit down.'

Lukas introduced himself, described the criminal division to her, then invited Peiperová to tell him about herself.

'Where shall I start, sir?'

'Hm? Oh, birth, I think. I like to know all I can about the staff here.'

Peiperová launched into a description of her life and family, though Lukas was using the time to think about whom she could be attached to. It was, of course, asking too much of Slonský to babysit two young officers. On the other hand, he could not think of anyone else to whom to allocate her. With a start he realised that she had stopped speaking.

'Excellent. First class. Well now, before we assign you permanently, I thought it would be best if you spent a few days with people you already know,' he improvised. 'I believe you've worked with Lieutenant Slonský and Officer Navrátil before.'

'Yes, sir.'

She smiled, which lit up Lukas' rather forbidding office. It disconcerted him and he lost his thread.

'Where was I?'

'Lieutenant Slonský, sir.'

'Ah, yes. Good man, Slonský, with a long record of distinguished service. You'll find him honest, intelligent, observant, but also inclined to cut corners. Shocking approach to administrative tasks. Don't be infected with his lax view of record-keeping. He has done wonders with young Navrátil, who has the makings of a first class detective.'

'I'm sure I'll learn a lot, sir.'

'I'm sure you will,' agreed Lukas, hoping fervently that the things she learned from Slonský would be of a kind that he would approve. 'Unfortunately I can't introduce you just at the moment, because they're out following up a lead somewhere. That's another of Slonský's foibles. He keeps his cards close to his chest, especially when it comes to telling us where he is. But it seems to be somewhere with a poor telephone signal. Well, shall I take you to the canteen and we can have a coffee before I get Sergeant Mucha to find someone to take you over to the barracks?'

Lukas tried to sneak a peek at his watch surreptitiously. He could see it was quarter to something or other, but without pulling his sleeve back he could not quite see the hour. Where was Slonský?

Admittedly he had forgotten to remind Slonský that Officer Peiperová would be reporting for duty that day, but that was not the point. It was part of Slonský's general sloppy approach that nobody knew where he was and his mobile phone was switched off.

The object of his wrath was sitting on a stool putting himself outside a large *párek* and wincing at the disgusting muck that passed for coffee there.

'I almost wish we'd gone to the burger bar,' he muttered.

'They're not as bad as you think. Have you ever been to one?' asked Navrátil.

'Yes. That's why I only almost wish we'd gone there. I know what we've been spared.'

'Your phone is ringing.'

'No, lad, it isn't ringing because I've turned the sound off. But I'll grant that it is flashing and vibrating.'

Having spotted the name Mucha on the screen, he deigned to answer.

'Discount Funeral Parlour.'

'Slonský, Lukas is going ape here. Where are you?'

'Investigating a murder in Ruzyně.'

'Which murder in Ruzyně?'

'The one in 1976.'

'Have you just found the paperwork on your desk?'

'I'll treat that remark with the contempt it merits. I'd hang up on you if I didn't want to hear more about Lukas throwing a wobbler.'

'He's got that young woman from Kladno here and nobody to take her off his hands. He thought you'd be here to show her the ropes.'

'That arrangement might have worked better if he'd asked me about it.'

'It must have slipped his mind. Anyway, that doesn't mean you won't cop it if you don't get back here sharpish.'

'Hang on — I'll have to consult my social diary to see what I'm doing this afternoon.'

'You're free. Now get your backside over here, Batman — and best bring Robin with you. She's asked for him and if you aren't careful people will wonder how she knows him.'

'We're on our way,' announced Slonský, fearful that his brilliant ruse was about to be rumbled.

He slurped the last of his coffee on the principle that he had paid for it, however vile it proved to be.

'What did Mucha want?' asked Navrátil.

'There's a beautiful princess back at the office looking for a frog to kiss,' said Slonský. 'You'll do.'

Lukas had never been happier to see Slonský. If he had possessed a tail it would have wagged violently as the old detective eased through the doorway of Lukas' office. Springing to his feet, Lukas introduced Peiperová, then recalled that Slonský had recommended her, so they must have met already. He asked Slonský to look after Officer Peiperová for a few days until proper arrangements could be made.

'Of course, sir,' said Slonský. 'It will be my pleasure.'

This was untrue. Slonský did not want Peiperová around because she had such a profound effect on Navrátil, whose mouth dropped open when she passed by and who was prone to dribbling if she bent over to pick something off the floor. At that moment Navrátil was in the toilet examining his appearance in the mirror and wishing he had brought a spare shirt that did not look as if wrestlers had spent an hour rolling over it.

It occurred to Slonský that Lukas was so delighted to see him that there was mileage in asking for something he would not ordinarily get. The trouble was that there was nothing he particularly wanted. He hated taking holidays, his expenses were all up to date and he did not have space for a bigger desk. Nevertheless, there were expectations of a man in his position, and he would never forgive himself if he did not take advantage of the situation.

'Will Officer Peiperová be sharing our small office, sir?' he asked.

Lukas smiled fixedly, though plainly uncomfortable with this discussion.

'That's the plan. For now.'

'Very good, sir. Then we'll need an extra chair.'

Lukas breathed a deep sigh of relief. He had anticipated a request for at least one more office, or a conference table. A chair was easily arranged.

'Of course, Lieutenant. I'll get Mucha to find you one.'

'Thank you, sir. This way, Peiperová.'

Slonský led the way to his office and held the door open, bowing his head slightly as she preceded him into the dark, utilitarian space. Navrátil performed his jack in the box impersonation, bounding out of his chair with such dispatch that his knee hit the edge of the desk and he had to bite his lip to conceal the pain.

'You know Officer Peiperová, of course.'

'Yes, sir. Good day, Officer Peiperová.'

'Good day, Officer Navrátil,' she replied.

Slonský took his seat with a broad grin.

'Well, isn't this nice?' he said. 'I love it when children play happily together. Of course, I'm aware that you two have each had one of Cupid's little arrows in your backside and that despite the formal greetings you're probably hoping I'll leave the room so you can attack each other like limpets.'

He leaned forward and fixed each in turn with a hard gaze.

'If you do anything like that on duty, I will send you, Peiperová, back to Kladno licketty-spit, and you, Navrátil, will find yourself on point duty in the busiest crossroads I can find. Is that clear?'

'Yes, sir,' they chorused.

'Outside hours, I do not care if you fornicate yourselves into a stupor and wreck half the beds of Prague, so long as I do not hear about it. Is that also clear?'

'Sir!' Navrátil began, 'Miss Peiperová and I have never…'

'No doubt!' said Slonský. 'And it's none of my business anyway. Just make sure that it stays none of my business. Whatever you do, don't do it here. And whatever you don't do, don't do that here either.'

'Yes, sir,' Peiperová replied.

'Do I have your agreement too, Officer Navrátil?'

'Yes, sir.'

'Good. Then let's not talk about that again. Peiperová, I recall that you make a good cup of coffee.'

'I make coffee too, sir. It's not just women's work,' protested Navrátil.

Slonský turned slowly towards his assistant. 'Did I say it was?' he asked quietly.

'No, but…'

'No, I didn't. Perhaps Peiperová does it better. Perhaps I want to have a man to man chat to you behind her back. Perhaps as soon as she is gone I plan to leap over the desk and strangle you with my shoelace. But if she doesn't go and make some damn coffee we'll never know, will we?' he roared.

Along the corridor Lukas looked up. It was unlike Slonský to raise his voice like that. He hoped he had done the right thing, but then contented himself with the reflection that since he had no other options, it must have been the right thing.

Chapter 4

Holoubek patted each of his pockets in turn to ensure that the contents were in order. House keys in the left pocket, handkerchief and comb in the right, bus pass in the breast pocket, identification in the inside jacket pocket over his heart, wallet in the other inside pocket. There were a few coins in the right lower jacket pocket and a small packet of sugar cubes picked up in a café in the other lower jacket pocket in case he felt tired. At 14:27 he left the house, knowing that his normal stride would take him to the tram stop without having to rush but without a long wait either. He had something to tell Slonský. It could have been done over the telephone, but Holoubek's hearing was not as sharp as it had been and he found the telephone difficult sometimes, to the point of having had it removed. Besides, if he still had the phone his son would call from time to time, but he would never see him. This way Ondřej had to show his face once in a while. He was a good boy, really. He just did not have a sense of family. That's why his wife turfed him out. That, and the incident with the gym teacher. She was a bit of all right, though. Nothing between the ears but if you wanted someone who could do a handstand in the shower, she was your girl. Of course, once he was available she went off him. Forbidden fruit and all that, thought Holoubek.

The tram arrived, and Holoubek boarded, waving his pass at nobody in particular. Fortunately no-one tried to strike up a conversation with him, and after a change of tram he arrived at police headquarters and was pleased to see the same desk sergeant was on duty.

'Holoubek, Edvard, to see Lieutenant Slonský.'

'If you'll take a seat, Mr Holoubek, I'll check he's in his office.'

Mucha rang Slonský's extension.

'Slonský.'

'Good, that's who I hoped you'd be. Mr Holoubek is back to see you.'

'He can't.'

'Why not?' hissed Mucha, who was dreading having to tell Holoubek that Slonský would not see him.

'Because I've only got three chairs and we're sitting on them. Unless, of course, he brings one up with him.'

Mucha counted to ten under his breath.

'I'll bring one with me, shall I?'

'That would work,' agreed Slonský.

A few minutes later Mucha and Holoubek arrived at Slonský's office. Holoubek now understood why Mucha was carrying a chair, which he offered Slonský with a flourish.

'Your chair, Lieutenant.'

'Thank you,' said Slonský politely. 'Just a minute.'

He fished in his pocket and gave Mucha a five-crown coin.

'God bless you, sir,' said Mucha, tugging his forelock. 'May you live for a thousand years.'

'Thank you,' said Slonský again.

'And have piles for nine hundred and ninety-nine of them,' continued Mucha.

Slonský kicked the door shut behind him.

'Now, Mr Holoubek…'

'Edvard.'

'Edvard. What can I do for you today?'

'Who is the young lady?'

'That is Officer Peiperová. She has just joined us today.'

Holoubek stood and offered his hand, which Peiperová accepted and shook firmly.

'We didn't have women officers in my day,' he said. 'Except the ones we used to trap Western diplomats, of course.'

Slonský coughed long and loud, causing Navrátil to go for some water. By the time he returned, Holoubek had forgotten the subject and had passed serenely to the question of his recent discovery.

'I went home after I saw you,' he said, 'and it occurred to me that I'd given you the copies of the official notes, but I hadn't given you these.' He pulled an old exercise book from the inside of his shirt. It was warm. 'My notes. I'm afraid they're not systematic — I just jotted things down as I discovered them. And there isn't much there you don't already know. But I tracked Válek down to his new flat in Karlín, so the address is in there. I was also suspicious about what happened to Vaněček.'

'When he died?'

'Well, that as well, though I couldn't find anything about that. But the case that he was alleged to have fouled up.'

'Why do you say "alleged"?'

'Oh, someone messed up, there's no doubt about that. Unlikely to be Vaněček, of course, because he never did anything, so how could he mess up?'

'Surely the buck stops with the man in charge?'

'Yes,' Holoubek accepted, 'but Vaněček had winkled his way out of that before. This time he couldn't do it. I was in Prague at the time, so I heard the rumours. They said that he had crossed an StB operation and unwittingly exposed an agent.

Well, if he did, he wasn't the first. It was an occupational hazard, because StB didn't tell us what they were up to, so how could we keep out of their way? Like we said the other day, Tripka was supposed to prevent it, but he was as much use as a glass hammer. Anyway, when the dust had settled I asked a few folks I thought might know, and they told me that Tripka had actually warned Vaněček off, but Vaněček pressed on because he wanted to nail an American diplomat for currency smuggling and, according to Vaněček, that was an ordinary crime such as his police should deal with.'

'He had a point,' remarked Slonský.

'If he said it. But I knew Vaněček. He'd never said anything remotely like that before. As far as he was concerned, once StB moved in, he shipped out. He warned us many times not to interfere with their "work of the highest national importance". So I found out where he was living and went to see him. He wouldn't talk to me. At least, not about that. I think he was worried that his house was bugged, because as I left he walked me up the garden path to the gate and whispered that he couldn't tell what he knew, because that was the deal he'd had to make with *them*. And a fortnight or so later he had his accident. I've often wondered if the two events were connected. Did he fall on the fence post because someone thought he'd spoken to me? If so, he was really shafted, because he didn't speak to me and they bumped him off anyway.'

'Did those things really happen then?' asked Navrátil.

'Oh, yes,' said Slonský. 'It didn't do to cross the secret police, even if you were in the business. There was a fellow I worked with called Zeman. He arrested a French embassy junior of some kind for indecency in a public place, and since he was a bright lad, he rang the StB and told them he'd got a hold over a foreigner. That was what we were meant to do. They ambled over, took the Frenchman away, told Zeman what a good job he'd done and he could expect a bit of a bonus. The bonus didn't arrive, so Zeman mentioned the incident to his boss one afternoon. Next evening, four heavies kicked the living daylights out of him in an alley not far from here. He lost the sight of an eye and was invalided out. And his boss was packed off to hold back any invading Hungarians at a customs post.'

Holoubek nodded. He knew some similar stories, but out of the corner of his eye he could see that his tram left in eight minutes.

'Are you getting anywhere?' he asked.

'We've spoken to Kopecký, who —'

'— found the body. I know who Kopecký was. He's still alive then. Must be some age.'

'Eight years younger than you, I think. But you're wearing better. The old chap's memory isn't good. But he remembers 1976 like it was yesterday.'

'Don't we all?' agreed Holoubek. 'Will his testimony be any use in court?'

Slonský considered carefully.

'I believe him. I wouldn't trust him to tell me what he had for lunch today, but take him back thirty years and his memory is sound as a bell. But a good defence lawyer would just tie him in knots and invite the judge to chuck him out. It's the perennial problem with cold cases. How much can you rely on elderly witnesses? That's my problem with these Nazi hunters. Those Nazis deserve to be punished, but how can you get a safe conviction? Anyone who was old enough to understand what they were witnessing is going to be over seventy now.'

'We're not all gaga, you know,' Holoubek bristled.

'Not all. But some are. That's why Navrátil and I have picked it up. If Jana Válková's killers aren't found now, they never will be. I don't know if Captain Lukas is going to let us take it on, but we're doing the spadework to build the best case we can to convince him.'

Holoubek pushed himself upwards with a great effort.

'Well, I wish you luck. I asked you to try, and you're trying. I can't ask for more. I should have done more myself.'

He waved a hand at Navrátil and Peiperová and headed for the door, stopping as he reached the handle.

'Keep me posted,' he ordered.

'I can't promise there'll be more to report, but if we're allowed to carry on, I'll let you know,' Slonský replied.

Holoubek nodded his appreciation, and smiled gently as he left. Navrátil followed to see him safely down to the front door.

'He seems like a nice old man,' said Peiperová.

'You think so? No better, no worse than the rest of us. You'll have to learn that those of us who have been around for a while have skeletons in our closets. The state put them there. We had to do things that we ought not to have done. Suspects beaten up, witnesses intimidated, evidence concocted, we've all done it. The generation coming to the fore now is the first one with the possibility of having clean hands. Of course, some of them haven't because they're grasping, conniving, devious, unprincipled ordinary human beings. So the torch passes to your age group. I want to live to see a police force I can be proud of from top to bottom, and I'm relying on you to give me one.'

Peiperová smiled. 'Me personally, sir?'

'Why not? Just promise me one thing. If you make it to Director, make sure you give Navrátil a hard time.'

'Why do I deserve a hard time?' asked Navrátil as he re-entered the office.

'Karma,' answered Slonský. 'And probably your Feng Shui.'

'I thought only buildings had that.'

'Look at you, lad. Full of untidy angles. Whereas Peiperová doesn't have a sharp corner on her. Altogether much more soothing to look at. Now, either come in or go and get some coffee from the canteen. Better still, let's give our new colleague a tour of the neighbourhood, starting with the bar on the corner. Peiperová, have you brought any other clothes? You're a detective now, and we only wear our uniforms on special occasions — parades, national holidays and disciplinary hearings. At least that's when I wear mine. Nip back to your room and change into civvies and meet us downstairs at the desk.'

Peiperová stood up and began to raise an arm.

'If that's a salute I'll break your elbow.'

'Just about to scratch my ear, sir.'

Peiperová looked around her and sipped the drink Navrátil had bought her without having to ask what she wanted. Slonský detected cranberry juice and ice in it, and that was enough for him to decide he wanted to know no more. At least Navrátil was still drinking beer.

'It's nice here,' Peiperová decided. 'Lively.'

'On the plus side, it's near the office,' Slonský said. 'But that brings us to the minus side, which is that it's always full of police.'

'Is that so bad?' she asked.

'I don't mind working with them,' Slonský replied, 'but that doesn't mean I want to hang around with them. There are some of them I wouldn't trust as far as I could spit them.'

Peiperová laughed. In her blouson jacket, white sleeveless top and jeans, with her blonde hair released from whatever implement of restraint held it under her hat during the day, she looked completely different. Slonský was enjoying sitting with her, once he had got over the shock of having, for the first time in his life, a colleague who wore makeup.

Navrátil had restrained himself long enough.

'Can we talk shop a moment, sir? Do you think Captain Lukas will let us investigate the Válková murder properly?'

Slonský rolled a mouthful of beer round his gums before replying.

'Not a snowball's chance in hell. And if I were in his shoes, I wouldn't either. To take up a cold case you need new evidence and a realistic chance of a conviction. Even if Kopecký told us anything new today, how credible a witness would he be?'

'He's not exactly demented, sir. Just a bit of short term memory loss. His long term memory is fine.'

'I believe you, but how would you prove it? The natural tendency is to forget things, Navrátil, and the more time passes the more we forget. Kopecký is unusual in having — apparently — been frozen in time. But it's hard to prove. Old men

235

forget; it's what they do. So unless we find something else, we'll be told to stop wasting time and get back to the present day.'

'But an innocent man was hanged, sir.'

Slonský frowned.

'I'm not sure he was innocent, lad. None of us are. We've all done something deserving of punishment. But I grant he didn't do what they strung him up for.'

'Then we ought to clear his name. More to the point, we ought to find who really did it.'

'I admire the sentiment, son, I really do. But even if we find them, I doubt we'll get enough evidence to convict.'

Navrátil hesitated. He knew he had a convincing argument, but he was unsure that he dared to use it.

'Who cares about conviction?' he answered. 'If they know that we know they did it, that's enough for me. Conviction if we can get one, of course, but that isn't everything. We've worked on a case where we knew we wouldn't get a conviction, but we didn't let that stop us doing what we thought was right.'

Slonský looked grave.

'I didn't let it stop *me*,' he said. 'You keep yourself out of it.'

Turning to Peiperová he explained Navrátil's allusion.

'Navrátil is reminding me that we knew we couldn't get a conviction in the Sammler case. I kept the pressure on him in the hope that he would confess, but he didn't. At least, not in a way we could use.'

Navrátil was not giving in that easily.

'But you will ask Captain Lukas, sir?'

'Yes, I'll ask. I promised Holoubek I'd ask. But I also warned him that we might not be allowed to continue. And this is not a case we can pick up in our spare time, Navrátil. If you want to be useful, make me a list of loose ends we could still investigate. Now, can we talk about something else?'

'Yes, sir. What would you like to talk about?'

'Well, for a start, I'd like to know what Captain Lukas said to our new recruit here, because he's said damn all to me about what I'm meant to do with her.'

Peiperová shook her head. 'I've got no idea, sir. He said he hadn't decided exactly where I should be placed, and the people he wanted to talk to about me weren't around for a few days, so he thought I could start with you since we'd already met and you'd been the one who put my name forward. By the way, sir, thank you for that.'

'No thanks necessary, young lady. Unless I need a favour, in which event I'll remind you of my help loud and clear until it gets across. So, if the people are away that gives us two candidates straight off. Lieutenant Dvorník is on holiday in Bavaria with his chubby little wife and his rosy-cheeked little offspring. And if I remember correctly Lieutenant Doležal is on a course in Brno swotting up on character profiling or some such tosh.'

'What are they like, sir?'

'Dvorník's all right, if you don't like excitement in your life and you want endless discussions about his mother's cooking and the best types of dumpling. His wife is allegedly a good cook, which, he says, is why he married her.'

'Why didn't he just hire her as a cook?' asked Navrátil.

'Yes, we wondered that. Wives are much more expensive. On the other hand, cooks don't commonly have three children for you, especially after they've seen the first globular little horror. I've forgotten his name, but Dvorník used to bring him in to show him off, wedged in a pushchair. Doležal couldn't be more different. Mid-forties, probably sleeps in his suit, unmarried. Stamp collecting is his thing.' He leaned forward confidentially and dropped his voice. 'People say he listens to classical music. I've never caught him at it but he shuts his office door when he's working, so who knows. Peiperová, we're relying on you to discover if those rumours are true.'

'I'll do my best, sir. Do they specialize in anything?'

'Dvorník doesn't like burglaries. If he had his way he'd only do murders, but as senior lieutenant I get more of them. Doležal specializes in dullness. Even Klinger in the fraud squad says Doležal is boring company, and if Klinger says someone is boring, you'd better believe it. He isn't exactly a sparkling companion himself.'

'Do they have vacancies for an assistant, sir?'

Slonský had not considered that and it was a moment or two before he felt able to reply.

'Dvorník already has Hauzer. Doležal has an ex-academy lad like Navrátil here, but from the class before.'

'That must be Rada,' Navrátil chipped in. 'Tall, thin chap who wears a lot of black.'

'That'll be the one,' agreed Slonský. 'Looks like a professional mourner.'

Peiperová looked perturbed.

'So if they've got assistants, and you've got Officer Navrátil, maybe there isn't a place for me at all.'

It was at this point that Slonský opened his mouth without thinking. Looking back later, he had no idea why he did it, because it had got him into trouble before and was about to do so again.

'Don't you worry,' he said. 'Your Uncle Josef will take care of you.'

Peiperová jumped up and hugged him.

'Thank you!' she squealed.

Everyone turned to look at her. Those who recognised Slonský were astonished. Nobody had ever thought that an attractive young woman would be moved enough to make physical contact with him voluntarily. It was one of those moments they would describe to disbelieving colleagues for some time to come. Their memories of the incident would, no doubt, become embellished with time, because memories do that to us. They sneak in little snippets of falsehood that make the overall picture more convincing. For example, more than one observer would swear that Peiperová was visibly drunk. Another would claim that Slonský's right hand cupped her bottom. This was untrue. Slonský's hands were extended sideways like a hockey defender claiming he didn't bodycheck an opponent. Eventually he patted her gently on the back in the belief that she would not release her grip until he did so.

'I've never been embraced by a subordinate before,' he explained as Peiperová returned to her stool and he straightened his tie in a belated attempt at recapturing his dignity.

'No,' agreed Navrátil, 'I'm not one for hugging the boss.'

'Sorry, sir,' said Peiperová. 'It won't happen again.'

'Well, we needn't go that far,' Slonský answered. 'Just give me a bit of warning. I'm a trained killer, you see. It's lucky I controlled my reflexes before I broke your neck.'

'Yes, sir.'

'We'll say no more about it. Whatever that disgusting red muck is in your glass, would you like another one?'

'Thank you, sir.'

'Navrátil, wave the waiter over and tell him what it was that you bought before. I can't bring myself to say it, even if I knew what it was called.'

Navrátil glanced around him.

'I can't see one. I'll go up to the bar and organise it.'

Slonský watched Navrátil push through the crowd, then spoke rapidly to Peiperová in a low voice.

'Peiperová, I know Navrátil is fond of you. I assume you're fond of him too.'

She hesitated, unsure how to answer.

'It's not my business unless it interferes with your work. But don't insult my intelligence by pretending there's nothing going on between you unless there really is nothing going on between you. I hope it works out. You're a nice pair. But if it doesn't, please tell me so I'm not left floundering around in the dark like an idiot. Deal?'

'Deal, sir.'

'Good. He's going to be a good cop. Of course, he has the great advantage of having me to show him the ropes. But you can't make a silk purse from a sow's ear, and he's got something about him. I think you have too. Don't prove me wrong.'

'No, sir. I'll try not to, sir.'

'Trying isn't good enough, Peiperová. Make it your business to succeed. What are you gawping at, girl?'

'It's Navrátil, sir. I think he's trying to attract your attention.'

Slonský turned to look. Navrátil was fighting his way back through the thirsty masses, his arms unencumbered by drinks, but with something in his hand. As he reached them Slonský could see it was a mobile phone.

'Sergeant Mucha rang, sir. He says would I tell you to turn your bloody phone on and get yourself back to the station pronto. He emphasised the pronto.'

'Did he say anything else?'

'Yes, sir. It involved his boot and both our bottoms, only he didn't express it quite that way.'

'Right, he obviously means business. And since it is business, you two had better come too.'

Ignoring the traffic lights and the legitimate claims of drivers to unrestricted use of the road, Slonský barged across the lanes of traffic, holding his badge up like a wizard's wand, and pushed the door open without bothering about the possibility that someone might be behind it. He could see at once that whatever it was, it was important. Mucha looked unusually agitated, but he did not speak until the three detectives were close enough to be the only people who heard him.

'It's Holoubek,' he announced. 'He's been killed.'

Chapter 5

'How? When?' asked Slonský.

'Don't know,' replied Mucha, 'but the call came in and I thought you'd want it. So why don't you get yourself over to Nusle and take charge?'

'Where in Nusle?'

'At the tram stop. It sounds like a hit and run as he got off the tram after seeing you. But I only know what the City Police told us, so stop rabbiting and get over there before the duty officer wonders why I haven't given this one to him. I've logged that you were already out in a car so I diverted you there. Now go!'

Slonský came very close to running. An observer could have followed Slonský's career for a very long time without seeing the like. Certainly he had run during his army service; people shooting at him tended to encourage that activity. He had occasionally run in his younger years. But it was a long time since he had skipped down the steps in threes, and by the time he reached the car the younger officers were in their seats. Navrátil put the lights and siren on and hammered the accelerator to the floor as they headed to Nusle, while Slonský struggled to get enough breath back to allow him to speak coherently.

They screeched to a halt on Táborská in front of a stern officer holding his traffic paddle aloft.

'We're in luck,' Slonský announced. 'That looks like Štajnhauzr.' He pointed at a tall, fit-looking City Policeman who wore an entirely unofficial black bodywarmer over his black shirt. The bodywarmer was apparently crammed with useful articles, many of which other officers did not feel the need to carry. Although summer uniforms were in use, Štajnhauzr had not worn his pale blue shirt, presumably because black suited his action lifestyle rather better.

Slonský strode towards him, waving his badge to head off any other city police who might have been thinking of intercepting him.

'Štajnhauzr!'

The object of the cry turned and waved in a gesture that approached a half-hearted salute.

'Lieutenant,' he acknowledged.

'Officers Peiperová and Navrátil. What happened here?'

'There are quite a lot of witnesses, sir. I've sat them down over there on the steps of the building. Officer Krob is watching over them. Basically, they tell a similar story. The deceased stepped off the tram onto the island that separates the tram lane from the car lane. As he crossed the car lane to get to the pavement, a dark blue van raced up and smashed into him. He was knocked forward several metres and the van kept going, ran over him and sped off.'

'Anyone get the registration?'

'A good partial from a cyclist and a few other partials. I've phoned it in to traffic and they're trying to match it.'

'Good. Time?'

'Whatever time the tram came. Don't know for sure. The tram driver didn't see anything happen but the van swerved across in front of him to take a left at the junction into Pod Sokolovnou. I've got someone checking the traffic cameras to see if they can plot its course from there.'

'Why that way? If you want to get out of the city, you go straight on or you turn left a block further down at Na Květnici.'

'Could be opportunistic, sir. Maybe there was just a break in the traffic. And Pod Sokolovnou is a one way street. He wouldn't meet anyone coming towards him.'

Slonský nodded. The city boys did not investigate crime but they knew the traffic system inside out. As soon as he arrived, Štajnhauzr would have put out a message to all the traffic police to watch for a dark blue van with any match to the partial registration.

There was a crackle from Štajnhauzr's radio. He listened intently.

'Van seen heading south on Michelská near the District 4 station, sir. We've got a couple of patrols out looking for it and they're going to rig the traffic lights on Videňská to hold him up. He may not go that way, of course, but if he wants a quick route out of town, that's favourite.'

'Good work. Why did you phone the criminal police?'

'Obvious hit and run, sir, but also because I went through his pockets to establish his identity and found a piece of paper with your name on it. There was also an envelope. It makes no sense to me, but it might to you.'

He handed over a thin manila envelope. It contained a copy of Vaněček's autopsy report, apparently made with a camera. There was also a grainy black and white photograph of a small house.

'Why didn't he give us these, sir?' asked Navrátil.

'I don't know, lad. You could try asking him but I doubt you'll get anywhere. Maybe he just forgot. That's what old people do.'

'Holoubek didn't, sir. He didn't seem to forget much at all.'

'Then maybe he didn't know what to make of this and wanted to look into it a bit more.'

Peiperová interrupted excitedly. 'Sir! Isn't this an address on the back of the photo?'

'Not easy to read, but I think you're right. Zdiby.'

'Zdiby? Where's that?'

Štajnhauzr supplied the answer. 'North of the city heading towards Klecany. Not a big village. Half an hour's drive round and you'll find this place, if it still exists. It's an old photo, after all.'

'Right!' Slonský shoved the photograph in Navrátil's hand. 'Before it gets dark, get yourself over to Zdiby and see if you can find this house. Save yourself some driving — ask at the district police or council office first. Peiperová, you're not doing anything tonight that stops you staying on a while?'

She glanced quickly at Navrátil, but he was already running to the car. 'No, sir.'

'Good. Get over there and interview all the women. You'll recognise them by their lumpy fronts. Get names and addresses and the facts. We don't need formal statements just yet. Start with the ones with small children. I'll join you to tackle the men as soon as possible.'

A man with thick glasses and a neat beard was crouched over the crumpled body of Holoubek making notes and directing a photographer to take a large number of images. Slonský approached him but was stopped by a peremptory command.

'Stop! Make a wide arc and approach from the head end. I haven't checked that bit of road yet.'

'That's a bloody mess,' Slonský said.

'True, literally and figuratively. If there's a plus point in this, I suspect he was concussed by the first impact and probably didn't feel much after that.'

'That's not much of a consolation to me or him,' said Slonský, 'and it doesn't change the fact that someone ran over a man of ninety.'

'No, it doesn't,' agreed Novák.

Dr Vladimír Novák was a pathologist, and a good one at that. He and Slonský enjoyed working together, though it was a matter of professional honour to both to conceal the fact.

'Are you going to tell me it's natural causes?' asked Slonský.

'Only if you want to enhance your reputation for rank stupidity. It's a classic blow with a blunt object, in this case a dark blue Volkswagen Multivan.'

'How can you tell that?'

'Because that guy in the motorbike leathers told me it was a dark blue Volkswagen Multivan. Certainly a dark blue vehicle. There's a flake of paint on his arm where it must have flailed down the wing as it rolled him over.'

'So the van was damaged?'

'He's an old chap and he's frail, but you can't hit a human being without doing a bit of damage to the vehicle. He was dragged along under the van, so the bumper is likely to be scratched or dented. And that looks to me like a corner off a number plate. We'll do all we can here and then take him back to the mortuary. I'll work him up first thing in the morning. No point in working overnight. I don't think forensics are going to be the key to solving this one somehow. Slonský, if your colleague is going to faint, could she fall in the opposite direction so she doesn't contaminate the crime scene?'

Slonský had not noticed Peiperová's return. She looked pale and was staring at Holoubek as if fascinated by the sight of an old man dumped on the road.

'What do you want?' Slonský growled.

'Sorry, sir. I thought you'd want to speak to that lady with the brown coat on. She says the blue van had been around for an hour or so before the accident.'

'It wasn't an accident, Peiperová. Find another word for it. But thank you, I'll come now.'

Peiperová nodded and returned to her interviews.

'Looks like murder, then,' said Slonský.

'Yes, it does,' said Novák. 'But that's not a professional opinion, before you hold me to it. Now push off and annoy someone else.'

Slonský walked across the road to the small knot of people whom Officer Krob was trying to keep from wandering off. Not for the first time, Slonský wondered whether the inhabitants of Prague were different to those of other cities. Here, there were two common responses to an incident like this. Some would not want to get involved, and would try to sneak off if the opportunity arose. Krob had deployed a lot of crime scene tape to create a sort of pen for the witnesses, and, in a masterstroke of improvisation, had managed to persuade someone to bring coffee and biscuits for them. Indifference to the plight of others was something of a Prague tradition, but you can't argue with free coffee and biscuits.

The second response was to concoct evidence designed to ensure that the right person was convicted. In this case, 'right' did not mean guilty. It meant morally deserving of punishment, often as a result of some other characteristic of the accused. Being Roma was usually a good start, though many a German motorist had found himself accused of a misdemeanour once his D plate was spotted on the rear of his car. This habit was time honoured. As a very young policeman under the Communists, when cars were rationed and you had to be someone to get hold of one, Slonský had been solemnly tutored by his sergeant to understand that in any road accident involving a car and a pedestrian, it must have been the pedestrian's fault. Similarly, any collision between two cars was easily explained once you knew which car was the larger one, because its driver could not be culpable. While this was very clear to any policeman, it was difficult to maintain in the face of the united testimony of passers-by that the larger car had reversed at speed into the smaller one, a view expressed all the more vehemently by those who could not possibly have seen the incident in question.

Eva Urbanová had made no effort to slink away. A woman in her late fifties, she stood squarely facing him. Square was a good adjective for Urbanová, who was around one metre fifty tall and roughly the same across. She wore a cheap brown raincoat and flat shoes with no stockings or tights, and had the corned beef legs of a woman who likes to sit close to the fire on cold evenings.

'Good day, madam,' Slonský began.

'Are you in charge of this shambles?' she asked.

'It won't be a shambles now I've taken charge,' he replied smoothly. 'Lieutenant Slonský, Josef, Criminal Police.'

'Urbanová, Eva,' she replied, in the formal manner that had characterized the country since the days of the Austro-Hungarian Empire.

'I understand you've seen the van earlier today,' Slonský said.

'Yes. I told that young bit that. I'm pretty sure it turned up around four o'clock. The driver pulled in down the road and just sat in the cab.'

'What made you notice him?'

'I've been waiting for the landlord to send a plumber. It looked like the sort of van a plumber might have. Of course, I've been waiting a week already, so why I thought that might be him I don't know, I'm sure. Anyway, he never budged. Just sat there looking in the wing mirror.'

'You didn't see his registration number, I suppose?'

'No. I can't read it at this distance. That's my window up there.' She pointed vaguely over her left shoulder.

'Where did he park?'

'Opposite side of the road in the dotted area.'

'And nobody moved him on?'

'Never a policeman around when you need one. Of course, the place is crawling with them now that old gent's been knocked over, and look at the parking now.' She gestured down the road. The parking was impeccable.

'Did you see the old gentleman being run over?'

She shook her head. 'You couldn't see because the tram was in the way. He must have got out at the middle doors. Then I heard this loud engine noise like a racing car, and the van came charging down the far lane. There was a shout and then a loud thump, and some screaming, but I didn't see anything until the van swept across the front of the tram and turned left.'

'The tram was moving by then?'

'Just started off. There wasn't a lot of space for the van to get in front, but he wasn't going to stop anyway, I reckon.'

Slonský had never had much success with young women in his life, but he was something of a charmer of women of a certain age, so he chanced his arm with Mrs Urbanová.

'My old mother wasn't very good on her feet, but she made sure she knew what went on in her street.'

'I know the type,' Mrs Urbanová said. 'Liked a chat, did she?'

'Not nosey, you understand,' said Slonský. 'Just keen to find out if she could help anyone with anything.'

'Public spirited. Not enough of that about.'

'Have you seen the old gentleman before?'

'Oh, yes!' she said, 'many times. He always got off at that stop. He must have lived in those blocks down the road.'

'Which ones are those?'

'See where this road joins the next one at an angle? If you cross to your right there there's a sort of little oblong with flats around. Then you can walk through to some more. I think he must have lived somewhere there.' A shocked look came over her face. 'You don't think his poor wife is still sitting there waiting with his tea?'

'He was a widower, I think.'

Urbanová crossed herself.

'Just as well the poor woman went first. It'll be a comfort to her, God rest her.'

'That's one way of looking at it,' agreed Slonský. 'You didn't get a good look at the van driver, I suppose?'

'What do you think I am, a ruddy eagle? I'll tell you what, though. On this side of the road, not far from where he was parked on the far side, there's a girl who does hairdressing. There's nothing much goes on that she doesn't see.' She gripped his arm and pulled down on it so he had to bend to follow it. 'Not official hairdressing, you understand, so don't say I said anything.'

'I won't mention it. I'm not interested in someone earning a bit of pin money. Would you mind walking me along a bit and pointing at the right door?'

Mrs Urbanová did just that. It was around fifty metres so she only needed to stop once to catch her breath.

'Up one flight of stairs,' she said.

Slonský climbed the stairs and knocked on the door. It was opened by a blonde woman wearing a pink polyester housecoat. He knew he had come to the right place because there was a strong smell of setting lotion.

He showed his badge.

'Can we have a word, miss?'

She looked reluctant.

'It's a bit awkward at the moment...'

'I know,' he said. 'You're in the middle of a perm and the timing is important. You carry on. We can talk while you work if that's okay.'

She nodded and he followed her in. They turned into the front room where a woman was sitting in a chair swathed in a blue plastic cape. Slonský exchanged greetings with her.

'You may have heard that an elderly man was knocked down and killed in this street this afternoon around five o'clock. It wasn't an accident. It looks as if the van that ran him over waited for him for over an hour.'

'That's awful,' gasped the woman in the chair. 'If that kind of thing can happen we could all be murdered in our beds.'

'It's my job to see you don't get murdered in your bed,' Slonský explained, 'and that will be less likely if we can put the driver away for life.'

'Better if you hanged him,' said the woman in the chair. 'You hang them once and they don't kill twice.'

'That's as may be…' began Slonský.

'And I'd castrate them first. They won't need them bits again and it means they wouldn't breed more criminals to murder us in our beds.'

'You're right there, Mrs Musilová,' said the hairdresser. 'And rapists too. They should get the chop.'

'Goes without saying,' agreed Musilová. 'And them podiatrists.'

'I think you mean paedophiles,' Slonský interrupted. 'Podiatrists look after your feet.'

'Yes, them too.'

'There's a lot of men would be less trouble to women if they didn't have hormones running through them,' continued the hairdresser.

'The law doesn't let us hang them,' Slonský explained, 'whatever our personal views on the subject. And the Czech Republic, almost uniquely, does castrate sex offenders, if they consent.'

'Fancy that. But I wouldn't worry about consent,' said Mrs Musilová.

'Well, I'd ask,' said the hairdresser, 'but if they said no I'd do it anyway.'

'That's not quite how consent works … anyway, to get back to the reason for my visit, the van that ran him over was parked opposite for about an hour from four o'clock. Did you see it there?'

'Dark blue van?' the hairdresser asked.

'That's right.'

'Yes, came just as my three o'clock left — say, around ten to four — and was there quite a while. Of course, while I'm working I have my back to the window.'

'You didn't get a good look at the driver, I suppose?'

'Yes, I eyeballed him. Black hair, not too long but not short either. Quite thick, straight, not dyed. I notice hair, you see, being a hairdresser. Parted on the left. Just lapping over his ear. He had a small earring in too. It caught the light.'

'Good. His face?'

'Didn't really see. Clean shaven. Sharpish nose. Heavy black eyebrows. I thought he could do with them plucking. Thin them out a bit. Not a bad-looking lad actually.'

'A lad? Quite young, then?'

'Younger than me,' laughed the hairdresser.

'Twenty-five?' Slonský offered.

'And the rest, love. Thirty-five to forty, I'd say. No wedding ring.'

Slonský glanced out of the window.

'You could see that from here?'

'I can see a wedding ring from a long way off, love.'

'Can't we all, dear,' agreed Mrs Musilová.

Navrátil had found the district police office in Zdiby just before the duty officer shut the door and went home for the night.

'I've got an old photo that appears to show a house here, and I was hoping you could tell me where I can find it, if it's still standing.'

'If it isn't still standing you won't find it whatever I say,' replied the district policeman, who, under direct questioning, was prepared to reveal that his name was Majer.

'That's my name, not my rank,' he expanded.

'I realised that,' Navrátil replied. 'It's unlikely that a major would be locking up a little police station.'

'We're not that little. We have a dinghy and a motor scooter.'

'I'll bear that in mind. Now, this picture. Does it mean anything to you?'

Majer frowned as he studied it.

'Yes.'

'It does?'

'I just said so, didn't I?'

'And it's still standing?'

'It was when I last looked.'

'How do I get to it?'

Majer stared into the distance as if this would help him to focus on the question in hand.

'You've got two choices,' he finally announced. 'You can carry on down this road and turn right. Alternatively, you can go back to the junction, take the main road, and turn left. It's about halfway down the road. Or up the road, depending which end you come from.'

'And it's easily recognised?'

'It should be,' Majer smiled. 'You've got a photograph.'

Each man headed for his car. Navrátil opted to take the first alternative, staying on the road and turning right. As is often the case on country roads, the inhabitants had parked at all kinds of angles, not anticipating that anyone would actually want to use the road, so Navrátil crawled along, carefully watching both wings to avoid damage to the car. After a few minutes he saw a house on the left that was a possible candidate, so he pulled in and stepped out of the car to get a better look.

It could have been the one, but then so could the next one or the one after that. Three very similar houses differed only in the decoration applied to them. Looking closely at the photograph, Navrátil ruled out the centre house, whose front path curved rather than following a straight line between gate and front door, and had finally decided the third house was the likeliest candidate when a police car came to a halt beside him and Majer climbed out.

'Hello again,' said Navrátil. 'Come to tell me which one it is?'

'No,' said Majer, looking as if the idea of further assistance had not occurred to him. 'I live here.'

'You live here? Why didn't you say?'

Majer shrugged. 'You didn't ask.'

'But weren't you curious about why I'm walking about with a picture of your house?'

'That's not my house. I live in the middle one. It has a curved front path, do you see?'

Navrátil counted to five before replying. 'Yes, I noticed that.'

'Your picture is the house next door.'

'I'd worked that out too. Who lives there?'

'My neighbour, Mrs Grigarová.'

Navrátil was losing patience. It would soon be dusk and he was keen to get out of the village before night fell. He had seen too many films in which people like Majer became zombies and feasted on the flesh of visitors once darkness arrived.

'Look, I don't suppose you ever met him, but we think this is the house where a policeman called Vaněček lived. Can you think of anyone who lived here around 1979 and might be able to confirm that for us?'

'Yes. My dad.'

'Great. Where will I find him?'

'Here. He lives with us. Come in and I'll introduce you.'

Navrátil followed Majer into the centre house, and was surprised to see that the hall was covered with photographs of people in police uniforms. He paused to look at them, which Majer took as an invitation to describe them all.

'That's me, obviously. That's Uncle Viktor. So is that. That's Uncle Ivo — he's on my mum's side. That's Mum in her first uniform. That's Ivo again, receiving his medal for rescuing a little kid who fell in the river. Now this one is unusual, because both my uncles are in it. You can't tell because of the riot shields, but the third from the left is Ivo and Viktor is the one putting his helmet back on after someone lobbed a brick at it. And that's Dad when he first came here.'

'So he was in the police then?'

'Man and boy his whole life. Until he retired, of course.'

Majer motioned Navrátil through to the front room where Mr Majer senior was reading a magazine about sporting guns. Introductions having been made, Navrátil decided to get to the point and avoid anything approaching small talk.

'Mr Majer, we're investigating a death this afternoon in Nusle. An ex-policeman was the victim of a hit and run.'

'Call me Benedikt. It'll be confusing otherwise. What was his name?'

'Holoubek. Edvard Holoubek.'

Benedikt looked pained.

'Did you know him, sir?'

'Only slightly. But a hit and run is a bad way to die, and it's doubly bad at his age. Holoubek was a good policeman. One of the few you could trust to be completely straight with you. Of course, I'll do whatever I can to help.'

'When he was killed he had this photograph in his pocket.'

'That's the house next door. Why did he have that with him?'

'We can't be sure, sir…'

'Benedikt.'

'Benedikt. But it seems likely that it was connected with a case from the past that he worked on. We believe the house in the photograph may have been that of another policeman called Vaněček.'

'No doubt about it. Though it's stretching the truth a bit to call him a policeman.'

'That seems to have been Holoubek's opinion too, sir.'

'It would be. Vaněček was a deadweight. He minced around in his dress uniform any chance he got — hang on, I'll show you what I mean.'

Before Navrátil could stop him, Benedikt had pushed himself out of the chair and could be heard rummaging in a cupboard. He returned after a couple of minutes with a dog-eared paperback book with a slate blue cover.

'Police handbook from the seventies.' He flicked through the first few pages. 'There you are. Nineteen seventy-two. There's Vaněček.'

Navrátil found himself looking at a passport-sized photograph posed in the classical Communist portrait position, with the left shoulder nearer the camera, the head turned slightly to the subject's left as if looking beyond the photographer's right shoulder. The cheap paper made the photograph look slightly blurred, but Vaněček proved to be a rather portly man with plenty of space on his chest for his many medals.

'What did he get all those awards for?' asked Navrátil.

'God knows. Shutting up and keeping out of the way would come high on the list. How he managed to stand upright with that lot dangling off his front I don't know. They had specially stiffened uniforms, you know, to take the weight of the metal without tearing.'

'And he lived next door.'

'Not while he was in the service. He was retired before he came here, and not voluntarily either. Some kind of cock-up on his watch, it was said. Of course, Vaněček was very keen to give me his side of it, and I was just as keen not to hear it. I knew his sort. They'd put good men at risk by their carelessness. It didn't surprise me if the stories were true and he'd done the same. He said he hadn't.'

Benedikt rubbed his chin thoughtfully.

'One funny thing, though. He didn't seem to care much what the other villagers thought, but he was very concerned that I should believe him. At the time, I didn't.'

'And now?'

Benedikt looked at his hands, inspecting the backs of his knuckles carefully as he thought.

'It's not evidence, of course, but his death was very peculiar.'

'That's what we're really interested in. The autopsy report said he fell on a fence and penetrated his chest.'

Benedikt laughed out loud and stood up, causing Navrátil to follow suit.

'Follow me, young man.'

They walked together to the back door, which Benedikt flung open. He stepped into the garden and invited Navrátil to do likewise.

'Tell me — where in these gardens can you see any fence you could fall on? It's barely changed these thirty years. The only fence I can see next door has wooden rails running horizontally across the posts. It's as smooth as a baby's bottom. I don't doubt for a minute that Vaněček fell on a fence somewhere — it's too daft a story not to be true — but it wasn't in his garden.'

'Did you know the StB had come for him?'

'Officially, no. They wouldn't tell a district policeman like me. The first I heard was when one of my men came tearing into the office to see if I was still there. He'd seen the car going down this street and he couldn't think of anyone else the StB would want to talk to. I, on the other hand, was concerned about my wife and son. Those swine weren't above getting to a man by arresting his family, so I got myself over here as quickly as I could. They were helping Vaněček into the car. Odd, isn't it, how police put a man into a car? They push gently down on his head so that he won't bang it on the roof, then they take him away and kick him to death, hang him or throw him onto a stake. He looked at me very briefly, and I've never seen a man look so terrified. I didn't see him again. But it's the fact that the StB came for him when he'd been retired for a while that made me wonder if there was something in his story.'

'Which was?'

'I didn't pay it much attention, because in those days the truth was irrelevant. If those above you disciplined you, it was pointless spending time on proving yourself innocent. It only annoyed them. I thought Vaněček should just get on with his life and stop trying to change his history. But, for what it's worth, and bear in mind that I know none of this first hand, he claimed that he had been tipped off that a group of students were producing pornography. He raided a clandestine press and it turned out that they weren't producing pornography, but political pamphlets, and one of those he arrested was an StB operative who had to blow his cover to get out of the cells. Some of those involved were foreign students. Now, normally anything involving foreigners would go straight to StB, but he said nobody told him foreigners were involved. Vaněček protested his innocence but Tripka produced a memo that he said should have alerted Vaněček. Do you know Tripka?'

'I've heard of him. StB liaison, I believe.'

'At the time, yes. He came back into the mainstream and was a deputy director of police when he retired. Well, the memo was a turgid thing, but it was the usual story — a line at the bottom of page nine that might have been relevant. Vaněček wasn't convinced and argued that the sentence referred to something quite different. He wouldn't let it drop, and after a few months they came for him. He was writing letters to the Party hierarchy, talking to journalists and so on. Stupid of him, because the journalists were all good Party members too. That's all I know.'

'Is his wife still alive?'

'I don't think so. She only stayed on here for a month or so, then the house was reallocated. After all, he qualified for it, not her.'

'Any other family?'

'Never heard of any. Certainly no children.'

Navrátil inspected the photograph again.

'I'd love to know why Holoubek thought that looking into Vaněček's death was worthwhile. They barely knew each other, according to his account.'

'Why do we do anything? To revisit our past. To set the record straight. You see, you young people think that history is fixed but your future can be changed. Actually, those of us who lived through Communism know that the past can be rewritten any number of times but your future depends on things you can't change. And because the past may change, it's important to learn how to forget. As I get older, I find it becomes easier. Nowadays I forget all sorts of things.' Benedikt smiled with a touch of resignation. 'Sometimes it's good to forget,' he added.

Chapter 6

Štajnhauzr was an impressive sight, waving his arms energetically to direct other policemen, pedestrians, onlookers and the television crew which had just arrived. He saw Slonský returning and marched across to him.

'Do you want the good news or the bad news first, Lieutenant?' he enquired.

'Let's get the bad news out of the way.'

'It won't make any sense unless I tell you the good news,' Štajnhauzr replied. 'The good news is they've found the van. The bad news is that it's in flames. However, there is potentially some *very* good news.'

'Has anyone ever told you you're an aggravating little sod?' asked Slonský.

'Yes, quite a few, but I ignore them. One of the officers who arrived first decided he couldn't put the fire out, but he might be able to preserve some evidence, so he used his toolkit to get the steering wheel out of the van.'

Slonský was astonished. 'It could have exploded at any time,' he gasped.

'Yes, but that's Officer Trousil for you; full of guts, or no brains at all, depending on how you want to look at it. Anyway, he's bringing the wheel over to give to the forensics team.'

'Team? What team? There's Novák, but I haven't seen any others.'

'I assumed there'd be more coming.'

'I don't think there are any more. And if there were, I bet Novák wouldn't pay them overtime.'

Peiperová coughed gently.

'I've got names and addresses, sir, but there's not much useful from them, and the officer is asking if he can get them more coffee.'

Slonský glanced across at the makeshift pen where Krob was dealing manfully with the small crowd he had enclosed with his tape. The old detective motioned to Peiperová to follow and walked slowly across to see Krob.

'Officer Krob? A word, please. Peiperová will look after these people for a few minutes.'

Krob looked hugely relieved.

'Sir?'

'A job well done, lad. Very resourceful of you. Did you pay for the coffees yourself?'

'I got the coffee free, but I bought the cookies.'

'Got the receipt?'

Krob produced a sliver of paper from his notebook. Slonský took it, glanced at the total and repaid Krob for the biscuits.

'I'll get my expenses quicker than you, and with less argument.'

Slonský tried to address the witnesses, but they were too busy haranguing Peiperová. Some wanted to go, whereas others were happy to stay if further coffee was likely to be forthcoming.

'Quiet!' yelled Slonský. 'Thank you all for your assistance. The ladies can all go. Officer Peiperová and I will talk to each of the men as quickly as possible. Please give your names and addresses to Officer Krob while you're waiting.'

Krob wondered whether this meant he had been involuntarily transferred to the criminal police, but the truth was much more prosaic. Slonský had merely taken his assistance for granted.

The crowd was dispersing. They had been questioned, and it was getting too dark for them to see what was going on in the road, so there was no point in staying. Novák had completed his work and had supervised the removal of Holoubek's body. Despite Slonský's scepticism a trio of scenes of crime technicians had appeared and were combing the road surface. The traffic diversion was working as smoothly as could be hoped so Štajnhauzr was ready to leave the scene and belatedly end his shift.

'Štajnhauzr,' Slonský called. 'Could you do me a favour?'

'If I can, Lieutenant.'

'Could you drop Officer Peiperová back at her barracks? She'll give you the address.'

Štajnhauzr agreed readily, and Peiperová thanked Slonský. Although exhilarated by her first real case, she was dead on her feet.

'I'll see you at seven,' said Slonský. 'Wear civvies. We're going to find Holoubek's flat and search it, so dress appropriately.'

'Yes, sir.'

Peiperová was about to salute, but recognised just in time that saluting when you are in plain clothes looks silly. She followed Štajnhauzr to his car and left Slonský to have a few words with Novák.

'Anything useful on the wheel?'

'Yes, a plastic bag, and it's staying that way until I can get it back to the lab.'

'Come on, Novák. It wouldn't be hard to do a quick test for fingerprints.'

'No, it wouldn't,' Novák conceded, 'but it might ruin other trace evidence, spoil the evidence trail, introduce contamination and make me even later for my supper than I already am.'

'Do you want to pack up and join me for a beer and sausage somewhere?'

Novák looked Slonský in the eye. 'Do I look like the sort of person who is devoted to beer and sausage?'

'No,' said Slonský, 'but you could slum it for once. We don't all sip kabinett Riesling and suck anchovies for fun.'

Novák looked at his watch.

'All right. Just the one. You can have what you like, but we're going somewhere that does a decent glass of red, and you're paying.'

Slonský draped an arm round Novák's shoulders.

'Of course, old friend. You'll enjoy it, trust me.'

'Trust?' stammered Novák. 'You?'

'I thought I might find you here,' said Navrátil, who could not help noticing a number of beer glasses on the table, along with Novák's head. 'What happened to Novák?'

'He's tired,' Slonský explained. 'It's lifting all those heavy glasses.'

'Novák drank this much?'

'No, Novák drank two glasses. With a teeny-weeny double schnapps in each.'

'You spiked his drink?'

'Of course not, Navrátil. What do you take me for? I ordered and he said "I'll have what you're having", so he only has himself to blame.'

'I thought Novák only drank wine.'

'And from now on he probably will. But it's been educational for him. He now knows what a beer tastes like.'

'No, he doesn't,' said Navrátil. 'He knows what a beer tastes like after it's been spiked with a double schnapps.'

'Good point,' agreed Slonský. 'Now, are we going to engage in Jesuitical debate all night or have you got something for me?'

'It was Vaněček's house. He told his neighbour — a policeman called Majer — that he had been stitched up for crossing an StB operation.'

'Holoubek said that.'

'So he did. But the story Holoubek had isn't the same as Majer tells. Holoubek said it was to do with currency offences, whereas Majer says it was an underground publishing press.'

Slonský shrugged his shoulders expansively. 'Does it matter? And do we have any reason to favour one story over the other?'

'Majer has a more detailed story.'

'Maybe Majer just has a better imagination. Anything else?'

'Majer doesn't think Vaněček died in his garden. There's no fence he could have fallen on.'

'Isn't now or wasn't then?'

'Both.'

Slonský gulped a large, satisfying mouthful.

'I knew it. So who came for Vaněček?'

'Probably StB. Majer knew nothing about it beforehand, so it's unlikely to have been ordinary police.'

'Hang fire, young Navrátil. We'd tell them now, but it didn't always happen then. It's suggestive, but not conclusive.'

'Fair enough. But they came for him after he'd been retired a few months. He was telling everyone he'd been hard done by.'

'Are you going to sit down? If you are, I'll give you a hand to shift Novák.'

'It's all right, sir. I'll get a stool.'

A waiter glided alongside the table.

'A large glass for my young friend. Novák says he has had enough. And if you can persuade the horse to give another sample, you can refill that.'

Navrátil had his notebook open.

'I wasn't going to have a drink, sir.'

'Nonsense. You can't watch me drinking. I'll feel lonely. And, as you know because I've told you so, beer is the essential lubricant that moves the cogs of the Slonský brain. Even that example of farmyard urine. Now, exercise your own brain. What could have provoked the StB to come back for Vaněček after he had retired? For some reason, they wanted him removed. They'd be pushing on an open door with the police force then, because that's what most police seem to have wanted too. But they'd achieved that. Why do they need to beat him up and kill him?'

'Was the killing an accident, or deliberate?'

Slonský mulled it over.

'Holoubek didn't voice any suspicions, and he knew more than we do. Maybe it was just an interrogation that went wrong.'

'And the suspect ended up dead?'

'Oh, it happened all the time, lad. You didn't know he had a dicky heart, or sometimes they did themselves in for fear of further pain.'

'How could they do that? Weren't they searched for anything that could harm them?'

'Yes, but I've known one throw himself down a stairwell. Mucha will recall that one; if I remember rightly he was at the foot of the stairs when the fellow landed. Do we know where Vaněček was buried?'

'No, sir.'

'Find out first thing tomorrow. If it's a grand affair it was probably an accident. When it's deliberate they don't care what people think of the headstone.'

Navrátil noted the order on his pad.

'So they remove him,' Slonský continued, 'but they give him a smart house in the country outside Prague. That looks to me like an endgame. That's saying to Vaněček "This is where it stops, so make the most of your new home, because

255

you're history now." Then two or three months later they're back to give him a hard time.'

'Majer says he'd been writing letters and mouthing off trying to get himself reinstated.'

'Then he really was as big an idiot as Holoubek said. But they could have ignored that. In those days he wouldn't get an audience if they didn't want him to. So we're drawn to the conclusion that Vaněček knew something and was threatening to reveal it. And that might be about the Válková case, or it might not. We'll have to see what Vaněček was up to during that time that could account for it. First thing tomorrow see if his personnel file is still in existence. I doubt it, but these things get overlooked.'

'I thought I was looking for his grave first thing tomorrow?'

'You are. And you're looking for his personnel record. You'll have to learn to multitask if you're going to make it to the top, lad.'

'Can you multitask then, sir?'

'Yes. I can drink coffee and write out your dismissal notice at the same time. Now, drink up your beer and then you can help me get Novák to your car. You can drop him off on your way home.'

'Where does he live, sir?'

'I don't know, Navrátil. You'll have to find out. That's what being a detective is all about.'

Chapter 7

It was ten to seven, and Peiperová was standing in front of Slonský's desk.

'Sit down, girl, and stop making the place look untidy. Untidier than it actually is, anyway.'

'Thank you, sir. Where, sir?'

'Have Navrátil's chair. He's going to be a few minutes late today. It seems one of his drinking companions spent the night on his sofa and he has to take him home first.'

Peiperová's face betrayed her thoughts.

'It's all right, Peiperová. Navrátil was the essence of sobriety. I was with them myself.'

Peiperová relaxed.

'Sober, assuming Navrátil went straight home, that is. Now, young lass, we have to find Holoubek's flat, get the key, and search it. Navrátil has his own list of jobs but will doubtless want to come and play with us later.'

'Do we have any leads, sir?'

'No, Peiperová, because this is not a dog-walking club. You've been watching too many detective shows on television. In real life you have to go out and find your own leads, because nobody gives them to you. We know the tram stop he normally gets off at, so we can assume it's easier to get to that one than any other. We also, thanks to the little woman shaped like an outdoor privy that you found, know which direction he walked in after he left the tram. But our best clue is that he was a policeman, and therefore probably drew a policeman's pension, which, pitiful as it is, is still enough to keep his old body and soul together. Until they were separated by a dark blue Volkswagen Multivan.'

'Were there any clues in the van, sir?'

'A very good question, Peiperová, and one I shall be pursuing with Novák when he sobers up. In the meantime, here's a telephone number. Do you have a mobile phone?'

'Yes, sir.'

'Good. Then let's exchange numbers. I'll get you a police issue mobile as soon as Captain Lukas signs it off. The police pensions office won't be open yet, so you can call in a little while. When you get the address off them, give me a call. We'll see if the local council have a name for the landlord.'

'Couldn't he own it himself, sir?'

'Peiperová, where's your sense of history? When Holoubek was earning, private property was a no-no in the Czech Republic, remember? And when it became possible to buy flats again, I doubt if anyone would give a mortgage to a retired man living on a pension.' Slonský shook his head sadly. 'How soon they forget,' he murmured.

Whatever he was about to say to Peiperová, he was interrupted by the sound of his telephone ringing.

'Slonský,' he answered.

'Bastard,' said the caller before hanging up.

Slonský replaced the receiver carefully.

'Sounds like Novák has made it to his office,' he said.

Peiperová had departed, and Slonský had managed to catch Lukas as the latter was hanging his coat up.

'All going well?' he asked.

'Not really,' replied Slonský. 'An old man has been run over deliberately, perhaps because he was trying to reopen a dodgy police enquiry from thirty years ago, the van that did it has gone up in smoke, a second death from the past appears to be very suspicious though the police didn't think so at the time, perhaps because they did it, I'm baby-sitting two officers with a combined age of about eighteen who keep looking at each other like rabbits, and Novák is abusing me down the phone because he lost count of his drinks last night. Apart from that, everything's fine.'

'Good, good,' said Lukas. 'I can't do much about Peiperová, but she's a bright girl and no doubt she'll be a considerable help to you.'

'Actually, she already is,' agreed Slonský, 'and she'd be even more help if she had a mobile phone so I can find her.'

Lukas opened his drawer and signed a chit.

'I can trust you to fill in the details, I hope?'

'Of course, sir.'

'But I've taken the precaution of specifying a single mobile phone in case you were planning to take a market stall this weekend.'

'Very wise of you, sir. My police salary doesn't go very far.'

'Join the club. And you don't even have daughters.'

'Yes, sir. How are … they?' asked Slonský, who had utterly forgotten their names.

'Both well, thank you. Eva has completed her teacher training now, and Eliška is studying the viola at the conservatory. Of course, neither has an income, so they both depend on their poor father.'

'It's just as well you're a captain, then, sir. On a lieutenant's salary, one of them would starve.'

'I was a lieutenant once, Slonský. You can manage if you're prudent.'

There was a gentle rap on the half-open door, and Navrátil poked his face into the office.

'Just letting you know I've delivered Dr Novák, sir, so I'm here now.'

'Well, why are you here, Navrátil? Aren't you supposed to be finding Vaněček's grave and his personnel record?' asked Slonský.

'Yes, sir. I'll set off now.'

'Just a minute, Navrátil,' Lukas exclaimed.

'Sir?'

'I just wanted to congratulate you on those burglary statistics. A first class piece of work. Of course, it bore out my contention that things are getting better in the face of some ill-informed comments from local politicians, but it's good to have hard facts to back up one's argument. Well done, young man.'

Navrátil blushed, which Lukas interpreted as embarrassment at being praised, rather than sheepish acknowledgement of the fact that they were the fruit of his imagination, as Slonský was quick to remind him obliquely.

'Yes, well done, Navrátil. I don't know how he did it so quickly, sir.'

'A keen head for figures, no doubt,' chuckled Lukas. 'We'd better watch you closely, Navrátil. If you're this good with statistics Klinger will have another try to seduce you into joining the fraud squad.'

Navrátil forced a smile as he left. Klinger had, indeed, made a previous attempt to persuade Navrátil to join him upstairs, but the young detective, while flattered to be asked, found Klinger's obsession with order and detail too wearing to contemplate working there. Klinger was a man who folded sheets of paper precisely in half with the care of an origami adept before shredding them, and Navrátil found that just a little spooky. Well, quite a bit spooky actually.

'Did you know an officer called Vaněček, sir?' Slonský asked.

'I didn't really know him. Knew of him, of course. Came to a sticky end.'

'Allegedly impaled on his garden fence, sir.'

Lukas winced.

'I meant his career, actually. I didn't know about his death.'

'The snag with the police report from 1979 is that he apparently died on a fence that wasn't there.'

'Some mistake, surely.'

'A fairly elaborate mistake, if you ask me. We'll try to retrieve the file, if it still exists. I'll add that to Navrátil's list. What do you know about the incident that led to his dismissal, sir?'

Lukas paused to collect his thoughts before speaking.

'He had been having a bit of difficulty with the StB for some time. Vaněček had his deficiencies as a policeman, but he was quite clear that we couldn't do our jobs if the security forces didn't keep us informed. He had complained a couple of times that Tripka was too much in the StB's pocket. That was Colonel Tripka's father, of course.'

'And Major Tripka, as he then was, was the StB liaison officer for the police.'

'That's right. But that's the point. He was supposed to be "for the police"; our man in their camp. There were suspicions that he was more like their man in our camp. Anyway, there was a crime reported by a hotel. I think a guest's briefcase had been forced open and important papers taken. Vaněček launched an inquiry, only for Tripka to announce that the case had been opened during an StB raid. Vaněček was livid. He complained to his superiors that his men had wasted valuable time, and — more to the point — the guest was a foreigner who would go home with a poor impression of the Czech police if they didn't make a real effort to restore his property. The interior ministry ordered the StB to return the papers so that Vaněček could give them back to the foreigner, but Vaněček was instructed to say that they had been stolen by an opportunist who didn't speak English and didn't realise what he'd taken. I remember that case quite well, because I was one of the policemen who had to interview all the hotel staff. I wasn't around when the StB got their own back, but none of us was in any doubt that that was exactly what they had done. It was several months later, and they claimed that Vaněček had fouled up one of their operations. He was removed and forced to retire.'

'According to his ex-neighbour, who was also a policeman, Vaněček refused to go quietly and that's why the StB came back for him a few months after retirement.'

Lukas said nothing for a few moments, and Slonský had no intention of filling the silence, believing that there may be more to tell.

'If he did,' said Lukas, 'he was stupid. The StB wouldn't let him tell his story. The snag is that we don't really know what that story was — or do we? Are you keeping something up your sleeve?'

'No, I'm not. I genuinely don't know what to think. Even if Vaněček was hard done by, I don't see why he needed to be eliminated. They could have ignored him. Unless, of course, he had hard evidence. But if he did, I don't know what it could be or where he kept it. I'll bet the StB took that house at Zdiby to pieces looking for it.'

'So where do you start?'

'My head tells me to start with Holoubek. He's the most recent one by thirty years, and we've got forensics to help. But my heart says it all starts with Válková. She's the innocent one in all this. You can argue that Vaněček brought it on himself, and that Holoubek did the same by trying to reopen the case.'

'He was ninety years old, for goodness' sake, Slonský. Whatever he knew, he didn't deserve to end his days under a truck.'

Slonský smacked his fist into his cupped hand.

'No, you're right, sir. He didn't. No-one does.'

Lukas rose from his seat and walked round to perch on the corner of the desk.

'I would back you to find the killer of Jana Válková if anyone can. You're an obstinate, insubordinate, disorganised nuisance and the bane of my life much of the time, but you're also the best detective I've got. Now, get your chin up and tell me how you're going to do it. Who is doing what?'

'Novák is doing the forensics. Peiperová is looking for Holoubek's flat so we can search it. Mucha is trying to find the original file on the Válková killing. I'll ask him to try to find Vaněček's too. Navrátil is hunting out Vaněček's grave and his personnel record.'

'Why his grave?'

Slonský shrugged. 'It helps me.'

'Fair enough. It sounds like a good plan. But I need hardly remind you to be careful. Someone who would kill a ninety-year-old won't baulk at further violence.'

'You needn't worry about me, sir.'

'I wasn't. I was reminding you to worry about Navrátil and Peiperová.'

'Oh. I do, sir, I do.'

When Slonský set out to join Peiperová he found Mucha at the front desk hanging his coat up.

'Got something for you.'

'Two plane tickets to Jamaica? The keys to a new BMW?'

'Better than that.'

Mucha offered a dog-eared dusky red folder. A paper label gummed to the top right hand corner described its contents.

'I can't read this here. Let's go to my office.'

Slonský could hardly contain his excitement and bounded up the stairs in pairs, while Mucha ran along behind, vainly trying to get his second boot off. The first was behind the front desk.

'Now, what have we here?'

Mucha pointed to the first page.

'List of contents.'

Slonský leafed through the sheets, skimming each briefly before moving on. After a few moments he paused, frowned, and began again. Without commenting he unlocked his desk drawer and took Holoubek's folder out, reading from each of the folders in turn.

'This is odd. Holoubek has copies of pages that aren't here.'

'Do you know when he made them?'

'Shortly after the sentence was passed. Do you know the file history?'

'Yes, I checked that while I was up at records. The file was taken into permanent store on 8th September, 1976.'

'That's less than eight weeks after the crime. The investigation and trial whizzed along.'

'It's the day after Bartoš was executed. See the last page for a copy of the warrant.'

'Has it been taken out since?'

'Who knows? We've got records since 1990, and it hasn't left the building, though that doesn't preclude someone consulting it at the library desk. But here's an odd thing. Count the pages.'

Slonský hurried to obey.

'Fifty-three.'

'Now look at the 1990 cataloguing docket on the front.'

'"Number of pages: fifty-nine." Someone's had six since 1990.'

'Apparently without taking it out, and right under the eyes of the library staff.'

Slonský pushed the files to one side so he could get his feet on the corner of the desk.

'Curiouser and curiouser. The only people who could go to records and get their hands on this file are police officers. If anyone took six pages out, it has to be a police officer. But why?'

'I was sort of hoping you'd want to know who.'

'Well, who and why, I suppose. Find out why and we'll know who.'

'Find out who and you might know why.'

'I'll have to read this closely and see if I can work out where the pages have been taken from.'

'I found one. The account of the first interview with Bartoš in prison is missing page five. The pages are numbered in the bottom corner.'

Slonský checked for himself.

'Not only that, old friend, this front page is either a ringer or there was a fib in the original papers. This is described as the first police interview with Bartoš, but it says it took place in Prague, whereas we know that Bartoš was first interviewed in the remand prison in Olomouc. And that interview isn't here at all. How did you get this?'

'I tried the truth. Honesty is always the best policy, my old mother used to tell me.'

'I'm surprised you've got on in this police force, with an attitude like that.'

'It's obviously held me back, because I'm just a sergeant and you're a mighty lieutenant.'

'I think that has more to do with your legendary refusal to apply for promotions.'

'I applied while I was getting them,' Mucha objected. 'It's just that once they turned me down I didn't want to face that disappointment again by reapplying.'

'Three of the pages Holoubek copied aren't here. Then we know page five of the prison interview is missing. So that leaves two more we don't know about. Not yet, anyway.'

'Why not just take the whole file?'

'You're checked for files when you leave, aren't you? It wouldn't have been easy to get a whole folder out. Besides, if it was missing altogether it might have provoked comment one day. With the incriminating pages removed, it's less of a threat, and there's just a chance we'd flick through it, not notice the editing and put it back.'

'Bit daft leaving the label on the front, then.'

'Who would count the pages?' asked Slonský.

'Well, me for a start,' replied Mucha. 'And Klinger would.'

'That's true,' admitted Slonský. 'Klinger would count them, line them up and straighten the edges. But we knew it had been edited because we had pages that weren't here and should have been. Our murderer doesn't know what Holoubek gave us.'

'Then why kill Holoubek?'

'Ah, good point. Though he might kill Holoubek because he feared Holoubek knew more than he actually did. The truth is unimportant. It's what the murderer *thought* Holoubek knew that caused his actions.'

Mucha picked up his boot.

'Too deep for me. I'm going back to vegetate at the front desk.'

'So we've signed this out for use in an investigation?'

'I said you needed it because the case was being reviewed for reopening.'

'That's good. So I can keep it as long as I need.'

'Yes. But even if I hadn't said that, you would have kept it as long you wanted anyway, wouldn't you?'

Left alone, Slonský concentrated on the file Mucha had brought him. Naturally indolent, Slonský rarely exerted himself, but these were precisely the circumstances that triggered his fastest work. Within a few minutes he had compared the watermarks in the paper and concluded that page one of the Bartoš interview report had been retyped after the other pages. The paper was old, but it was made by a different factory. That was not quite conclusive, because he knew that officers like himself might grab fresh paper from other people's shelves in a hurry, which might be a different batch, but it was a hint that someone might have removed something of importance. There was nothing in the file to indicate that Bartoš had ever been in prison in Olomouc, but then Slonský realised belatedly that he only had Holoubek's word that he had been there, so he made a note to get Navrátil to check that too. A few sums led him to conclude that Bartoš might yet have family living somewhere. His mother would be in her early eighties, if not older, but it would be worth tracking her down if she were still alive. He allocated that job to Peiperová, then decided that Navrátil would do it better. On the other hand, Peiperová had to start somewhere.

No sooner had he thought of her again than his telephone rang and he found that she was calling him.

'I wondered when you expected to get here, sir.'

'Where is here?'

'Holoubek's flat, sir.'

'When you tell me where it is, Peiperová,' Slonský replied testily.

'I left a message on your answerphone about an hour ago, sir.'

'I don't have an answerphone.'

'Yes, you do, sir. Is there a little red light flashing at the top of your phone?'

'Yes.'

'That's to tell you I've left you a message.'

'The flaw in this plan, Peiperová, is that I have no idea how to retrieve it.'

'When I hang up, sir, just press the message key. It'll ask for your PIN number. Put that in, and it will play my message back.'

'But I don't have a PIN.'

'Then it's probably the factory default, sir. It might be 0000, but Sergeant Tomáš's phone was 2512.'

'I've got a better idea, Peiperová. Why don't you just tell me what the message was?'

'Very well, sir. I've found his flat. If you come to the end of Táborská where we found him, I'll show you where it is.'

'That's better, officer. I'm on my way. Meanwhile, you can do something very important for me.'

'Sir?'

'Find me a coffee and a pastry and keep them warm.'

Peiperová was waiting patiently by the front door with a small carrier bag in her hand.

'Didn't you want one?' asked Slonský.

'I didn't see any point in letting it go cold, sir.'

Slonský tried the coffee. It was still warm.

'Got the key?'

Peiperová held it up.

'You can do it. I've got my hands full. Nice pastry, this. You made a good choice.'

Peiperová placed the key in the lock, stepped outside the door frame, and turned it.

'And what was the point of the little sidestep, pray?' Slonský enquired.

'In case it was booby-trapped, sir.'

'I see. So if it exploded you would only lose a hand instead of being killed.'

'I suppose so, sir.'

'Whereas I would be decorating the passageway because you didn't think to tell me of your precaution.'

'Sorry, sir. I thought you would know what I was doing.'

'I never know what anyone else is doing, Peiperová. Always assume that I'm completely ignorant, then make it your job to ensure that I'm not ignorant.'

'Yes, sir. Shall we go in? Watch the rug on the polished floor.'

Slonský followed her into the flat, and watched with approval as Peiperová donned evidence gloves before touching the door handles. He closed the front door by nudging it with his rear end.

'Nice flat. Small, but neat. Let's treat this as a training opportunity, Peiperová. What do you deduce?'

'About what, sir?'

'About Holoubek.'

Peiperová looked around slowly.

'He's been widowed a long time. There's no sign of a female touch. No flowers or bright colours. But his clothes are all hung up and there are shoes in the cupboard in pairs. He took a pride in his appearance. There's very little dust, so he must have had a cleaner.'

'I doubt it. A policeman's pension doesn't run to a cleaner. And cleaners don't organise your pantry like that.' He pointed to a series of jars with large handwritten labels.

'Everything is well looked after. The radio is old but still working and I haven't seen a television like that for years.'

Slonský knelt behind the television with his pastry jammed in his mouth to free a hand. When he stood up, he had a broad smile.

'The crafty old codger,' he said admiringly.

'Sir?'

'Come along, girl. You've got eyes. What do you see?'

'An old television.'

'And?'

'Is it broken? It isn't plugged in like the radio was.'

Slonský plugged it in and turned it on.

'Evidently not broken, then.'

He turned the television back off and removed the plug from the socket.

'I'm sorry, sir. I don't know what you're hinting at.'

'The television works, but is unplugged. There could be lots of reasons for that. But when I see a screwdriver on the shelf behind the television — and the television has been moved forward to let someone as big as me get behind it — coupled with my knowledge that Holoubek was a policeman who must have searched hundreds of houses, I draw a definite conclusion. He unplugged the television so as not to kill himself, because he used the screwdriver to take the back off it, and he did that because he used it as a hiding place for something he didn't want anyone to find. What more natural than to guess that this is where those copies he gave us have been kept? He retrieved them just before he came out and if he'd made it back home he'd have put his room back in good order.'

'Why hide them, sir?'

'Habit? Fear? A belief that they're still being looked for by others? Who knows? Now, it would be a dereliction of duty if we didn't take the back off and look for ourselves.'

Suiting action to the word, he swallowed the last bite of pastry, took a slurp of coffee and knelt behind the television.

'Adhesive tape residue on the inside of the upper surface, but no more papers. Now then, Peiperová, we have to take this place to bits. And in view of our discovery, that means taking bits to bits too.'

People told Peiperová that Slonský was idle, but his assiduous searching gave the lie to that. They had found nothing to do with the case, but Peiperová found an address for Holoubek's son.

'We'd best stop and tell him the sad news. It's not too far away. No need to take your car.'

'Just as well, sir. I haven't got a car.'

'So how did you get here?'

'By tram, sir, the same way Holoubek got to our office.'

'So how do you plan to get back?'

'In your car, sir.'

'I haven't got a car either. Or, more accurately, I haven't brought one with me. You can never park the thing anyway. Come on, we'll walk.'

They were still on their way when Slonský's mobile phone rang. He glanced at the screen.

'Novák. Must be important. He never rings me.'

Slonský ducked into a doorway to answer the call.

'Have you rung to swear at me again?'

'No, business before pleasure, Slonský. I thought you'd like to know that the steering wheel came up trumps. We've got a lot of prints including a nice clear set from the right hand and some partials from the left.'

'Excellent. Have we got a match—'

'Yes. It goes on getting better and better. They belong to a man called Roman Pluskal.'

'What's on his record?'

'Everything apart from murder and riding a bike without lights. He was a rent collector for some local bad boys. It'll probably mean more to you than to me, but he sounds like just the sort of person who would do a bit of driving for someone.'

'Good work, Novák. I owe you a drink.'

'No, thank you,' replied Novák primly, and hung up.

Ondřej Holoubek was at work, but a neighbour knew the school where he taught. The principal sent for Ondřej and lent the detectives his office so they could speak undisturbed.

'Dead? How?'

'He was run over by a van driver, I'm afraid. The doctor says he didn't suffer.'

'Poor Dad. To make it to his age and then…'

'Are you all right, sir? Can I get you anything?' asked Peiperová.

'I'm fine, thank you. But poor Dad. Poor, poor Dad.'

'Did you know he'd been to see us twice recently?'

'I knew he'd been once. He told me he went the other day. I didn't know he'd been back.'

'Yes, sir, yesterday. He was killed as he returned home. I'm afraid it wasn't an accident.'

Ondřej sat up as if an electric shock had been passed through him.

'Not an accident? You mean it was deliberate? Someone murdered him?'

'Yes, sir. We're working on the basis that the motive for killing him was connected to his visit to us. Do you know what he wanted to tell us?'

'Yes. At least, I know the general story, but not the detail. He was obsessed with a case from thirty years ago. He believed an innocent man was hanged and he wanted to put that right.'

'There's not much you can do for someone who's been hanged, sir.'

'You can restore their good name, Lieutenant.'

'What more did you know, sir? Did he discuss his plans with you?'

'No, he didn't. To be honest, I'd have tried to discourage him. I'd probably have failed, because he was a stubborn old devil, but I'd have tried.'

Slonský gave Ondřej a card.

'If you come across anything that could help us, I'd be grateful for a call.'

'Of course. Thank you for coming to tell me in person. Where is he now?'

'He's at the mortuary. I'm afraid we have to conduct a post-mortem on him, but as soon as we can we'll release him to you.'

'Can I see him?'

'I'll make a call to see where we stand on that, sir. Will you excuse me a moment?'

Slonský retired to the corridor to ring Novák, who said that the body would be ready to view by the time Ondřej got there. Slonský rang for a car to pick them up and take Ondřej to the mortuary and then home again.

Slonský was impatient to ask questions but Novák was determined to take Ondřej into the viewing room personally. However, as he ushered Ondřej through the door, Novák handed a printout to Slonský.

'This is interesting,' said Slonský. 'Pluskal has a varied record. Assault, drunk and disorderly, assault again, assault when drunk and disorderly, possession of narcotics with intent to supply, assault, obtaining money with menaces and another assault. Connected with the Griba gang.'

'Who or what is Griba?' Peiperová asked.

'Good question. Griba runs a mob who do all sorts of naughty things, chiefly involving drugs, illegal gambling and prostitution. They also run a little protection racket.'

'So if we know all this, why haven't we stopped them?'

'Well, there you are. The courts keep asking for evidence. I've complained about it, but I get nowhere. And the evidence we get never quite stands up. Witnesses change their minds, exhibits get lost or damaged, people unexpectedly emigrate — you know the sort of thing. You stay here and see young Holoubek gets home. I'll call you with instructions in half an hour or so.'

'Where are you going, sir?'

'I'm off to see a hairdresser.'

Armed with confirmation from the hairdresser that the person she had seen in the van was Pluskal, Slonský called Mucha to arrange for all officers to be alerted to watch for him.

'Tell them not to try tackling him single-handed,' said Slonský. 'It could be dangerous.'

'Don't worry,' Mucha told him. 'As soon as they see the word dangerous the risk that they'll try to arrest him will drop to zero.'

'Any ideas where he might be?'

'I'd be surprised if the drugs squad weren't well informed on Griba and his men. I'll ask Tripka.'

'You do that. Has Navrátil returned yet?'

'Yes, a couple of hours ago. I looked in on him and I'm pleased to report he isn't sitting in your chair, even though you aren't there.'

'Is he doing anything useful or is he gazing at a photo of Peiperová?'

'Are they an item, then?'

'Heading that way. He's young. He'll learn.'

'Isn't young love wonderful?'

'Not just wonderful, but nauseating. Don't let him leave till I get there. Use reasonable force or hide his shoes, whichever works better. What about Peiperová?'

'No sign of her.'

Slonský rang Peiperová and directed her back to Holoubek's flat to continue the search. Since time was of the essence during a murder enquiry he restricted his coffee break to twenty minutes, during which he fortified the inner man with a *párek*, having been bewitched by the smell of sausage when attempting to walk past the stall.

Navrátil was on his knees on the floor of the office. The contents of a folder were strewn around him, and he was busy affixing sticky notes to several of the pages.

'Anything of interest, Navrátil?'

'It seems that Vaněček was cremated and his ashes were scattered because no family could be traced.'

'But Majer said that Mrs Vančková moved out after Vaněček's death, so why didn't she try to claim the body?'

'Is it possible the record is wrong, sir? Wouldn't she have kicked up a stink if we hadn't given the body back?'

'Privately, but she wouldn't have any mechanism to do so under the old regime. If the StB didn't return a body, who could you complain to?'

Navrátil digested the information and pondered over it for a few moments.

'Sir, didn't Vaněček have friends in high places?'

'He must have done at one time. But it's amazing how quickly they forget you when the StB reels you in.'

'But wasn't there anyone among them who wouldn't be scared of the StB? Wouldn't anyone speak up for him?'

'Not a snowball's chance, lad. In a Czech popularity list he would have come just below Heydrich once he was in custody. But where did you get your information?'

'His personnel file, sir. I've marked the relevant pages. He left the service in May 1977. It says that he was disciplined for interference in a security operation, demoted to Major and retired with a pension. That sounds harsh to me.'

'It sounds bloody generous to me. A lot of people wouldn't have stayed out of jail, kept any rank or got a pension.'

'He moved to Zdiby and then it records that his pension ceased after he was arrested for disseminating anti-State propaganda, whatever that means.'

'It means moaning, lad. Any date for that?'

'Pension ceased 24th May 1979.'

'Anything else useful?'

'Two things, sir. He died at Pankrác Prison, so he may be in the records there. And between the end of the Bartoš case and his demotion he was working on a profiteering enquiry.'

'No more details?'

'No, sir. It just says it was bourgeois anti-social profiteering.'

'Aha!' Slonský cried, causing Navrátil to jump a little. 'You don't speak the lingo, Navrátil, but that's a sort of code for anti-corruption work. He was tracking down people who counted who had lined their pockets. That won't have made him popular either. We need to find out if anyone was prosecuted as a result of that investigation. A lot of the old StB files are still around and we'll have to check whether any of them mention him. That's a big job, so get the address and a pass from Mucha and stay there till you've checked it out.'

'Yes, sir. Do you think I'll find anything, sir?'

'I don't know. That's why you need to look. Generally speaking, Navrátil, I don't ask you to do things when I already know the answer. Unless you've annoyed me with stupid questions and I feel like wasting your time, of course.'

'Yes, sir. Sorry, sir.'

Slonský flopped into his chair.

'No, I'm sorry, lad. It wasn't as daft as I made out. Besides, I'm going to spoil your plans for a day or two. I'm going to take Peiperová on a long trip.'

'I thought I was your assistant, sir.'

'So you are, and it's a compliment to you that I think I can leave you to look through the StB archives without having to hold your hand. Peiperová is coming because I'm planning to look for Bartoš' family and I may need a female officer. I suppose the Slovaks might give us one, but it's safer to take my own. I'm planning to go tomorrow, spend a day or two on it and come back at the weekend. Don't worry, I'll make sure Peiperová has her own room in the hotel.'

'I'm sure I can trust you, sir.'

'Yes, that's the sad thing. You can. Twenty years ago … who knows?'

Lukas looked doubtful.

'I hope this is an efficient use of our resources, Slonský.'

'So do I, sir.'

'I can understand the need to speak to Mrs Bartošová if she is still alive…'

'I've checked with the local council, sir, and she is. She still lives in the same house as she did when Bartoš was hanged, in the country to the north of Dolný Kubín.'

'Couldn't we ask the local police to go?'

'They don't have enough background, sir. Besides, I like to see the whites of a witness's eyes when I question them.'

'Well, is it necessary to take Peiperová? That means two hotel rooms.'

'We could always share, sir, but she may snore.'

'Slonský! There is no question of your sharing a room, under any circumstances. Do I make myself clear?'

'Perfectly, sir. Thank you — she's a fit young woman and I'm not sure I'd be able to fight her off if she jumped on me.'

A tiny smile flickered on Lukas' face.

'I think the expression I'm looking for is "in your dreams", Slonský.'

'You may be right, sir, though I don't have those dreams anymore.'

Lukas scrawled a signature.

'Very well. But tell the Slovaks what you're up to, do it all by the book, don't upset anyone and come straight home afterwards. How is it going?'

'Peiperová is searching Holoubek's flat now, sir. I'm going to join her. Navrátil has Vaněček's personnel file. We know he was investigating corruption when he was sacked.'

'That's suggestive. Do we know whom he had in his sights?'

'Not yet, sir. While we're away, Navrátil will check the StB archives, but it's a long shot. The chances are that the villain was one of us, but we might strike lucky. And we know Vaněček's ashes were scattered, allegedly because he had no family, though we know his wife was still alive.'

'You know what that means, Slonský. The body was so badly damaged they couldn't risk letting his wife see it.'

'That explains the cremation, sir. It doesn't explain the scattering. A convicted criminal might be scattered, but Vaněček wasn't convicted. And as Navrátil points out, he must have had powerful friends. The StB can't have known how powerful. Surely they wouldn't want to risk upsetting anyone in high places.'

'I doubt if they cared. They were almost untouchable. And they'd have gauged the reaction to his arrest. I assume they'd have held him for a few days. Firm intervention might have saved him, but I'd hazard a guess that nobody lifted a finger. And when nobody made a fuss, they proceeded to maltreat him.'

'It would be interesting to know who Válek called to get Vaněček brought in, sir.'

'So it would, but you'd have to find Válek first.'

'I've got his address, sir. Holoubek found him.'

Lukas glanced at his watch.

'You've just got time to go and see him this afternoon.'

Navrátil was a little surprised to be told to leave Vaněček's personnel folder and fetch the car, but Slonský disliked driving around Prague if he could persuade someone else to do it.

'Shouldn't we ring first, sir?'

'No, Navrátil. We want to surprise him so he doesn't have time to make up a story.'

'It'll certainly be a surprise, sir. It's been thirty years since his daughter died.'

'I think we need to approach this interview with the maximum of tact, lad. Leave all the talking to me.'

Navrátil managed to stifle his response, but the keen observer would have seen his mouth drop open.

'Eyes on the road, lad. Bear right here and then left at the next junction.'

They found the apartment block and Slonský led the way up to the third floor. They knocked on a door that had once been cream but now looked slightly yellow. After a few moments and a lot of noisy shuffling the door was opened by a large old man walking with a crutch attached to his right elbow.

'Mr Válek?'

'Yes.'

'Lieutenant Slonský and Officer Navrátil.'

'Come in. The neighbours will have a field day if they see policemen here.'

'Are they inquisitive, then, sir?'

'Nosey bitches. Especially her across the corridor. Old cow.'

Válek sank into an armchair and indicated a similar chair and the sofa. Slonský took the chair.

'I'm sorry to bring this up after all this time, sir...'

'Jana. You've come to talk about Jana. Have you found the other man?'

'It's more complicated than that, sir. You'll recall that a man called Bartoš was hanged for killing her.'

'Yes, I remember. How could I ever forget? He took my precious girl from me.'

'That's the problem, sir. He didn't.'

Válek reddened and glowered at them.

'Don't talk nonsense. He was convicted and hanged. He did it.'

'I'm afraid he can't have done, sir. He was in prison for something else at the time.'

Now Válek blanched.

'In prison? But surely you knew that?'

'We did, sir. I'm trying to find out why we ignored the fact. But, more to the point, we've reopened your daughter's case and I've been assigned to finding her real killer.'

'Killers, Lieutenant. There were two of them.'

'That's my first question, sir. Why did they stop looking when they charged Bartoš? You knew there were two, and they must have known there were two as well. Didn't you press them to keep looking?'

'I certainly did. That fat pompous officer — what was his name? — the one my wife persuaded them to appoint.'

'Vaněček.'

'Vaněček! That's him. Bloody useless. We'd have been better off keeping that stringy one who was on it at first. At least he was a proper detective. Vaněček couldn't find his own backside with a map.'

'May I ask, sir, how your wife had Vaněček appointed?'

Válek rubbed his hands together as if he were washing them.

'Her sister was married to an army general. My wife rang her sister to tell her what had happened, and my sister-in-law said her husband would make sure the best man was put on the job. He'd served with Vaněček in the army, so he rang him for suggestions, and Vaněček said he would take it on himself. At the time we thought that was the best possible arrangement. It soon became clear that he was a clueless imbecile.'

'Are your sister-in-law and her husband still alive, sir?'

'No, neither of them. General Mikula died ten years ago, and my sister-in-law followed last year.'

'I'm sorry to hear that, sir. You were going to explain why the search was stopped.'

'It was Vaněček. He told us he'd got a confession from this man Bartoš, but Bartoš had given a statement that didn't mention an accomplice. It was therefore clear that Kopecký must have been mistaken. He advised us not to mention the second man because if the court thought the confession was wrong about that the judges might throw it out altogether and then Bartoš would go free.'

'Did you believe that, sir?'

'I'm not a lawyer, Lieutenant. I can't argue with people who know how the courts work. But I have to admit that I didn't think Kopecký would be wrong. He was an interfering busybody but he had eyes like a hawk.'

'In what way was he interfering, sir?'

'He wanted the street kept exclusive. He started a residents' association and we had all kinds of rules about when the garbage had to go out and where it could be put. All that sort of thing. But he was an honest man and his wife was lovely with Jana. Are they still around?'

273

'Yes, sir. We met them a few days ago.'

'I should give them a call,' muttered Válek. 'They were good neighbours.' He raised his voice. 'Not like that interfering woman across the hall.' He mopped his face with a large white handkerchief. 'Sorry. I'm all alone in the world now, you see. No-one to fight my battles for me. Wife's dead, poor Jana's dead, I've got nobody. The Kopeckýs were good friends. I just didn't appreciate that at the time. I'd like to talk to them again.'

'If you want to give me your details, I'll ask them if they want to make touch, sir.'
Válek nodded his thanks.

'If it's not too painful, sir, it would help us if you would talk us through the night your daughter was killed. I know it's a long time ago, but...'

'I'll never forget it, don't you worry. You can't forget a minute of a day like that. Memories don't work that way. My wedding day went past in a blur, but the 16th of July, 1976 is in my head forever.'

Válek closed his eyes for a moment while he decided where to start.

'I was manager of a kitchen electricals factory. We were close to sealing a deal to provide irons and toasters to Hungary. They were paying for them with hi-fi equipment, of all things. Goodness knows how I was meant to sell those, but that's what the ministry had agreed. The Hungarians were in town and the ministry threw a dinner for them. All of us who were negotiating deals were told to go. I didn't like going out on a Friday, but I didn't have a choice.'

'And you left Jana alone?'

'She sometimes went to a youth club on Friday nights, but I told her I didn't want her walking back home from the tram stop on her own. To be frank, I wasn't convinced that she would come home at the normal time if she knew we were out. She wasn't a bad girl, you understand, but you know what teenagers can be like. So I confined her to the house. She complained and asked if she could have some friends round. My wife agreed, thinking she meant the girls she used to hang around with.'

'But in fact she invited boys.'

'She must have done. She let them in and they had some beer together. The boys must have brought that. It wasn't mine. I didn't know Jana ever drank. She was only just seventeen.'

Válek's eyes were glistening as tears filmed them over. He paused to wipe them away with a thumb.

'We didn't know that she was friendly with any boys. Of course, we asked her best friends, but they swore they didn't know of any boyfriends either. There were one or two who lived nearby, but they didn't fit the description Kopecký gave. They all had longish hair. It was the fashion then.'

'So you have no idea who they were?'

'No, none at all.'

'Surely you didn't believe that Jana would have let Bartoš in and shared a beer with him?'

Válek nibbled his thumb in agitation.

'I couldn't see how they could possibly have known one another. They just wouldn't move in the same circles. And he was a dozen years older than her at least. But Vaněček was very persuasive. He told us we obviously knew very little about our daughter's private life so how could we say that she didn't know Bartoš?'

Slonský checked that Navrátil was making notes of the conversation.

'So you went out, sir, and you came in — when?'

'About half past one, I think. We were brought back by car because I'd been drinking so many toasts to those damn Hungarians. When we turned in to the road we saw the police cars and noticed that our front door was open. I ran in — a couple of police tried to stop me, but I pushed them off and told them I lived there — and I heard talking in the bathroom. When I ran in there I found Jana. It was horrible. That skinny policeman pushed me outside and sat me down in the lounge with my wife. He told me what had happened. That's it, I think. I remember the policeman went outside and yelled at the pair by the front door. Something about sending them to the tiniest police station in the Tatra mountains. After a while they let us go in to see her. They had put her on a trolley and covered her with a sheet so only her face was showing.'

'Did you go to the court hearing, sir?'

Válek nodded.

'I wanted to see the murderous monster who took my baby. He looked such an insignificant little squirt. But he was only there for a few minutes. When they read out the charge he went berserk. I didn't catch what he shouted — he had quite a strong Slovak accent — but it was something about the police having tricked him into confessing. The judges ordered him taken away and they carried on without him.'

'Didn't his lawyer object to that?'

'His lawyer barely said a word. Mind you, he only looked like a kid himself. I don't know where they got him.'

'He doesn't seem to have known that Bartoš was in prison when the crime was committed. And when he was told, he doesn't seem to have made a fuss about it.'

'That figures. I don't think he would have known how. He was a novice.'

'You don't recall his name, by any chance?'

Válek hoisted himself out of the armchair without a word, and limped out of the room. When he returned, he had a large black loose-leaf folder.

'My scrapbook of the trial.'

Slonský and Navrátil goggled at each other.

'You've got a scrapbook? May we read it?'

'Be my guests, but I'd rather you didn't take it off me. I'll go and put the kettle on.'

Slonský flipped the cover over. There was a newspaper article and a photograph of Bartoš being bundled into court. The witnesses were right; he was very slightly built, almost like a jockey. There was a large man in uniform a couple of steps behind him.

'Isn't that Vaněček?' asked Navrátil.

'I think so.'

Slonský scanned the preamble rapidly. Suddenly he prodded the paper with his forefinger.

'There, Navrátil! Look who was lawyer for the defence.'

Navrátil gawped at the page.

'Here we go again,' he said.

Chapter 8

Lukas spat his coffee across the room.

'You need to interview whom?'

'The Minister of the Interior, sir.'

'Slonský, are you going to make a habit of this? Need I remind you that you arrested a Minister of the Interior and charged him, quite incorrectly, with murder?'

'That was the last one, sir. I'm not planning to charge this one.'

'I'm delighted to hear it. By the way, why are you still here?'

'Why are any of us here, sir? It's puzzled better minds than mine.'

'It's not a philosophical enquiry, Slonský. I thought you were going to Slovakia.'

Slonský had the grace to look embarrassed.

'It's Peiperová, sir. She needs some time to get herself ready.'

'Well, I'm very surprised. I thought she would be an organised young woman.'

'Yes, sir.'

'So why isn't she ready to go?'

'She's sleeping, sir. I may have overlooked telling her to knock off last night.'

'You left her searching Holoubek's flat all night?'

'It never occurred to me that she wouldn't stop when she'd done a full day, sir.'

'She's under your command, damn it! Of course she won't stop until you say.'

'She could have called me to remind me, sir.'

'She shouldn't need to.'

'And it wasn't all night, sir. She caught the night bus back to the barracks.'

'The night bus doesn't go to the barracks, man. She must have walked quite a distance, alone, at night. I'm surprised the guards let her in.'

'They didn't at first, sir. She doesn't have a Prague identity card yet and they wouldn't let her in with the one issued in Kladno. Fortunately Navrátil was able to vouch for her.'

'And I suppose he was just passing?'

'I believe she rang him, sir.'

'I'm very close to speechless, Slonský. I trust there will be no repetition of this shocking episode.'

'I'll certainly try my best, sir.'

'No, Slonský, you will not try. You will succeed.'

Slonský adopted his most innocent expression, as if to convey his extreme willingness to please.

'Don't do that, Slonský. You look like an illustration from *The Good Soldier Švejk*.'

'Yes, sir. Sorry, sir.'

'So explain to me why you want to interview the minister.'

'Dr Pilik was the defence lawyer when Bartoš was on trial, sir. He doesn't seem to have made much effort to keep him from the noose, and I'm curious to know why.'

'We need more than curiosity, Slonský. Are you alleging corruption?'

'Do you think I should, sir?'

'You don't have any evidence, Slonský,' yelled Lukas in exasperation. 'I grant it looks bad, but his client had confessed.'

'His client had allegedly confessed, sir, but since said client could not read or write, you'd have thought a lawyer might have questioned the confession. Not to mention asking about the missing accomplice, or what Bartoš was shouting about when he was manhandled out of the court, since he is said to have claimed that he had been induced to sign a false confession following promises made by a police officer.'

'Vaněček?'

'No, and that's another thing I want to ask him about. The statement was taken in Olomouc by another officer. Vaněček processed it, but who gave it to him, because he didn't go to Olomouc, and the statement arrived here before Bartoš did? The statement in the file is alleged to have been made in Prague, but I suspect it's the Olomouc one retyped.'

Lukas threw his pen petulantly onto his blotter.

'I suppose there are sufficient irregularities there to warrant an interview. We will go together. I'll clear it with the Director of Police and make an appointment. You'd best stay in Prague until we know when that will be. In the meantime, give the girl the day off. It's Friday and she'll probably want to go home to see her family for the weekend.'

'Yes, sir.'

Slonský made for the door.

'One last thing, Slonský. The last time you persuaded me to see a minister with you, you came close to wrecking both our careers. If you do anything untoward this time, I will leave you to sink on your own. In fact I'll hide the lifebelts. Is that clear?'

'It certainly is, sir. No lifebelts.'

Slonský telephoned Peiperová, apologising for waking her and telling her she could have the day off since she had worked seventeen hours on the day before. He told her he would collect her from the barracks at 07.00 on Monday morning, when she should be ready to go to Slovakia. If plans changed he would call her. Peiperová thanked him and rang Navrátil, which explained why it was that Navrátil was both well-informed and grumpy when Slonský told him about the plans for the day.

'What shall I do, if you have to stay here, sir?'

'You can get yourself across to the National Archives and look out anything in the StB records that looks useful. I only have to stay in Prague. And I suppose I'd better put my mobile phone on. It's been a tense morning, Navrátil. I could do with a beer.'

'It's only half past eight, sir.'

'Is it? It seems later than that. I suppose we'd better settle for a coffee. Come along, lad. I'll pay.'

Slonský left the room, leaving Navrátil checking his hearing by placing a finger in each earhole. No, he couldn't hear any voices. It must have been real.

Lukas rang to tell Slonský that Pilik would see them briefly at eleven o'clock, by which time Slonský would no doubt have polished his shoes, ironed his shirt and generally smartened himself up.

'Have I got time to book into a clinic for a facelift, sir?'

'Don't be facetious, Slonský. We must make a good impression on the new minister.'

'If he's done anything corrupt I could ensure he's impressed by how quickly I get his carcass into a cell.'

'He's not a suspect, Slonský. He is an involved party, that is all. Don't annoy him.'

'Don't worry, sir. I won't. Unless he's done something, of course. Then I'll annoy him a lot.'

As Slonský and Lukas were shown in Slonský found himself wondering if the office would have changed at all since Dr Banda occupied it just three or four months before. He soon discovered that the changes were minimal. The computer and telephone had been moved to the other side of the chair because Pilik was right-handed, so the visitors' chairs had been inched sideways a little to keep both in sight. The same snooty secretary showed them in, offered them the same execrable coffee and once again bypassed Slonský to serve Lukas first.

'I understand you wish to speak to me about an early case of mine,' Pilik began.

'Yes, minister,' agreed Lukas. 'The defence of a man named Bartoš.'

Pilik nodded in recognition.

'Not a case I like to remember.'

'I'm not surprised,' said Slonský, earning himself a stamp on the instep from Lukas.

'You'll realise it was a long time ago. One of my very first cases, in fact, and the only client I've ever had executed. And, of course, since the Czech Republic no longer has capital punishment, the only one I will ever have.'

'I suppose as Minister of the Interior you could bring it back, sir.'

'I could try — if I had the inclination, which I haven't. I haven't had it since Bartoš hanged, in fact.'

Lukas did not like the turn the conversation was taking, and intervened to bring it back to safer territory.

'May I ask how you were appointed to the case, minister?'

'I'd been in practice only a few months. I had a telephone call saying that Bartoš needed a court-appointed lawyer, and I was next on the list of possibles.'

'Surely a more experienced advocate should have been selected for a murder trial, sir?'

'But it wasn't a murder trial,' Pilik explained. 'When I was appointed it was about a series of burglaries. Bartoš was living in Olomouc, but it seemed that he had come to Prague and conducted a string of break-ins. He admitted some but of course he had no real idea where he had robbed. He just walked around the streets looking for likely targets. The police tried to get him to confess to a list of places. Bartoš was sent over to Prague and I went to see him. I think I was allowed about fifteen minutes with him.'

'That's not very long, sir.'

'No, it isn't, Captain. He agreed that he had confessed to burglaries in a couple of places and he hoped I could get him some allowance for having pleaded guilty. I said I would try, but that wasn't guaranteed — some judges would inflate the sentence so that they could take off the allowance and it would make no real difference. Then I had a message to say the trial would start in two days and that Bartoš had been charged with murder because a young woman had been killed at one of the houses he'd confessed to burgling.'

Slonský pulled his chair forward to get nearer to his prey.

'How could he confess, sir? He couldn't read and write.'

The minister looked acutely uncomfortable.

'I didn't know that then. I'd never had a client who couldn't read before. And he didn't say anything about that. It was only after he had been sentenced that one of the policemen asked me why I hadn't questioned the confession.'

'That policeman wasn't a man called Holoubek, was it?'

'I don't know. It may have been. The name rings a bell.'

'The newspaper accounts of the trial say that Bartoš kicked up when he heard the charges. Was that the first he knew of them?'

'Probably. I hadn't been allowed to see him again. Bartoš can't have known that I'd tried. He shouted one or two very unpleasant things at me.'

'I'm not surprised, sir. The prospect of getting your neck stretched tends to put social graces out of your mind.'

'I did the best I could, Lieutenant. I'm not saying I wouldn't do better now, but given the poor hand I was dealt, I tried hard to shake the police case. But the judges kept coming back to the confession. The verdict was inevitable. In those days it was often decided before you got into court anyway.'

'And when Holoubek told you about the confession, what did you do?'

'Well, of course I went straight to the President of the Court. He was a monster. He said it would be an unnecessary embarrassment to socialist justice if the verdict were shaken in any way, and that for the sake of my career I should let things lie. In any event, he said, it was futile because he happened to know the execution had been carried out. I protested that the date set was still a few days away, but he said that the date was "an administrative decision" that the governor of the jail could vary. Pankrác needed the space so the governor had cleared the cell.'

'"Cleared the cell"? Is that what they called hanging an innocent man then?'

Pilik was now acutely uncomfortable.

'It's not my choice of words. And while he may not have signed the confession, we don't know that he didn't do it.'

'Yes, we do,' Slonský snapped. 'He had the best possible alibi. He was already in jail when the murder happened.'

Pilik went pale. Lukas wondered whether he was about to faint and looked around for a bottle of brandy.

'In jail?'

'In Olomouc.'

'But surely the police must have known that?'

'They did. Why didn't you?'

'Nobody told me,' wailed Pilik. 'They just told me he'd been arrested there and returned for questioning. They didn't tell me he had an alibi.'

'Well, they wouldn't, would they, sir? Even a complete beginner like you might have got him off if they had.'

Pilik winced involuntarily.

'I recognise that this incident doesn't show me in the best possible light,' he began.

'No, you're right there, sir,' Slonský confirmed.

'But it was a long time ago. Things have changed here since. You're old enough to remember what it was like. If someone wanted him convicted there wasn't a lot I could have done.'

'No,' agreed Slonský, 'but you could at least have tried.'

Lukas was starting to feel a little wan himself, and he still could not see any brandy. He ran a finger inside his collar which felt rather tight.

'The thing is, sir,' Slonský continued, 'the case has been reopened and is likely to be quite a sensation in the press. Whatever we think of what happened, you should prepare yourself for some awkward questions from the media.' He stood abruptly, causing Lukas to follow suit. 'Thank you for your time, sir. We'll see ourselves out.'

As they walked back to Lukas's car Slonský strode out forcefully, causing Lukas to trot at intervals to keep up.

'Do you really think the press might get hold of this?' Lukas enquired.

'I'm sure of it, sir. You know how they like embarrassing people in power.'

'Of course, we must not fetter the press,' Lukas mumbled. Slonský knew what was coming next. 'But the police don't come out of this too favourably either. How will we handle that?'

Slonský stopped. 'I could brief the press first, before they hear somewhere else.'

'Out of the question! We can't draw attention to this. Most embarrassing.'

'How about I prepare a briefing sheet that throws all the blame on the StB? Just in case.'

'Do you think we could?'

'Well, they get the blame for everything else. They'll be used to it by now, sir.'

'But do the facts bear that interpretation?'

'Oh, I think they could, sir.'

'Well, Slonský, let's hope that the press show no interest. We'll have to keep our fingers crossed.'

'Yes, sir. Fingers crossed.'

'This is good stuff,' agreed Valentin. 'Minister of the Interior lets a client hang because he forgets to ask if he can read and write. I can see the headlines now — "What kind of nincompoop do we have running Law and Order?"'

'That's good. I like that,' said Slonský. 'Another?'

'Go on then, if you're paying.'

'I thought you were taking your earnings to the bank twice a day in a wheelbarrow now.'

'Things are better, there's no denying it. But the big money is in television. I do all right. And this little beauty should snag me a bit extra.'

'Just hang on until after Monday so I get to Bartoš' mother first. I want her to hear from me before she reads anything in the papers.'

'It's a deal. Though if he couldn't read, what's the chances that his mother will be able to?'

'Fair point.'

'How are your little turtle doves?' Valentin asked.

'I'm keeping them apart. Navrátil is at the Archives wading through mountains of StB papers. That should occupy him for a day or two. Peiperová has gone home for the weekend. I try to keep her out of the office. That way I don't have to look at Navrátil's bushbaby impersonation. Plus she doesn't actually have a desk.'

'Cunning,' said Valentin approvingly.

'I like to think so,' Slonský smiled.

Chapter 9

The Slovak police were fascinated to hear from Slonský. In no time at all he was put through to the chief of the City Police, who was polite and keen to be helpful, qualities that would have rendered him utterly unsuitable for employment in Prague.

Slonský asked whether they could ascertain if Mrs Bartošová were still alive and still lived at the address Slonský had. Within moments both had been confirmed. Slonský was impressed with their filing system, until the chief explained that the Bartoš family were well known to the police, having been what are euphemistically called 'service users' for many years past. Every policeman in Dolný Kubín knew where the various Bartoš family members lived. They actually lived a little way out of the main part of town, which was a blessing because there was only one route they could reasonably take to get home with their swag. The chief had heard of the hanging but it did not seem to have changed the family's ways.

'I need to interview Mrs Bartošová about her son's conviction. Would you be able to send an officer to ensure everything is done properly?'

'Of course. Drop in at the police station as you go through and I'll send someone to guide you and interpret.'

'Don't they speak Slovak?'

'Yes, they speak Slovak, but they'll probably pretend they don't understand Czech. And their dialect is a little difficult to follow sometimes. If you shake hands with them, count your fingers afterwards.'

'Thanks for the tip. I'm bringing a young policewoman with me, Officer Peiperová.'

'Tell her to wear trousers. The Bartoš house is no place to wear a skirt.'

'Then I'll change my wardrobe plans. See you on Monday afternoon.'

Navrátil had expected his search of the StB archive to be achingly boring and unproductive, and he was not disappointed. For a few hours he found nothing but dead ends. It was clear that Vaněček and the StB were not on each other's' Christmas card lists, because the files held a number of vituperative and pompous memoranda from the former and some frosty replies from the latter. There were also some notes from various StB personnel to Tripka asking him why he could not control Vaněček better. Tripka replied to one that he was in a dilemma, because Vaněček was a superior officer but he did not always appreciate the wider importance of StB work, so he had consciously withheld some operational material from him for fear that he would impede the investigation. When Vaněček found this out, there had been a very difficult interview with Tripka being threatened with a transfer to the border police. Another exchange caused Navrátil more concern. It looked as if the StB had flooded an area of Prague with prostitutes in order to trap Western businessmen attending a large conference, but Tripka had not told Vaněček. There had been a sharp increase in pickpocketing and Vaněček, who was looking after security for the conference, had ordered the area cleared. The prostitutes were rounded up and taken into custody. The StB had protested and Vaněček, instead of answering them, had taken his complaint directly to the minister, arguing that these tactics would give the Communist system unwanted bad publicity in the West and should be outlawed. To the StB's surprise the minister, who — as Vaněček knew well — was something of a puritan, had agreed and had instructed them that this sort of provocative action must cease at once. However, his letter had been annotated 'Be more careful!' by some StB hand and there was no sign that the security police had paid any heed to it.

It was not until late afternoon that Navrátil finally located a file that related to the arrest and interrogation of Vaněček in 1979. It was surprisingly thin, but that proved to be due to substantial editing over the years that had removed some of the pages. Nevertheless, he settled down to read it and make some notes.

The top of Navrátil's pencil was soggy, always a sign of deep cogitation. He had scoured the files and kept coming to the same conclusion. There was no reason in those files for anyone to arrest Vaněček. Certainly that had changed. There were a number of file notes concerning 'Statements made by the witness Vaněček' which later became 'Statements made by the prisoner Vaněček', but those were things he had said after he was detained. Navrátil could find no reason why he might have been arrested in the first place. There was no warrant, no preparatory papers, and indeed the matter did not seem to have been discussed beforehand.

'So they just pulled him in?' said Slonský.

'It looks that way.'

'Well, there's a conundrum, then. Even in those days just arresting people at random and beating them to death in custody was frowned upon a bit.'

'Sir, was he arrested? This bit about "the witness Vaněček" puzzles me. Did he come in voluntarily as a witness?'

Slonský considered for a few moments.

'He'd have had to come in voluntarily a few times, wouldn't he? He doesn't become "the prisoner Vaněček" until the fourth or fifth statement. But I suppose he might have made a complaint that was turned against him. What are the statements about?'

'In the later ones, it looks like Vaněček is defending himself against a suggestion that he has deliberately fouled up StB operations. He keeps saying that he didn't do

A, B or C. But in the first couple it's about what he was told and when. There's a piece here where he's arguing that these allegations have already been investigated and he was exonerated.'

'And was he?'

'Nobody seems to have checked.'

'But is there ever a specific charge mentioned — any hint that they planned to take him to trial?'

'Not a thing.'

'And no report on his death?'

'Just a file note to say that it happened. 24th May, 1979.'

Showing an unaccustomed display of energy, Slonský picked up the phone and dialled a number he must have known by heart.

'Novák.'

'You certainly are. You know you're my favourite state pathologist and I've often said you are a pivotal figure in our fight against crime?'

'What do you want?'

'Your inestimable assistance once more. A policeman called Vaněček died on 24th May, 1979. He allegedly had an accident in his garden, which we know can't have happened. Presumably an unexpected death would have triggered an autopsy?'

'I know where you're going. It would only have triggered an autopsy if he was found in his garden. If something happened to him in custody they wouldn't have called us, would they?'

'No, I grant that. But why come up with the garden story — which, incidentally anyone with half a brain would know was untrue; even Navrátil spotted that — unless they intended him to be found well away from StB headquarters in some safe place like, say, his garden?'

'Then the local police would have taken a look at it, and called your lot if they were suspicious.'

'And if they were too thick to be suspicious?'

'They'd have called us, I suppose. Or, conceivably, just sent for an ambulance to shift the body and the hospital he was taken to would have called us.'

'Then, just possibly, somewhere in your archive...'

'Slonský! Do you have any idea how many files there are in our archives?'

'No,' said the detective. 'I bet you haven't either. Let me guess — a hundred and two?'

'More than that.'

'Two hundred and sixty-eight?'

'Stop playing games. It'll take an age.'

'You've got a name and a date. Presumably there's an index. And young Navrátil is sitting here looking bored and would be very happy to come down and help you find it.'

There was the deepest of sighs at the end of the line.

'I'll see what I can find. I'll call you back.'

'Wonderful. Don't forget Navrátil goes home at five.'

Slonský dropped the receiver and beamed at Navrátil.

'When do I ever get to go home at five?'

'Poetic licence. And I didn't say whether it was p.m. or a.m.'

'Are you going to make me work all night like you did…'

'Enough. That was a mistake. And the girl has a tongue in her head, as I suspect you're set fair to discover for the rest of your life.'

'Nothing like that is planned. We're still getting to know each other.'

'Can she cook?'

Navrátil was nonplussed.

'I don't know.'

'You don't know? The single most important fact about a future wife and you don't know?'

'It's not been high on my list of priorities.'

'Then bump it up, lad. Looks don't last, but cookery skills do. When everything is beginning to sag and she's covered in crow's feet you'll be able to content yourself with the thought that she can still turn out a good *svíčková*.'

'She's a long way from sagging yet, sir.'

'Ah, you think that, but it creeps up on you, son. That's the odd thing about Czech women. For years they're tall and blonde and good-looking, then you go out for a beer and when you come back they've dropped ten centimetres and developed a backside like a carthorse.'

'Sir, you can teach me about a lot of things, but I'm not sure you're an authority on Czech women. After all, you've been divorced a long time.'

'I haven't played hockey for thirty years but I still know what a goal looks like. Look out of that window and show me a single good-looking older Czech woman.'

Navrátil accepted the challenge. He watched patiently for a while before triumphantly pointing along the street to his left.

'There! The woman in the wine-coloured coat.'

Slonský took a brief look and sniffed.

'Obviously a foreigner, Navrátil.'

He left the room before Navrátil could argue.

Slonský was in a quandary. The canteen had run out of anything containing meat. There was an egg roll, and several types of salad, some of which contained bits of meat, but he risked inadvertently eating something green in trying to pick them out. Not only that, but the lady behind the counter advised them not to touch the pastries, which were two days old.

'The salad is very fresh,' she said.

'I went straight from breast milk to meat,' said Slonský.

'Well, I'm not giving you breast milk and we're out of meat,' came the reply.

The queue was growing restless. There was only Navrátil in it, but he was restless enough for any number of others.

'Out of meat? What sort of canteen runs out of meat?' whined Slonský.

'Wait here,' said the assistant, and returned in a few moments with a hunk of salami and a bread roll.

'Bless you, Anna,' Slonský whispered. 'I was just telling Navrátil that a good Czech woman looks after her man's stomach.'

Anna smiled.

'You also said that Czech women sag — ouch!'

'I'm sorry, Navrátil. Was that your shin? Don't hold the queue up, lad. Grab your coffee and pay up.'

No sooner had they taken their seats than Mucha beckoned from the doorway. Slonský beckoned him in return. This continued until Mucha gave in.

'Novák says you're to come and get it.'

'The little devil. Usually he plays hard to get.'

'He also says he can't take it out of the building so get your backside in gear and get over there before he goes home at five.'

'Clock watcher. Navrátil, ask Anna to put these coffees in a takeaway cup. I'll eat my sandwich while you're driving.'

'And what will I do with this?' asked Navrátil, indicating his half-eaten egg roll.

'If you've got any sense you'll heave it in a bin and get something edible. Come along, lad, we can't keep Novák waiting.'

Novák peered at them over his glasses.

'There's more to this than meets the eye.'

'I'm the detective,' said Slonský. 'You're not trained for it.'

'True. But if I'm signing stuff out of the archive that has a bad smell about it I want to know what it's all about before I hand it over. And I have the upper hand because I have the file.'

Slonský reached inside his coat and pointed his gun at Novák.

'And I have this.'

'You wouldn't pull the trigger,' Novák scoffed.

Before Navrátil could stop him, Slonský pulled the trigger.

There was a loud click.

'You complete idiot!' yelled Novák. 'It's just as well I've got iron bowel control. That could have been loaded.'

'It is loaded,' said Slonský. 'But the safety catch is on.'

Novák snatched the gun.

'Slonský, the safety on this model disengages when you grip hard and pull the trigger.'

'Does it? I forgot that. Just as well that I also forgot to load it, then.'

Novák held it sideways to remove the magazine, and was rewarded by seeing Navrátil dive towards the ground.

'Navrátil? What are you doing?'

'Saying a Hail Mary,' was the reply.

'I've been shot,' Slonský announced, 'and it's not so bad.'

'You have? Where?'

'In a warehouse,' said Slonský. 'And I was not running away from the enemy, whatever anyone tells you. It was a ricochet.'

Novák handed the disarmed gun back.

'It wouldn't be a great feat of marksmanship to hit your backside, Slonský.'

'No,' agreed Slonský, 'but it was round a corner. I wouldn't have minded, but it was a police bullet. And they wanted to charge me for a new pair of trousers.'

Novák opened the dog-eared file.

'First things first. He didn't die on 24th May. It was the 28th.'

'But his police file says he died on the 24th.'

'No doubt it does. But the local police at Zdiby found him in his garden on the 28th.'

'Couldn't they tell he'd been dead four days?' asked Navrátil.

'Apparently not. They remarked on the absence of rigor mortis, but that had passed off by the time he was found. The photographs of the body are monochrome, but you can clearly see that his face is livid. There's simply no way he could have died in the posture in which he was found, propped up on a loose fence post, which, incidentally, doesn't match any of the others in the garden. He died lying face down. I'd guess he was injured and thrown on a cot with his head hanging over the edge. The actual cause of death was a series of blows to the chest. The fifth to seventh ribs on the left side were all broken and the skin was pierced. But you can see from this picture that the skin was pierced from the inside by a piece of rib, rather than from the outside by a fence stake. It looks as if he suffered from a flail chest. The ribs broke in two places so that whole segment of ribcage wouldn't move when he breathed. There's a pleural tear as well.'

'Is that bad?'

289

'The pleura is the sac inside the chest. If the broken rib rips it, the lung on that side has trouble filling and air can enter the chest cavity. It's painful and it's life threatening. Without serious medical care he'd have less than a fifty-fifty chance of surviving.'

'And the cover story is nonsense?'

'Unless the fence wore boots, complete bunkum. I'd say Vaněček was kicked repeatedly while he was lying on the ground, then dumped on his bed to die.'

'And the pathologist said that too?'

'That's the interesting bit. He obviously knew the truth, but he didn't dare tell it, so he was crafty. He wrote what he was told to write, but he left plenty of clues to those of us who know these things so we could see plainly that he knew what really happened. Look here, for example. He measured the top of the fence post and notes that it was eighty-three millimetres in diameter. But he puts that in table 5 and immediately below he notes that the wound he labelled C measures 117mm across. He's telling us that the post can't have made that wound. Again here, he notes that the body was found on 28th May and that death must have been a little before that, but he says he knows this because there were only early signs of skin blistering. But skin blistering happens around day five after death. He knows the death occurred on the 23rd or 24th.'

'Wasn't that a risky thing to do, sir?' asked Navrátil.

'Very risky,' Novák replied. 'He must have known that his work could be reviewed by a second pathologist who could have shopped him. But if it was, nothing seems to have been said. The file was put away, and until today that's where it has been.'

Slonský was leafing through the file slowly.

'Bastards,' he said finally. 'This wasn't an interrogation. This was a punishment killing. I thought they'd accidentally killed him, but it's clear they didn't expect him ever to leave alive. They wanted it to look like an accident, but you can't accidentally kick a man to death. They didn't want him to go to trial, so they didn't need to charge him, because a charge would be irrelevant anyway. Whatever Vaněček was saying, they weren't going to let him go on saying it.'

'Who are "they"?' demanded Novák.

'Good question. But we've got some names.'

'Have we, sir?' asked Navrátil.

'We know who signed the witness statements. That's your next job, lad. Decipher the signatures and see if they're still alive. The pensions office may help again.'

'Surely you'll never get a conviction after all this time, Slonský,' said Novák.

'Perhaps not. But when I look them in the eye, they'll know that I'll know, and I'll make sure they never forget I know. I want them to toss and turn every night for the rest of their lives.'

Slonský marched through the door and indicated the clock over Mucha's counter.

'Time you went home, lad. Have the weekend off. On Monday, find those StB hoodlums. And have a look through that file Mucha gave me. You may spot something I've missed.'

'Thanks, sir. Have a good weekend.'

'I won't. Remind Peiperová I'll see her at seven to drive to Slovakia.'

'I will if I see her, sir.'

'"If I see her"? Of course you'll see her. Around six o'clock on Sunday evening, I'd guess.'

'How…?'

'Because she won't be able to escape from her family until late on Sunday afternoon, but her mother will accept that she wants to get back to Prague before dark. Then all you need is a knowledge of the train times from Kladno and it's pretty elementary, really.'

Mucha coughed loudly.

'Sorry, Navrátil, one of the servants is trying to attract my attention. What is it, Mucha?'

Mucha adopted the fawning posture of a peasant addressing his lord, his eyes fixed on the floor and his head bowed.

'Begging your pardon, sir, but there's somebody waiting here to see you.'

'Who is he?'

'It's a lady,' said Mucha, tipping his head to one side to indicate a woman in a cheap raincoat sitting on the bench against the wall.

Slonský scrutinised her closely.

'That's not a lady. That's my wife.'

Chapter 10

Věra Slonská stirred her coffee slowly. It contained more sugar than was good for her.

'Still got your sweet tooth, then?'

'I suppose so. It's my only vice.'

'Apart from running off with second rate poets, that is.'

'Keep your voice down. No need to tell everyone.'

'Really?' Slonský boomed. 'Don't you want people to know you dumped your husband to shag some greasy slimeball?'

'All right, I can understand you're upset.'

'Upset? I lost two years of my life to the bottle. I finished up in a one-room flat on my own for thirty-five years so I think I'm entitled to be upset.'

'You could have found someone else. Someone better than me.'

'That's true. There's no shortage of women better than you, but I didn't realise that at the time. I was heartbroken and you didn't care.'

'I didn't mean to hurt you.'

'You mean you were dancing in the nude and accidentally fell onto his penis?'

Věra pulled a handkerchief from the cuff of her blouse and dabbed her eyes.

'I know I did wrong. I'm sorry. This isn't easy for me. Can't we be a bit more civilised about it?'

Slonský bit his lip.

'I'll try. Why hunt me out now after all these years?'

Věra sipped her coffee and replaced it delicately on her saucer before speaking.

'I haven't been entirely honest with you.'

'You mean it wasn't just one out of work poet but an entire writers' workshop?'

'No.'

'You were always a lesbian?'

'Of course not.'

'I give up.'

She took a deep breath. The canteen was a very public place for this sort of discussion but Slonský had refused to go anywhere more private, claiming that she would pretend to have been attacked if there were no witnesses.

'My relationship with Petr didn't last long.'

'How long?'

'A bit less than a year.'

'And after that?'

'After that? Nothing.'

'Nothing? Nobody else?'

'I was wounded. I understand what I did to you because he did it to me. He took me skiing in the Tatras and walked out. I had to find the money for the hotel bill. I sold my wedding ring.'

'Some justice in that, I suppose.'

'Josef, I was miserable. Have some compassion. I knew you wouldn't have me back and I knew I'd been incredibly stupid and ruined it all.'

Slonský pushed a crumb round his plate with his fingertip.

'You don't know that because you didn't ask.'

'I didn't need to ask. You made it very clear what you thought of me when I was packing. As I recall words like slut, whore and scumbag were used.'

'Nothing personal. I say that to all the wives who leave me.'

'I got a job as a filing clerk and tried to start again. But I never found a man to settle down with. They just wanted a fling. I wanted to put down roots.'

'Was this in Prague?'

'Not at first. I worked in Slovakia for a while, but my mother was ill, so I came home to Prague. I thought I might go to one of the places we used to go to see if I could bump into you, but then I remembered how angry you'd been and it didn't seem like a good idea. After Mum died, I moved out of town and got a flat.'

'So what made you come back now?'

'I saw an article in the newspaper about you and that German banker. There was a photograph of you. You haven't changed much.'

'Of course I have. I'm around fifteen kilos heavier for a start.'

'Twenty-five, probably. But your eyes are the same. And while I said some spiteful things about you, I knew you were one of the few honest policemen in town. I never doubted that, Josef.'

'Thank you. I appreciate your endorsement. But it still doesn't explain why you came to find me.'

'I have a confession to make. There's something I didn't tell you that you have a right to know.'

'You're not going to tell me I've got children?'

'No, of course not. The thing is, we're still married.'

'What?'

The small number of diners in the canteen turned instinctively to see what had happened.

'What do you mean, we're still married?'

'Simple statement of fact, Josef. When Petr deserted me, our divorce had not come through, and I never completed it. Actually, I never got round to asking for one. I told you I had, but I hadn't. You can check if you want.'

'Don't worry, I will. And you're not getting half my pension.'

'The only way I'd get anything is if you were killed in service, and then it wouldn't matter to you.'

'I'd rise from the grave to put a stop to it. Just because I'd be dead doesn't mean I wouldn't be bloody furious.'

'I don't want your money. I wanted to tell you where we stood in case you'd found someone else and had inadvertently been a bigamist. I'd have put things right for you if I could. Then I'd get out of your life again. Josef, I'm sorry for what happened and I know I can't put it right now. I'd like us to be friends if we can, but I understand if that's too difficult for you.'

'Difficult? I wish it was impossible.'

'You loved me once, Josef.'

'I loved bootleg Barry Manilow recordings once, but I've grown up.'

'Well, I've tried…'

Věra picked up her handbag and turned to say goodbye, but Slonský was running to the door.

'Stay there,' he barked. 'I'll be back soon.'

Slonský was gone about twenty minutes, and when he returned he was flushed with excitement.

'Sorry. Just needed to check something. Look, I need to get back to work. I really don't know where we are. This has all come as a big shock to me. Leave me your address or phone number and I'll give you a call in a few days. I've got a big case on and this isn't the time to be making important decisions. Once it's over, I'll give you a call.'

'Promise?'

'Promise.'

Věra wrote her telephone number on a paper napkin, then put her coat on and picked up her handbag.

'It's good to see you. I thought you might hit me.'

'I've never hit you. I don't hit women and I despise men who do.'

'I know. But nobody ever provoked you like I did.'

'True. But that still doesn't justify hitting a woman. You know what I always used to say. A gentleman wouldn't hit a lady, so any man who does can't be a gentleman, therefore…'

'He doesn't deserve to keep his gentleman's parts. See, I do remember. Goodbye, Josef. Don't forget to call.'

'Goodbye, Věra.'

He walked her to the door, waved one last time, and walked back to his office, lobbing the crumpled napkin into a waste bin as he did so.

Personnel would have a lot to answer for if Slonský were in charge. Fancy leaving a door unlocked. Well, not unlocked exactly. Just locked with a lock that was so basic a passing stranger with a picklock could open it really easily.

Slonský had been here a few times on disciplinary matters, so he knew his way round quite well. The filing cabinets filled a wall in the back office. Although all new records were kept electronically, they had never quite got round to entering all the old paper records into the computer system. Slonský's own record was still partly on paper, but he resisted the urge to edit it. However you looked at it, his presence in the personnel department after hours with the lights off would take some explaining. He would come up with something — he always did — but it was not easy to think what that might be.

He found the folder he wanted and scanned the postings its subject had held. From 1972 to 1974 he had been at a listening station keeping an eye on the Americans. It was obvious, once you knew what to look for.

He returned the folder to its drawer, switched off his flashlight, and opened the office door just enough to slip outside, shutting it with a gentle click as he did so. He finally exhaled, turned, and found himself face to face with Navrátil.

'Jesus Mary! You made me jump. What are you doing here?'

'Wondering what you're doing creeping around personnel with the lights off.'

Slonský drew himself up to his full height and his chin jutted out defiantly.

'There is a perfectly good reason but I decline to give it.'

Navrátil shrugged.

'Fair enough. It's not my place to question your actions. But if anyone saw you, what are you going to tell them?'

'Who saw me?'

'Nobody. I stayed here to keep a lookout.'

'So did you follow me?'

'Follow is too strong a word. I came to talk to you but you were so preoccupied you ignored me.'

'Then I must compliment you on your shadowing technique. I had no idea I was being followed.'

'From the look on your face you wouldn't have noticed if the Presidential Guard and its band had followed you. So what have you found out?'

'I don't know just yet. A germ of an idea is forming in my head but I can't quite see how it all fits.'

'And what did your ex-wife want?'

'Private business.'

'It was private till you bellowed at her in the canteen, sir. After that it was all a bit public.'

'We've got something to work out, that's all.'

'If you want any advice about handling women…'

'I'll ask someone other than you, thank you. Now, go home, Navrátil, as I am about to do.'

Slonský strode off along the corridor, leaving Navrátil musing about the events of the evening as he smoothed out a crumpled paper napkin.

Chapter 11

It was a chilly morning so Peiperová was wearing a winter coat and boots. She almost walked past the blue Octavia that Slonský was occupying, but he wound down the window and called her.

'Sorry, sir, I thought we were meeting inside.'

'And waste five minutes going in just to come back out? Get your seat belt on and make yourself comfortable. It's a long way to Dolný Kubín.'

Peiperová began unbuttoning her coat.

'I wouldn't bother with that, lass. You'll be glad of it when you get out to fetch us some breakfast when we're out of town.'

Slonský drove at his usual speed, around five kilometres per hour over the speed limit. They drove through the city and headed south-east on the road to Brno.

'Good weekend?' Slonský suddenly asked.

'Yes, thank you, sir. Yours?'

'You already know about mine, don't you?'

'Yes, sir. Some of it anyway.'

'How much did Navrátil tell you?'

'That your wife turned up and there was a bit of a scene.'

'"A bit of a scene"? If you think that was a bit of a scene you should have been there when she said she was leaving.'

'I'm really sorry, sir. It must have been difficult for you.'

Slonský looked confused as if the idea that it might have been difficult had not occurred to him before.

'Thank you, Peiperová. It's good to know someone appreciates my position.'

'So what will you do now, sir?'

'Now? I think I'll pull over by that bakery so you can get us some breakfast.'

Peiperová was driving as they entered Dolný Kubín and looked for the police station.

'There it is,' said Slonský. 'Pull in at the side of the road.'

They entered the station and effected introductions. A young man in motorcycle gear was detailed to lead them to the Bartoš house. He introduced himself as Officer Jakubko.

'I'll ride ahead, sir. It's not too far. Just so I know, am I going to have to arrest them?'

'Not that I know of. They haven't done anything in the Czech Republic.'

'Very good, sir. They don't have a good name around here, I'm afraid.'

A few minutes later Jakubko signalled a right turn and pulled into a small yard. There was a long, low building on one side that had seen better days, a hen house and a fenced compound containing some unpleasant-looking dogs. Jakubko put his motorbike on its stand and smoothed out his uniform, stowing the helmet in a pannier and donning his uniform cap.

'Shall we go in, sir?'

They walked towards the door, which opened to reveal a scruffy man in a tattered vest who was chewing on a corn cob.

'Whatever it is, we ain't done it.'

'Nobody is accusing anyone of anything, Viktor. These officers are Czechs. They've come all the way from Prague to see your mother.'

'Why should she want to talk to them?'

Slonský intervened. 'Because we want to get justice for your brother Ľubomir.'

Viktor considered this as he chewed.

'Bit late. You hanged the poor bugger.'

'Yes, and I don't know why. But if I could talk to you all inside, we might get some clues.'

Viktor turned and held the door open behind him with his foot.

'Ma, these folk are from Prague. They want to talk to you about Ľubo.'

An old woman was sitting by a potbelly stove peeling potatoes.

'What about Ľubo? You can't pick on him anymore.'

'I know, Mrs Bartošová,' Slonský replied. 'I want to find out why he was hanged.'

'There's no reason. They just did it.'

'Mind if we sit down?'

'If you like. It'll make a change to have someone to talk to other than Viktor. I don't get out now, what with my legs.'

She indicated the limbs in question. There was no obvious problem with them.

'Who's the maid?' she asked.

'This is Officer Peiperová.'

'Married? My Viktor's going spare.'

'I'm spoken for, I'm afraid,' said Peiperová, causing Slonský to do a double take.

'Shame. You look like you wouldn't take any lip from a man. He can be a bit mouthy, our Viktor. Gets him into trouble sometimes, don't it, Jako?'

Officer Jakubko agreed that it did.

'That, and the vodka,' the old lady expanded.

'I had the impression you had a big family,' Slonský began.

'I have, but they're all married and away now, except Viktor. And Ľubo of course.'

'I'm Lieutenant Josef Slonský. I was visited a little while ago by a retired policeman called Holoubek. He was involved in investigating the murder your son was convicted of. Holoubek told me he had discovered too late that your boy was already in jail in Olomouc when the crime was committed.'

'That's right. He came over to see me. It was too soon after. I sent him packing. It does you no good to hear your boy's innocent when they've just hanged him.'

'Holoubek was murdered himself a few days ago. I think he was killed because he was trying to get your son's case reopened.'

The old lady stopped peeling for a moment.

'That's a shame. He was a decent man, for a policeman.'

'What I don't understand is why someone in the police came to Olomouc to get your son. Why pick him out? He must have known him already, but I can't see how. I mean, your son had been run in any number of times around here, but I can't work out why the villain thought he was the best person to frame. Tell me what your son did after he left here.'

She resumed peeling.

'He'd been banged up too many times here. I thought if it happened again he'd get a long sentence. He wasn't a bad lad, just not very bright. He couldn't read, you know. They thought he was thick, but one of my grandsons is just like him. I don't know what they call it, when they can't make out letters to spell words.'

'Dyslexia?'

'That's it. That's what the school said. Dyslexic. The grandson gets special help, but poor Ľubo didn't. He just got written off as an idiot. Couldn't get a job, so he did odd bits here for me, then he discovered he could climb. That's when he took to cat burgling. He got himself a bike and he used to go off places to burgle for a few days, then he'd come back here. But he couldn't get shot of the stuff, so he said he'd have to move. He went up to Bratislava, then when that got too hot for him, he crossed into the Czech bit of the country to live in Olomouc. It was all one country then, you remember.'

'But how did he come to the attention of a policeman in Prague? I can't find anyone connected with the case who had ever worked in Olomouc.'

'Just before they hanged him, he said he'd try his luck in Prague. Bratislava was a poor place then, but he thought people were better off in Prague. They'd have stuff worth nicking. So that's what he did.'

'Why did he get caught?'

Mrs Bartošová sighed.

'He couldn't read, could he? He broke into a few houses. At one of them, he stole a medal. He didn't realise it was some special Russian thing they'd given a bigwig. Shouldn't be accepting medals off Russians anyhow. But he got caught trying to flog it in Olomouc. They picked him up and charged him with burglary. He co-operated, mind. When they took him back to Prague he showed them where he'd been. He didn't know they were important people's houses. He just thought they looked posh.'

Slonský thought for a moment.

'You don't know anyone else he burgled? Did the owners get their property back?'

'I don't know. He'd spent the money, of course.'

'What money was that?'

'He found some money in one of the houses. Quite a stash by all accounts. But it wasn't crowns. It was some other sort of money. He had to find someone to swap it with. I think they ripped him off, because he said he only got about a tenth of what it was worth, but he couldn't argue because he didn't know where else to trade it and he didn't want to be found with it on him. They didn't charge him over the money, because he didn't have it any longer when he was taken in. I think it was just the eight burglaries. He pleaded guilty, but then they said he'd killed a girl doing one of the robberies and next thing we knew he'd been strung up.'

'Jana Válková.'

'Was that her name? Well, I'm sorry for her parents, but I knew my Ľubo. He wouldn't hurt a girl. Might chance his arm with her, see if she was interested, but he wouldn't force her.'

'The odd thing is that Mr Válek didn't report a robbery, so Jana can't have been killed during one.'

Peiperová had her index finger raised as if wishing to discreetly catch Slonský's eye. He nodded to her to continue.

'May I ask if your son always worked alone? Could anyone have known of his plans?'

'Always alone so far as I know. What kind of help could anyone give a cat burglar?'

'But it sounds as if you knew his plans.'

'Only the gist of them. He kept himself to himself. He said he didn't trust others not to blab. He told one of his brothers once that he was planning to rob a place nearby and it got out. He didn't half give his brother a hiding. After that, he got even more tight-lipped. He only told me so I would know where to start looking for him if he didn't come back. He said if he fell, he'd probably wind up unconscious in hospital somewhere and they wouldn't know who he was, so we needed to come looking for him.'

Slonský picked up his hat and stood to indicate they had asked all their questions.

'Thank you, Mrs Bartošová, Mr Bartoš. You've been a big help.'

'Are you actually going to do anything or was this just for show?' asked Viktor.

Slonský's eyes blazed for a moment, and Peiperová held her breath in anticipation of the angry riposte, but Slonský recovered himself.

'No, I want to find out who framed your brother, who really killed Jana Válková, and who killed Edvard Holoubek.'

Mrs Bartošová resumed her peeling.

'Mr Detective, if you do find out who it was,' she said, 'I hope you'll tell us so Viktor and his brothers can take a trip to Prague and beat the living daylights out of him.'

'Unfortunately,' Slonský responded, 'we're expected to guard our prisoners so that doesn't happen to them. Weird, isn't it?'

'It's not that weird,' she added. 'You gave Ľubo a medical to check he was fit before you hanged him.'

Jakubko was torn between two conflicting instructions. He was under orders to facilitate the Czech guests' visit in every way so that they would finish and go home as quickly as possible, and he had been told to do all he could to make them welcome, so when Slonský asked for a recommendation for a café, the young police officer had to decide whether to tell them there were better coffee places elsewhere, or take them to his aunt's little place which, while small and something of a sixties time warp, did a really good coffee and a nut and poppyseed cake to die for. The conflict did not take long to resolve, and soon the motorbike was propped against the decaying plasterwork of a café while Jakubko, Slonský and Peiperová tackled a large piece of cake each.

'Is it good?' he asked.

'Yes, very good,' said Slonský. 'Are there any vacancies for an experienced detective in your force?'

Jakubko laughed.

'We don't have one. We have to send to Žilina if we want help.'

'Does it happen often?'

Jakubko pondered.

'Not since we've had all these cameras in the town. We had a bicycle stolen a while ago, but we solved that ourselves.'

Peiperová delicately replaced her coffee cup on her saucer.

'Sir, did that really get us anywhere?'

'Not really. I mean, it probably solved the crime for us, but apart from that, it was a bit of a waste of time.'

Peiperová and Jakubko gazed at him in surprise.

'Solved the crime? How? Who?'

'I'm saying nothing till I've checked it, but I now have a hypothesis to test. And that's one more than I had when we came. Now, shut up and enjoy your cake. Actually, I might just have another piece, seeing as Jako's aunt went to all the trouble of cooking it.'

'What time will we get back, sir?'

'That depends on how fast you drive, Peiperová. If you press on that pedal under your right foot, the car goes faster.'

'I know, sir. I just don't know the roads very well.'

'Like the Slovaks themselves, lass, they're often dark and twisted.'

'Sir! That's really prejudiced of you!'

'Joke, girl, joke. It doesn't represent my real view of Slovaks. Given that they don't have our advantages and the beer is maiden's water, I admire their sturdy independence. Jakubko was a nice lad.'

'Yes, he was, sir.'

'I hope Officer Navrátil isn't the jealous type. I don't want him driving up here and challenging Jakubko to an inter-force duel.'

'He has no reason to be, sir. You're just stirring things.'

'You know, you're very wise for one so young.'

'Thank you, sir. To return to my original question, when will we get back?'

'If we drive non-stop, a little before nine o'clock. However, that nice Captain Lukas has approved an evening meal for us, so we could stop somewhere and eat at public expense at a reasonable time, rather than grabbing some fast food just before bedtime.'

'Sounds like a plan, sir. I'd be happy with that.'

'Good, because the alternative was that you sat in the car until I'd eaten mine, and I might have felt slightly guilty about that. If I ever felt guilty, which I generally don't. Now, I'm going to snatch forty winks. Wake me up just before you hit anything.'

Instructed to find somewhere to eat around halfway, Peiperová spotted an inn about forty kilometres east of Brno and pulled off the road. It turned out to be an excellent choice, and by the time Slonský had filled himself with home-made venison sausages, dumplings of various kinds and a litre of the local brew, he was feeling benign. Peiperová had expected to switch seats, but Slonský had other plans.

'You'll be nicely rested after that break, so you may as well carry on driving for a bit.'

As they drove along they chatted about police life, promotion prospects, Prague, promotion prospects, inside information on other officers that they might not want made public, and promotion prospects. Slonský found himself experiencing an unexpected feeling. Having regarded Peiperová as a supplementary nuisance, over and above his existing necessary nuisance, he now found himself thinking that keeping her around would make life more interesting. This was strange, because it was only a little over three months before that his arm had been twisted to take

Navrátil under his wing. Officers assigned to work with Slonský seemed to have an above average sickness rate, and eventually Lukas had run out of options. However, the academy was sending Navrátil to him for further in-post development, and someone had to supervise him. While the idea that Slonský could supervise anyone made the average senior officer gulp, Lukas was in a position to exert pressure. It was Navrátil, or work on your own, so Slonský took Navrátil, having been assured that he could work a kettle. As Lukas had suspected, Slonský enjoyed having a captive audience. Navrátil laughed at his jokes, was impressed by his successful deductions, made or fetched coffee on demand and was happy to do some of the tedious grunt work that Slonský detested. Lukas also suspected that Navrátil might have been doing some of Slonský's paperwork, the quality of which had improved markedly in the last three months. Tackled on this point, Slonský claimed that it was because he felt an increased responsibility to do it well. Lukas noted waspishly that this increased responsibility seemed to run to numbering his list entries consecutively, indenting his paragraphs in a consistent way and no longer typing random headings in a completely different font.

Thus the partnership between Slonský and Navrátil had flourished, and now Peiperová had come along. By skilfully keeping them apart, Slonský had avoided the worst of Navrátil's impersonations of love's young dream, and there was no doubting the fact that Peiperová was clever, conscientious and very, very ambitious. It was undeniably true that three people could do more work than two, and nowadays Navrátil needed much less supervision. In fact, Slonský belatedly realised, Navrátil was the best policeman he had worked with for a long time, despite his youth, and one day this pair of puppies would become top dogs in the Czech police. He only hoped he had retired by then so he never had to work for them.

Slonský suddenly realised that Peiperová was talking to him.

'I'm sorry, Peiperová. What did you say?'

'I asked if the link you found earlier was that Bartoš had robbed someone important who got their own back by framing him.'

'Well done, girl. It seems very petty for people in high places, but the obvious one was whoever had the dollars or marks. They probably shouldn't have had them, so they couldn't report them missing, so they had suffered a real loss. Alternatively, perhaps they were entitled to have them, but it was government money and they'd have to describe how they lost it, which would have been difficult. Either way, they'd be cheesed off with Bartoš.'

'Annoyed enough to have a man killed?' There was genuine wonder in Peiperová's voice.

'I've known people killed for less. And I've known people who thought nothing of settling scores with a bit of murder. If there's one thing that I learned from living for forty years under Communism, it's that you should never underestimate the sheer pettiness of people in high places.'

'But even if we allow that he would want to do it, how could he actually effect it?'

'Well, we're entering into the realms of supposition here, and that's a very bad thing for a detective to do. After all, we're meant to work out our solutions from the data. If we start working out our solutions, then looking for the data, we might bias our investigation. I'm surprised at you for even suggesting it, Peiperová.'

'I'm sorr—'

'However, I can envisage a world in which the murderer takes advantage of the fact that the investigation has been left in the hands of a complete nincompoop like Vaněček, under which it would soon grind to a halt. The murderer knows by now that Bartoš is under lock and key. He goes to see him, gets the signed confession — worthless because Bartoš can't read it anyway — and drops it into Vaněček's lap. Vaněček breathes a sigh of relief. Just to make sure, our man has had Bartoš brought to Prague, signing the paperwork in Holoubek's name to cover his trail. If Vaněček sees the signature, he'll think Holoubek has given him a discreet hand, or maybe it was a line of inquiry Holoubek started before he was removed from the case.'

'So taking Bartoš round Prague looking for the houses he burgled was a charade?'

'It may have been. Or maybe the murderer wanted to check he'd got the right man. After all, there wouldn't be much satisfaction in getting Bartoš hanged if you discovered afterwards that the real villain was still out there.'

Peiperová suddenly pulled in to the side of the road.

'What are you doing?' snapped Slonský.

'Sorry, sir. I can't drive and argue at the same time. We haven't asked a key question. Just who took Bartoš around? It's our murderer who has most to gain from it, and from what we hear about Vaněček, he's unlikely to have come up with the idea. If he did, the murderer must have prompted it. If we can find that out, perhaps we'll have our man.'

'Yes,' agreed Slonský, 'and if Navrátil has been reading the investigation files properly, perhaps he'll tell us tomorrow.'

Chapter 12

Navrátil was already at work when Slonský breezed in one minute late.

'Productive day yesterday?'

'Not very, sir. I've got some possibilities. How was your day?'

'Very good. I think we may be slowly knitting together a case.'

'I tried deciphering the signatures but without names to start with, it's almost impossible. They've faded anyway. Personnel found me an internal handbook from around 1979 that lists some of the staff in the StB, and they're busy trying to compile a catalogue of those known to have been with the StB in Prague then, but they say it will be incomplete because the StB deliberately destroyed some files.'

'The StB destroyed a lot of files about informers, but it's difficult to destroy pay records. They've just got to look in the right place. You'd think a police personnel department would know how to conduct an inquiry, lad. Of course, if they were any good at running inquiries they wouldn't have been sent to personnel, I suppose.'

'Did the Slovaks give you anything useful?'

'Yes, I think so. It seems that Bartoš robbed some big houses in Prague and got off with some foreign currency. Now, what sort of person would have been able to amass a stash of foreign currency in those days?'

'A black marketeer? Organised crime?'

'Our crime was strictly disorganised in those days, son. There were currency speculators, and there were black market traders, it's true, but none of them could have known that Bartoš was in jail in Olomouc and none of them could have arranged for him to be taken round Prague pointing out the houses he'd burgled in exchange for a supposed reduction in his sentence. I'd like to know who suggested that to our friend Vaněček, because I'll bet he didn't come up with it himself.'

'Anything else, sir?'

'Yes, but it's probably going to involve some more work in the archives for you. You'll be getting a taste for it now.'

'I hate it, sir, but if it has to be done to find the murderer —'

'Murderers, lad, plural.'

'We know that?'

'Perhaps "know" is a bit too strong, but it's highly likely. After all, we're looking at murders spanning thirty years. There can't be too many men who have been active all that time.'

'You have been, sir.'

'Yes, Navrátil, but I'm not a murderer, am I? Despite extreme provocation.'

305

'I only meant, sir, that someone of your age would fit the bill.'

'Don't go getting ideas, Officer. If I go down, I'm taking you with me.'

'What do you need me to do, sir?'

'I've just changed my mind. You've spent enough time in the archives. Let's give this one to Peiperová.'

Slonský glanced at his watch.

'If she ever turns up, that is. Six minutes late. When she gets here, she can have a look for Czechs who received Soviet honours. Somebody had a Soviet medal stolen, but I don't remember seeing that mentioned in the papers anywhere? Do you?'

'No, sir. Why would a Czech get a Soviet medal?'

'International solidarity, the joint struggle against capitalism, stitching up other Czechs, the list of possibilities is endless. But there can't be that many Czechs who got one, and whoever it was got burgled, because it was when he tried to sell the medal that Bartoš got picked up. Whoever got the Order of Lenin or whatever it was would be the sort of man who had the clout to get a Slovak cat burglar hanged, evidence or no evidence. As for you, I want you to follow up on Roman Pluskal. Nobody has turned him in, and no officer has clapped eyes on him. I wonder why? Let's see if he has a credit card or mobile phone, where he's using them, what state his flat is in, all the usual things we do when we really haven't got a clue what else to do. Meanwhile, I'll do the really important bit, and get us some coffee.'

Slonský had just reached the door when his phone rang. Since he had never quite mastered the black art of transferring a call to Navrátil's extension, he picked it up himself.

'Slonský.'

'If you want to see your niece again, drop the Holoubek enquiry,' said a male voice.

'Who is this?' asked Slonský, before realising that he was talking to a disconnected line.

'What is it, sir?' asked Navrátil.

'Someone threatening my niece, but I haven't got a niece,' replied Slonský, feeling more than usually confused. It took him moments to realise that Navrátil was quicker on the uptake. The young detective was sprinting down the hall.

'I'll try her room, sir.'

Slonský realised that someone must think Peiperová was his niece, though he was unclear why. On the other hand, they did not apparently realise she was a policewoman, perhaps because she did not wear uniform and had spent very little time in the office since she arrived. He was also perplexed by the fact that someone apparently knew it was worth ringing his desk at 07:07, rather earlier than some of his colleagues would have been there. Through the bafflement he could see one important step he had to take, so he walked to Navrátil's extension and dialled a number.

'Technician First Class Spehar.'

'Slonský. I'm glad you're there. I need a phone call tracing urgently. Who do I call?'

'You just called him. I'll get Ricka on it straight away.'

'Is he good?'

'Well, he's better than me and you've only got two of us to choose from at this time of the morning. Now please tell me the number that was called and leave us to it.'

Slonský's mobile phone tinkled quietly, evidence that he had either changed the ringing volume by accident again, or had forgotten to charge it.

'Yes?'

'She hasn't slept here, sir. Her bed is made and it's cold, and nobody I've met yet recalls seeing her this morning. When did you last see her?'

'I dropped her off at the car pound last night about half past nine. She said she wanted to walk back.'

'I'll plot the street cameras and see if there are any on her route.'

'No, Navrátil, you come back and get on with finding Pluskal.'

'But sir —'

'You're too close to it, lad. Trust me and your other colleagues to do all we can for her. Meanwhile, we've got a murderer to find, and that's what you'll do. I'll go and ask Lukas for some extra manpower to find Peiperová.'

'I want to help, sir.'

'I'm sure you do. But your emotions are involved, and emotions make for bad policing.'

'Don't you have emotions, sir?'

'Of course I do. I want her back safe and well. But I can control mine better than you'll control yours. Now stop yapping and get on with finding Pluskal. And that's an order.'

Ricka proved to be a snowman-shaped lump with thin, straight hair cut like a moth-eaten mop. His fingers flew across the keyboard as he scrutinised four monitors in front of him. So far as Slonský could make out, one was filled with zeros and ones, while another had a green bar that lit up lines in turn and travelled up and down the screen. Ricka did not seem interested in these. His attention was focused on another that had pop-up boxes appearing and vanishing in quick succession.

'Have you got anywhere?' Slonský asked.

'The mobile number you gave us isn't helping. It's switched off now and no calls have been made from it since last night. Your call came from a public phone booth at the main train station. Did you recognise the voice?'

'He said so little. No obvious accent.'

'Our phone system here has been improved a lot recently. Who knows your extension?'

'I don't know. Who knows yours?'

'Not many. But your caller didn't get switched by switchboard. He dialled your extension directly.'

'That figures. He also knew I was leading on the Holoubek case.'

'But that was in the papers and on the television. He went to a public call box, and he dialled directly to you. I think you know him.'

'I don't hang around with criminals.'

'Yes, you do, it's your job. You have to spend time with them to arrest them.'

'Tell me, why didn't they accept you in the diplomatic service?'

Ricka frowned.

'Why would I apply to the diplomatic service?'

'Never mind. My mistake. Can you identify the exact box?'

Ricka passed him a slip of paper.

'That's the number. The station master should know. It would be good if there was a camera looking at it.'

'It would be good if there was a camera looking at it,' said the station master, 'but we don't have enough of them to cover everything.'

'Is there a camera anywhere near it?' asked an increasingly exasperated Slonský.

'This one covers the nearest corner, but the actual boxes are out of sight.'

'Never mind. Wind it back to 07:00 this morning and let's see if anyone heads towards those boxes.'

They sat tensely, watching the milling crowds. It was impossible to track where everyone went, but nobody walked purposefully towards the phone booth.

'Okay,' said Slonský. 'If they didn't go to the booth on the way out from the trains, maybe they went on the way in. Where's the nearest entrance?'

The station master found the appropriate recording and played it. Slonský threw his hat on the ground in annoyance.

'What earthly use is that? All you can see is the top of a lot of heads.'

'Well, we only need it to watch for blockages. We don't need to know who the people are, just that they can get to the trains.'

Slonský could feel the rushing sound in his ears again. The doctor had told him that was a bad sign. When it happened, he was supposed to calm down. In fact, he found it helped more if he let rip.

'Is there no way of finding out who used that damn phone at 07:07?' he snarled.

The station master relaxed. If that was all they wanted to know, why hadn't they said?

'There's Jiří.'

'Jiří?'

'The guy who sells the papers at the entrance.'

Slonský bounded down the steps and strode through the station hall. As he passed the phone booth he could see a trestle table laden with newspapers and magazines.

'Jiří?' he asked.

An upright bundle of rags stirred and a face poked out.

'Who wants to know?'

'Slonský, Josef, Lieutenant in the Criminal Police. Just past seven o'clock this morning, someone made a short phone call from that booth.'

'I know.'

'You know?'

'Yes. I wondered what anyone could possibly say in so short a time.'

'Can you describe him?'

Jiří stroked his chin.

'Any chance of a drink out of this?'

'Help me find the guy and there's a bottle in it. Not to mention you won't get your fingernails pulled out like he might.'

'Like that, is it? Important to you.'

'Very. A young woman has been abducted and he was involved.'

'Oh, so it was a ransom demand? That makes sense.'

'Can we get on? What was he like?'

'Black hair, plenty of it, jeans, dark jacket over a navy t-shirt or jumper. And he had a mobile phone.'

'A mobile?'

'Yes, that's what I thought was odd. He'd got a phone, so why use a public call box? But of course if he was up to no good, he wouldn't want the call traced to his phone.'

'No, he wouldn't. So someone called him?'

'That's right. He stood there smoking for about ten minutes, waiting for a call. I mean, he had the mobile in his hand all along. Then it came, he just listened, put the mobile away, and walked over to the booth. Then he made his call and in no time he was gone.'

Slonský had a bad habit of not emptying his pockets very often, but it came in handy now and again. He suddenly recalled something in his jacket pocket and paid it on Jiří's table. Jiří inspected the photograph cursorily.

309

'That's him. Well, if you know who he is, why are you wasting my time asking me all these questions?'

Slonský dropped a banknote as he retrieved the photograph.

'That should cover your time, unless you're an off-duty lawyer.'

Jiří indicated his threadbare coat and scuffed shoes.

'Do I look like a lawyer?'

'Not really,' agreed Slonský. 'Not slimy enough.'

Lukas cornered Slonský on the stairs.

'Why didn't you tell me about Peiperová?'

'I was going to once I knew for sure what had happened. I thought the most important thing was to get the search under way.'

'Have we any clues?'

'An identification of the man who phoned me. Roman Pluskal, the same thug who ran Holoubek down.'

'The link was already there, I suppose. It's natural that he would want the inquiry halted.'

'Wouldn't all criminals? May I ask how you know about this, sir?'

'Navrátil came to ask me to overrule you.'

'I see. And did you?'

Lukas sighed and draped a heavy arm round Slonský's shoulders.

'Josef, there is no danger that I would do that to my best detective. Unless, of course, this gets too much for you. I don't have a lot of spare manpower but I'll see who I can borrow. When it's one of our own…'

'Thank you, sir, but I can cope.'

'You've lost Peiperová and you excluded Navrátil from this case. That leaves you precisely one person, yourself.'

'Not quite, sir. I told Navrátil to get on and find Pluskal. That's doubly important now. And if he finds him he'll be making a major contribution to this case.'

'I could recall Doležal from his course. Ah! No need. Dvorník came back from leave yesterday. He could help you.'

'Dvorník does murders, sir. I sincerely hope this isn't one.'

'No, Josef, Dvorník does what I tell him. He's a competent officer.'

Lukas lowered his voice before qualifying his assessment.

'Not, perhaps, inspired, but certainly competent. More or less.'

'Very well, sir. If you insist.'

'I'll make plain to him that this is your inquiry. And I'll see who else is free to help you. Good luck, Josef. It's a horrible thing to have happened, but there's no-one better to have looking for her than you.'

'Except Samson.'

310

'Samson?'

'Dog I had as a boy, sir. He could sniff out a bone at the bottom of a coal mine.' Lukas turned to walk away.

'Then get yourself some dogs, man. If she walked, she may have left a scent.' Slonský took the stairs two at a time back down to the lobby.

'Mucha, where can I get some sniffer dogs?'

The van disgorged its contents. Slonský was unimpressed.

'What is that?'

'It's a kopov, sir.'

'A what?'

'A Slovakian hunting hound. These things trap wild boar, sir,' his handler proudly announced.

'Wild boar don't abduct police officers and make threatening phone calls, so some use this will be.'

'Trust me, sir, when Malý here gets a scent, he'll follow it to the end.'

'We'll see, Officer…?'

'Malý.'

'Malý? The dog's named after you?'

'Makes it easier, sir. His kennel club name is something awful.'

'Right, then, Malý. Let's see what Malý here can do.'

'Have you got something of hers, sir?'

'Navrátil says she was wearing this scarf on Sunday evening.'

'Very good, sir. Sniff! Not you, sir, I was talking to the dog.'

'I guessed you were.'

'He's got something, sir. It's been dry overnight, which helps. And I expect she was wearing some sort of scent.'

'I didn't notice, but then my nose isn't as sensitive as his, or I'd be on the end of your leash and he'd be redundant.'

The hound trotted along the pavement. So far so good — Slonský had seen her head this way. The dog also correctly spotted the point at which she had crossed the road. He led Officer Malý to the far side, then turned right and continued along the street to the next corner. Slonský followed close behind, but had to wait for a break in the traffic, so he was a little concerned that they might have slipped out of his sight.

When he caught up with them around twenty metres from the corner he found Malý turning circles at the kerb.

'Is he having a fit?'

'No, sir, the trail's ended here. She was snatched right at this spot.'

311

Slonský cursed. There were no cameras here, but he could put Dvorník onto looking at the nearest one to get a list of large vehicles that might have come past here just a few minutes after he dropped Peiperová the previous night.

'Well,' he said, 'we've got a place, and that tells me the time. I don't suppose Malý here can sniff a licence plate number?'

Lieutenant Dvorník's office was small anyway, but the man himself made it look even smaller. He was described by his wife as cuddly, an overly kind epithet but just about plausible if she had long arms. He had the same amount of furniture as Slonský, but less area to accommodate it, so the free floor area was not great even when he was sitting down, and almost non-existent if he stood. A large number of the available surfaces were covered in photographs of his offspring.

Navrátil stated the obvious.

'He's not here, sir.'

'No, even on my worst days I can detect a Dvorník, and there isn't one here.'

'Are all those his children, sir? I thought you said he only had three.'

'He and his wife have been married before. He had two or three with his first wife, and I think his new partner had a couple, and then they've had three more since. I'm not sure of the running total, but it's high time he found some other hobby. At least when you look at his children there's no need for genetic testing. They all tend towards the fuller figure.'

'I'd better go look for him, sir.'

'No need. He'll be in the canteen. Come along.'

In fact, they met Dvorník in the corridor on his way back from the canteen. He had a coffee in his hand, upon which he had balanced a torpedo roll containing a substantial share of a pig. Slonský explained the job he wanted doing. Since it involved remaining seated, Dvorník was content, though still slightly resentful at playing second fiddle to another lieutenant.

'Now, lad,' Slonský continued, 'how are you going to find Pluskal?'

Navrátil felt obliged to sound decisive, though he had been wondering about that himself.

'Money, sir. Everyone needs money. He must use cash machines or credit cards.'

'Worth a try. But Griba's gang will deal largely in cash. They get lots in, and they can't bank it without questions being asked, so they work almost entirely in cash.'

'Driver's licence?'

'Well, we know he can drive, so he probably has one. Whether the address is up to date may be another matter, but give it a go.'

'I can see if any vehicles are registered to him while I'm at it.'

'I doubt it. He probably drives some of Griba's. Though of course there's one less now that he torched the Volkswagen.'

'Won't Griba be angry about that?'

'No,' Slonský answered with a touch of scorn. 'Griba probably told him to do it. So far as I know, Griba had no grudge with Holoubek, so he was probably paid handsomely to arrange it. He can stand the loss of an old Volkswagen van.'

'Who is this Griba, sir?'

'We don't know a lot about him. Griba is a nickname, and we don't know where it comes from. Someone told me it's a Hebrew word meaning wonderful, so perhaps he's Jewish. There's a synagogue somewhere called Griba. He just appeared in his late twenties and he's been a blight on Prague ever since.'

'Like Moriarty and Sherlock Holmes?'

'Not that high level. Griba doesn't bother with big, high-risk things, just a lot of protection rackets, prostitution, gambling, smuggling, probably some trafficking and plenty of drugs. That reminds me — let's find Mucha. I asked him to have a word with Colonel Tripka about Griba.'

'Nothing.'

'Nothing?'

'Nothing. Nada. Rien du tout,' asserted Mucha.

'But we know he has a finger in all those pies.'

'According to Tripka, they know it, but they can't prove it. Nobody will finger him and because he employs people with bad records, it'll stay that way.'

'Even by Tripka's standards, that's a stupid comment,' Slonský growled.

'He means that Griba takes on people who have every reason not to want to get back in front of a court. As witnesses against him, they'd be useless. A defence lawyer can shut them up very easily. They make a good living only because Griba helps them commit crimes they were too stupid to get away with themselves, so of course they're loyal.'

Slonský sighed. 'Like the Personnel Department.'

'That's right,' agreed Mucha.

'I don't understand,' protested Navrátil. 'What has our personnel department got to do with organised crime?'

'More than you'd think, except for the word "organised",' said Slonský, 'but I'm not talking about our personnel department. I'm talking about *The* Personnel Department. It was a setup from the early eighties. A disaffected underling in the Department of Justice hit on the brilliant idea of contacting criminals who had just left prison and couldn't get jobs. He'd offer them work in his scams. They got their instructions by telephone from "The Personnel Department", so they couldn't betray him because they didn't know who he was. Only one man knew, whose job it was to recruit them and hand over the wage packets. Working in the justice system meant the villain managed to screw up any number of investigations with fake alibis, lost statements and so on. Mind you, we could have done that ourselves in those days.'

'Yes,' added Mucha wistfully, 'those were the days. Do you remember that captain in Jihlava who took a statement from someone who'd been shot dead in a raid three days earlier?'

'Didn't even get disciplined. Just moved to a border post near Poland, which admittedly wasn't the best career move, not to mention being bloody cold in winter. So is Tripka even trying to nail this Griba character?'

'He says nothing would give him greater pleasure. He's convinced that Griba is probably behind one of Prague's biggest cocaine distribution networks; perhaps not the most valuable, but the widest reach. Of course, he says, his predecessor wasn't vigorous enough, which allowed Griba to get a toehold.'

'He would say that, wouldn't he? Everyone's predecessor was always too lax. It may be true in Tripka's case, but he hasn't exactly cranked up the action in the last couple of years since he's been there.'

'There was that big heroin seizure last winter.'

'Yes, but that had nothing to do with Tripka. The smugglers fell out and one of them snitched on the others. Even then, if he hadn't driven the van into the police station car park we'd probably never have found it.'

'You have to admit, Tripka falls on his feet. Luckiest officer I've ever known,' opined Mucha.

'I wonder how much is down to his father's reputation. Tripka himself is no great shakes.'

'But he's a colonel,' protested Navrátil. 'If he was an idiot they wouldn't have promoted him to colonel.'

'They would if they were bigger idiots,' Slonský pointed out. 'And rumour has it they wanted him out of ethics and internal affairs so when he applied for the leadership of the Drug Squad, everyone breathed a sigh of relief.'

'What did he do wrong in internal affairs?' asked Navrátil.

'He did nothing wrong because he did nothing at all, lad. No case ever seemed to have enough evidence to actually go anywhere.'

'To be fair to Colonel Tripka,' put in Mucha, 'he started unluckily when he charged a sergeant in the drug squad with graft and someone completely different turned up in Morocco with a large amount of cash. He took a lot of flak for that, but many of us thought he might well have had the right man. It made him ultra-cautious after that.'

Slonský was standing open-mouthed.

'What's the matter with you?' asked Mucha.

'I'm speechless,' said Slonský. 'I can't believe my own ears. "To be fair to Colonel Tripka"? When did we start being fair to people like Tripka?'

'I'm sorry,' muttered Mucha, 'I don't know what came over me.'

'I'm all for fair play and decency,' continued Slonský, 'but I never thought I'd live to see the day when you'd want to extend it to a nonentity like Tripka.'

Mucha took the hint.

'I'll go now.'

'I think you should,' agreed Slonský. 'I'll allow you to buy me a beer later to restore our friendship.'

'That's very good of you, sir,' said Mucha. 'Will I be allowed to stand in the same bar and watch Your Lordship drink it?'

'If you're good. Now, Navrátil and I have serious work to do. We've got to find Peiperová.'

'I'll send out an All Stations alert. Have we got a photo of her?'

'There's one in her personnel record.'

Navrátil fished in his inside breast pocket.

'This is a better one. Can I get it back?'

'Of course,' said Mucha.

'Excuse me,' Navrátil stuttered, and ran off along the corridor.

'Taking it hard,' Mucha commented.

'Yes. But it doesn't help find her. Let's get that alert out.'

'Right away. What's her first name?'

Slonský looked perplexed.

'Officer?' he offered.

Chapter 13

Navrátil looked miserable.

'We should be doing something,' he said.

'We are,' replied Slonský. 'We're having an early lunch so we can devote all our afternoon to finding Peiperová. Don't you want that?'

'No appetite.'

'Give it here, then. She'll be fine, lad. So long as we're looking for her, we're not working on the Holoubek case, and that's what the abductor wants. He has no reason to hurt her. If he does, he loses the only weapon he has.'

'How can you eat at a time like this?'

Slonský put Navrátil's sandwich down.

'If I don't eat that, how does that help find Peiperová?'

'It doesn't.'

'Thank you,' said Slonský, picking it up again. 'My point exactly. There's enough misery in this without letting good food go to waste.'

'I'll have to tell her parents.'

'Ah. Yes, we should.'

'We. Or me?'

'No, it's my job. Give me their number and I'll ring them.'

Navrátil tore a page from his notebook and copied the telephone number from his mobile phone.

'There.'

Slonský picked up his sandwich and his coffee.

'I'll do it now. You bend your mind to finding Pluskal. Wherever he is, she is.'

The phone rang. It was Valentin.

'I wondered what had happened to you,' said Slonský. 'I thought maybe you were too busy signing autographs to do the little favour you promised for me.'

'It wasn't a little favour. It was a thumping big mega-favour and it cost me a bomb in phone calls.'

'You'll get it back.'

'I certainly will. Where can we meet?'

'Is it important?'

'I think so. But since you never tell me anything, what do I know?'

'Where are you now?'

'Across the street.'

'Valentin, why don't you come in here?'

'No chance. I get a shiver up my spine every time I walk past that place, let alone go inside. When they've frogmarched you inside with a sack over your head and kicked you in the cellars you tend to get clammy about a place.'

'That sounds painful — a kick in the cellars.'

'It was. And when you've stopped the cheap innuendo at my expense, get yourself down here.'

Slonský's voice became grave.

'Someone has snatched Peiperová.'

'The blonde girl? Why?'

'To get me to lay off the Holoubek case.'

'Then I'm right. You will want to hear what I've found out. And so will Navrátil. I don't know if you've noticed, but his eyes light up whenever you mention her. I think he may have a soft spot for her.'

'Actually he has an extremely hard spot, and I've told him to take some cold showers to get over it. But I'll give him a call and get him back here. Meet me on the steps in half an hour.'

As it happened, Navrátil was already coming back. The search of driving licences had been fairly pointless, because Pluskal had not amended the address on his record. The new inhabitants of the flat, a young architect and his pregnant girlfriend, had never heard of Pluskal. Navrátil was finding it hard to think of any new lines of inquiry. There must be some, but he simply could not think straight.

He saw Valentin on the steps.

'What are you doing here?'

'Waiting for you,' said Valentin. 'Now you're here, Slonský may deign to talk to me.'

Before Navrátil could open the front door, Slonský erupted from it.

'I've been a bloody fool,' he announced, before striding past them and heading for the café on the corner. Pushing open the door, he entered and looked around. It was almost empty except for a few hardened drinkers, some of them police officers. Navrátil and Valentin walked towards the bar, only to notice that Slonský was not with them. He had taken a perch on a high stool in the middle of the room and was turning from side to side as if bewildered.

'Something wrong?' asked Valentin.

No answer came. Instead Slonský closed his eyes and slowly revolved on the stool. When he had completed a whole revolution, he opened his eyes.

'What'll you have, sir?' asked Navrátil.

'Hm? Oh, coffee,' replied Slonský abstractedly.

'Coffee?'

'Yes, Navrátil, coffee,' answered Slonský, as if no other answer had ever been possible.

'Pastry?'

'This is no time to eat, lad. Valentin, come and tell us your story.'

They sat at the adjoining table. Navrátil and Slonský had a coffee each, while Valentin tackled a small beer with a brandy chaser.

'You asked me to check the reports of the Válková death,' Valentin reminded Slonský.

'Well remembered. And did you?'

'Yes, I did. At least, I checked our files, both published and unpublished. Nothing much in the unpublished, of course. Nobody keeps papers for thirty years. But there was something that struck me as odd about the published stuff.'

'Go on, we're listening.'

Valentin took a lubricating mouthful before continuing.

'The murder was late on Friday night, so it's no surprise there was nothing in Saturday's edition. There was nothing on Sunday either. The first mention is a report on Monday, but with no by-line.'

'Which means?'

'Probably that it was written by the state news service and just printed verbatim. It tells you nothing you didn't already know, but I've brought you a photocopy. There's nothing much for a few more days, then eventually the announcement of the arrest of the Slovak boy. And that's it.'

Slonský glanced over the copies.

'A brutal murder in Prague and that's all the papers say?'

Valentin smirked.

'It's all the Czech papers say. But I was doing a bit of internet searching and I discovered a report had appeared on Monday in a Hungarian newspaper. It was dated Sunday. Now, the story was filed by a chap called Möller. I knew him. He was quite an old man when I started out, but he was a good reporter. He would have done his homework, so I thought I had better get that story. To cut a long story short, our man in Budapest managed to trace a copy and get it translated. You owe him a couple of bottles of something nice.'

'A couple?'

'One for him and one for the translator. On second thoughts, you don't want to look mean. Our man probably ought to have two for himself.'

'Mug me, why don't you, and have done with it.'

'Believe me, you won't begrudge a single crown of it. Wait till you hear what he discovered.'

'Stop spinning out your part and get on with it, you irritating prima donna.'

'Coming from you that's a bit rich. When Möller heard about the murder he went down to Ruzyně himself. Kopecký wouldn't talk to him — that was the neighbour who found the girl —'

'We remember. You've got thirty seconds to get to the bombshell or you've had your last brandy off me.'

'Okay, keep your hair on, while you still can. Kopecký wouldn't talk to him, but Hruška would. You see, Hruška was an old man, an ex-civil servant. But he joined the civil service during the First World War. In those days, they did all their business in German, so he was a fluent German speaker, and so was Möller, who had been brought up speaking it in Hungary.'

'But Hruška was stone deaf. Interviewing him had been a waste of time.'

'Deaf, yes. Daft, no. He hadn't heard anything, it's true. And he hadn't seen anyone leave. But none of the police had asked him the right question, and Möller did.'

'How?'

'He wrote it down and Hruška wrote out the answer. It worked perfectly well. Hruška didn't see anyone leave, but he had seen people come, and he said so.'

Slonský leaned forward eagerly.

'Who did he see?'

'He didn't give names, but look what he said.'

Valentin traced his finger over the translation of the report, indicating a sentence in the middle of the page.

Slonský read it and smiled triumphantly.

'Soldiers. He saw two soldiers.'

'That doesn't appear anywhere else, and in the subsequent days it disappears and they just become two men, before finally they are transformed into Bartoš and he is hanged for it. But at the time of the first Hungarian report, they're soldiers.'

Back in the office, Slonský kept his coat on and walked straight past his desk to Navrátil's, where he opened the drawer. It took Navrátil a few seconds to realise that Slonský was inspecting his academy passing-out photograph.

'I thought you were going to give this to your mum.'

'I am. I just want to get it framed first.'

'You're taking your time.'

'It's expensive,' Navrátil explained. 'The police don't pay me enough to do it properly, so I'm saving until I can.'

Slonský turned to face his young assistant. The smile on his face was reminiscent of a deranged cherub.

'Let me pay for it as a graduation present. I insist.'

'Why would you do that, sir?'

'Because you're about to solve this case for me, lad.' Slonský laid the photograph on Navrátil's desk. 'Who was your best friend at the academy, Navrátil?'

Navrátil responded at once. 'Him.'

'The one next to your right shoulder?'

'That's right. His name was…'

'I'm not interested in his name, lad,' replied Slonský, who was out of the door in the blink of an eye.

Slonský was feeling lucky. His enquiry at the Army Personnel Office had produced a list of names.

'Do you know where any of these men are now?' he asked.

'Certainly,' said the clerk. 'We all know that one.'

'Zelenka?'

'Major-General Zelenka. He's upstairs. He's our boss.'

'I need to see him.'

'I'm sorry…'

'You will be, if I don't see him today. I need two minutes with him, absolute maximum.'

'I'll ask.'

'You do that. If he says no, keep asking until he says yes. That usually works for me.'

But Zelenka did not say no. A dour, humourless man, utterly unremarkable apart from the two stars on each epaulette. He did not have a photograph of his national service class there, but given a name to conjure with, he remembered him well, though wondering whatever became of him, because he would never have made a soldier. Asked who the man's best friend was, he volunteered another name on Slonský's list.

'I probably have that photograph at home,' said Zelenka. 'I could send it on.'

'If you can, sir, that would be good. But all I need to know is whether those two are standing next to each other.'

'I'd be surprised if they weren't,' said Zelenka. 'They were like a man and his shadow. Big man, smaller shadow.'

And in that moment Slonský knew who had killed Jana Válková. Now all he had to do was prove it, thirty years later.

Chapter 14

Dvorník had scoured hours of video footage but had not seen a van that could definitely be identified as the one that collected Peiperová. However, being a man of a mathematical disposition, he unrolled a map of Prague, marked the kidnapping point, and then drew pencilled circles showing the distance that would be covered by a vehicle driving at 50 kilometres per hour, on the basis that anything faster might trigger a speeding fine. The first circle was set at around 1667 metres, the distance it might have covered in two minutes; the second was a further two minutes beyond that, and there was a third one two minutes further out. It was, of course, possible that the driver had doubled back or turned off, but Dvorník had a hunch that the driver would want to get out of the city centre by the most direct route. The van had probably been waiting for Peiperová, so there was no point in looking for the inward journey, but by knowing where the van could be expected to be on the way out of town he could narrow his search.

After a couple of hours of scanning video, he saw it. Not wishing to trust his line of thought he fetched Navrátil, explained what he was doing, and ran the footage again.

'You see there? At the end of the bridge, going along the river. That's around four minutes after Peiperová was snatched, if Slonský's timing is right. But the main reason for thinking this could be the one is what happens at the traffic light a little later.'

Navrátil watched closely. The video was apparently taken from an office building near the Hilton hotel. The van was about to enter an underpass and suddenly swerved between lanes.

'See that? That's a change of plan. If he hadn't done that he'd have been sitting at the red signal right opposite a police car. Instead he turned right, jumping the light to do it. And notice the back windows of the van are obscured.'

'Good enough for me,' said Navrátil. 'Can we get the registration number?'

'It's a bit blurry, but if we go through frame by frame we may get all the digits.'

They pieced together a registration and rang it through. A few minutes later their call was returned.

'Registered to the Silver Rings Gymnasium and Spa. Mean anything to you?'

'I think it's one of Griba's places,' said Dvorník. 'Tatty as hell outside but well set up within.'

'I'll get a message to the patrol cars to keep an eye out for it. Should we go to the gym, lieutenant?'

Dvorník thought for a moment.

'It's Slonský's case. I know what I'd do, but we'd better ask him.'

'I don't know where he is.'

'Neither do I. Stuff it, let's go.'

Slonský was reflecting on a successful day. If he was honest, he was finding Navrátil a bit of a trial at the moment. Granted, he had not yet found Peiperová, but there was no logical reason for anyone to harm her. Then again, criminals were not the most logical of people. Free from distractions, Slonský would do what he did best; drink and think.

A large beer before him, a plate of salami and bread and a selection of pickles at his right hand, his hat on the bar counter, Slonský began to piece together the jigsaw of clues. Like a master symphonist, he looked for themes.

First theme: Válková's death would be brought home to somebody — let's call them A and B for the moment — but who had stalled the investigation by pulling Holoubek off it? We know Válek's sister-in-law took the credit but in fact the conspirators must have been able to influence that somehow.

Second theme: Bartoš comes into the story. He had stolen some money from someone in high places who wanted revenge, and whoever it was knew where to find him because the nincompoop tried to flog an Order of Lenin or something similar in Olomouc, so he was a sitting duck. Already in jail, with a criminal record, he could be set up. And whoever it was who set him up did so either to get cheap revenge, or to distract from the real culprits, or both.

Third theme: Vaněček, who had been conned during the Válková investigation, and should have known it thanks to Holoubek, suddenly starts mouthing off about something that leads to his death in police custody. But what triggered that? He had kept his mouth shut for three years, so why blurt it out now? Was it just the compulsory retirement? Or did something happen that stirred even Vaněček into action? And who had the standing to order his arrest on pretty vague grounds?

Fourth theme: Old Holoubek, whose conscience was troubling him, is run down in broad daylight while crossing the road. We know who did this one — Roman Pluskal — but who put him up to it? Presumably somebody was scared of what Holoubek might know, but the events Holoubek knew about were thirty years old. Why leave him alive all that time, but kill him now? The obvious answer was because he was trying to get Slonský to reopen the case, but the killers cannot have known that Slonský would take it on, or that he would get anywhere if he did. The reason has to be fear. There must still be evidence out there that the killers know about but cannot secure, but what can that be?

Fifth theme: as a mark of respect to Slonský's investigative powers, they kidnap an assistant to get him to back off. Admittedly they seem to have thought she was a family member, but the principle holds true. But that's a sign of desperation. If they hurt her, they lose their hold on him, and earn his perpetual hatred which would, in due time, probably cost them a few broken ribs for starters. Against that, if he holds back for a while and they let her go, they must know that he would just start up again. After thirty years, waiting another year or two would not be an issue. And how would they know that he had backed off? He could tell them anything, if they bothered to contact him again, and he was not convinced that they would.

Sixth theme: what is the link between the killers and Griba? He seems prepared to do a lot for them, considering that he was not active in crime when the early events took place. Slonský tried to recall the crime history of Griba in his folder. He did not remember a contract killing. Certainly some enforcement, a lot of graft, some "teaching of lessons", but no killing; so why had Griba accepted this job? Was it just money? Pluskal would eventually go to jail and Griba could not prevent that, but until he brought Pluskal in he would never know who persuaded Griba, and how Griba persuaded Pluskal to risk a long sentence.

Slonský poured the last of his beer down his throat. It was time to find Pluskal. Do that, and all the rest would fall into place. Find Pluskal, and he explains what Griba was doing. Find Griba, and we discover just who has the clout to push him around. Find that person, and we have our murderer, and he will lead us to his mate.

Dvorník and Navrátil pushed open the swing doors and looked around the gymnasium. Seeing them standing there in their street clothes, including Dvorník's overcoat, since he felt the cold cruelly, a young woman in a vest top and tracksuit trousers marched towards them.

'Come to sign up?' she asked, tilting her head to one side as if well aware that the simple answer was no, but there might be a more interesting one.

'Never in a million years,' said Dvorník, who had instructed Navrátil to let him do the talking. 'We've come to collect Roman Pluskal.'

'Who?'

'Roman Pluskal.'

'I'm sorry, there must be some mistake. We don't have a Roman Pluskal, unless it's the name of one of these members.'

'No, love, he's staff.'

'Not here he isn't. And who are you anyway?'

Dvorník silently showed his badge.

'Police? Look, whatever this Pluskal character has done, it has nothing to do with us.'

'Really?'

Dvorník unfolded a piece of paper taken from his inside pocket.

'That's Pluskal driving the van. And that van is registered to this gym.'

The young woman inspected the photograph carefully, chewing her lip as a sign of perplexity.

'I didn't know we had a van. God knows I'd have used it to move equipment if I had. And I don't know this guy at all.'

Dvorník reclaimed the picture and folded it carefully before returning it to his jacket.

'You see, I'd like to believe you, but frankly I can't take the chance. This man snatched a policewoman and we want her back, unharmed and soon. So if you have a head office or a contact with Griba, you might pass the message to him that he had better do as we want.'

'Griba? Who is Griba?'

'Okay, have it your way. I'll give you the benefit of the doubt and assume that you really don't know anything about the drugs, protection rackets, sex trafficking, prostitution and illegal gambling that goes on in this organisation, because you're young and innocent. But if anyone asks what we wanted, you'll be able to tell them, won't you?'

Dvorník turned to leave and motioned Navrátil to follow. The woman watched them for a few metres, then walked away.

Slonský waved for a waiter to get refills for Navrátil and himself.

'Dvorník moves in dirty circles and he can take care of himself. They'll respect that. Of course, it means they'll shoot first and warn him later. I'm more concerned that if Pluskal didn't know we were on to him, he may now. And I hope she wasn't lying, because if Griba is under threat he may get nasty.'

The waiter was hovering, tray poised to remove the empties.

'I don't know what you put in my glass, but that horse isn't fit for work. We'll have two more from the barrel you opened last. Got any sausages?'

'We will have when the chef catches that horse,' said the waiter.

Slonský laughed and punched him playfully on the arm.

'You topped me,' he announced. 'But some sausage and bread would be good.'

Navrátil sat hunched and dejected.

'They could be doing terrible things to her and we're laughing and joking.'

'How many times do I have to tell you they have no reason to hurt her? And we're making headway. We just need them to make contact again so we can find anything we can about them. And don't forget every policeman in Prague is keeping an eye peeled for Pluskal. If he steps outside, we'll hear about it. Now, the best thing we can do is force down a bite to keep our strength up, keep well hydrated, and get a good night's sleep. Tomorrow could be a long day.'

'I'm off to bed then,' said Navrátil. 'I'll get in at six to get started right after dawn.'

Slonský sighed.

'And of course I'll do the same,' he replied reluctantly.

Chapter 15

Slonský's hand snaked out and batted the top of the alarm clock, but the ringing did not stop. A second clout knocked the clock on the floor, but the ringing continued brightly. It was only then that Slonský realised that it was the telephone.

'Slonský.'

'You want to be here, sir,' said Navrátil, who sounded feverish.

'You're wrong there, lad, that's the last place…'

'Peiperová rang you.'

Slonský sat up with a start.

'Rang me? How?'

'With a phone, I suppose.'

'But Ricka said her phone was out of service. What did she say?'

'She doesn't know where she is, but she left us a few clues. She rang your answerphone so the message is still there.'

'Right, lad, call Ricka and get the lout out of bed on my orders. I want to know where she called from and when. I'm on my way. Whatever Ricka says, do it. I want this particular lemon squeezed till we've got all the juice out.'

Ricka was strangely compliant. It seemed that he needed very little sleep, possibly because the most strenuous thing he did all day was to prise the top off his yogurt at lunchtime. He appeared in the office within fifteen minutes carrying a couple of laptops.

'This phone?' he barked.

Since it was the only one with a flashing red light, Navrátil saw no need to respond positively, but it was of no importance because Ricka started hooking up cables to the phone socket anyway. Before he had finished Slonský erupted into the room with the appearance of a man who had dressed himself by letting his wardrobe topple over onto him.

'Don't touch!' yelped Ricka. 'Just a minute more.' He produced a little silver box and connected it to one of the laptops. 'Got any more plug sockets?'

Navrátil pushed a waste paper basket aside to expose one by his desk.

'Great. We're away. First off, I'm going to play the message and record it so we can't lose it. Ready?'

The others nodded. Slonský had never been big on patience and he had already held his tongue longer than it had ever been held before in like circumstances. He rapped his fingertips impatiently on the filing cabinet. The message began to play and they could hear Peiperová's whispered voice.

'Sir? Sir? It's Kristýna.'

So that's her name, thought Slonský. Must try to remember that.

'They drove me about twenty minutes. I'm one floor up in what sounds like a warehouse. There's no activity inside but there's a bit of traffic noise. They took my phone but they stopped looking before they found the mobile you gave me. I'll turn it off to save the battery but I'll try to put it back on for a few minutes after eight o'clock. I can't see what the time is now — there's no light. I'm okay, they're treating me all right, but it's cold and my hands and feet are tied. I hope you get this. Don't know what else to say. Tell Navrátil I'm looking forward to seeing him soon. And you of course, sir. Oh, the window must face south because the sun comes in at midday. Right, I'll phone later if I can. Bye.'

They stood in silence until they were sure there was no more. Slonský gave a little cough.

'Load of waffle. She could have said that in half the time.'

Ricka was tapping at his keyboard like a deranged woodpecker.

'Okay, call made at 02:04. We've got the number she used but you probably already know that.'

'I didn't know she had a police mobile phone,' said Navrátil. 'I haven't.'

'This is no time for sulking, Navrátil. I'll get you one if it stops you pouting. What else can you tell us, Ricka?'

Ricka had switched to the second laptop. Around two-thirds of the screen was taken up with a map.

'Right, stage two,' he announced. 'The phone company will have strength of signal data for its masts. I'm going to suck those down and it will display on this map as circles of different sizes related to the signal strength centred on each mast. Where the circles intersect is where she was when she made the call. But it'll only be accurate to around fifty metres at best, so don't get too excited. It'll take me five minutes or so.'

'Fine,' said Slonský. 'Navrátil, go and get some coffees, rolls, whatever. Here's some cash. I'm going to call Captain Lukas and tell him what has happened.'

Navrátil reappeared with a tray. Either the canteen felt generous or it was unsold stuff from yesterday but it would do. Ricka was reciting a series of numbers to someone via his mobile phone and then the screen started to fill with pale blue circles. After a few moments a selection of them darkened and a couple began to expand.

'Just a moment,' said Ricka. 'We have to wait for them to stop pulsating.'

The images steadied.

'That's a bloody mess,' opined Slonský.

'We can tidy it up,' said Ricka. 'I'll take away the masts that had a minimal signal.'

One by one the circles disappeared until four were left.

'Now I can make them more transparent so we can see the map underneath,' he continued. 'And finally we enlarge the intersection like this.'

Slonský lent so far forward that neither of the others could see the whole screen.

'What's that big rectangle?'

'Switch to "aerial photograph" and we'll see,' said Ricka. 'There you are — you're in luck. It's one big building with a lot of space round it.'

'Certain that's the place?'

'Over 99.98% certain.'

'Can't you just say yes?'

Ricka raised his palms apologetically.

'That's south of the city, sir,' Navrátil observed.

'Yes. And what makes me feel happier about it is that it isn't too far from the place where Pluskal torched the Volkswagen. He knows his way round that district.'

Slonský pointed to a piece of wasteland. 'That's where the van went up. How far is that?'

Ricka measured the distance against his thumb and then laid the thumb on the scale.

'Perhaps six hundred metres, maybe a little more.'

Slonský clapped Ricka on the shoulder.

'Good work. Navrátil, let's go and get her back.'

'Shouldn't we get backup, sir?'

'Element of surprise, lad. Besides, they're all in their pits. I'll tell the desk sergeant what's happening and Dvorník can get some help on its way. We'll just get over there and keep watch. See if we can check that she's in there before we go in with guns blazing.'

'Guns? Isn't that dangerous?'

'It's a damn sight more dangerous if the bad guys have guns and you haven't. Can we leave you to tidy up, Ricka?'

'Sure. I'll print these out and leave them on your desk.'

'Fine. Can you spin your magic at eight o'clock when she switches it back on and phone me if anything has changed? Come on then, lad. Polish your shining armour and let's go rescue the damsel.'

It was surprising how fast Slonský could walk, thought Navrátil, finding it difficult to keep up despite breaking into a trot.

'One thing, lad; how did you know it was Peiperová?'

'Sixth sense, sir. That, and she told me the code to your voicemail.'

Slonský stood still, hands on hips and a scowl on his face.

'Does everybody know that damn code except me?'

On Slonský's orders, they parked the car a block away from the warehouse and continued on foot. The removal of any markings made identification of the building difficult, but where the letters of the sign had been removed the paint was a darker green, allowing them to make out a word that could well have been "turbine". The building was broadly rectangular with a large double door in the nearer short side. There was a forecourt of around twenty metres between the door and the road. Navrátil made for the main door, but Slonský grabbed his arm and dragged him to one side.

'Keep in the shadows, lad. When we open the door, don't stand behind it. You'll be silhouetted against the light and make an easy target. If she's here, she's probably at the far end of the upper floor.'

'How do you know that?'

'She said the sun came in at midday, and that's the south end. Are you happy you know the plan?'

'What plan, sir?'

'Breathtakingly simple. We open the door, sneak in, rescue her, arrest Pluskal, and live happily ever after.'

'I thought we were going to wait for backup.'

'We are, but if I know Dvorník he'll arrive with all the sirens going and all hell will break loose. We need to be in position when that happens. Come on. Keep it quiet, and when we get inside head for the darkest corner.'

They crept to the door and Slonský gently rotated the handle. It was locked.

'Damn!'

Navrátil dropped to his knees and squinted under the door. He selected the corkscrew attachment on his knife, spotted a piece of cardboard and slipped it under the door, and jabbed the corkscrew into the keyhole. There was a gentle clink as the key dropped on the card and Navrátil pulled it back under the door. He smiled triumphantly at Slonský.

'Beginners' luck,' whispered the older man. He turned the key and they slipped inside, bearing to the left to get under the east windows where light was dribbling in half-heartedly.

'Let your eyes get used to the gloom,' said Slonský.

There was a staircase that started about a third of the way into the building and ran upwards along the west wall. At the far end there was a second staircase that doubled back on itself in a tight spiral.

'Okay,' hissed Slonský, 'you're quicker than me. Can you get to the far end and position yourself on the stairs to block anyone running away? Keep your head down. I don't think there are lots of them — they couldn't stay this quiet. If you're sure it's safe, start creeping up the stairs. If you spot anyone at this end, don't shoot. It'll probably be me.'

Navrátil nodded and slid along the wall. It was necessary because the nearer part of the upper floor was in the form of an atrium, so someone at the top of the stairs or on the gangway might have seen him. He relaxed as he passed halfway and found his way to the foot of the rear stairs. It was difficult to see Slonský, who had secreted himself in the shadow at the far side of the staircase, but Slonský must have been able to see him, because he waved his gun and started to climb the stairs slowly. Navrátil tried to keep pace, but it was tricky to judge how quickly to climb given that he had to keep looking upwards to watch for Pluskal or another of Griba's goons.

Navrátil reached the top of the stairs and gingerly raised his head. He was looking at a large room, almost square. The wall furthest from him did not exist; what he had taken to be a companion-way was simply the edge of the upper storey. The stairs met it at the left side and there was a double safety rail from there to the wall on the right. Peiperová was sitting against the wall to his right on a grubby mattress, her hands and feet tied with duct tape and cable ties and she had another piece of tape across her mouth. Navrátil briefly wondered how she had made the call, but then decided to puzzle that out later. He ducked his head again and found his penknife, extending the blade in readiness to cut the tape. His chief concern was that he could see no sign of Pluskal or anyone else, but he was sure that someone must be there.

Slonský had climbed two-thirds of the way up the stairs when hell was unleashed. So far as Navrátil could make out, it began when Slonský's mobile phone rang. Slonský fumbled in his pocket for it, just having time to register that it was Ricka before Pluskal erupted from a pile of blankets that Navrátil had mistaken for rags. Pluskal dived down the stairs and Slonský's gun was jarred out of his hand. Navrátil was torn between helping Slonský and rescuing Peiperová, but there was no real contest, so he fell to his knees and began sawing at the tape and ties with his penknife. Once her hands were free, he pulled off the tape over her mouth and gave her the knife to finish the job. Navrátil decided that the best plan would be to get back downstairs and form a second line of defence behind Slonský, so he plunged down the stairs again and started running the length of the building. To his horror, he could see an elderly tourist silhouetted in the doorway. He was wearing a backpack and was consulting a map, apparently unaware of the danger he was in. It meant that Navrátil did not dare to use his gun.

Pluskal had barged past Slonský and despite a ragged tussle on the stairs, he had managed to free himself. He raced for the doorway with Navrátil about twenty-five metres behind him, and made to push past the hiker. As he sprinted through the doorway the old man took a step to the side and jabbed his walking pole into Pluskal's ankle, causing him to tumble to the ground. With an inelegant flop, the man finished up sitting on Pluskal's back, and Navrátil was able to throw himself on top of the criminal to pin him down. It was only then that Navrátil realised that he was looking at Captain Lukas.

'Quick, man, your cuffs!' Lukas barked. 'There are spares in the rucksack.'

Navrátil unzipped the rucksack to discover a clanking mass of ironware. In addition to half a dozen revolvers, there were several pairs of handcuffs, a baton or two and a coil of fine rope. It was a surprise that Lukas could walk with it on.

Slonský arrived, panting heavily and bleeding from the knuckles of his right hand. He applied another pair of cuffs to Pluskal's ankles and took the opportunity to give him a sly kick in the ribs while he was lying on the ground.

'Perhaps you would help me to my feet,' said Lukas.

'Of course, sir. Thank you, sir,' said Slonský. 'Navrátil, help the captain up.'

Peiperová had limped down the stairs and was walking towards them, her legs still numb from the binding. She was dishevelled, in need of a good wash and rather embarrassed because she knew she smelled of urine.

Lukas straightened his clothing. He was wearing a gaudy tropical shirt such as nobody would have believed that he might own.

'Don't stare,' he snapped. 'I got it from the lost property box. Now, Slonský, perhaps you would explain to me why you didn't wait for back-up?'

'We were just conducting a reconnaissance when my phone went off, sir. Ricka is a genius but has no common sense. The ringing alerted Pluskal and it all happened from there.'

'I see,' said Lukas, apparently unconvinced. 'It's as well that the desk sergeant gave me your message instead of Dvorník, so I gathered together a few guns just in case and threw them in this malodorous backpack, thus showing, if I may say so, considerably more foresight than you.'

'Yes, sir,' replied Slonský, who had divined that a display of abject contrition was his best policy. 'But you were taking a chance, sir. You put yourself in great danger.'

'Not really,' said Lukas, and swept his arm behind him. Now that he drew their attention to it, Slonský and Navrátil could see the detachment of four police marksmen with their rifles trained on the doorway.

Peiperová had reached them, and threw herself against Navrátil's shoulder. She cried quietly for a few moments as he stroked her hair, and then she pulled away and looked at Pluskal lying face down on the concrete.

'Has he been arrested, sir?' she asked.

'Not yet,' said Slonský. 'But it's a fine distinction.'

Peiperová nodded, then kicked Pluskal at the side of the knee. He yelped with pain.

'That'll teach him to resist arrest,' said Slonský.

Lukas looked away.

'I'm glad I didn't see anything,' he said, 'but I'm sure you will treat the prisoner with respect henceforth. Now pick him up and get him over to the cells before his masters realise what has happened.'

As Lukas had noted, there was a certain urgency in getting information out of Pluskal before the villains realised that Peiperová had been freed, so Slonský was prepared to forego his usual degree of delicacy during the questioning.

'Here's the thing,' he said. 'I've got evidence proving that you were driving the van that killed Holoubek.'

'As if,' Pluskal said scornfully.

'Please yourself,' said Slonský. 'Navrátil, show him the steering wheel from the Volkswagen with his prints on it. Now, we can link this van to the killing of Holoubek and I have two eye-witnesses who can identify you. Wriggle all you like, but you're looking at forty years inside. Courts take a dim view of killing old age pensioners and policemen, and Holoubek was both, so you're doubly stuffed. They'll probably give you great medical care to make sure you stay alive for every day of your sentence. You'll be an old man when you get out. *If* you get out, that is.'

Pluskal snorted. Slonský took two large strides towards him, grabbed him by the front of his sweater and hoisted him to his feet. It was an inelegant move because Pluskal was handcuffed to the chair, but eventually he was upright and Slonský was undoing the handcuffs and refixing one end to his own wrist.

'Come along!' he growled, and dragged Pluskal into the courtyard at the back of the cells.

'Navrátil, cuff him to those window bars,' said Slonský. When that was done Slonský unfastened his own cuffs and put them back in his pocket.

He stood in front of Pluskal and lifted the prisoner's chin so he could glower into his eyes.

'Forty years. Have you got any idea what forty years in jail will be like? Look up. Go on, look up!'

Slonský yanked Pluskal's head back.

'See that blue stuff? Last time until 2046. You'll be — what? Seventy-nine? Make the most of it. Breathe in the fresh air. It may never happen again. In fact, maybe forty years is too few. Perhaps we'll ask for forty-five. What's an extra five years between friends? Of course, if you helped us I could get five years off for you. Thirty-five instead of forty. What difference will five years make, you wonder? Ask yourself again when you've served thirty-four and a half. There may not be much between thirty-five and forty, but there's a world of difference between six months more and five and a half years more. You're not looking at the sky.'

Pluskal felt his head being pulled back again.

'Got kids? They'll be middle-aged when you next hug them. You won't have to pay for a daughter's wedding, because you won't have done a quarter of your sentence by then. If she has kids, you won't see them till they're adults.'

Slonský grabbed Pluskal by the chin and squeezed his cheeks.

'My only regret is that I'd have to make it to a hundred to enjoy every last day of your imprisonment. But if I can, I'd love to. It would be worth the effort.'

Pluskal made the mistake of smiling.

'Then we've got kidnapping a police officer to add in,' continued Slonský. 'That should be good for an extra fifteen years. Consecutive, of course. There'd be no fun in a concurrent sentence. And maybe we can add some more.' He gripped Pluskal firmly by the ears so he could maintain fierce eye contact. 'Did you touch her? Did you?' His voice was quiet, conspiratorial, menacing. Pluskal tried to pull away. 'I bet you did. Pretty girl like that all tied up, how could you resist? Cop a quick feel, did you?'

Slonský was taken by surprise by the punch. And even more by the second, third, fourth and fifth punches. He grabbed Navrátil by the upper arms and wheeled him away. Navrátil's baby face was contorted with anger.

'It's his skin I'm trying to get under, not yours,' bellowed Slonský.

'If he did … if he laid a finger…'

Slonský trapped Navrátil against the wall and lowered his voice.

'Look, she didn't mention it, did she? If he'd molested her, she would have said.'

'She kicked his knee pretty hard.'

'Yes, she did,' agreed Slonský, 'but she's a well brought up Czech girl. If he'd groped her, she'd have rammed her knee in his groin.'

'Yeah, I suppose…'

'Go and see how she is. She won't want to be alone when she wakes up. Take her to get some new clothes, have a hairdo or some other treat. If she wants to talk, you can listen. Now go. You can give me a call later and we'll make plans for tomorrow.'

Navrátil nodded and went back inside. Slonský straightened his jacket and took a couple of deep breaths to get back into inquisitorial mode.

'Sorry about that,' he said to Pluskal. 'Now, where were we? Ah, I remember. We were calculating the length of your sentence.'

Pluskal chuckled. 'Your maths is bad. I'll be out long before that.'

Slonský sat on the windowsill.

'Now, that's where we disagree. I know you'll be gone much longer than you think, and actually you know it too. This is all just bravado. It's a shame Navrátil has gone. It stops us playing good cop, bad cop with you, though actually we're more bad cop, bad cop. As you saw, Navrátil believes in direct action, while I'm hot on sarcasm and humiliation. We're a good team.' He fished in his pocket for something. 'Did you ever play rock, scissors, paper as a boy?' he asked.

'Yes.'

'Me too. I have my own version we could play. It's called testicles, cheese wire, confession. Cheese wire cuts testicles; confession stops cheese wire.'

'I'll go cheese wire.'

'That's where my version is different.' He opened his hand to show what he had taken from his pocket. 'You see, I always have the cheese wire in this game. The only choice you have is between offering testicles or a confession.'

'You wouldn't dare. They'd lock you up too.'

'I don't care. I promised Holoubek I'd finish his work, and if that's what it takes to get what I want off you, it's a small price to pay. I'm getting on and I'm on my own. At least in prison I won't have to pay for heating, it's dry and I'll get my meals provided. And anyway, some consolation it would be to you. I'll be sitting in jail but you will too, and only one of us will still have balls. Have a think.'

Slonský walked inside and left Pluskal chained to the window bars. It was just starting to rain.

The young soldier was standing so rigidly that Slonský thought his spine might snap.

'Are you waiting for me to tell you to stand easy?' he asked.

'I'm to invite you to make a copy and then to take the photograph back to the general, sir.'

There was a barrier to the successful completion of that task. Slonský had no idea how to use the new photocopier, but he had no intention of letting the soldier know that.

'Come with me, young man,' he ordered, and marched him down to the front desk, where he handed the photograph to Mucha.

'Make some copies of this,' he said, 'then give the original back to the Good Soldier Švejk here.'

'Certainly, O Master,' replied Mucha. 'And where would you like me to put the copies?'

Slonský told him, and walked away.

Pluskal was unhappy, and let Slonský know it.

'I'm soaked. I'll catch my death.'

'That'll shorten your sentence, then. They turf you out of your cell when you die. At least now your family gets your body back. In the old days, they cremated you and used the ashes to melt the snow on the roads.'

Pluskal dried his hair with the towel Mucha had brought.

'Five years, you say?'

Slonský understood, though Mucha looked puzzled.

'Yes, I reckon I can get you five off if you co-operate.'

'I can get my throat cut too.'

'Not by us. And I'm not asking you to be a witness. I just need a link.'

'What good is that without testimony?'

'I'm not stupid, Pluskal. I know nobody is going to finger Griba unless they know he's going behind bars.'

'Griba? Forget it.'

'You know him. I'm pretty sure that he ordered you to run Holoubek down. I just don't know why.'

'I don't know why. Griba doesn't tell you why.'

'Only a handful of people see Griba, I'm told. Everyone else deals through intermediaries. You're one of the privileged few, aren't you? That's because you do some of his bodyguarding.'

'I'm saying nothing.'

'All right,' said Slonský. 'Let's try it another way. You don't have to say anything. I'll tell you, and you can tell me if I'm right.'

Pluskal made no reply, but watched as Slonský unrolled the sheet of paper. He carefully placed his finger on it, then moved a fraction to the left. Pluskal nodded once, briefly, and Slonský rolled it up again and smiled.

'Five years, remember?'

'I'm feeling generous. If this comes off, I'll give you ten and settle for thirty.'

Outside Mucha was curious.

'Are you really going to ask for thirty years?'

'Yes,' said Slonský. 'I'll tell the prosecutor I've agreed it with the suspect. It'll come as a shock, because he was only planning to ask for twenty-five.'

Major Klinger, head of the fraud squad, scrutinised the photograph closely without touching it.

'I don't know why I'm doing this, Slonský. I have no idea what Griba looks like.'

'But the fraud office came closest to building a case against him, didn't it?'

'It's still live, but we're running up against the time limit for action.'

'We've got an identification.'

'Have you, by Jove? Well, that's a great leap forward.'

'Navrátil arrested one of Griba's bodyguards this morning, and he's prepared to identify Griba in exchange for a reduction in his sentence.'

'Sentence? For what, pray?'

'Murder and kidnapping a police officer.'

'That young woman of yours? I heard about that. It's obviously a risky business working for you. High time you handed that bright young chap of yours over to me. He's made for financial work. He's meticulous, you see. You'll ruin him if he isn't separated from your influence soon.'

'If Navrátil wants to go, I can't stop him, but he's only been in the criminal division for three months.'

'That's long enough to suffer your supervision. Goodness knows what he'll be like after a whole year.'

'Look, I want to pool what we know about Griba. Every little helps.'

Klinger produced a folder from his filing cabinet. Like all his folders, it was immaculate, with coloured stickers on some of the pages. The manila cover was unblemished, primarily because Klinger threw them out if they became creased.

'He first came to our notice in the late eighties. You'll recall that the Albanians appeared around then. When the Wall came down, the Albanian mafia became really active. There are numerous tales of sex trafficking, drug running, prostitution and arms trading in which they were involved. We had some CIA people here for a while helping us clear them out.'

'I remember.'

'Griba arrived sometime then and was initially a very minor player, but it seems likely that at some point he executed a remarkable double cross and eliminated one of the key Albanian leaders. Of course, the Albanians are still around, but they don't cross Griba who, incidentally, speaks Albanian and Czech fluently. He can be ruthless if he needs to be.'

'Is he still running all the businesses?'

'That's the interesting thing. He still trades in drugs and prostitution, but we're told he no longer touches arms. I assume his supply dried up when the fighting in the Balkans ended. Now, why am I looking at your old National Service picture?'

'Because, if our prisoner downstairs is to be believed, that man there is Griba.'

Klinger stared intently at the picture.

'So he speaks fluent Czech because he is Czech.'

'Precisely. Not an Albanian at all. Though, as an hour in the library told me, Griba is an Albanian word meaning rake or comb. It's a nickname he acquired at some time. And thanks to Major-General Zelenka, I now know his Czech name.'

Chapter 16

Navrátil ran up the stairs as quickly as he could, straightened his tie, and knocked on the office door.

'Come!' commanded Lukas.

Navrátil was not a great reader of facial expressions, but he knew relief when he saw it, and he saw it now on Lukas' face. Peiperová's parents were sitting in front of the desk and turned to see who was entering. Mrs Peiperová gave a slight smile of recognition when she saw Navrátil, whom she vaguely recalled having been told about when he was in Kladno though Peiperová refused to bring him home for tea. Mr Peiper had never been one for small talk or bothering to remember people, so he shook Navrátil's hand with the formal movement of a first encounter. There was no antagonism; it was just that you meet a lot of people in a lifetime and it stretches the brain a bit to try to recall them all.

Navrátil had forgotten that Slonský had telephoned them to tell them of Peiperová's kidnapping, so he had not mentioned it to Peiperová, who assumed that her parents knew nothing of her adventure.

'Navrátil, I believe you've just come from Officer Peiperová's barracks. I hope she is getting some rest.'

'Yes, thank you, sir. She's sleeping. I said I would be there when she woke up, if you don't mind.'

Lukas glanced quickly at her parents. Mrs Peiperová had tensed slightly until she realised that there was more than one construction that Navrátil's words would bear.

'Yes, indeed. It's very good of you to provide support for her after her ordeal. Has the doctor examined her yet?'

'I believe so, sir, before I got there. She has some minor cuts on her arms where she was tied, and a few bruises, but no other physical injuries. It's mainly the stress and shock. And of course, she didn't sleep well.'

'Of course. I wonder, would you be kind enough to take Mr and Mrs Peiper to see their daughter? I have promised them that she will be given time to recover before she returns to duty.'

Navrátil agreed, though now he was concerned that they would take her back to Kladno and she might never return to Prague again.

He held the door open and invited them to follow him to his car. They were happy to walk, partly because they wanted to see where she was kidnapped.

'Imagine!' Mrs Peiperová said. 'What a place Prague must be! They snatched her there in broad daylight.'

Navrátil resisted the temptation to point out that ten minutes to ten at night was hardly broad daylight, but hastened to assure her that such kidnappings were extremely rare. It was then that he had the misfortune to meet Slonský who was returning from Klinger's office with a jaunty air.

'Heigh-ho, Navrátil,' he boomed, 'and what have you arrested this pair for?'

Navrátil winced inside.

'These are Officer Peiperová's parents, sir. Mr and Mrs Peiper, may I introduce our boss, Lieutenant Slonský.'

Without a missed beat, Slonský took each by the hand and expressed his delight with their daughter's performance since she had been under his tutelage, and his firm conviction that she might well be the first female Director of Police.

'That's as may be,' said Peiper, 'but not if it puts her in danger like this. It's not worth it.'

Despite nearly four months with Slonský, Navrátil had no idea how the old detective would overcome this observation, particularly since he had said the same thing himself on more than one occasion. To his surprise, Slonský dealt with the objection with a flamboyant impatience.

'I can understand that view, sir, but I'm sure that if you ask your daughter she will tell you that we who serve the public do not worry about the dangers. It's a measure of the helplessness to which we have reduced the criminals that they felt compelled to try something this desperate. They intended your daughter no harm, of course. Any mishap to her would have wrecked their last chance of avoiding imprisonment. Your daughter willingly allowed herself to be abducted, having cleverly concealed a second telephone about her person which she used to contact me on the night after they fell into our trap.'

'A trap? So this was planned?'

Slonský carefully avoided answering the question.

'When dealing with the criminal mind, you can't plan like you can with ordinary people, but we made it possible for them to take this rash step. It's greatly to Officer Peiperová's credit that she came up with such a daring idea. I shouldn't be surprised if an official commendation came her way.'

'But you sounded so concerned when you rang us,' protested Mrs Peiperová.

Slonský gathered them in so that he could speak quietly.

'As will become clear in a few days, there was a good reason to give that impression. I can say no more until further arrests are made.'

'Further arrests?' said Mr Peiper. 'Then someone has been arrested?'

'Certainly,' said Slonský. 'Captain Lukas and young Navrátil here fearlessly captured the kidnapper at the scene. He has implicated others, but I'm afraid I can say nothing about that at the moment.'

Evidently not even to me, thought Navrátil, since I haven't a clue what you're talking about. And I bet you haven't either.

Mrs Peiperová pointed at the bandage on Slonský's grazed knuckles.

'You were injured too.'

'A mere flesh wound,' he replied with the air of someone downplaying a serious incident, whereas to describe it as a flesh wound was itself hyperbolic. 'A week or two and it should be back to normal. I'm very lucky,' he added with an attempt at a brave smile as he ushered them towards the canteen. 'Let me give you a coffee and describe this morning's events more fully while Navrátil runs ahead to tell your daughter the good news that you're coming to see her. It'll give her a minute or two to tidy herself up, then I'll take you there personally.'

'Are you sure you can spare the time?' asked Mrs Peiperová.

'Tsk!' replied Slonský. 'What is more important than my staff's families?' He looked steadily at Navrátil. 'No doubt Navrátil will bring dear Kristýna up to date with developments,' he added meaningfully.

Navrátil could hardly believe his ears. A few hours ago, Slonský didn't know her name, and now he was speaking of her like a child of his own. The poor benighted parents were ready to sign up to the Slonský fan club, while he was left to explain to Peiperová that while she may have thought she was being kidnapped, in fact it was all a cunning plan that she had sprung with herself as bait.

To his surprise, she was more than happy to adopt this account, since it offered the best chance of being allowed to stay in Prague. Although part of her was worried about the possibility that this might happen again, she could not face having to return to Kladno and listening to all her mother's friends telling her that they had told her so. Besides, if Slonský meant what he said about a commendation, that was not to be sniffed at.

'If you're sure…' said Navrátil in tones betraying his own uncertainty.

'I am,' Peiperová said. 'When all is said and done, my parents still have their child, which is more than can be said for poor old Mrs Bartošová. I'll have a shower and we'll put on a brave face for Mum and Dad.'

Navrátil was unconvinced that she could recover as quickly as that, but if she wanted to try, he would go along with it. But he could not help feeling that it was lucky he was around to keep an eye on her, and it was in her interests if he set about making that a permanent arrangement.

Slonský had taken the Peipers to the barracks and then excused himself by saying that no doubt they would want some family time together. Navrátil showed every inclination to stay until Slonský announced loudly that they had a witness to interview, and then announced even more loudly that they would do so together.

'Who is the witness?' asked Navrátil, 'or was this a subtle way of getting me out of there?'

'Well, a bit of both. We have got a witness to speak to, and there's no point in delaying if it helps to get the villains behind bars. On top of that, we don't pay you to sit around gawping at young women.'

'I'm not gawping. I'm supporting her after a really frightening ordeal.'

'Of course you are, but the two aren't mutually exclusive, as you've just been proving. I saw the look on your face. Look, I'm not knocking it. Just saying you can't shield her from the world forever.'

'Maybe not forever, but I was hoping for more than six hours.'

'Her family are with her now, and that's as it should be. She'll need you again when they're gone.'

'That reminds me, sir, where did this masterplan to get Kristýna kidnapped come from?'

'It's Officer Peiperová to you during working hours, lad. It set her parents' hearts at rest and it didn't do her self-esteem any harm. Who is hurt by it?'

'The truth comes to mind as a victim.'

'I seem to remember that someone important once asked "What is truth?" and shot off without waiting for an answer.'

'Pontius Pilate, I think.'

'I rest my case. What kind of policeman was he? He only had one case and he fluffed it.'

'Which way now?'

'Out to Ruzyně again. We're going to see Mr Kopecký.'

The old man was wearing a particularly startling pullover of his wife's devising with red and white diamonds on the front and back and a zigzag design down each sleeve.

'You could get migraine looking at that,' whispered Slonský as they waited for Mrs Kopecká to return with coffee and sufficient cakes and pastries for six ordinary people and place them in front of Navrátil who, she thought, might have lost a little weight since he was last there.

When they were all provided for Slonský unfolded the paper he had brought and explained their purpose.

'I want you to think back to the day Jana Válková died.'

'We talked about that,' said Mr Kopecký.

'Indeed we did, and you said you saw a couple of men running away. I know you only caught a brief glimpse, but we think they may be in this photograph. Take your time, and see if you can identify them. It doesn't matter if you can't.'

Kopecký hunched over the photograph and inspected each figure in turn. Finally he stabbed at a man near the right edge.

'That's the big one who got in the front seat,' he said. 'The littler one who got in the back may have been this one beside him. It's a bit hard with a black and white photograph, but if his hair is fair, I'd say he was the one.'

Slonský smiled. 'Excellent. Navrátil will just put that into a statement that you can sign, if you will.'

'Did I pick the right ones?'

'You must pick the people you think were there, sir. It's not for me to say whom you should point out. But those were the two I thought it would be. It's a shame your neighbour isn't around to confirm it, because he got a better view in daylight.'

'Mr Hruška?' said Mrs Kopecká. 'He never said.'

'Nobody asked him properly. The chances are that they found his deafness too much of a barrier or that he didn't hear the question properly.'

'That's very likely,' said Mrs Kopecká. 'When I took food in to him, we had a conversation of sorts, but I never felt he knew what I'd said. I think he just answered the question he expected you to ask.'

'A reporter conducted an interview with him by writing down the questions. Mr Hruška said he saw two boys arrive. He thought they were soldiers.'

Kopecký took a sudden interest.

'Do you know, I believe he's right. I thought they might have been policemen, but they may have been in fatigues.'

Slonský understood. In the dark there had not been much difference between the uniforms in those days.

'And of course, it was a police car they got into,' added Kopecký.

Slonský came close to taking a bite out of his cup.

'A police car? You didn't mention that.'

'Didn't I?' said Kopecký. 'I must have forgotten. I do, you know. It's my age.'

'No, I mean you didn't mention it at the time.'

'I'm sure I did. I don't mean it was one of the green and white things. It was like a staff car. You know the kind. The ones they come to take you away in.'

'An StB car?'

Kopecký became agitated. 'Keep your voice down! We don't want to upset them.'

'But those cars were unmarked. How did you know it was a police car?'

'Well, because the man who got out was in police uniform. I was surprised he drove himself, because he had a fair amount of decoration on his jacket.'

Slonský needed to get this straight. 'Who got out, and when?'

'The car came into the road and turned round with a big loop at the end of the cul-de-sac before it pulled up by the Váleks' house. It was on the wrong side of the road by then, facing back to town. The driver opened the door and started to run towards the house, but the two boys must have seen him and ran out. The stocky one got in the front so the little one got in the back. The driver was an older man. He put his cap on as he got out but I could see he was quite grey.'

Slonský understood now. He had already guessed that this must have happened, but he was surprised that the driver had come in person, at some risk to himself. Navrátil had written out a statement which Kopecký signed, then they took their leave, Navrátil politely declining a bag of buns.

Mrs Kopecká saw them to the door.

'Mr Válek visited the other day. He's not well, the poor man, but it was good to see him. I don't think he'll come again. It upset him too much to see his old house. Bad memories, I suppose.'

'You could meet up in town,' suggested Slonský.

Mrs Kopecká shook her head. 'I doubt it. My husband doesn't go out much. But perhaps when he has a hospital appointment in town we could see what is possible.'

They sat in the car in silence for a few moments.

'Surely if he'd mentioned a police car...' said Navrátil.

'I think he did. He mentioned it to someone who didn't want to hear. When Holoubek visited he didn't think he needed to say it again because it would already be in the file, but whoever it was mentioned to didn't make a note. And I bet that wasn't an accident.'

Navrátil started the engine.

'Now where, sir?'

Slonský lifted his hat and scratched his head.

'I suppose we may as well go and arrest the killers.'

Chapter 17

'You know who they are?'

Both men exhibited surprise, Navrátil had no idea that an arrest was imminent, and Slonský had not realised that their identity was not as blindingly obvious to Navrátil as it was to him.

'You really don't know?'

'Not a clue.'

'Are you pulling my leg?'

'No, sir. How long have you known?'

'I knew one of them almost from the start. The other one, I wasn't certain about until I saw Zelenka's photograph. There's just one little bit I'm having to guess. Never mind, I'll explain when we get there. In the meantime, put your foot down. I want to arrest him at work.'

'It would help if you told me where we were going, sir.'

'What? Oh, park the car at our station. We'll go the rest of the way on foot.'

On arrival, Slonský instructed Navrátil to see to the most pressing matter on their agenda by fetching two coffees and any non-toxic edible material that the canteen might be stocking, with a stern warning that Slonský did not regard any kind of vegetation as fit food for human beings. Fortunately, there was still some sausage left, so the kindly canteen lady piled some into a roll and wrapped it with care once she knew it was for Slonský. Although Slonský had never been one for flattering any authority figure, he laid it on with a trowel where the canteen ladies were concerned since, in his view, the canteen was the hub of the Czech police force and it was impossible to detect on an empty stomach; or, indeed, a stomach filled with lettuce, which was more or less the same thing. In this opinion, he was at one with Dumpy Anna, who believed that men need meat and that a lot of the young officers she served were much too fussy about their diets. She exempted Dvorník from this criticism, since he was prepared to eat any part of an animal that did not have hair on it and had a particular fondness for tripe stewed with onions, as she did herself.

Slonský had closeted himself with Lukas. When the door opened and both men emerged, Lukas looked very grave.

'I'll make some calls to explain the situation,' he said. 'Don't assume they'll come quietly. Put your vests on.'

Slonský agreed to do so, though he hated wearing the bulletproof vests, since he hated being shot too. He ate his roll in silence and with an intensity in his gaze that Navrátil found intimidating.

'Ready?' barked Slonský.

'Yes, sir.'

Navrátil reached for his coat.

'You won't need that,' said Slonský, and led them down to the front desk, where he exchanged a brief word with Mucha.

'I think cell 7 is available at present,' Mucha confirmed. 'Will sir be requiring it for just the one night?'

'Probably a few. We'd better remove any of the frills and extras in there.'

'Of course,' replied Mucha. 'I've got a leaky slops bucket if that suits.'

'Excellent. And don't give him the wooden seat for the top. Don't stand with your mouth open, Navrátil, people will think the police are employing simpletons.'

'We do,' protested Mucha.

'Yes,' agreed Slonský, 'but not usually at Navrátil's rank.'

'That's true,' Mucha agreed. 'You need a lot of experience to be truly clueless.'

Slonský marched across the foyer to the double doors leading into the other wing of the building and climbed the stairs with vigour, Navrátil trying to keep up despite his shorter legs. On the upper floor, they passed through the swing doors into a corridor equipped with a thick carpet. Navrátil could not help noticing that the office doors were polished hardwood and had name plaques on them. Slonský pushed one of these open and marched past the secretary's desk.

'Is he in?' he asked, without waiting for an answer.

'You can't…' she began to reply, but stopped when Slonský turned to face her and she saw the fire behind his eyes.

'Isn't it your coffee break?' he asked.

Without a word, she slipped from the room, and Navrátil heard her begin to run as she left them. Slonský stared after her then, when he was sure she was not going to turn back, he jerked the handle of the inner office and entered.

Colonel Tripka was signing papers and looked up only briefly.

'Don't you knock?' he asked.

'Not when I'm arresting people, no,' replied Slonský.

You had to admit that Tripka was impressive, thought Navrátil. He carefully replaced the cap on his fountain pen, laid it on his blotter, and fixed his eyes firmly on Slonský's.

'You had better explain yourself,' he said, without inviting them to sit.

Slonský sat anyway.

'It's really quite simple. Me good guy, you bad guy. Good guy puts bad guy in jail.'

'On what charges, pray?'

'Conspiracy to murder, corruption, conspiracy to kidnap, dereliction of duty in a public official and probably a few miscellaneous other bits we'll find out as we go along.'

'That's ridiculous,' snorted Tripka. 'Now get out of my office before I get annoyed and stop treating this like the joke it is.'

Slonský grabbed Tripka's arm and turned it palm upwards.

'Lesson eighty-six, Navrátil. You can't control your nervous system. See the sweaty palm. The Colonel — or should I say, soon-to-be ex-colonel — is under stress.'

'This is a career-ending move you're making,' Tripka snapped.

'It certainly is,' agreed Slonský, 'but not for my career. This all starts when Holoubek came to see me. He wanted to reopen a case from 1976, the murder of Jana Válková. Remember her?'

'Is there any reason that I should?'

'Actually, a lot of reasons. The simplest is that you'd met her. Her father remembers thinking you'd be a good catch for her when you came to her birthday party in February. He didn't think you'd shown any interest so when he was asked about boyfriends he didn't mention you. But he'd have been delighted. After all, your father was an officer, if not quite a gentleman. And you were destined for high things. You just had to get your national service out of the way, like we all did, by which time Jana would be old enough to get engaged. Then you'd start your long climb up the greasy pole that would elevate you to your current status. He wasn't wrong, was he? You'd have been a good catch for Jana. In some ways, that is.'

Tripka was clearly furious. His fists were clenched and the knuckles were showing white.

'Anyway, Holoubek had investigated her murder and had proof — absolute proof — that the wrong man had been hanged. Not only that, but people in the police had known he was the wrong man before the life was choked out of him. It wasn't much of a life, Tripka, but it was the only one he had and he was entitled to keep it. Normally I'm opposed to the death penalty but I would be willing to make an exception in your case.'

Navrátil tensed, hoping that Slonský was not going to produce a gun, but he seemed content simply to talk.

'Holoubek returned to see me, and the same day he was creamed by a van driven by a thug called Pluskal. We've got Pluskal downstairs by the way. He doesn't have much of a brain but he does have eyes and ears, and I don't doubt he'll tell us a few juicy snippets once we've loosened his tongue. Pluskal is employed by Griba, and don't tell me you don't know who Griba is.'

'No, I know who he is. One of Prague's foremost criminals.'

'That's right. A man you're paid to try to stop. After all, you're in charge of our anti-drug efforts, and he sells drugs. It sounds like a good fit. And yet although everyone knows what Griba does, our attempts to stop him have been remarkably ineffective. I wonder why?'

'That's an offensive insinuation.'

'Hold on to it. I have plenty more. So, who knew Holoubek had been to see me? You see, Pluskal was waiting for the tram. A brighter villain would have followed Holoubek and killed him in his flat, but Pluskal's orders were to make it look like an accident. Fortunately, he has no idea what an accident should look like. He also left his fingerprints all over the van and some were retrieved before he set fire to it. He's going to plead guilty to the murder of Holoubek, I believe, but he may try to reduce his sentence by being very cooperative about naming others. Needless to say, he doesn't know many others, because Griba likes to keep his secrets, but as a personal bodyguard Pluskal knows a few things others might not know. Things like who Griba meets, for example. Oh, and to answer my own question, there's one person we know for sure knew that Holoubek was here. He asked me what you were doing now, because he'd seen you downstairs. I thought perhaps his son had let the news of his father's visit slip out, but Ondřej only knew about the first visit. He didn't know his father had come back, so he could hardly have told anyone. In the time Holoubek was here, someone organised his death. There's barely time for an outsider to do that, is there?'

Slonský paused and draped one leg negligently across the other so his ankle rested on his knee before continuing.

'Let's go back to Jana Válková. Her parents were going out for the evening. You knew that, because your father had been involved in the security arrangements for the banquet, so you'd seen the guest list. It was Friday night, so you got yourself some passes and made your plans. You'd take some food and a lot of drink and have some fun with Jana. You liked her, she liked you. It could have been a good evening. The snag was that you didn't go alone. I have an eye-witness who has identified you and your companion leaving the Válek house on that evening.'

'Surely it was thirty years ago? You'd never get a conviction based on digging up someone who thinks they might have seen me thirty years ago.'

'We'd have to let a court decide that. But he's a good witness. His memory is stuck. He doesn't remember many new things, but he doesn't forget many old ones either. Memory can work like that. You wanted people to forget, and he can't forget. He doesn't know it was thirty years ago, but he knows it was you. And he has also identified your friend Sedláček.'

Tripka could not conceal his surprise. There was an involuntary stiffening of his shoulders that showed that the name meant something to him.

'I see you know who I mean. Not that you could deny it. Just as Navrátil here is standing next to his best friend in his class photo, so you're next to Sedláček in your national service group photo, which Major-General Zelenka was kind enough to lend us. And he remembers the two of you as best buddies — or are you going to tell me the Major-General is feeble-minded too?'

'No, Sedláček was my best friend. But it was a long time ago.'

'Strange how you never really know someone, isn't it? I suppose if you'd known about the stuff Sedláček had in his pockets you might not have taken him. Because it was Sedláček who started it all, wasn't it? He took his drugs and turned nasty, didn't he? He raped Jana and started torturing her. And you didn't stop him.'

The statement was greeted with silence.

'I said you didn't stop him, did you?'

Tripka reached for the telephone.

'I think I'd like my lawyer here now.'

Slonský threw it on the floor.

'All in due time. All the lawyers you want. You can fill your cell with lawyers. But first I'm going to tell you what a spineless little worm you were. You tried to stop her bleeding with a towel. But it had already been going on a long time by then. You'd enjoyed it at first. You'd even joined in. The forensic report tells us that two different hands had done the stabbing. Did you take the drugs too? Or were you perfectly sober when you sliced into her arms and belly? You were sober enough to ring Daddy for help, weren't you? The telephone record vanished but you rang the hotel where the banquet was taking place, and your father came to fetch you. You were seen arriving by the old man across the road, and another witness saw you climb into a car driven by a senior policeman. Just to convince you he knows what he saw, I'll tell you Sedláček climbed into the front and you rode in the back. I don't know if Jana was actually dead by then. Can you tell me?'

'I want a lawyer,' Tripka croaked.

'No, you want a long pointy stake up your backside with plenty of splinters sticking out. But all in due time. Let's go on with the story. It was your great good fortune that Válek's wife wanted a senior officer to take over the case, so they replaced Holoubek, who might have discovered the truth, with Vaněček, who wouldn't have seen the truth if it was painted on a buffalo and paraded through Prague. He was floundering, and then a colleague gave him a bit of help. He produced a ready-made confession from Ľubomir Bartoš. Bartoš was in jail in Olomouc after trying to flog a Soviet medal, so Vaněček didn't even have to find him. What wasn't said, and Vaněček didn't ask about, was that Bartoš had been in jail at the time of the murder, which is usually reckoned to be a pretty good alibi. Even in those days, we didn't let prisoners out to commit murder and then let them back in again afterwards. Now, here's the bit that was a stumbling block for a while.

I can understand the need for a scapegoat, but why Bartoš? What had he done that put him in the frame? The man was a cat burglar with no record of violence at all, but someone went to a lot of trouble to frame him.'

Slonský retrieved a bundle of papers from his pocket, selected one, and unfolded it so Tripka could read it.

'There's your answer. The list of houses Bartoš burgled during a spree in Prague. Your dad helped to compile it by driving him around town, but your father was only really interested in one. Your old house is on it. But even that isn't much of a reason to see someone hanged. However, when you add to it with his mother's testimony it becomes clearer. Bartoš stole some money, but not Czechoslovak money. It was dollars. Quite a bundle of dollars. And in those days ordinary people couldn't get dollars. It wasn't even allowed for most people in high places to hold dollars, but your father had access to them. He'd sneaked a few here and there and built a little stash, and now it was gone. No wonder he was mad. He couldn't report them as stolen because he wasn't supposed to have them in the first place, so if he couldn't have redress, he'd have revenge. And that's why Bartoš hanged. Your father went to Olomouc, persuaded him to sign a confession — which, by the way, he couldn't read — and dumped him in court to face the music. I can't prove it but I suspect he squared the judge to throw Bartoš in the cells and proceed in his absence so he couldn't deny anything. Poor Bartoš didn't know what had happened, but he did give us one good clue. He told the chaplain that the police officer who took his confession knew Mandy.'

Tripka tried to remain stone-faced, though the strain was showing.

'That had me foxed for a while,' Slonský admitted. 'I couldn't think of anyone called Mandy who featured in the case. I thought the priest must have misheard. Perhaps it was Mandl and we were looking for someone Jewish. Then my dear ex-wife, God rot her soul, came to visit me and the light dawned. We weren't looking for a person. Bartoš had been talking about a song. We didn't get to hear a lot of American music then, but somehow this policeman had picked up all the words of the song and could sing it in English. You'd have to listen to it quite a few times to do that, wouldn't you? It's the kind of thing someone who worked at a counter-espionage listening station near Český Krumlov from 1972 to the end of 1974 might have done, don't you think? I got that from your dad's personnel record, by the way. Bartoš couldn't read, but he had a good memory for a tune. It was the only way he could identify your father, the man who stitched him up. There have been four killings in this case and I can't decide which is the most revolting. What do you think — slicing Jana Válková to death slowly like you did, or hanging an innocent half-wit who stole what you stole, like your dad did? Or perhaps it was having a ninety-year-old man run over, like you did, as opposed to kicking a fellow policeman to death like your dad did? The score is two each, but you're still active and unfortunately, your father isn't. That's a shame, because we don't get many father and son murder trials. The public gallery would have been packed with geneticists wanting to run tests on such a pair of psychopaths. Now you'll have to stand there on your own, which is a shame. It's good for a father and son to have a shared interest, provided it isn't mindless violence.'

Tripka winced. His former bluster had seeped away under Slonský's angry onslaught.

'Let's come on to Vaněček. I'm not going to pretend he was a great policeman. In fact, he was a walking disaster area. Forcing him into retirement was possibly a great blessing for us all. Of course, he was furious. Your father had him thrown out and despite Vaněček's contacts he couldn't prevent it. He lost his nice house and finished up in a small place in Zdiby, brooding in his garden and waiting for a chance to take his revenge. And he thought he'd got it, didn't he? That's why he wouldn't go quietly. He'd found new information and thought that it would see him reinstated and your father retired or worse. But that was Vaněček's weakness, wasn't it? He wasn't ruthless enough. He said his piece to the wrong people, and your father had it characterized as a piece of vicious gossip. Vaněček was taken in for questioning and kicked to death. There wasn't even the spurious dignity of its being labelled as an unfortunate accident. No pretence at all — just a series of boots in the ribs until he died. It was all so panicky and rushed that they didn't even construct a good cover story. He was alleged to have fallen on a fence post, except that his garden didn't have one. They had to deliver a fence post when they took the body back. And his neighbour, who was, after all, a policeman, thought it was suspicious, but he knew better than to raise his head above the parapet. Look where it got Vaněček. I wonder, by the way, what that new information was? I haven't been able to check that out, but I'm struck by the coincidence that Sedláček hurriedly left Czechoslovakia in 1979, just before Vaněček was murdered. Did Vaněček recognise the method in another killing? We'll never know, unless you tell us. No, I didn't think you would.'

Tripka unfastened his jacket and ran a finger around his collar.

'Let's come to your first big mistake — other than being born, that is. That mysterious phone call I received when Peiperová was kidnapped. Why would anyone think she was my niece? Then I remembered an incident on her first day. We were in the place on the corner of the street and for some reason I said to her that Uncle Josef would look after her. You remember that, Navrátil?'

'Yes. And she gave you a hug.'

'And that's the only time anyone has ever done that to me. So whoever thought she was my niece was there. And when I close my eyes and picture the scene, lo and behold you're sitting reading your newspaper at the round table by the pillar about four metres away.'

Navrátil was astonished. He was no student of body language, but even he noticed that Tripka was shrinking in his seat.

'Arranging for Peiperová to be snatched wasn't too difficult. She didn't work here in the intervening period so your mistake wasn't obvious. I thought Pluskal was watching the station, but in fact he tells me he was keeping an eye on the bar because that was the only place they thought she might turn up. Griba told him to pick the girl up and take her somewhere safe. Then he had to phone me with the message, but how did he know when to phone? I arrived at work early and within a few minutes the phone rang. If it had been a bit later, when we were all there, I could have understood it, but somebody must have told him I'd arrived. In fact, an eye witness said Pluskal was phoned and then phoned me. So, who phoned Pluskal? It must have been someone watching this building. Someone who was so panicked by my inquiry that they didn't dare leave me an hour in case I made a breakthrough. They wanted me warned off as soon as I arrived. So much so that they took a big risk. They used their own mobile phone to ring Pluskal, as his account records show. I don't remember the whole number but it ends one-six-five. Oh, look, so does yours! I don't know why I feign surprise, because I checked it beforehand. You saw me arrive, and you rang Pluskal. Navrátil, meet the man who kidnapped your girlfriend. Feel free to give him a sound thrashing.'

'I'd like to, sir, but it's against the rules.'

'I'm sure I saw him attempting to resist arrest.'

'Well, in that case, sir…'

Navrátil landed a beauty on Tripka's cheek before wheeling away to hold his fist in pain.

'There's a water cooler in the outer office, lad. Run it over your hand. Don't worry about getting the carpet wet, they'll be burning it all anyway in a few days to eradicate all traces of the previous occupant. Now, are there any loose ends? We've explained how you murdered Jana Válková, how your dad set up Ľubomir Bartoš to take the rap for that, how he had a former colleague kicked to death when it looked like it would all be reopened, and how you asked Griba to have Holoubek killed when he was trying to do the same thing. Ah, yes — why would Griba, a hardened criminal and one of our most wanted villains, do a favour for you, the head of the anti-drug office, given that you're trying to shut him down? Except, of course, that you aren't really trying, are you? He's pretty immune. Evidence goes missing, witnesses are bumped off, and if anyone inside his circle tries to betray him word somehow gets back to him. Pluskal is very voluble on the subject. He didn't know who the police informant was but he was sure that there must be one, and if even someone like Pluskal with the IQ of a retarded amoeba has come to that conclusion there must be something in it, wouldn't you say? Griba has the best

350

possible insurance policy, hasn't he? He has the head of the anti-drugs squad by the short and curlies because on a July evening in 1976 they murdered a girl together.'

Tripka closed his eyes and pinched the bridge of his nose.

'Griba and Sedláček are one and the same, aren't they? He escaped in 1979 and made his way to Albania. In the mountains, he was safe because the government couldn't make its writ run up there. He was a good shot and he made a first class bandit. That's what Vaněček discovered, I think. There were intelligence reports from Yugoslavia that mentioned a Czech working with the Albanians who raided over the mountains into Kosovo. When the Albanian mafia started muscling in on Prague, Sedláček was the ideal front man. He just needed a new identity, and he got himself one. Just to keep the pressure on you, he picked a good one. He passed himself off as your brother. You couldn't refuse to acknowledge him, or he would bring you down, so to those who know him he's your little brother Vladimir who has been so lucky in his property dealings. Mind you, I only discovered that when I saw a photo of him taken by the fraud squad. They have an innate suspicion of recluses, you see. Give Klinger his due, he's a good fraud officer. When I said I was investigating you, he volunteered the opinion that it must be difficult for you to live in the shadow of such a successful brother and told me all about little Vladimir. He's lost a kilo or five, but he's still the cheeky little chappie in Zelenka's photograph. I don't suppose I need to tell you that I wasn't surprised that your father made no mention of having two sons in his personnel record, or that your mother would have been astonished to discover that she'd given birth to two sons just four months apart. You see, Griba kept his real date of birth when he had his new papers forged. It's easier to remember then, isn't it? The fewer lies you have to remember the easier it all is.'

Slonský reached across the desk and gave Tripka a slap.

'Resisting arrest again, eh? Did you see that, Navrátil?'

'Yes, sir.'

'Let's get the cuffs on him and take him down to the cells, lad.'

Tripka straightened his collar and brushed his jacket with his hand.

'Perhaps you'd give me a minute or two to put my personal effects in order.'

Slonský dived forward and slammed the desk drawer shut.

'No, you don't. There's no easy way out for you. Navrátil, put the cuffs on him and I'll take his gun from the drawer. Tripka, I won't be satisfied with anything other than your complete and utter humiliation. I want you to be treated with universal contumely. I want Prague mothers to substitute your name for the bogeyman's when they're telling their children off. I want to watch as they rip your epaulettes off and write you out of the police service's history. And I want to see you taken down after your trial. Just think how warm a welcome a one-time police colonel is going to get in prison. I'll have to make sure they know I'll take it amiss if anyone kills you too quickly. Navrátil, hold the door open, please.'

Slonský marched Tripka to the door. The secretary had crept back to her desk and was watching goggle-eyed as her boss was led away in handcuffs. In the corridor Slonský was surprised to come face to face with Captain Lukas, who was in full uniform. He ignored Slonský and addressed Tripka.

'I came to tell you in person,' he said, 'that I think you're a complete shit.' He seemed to have run out of things to say, and simply muttered 'Pardon my language' before returning to his office.

Slonský and Navrátil had never heard Lukas use a word like that before. They looked at each other for confirmation that they had not dreamed it.

'It's impressive,' said Slonský, 'how sometimes a man is able, in a few short words, to sum up the thoughts of his entire nation.'

Chapter 18

Tripka was a picture of misery. Slonský had insisted on removing his uniform, leaving him sitting in a bright orange jumpsuit with one leg chained to the table. His rank had vanished too, leading to his being addressed as Prisoner Tripka, and in a further flourish his wife had been telephoned to be told that he was under arrest and was unlikely to be returning home. She arrived at the station to speak to him and instead found herself sitting opposite Slonský.

'Surely there is some mistake,' she protested.

'Certainly,' replied Slonský, 'and your husband made it. He is being charged with one count of murder, one of conspiracy to murder, one of kidnapping, one of obstructing a public official in the execution of their duties — need I go on?'

Mrs Tripková dabbed at her tearful eyes.

'But he's a good man,' she cried.

'He's good at having people killed, I'll give him that. And apparently he's good at pulling the wool over your eyes for thirty years. All the time you've known him, he's had a guilty secret. He murdered his first girlfriend.'

'I refuse to believe that,' she shouted. 'Let me speak to him.'

'I'm afraid we're still questioning him. I can't allow you more than a few minutes and one of us will have to stay in the room.'

He led Mrs Tripková down to the interview room, which was what they called cell 8 when they wanted to impress people. Tripka was led in, and his wife tried to embrace him, but Slonský and Mucha intervened.

'No touching, I'm afraid, madam,' said Mucha.

Mrs Tripková attempted to make eye contact with her husband, but he found it too painful.

'Tell me it isn't true,' she pleaded.

Slonský decided to be helpful.

'You're not under oath,' he said. 'You can lie and tell her you didn't do it, if you've got the brass neck.'

Tripka remained silent. His lip was quivering and he looked ashen.

'Perhaps you'd like to tell Mrs Tripková about your brother,' Slonský suggested.

'He hasn't got a brother,' she replied.

'No, but he lets people think he has, when it suits him. Isn't that right?'

'What's going to happen to him?'

'Hard to say,' Slonský answered. 'If he gets a lenient judge he could be out in twenty-five to thirty years. Of course, prison is a difficult place for ex-policemen. There are a lot of inmates with scores to settle. There may even be some that he put away. I doubt it, because he hasn't actually solved much crime for years, but you never know.'

Tripka's head dropped. He was openly sobbing now.

'You'll have to think carefully about whether to let the children visit,' Slonský added, in what he hoped was a concerned tone. 'It can be very distressing for them.'

'What have you done to us?' his wife screamed.

Tripka just shook his head and continued to cry.

'Technically, he's only suspended at present,' said Slonský, 'so there'll be some money this month. I don't know how long it will take for his wages to stop but at least you've got some time to adjust to your new standard of living.'

'Are you enjoying this, you monster?' spat Mrs Tripková.

'I wish it had never happened,' replied Slonský, 'but your husband made his bed and now he has to lie in it. All we're doing is turning the sheets down.'

Lukas received an unexpected phone call.

'I have Dr Pilik on the line for you,' announced a sepulchral voice. Instinctively Lukas combed his hair and straightened his tie before sitting to attention to take the call.

The minister was delighted. He must have been, because he said it at least four times.

'I shall look forward to these villains appearing before the court. Of course, one is above revenge, but I can't forget that they have caused me some personal embarrassment in the matter of Bartoš.'

Lukas was confused as to whether the minister realised that the identification of Bartoš as the murderer was the work of old Tripka rather than the one in custody, but he let it pass.

'I shall have a word with the prosecutor's office,' Pilik continued. 'We must not show any weakness in dealing with errant police officers.'

'Certainly not,' agreed Lukas.

'There must be exemplary sentences.'

'Certainly.'

'Are you likely to arrest the other conspirator soon?'

'We have identified him, minister. He will take some finding.'

'If you need extra resources, please ask the Director of Police. I shall instruct him accordingly.'

'Thank you, minister. At present we are building our case methodically,' Lukas responded, hoping that it was actually true.

The difficulty with putting the pressure on Tripka was that he had collapsed mentally and was proving impossible to interrogate because he would not stop crying. Eventually the police surgeon was called to give him a sedative.

'I hope it's a placebo,' muttered Mucha.

'I just hope it's painful,' replied Slonský. 'We're not going to get any more out of him. We'll have to make our move soon before Griba knows what has happened.'

'I wouldn't be surprised if he knows already. You know what this place is like for gossip.'

'Yes,' agreed Slonský, 'but you and I start most of it and I haven't said a word.'

'Me neither.'

'It should all be fine, then. Peiperová says she wants to be in on the arrest seeing as Griba ordered her kidnapping.'

'Is she up to it?'

'She's a tough girl. Besides, I wouldn't want to try telling her she can't. She needs it to wrap the whole thing up in her head.'

'Griba was at Tripka's beck and call just as much as the other way round, wasn't he? Tripka was the one person who could lead the police to him.'

'Yes. When Tripka said it was necessary to kill Holoubek, Griba didn't argue. He just did what he was told. He only had an hour or so to arrange it.'

'Do we know where to find Griba?'

'Yes, now that we know he's Tripka's so-called brother. But it's a high security site and it's going to be difficult to get in.'

'So do we wait until he comes out?'

'The trouble is he could land a helicopter in his garden and escape us. I toyed with arresting him at night, just for old times' sake really, but the best bet is to walk calmly up the drive at breakfast time. I've got a rifle squad having a look round for points of entry.'

'So what now, old friend?'

'Now? The only fixed points in a changing world — a beer, some sausages and a good night's sleep.'

It was 06:30 and Slonský, Dvorník, Navrátil and Peiperová were in their car. Navrátil was driving.

'The gate is under CCTV so we'll all have to enter together and just hope nobody is paying it much attention. Navrátil and I will go to the front, while you two make your way to cover the back. Watch out for dogs or security guards. If you meet any you're entitled to disarm them. Security guards, that is — never try to disarm a dog. So far as we know, he and his wife live alone here. There'll be staff around but they don't live in. Any questions?'

'Do you want him taken alive?' asked Dvorník.

'Ideally. But don't put yourself at risk. I've divided us this way so there's one experienced officer in each pair. If anything happens to me, Dvorník takes charge.'

'What about if something happens to you and Dvorník?' asked Navrátil.

'Then you'd better run like hell, because you'll be in real trouble,' Slonský told him.

They could hear a deep rumbling sound not too far away.

'What's that?' asked Peiperová.

'That,' replied Slonský, 'is as subtle as a spade round the back of the head. That's an armoured car moving into position. If a gunfight starts they'll take out a chunk of the perimeter wall and the army boys will move in. If that happens, we all come back here and sit in the car. No point in heroics.'

They climbed out and wrapped their coats around themselves in the chill morning air. It was bright, but in the lee of the trees there was a definite coldness and their breath fogged in front of them.

'Best leave the car unlocked,' said Slonský. 'We don't want to be unable to get into it if we have to run back.'

'Should I leave the keys in the ignition?' asked Navrátil.

'Better not. There may be criminals about who would steal it, and how stupid would we look then? Tuck them in the glove compartment.'

Navrátil obeyed. Slonský asked each of them to show their gun and check it was loaded, just in case. He also suggested that they should verify that the safety catch was on, now that Novák had shown him how easy it was to disengage it. In fact, it was so easy that Slonský was very careful as he put it back in his holster in case he shot himself in the foot.

'Right. On we go.'

At the gate, Slonský pressed the buzzer. A voice asked who he was.

'Detective Lieutenant Slonský and Officer Navrátil. We'd like a word with Mr Tripka away from his office, please.'

The gate opened and all four walked through. Dvorník and Peiperová slipped off to the left behind some bushes and made their way round the perimeter, hoping there were no cameras watching them. Meanwhile Slonský and Navrátil marched boldly up the drive, and were met at the front door, where they showed their badges.

Griba was still a square man, perhaps not as nakedly powerful as in his youth, but nevertheless quite impressive. He wore his hair in a steel grey crewcut and was dressed for a day at the office.

'What can I do for you?'

'I'm afraid there is some embarrassing family business,' said Slonský. 'Your brother has been arrested for corruption and he has mentioned your name several times in questioning.'

Griba did not flinch or twitch. He chewed something slowly and finally responded.

'I'm sorry to hear that. What has he been saying?'

'He says that he did some of the things we discovered because you put pressure on him.'

'That's nonsense. What pressure could I possibly put on my big brother?'

'Well, that's what we thought,' said Slonský, 'but you can understand that we had to ask.'

'Of course.'

Griba's wife appeared in the hallway.

'What is it, darling?' she asked.

Griba answered without looking at her.

'It seems my brother is suspected of taking bribes or something of the sort.'

'Never! I don't believe it.'

'Neither do I,' Griba said, 'but these gentlemen wouldn't be here unless something needed explaining. I hope he's able to satisfy them.'

Slonský smiled his simplest village idiot smile.

'He's certainly being very talkative. I don't doubt he'll tell us everything in the end. For example, he has already told us you're not his brother, Mr Sedláček, and implicated you in a murder you jointly committed. Not to mention fingering you for another murder and a kidnapping.'

Griba tried to shut the door but Slonský had jammed his foot in the way. Springing back, the criminal seized his wife by the shoulders and held her in front of him as a shield.

'Get back,' he said. 'Retreat down the path. We're going to walk calmly to our car and drive away and no-one gets hurt.'

To illustrate how someone might get hurt, he flourished a flick-knife he drew from his pocket.

'I don't think so,' said Slonský, drawing his gun and levelling it at Griba. 'We seem to have reached a bit of an impasse. If you cut her throat, that just adds another to your catalogue of victims. It's no skin off our nose.'

Griba's wife was whimpering. It sounded as if she was on the verge of an asthma attack.

'I think your wife is finding this a bit stressful,' Slonský commented. 'It must be difficult to discover your husband has an assumed name and you've been living for twenty years with a murderer. Since I may not get the chance to ask her later, do you mind if I ask her whether you've carved a cross on her nipples too?'

'You're very cocky, Mr Detective, but I only have to wait a minute or two, and then my men will be here to even up the fight.'

Griba opened his left hand to show a panic button.

'They're on their way even now,' he gloated.

Suddenly there was a loud noise and Griba's wife slid to the floor, blood running from her shoulder. Griba let her slip and stood stunned as his white shirt sleeve reddened. Navrátil kicked the knife from his grasp and pushed him against the wall as Slonský stood transfixed and uncomprehending, until he was able to see past Griba and saw Dvorník and Peiperová in the kitchen doorway. Dvorník's gun was levelled and smoking.

Slonský showed his gratitude in his usual way.

'You could have bloody killed us,' he growled.

'Could have, but I didn't,' said Dvorník.

'You shot his wife.'

'Just a flesh wound, I expect. The bullet went through his arm and smacked her in the shoulder. Small price to pay if you ask me. Better than getting your throat cut, anyway.'

Slonský paced to the kitchen door, completely ignoring the scuffle as Navrátil and Peiperová subdued Griba and tried to get handcuffs on him.

'You had a lot of confidence in your aim, I'll give you that.'

'Belong to a gun club,' Dvorník smirked. 'If I can't hit an arm at ten metres, there's something wrong.'

'Sir,' Navrátil interrupted, 'shouldn't we tell the boys outside what's happening and warn them that a bunch of armed guards may be coming?'

Slonský sighed.

'I suppose so. Don't want the health and safety people onto me.'

Chapter 19

'Of course, there'll have to be an enquiry,' Captain Lukas announced.

'I don't see why,' replied Slonský. 'Dvorník didn't shoot at Mrs Tripková. He just happened to hit her after he hit her husband. You could argue that it was her husband's fault for not stopping the bullet properly.'

Lukas was having none of it.

'You know as well as I do that there is an enquiry every time someone is shot by the police. The mere fact that there is an enquiry does not imply guilt. It means that we have nothing to hide.'

'We have plenty to hide,' argued Slonský, 'but not involving bullets. The amount the fraud squad spends on disinfectant thanks to Klinger's obsession with cleanliness comes to mind. And doesn't the fact that we're charging the head of the anti-drug centre with murder suggest that we have nothing to hide?'

Lukas became grave. 'I hope we can get a conviction. A confession would be helpful, but I rather fear he's going to claim that he isn't fit to stand trial.'

'So he was fit to head the drugs squad at half past three, but by four o'clock he wasn't fit to be held to account for what he did thirty years ago? Of course, there are some of us who believed he was out of his tree for much of the intervening thirty years, but that's just prejudice, not a psychiatric evaluation.'

'What about Griba? Do we have enough on him?'

'Pluskal began to sing like a lark once he heard that Griba was in the cell across the way. I explained to him that he had a free choice whether to grass on Griba or not, but since Griba was going to believe that he'd informed on him anyway, Pluskal had every reason to make sure Griba stayed behind bars for the sake of his own future safety.'

'And he bought that argument?'

'He isn't very bright, but he understands a threat.'

'He can't be bright if he doesn't realise Griba isn't there.'

'That's because I've let him believe Griba is. We threw a blanket over Dvorník and kicked up a bit of a fuss as we locked him up.'

'And how is Griba?'

'Sore arm, no doubt. Being shot does that for you. But the surgeons sorted the wound and gave him enough sedative to keep an ox docile, so as soon as they give us the nod we'll throw a blanket over his head and repeat the manoeuvre.'

'There's no danger that he'll be liberated from the hospital?'

'I've got four marksmen standing guard and we've manacled one of his legs to his bed frame.'

Lukas indicated the chair and motioned Slonský to sit. The word "retirement" began to form in Slonský's mind.

'How is Peiperová?'

'Better for having come back to work, I think. Navrátil is good for her. I don't know why, because some days he irritates the hell out of me, but she seems to enjoy his company.'

Lukas made a steeple from his fingers and held it to his lips for a few moments.

'I'll reach retirement age around the same time as you. There'll be a captain's job going. If you wanted, I'd go before you so that you can get the rank for a few months and bump your pension up. Not that I can guarantee you'd get the job,' he added hurriedly.

'Thank you, sir, but I don't think I'm captain material. I'm happy being a lieutenant.'

Lukas would normally have approached this objection obliquely, but since Slonský did not appear able to understand anything less subtle than a simple declarative sentence, he tried the more direct approach.

'If you don't take it, it will probably go to Doležal.'

Slonský twitched. It was just a reflex, he told himself, something that he would learn to control.

'In that event, perhaps I've been too hasty, sir. I'll give it some thought.'

'You do that, Josef. You do just that.'

Tripka sat on his cot, rocking slowly and cuddling the pillow in front of him.

Slonský opened the door, closed it behind him, and leaned against the wall.

'How are you enjoying your stay? The food is hardly cordon bleu, but then you're getting it for free. And I managed to wangle you your own cell. Not much of a view but better than Griba has across the corridor.'

Tripka did not respond, so Slonský straddled the chair facing him. This allowed Slonský to slouch forward, but also protected his genitals in case Tripka had a fit of the habdabs.

'He's not many metres away. Would you prefer to share?'

Tripka's eyes widened.

'Ah, you understand. You see, we're always short of space here. In your wing you've got that big cell because it doesn't matter if you put twenty whores or junkies in together. If we did that, there'd just be a few bones left in the morning. But there would be a certain poetic justice in locking you up in your old department's cells, because then we could put Griba and Pluskal in with you. It would be like a reunion, just like old times. What more could a man want than to die surrounded by his friends?'

Tripka refused to speak, but his eyes betrayed his fear.

360

'If you want to stay on your own, you'd better start talking. In the normal run of things, I would regard you as the grubbiest, nastiest, most despicable, loathsome lowlife we've ever had in here, and believe me we've had some who would give you a good run for that title. There was that chap who liked beheading nuns, for example. And then there was the one who stabbed a teenage girl so she bled to death slowly. Oh, no, hang on — that was you. Scrub that example, then; I'll find a better one. The key is that I'm coming under pressure from others to get you a bit off your sentence if you ensure that Griba stays in jail so long he'll leave in a cherrywood urn. Can we do business? Don't dither too long, or I may take the offer across the corridor and see what Griba is prepared to offer to keep you inside for the rest of your days. Personally I'd prefer that. He's a mere sex trafficking drug dealing pimp, extortionist, kidnapper and multiple murderer, whereas you're a corrupt policeman. The distinction is that if you were both on fire, I would be prepared to pee on him to put him out. But if you were to make a clean breast of the whole thing, save us a lot of police time and ensure that Griba is taken off these mean streets, I can be magnanimous. So here's a pencil and paper. Get writing. An hour from now I take them away and give them to Griba instead.'

Navrátil opened the door in response to Slonský's knock. As they walked back to the main desk, Navrátil asked a question that had been puzzling him.

'You know you talked about mean streets. Does Prague have mean streets, then?'

'Oh, yes,' replied Slonský. 'Not to mention some tight corners and some really stingy alleyways.'

Dvorník was ecstatic. Slonský no longer needed him, and he was restored to his normal freedom of action. On top of that, he was the man who had shot the fearsome Griba, and he would be the recipient of many a free drink over the next few weeks on the strength of that. Admittedly he was also the man who had shot Griba's wife, but you can't have everything, and she was recovering well in hospital. The surgeon had spoken to Lukas and assured him that her shoulder blade would be good as new, if you overlooked the hole in it which he might try to fill with some mashed up bone and cement. Despite Lukas' scepticism it appeared that this was perfectly respectable medical practice, according to Dr Novák, and not a species of mumbo-jumbo akin to chicken entrail inspection.

'It was a good job, there's no denying it,' said Slonský to him. 'Should I have heard a warning?'

'Of course not,' said Dvorník. 'A warning would only … well, warn him.'

'That clarifies things,' said Slonský. 'I wondered why standing orders said we had to shout a warning before we shoot someone, but now I see that the idea is that he won't get a nasty surprise when the bullet hits him.'

'Next time I'll let him cut her throat, shall I?'

'No, no need to get defensive. I'm not judging you. Given half a chance I'd have done the same myself. I just want to sort out what we're going to say to the investigation team.'

'How about "It happened. No regrets. Get over it."?'

'Perfect.'

Slonský breezed into the cell. Tripka pushed the paper wordlessly towards him.

'Let's have a read of this, then,' said Slonský. 'Nice handwriting.'

I, Bohuslav Tripka, make the following statement voluntarily.

I first met Jana Válková at a camp organised by the Pioneer movement. She was about eighteen months younger than me but I was immediately drawn to her. However, she was too young to show an interest. On the occasion of her seventeenth birthday, which I believe was in February 1976, I was surprised to receive an invitation to her party. I had not realised that this invitation was extended to a number of those she had met at the camp, as well as schoolfriends. As a consequence, I knew very few people there and I found myself talking to her mother, Mrs Válková. Although I believe that she did not know my father personally, she knew of him and asked me a number of questions about him. She said she hoped they would see me there again when the house was less crowded. From these remarks I deduced that she approved of me as boyfriend for her daughter.

However, no further invitations arrived. We met briefly at another camp and Jana was friendly and remembered me by name. When the time came for me to do my national service I found myself doing my initial training not too far from her house — we lived in the centre of Prague at the time.

My best friend in the army was called Sedláček. He was physically bigger than me and boasted of his success with girls. When we came to know each other well, I asked him for some advice and told him about Jana. He suggested that we went to see her together and he would put in a good word for me. He said that she would know I was respectable and safe, but that young women wanted adventure and danger, and that was why bad boys like him had so much success with girls. I should show her that I knew how to have fun.

At my parents' house, I discovered a guest list for a banquet and saw that Jana's parents were invited. Since it was a Friday night, I was able to obtain a pass to go out of barracks and Sedláček and I took a bus out to Ruzyně. He had some beer and some food in a canvas bag. I did not know that he also had some illicit drugs. To this day, I do not know exactly what it was. It may have been cocaine, because after we had some drinks, he opened the bag and put some crystals on his hand so he could sniff it like snuff. He then rubbed some on his gums, after which he became louder and more aggressive. He wanted us to try some. I used a little but the powder made me sneeze so I think I absorbed very little. My nose tingled but I cannot say that I noticed any other effects. Jana at first refused to try any, but after some coaxing from Sedláček she agreed to place a little on her tongue and lips. After a while she said her lips were numb. Sedláček told her he did not believe her, and kissed her before asking if she could feel it. After that we took it in turns to kiss her. Sedláček used more of the powder and he became rougher. At one point I noticed he had pushed his hand inside her top and she was telling him to stop, though she did not really seem annoyed.

We had some more beer, then Sedláček passed round his powder again. This time Jana seemed disorientated or intoxicated and she made no protest when Sedláček started to undo her clothes. She slipped off the sofa onto the floor and Sedláček told me to hold her shoulders so she would not keep moving. I did not realise what he had in mind, but soon he was raping her. She started to shout so he turned the music up then pushed her jumper into her mouth and slapped her. She stopped protesting after she was hit. I remember Sedláček telling her she was one of those girls who liked being bullied. She disagreed, but he hit her until she agreed to say that she liked him doing it. He told her she would like pain, and she agreed, probably because she thought he would hit her again if she didn't.

He produced a penknife and prodded her arm. He didn't pierce it, but it dented the skin. He repeated this several times, but on the fifth or sixth occasion he drew blood. He gave me the knife and told me to see how hard I could push before I penetrated the skin. Next he tried throwing the knife to see if it stuck in. Finally he started slicing into her skin. He said he wanted to see how many cuts she could tolerate before she passed out.

Suddenly I became aware that her arm was bleeding badly. I told Sedláček we needed to give her first aid and together we carried her to the bathroom, where we tried to stop the blood with towels and a curtain. I tried to make a tourniquet but Sedláček just kept giggling and when I finally got the bleeding from her right arm to stop, he laughed "That was fun. let's make another one" and cut into her left biceps and armpit. There was a lot of blood and I wanted to send for help but Sedláček said we could fix it.

I don't know when I realised that she was dying. I felt completely sober and I was shaking Sedláček to make him stop playing his silly games. He punched me quite hard and I knew then that I could not stop this by myself.

I rang the hotel where my father was at the banquet and asked to speak to him. When he came to the phone he told me to calm down and he would come over at once to sort things out. I don't know how long he took. It seemed to be hours. By the time he came Jana was dead and Sedláček was less aggressive. We ran out to the car and father drove off. He took us to his house and made us shower and change our clothes, then he returned us to the barracks and ordered someone to issue us with some new kit. Although he was in police uniform, he was a major and the quartermaster felt he should obey his orders.

Father told us to say nothing to anyone, and not even to discuss it ourselves in case anyone overheard. After a few days he said that he did not think we were likely to be arrested because the investigation had run out of steam and in any event an incompetent officer had been placed in charge, but he said the best way of ensuring our safety would be if someone else had been convicted of the murder. I did not realise that he was going to make that happen.

I knew that our house had been burgled earlier in the summer and I remember father being very angry because something had been taken and he could not recover it. I heard him say to mother that even if it was found, he could not claim it was his. I heard later that he found the culprit and decided to make an example of him. I knew nothing of this until a Slovak man was hanged for the murder of Jana Válková.

After that I tried to forget the whole episode. Sedláček said we would have to watch out for each other and that this would make us even better friends now that we had a shared secret.

A couple of years later I had completed my service and joined the police. Father told Sedláček that he wasn't suitable, and suggested that he should stay in the army. He used his influence to have him accepted in a commando unit. I had occasional letters from him telling me how much he enjoyed it. He especially liked mountain training and camping outdoors. I don't know exactly when it happened, but within a couple of months there were two serious developments.

First, we heard that the police officer who had investigated the murder had discovered proof that the wrong person had been hanged. Father was worried because this officer, whose name I have forgotten, was blaming him for having provided evidence against this Slovak which had now been shown to be false. Fortunately the officer had left the police and he confronted my father personally. My father was able to use his influence to have the officer neutralised before questions were asked.

After that, Sedláček got into trouble with the army. He wounded an officer in a quarrel and I do not know if he was discharged or just ran away. He made his way to Albania where he found a welcome amongst the mountain people who prize a good fighter. He stayed there for over ten years and made a number of firm friendships. I did not hear from him during this time.

When Communism collapsed, he heard that Albanian gangsters were coming to Prague to set up various illegal operations and offered his services as an interpreter and guide. He returned covertly to the Czech Republic and obtained new papers. I did not know that he had created a new identity as my half-brother. He claimed that we had the same father but that his mother had been my father's mistress. This explained how he was almost the same age and why nobody had previously known of him. By this time, my father was dead and unable to disprove the story.

Over a period of time he took over a large part of the illegal Albanian activity, masquerading under the codename Griba. The Albanians had given him this name because he was skilled at finding and defusing mines, so they called him "The Rake", like the garden tool.

From time to time our paths crossed, and Sedláček would remind me that he had not forgotten our past, and if I wanted to keep our secret I must ensure that he knew if the police were planning to move against him. When his staff threatened to leak information to the police I would let him know, and he would take whatever action was needed to keep them quiet. In this way he remained immune from prosecution. I admit now that I gave him this information.

However, I did not protect him as has been alleged. I wanted nothing more than to have him arrested. I did not fear this because once he was in prison he would no longer torment me. If he had tried to tell anyone what had happened to Jana Válková, I would have argued that it was fantasy with no evidence and it would have been my word as a police officer against that of a known criminal and fugitive. In my view, I had nothing to fear from his arrest.

This changed when Holoubek began to interest the police in reopening the case. We knew that Holoubek had some information, but despite burgling his flat we could not find it and did not know exactly what it was. As a result of Holoubek's meddling, we were no longer secure.

I discovered that he had been to see Lt Slonský. I also determined that Lt Slonský had requested some relevant files from the archives. I had been able to remove a few incriminating pages in the past without being noticed but I worried that Lt Slonský might still find something that I had overlooked. I therefore suggested to Sedláček that we should take steps to get the case dropped.

I did not realise that Holoubek would be killed, particularly in so brutal and public a manner. When I heard what had happened I felt quite sick. It was also counter- productive, because it encouraged the said Lt Slonský to investigate more thoroughly, and he is a more formidable adversary.

Sedláček suggested that we had to find some way of deterring Slonský personally. Since we knew nothing dishonourable about him and we did not think that we had any credible threat against him personally, we did not at first know how to do this. Then I remembered that he had brought a young woman to a bar, and that this young woman had addressed him as "Uncle Josef". Since Slonský has no other family and very few friends, we thought a threat to this woman might deter him. We did not realise that in fact she was a member of the police force newly arrived from some other city.

I wish to state that I made it very clear to Sedláček and his men that this woman was not to be harmed and that she should be held only until Slonský dropped the case.

I am prepared to co-operate to the full with any enquiry.

Slonský put the papers down and looked at Tripka, who was waiting apprehensively for Slonský's comments.

'I should put your name down for a creative writing course when you get to prison. You have a definite talent. Of course, I doubt you can string it out for thirty years, but it'll give you an interest. That said, I'm afraid I can only grade this as a B minus. You haven't really put the effort in, you see. For a start, there's no mention of the fact that you stabbed Jana Válková too. If you didn't rape her it can only have been because you weren't up to it. Remember we have forensic evidence that two different people did the stabbing, and it was more than just testing to see how hard you could push before the skin popped open. You participated to the full, didn't you? You're not giving yourself credit for the part you played. That's why there was a cross on her nipple, wasn't it? Sedláček made one cut and you made the other.

'Then there's the choice of language. The officer was neutralised, was he? It sounds like you took him to a vet. He wasn't "neutralised"; he was kicked to death in cold blood. And it's very good of you to feel sick about the killing of a senior citizen and former colleague. Do you know what a body looks like when a van runs over it at high speed? But the bit that really offends me is that nowhere in this self-justifying trash is there the word "sorry". Nowhere is there any acceptance of any responsibility for what happened. Jana was killed because you took some drugs and were too spaced out to realise what had happened, then you were too weak to intervene. How many times do you say that you didn't realise, you didn't know, you didn't approve? Actually the thing you didn't do was give a toss. That nasty Sedláček put you up to all this, did he? Your father could sort all the rest out for you — a scandalous misuse of his office and rank, by the way — but he couldn't sort out Sedláček? Tell me, where is your father's headstone? I may want to relieve myself later.'

Tripka had taken refuge in tears again.

'You've got some paper left. I'll sharpen your pencil, and you can start from scratch. And if you don't tell me the truth I'll put you in Sedláček's cell and show him this account in your handwriting that lays all the blame on him. You know him better than I do — how do you think he'll take it? Laugh it off, will he? I can picture that winning smile of his as he gouges your eyes out. Now, start writing and this time tell the whole story.'

'You're sure you want to do this?' asked Lukas doubtfully.

Slonský merely nodded.

'It'll surprise a lot of people,' Lukas went on. 'It's been a shock to me.'

'Things change,' Slonský shrugged. 'Ideas you used to be certain about become less definite and then you find yourself thinking exactly the opposite.'

'That's obvious. Well, if you're absolutely sure this is what you want I'll put the wheels in motion. But once I've done it, you realise there's no going back. You can't have thought about this for long.'

'I'm going with my gut feeling,' Slonský explained. 'It's rarely let me down over the years.'

Lukas looked into Slonský's eyes for any sign of doubt, then, seeing none, he reached for his pen, uncapped it, and signed the sheet of paper.

'I'll keep it in my desk until the morning in case you change your mind,' he said.

'I won't,' replied Slonský, 'but thanks for the thought.'

From his adolescence, Navrátil had pictured what happened when you got engaged. He had replayed the scene many times in his head. He would take his intended for a quiet dinner, the best he could afford. Afterwards they would walk in the woods or along the river, just the two of them, ignoring anyone else who came near their space, and at some point he would invite her to sit on a tree stump or a bench, kneel in front of her and announce his undying love, simultaneously producing a ring from his pocket. He had even practised removing a ring box from his jacket and talking at the same time, just to prove this particular act of multitasking would not be beyond him. If she said yes, he would give her a passionate yet chaste kiss. If she said no, he would give serious thought to romantically heaving himself in the river, because that was how you showed your disappointment.

Peiperová wanted to go to the cinema, to lose herself in another world for an hour or two. The movie was not the sort he would have chosen, since it seemed to consist mainly of young women in their pyjamas talking a lot and he wanted to shout at the screen that the best way of finding out if the journalist loved the blonde one was simply to ask him instead of talking about it to her friends for eighty minutes. It was too late for dinner when they came out, but Peiperová said she would like a *párek* so Navrátil bought a pair at a stall.

'Slonský would be proud of you,' he said. 'His world revolves around sausages.'

'And pastries.'

'And beer. Especially beer.'

'Do you think he'll see his wife again?'

'There's a lot of anger there for him to overcome. I can't see it. He's getting on and he won't change now. He's a nice man, a good man, but I fear he's going to finish up living in one room on his own. When they eventually kick him out, that is, because he'll never retire voluntarily.'

Peiperová nodded. 'We're like a family, aren't we? It's one of those discussions my parents used to have — "what are we going to do about granddad?"'

'I feel a responsibility towards him, and I've only known him four months or so.'

'So do I, and I've only been here a fortnight. The most exciting fortnight of my life! What more can possibly happen?'

'Marry me,' Navrátil blurted out.

Peiperová froze, the sausage halfway to her mouth.

'What did you say?' she asked.

'Marry me. I hadn't planned to ask like that, and I haven't got a ring, and I've probably messed it all up now. You haven't even met my mum yet and I should have told her about you but it's just that when I saw you hogtied like that...'

'I hope you're not one of those boys who gets turned on by tying up women.'

'Certainly not! I only meant that I realised I wanted to take care of you forever.'

'We've only known each other a short while. Are you sure?'

'I'm sorry, it was a dumb question, forget I asked. I—'

'Yes.'

'Yes what?'

'Yes, it was a dumb question. But yes, I think I'll marry you. Not yet, but I will.'

'When?' asked Navrátil, his voice breaking with excitement.

'Can I finish my sausage first?'

'Not really,' said Navrátil. 'It dropped out of your bun when I asked you.'

Slonský had a few glasses in front of him, while Valentin looked more like the disreputable and dishevelled specimen he used to be before dreams of television stardom induced him to comb his hair more than once a week and wear matching socks.

'It worked out all right, old friend,' said Valentin.

'We've got Tripka. And I think there's enough to nail Sedláček too. A confession would be good, but I doubt he'll be that obliging. I just need to get Tripka to own up to what he did so the judge doesn't think he put the blame on his mate to save his own skin.'

'But he did.'

'That's why I need him to rewrite his confession. At the moment you'd think the pair of them were Adolf Hitler and Mother Teresa. I'm hungry. Do you think they'll have any sausages left?'

Slonský was in luck. The waiter soon returned with a plate of sausages, sauerkraut and onions. While these last two were technically vegetables, Slonský was prepared to eat them as necessary accoutrements to a good sausage, provided he had enough beer to wash them down.

'When did you know it was Tripka?'

'I was sure it was a policeman when Holoubek was killed so soon after seeing me. I settled on Tripka after Peiperová was kidnapped.'

'But the other one had been around Prague for ages. Didn't anyone recognise him as Sedláček?'

'It had been over ten years when he came back, and it was a few more years before he started making serious money. He'd gone grey and lost a bit of muscle.'

'So what put you on to him?'

'That newspaper story you found. I'd been trying to find one killer for all the victims, but then it struck me that it didn't have to be the same one. The fact that Hruška saw soldiers confirmed the way I was thinking. I'd realised that when Válková was killed young Tripka would have been doing his national service. And I'd also realised that the dislike between old Tripka and Vaněček was such that Tripka could well have engineered Vaněček's killing. I just couldn't see who would have helped Vaněček by framing Bartoš. Of course, if you want to get off a charge, finding someone else to carry the can is a good move, but I couldn't see why it had to be Bartoš until his mother mentioned the money. After that it was clear in my head. Young Tripka had to be involved in the killing of Jana Válková, and the old man had covered it up and found a scapegoat. I started by believing that the spat with Vaněček three years later must have been about something else, and that eventually Tripka had eliminated him, but why take the risk of killing someone who had lost anyway? Then it dawned on me that it must be fear that the case was going to be blown open. That would cause a killing, because it was the only way the

Tripkas would ever be safe. The Mandy thing was a confirmatory detail — plenty of us listened secretly to Western radio, but only an StB agent would sing American tunes publicly. I still need one or two more things ironing out, but we're almost there now.'

'A job well done, Josef. You must be very pleased.'

'Actually, old friend, I'm feeling flat, dejected, tired, old, you name it. Get your thesaurus out, because I've run out of adjectives. Young Tripka had done all this and he was still one of the police force's top men. Why hadn't we spotted him? How many others are there in high places with dirty pasts? When Communism fell I thought we'd clear all these villains out and I'd see a proper, honest police force doing what I joined the police to do — to sort out crime and keep people safe. Here I am, coming up to retirement and we haven't finished the job. Thank God for the likes of Navrátil and Peiperová who may just be good enough to complete the spring cleaning.'

'They're bright kids.'

'They're the future, and I'm ancient history. Come on, old friend, I'm getting maudlin. Put me on the night bus and let's go home.'

Chapter 20

The morning dawned bright and cheerful, and the sun slanted down on a police headquarters that was missing Josef Slonský. During the night an idea had occurred to him, and he was therefore moving from office to office collecting signatures and permits. It might have been helpful if he had communicated his intentions to his increasingly frantic boss, who was unsure whether to tear up the paper in his top drawer, or go ahead with it. It also crossed his mind that Slonský might have been seized by Griba's men with a view to swapping him for the criminal. If that happened the official policy of the government was that the captors would be told that no deal was possible and they must do their worst. Lukas would have felt very uneasy about condemning Slonský to death in that way, the only mitigating factor being that Slonský would undoubtedly have done the same if the roles were reversed. Indeed, if a deal were to be done, Slonský himself would probably repudiate it. But that did not make it any easier for his bemused superior.

If he had only thought to ask Mucha, his mind might have been set at rest, because Slonský had consulted the desk sergeant before beginning his quest, and a small smile was flickering across Mucha's lips even now as he stood arranging the staff roster for the next month. Its cause was not the thought of giving himself a weekend shift when his wife's sister was coming to stay, nor even of the pleasure he would derive from making that slimy little toad Bureš work on his birthday, but of the lengths Slonský was prepared to go to in order to ensure a conviction. His plan might not work, but you had to admire the fact that he was even bothering to try.

Tripka looked up as Slonský and Navrátil entered the interview room. Slonský sat opposite the disgraced policeman and placed a box on the table. Removing the lid, he carefully lifted the contents out and stood it in front of him.

'Recognise this? I thought you'd like to see your dad again.'

'What do you mean by digging him up? What has this to do with him?'

'I've brought him in for questioning in connection with a very serious offence that he may have committed. He's just as guilty as you, so this way you both get to spend thirty years behind bars. I admit it probably won't worry him as much as it will you, but you'll enjoy each other's company. Unless you'd prefer me to scatter him in the exercise yard?'

'No! You can't do this. It's inhuman.'

'Inhuman? That's rich coming from someone who held a teenage girl down while his mate raped and slashed her. What's inhuman about scattering ashes? It happens all the time. What would be inhuman would be if I took this urn and emptied the contents down the toilet, but fortunately you have an hour to prevent that.'

'You wouldn't dare.'

'Wouldn't I? Now that's where you're wrong, because I've done a lot of stupid things as dares in the past. Running across the railway line when the express was coming, skiing over a blind jump, eating sushi — this would just be another in a long line. Now, you give a fresh statement to Navrátil while I go and pick the wax seal off the lid of the urn.'

'You're a monster, Slonský. We're the same vintage. We've worked together for years. You know what the old days were like. Why couldn't you just let me take the best way out, for old times' sake?'

Slonský leaned menacingly over the table and spoke slowly but with passion.

'Because you're an ordinary criminal, and ordinary criminals don't get to avoid a trial by shooting themselves. Because we were never that close anyway and I've despised you for many years. It was probably unfair of me because I disliked you because of what your father was, but that's how I felt. Because Jana Válková and Edvard Holoubek deserve to be avenged for what you did to them. They weren't offered a clean, quick death with a pistol. Because if I don't put you in the dock I'm as bad as you are, and I have enough on my conscience already without doing anything else that I shouldn't.'

Tripka closed his eyes and seemed to be composing himself.

'I didn't go to Jana's house intending her any harm. If I'd known what Sedláček was going to do I'd never, ever have taken him. I let my loyalty to a friend get in the way of what I should have done. You have to remember I was very young.'

'Young, but not an idiot. You knew right from wrong.'

'Yes, and it was wrong. There, I've said it. I did wrong. I should have stopped him. I should have owned up. I didn't know what my father would say when I phoned him. I suppose I hoped he'd stay with me while I was being questioned. It honestly didn't occur to me that he would cover it all up. Even if he'd wanted to, I didn't think he could. If he'd been caught he'd have been disciplined and disgraced.'

'He'll be disgraced now. Like father, like son, eh?'

'I accept that I bear some of the blame for what happened to Jana. I also regret what happened to Holoubek. I didn't really know what I thought Sedláček would do when I asked him to stop Holoubek asking for the case to be reopened. I can't say it didn't cross my mind that he might kill him, because nothing crossed my mind. I panicked, and I didn't think. I was wrong and I deserve some of the blame. What proportion of the guilt is mine, I leave to others to decide.'

'The greater the share Sedláček has to carry, the less there is for you. For what it's worth, I believe you when you say you didn't plan to hurt Jana. You liked her too

371

much. And if Holoubek had left well alone you'd have left him alone. But he didn't and you didn't. Now, the last chance you have to redeem a bit of honour for yourself is to tell the whole story, stop Sedláček getting off and take your punishment like a man.'

Tripka took a deep breath and inspected his hands for some time. When he spoke, his voice was barely above a whisper.

'In my house, there's a crawlspace in the eaves alongside the guest bedroom. In there, there's a metal toolbox. It's painted blue. If you lift the top tray out you'll find a bundle of letters from Sedláček that he wrote while he was in the army here. In a couple of them he talks about what happened to Jana. He says he enjoyed it and wanted to do it again. He recalls how she tried to shake him off her despite having her hands tied. I kept them so that if he ever tried to incriminate me I could turn the tables.'

'You're not very trusting, are you?'

Tripka raised his head, and his sad brown eyes met Slonský's.

'Only a fool trusts Sedláček. I may be a fool, but even I'm not that stupid.'

Slonský acknowledged the truth of this statement with a cursory nod.

'We'll go and get the letters. If you're right, we can start talking about mitigating your sentence.' He started to walk to the door, then turned back, picked up the urn, and handed it to Tripka. 'Villain or not, he's still your dad. Take care of him.'

Slonský was no psychologist, but he could detect a certain amount of latent hostility in Sedláček's attitude to him. For a start, the hoodlum was slightly put out that he had been shot.

'When I get out, you'll regret that,' he said.

'When you get out, I'll be sitting on a cloud with wings,' Slonský corrected him, 'or I'll be over ninety. I suppose you'll run me over like Holoubek, now that you've got your eye in and you know exactly how to take out old age pensioners with a van.'

'I'm not going inside. What sort of evidence have you got that would hold me?' Sedláček asked scornfully.

'I'm sorry,' said Slonský, 'I'm not allowed to discuss whatever evidence we have in detail. But I can tell you that Tripka will tie you to the murder of Válková, Pluskal will say you ordered the killing of Holoubek and the kidnapping of Peiperová, and some Albanian acquaintances of yours have been queueing up to give us evidence on a range of other events in recent years.'

'Losing rivals can't be trusted to tell the truth,' Sedláček replied.

'That's fair comment, but I don't think they're too worried about whether it's the truth, so long as it puts you away for a long time. Come to think of it, I agree with them. Whatever they're fabricating, I hope it stands up in court.'

Back at the office, Navrátil voiced their shared concern.

'Have we got enough to hold him?'

'The prosecutor says so. He reckons he'll get convictions on the murder of Holoubek and the abduction of Peiperová without much difficulty. The murder of Válková is more problematic, but we've got an eye-witness, Sedláček's letters and a conspirator's sworn statement. Either way, you'll be close to retirement when he gets out.'

Peiperová and Navrátil came to stand in front of Slonský's desk. As their shadow blotted out the feeble light from the bulb overhead, he looked up to see them standing side by side to attention.

'May we have a word, sir?' Navrátil began.

'If I say no?'

'I'll ask instead, sir,' Peiperová explained.

'I take it the use of the word "we" is significant, in view of my warning that there mustn't be a "we".'

'It is, sir. We've become a "we",' Navrátil explained.

'Congratulations. Are you still standing there because you're expecting a present?'

'No, sir,' Peiperová interjected. 'We're wondering what happens to me now. Plainly I can't stay here if Navrátil and I are engaged, and I'm only with you temporarily anyway.'

'Not so fast, young lady. How do you know I won't keep you and give Romeo here the elbow?'

Peiperová looked anxiously at Navrátil, who was definitely flustered by this turn of events. His face was reddening and he had the facial expression of a frog with dyspepsia.

'Because that wouldn't be fair to Navrátil, and you're a fair man, sir.'

'If you believe that you're a shocking judge of character, my girl. I think there's something you should both know.'

'Sir?' they chorused.

'I went to see Captain Lukas yesterday to talk about my future. Let's go and find him so he can tell you what he has decided.'

If Lukas' office had possessed a back door, he might well have disappeared when he saw the three of them approach, but he was trapped. He invited them all to sit.

'Now,' he asked, adopting his most avuncular manner, 'what's all this about?'

Slonský motioned Navrátil to speak.

'The thing is, sir, that Officer Peiperová and I—'

'How are you, Peiperová? Recovering well?'

'Yes, thank you, sir.'

'Good. First class. Sorry, Navrátil, you were saying?'

'Well, sir, when Officer Peiperová was kidnapped, it made me think that perhaps, in the fullness of time, she might possibly not be averse—'

'We're engaged, sir,' Peiperová interrupted.

'Excellent,' Lukas responded. 'I'm pleased for you both.'

'Thank you, sir. However, we're aware that there are rules about couples working together and we weren't clear how separate we have to be. For example, can we work in the same department under different lieutenants?'

'Ah, yes. Very good question.'

They sat in silence for a moment or two, until it dawned on Lukas that the only one who could answer that very good question was him.

'There is a difficulty. Undoubtedly, having married — or even engaged — people working together can be tricky for their colleagues and is therefore frowned upon, but in the present circumstances I don't have anywhere else to assign you. Dvorník and Doležal both have assistants already.' He paused and looked squarely at Slonský. 'You haven't changed your mind, Lieutenant?'

'No, sir,' said Slonský stiffly.

'Very well. We must deal with matters as we find them. Lieutenant Slonský has decided that if I am prepared to grant permission, he would like to have two trainees to look after. He says that he will not find that your relationship causes him any concern. Is that right, Slonský?'

'Yes, sir, because I'm going to ignore it completely. In the event of untoward canoodling by either party, I shall put some bromide in Navrátil's coffee or describe my prostate operation. Either of these steps should suffice to cool their ardour.'

Lukas did not reply at first, since he was contemplating his own prostate's performance and his doctor's plans for it, and feeling more than a little uncomfortable as a result.

'I've signed the forms,' he finally announced. 'Officer Peiperová, you are now formally attached to Lieutenant Slonský.'

'Though not in any physical sense,' Slonský quickly added.

'This calls for a celebration drink,' Slonský announced. 'We can raise a glass to your future at the same time as we celebrate a job well done in putting Sedláček and Tripka behind bars for years to come.'

'I thought you'd be anti-marriage, sir,' said Navrátil.

'Me? No, marriage is a fine institution. For everyone else, that is.'

'Forgive my asking, sir, but did you call Mrs Slonská as you promised?'

'Ah, now, the thing is, I lost the number.'

'No problem, sir. I found it. Here it is.' He handed Slonský the crumpled napkin.

'Maybe I'll call later.'

Navrátil handed him his mobile.

'Be my guest, sir. We'll be at the bar.'

BOOK THREE: DEATH ON DUTY

Chapter 1

It was as close as Lieutenant Josef Slonský had ever come to an ecstatic religious experience. He had to admit that in the six months since Officer Kristýna Peiperová had arrived to join his team, there had been a number of changes. For example, she had instituted the Grand Night Out, when they all went out together once a month to enjoy ballroom dancing, bowling or skating. Slonský did not especially enjoy any of these, but he approved heartily of the principle, even though it meant spending the evening with a bunch of teetotallers, which in Slonský's definition meant anyone who drank less than two litres of beer in a day.

Another change had been the marking of people's name days or birthdays. For a long time nobody knew when Slonský's birthday was, and he was still unsure how they had found out. Of course, Officer Jan Navrátil now had the telephone number of Slonský's ex-wife — or, more accurately, the wife who would be an ex-wife but for a small clerical error when she failed to sign and return the paperwork — so that was a possibility. And Peiperová had a gift of winkling information out of people without giving the impression that it was anything other than idle chatter. Either way, it had been wonderful enough when they had given him a ticket to the All-Moravia Artisan Sausage-Making Championship, but when he was co-opted as a substitute judge after one was taken ill, he was as close to heaven as he ever expected to get.

He had found a nice little inn with the intention of making a weekend of it and after a simple lunch of beer and hunter's stew with dumplings, he was busily contemplating entry number twenty-five, for which he scored a seven, being concerned that the skin was insufficiently extruded and therefore played too great a role in the overall chewing process. The meat content was good, though, and he would have given high marks for the seasoning. Moreover, unlike entry number eight, there was no foreign matter in it. Slonský had been shocked to discover that anyone would sink low enough to bind their sausage together with egg, which in his view made it a type of omelette. His indignation was fanned by the discovery that the other judges felt the same way, and he was fairly sure that the retired butcher who was chairing the panel would have hanged the man on his own meat hook, but they had tempered justice with mercy on the grounds that the evildoer was half-Hungarian and therefore could not be expected to know better.

Entry twenty-seven was chunky, a good colour, but perhaps a little heavy on the garlic. Slonský felt he had to deduct a point or two for the failure to let the flavour of the meat flow through, and was just marking his card when it occurred to him that he had not seen number twenty-six.

He sought out the nearest judge to compare notes. He, too, had not sampled number twenty-six, nor had any of the other judges, although the sausage-maker in question had registered on arrival earlier that day. The organisers were perplexed, because they knew that Mr Mazura was a keen competitor and highly fancied by the sausage-making cognoscenti to come away with a prize. He had been seen as the tables were being set up, but his post was now unmanned and his ingredients were hopelessly overcooked.

A search was instituted in case he had been taken ill somewhere, and after about a quarter of an hour a series of loud cries announced that the quest had been successful. Mr Mazura was found gagged and tied to a post in a barn on the outskirts of the village, a placard round his neck proclaiming that he had been seized by a party of militant vegetarians for crimes against the animal kingdom. There was uproar, and a number of persons worthy of investigation were denounced to the local policeman, who appealed to Slonský for help in detecting the perpetrators.

Slonský had been hoping to have a weekend free from consideration of crime, when a second series of cries proved how cunning the whole thing had been and how unlikely it was that his ambition would be fulfilled.

'The trophies!' yelled the chief judge breathlessly. 'They've all gone!'

Mr Mazura was shaken by his experience, but answered the question Slonský put to him, after which the detective showed no interest in him, but went off to make a couple of phone calls.

Mazura had managed to see that the van he was bundled into was small and red with a registration number ending in -56. Slonský rang police headquarters in Prague and asked for a search for such a vehicle, starting from the assumption that a local gang was most likely to be the culprits. Within a few minutes a police patrol reported seeing such a van on the road towards Vsetín.

'I hope he can keep them in sight until a car gets there,' Slonský said.

The local police officer smirked. 'The way Marek rides that bike, there's no car on earth could get away from him,' he said.

Traffic control rang back with a couple of names and addresses.

'Any chance of a lift to Vsetín?' Slonský asked. 'It seems there's a van fitting that description registered to a young man there.'

The occupants of the van had tried hard to lose Marek, but to no avail, and when they pulled up in Vsetín he was right behind them. They fled the scene, allowing Marek to confirm that the load area was filled with cups and shields. He shut the door and sat by the van to wait. Around twenty minutes later Slonský and Officer Limberský arrived.

Slonský introduced himself to Marek and showed him the address he had written down. 'Know where this is?'

Marek pointed through the trees to a couple of white buildings. 'It's one of those,' he said.

'Good,' said Slonský. 'Let's go for a little walk.'

Marek rapped on the door. After a few moments it was opened by a young man who yawned and stretched as if he had just woken up.

'Pavel Baránek?' asked Slonský.

'Who wants to know?'

'Lieutenant Slonský, criminal department, Prague, and Officer Marek.'

'Yeah, I'm Baránek.'

'Where's your van?'

'Isn't it outside? Oh, my God, it's been stolen!'

'Just as well we're here, then. I'll be happy to look into it for you. Mind if we come inside?'

'Well...'

'Thanks,' said Slonský as he pushed past. 'In bed, were you?'

'No, asleep in the chair.'

'All afternoon?'

'I must have been.'

Slonský nodded. 'That figures. You're asleep over there, so you don't hear your van starting up outside.'

'That's right,' agreed Baránek.

Slonský walked over and felt the seat cushion. 'Are you a reptile, sir?'

'How do you mean?'

'Reptiles are cold-blooded. They take in heat from their surroundings. That would explain why this seat you've been in all afternoon is stone cold. By the way, one of our colleagues is getting your van fingerprinted.'

Baránek did not flinch. 'Of course it'll have my fingerprints on it. It's my van. And I bet the thieves wore gloves.'

'Thieves, sir? So you know it was more than one?'

'Just guessing.'

'Good guess, then. Perhaps you'd like to tell me who the other two were. After all, there'll be prints all over the metal trophies, won't there? At least one of you wasn't wearing gloves.'

Baránek flopped in a chair, crestfallen and defeated. He offered a couple of names.

'Abduction, theft, driving without due care and attention, and coming between me and the sausage experience of a lifetime. I should think that might well earn you around two and a half life sentences. Officer Marek will book you now, then we'll haul you off to clink and I'll return to the contest. The length of your sentence may well depend on how many sausages I've missed.'

Slonský need not have worried. When he arrived with the trophies, he was the hero of the hour and was feted in the village that evening. He finally crawled into bed around 2 a.m. with his wallet unopened all night, his stomach filled with sausages of all conceivable kinds, and the makings of the mother of all hangovers.

Chapter 2

Sunday was a painful day. Slonský was reduced to drinking water until he found some Polish beer which, he thought, was pretty much the same thing and should rehydrate him adequately. He spent the morning writing his report on the previous day's events, then took a walk before lunch to work up an appetite. A rather slower walk after lunch filled in the time until his train to Prague departed in the late afternoon.

Peiperová and Navrátil were both disgustingly bright and cheerful on Monday morning. In any other young couple, Slonský would have suspected that this was a prolonged bout of post-coital merriment, but it was clear that Navrátil had views on that kind of thing. Whether Peiperová shared them was a matter of debate, but Slonský was inclined to give her the benefit of the doubt on that matter — or indeed any other.

Slonský recounted the events of his trip, playing down the detection element but majoring on the defects in parts of the artisan sausage industry, particularly of the semi-Hungarian variety, while making it plain that this had been a thoughtful and acceptable present that he would be happy to receive again. He asked politely about their weekend, and Peiperová recounted tennis matches, walks, dinner in a riverside restaurant and a considerable amount of laundry. Navrátil was quick to point out that he attended to his own laundry, and that after church he had engaged in vigorous shoe-polishing. Slonský glanced downwards, and observed that Navrátil's shoes were highly buffed. This was not a description that anyone would have applied to his own, which had quickly acquired a matt finish and were scuffed in a number of places.

'What would you like us to do today, sir?' asked Peiperová.

'I think a division of labour is called for,' Slonský opined. 'One of you can fetch coffee, while the other can help me with my groundbreaking report into the criminal activities of expatriate Bosnians in Prague.'

'Are there any criminal Bosnians in Prague?' asked Navrátil.

Slonský adopted his most pitying tone. 'We won't know until I've written my report, will we? So far as I can make out, this has arisen because the police there have lost track of a bunch of desperados and are hoping that if they ask enough people someone will tell them where they've gone. I haven't seen any sign of them in Prague but in an hour or so we'll venture into these mean streets to find one of our informers who'll tell us what he knows.'

'Why not go now, sir?'

'Because, Navrátil, he'll still be in his pit. We won't see him much this side of lunchtime, especially in November when there are fewer tourists to rip off. So we have time for a leisurely coffee and then we'll wander down to the corner by Kafka's birthplace and keep our eyes peeled for Václav the Storyteller.'

'He sounds like a character from a fairy tale.'

'Obviously it isn't his real name, Navrátil. We have to observe confidentiality when it comes to informers. The key thing is that Václav is a nosey so-and-so who seems to know what is going on.'

'Why don't we use him more often then, sir?'

'Think about it, lad. If he tells us too much, everyone will know he's the squealer. Even meeting us is taking a chance for him, so there's a certain etiquette to be observed. Try hard not to look like a policeman. Make it as short as possible, and when he decides it's over, we let him go and head in the opposite direction, even if he goes the way we were going to go. Now, we need a newspaper and then we're ready.'

'A newspaper, sir?'

'Yes, one of those things they print every morning with news in it. We tuck a small monetary token of appreciation between the front page and page three, fold the paper and negligently leave it on the table in front of us. If we leave first, he picks up the abandoned paper. If he legs it, he takes the paper with him.'

'But how do we know how much his information is worth?'

'We don't, so we keep tight hold of the paper until we've ascertained that. If it's really juicy we may have to leave a note on the table, but that's risky if anyone is watching.'

'How will we find him, sir?'

'If he's around, he'll find us. Believe me, once he sees me standing by Kafka's birthplace with a folded newspaper in my hand he'll make himself known.'

Peiperová looked less than happy. 'Do I take it this means I'm fetching the coffee?' she asked.

'Ah, I have an alternative task for you,' said Slonský.

'Yes, sir — which is?'

'I'll tell you when you get back with the coffee.'

Peiperová set off on her quest. As soon as the door closed behind her Slonský whispered urgently to Navrátil, 'Quick, lad! Think of something she can do, or our lives are going to be hell for a day or two.'

Peiperová had been taken aback. No sooner had she placed a coffee in front of each of her colleagues than Slonský had lent forward as if about to impart a great secret.

'I don't think we take Christmas seriously enough here,' he said.

'No, sir?'

'Oh, no. It's been bugging me for a while and I've come to the conclusion that no-one else in this department is going to do anything about it, so we'd better take the bull by the horns and organise Christmas ourselves. Oh, I suppose Mucha will put a few streamers up downstairs and there might be a small tree, but I'm more concerned about the social aspects.'

'Social aspects, sir?'

'Yes, Peiperová. Are you going to repeat the last couple of words of everything I say? Navrátil does that, and it's one of his most irritating habits.'

'Sorry, sir.'

'You usually tell me it makes me sound stupid,' Navrátil interjected helpfully.

'Yes, but Peiperová is bright enough to realise for herself that it makes her sound stupid, Navrátil. She doesn't need me to tell her. Now, where was I?'

'Social aspects, sir. I'm not quite clear what social aspects are, sir.'

Slonský looked aghast. 'Navrátil, explain to Peiperová about social aspects.'

'I'm not entirely clear...'

'Just tell her what we were talking about while she was fetching coffee, lad.'

'Oh! I asked what we were doing about the staff Christmas party.'

'And I said...?'

'You said we don't have a staff Christmas party but you've always thought we should and maybe Peiperová and I could introduce some Christmas spirit into the miserable bunch of killjoys that inhabit these offices.'

'Exactly! Social aspects. I'm sure Captain Lukas will agree.'

Slonský had not asked Captain Lukas, because the idea had only just come to him, and was banking on the probability that Lukas would not want to dampen the enthusiasm of two young officers, and the fact that it was only six weeks until Christmas which would not allow Lukas to conduct his usual degree of in-depth dithering.

'I'm not sure we'll get any money from the department, but perhaps a nice lunch together, or an hour of cocktails? I leave it in your hands to organise. But there isn't a lot of time, so while Navrátil and I do this tedious interview with the informer, why don't you pass a couple of hours scouting out the possibilities in the restaurants and pubs nearby?'

'Shouldn't I do it in my own time, sir?' asked Peiperová.

Slonský had not anticipated that objection. He knew of very few police officers who offered to do anything in their own time. Lieutenant Dvorník had once offered to question a suspect when everyone else had gone home, but somehow he did not think it was quite the same thing.

'The main organisation, perhaps, but these places will be busy when you finish at the end of the day. No, much better to visit them in a quiet time.'

'Very good, sir. And it's all right for me to do this without Navrátil, although he is organising it with me?'

'Certainly. If it's left to Navrátil we'll probably wind up in some lap-dancing club.'

Navrátil spluttered a protest.

'Joke, lad, joke.'

Slonský and Navrátil sauntered across Old Town Square and paused for a few moments in the corner nearest to Kafka's house before continuing their walk in the general direction of the old Jewish quarter along Maiselova. There was a café on the left hand side that seemed quite empty, into which Slonský turned. They took their seats against the wall, and Slonský ordered three coffees.

'Three?' asked the waitress.

'Yes, three,' said Slonský. 'Our friend will join us in a minute.'

As the coffee arrived a man in several layers of ragged clothing pushed open the door and took the seat opposite Slonský.

'Something to keep the cold out?' asked the detective.

'Civil of you. Wouldn't mind.'

'Navrátil, you'll have gathered this is the man we've come to meet. I told you he'd see us.'

'But you must have seen him too, sir, or you wouldn't have ordered three coffees.'

'I did. But I knew where to look, didn't I, Václav?'

'A warm doorway is a blessing in this weather. What do you want to know?'

'We're looking for Bosnians.'

'You'll have no trouble finding them. But I guess you're after some particular Bosnians.'

Slonský unfolded the fax. 'This lot.'

Václav peered closely at the pictures. He obviously needed spectacles, but presumably could not afford them. 'No, no, no, yes and no.'

'Which one is yes?'

'That one. Eldin whatever it says.'

'Savović.'

'If that's what it says.'

'Where have you seen him?'

Václav sneaked a peak over his shoulder. 'There's a red brick building not far from this side of the Charles Bridge. Head up towards the Art School and look across the road and you'll see the windows in the end wall. He goes in there with a bunch of fellows you'll know. They don't stay, but it seems to be his base.'

'Been there long?'

Václav shrugged. 'Three months maybe.'

'Any idea what he's into?'

'Bosnians usually have arms to trade. Small stuff mostly. They rent out big guys if you want scores settled. I don't think they're pimping or gambling types.'

'Anything else you want to tell me?'

'There's one time you'll catch him alone. He's got a sweet tooth, so he goes to the sweet stall in the nearby market. Likes to make his own choices, you see?'

'No protection?'

'Two big guys with black leather jackets won't be far away, but they switch off once he's at the stall. I've seen them go and get a hot wine at the kiosk. They can still see him, but an enemy could take him down then.'

'Does he have enemies?'

Václav stood up and finished his coffee. 'He's a Bosnian,' he said. 'Of course he has enemies.'

No wonder my digestion is troubled, thought Captain Josef Lukas. He took out his calculator and tried to decipher Slonský's expenses claim. Never one to provide excessive detail, Slonský favoured a terse approach to narrative.

'1 train journey — Kč.140.'

'A train journey? To where?' Lukas asked himself. 'Why?'

As if that were not enough, the page bore the unmistakable stamp of a wet beer glass in the top corner. It also seemed to have been written by someone using a stick of spaghetti dipped in ink and the numbers were abominably indistinct. Was that one hundred and sixty crowns, or one hundred and sixty-nine? Or possibly even one hundred and eighty-nine?

Latterly Slonský had discovered a new way to sow confusion. Possibly in order to safeguard Navrátil's pocket, he had taken to paying for both of them and claiming both sets of expenses on his form, while cunningly failing to make clear whether the costs were for one person or two. Thus his bill for lunch during a stakeout was quite reasonable if it was for both of them, but extortionate if he alone consumed it; yet the description did not make that clear, and Lukas was beginning to suspect that this was another of Slonský's irritating little schemes to win a small triumph over bureaucracy.

Finally Lukas gave up and signed the sheet, turning it face down on the pile to his left and shifting his attention to the requisition form in his in-tray.

'This is too much!' he exploded, marching down the corridor to see if Slonský could explain himself.

The only person in the office was Peiperová. It was unfair to expect a young girl to know what her boss was up to, but Lukas needed to share the burden with someone.

'Good morning, Peiperová. No, don't get up.'

'Good morning, sir.'

'Slonský not back yet?'

'He's seeing an informer, sir.'

'Goodness knows what that will cost us.'

'Sir?'

'Oh, nothing. You don't happen to know why Slonský wants some new uniform shoes when he doesn't wear a uniform, I suppose?'

'I'm afraid not, sir.'

'He hasn't mentioned it?'

'No, sir.'

'He's not planning on applying for a uniformed job? Mine, for example?'

'I didn't know there was a vacancy, sir.'

'There isn't, and you might remind Slonský of that when he reappears. Please ask him to see me when he returns so I can get to the bottom of this. What are you looking at, Peiperová?'

'Menus, sir. Lieutenant Slonský asked me to investigate a Christmas lunch for the department.'

'Did he? He hasn't mentioned it to me. Though I approve, of course. It can only serve to foster team spirit. Have you chosen a venue?'

'I wondered if this one might be suitable, sir.'

Peiperová offered Lukas a menu. It took him no time at all to find six dishes that he could not possibly eat, given the emphasis on cream and the frequent use of the word 'fried'.

'Splendid!' he said. 'Keep me informed. It's probably best if we keep this to staff only, rather than families. Dvorník's eight children are ... charming, but you can have too much of a good thing.'

'What now, sir?' asked Navrátil.

'I'm not sure. My head says have another coffee, but my heart tells me that a small beer would slip down nicely.'

'And what does your bladder say?'

'Good point. Perhaps we'll just take a stroll along the river and cast an eye over that building Václav mentioned.'

Slonský's idea of a stroll proved to be slower than Navrátil could have imagined. They dawdled to look in shop windows, and Slonský spent some time in a cheap souvenir store behaving like a yokel on his first visit to Prague.

'Sir, shouldn't we be getting over there?'

'Ten more minutes.'

'Why, sir?'

'Because, young Navrátil, seeing the building won't help me much. I've seen it thousands of times. I want to see who is coming and going. Of course, we could strike lucky, but given that we don't want to stand around for an age drawing attention to ourselves, we're just going to amble up one side, go round the block, and then go along the river again, and the time when we're likeliest to see someone is lunchtime, when no doubt at least some of the occupants will be heading out to put on a nosebag. Therefore, we want to arrive around lunchtime, and not at twenty to twelve. Ten minutes here, a gentle perambulation to the site, and a turn round the block should give us about half an hour of potential eyeballing of the men in the building.'

'Should we ask the City Police if they know anything?'

Slonský sighed. 'I suppose we should. They won't, of course, because they never do. Someone could snatch the statue of John Nepomuk off the Charles Bridge and it would be a fortnight before they noticed. Unless his dog was fouling the footpath at the same time, when they'd be on him like a shot, rubbing his nose in it.'

As luck would have it, two of Prague's police were taking an early lunch at a sausage stall as Slonský and Navrátil headed northwards. One was small, rotund, and had a cap that looked as if it belonged to a smaller man's head. The other was a familiar face. It belonged to Officer Krob, who had assisted Slonský once before during a hit and run incident.

Krob straightened himself and tried to look keen.

'Good day, Officer Krob,' began Slonský. 'Do you come here often?'

'The stall, or Prague?' came the reply.

'This part of Prague.'

'I've been on this beat for a month or so, sir. Vácha here has been around much longer.'

'Wonderful. Let me grab one of those sausages and then we can have a little chat. Navrátil, do the introductions.'

They sat on a bench facing the river, all thoughts of arriving at the building around midday apparently banished from Slonský's mind.

'This is just a friendly chat between ourselves,' Slonský explained. 'Nothing formal. Nothing that needs mentioning to anyone.'

Krob willingly agreed. Vácha seemed rather less convinced that such a promise was a good idea when he had not yet heard what was wanted of him, but nodded half-heartedly.

'Behind me to my right there's a large red building. We're told a wanted criminal from Bosnia works out of there. Any idea what might be going on?'

Vácha studied the building intently as if its inhabitants' names were about to be displayed in neon on the roof, but turned back reluctantly when he realised that it would not be so.

'We've seen Rudolf Smejkal there a couple of times,' Krob offered.

'Smejkal? Have you reported that?'

'Yes, sir.'

Navrátil felt the need to interrupt. 'Who is Smejkal?'

'He's what is politely termed a property developer. He buys old rundown buildings and stuffs them with tenants on the promise that he'll do some improvements. The improvements take an age to happen, despite the readiness of banks to lend him money to do the work. He uses that money to buy another building, and the cycle repeats. If anyone gives him a hard time he sends a couple of plumbers and a carpenter around to smarten up the worst of the places, then he goes back to normal.'

'So why would he be mixing with the Bosnian?'

'I don't know. Usually when Smejkal buddies up to people it's because the banks have cut off his line of credit and he needs some capital from people who don't want to have to explain where it came from. You see, lad, ill-gotten gains can be a real sod to invest. Banks ask awkward questions and everyone wants to know your business, so criminals may have money and no idea what they can do with it. Smejkal takes some of it off their hands. But Savović hasn't been here long enough to build up a stash.'

'He could have brought it with him.'

'He could, but the Bosnian police didn't mention it, and if they thought that was likely they'd have sent the fax to the fraud department. Since I haven't seen a hyperexcited Klinger stalking the corridors or asking us what we know about it, I deduce our colleagues upstairs aren't being informed.'

'Is there anyone else in the building Smejkal could be meeting?'

Slonský eyed his assistant and frowned. 'A remarkably percipient question. By your standards, anyway. Krob? Vácha?'

'Don't know, sir,' Krob replied.

Slonský rose to his feet ponderously. 'Fair enough. No reason why you should. Probably best if uniforms don't go rooting around there. Come along, Navrátil. Let's see who occupies those offices.'

'Sir? Couldn't it be dangerous for you?'

'Indeed it could, lad. That's why you're going in.'

They walked along the embankment, passing a woman disguised as a Greek goddess posing on a white plinth and a mediaeval knight with his sword drawn.

'I've no idea how they stand still all day, especially in this weather,' Slonský whispered.

'I think they move when nobody's watching, sir.'

'God is always watching, lad, or so my grandmother used to tell me when I was up to something.'

They crossed the road and walked past the front of the red brick building, turning at the corner and continuing along its side.

'Right, Navrátil, in you go. I'm sure you'll think of some story to find out who is in there. Meanwhile, I'm going to sit in the window of that bar opposite and strike up a conversation with any regular customer who may have a tale to tell.'

Navrátil resisted the temptation to protest that the bar could not be described as opposite the building, since it was forty metres along the street and a patron sitting in the window would only see who came and went if they stood on the table with the transom window open and their head sticking out. He took out his notebook, entering the building apparently deep in thought and writing a note or two.

A security desk was placed at the foot of the stairs where a doorkeeper sat with a large visitors' book.

'Seeing someone, sir?' he asked.

'Not necessary,' said Navrátil. 'Council environmental health department.' He waved his tennis club membership card in a cursory way before shoving it back in his pocket. 'We've had complaints that someone in this building has been putting their refuse out without closing it, with the result that rats from the river have been seen picking at it. That's an offence under section 238 of the law on refuse, you know.'

The doorkeeper looked pained. 'Rats? Where?'

'That's a bit vague. The complaint just says in the doorway, so whether that's this main doorway, or a side door, I'm not sure. Have you seen any evidence of rats?'

'No, certainly not. This is a clean building. All our tenants are respectable.'

'Perhaps I could have a list?'

The doorkeeper photocopied his list of telephone numbers and gave it to Navrátil. 'They're all on there. It tells you which floor they're on in the side headings, see?'

'Thank you. Usually when this happens we find the culprits are foreigners who don't know our waste disposal legislation like a Czech would. You don't have any foreigners here, I suppose?'

The doorkeeper looked around anxiously to check there was nobody in the lobby or coming down the stairs. 'They're all respectable, like I said. But there's an American gentleman on the third floor. He teaches English and writes for magazines. And there's a man from Yugoslavia on the floor above this.'

'Ah! Newly arrived?'

'Three months or so.'

Navrátil flicked over the pages of his notepad. 'Well, that just about ties in with the first complaint. You don't know his name?'

The doorkeeper made a mark on Navrátil's photocopy with his pen. 'That's him. Keeps himself to himself. Never gives me no trouble, pays his bills on time.'

'These Yugoslavs often have noisy friends though. We get a lot of complaints about noise.'

'No, nothing like that. All the visitors I've seen are Czechs. Of course, his driver is a Serb or Croat or something of the sort. And of course he doesn't live here. I dare say he has his wild parties in his flat.'

'I dare say. Well, thanks again. I'll give him a ring sometime just to wrap it all up and explain about the rats.'

Navrátil dashed out into the street, leaving the doorkeeper to wonder where he could buy a few traps and some environmentally-friendly rat poison.

'Come along, lad, we can't put it off any longer. We're going to have to go back to the office and do some work.'

'What about the other names on the list, sir?'

'How do you mean?'

'Well, there must be a reason why Savović chose that particular office building. How did he hear that it was available? Did somebody introduce him? And what does he need an office for anyway?'

Slonský rubbed his chin. 'There are some good questions there, Navrátil. Tell you what: you get some good answers, and I'll go back to the office and wait for them.'

'Where shall I start, sir?'

'Use your initiative, son. Or, putting it another way, I haven't a clue. Why not start by finding out who the letting agents are? Where do they normally advertise vacancies? Perhaps your mate on the door can give you a hand.'

'He thinks I'm an environmental health officer, sir. I can hardly go back asking about letting agents.'

'Of course you can. Even environmental health officers need offices somewhere. Tell him you need to find a new office, or your girlfriend wants somewhere to keep all her whips and black leather. In short, lad, fib. Spin him a yarn.'

Navrátil breathed deeply and pushed the door open. The doorkeeper glanced up and his face distorted in alarm.

'Not more rats?' he whispered.

'No,' said Navrátil. 'You were kind enough to give me a list of occupants, but I didn't ask if any rooms are empty.'

'Empty?'

'Yes. You see, rats prefer to sleep in places where they won't be found by a human. I've been thinking, and if they're anywhere in this building, they'd be in an empty flat or office.'

The doorkeeper snatched a ring of keys and used one to lock the front door, hanging a sign behind its glass to tell callers that he would be back in ten minutes.

'Third floor,' he said, 'but you're going in first.'

They mounted the stairs and the doorkeeper unlocked the suite and gingerly pushed the door open. Navrátil stepped inside. The room was completely empty.

'No hiding places here, then.' Navrátil commented. 'I'd better just check that the skirting boards are sound.'

'You do that,' agreed the doorkeeper.

'Where does the owner advertise these offices? I'm surprised a nice place like this is still empty. Maybe he's using the wrong people.'

'He uses a range of different folks.'

'I suppose people do see the advertisements,' Navrátil mused. 'After all, the Yugoslav gentleman must have seen one.'

'Ah, no, you're wrong there,' said the doorman. 'He was introduced by the man on the floor above.'

'The American writer?'

'No, he's on the top floor. The import-export company, they're the ones. Mr Nejedlý knew him.'

'It's Mr Nejedlý that runs that company, is it?'

'That's right.'

'That's very good of him, introducing a new tenant. Must be a kindly man.'

The doorkeeper eloquently failed to agree. After a moment or two Navrátil sensed a chill entering the conversation.

'You obviously don't agree.'

'It's not my place to comment on the tenants, sir.'

'I'm sorry. I didn't mean to put you in an awkward position, especially when you have to work with them every day.'

'That's all right, sir. Mr Nejedlý is a nice enough man himself. It's the company he keeps that concerns me. They can be very impolite.'

'I know what you mean,' Navrátil replied, even though he did not. 'Well, I'm satisfied this suite is rat-free. I think we can safely conclude that the rats are outside. Perhaps you could just remind tenants to seal their bags properly when they put them out.'

'I will. We don't want rats around here.'

Major Klinger, head of the fraud squad, was much more interested in Navrátil's report.

'Nejedlý. Yes, that rings a bell. That would be the Double Arrow Import Export Agency.'

'That's right,' agreed Navrátil.

'And what exactly do they import and export?' Slonský asked.

'Girls. Women for the bars and clubs, and probably for the streets. They're also one of our biggest importers of plums, though I suspect jam-making isn't nearly as lucrative.'

'Where do they import these girls from, as if I couldn't guess?' continued the lieutenant.

'Bosnia, Kosovo, the less affluent parts of the Balkans. I'm by no means an expert, but it isn't easy to explain why you would route plums through Serbia, Romania and Hungary to enter the EU. On the other hand, that would be a very good route if you had a truckful of women. There are lots of places where you can sneak across the borders.'

'So that could be our link with Savović,' Navrátil interjected.

'Who knows?' Slonský replied. 'The Bosnians haven't told us why they want him, largely because we haven't told them he's here. That's the next step. But that still doesn't tell us why he would be meeting up with Smejkal.'

'No, it doesn't,' agreed Klinger. 'Smejkal has his finger in many pies, but this is not one of them so far as I know.'

'And you would know, I suppose,' Slonský teased.

'Start from the working hypothesis that I know everything, and you won't go far wrong,' said Klinger. 'Now, if you've finished cluttering up my office, I believe you have a telephone call to make to Sarajevo.'

Slonský pushed Lukas' door open and poked his head in.

'Can you spare me a minute, sir?'

'Of course. Take a seat.'

Slonský summarised the day's events while Lukas nodded in what he hoped looked like a sage manner. 'I see. And what did the Bosnian police say?'

'That's the really puzzling bit. They want to find Savović, but they don't have any evidence tying him to any crimes.'

'That's nonsense. What they mean is that they have evidence they don't want to share. Do they want us to arrest him?'

'On what charge? So far as I can make out they're really pleased he's left the country. They didn't even want to send someone to talk to him.'

Lukas spread his hands expansively. 'Then we drop it. We've done what they asked. However much it piques our interest, we don't have time or manpower spare to investigate people out of idle curiosity.'

'That's what I thought, sir. Until someone alleges a crime, I don't see what we can do.'

There was a sharp knock at the door. Navrátil entered without waiting for an invitation. 'Sir, we've had a call. There's been a murder.'

'Where, lad?'

'That's the point, sir. It's where we were earlier, down by the riverside. Someone has killed the mediaeval knight.'

Chapter 3

The knight was kneeling as if in prayer, his sword planted firmly in the ground before him and his head resting on the pommel at the end of the hilt. His arms had presumably been grasping the crossbar but now dangled in front of the sword. His position was so stable that he had not fallen to the ground, but remained kneeling in death.

'He'd have to be stable to hold that position for so long. Where's the wound, Novák?'

The diminutive pathologist, Dr Vladimír Novák, blinked through his bottle-bottom glasses.

'And good afternoon to you too, Lieutenant. He was stabbed at the back of the neck. A fine blade. It may have severed the spinal cord, or it might have pushed upwards into the medulla oblongata — the brain stem to you. I won't know until I peel the skin back.'

'Looks like it was pretty quick.'

'He'd probably never know it happened. He'd die within moments.'

'Time?'

'About an hour ago, give or take. The place was swarming with people, Slonský. It's incredible that nobody noticed someone walk up behind a praying knight and stab him in the nape of the neck.'

'Could it be a flick-knife?'

'Probably a triggered knife of some kind, with a very narrow blade. This isn't easily done, Slonský. This is the sort of technique a Special Forces soldier would use.'

Slonský turned to look for the Greek goddess who had been standing beside the knight at lunchtime. She was sitting on a bench crying and shivering.

'You didn't see anything?' he asked her.

'No, not a thing. When I'm in position, he's slightly behind me. I can't turn and look. I didn't know anything about it until it came to five o'clock. We usually stop then for something to eat and to decide if it's worth carrying on into the evening. I stepped off my pedestal and came to talk to him, and when he didn't answer I lifted his head a little. I never dreamed he'd be dead.'

'It must have been an awful shock for you. Can you tell me anything about him? His name would be a good start.'

'Pavel. I don't know his surname.'

'Had he been coming to this patch for long?'

'About a month, I think. He asked me if I minded, because I was here first. To be honest, we do better when there are a couple of us. It encourages people to stop and look, so I didn't mind at all. Better than having a musician or a juggler next to you, when they get all the attention.'

'Did he tell you anything about his past?'

'He said he'd done this when he was a student. He was good. People used to say how steady we were. Anyway, he'd lost his last job and decided to give this a try.'

'Thank you. Officer Peiperová will take you somewhere warmer and get a statement from you, if you don't mind.'

The goddess nodded and allowed herself to be wrapped in Peiperová's enveloping arm and led away.

Slonský turned back to Novák. 'You must have something else for me. You always have.'

Novák sucked his lower lip pensively. 'I could give you an estimate of the murderer's height,' he offered.

Navrátil took out his notebook and stood with his pencil poised.

'I'm pretty confident he's more than a metre tall, or he'd have had to reach upwards to stab this chap in the back of the neck.'

'Damn!' said Slonský. 'We'll have to let all the dwarves go. If you don't have anything useful to tell me, stop taking the mickey.'

'Then stop asking damn fool questions and let me do my job. Why don't you go and talk to that other policeman?'

'What other policeman?'

'The one getting out of that police car.'

Slonský followed his gaze and fixed on a heavy-set man in a brown belted raincoat and chocolate-coloured fedora who was walking towards him.

'Have we run out of silver bullets?' he asked Navrátil.

The new arrival looked at the knight and grimaced.

'Do you know who he is?' asked Slonský.

'Yes,' came the answer. 'He's one of my men.'

Slonský pushed his hat to the back of his head so he could scratch his brow. 'I know we've cut back on overtime, but surely your officers don't have to moonlight to make ends meet.'

The newcomer winced again. 'It's a long story.'

Slonský pointed at the body. 'Well, he's got all the time in the world now. By the way, this is Officer Navrátil. Navrátil, meet Captain Grigar. He organises crime.'

'Not quite right, Slonský. I work in the Organised Crime team. This is Officer Hrdlička. He was working for me.'

'Covered in silver paint and wearing fancy dress?'

'It was his idea. He used to do it as a student. He said that a surveillance team would eventually be spotted, whereas he could stay openly in a good position in this disguise without anyone noticing.'

'He was wrong there, then,' said Slonský.

'It worked for a long time,' Grigar protested. 'He's been here over a month.'

'What's he watching?'

'Don't turn round. That red brick building opposite. We've been trying to found out who is based there.'

Slonský beckoned to Navrátil. 'Come along, lad, give the nice man your list.'

Grigar goggled at the photocopied sheet that Navrátil passed him. 'How did you get this?'

Navrátil had been brought up to believe that honesty is the best policy, so he told the truth. 'I asked for it, sir.' He explained the events that had produced the list for him.

Grigar was never the most animated of souls, but now he looked positively downcast. 'What now?' he asked.

'Well,' said Slonský, 'this looks like a murder to me, and murder is my province. Of course I don't want to mess up your investigation so you're welcome to hang around, but it's my show.'

Grigar nodded his assent.

'However,' said Slonský, 'it would be good to check out the inhabitants of that block as quickly as possible just in case someone has seen something, and no doubt you'd like to take a sly squint at the place, so how about we take a floor each? Since Navrátil speaks English, he'd better do the top floor. I'll do the middle floor with Mr Nejedlý at this side, and you, Grigar, can do the first floor, where the Bosnian gentleman hangs out.'

'And the ground floor, sir?' Navrátil enquired.

'Unless they've got x-ray vision, lad, they won't have seen through that brick boundary wall. The tenants at the far side probably won't have seen anything either, but let's make a note of their names for the future anyway.'

They crossed the road and marched into the red brick building, Slonský and Grigar flashing their badges. The doorkeeper goggled as they went past and hissed at Navrátil. 'What did you bring them for? I said I'd sort the rats out.'

Navrátil opened his mouth to explain, but Slonský got in first. 'There's been a murder on the river bank. Navrátil was discreetly checking whether the murderers were hiding here.'

'Murderers? Not rats?'

Navrátil shook his head sadly.

'Jesus Maria. Murderers!' mumbled the doorkeeper. 'That's probably worse than rats,' he added as he returned to his post.

Grigar found Savović sitting at a desk. Grigar explained what had happened, and Savović promptly displayed his passport, a residence permit, his lease and anything else Grigar could think of to enquire about.

'Have you noticed the knight outside?' he asked.

'Of course,' said Savović. 'He's good. Sometimes I've stood at this window drinking a coffee and he hasn't twitched all the time I was drinking it.'

Grigar distrusted the Bosnian's openness. The more innocent he appeared, the more Grigar felt uneasy.

'He's a police officer, and he's been stabbed. Did you see anything?'

'No,' Savović answered. 'If I had, I'd have called the police. But in any event I haven't been facing the window. As you can see, my desk faces into the room.'

Grigar nodded. 'May I ask what you do for a living, sir?'

'Entertainment. I'm a sort of impresario. I bring dancers to the clubs. There's no law against it, is there?'

'Not if they're legal immigrants and there's no coercion.'

'That's what I thought. I could give you names if you want.'

'That would be good.'

'I'll have a list put together and fax it to you. The police have a fax machine, I suppose?'

'Several.'

Navrátil was making heavy weather of questioning Mr Brown, the American gentleman on the top floor. Despite watching a lot of American films and police shows, Navrátil found Mr Brown's accent difficult to penetrate.

'Athens,' Mr Brown helpfully repeated. 'Not the one you're thinking of — the one in Georgia. And not the Georgia you're thinking of — the one in the United States.'

'And you are a writer?'

'A travel writer. I produce guide books mainly. I pay my way by teaching a little English when I can. But at the moment I'm working on a biography.'

'Whose biography, if I may ask?'

'You may, officer. A biography of your President Edvard Beneš. I know he died in 1948, but he isn't well known in my country, you see.'

Navrátil duly made a note.

'A person was stabbed on the bank outside earlier this afternoon, sometime between four and five o'clock. Did you see anything?'

'I saw the crowd gathered around the knight. Was it him?'

Navrátil nodded slightly.

'My word! How could anyone stab a person in broad daylight on such a busy street?'

'That's the question I have to answer, sir.'

Slonský had less luck. Mr Nejedlý was out. The doorkeeper produced a spare key on request, so the three detectives entered and fanned out to have a quick look round.

'And if Nejedlý returns?' asked Grigar.

'We're in hot pursuit of a murderer. He may be holed up in this building. That justifies checking every square metre, just in case. But we'd better not disturb drawers and cupboards.'

They walked around for a few minutes, then Slonský declared himself satisfied, so they locked the door and returned the key.

'I suppose he could have killed Hrdlička and then fled,' offered Navrátil.

'That's possible,' conceded Slonský, 'but it doesn't explain why he waited until we were on site before he left.'

'How do you know that?' demanded Grigar.

Slonský displayed his hand with a red mark at the base of his thumb.

'His kettle is still hot,' he explained. 'As I discovered when I touched it.'

Lukas frowned. This damn shoes business was beginning to get to him. He could not get a sensible answer out of Slonský to the perfectly straightforward enquiry as to why the latter needed uniform shoes. Slonský had grudgingly noted that although he had managed without them for some time, he had been acutely aware that when they visited important people he did not have a presentable uniform to wear. That was undoubtedly true, but it was also true of his civilian clothes, most of which would have disgraced a charity shop. Lukas had tried to arrange that Slonský was kept away from the powerful people of Prague, but since two recent cases had required him to question successive Ministers of the Interior that had not been entirely possible. Slonský was disrespectful, thought Lukas. He thought ministers were shifty, devious, lying scum. Unfortunately he was quite often right about that, but it did not do to say so, especially to them.

He was also concerned about Peiperová. One moment she was being used as some sort of domestic servant, fetching coffee and sandwiches and not doing real police work, and the next she had been sent out into some of the seediest areas of Prague to question the girls in the clubs. Slonský had justified sending her on her own by explaining that women were more likely to talk to women, and that Navrátil would be less than a hundred metres away in an unmarked car. Lukas could not help thinking that Navrátil, however game and devoted to Peiperová, was no match for the average pimp's team of thugs. Slonský acknowledged that, but pointed out that Navrátil was equipped with a sniper's rifle with a laser sight.

'Has he ever fired one?' asked Lukas.

'No, but it wouldn't help if he had. He doesn't have any ammunition, just in case he hits Peiperová. The idea is that if he gets the red light on their hearts they'll assume a bullet is on its way, so they'll be compliant.'

'And if they don't?'

'I guess he'll have to shout bang very loud and hope they don't realise he's bluffing.'

'I don't find that very reassuring, Slonský.'

'I could give the rifle to Dvorník, sir.'

Lukas winced. Lieutenant Dvorník had such confidence in his own firearms ability that he had shot a suspect who was holding his own wife hostage while Slonský was standing a couple of metres away. The thought of the things he might try with a sniper's rifle was acutely unsettling and Lukas began to feel another bilious attack coming on.

'Excuse me,' he muttered, and ran to the washroom.

Peiperová was beginning to doubt the idea of a universal sisterhood. The girls in the club had made it abundantly clear that she was about as welcome as a dose of thrush and they were unwilling to talk.

'I don't want to muscle in on your job,' she remarked.

'Just as well, dear,' one replied. 'You haven't got the boobs for it.'

Peiperová sat on a stool and waited. If it became clear she was going to sit there until she got an answer, perhaps they would cave in. Eventually, one did.

It was the tall girl with a beehive hairstyle who worked under the name of Medusa. She waited until the others had gone out to the dance floor before quickly responding to the question she had been asked fifteen minutes earlier.

'We don't have Balkan girls here. We've been offered them, but the boss knows they don't want to do it and he says they're miserable cows. They've got some at the Padlock Club. Know it?'

Peiperová confessed that she did not, so Medusa gave her some brief directions before following her colleagues. It was about a ten minute walk to the Padlock Club, which was anything but discreet. There were large windows that gave tantalising glimpses of the interior courtesy of large rotating mirrors carefully positioned so as not to identify any customers. As Peiperová approached the door a large man stepped from the shadows to block her way.

'Men only, love,' he announced.

'Isn't that discriminatory?' Peiperová asked.

'How do you mean?'

'Haven't I got just as much right to look at the girls as a man?'

The bouncer thought about this for a moment. 'If it was up to me, you would, but it isn't, and you can't.'

Peiperová issued a deep sigh. 'I was hoping not to have to be formal,' she said, 'but this is official.' She produced her badge. 'No doubt you'll know that impeding a police officer is a serious offence,' she continued. 'And I'm sure you don't want any trouble.'

'What do you want?'

Peiperová fished in her pocket and produced a photograph of Savović. 'Has this man been here?'

There was just enough hesitation to tell her the answer.

'I don't see everyone who goes in.'

'That's an unusual thing for a doorkeeper to admit. Tell you what — I'll come again with my boss in a couple of days. You have a good think about what you remember.'

Slonský inspected his watch. 'The big question is: do we turn the club over now, or have a mid-morning coffee first?'

'I'm not thirsty, sir,' Peiperová responded. Navrátil nodded vigorously, partly because it was true but mainly because he wanted to appear supportive of her.

'You don't want to go searching on an empty stomach,' Slonský announced, but then added, 'but I suppose we're only scouting out the lie of the land at the moment. Come on, then. Navrátil, make sure you lock the car properly. There are some shady characters around here.'

There was a different doorman standing guard at the Padlock Club. A brief glance at him told Slonský that he was unlikely to be a champion crossword solver.

'Good morning,' Slonský said cheerily, waving his badge. 'We've come to pay you a visit.'

The doorman seemed unsure whether to let them pass unopposed but it was taking him too long to make up his mind and Slonský was inside before he found his voice to protest. 'I'll have to tell the boss you're here.'

'No need,' Slonský told him. 'We'll find our own way round. You don't want to leave the door unguarded, do you?'

The doorman turned back, but a second thug had appeared from a small room off the corridor. He must have been watching the door on closed circuit television and stepped out briskly, as betrayed by the ketchup round his mouth.

Slonský grabbed Navrátil's arm. 'No, lad! Don't attack till I say.'

Thug B looked at each in turn. 'Him? Attack?'

Slonský was at his most affable. 'He's our best. You don't think someone that weedy could get by if he wasn't really good at it? Hands like lightning.'

Despite his best efforts, Thug B's face displayed a flicker of concern.

'You may find this hard to credit,' Slonský said in a stage whisper, 'but this lad is so slick with a flick-knife he can arrange which of your trouser legs your balls are going to drop down. I've never actually seen him do one each side, but he says he can.'

Now Thug B was convinced. He had a job to do, but with only a baton tucked in his belt he knew he was no match for a castration-fixated ninja with a conjuror's hands. 'What do you want?' he asked, semi-graciously.

'That's nice,' Slonský said approvingly. 'I always appreciate a public-spirited citizen who is prepared to help us in our never-ending quest to stamp out crime. We've been asked by our colleagues in Bosnia to find some girls who have been abducted. Our enquiries have led us here.'

'The girls aren't in yet.'

'I didn't think they would be, which is why we came early. That way you can take your time giving us a list of your girls' names so we can check them out and come back later with the warrants nicely filled in.'

'All our girls are...' He paused, searching for the most appropriate word. 'Volunteers.'

'You mean they dance for nothing? Actually, I can believe that. Your boss isn't a big payer, is he?'

'He's all right,' Thug B mumbled. 'Looks after us.'

'I bet you don't get private health insurance? No, I thought not. Not even free Metro passes.'

'Ah, we get them!' snapped the big man in black. 'We get the free trips on the Metro to get to work.'

Slonský leaned forward conspiratorially. '*You* might. I'm not so sure all your colleagues do.' He nodded towards the outer door. 'And if you're getting things others don't get, what do they get that you don't?'

That this had struck a chord was clear from the deep frown crossing Thug B's brow as he lapsed into something approaching thought.

'That list,' Slonský prompted. 'Peiperová will write it down for us. Meanwhile Navrátil will have a little look around just to see that none of the girls have sneaked in.'

On a signal from Slonský, Navrátil inched past his back and continued along the corridor.

'Oh, and Navrátil!' Slonský called. 'No unnecessary violence, please. Keep the choke chain in your pocket.'

Navrátil, though bewildered, nodded assent, noting with a little satisfaction that the hoodlum appeared very wary of him.

In the old days, mused Klinger, there was no freedom but there were lots of card indexes, upon which the maintenance of the communist state depended. In offices throughout Prague you could find banks of drawers containing millions of cards recording most aspects of people's lives.

Then the wall came down, liberty was ushered in, and the card indexes became a matter of history. Computers arrived, and now it was possible for him to check in just a few minutes how many times Smejkal had left the country and where his immediate destination was. In the past it would have taken him weeks to discover this, but such is progress, sighed Klinger.

The printer churned out a second list, this time for Nejedlý. Carefully selecting a lime green highlighter, Klinger set himself to comparing the journeys. There were several occasions when both Nejedlý and Smejkal had been out of the country at the same time, though they had never travelled together. But on the fifth of May Smejkal had taken a flight to Belgrade and had not returned until the tenth; meanwhile Nejedlý had crossed a land border leaving the EU in Hungary to go into Serbia on the seventh. Unfortunately there was no clear re-entry point for the return, but he had used a credit card to buy an Austrian toll road token on the ninth.

Klinger calculated the mileage and estimated the driving time. It was certainly possible for them to have met up. Was this the link they had been looking for? Savović finds the girls and passes them to Nejedlý. He knows the police are onto him so he wants to leave Bosnia for a while, so Nejedlý introduced him to Smejkal and they all meet up in Belgrade. A couple of months later Savović leaves Bosnia and sets up in Prague in a building that Smejkal frequents. *I wonder if he owns it?*, pondered Klinger.

Navrátil stared gloomily into his coffee cup.

'Cheer up, Navrátil! They'll give you a wide berth if they see you again.'

'More likely they'll shoot first and take no chances,' grumbled Navrátil.

'Well, there is that possibility,' Slonský conceded, 'but we'll cross that bridge when we come to it. Now, how does that list help?'

'I was hoping you were going to tell us that, sir,' Peiperová replied. 'I thought you had a reason for wanting it.'

'No, I just wanted the hooligan occupied while Navrátil had a look round. I thought anything involving writing was bound to be slow. What did you find, lad?'

'I didn't really know what I was looking for,' Navrátil explained.

'Well, did you find any girls?'

'No, there was nobody. There must be some Bosnians or Serb girls because there were women's magazines in the Cyrillic alphabet lying around.'

'Excellent!'

'None of them was dated after September.'

'Even better.'

'And there's a back door that opens onto an alley. As you come out, it's blind to the left but it opens alongside the front door.'

'Building opposite?'

'Looks like a shop with offices above. The offices have a door opening onto the alley.'

'Good. So if we need to sneak in the back way we know how to do it.'

'There's no handle on the back door from the outside, sir. Someone has to let you in. It's one of those fire doors with a push bar.'

'Damn.'

'But unfortunately someone has carelessly broken the peg at the top of the door that keeps it shut, sir,' said Navrátil, who curiously had that very peg in his hand and was displaying it for all to see.

'Navrátil, you are destined for high things in this police force. Peiperová, if you don't come to your senses soon and give him the heave-ho, you're going to spend your future sewing increasing amounts of gold braid on his uniforms.'

'Maybe he'll be sewing braid on mine, sir. It's an age of equality.'

'So it is, and quite right too.' Slonský leaned over and whispered to Navrátil. 'I bet *she* can get one down each trouser leg, lad. Watch yourself.'

Klinger was puzzled. The building was not owned by Smejkal, which helped to explain why it was in relatively good repair. Moreover, unlike Slonský he had managed to get some useful information about Savović from Bosnian colleagues.

'So basically they don't know why they're after him, but they just wanted to know what he was up to?' Slonský snarled.

'That's about it,' agreed Klinger. 'Savović is a well-known bad boy, who probably has a warehouse or two of ex-army supplies.'

'Weapons?'

'Weapons, but also an awful lot of canned food, I hear.'

'A useful person to know if you want to corner the cling peaches market, then.'

Klinger tipped the last of his espresso into his mouth with a flourish of his little finger. 'I think they're more concerned about the weapons than they are about the cling peaches, Slonský.'

'How times change. In the nineties they had plenty of weapons but cling peaches were like gold dust.'

'I wouldn't know. I'm not a devotee of canned food myself.'

'Not now, perhaps, but think of those decades when we lived on tinned sauerkraut.'

'I would very much rather not think of those decades and especially not of tinned sauerkraut.'

Slonský drained his mug. 'Where's your sense of Czech heritage, man?'

Klinger smiled thinly. 'I place more emphasis on Dvořák, Janáček and Martinů than on sauerkraut as components of Czech heritage, Slonský.'

'You can't have been as hungry as I was in the sixties. You can't eat a Dvořák.'

'Undoubtedly true, but irrelevant. Now, to return to the point, Savović has not cleared all his bank accounts, so our colleagues in Sarajevo plainly expect him to return at some point in the future.'

'Any idea how much he has grabbed?'

'Around four million Euros, they think, leaving about six behind him.'

'Four million Euros? You can buy a lot of tinned peaches with that.'

'A possible, but improbable, use of the money,' Klinger pronounced.

'So do you have any idea what he could be spending it on?'

Klinger made a steeple out of his fingers and held them in front of his lips for a moment to signify deep thought. 'Of course, there's always arms and drugs. But, speaking as an economist, those markets are already well-supplied and there are significant barriers to market entry.'

'He's got plenty of cash.'

'I was thinking more of the likelihood of being found in a ditch with a bullet through one's head. Savović has bodyguards but he could never win a turf war against the existing barons who would combine to stamp out interference in their nicely sewn-up market.'

'We know he's in cahoots with a sex trafficker.'

Klinger shook his head. 'We suspect, but we don't know. But even if he is, it won't give him a return on that amount of money. There just aren't enough people who want Bosnian women.'

'Not who are prepared to pay, anyway,' Slonský agreed.

'That leaves property. Savović could be trafficking with Nejedlý but using most of his money to bankroll Smejkal. Smejkal would have no difficulty in finding a profitable use for four million Euros, especially if they had not been declared to the tax authorities so the interest rate demanded is likely to be lower than the banks would expect to pay. Unless it's an interest-free, profit-sharing arrangement, I suppose.'

Slonský shook his head slowly. 'No, I can't see it. In time, perhaps; but I can't imagine Savović handing over that sort of sum to someone he can only just have met. How does he know Smejkal isn't going to run off with his cash? Even if he got a receipt, it's not going to help a lot when Smejkal is sitting by a pool in Mauritius.'

'He may not have handed it over yet. He may still be weighing up the deal.'

'So there could be a big sack of Euros under his bed?'

Klinger wiped his hands on a large white handkerchief. He always felt the need to do that when he came to Slonský's office. 'Actually, four million Euros doesn't need a particularly large sack. You can calculate the size of a pile of four million Euros.'

'I can't,' said Slonský, always a stickler for accuracy. 'You can.'

'Well,' Klinger responded, 'let's put it in simple terms for you. That box of paper by the printer holds two thousand five hundred sheets.'

'If you say so.'

'The label on the side says so, Slonský. Use your eyes. If each of those sheets was a five hundred Euro note, a stack as tall as the box would amount to one and a quarter million Euros. Now, we need to know the size of a five hundred Euro note. I don't suppose you have one?'

'Have one? I've never even seen one.'

'No matter.'

Klinger tapped a few keys on his mobile phone. '160 millimetres long by 82 wide,' he said. 'Whereas a sheet of A4 paper is 297 by 210 millimetres.'

'You must be a wow at parties, Klinger. Imagine having all this at the tips of your fingers.'

'I detect a measure of sarcasm in your tone which I shall ignore. Simple multiplication tells us that you could fit 4.75 such banknotes on a piece of A4 paper. Therefore that box of paper could contain the four stacks of banknotes necessary to constitute four million Euros.' Klinger rose from his chair. 'Slonský, however entertaining this demonstration, and however fascinating the whereabouts of that money may be to me, I don't see how it will help you find the murderer of poor Hrdlička.'

Slonský rocked back in his chair, which creaked alarmingly as the joints were strained. 'People don't generally kill other people for no reason. Somebody knew who Hrdlička was and why he was there. Somebody had something to hide. And the prime suspects must be Savović, Nejedlý and Smejkal. Find out what they were hiding, and we may discover why it was worth killing to keep it hidden.'

Klinger acknowledged the logic with a pursing of his lips and returned to his office, taking care not to touch the doorknob of Slonský's office with his bare hand, a ritual that Slonský found constantly entertaining.

'Obsessed with hygiene,' he muttered. 'I wonder if he's ever seen the showers in the basement?'

He took a pair of scissors, a sheet of paper, a pencil and a ruler and set about trying to prove Klinger wrong.

Peiperová and Navrátil had returned from their respective duties for a debrief at four o'clock as requested. Peiperová had managed to find and speak to some of the women on the list that she had compiled. None of them admitted to having seen Savović in Prague, but a couple were prepared to admit to having met him in Bosnia.

'Will they give evidence that he brought them here?' asked Slonský.

'Yes,' said Peiperová, 'but it won't help because they say he is just a travel agent.'

'A travel agent?'

'That's right. They gave him money and he organised bus tickets and the necessary paperwork. They crossed into Serbia, then Hungary, Slovakia and so to Prague.'

'What necessary paperwork?' asked Navrátil.

'False passports.'

'Isn't that an unusual service for a travel agent to provide?' asked Navrátil.

'It is,' Slonský conceded, 'but the offence doesn't sound like it was committed here, so we can't arrest him for it. We could deport the girls, but how does that help?'

'And I suppose he'll claim he didn't know they were being imported for immoral purposes,' Navrátil added.

'He'll probably tell us he thought they were a folk dancing troupe. Anyway, keep in touch with them, Peiperová. When they're ready to talk, they'll know who to come to. What sort of day have you had, Navrátil?'

'I tracked down Mr Nejedlý. He claimed that he had been at a business meeting on Kampa Island.'

'The other party confirm that?'

'He can't remember the other party's name exactly. And he says the other chap suggested the bar as a venue. And he isn't a frequent visitor to Kampa so he can't remember the name of the bar, though he could probably take us there if asked. So I asked.'

'And?'

'The barman couldn't swear to the time but was sure that Nejedlý was there at some time during the afternoon.'

'Did he see the business acquaintance?'

'No, they sat in one of the screened booths. He could see Nejedlý who was facing him, but not the other man. And he didn't see them leave.'

'That doesn't surprise me. They might not want to be seen leaving.'

'So where does that get us, sir?'

'I don't think it clears Nejedlý. A very uncertain sighting earlier in the afternoon within easy walking distance of the murder scene isn't convincing, lad.'

Peiperová broke into the conversation. 'If he was making it up, sir, surely he'd pick somewhere a bit further away than Kampa.'

'Bluff and double bluff, lass. Maybe he was banking on us being dim enough to think a real criminal would place more distance between himself and the scene of the crime, whereas actually if he was on the other side of Prague we'd wonder why he just happened to be so far away. Oh, I wish criminals wouldn't lie to us! It just makes a hard job completely impossible.'

Chapter 4

Slonský languidly stirred his coffee and glanced around the canteen. There was nobody he wanted to talk to, which was neatly symmetrical because nobody there wanted to talk to Slonský very much. Lieutenant Doležal was drinking a mint tea, which was the kind of thing you were reduced to when your doctor told you to cut out all forms of excitement, something which probably came easier to Doležal than anyone else. Even Klinger could get more animated, if he came across a particularly well laid out bank statement or a new shape of sticky thing to write notes on for his files.

Doležal paused in mid-sip, suddenly uncomfortably aware that Slonský was looking at him. Feeling some response was required, Slonský raised his cup in a silent toast, which Doležal acknowledged with a dip of his head.

'Dear God, don't let him come over and talk to me,' Slonský prayed.

Doležal finished his tea and left.

'My prayers are answered. Thank you, God,' muttered Slonský.

'That's very kind,' said Sergeant Mucha. 'It's always nice to be appreciated.'

'You're not the answer to anyone's prayers,' Slonský replied.

'Well, you're entitled to your opinion,' said Mucha, 'but my wife may disagree with you. She prayed for a lifelong scapegoat and here I am.'

'Ah, but why are you here?' asked Slonský.

'Why are any of us here? It's foxed better minds than mine. Personally I favour the hypothesis that God likes a laugh, but being omniscient he knows all the punchlines, so he put us here to give himself something to giggle over. Every so often he shakes things up a bit and then wets himself watching us trying to get out of the mess we're in.'

Slonský bit into his ham roll. 'Were you taught by Jesuits?'

'No. Do they go in for that line of thought?'

'I've no idea, but I thought I'd ask. The alternative was a discussion based in the real world where I live and you're an occasional visitor. So, I repeat, why are you here?'

Mucha sat down and leaned forward. 'The pertinent question is why you're here. I've been sent to fetch you because Dr Novák is upstairs waiting.'

'Damn! Forgot he was coming.'

'It's all right. He's talking to Captain Lukas.'

Slonský sprang to his feet. 'Novák talking to Lukas is definitely not all right. How can I keep the upper hand over them if they can gang up on me?' He pushed the roll into his mouth so he could carry his cup and open the doors on his way.

As he left, Dumpy Anna called to Mucha, 'I know it's only Slonský, but you'll get him to bring that cup back, won't you? Takeaway is in cardboard cups. China is for sit-downs.'

Mucha waved her concern away. 'Anna, tell him he's vegetarian till he brings it back and you'll have every cup in the building back here by nightfall.'

Slonský skipped up the stairs and nudged his office door open with his hip, putting the coffee and roll down and greeting Novák in one fluid movement before realising that Novák was not there. Navrátil looked up from his work and pointed down the corridor with his pen. Leaving the snack behind, Slonský strode purposefully to Captain Lukas' door, knocked and was at the side of the desk before Lukas had finished saying 'Enter'.

Lukas had a sour look about him. Although he was a very experienced police officer he had long been rather squeamish about the work of pathologists and preferred not to know what they got up to. All he wanted was a clear set of findings, and it looked as if Novák had some. The manila folder in front of him was commendably thin.

'Ah, Lieutenant Slonský, Mucha has tracked you down.'

'No mystery, sir. Just having a well-deserved ham sandwich.'

The dyspeptic look was intensified. 'Not one for ham, myself. Not police ham, anyway. Rather fatty for my taste. Anyway, we aren't here to talk about sandwiches. Dr Novák is about to tell us what he has found.'

Novák opened his folder and gave a light preparatory cough as if about to deliver a presidential address at a university. Slonský flopped into the vacant chair, where his attention was captured by a carrier bag at Novák's feet.

'You know all the details of the deceased,' Novák began, 'so I needn't recite those. He died as a result of a single stab wound to the brain stem. It was a narrow blade, perhaps one and a half centimetres wide, but at least twelve centimetres long.'

'Spring loaded?' asked Slonský, whose eyes were beginning to gleam as facts fell into his possession. He found such material enervating and needed very few hard facts to rouse from torpor and begin detecting.

'I can't rule it out,' said Novák, 'but if it was it was a straight spring rather than a side spring.'

'I'm sorry?' Lukas interrupted.

'Switch blades either swing out of one side or they strike like a snake straight forward,' Novák explained. 'If it was a spring loaded knife, it must have been the latter type, because having jammed it through Hrdlička's neck into his brain stem, the murderer gave it a pretty firm wiggle, and there's no sign of the blade trying to close, which I'd have expected a hinged blade to do.'

Lukas pressed a handkerchief to his lips. 'Wiggled? In the brain stem?'

'Yes,' continued Novák, completely oblivious to the peculiar waxy appearance exhibited by Lukas or the lip-licking that Slonský was performing. 'At the base of the brain there's a little tail that leads down to the top of the spine. Some of the most important parts of the brain are in the stem. You don't survive substantial damage to it.'

'So Hrdlička died quickly?' Slonský enquired.

'I can't say it was instantaneous, but his vital functions would have been disrupted severely. He would have been paralysed from the wound down, and he would have had difficulty in breathing because he wouldn't be able to fill his lungs. I think there's good evidence that the shock killed him but I've sent some blood samples off for analysis to confirm the point. His blood pressure would have fallen calamitously and I suspect he lost consciousness in moments and died very quickly. It's the same effect as a judicial hanging, just achieved another way.'

'Thank heaven for small mercies,' Lukas said, though it was difficult to hear him due to the muffling caused by the handkerchief in front of his mouth.

Slonský was thinking hard. 'But Hrdlička was a trained police officer. He'd done surveillance work for a long time. How did they kill him in broad daylight without any sign of a struggle?'

Novák beamed. 'Ah! A good question, and I may have an answer.'

'May have?'

'I can't prove it myself, but I may be able to do so with the aid of a willing volunteer. Not you, Slonský, I need to talk to you.'

Slonský turned to look at Lukas.

'Not Captain Lukas either,' said Novák. 'His head is too big.'

'That'll be due to the brains,' Slonský opined gravely.

'No doubt. Is young Navrátil about?'

'I'll fetch him.'

In this case, "fetch" meant that Slonský went to the door and shouted down the corridor. 'Navrátil! Come here and get murdered!'

Novák opened the carrier bag and produced a knight's helmet.

'Is that the one Hrdlička was wearing?' asked Navrátil.

'Don't be squeamish, lad,' Slonský answered. 'None of us is a homicidal maniac. You'll be quite safe.'

Novák handed it to Navrátil. 'Put it on and kneel with your back to us.'

Navrátil did so.

'You can pray if you want,' Slonský suggested. 'May as well use the time profitably.'

Novák produced a flat wooden stick. 'This tongue depressor will stand in for the murder weapon. Don't want to risk an accident, do we?'

Slonský rapped on the helmet with his knuckles, making it ring. 'You're all right, we're not going to use a real knife,' he bellowed.

Navrátil nodded an acknowledgement.

Novák pushed Navrátil's head gently forward.

'When he is upright, the cuff at the back of the helmet protects his neck. It wouldn't have been much use in the olden days if it hadn't. It's only when he tips his head forward in prayer that the murderer can stab him in the back of the neck under the helmet. Stabbing upwards at an angle — like this! — is only possible in the praying position.'

'But why didn't Hrdlička hear the assassin sneak up?'

'Because the assassin is a trained killer. Because he's on a busy road with plenty of traffic noise. And because Navrátil can't hear us very well with the helmet on, can you, Navrátil?'

There was no response, proving the point.

'I never liked the slimy little weed anyway,' said Slonský.

'Hrdlička?'

'No, Navrátil. And his girlfriend has spots and a lop-sided bottom. No, you're right, he can't hear us.'

Lukas was frowning. 'But Hrdlička's face was painted silver. Why bother if he was going to wear a helmet?'

Slonský wheeled round at speed. 'He didn't! When we saw him at lunchtime he wasn't wearing the helmet.'

Novák was smirking. 'Very observant, Slonský.'

He leaned forward and lifted the helmet from Navrátil's head, allowing the young detective to rub his neck.

'That's heavy,' he remarked. 'You wouldn't want to wear it for long.'

'No,' agreed Novák, 'you wouldn't.'

'So why did he?' asked Slonský. 'And your face tells me you know.'

'I don't know,' said Novák, 'but I can guess and you can check.'

He inverted the helmet and pulled back the padding that cushioned the inside around the temples. With a flick of a thumb he brought a small white object the size of a kidney bean into view.

'An earpiece?' said Navrátil.

'A wireless one. He was listening in to something when he was killed. That's why he didn't hear anyone sneak up on him; he was concentrating on the scratchy sound of a hidden microphone somewhere. The question for you is where that microphone is.'

'Maybe Grigar knows.'

'I doubt it, Slonský,' said Lukas, 'or he'd have mentioned it. The prime suspect would be the person they're listening to.'

'So can we find out when he put the helmet on? Navrátil, that's your first job. Ask that goddess if she knows when he fetched his helmet. Any ideas, Novák?'

'Found at five, dead around four.'

'So the next question is what provoked him to put the helmet on. Did he put it on at the same time of day every day, or did he see something that prompted him? That's your next job, lad.'

Slonský inspected the large map of Prague on the wall in front of Lukas' desk.

'If Hrdlička is watching the buildings opposite, then how could a murderer sneak out and get round behind him? Visibility is too good. He'd have to go quite a way up or down the river.'

Navrátil traced a route on the map. 'He could have set off in the opposite direction and taken the Metro over the river before walking back.'

'He could also have climbed up to the roof, strung a big piece of elastic between the chimneys and catapulted himself to the other side, which is just as likely. How long would it take him to do what you've suggested? Twenty minutes? How would he know Hrdlička would keep the helmet on that long?'

'But if Hrdlička is watching the boss, and the boss sends a man out to do the actual killing while he keeps talking, Hrdlička would concentrate on the wrong man.'

'That would work,' Novák agreed.

'Detectives detect,' Slonský growled. 'Pathologists … path. Well, whatever they do it isn't detecting. But the lad may have something. If they know they're being watched, the accomplice could slip out at any time of day and wait for a mobile phone call to tell him when to strike. That complicates things.'

'So someone in that red brick building could see that they were being watched and had someone outside to do their dirty work, sir?' Navrátil enquired.

'Not so fast. That's the likeliest explanation, but don't forget that anyone on that side of the road could have thought that they were being watched. If Hrdlička was careless, he could have raised suspicions in anyone with a guilty conscience. And you mustn't forget the person who has admitted being right there at the time of death.'

'Who, sir?'

'The goddess, Navrátil.'

'Sir! She can't be the murderer. She was so shaken by it all.'

'She's hardly going to show her icy coldness to you, is she, lad? She could be acting. Women do, you know. You'll find out soon enough. She could have stepped off the pedestal, and Hrdlička wouldn't have suspected a thing. She fetches a knitting needle, drives it into his neck and then calmly steps back on her pedestal and waits an hour or so to start wailing. Easiest thing in the world to arrange.'

'Knitting needle?' murmured Novák. 'Could be.'

'She didn't have a knitting needle on her when Peiperová brought her here to make a statement, sir.'

'Of course not. There's a damn great river just behind her. She takes the needle out and heaves it into the water. Not much point in getting divers in, though. It's too big a search area and the current may have carried it downstream by now.'

'Surely someone would notice a woman dressed as a Greek goddess chucking a blood-stained knitting needle into the Vltava, sir.'

'Navrátil, there are people in this city who wouldn't notice if King Kong scaled St Vitus' cathedral and swotted planes out of the sky. There are others who wouldn't tell us even if they saw the whole thing. I wouldn't mind betting...'

There was a dull thud behind them. To Slonský's surprise, Captain Lukas had disappeared from sight, as had his chair. It was Navrátil who first surmised that the reason might be that it had tipped over, and ran behind the desk to find Lukas lying on his side.

'Sir? Can you hear me, sir?'

Lukas grimaced but did not speak. His skin was clammy and the colour of an unripe grapefruit, and his fist was clenched in front of his chest.

Slonský realised that he would have to take command.

'Novák, do something!' he bellowed.

'Me? Why me?'

'Because you're a doctor.'

'Send for an ambulance, for God's sake.'

'Navrátil, tell Mucha to get an ambulance. Now, Novák, surely they taught you something at medical school?'

'It was a long time ago, Slonský. I don't deal with living patients nowadays.'

'Well, we could bump him off if it makes you happier, but there'll be a hell of a stink when the Doctors' Union hears about it.'

'This is no time for sarcasm, Slonský.'

'This is no time for hair-splitting, Novák. Do something!'

'Just shut up, Slonský, while I try to think. Is there any pain?'

'Any pain? He's bent double, man!'

'Well, where is the pain, Captain?'

Lukas gritted his teeth and took a deep breath. He banged his clenched fist against his breastbone.

'Is it your heart?'

'You're not meant to ask the bloody patient. You're supposed to know if it's his heart.'

'Slonský, you're not helping. How can I think with you yelling at me? Lukas, can you breathe properly?'

Lukas nodded.

'Is there any other pain?'

Lukas nodded again. He pointed over his shoulder.

'In your shoulder? Your right shoulder?'

'Behind … my … shoulder.'

Slonský leaned across. 'There's nothing sticking out,' he declared.

'I didn't think there would be,' Novak hissed. 'Help me get him on his back so I can examine his chest.'

As they rolled Lukas over he had a loud attack of flatulence.

'You'll feel better after that,' Slonský said.

Novák gently probed Lukas's trunk and was rewarded with a groan when he pressed near the liver.

'Of course! Cholecystitis.'

'What's that?'

'Inflammation of the gall bladder. Has he been unwell lately?'

'He's been sick a lot. Queasy sick — you know — chucking up.'

'Has he seen a doctor?'

'He's looking at you now and a fat lot of good it's doing him. Shouldn't you take it out or something? Have you got your scalpel?'

'Slonský, I haven't done surgery in years.'

'You carve some poor so-and-so up every day of your life.'

'Yes, but I don't have to put the bits back in the right place afterwards. My patients are past caring about that. It's best if we wait for the ambulance. I'll check his vital signs. Why don't you go and find a bowl in case he vomits?'

Navrátil reappeared at the door. 'Ambulance is on its way, sir.'

'Good lad. Now, fetch a bowl for the captain in case he's sick.'

'Anything else, sir?'

'Yes. I left half my sandwich on my desk. If you've got a spare hand…'

It defied any common sense, but Slonský stood to attention while he telephoned the Director of the Criminal Police to tell him what had happened to Lukas. The Director listened calmly, asked what investigations Lukas was overseeing, then suggested that everyone went home and got a good night's sleep.

'Can you carry on as normal?' he asked.

'Yes, sir.'

'Good. Let's see how it looks in the morning. I'll ring the hospital and then we'll see what's what.'

'Very good, sir.'

'In Lukas' absence, you can cover for him. No need to panic for a day or two, but we'll have to deal with his paperwork somehow.'

'Very good, sir.'

'Have you told his wife?'

Slonský groaned inwardly. He knew there was something he should have done. 'I'm on it now, sir.'

'Good man. I'll speak to you tomorrow.'

Slonský put the phone down. 'We'll have to tell Mrs Lukasová,' he announced.

'I rang her while you were putting him in the ambulance,' Peiperová responded. 'Navrátil has borrowed a car to take her to the hospital. If you don't need me, sir, I said I'd sit with their daughters until she gets back.'

Slonský sighed. He would never get the hang of this touchy-feely stuff.

Chapter 5

Lukas was slowly sinking into a pile of pillows. To Slonský's unpractised eye, he looked no better than before the operation, but the doctors assured him that he was making good progress.

'Just in the nick of time, then, sir,' Slonský said cheerfully.

'So I understand.'

'Within an ace of rupture.'

'Yes.'

'Could have been really nasty.'

'Yes. Could we change…'

'Just as well Dr Novák was there. Though he didn't actually do anything. But it must have been a comfort.'

'Yes. At least he could tell the paramedics what was wrong.'

'They were a bit flummoxed by the knight's helmet, sir, but once I'd explained he was a pathologist they seemed to think it was par for the course.'

'Really?'

'Yes. Are you feeling like eating yet, sir?'

'Er — no, Slonský. Not in the least.'

'The Director was very good, sir. Sharp man. Always liked him.'

'Yes, he is. He was good enough to ring this morning and leave a message for me.'

'A personal message. Very thoughtful, sir.'

'I'm going to be laid up for six weeks or more, so I need to make some arrangements to keep the department ticking over smoothly.'

In other circumstances Slonský might have disputed this use of the word "keep"; "start" seemed more appropriate, but this seemed to be neither the time nor the place.

'You're the ranking lieutenant, Slonský, so you're going to be acting captain.'

'I'm not sure…'

'It's not negotiable, Slonský. It was you, Doležal or Dvorník, and I refuse to leave my department in the hands of Dvorník.'

'He'd be good on the firearms training, sir. We'd all get plenty of time on the range.'

'Precisely why he isn't ready … yet. And Doležal is not really a team player.'

You can say that again, thought Slonský. Doležal would have shut the office door and not come out for weeks on end.

'That leaves you. And to tell you the truth, Josef, you're ready for this. I worry that you'll miss your chance. It's high time you put in for a captain's job. This will be good experience for you. Handy on your CV.'

Slonský did not want to aggravate a sick man by arguing. He just crossed his fingers out of sight to show that he did not agree.

'Don't worry, sir. Everything will be fine when you come back.'

'I'm pleased to hear it. I'll feel much happier knowing you're filling my shoes for now.'

'You're very kind, sir.'

'Now, get your notebook ready. The expenses forms have to be signed off after you've checked all the receipts are attached, then they go up to the third floor…'

Slonský was sitting at his new desk. He would much rather have been at his old desk, but the telephone lines could not be moved for at least two weeks, and then only if the Director signed some form TP one hundred and something. The Director had issued a memorandum to everyone explaining the temporary arrangement and adding that since Acting Captain Slonský was still an active detective, he would not be wearing uniform. Everyone was asked to do all they could to make his posting successful.

Anna in the canteen had been surprised to see him and immediately curtseyed.

'Cut it out,' he barked. 'Coffee and the stodgiest pastry you've got.'

Anna busied herself pouring his coffee. 'You know you can ring down and we'll bring this up to you,' she said.

'Yes. And I don't want that. I'll come down like I always have.'

'No, you haven't,' she said. 'Sometimes you send Navrátil. Or that pretty girl with the long blonde hair.'

'And I still will. Sometimes. But I'm not going to let my promotion get in the way of coming down here to see you, Anna.'

Anna paused in mid-pour and wondered if she was blushing. 'I'll send someone up to get that cup you stole the other day,' she said.

Navrátil had finally managed to find someone at police headquarters in Sarajevo who spoke English, which allowed them to communicate to some degree. It meant that the telephone call was quite long, but since he would now be explaining that to Acting Captain Slonský rather than Captain Lukas, he felt relatively comfortable. Whatever his faults, Slonský was not a penny-pincher.

Armed with his hard-won information, Navrátil knocked tentatively on the door to Lukas' office and was rewarded with a simple instruction, forcefully expressed.

'It's me, sir — Navrátil,' he replied.

'Ah — come on in, lad. I hope you don't want a day off, maternity leave, a pension booklet or anything like that.'

'I've come to talk about crime, sir.'

'That's good. Crime is the very thing we're meant to be doing something about. I like criminals. They don't waste my time asking about bicycle parking chits. Well, take a seat and tell me all about it.'

'Very good…'

'But before you start, let's get some coffee and a pastry. My blood sugar must be low. Is Peiperová around?'

Navrátil knew how Peiperová felt about being a coffee runner. 'I'll go, sir.'

'No need, Navrátil. Let's go down together, and you can tell me all about it on the way. I'll just leave a note on the door in case anyone wants me.'

Slonský scrawled a few words on the back of a circular and taped it to the door glass. Navrátil could not help noticing that it claimed that Slonský had just gone to Peru and might be some time.

They marched down the stairs side by side.

'Why Peru, sir?'

'Why not? First thing that came into my head. Besides, anywhere in this country and the pests might chase after me. They can't get to Peru unless I sign off their travel passes, which, of course, I wouldn't, being in Peru.'

Navrátil considered, not for the first time, what the world inside Slonský's head must be like, and decided again that he did not choose to live there any longer than was necessary.

'I rang Sarajevo, sir, to talk about Savović.'

'And what did the capital of Bosnia have to say for itself?'

'I told them we knew where Savović was, but I wondered what the relationship was between him and the other four. Did they expect them to be together?'

'Good question. Did they have a good answer?'

Navrátil produced the fax bearing the five photographs from his pocket. 'It seems that Savović and this one, Brukić, are old associates. It wouldn't surprise the Bosnians if Brukić had come here too. The other three belong to a completely different gang. The Bosnian police had heard rumours that the five of them were combining to make a play to take control of crime in Sarajevo. They anticipated a bloodbath, because the two sides have some heavy weaponry available to them.'

'That's what happens after a war. People never tidy up properly. There are always unwanted guns left lying around.'

'In this case, some hundred and fifty millimetre mortars and a certain amount of motorised artillery were mentioned.'

Slonský gave a low whistle. 'Thank goodness our local hoodlums aren't as enterprising. I take it that Savović doesn't have these in a shed somewhere?'

'Not in the Czech Republic, so far as we know. Anyway, the Bosnians decided the best way to deal with this was to tell each group what was known about the other's plan.'

'A fine example of police transparency. And the upshot was?'

'A nightclub owner found in a wheelie bin. At least, most of him was. They haven't found one arm and a bit of a leg.'

'He was dead, I assume?'

'Stone dead, sir. And the five took off that same evening and haven't been seen since. If they're scattered, the Bosnians are happy. Their concern is that they may be in one place plotting their return.'

'Whereas our concern is that we have enough villains of our own without importing them from other countries. Our second concern is that I've left my money in my coat so you'll have to get these, Navrátil.'

They collected their coffees and Slonský filled a plate with pastries before dumping it on a tray. Navrátil took out his wallet to pay at the till.

'Aren't you having anything to eat?' asked Slonský.

Some enquiries need a woman's touch, thought Peiperová. She was ostensibly looking in a shop window, though actually her attention was focused on the woman across the street whose reflection she could study.

Touring the streets by some dancing clubs, Peiperová's attention had been drawn to this tall, brown-haired girl. There was something about her street clothes that told Peiperová that she was an immigrant. Her boots were sound, but constructed for warmth rather than style. Although the girl glanced in the windows of the more expensive shops, she did not go in. Instead, she checked out department stores and some of the chain retailers. She bought some cheap underwear and stockings. Looking over her shoulder as she paid for them, Peiperová could see that there was little in the woman's purse. She permitted herself a wry smile as she reflected that not only would the men have failed to spot this woman's origin, but they could hardly have followed her inconspicuously around lingerie departments.

Peiperová had herself been followed by an inquisitive store detective. She had opened her badge and, holding it up like she was checking her make-up in a pocket mirror, allowed the detective to see it. To her credit, the older woman simply melted away, leaving Peiperová to pursue her quarry unmolested.

The dark girl sat on a bench and bit her nails. Perhaps not conventionally pretty, though undoubtedly statuesque, she marred whatever good looks she possessed by frowning. Her young face was disfigured by worry, which had etched some lines on her brow, and her eyes were purple with lack of sleep. Peiperová dropped on the bench beside her. 'Would you like a coffee?' she asked.

'I'm not like that,' the girl replied.

'Like what?'

'One of those. I'm not into girls.'

'Neither am I. I'm a policewoman.'

The dark girl tried to walk away, but Peiperová's arm linked through hers and bound them together. 'I'm not with immigration,' she explained. 'So we're just two girls out shopping together who decided to get a coffee. Okay?'

'Do I have a choice?'

'You always have a choice. We can talk a bit over a coffee or I can get heavy and take you to a station. But I guess you wouldn't feel comfortable in a police station.' She caught the other woman's inquisitive look and returned it with a smile. 'Besides, you look as if you could really do with a coffee.'

The girl nodded, so they walked together towards a coffee shop.

'Let's go inside,' suggested Peiperová. 'The seats out here are a bit public. You won't want to be seen talking to me.'

They ordered their coffees and sat in silence for a few moments. The girl played obsessively with a paper napkin, betraying her tension by worrying the folds with her fingernails.

'Have you got any papers?' Peiperová asked.

The girl shook her head. Her eyes were fixed on the table top.

'What about identification from your home?'

'Identification?'

The girl had a strong accent and pronounced the word in divided syllables as if it might be easier to understand that way.

'What's your name?'

'Suzana.'

'Is it really Suzana?'

The girl looked confused as if the idea of using a false name had not occurred to her.

'Yes. I'm really Suzana.'

'Fine. I'm Kristýna.'

Peiperová offered her hand. Suzana shook it cautiously.

'Where are you from, Suzana?'

'I come from Bosnia-Herzegovina.'

'How long have you been here?'

'Fifteen weeks and two days.'

'You don't like it, do you? Are you homesick?'

'Please, homesick?'

'Do you wish you were in Bosnia instead of Prague?'

'I miss my home. I miss my mother and father. I am ashamed for them.'

'Ashamed? Why?'

'They think I work in hotel. They don't know I have to dance here in such places.'

'Why did you leave?'

'There was no work for me in Bosnia. A man told me he had a little hotel here and he needs waitresses, girls for reception, cleaners. Together this makes ten girls. He sends a bus for us.'

'A Czech man?'

Suzana frowned and shook her head vigorously. 'No, Bosnian man. He says to our families that we will be trained here and not to worry but for some weeks we will be in hotel training so we cannot have telephones. This is normal, he says.'

Peiperová had heard this sort of thing before. The families would not try to contact their daughters for a while because the explanation seemed plausible.

'So he brought you here by bus?'

'Yes. But it is a long journey. First, we go to Serbia. Then we go to Hungary. We don't stop nowhere. Then we eat in Slovakia and at last we come here. In Slovakia a Czech man comes on the bus and stays with us. He teaches us to talk a little bit Czech.'

Suzana sipped her coffee. She took it with plenty of hot milk and sugar.

'Then when you arrived you found there was no hotel.'

'Yes, no hotel. The Czech man says this is no problem because he has other work. We are young girls, so we can be dancers. One of the girls says she has been a ballet dancer but he laughs and says it is not ballet. He has a cruel laugh.'

She bit her nails again.

'So they made you work in a club?'

Suzana's eyes were wet with tears. 'It is bad work. I don't like to take my clothes off. But he says if I don't dance, then there is only one way to earn my fare home, and I don't like this more. There is a Bosnian girl who says she don't dance, and they take her away. Next time I see her, she has bruises on face and she does big cry. She tell me men make her to go to bed. One holds her while the other does things then they change places. Then the cruel man tells her no-one will marry her now because she is spoilt. She can walk back to Bosnia but everyone will know she is bad girl who goes with men.'

'Could you introduce me to her?'

Suzana shook her head.

'I mean, could you take me to her?'

'No, is not possible. This girl is so sad she take knife and cut wrists in bath. The Czech man and the Bosnian have big words about this. The Czech man says now is big trouble for him but the Bosnian tells him he knows people and they can take her body away and nobody ever find it. He says is no big deal anyway. It is not crime for a girl to kill herself.'

She crumpled the napkin into a ball and used it to stifle her tears.

Peiperová suddenly remembered the fax that she had in her pocket. 'I'm going to show you some pictures,' she explained. 'I need you to look at them and tell me if you know any of the men you see.' She unfolded it, and the gasp that Suzana gave as she brought her hand to her mouth betokened recognition. Her hand shook as she pointed at one of the men.

But it was not Savović.

The desk phone rang. It was Sergeant Mucha ringing from the front desk.

'Who's a pretty boy, then?'

'You speak in riddles. Why am I pretty?' demanded Slonský.

'Well, you'd better be because a lot of egg-yolk is on its way up.'

Slonský hurriedly straightened his tie and rubbed each shoe in turn on the back of his trouser leg. The door was opened and the Director walked in. A uniformed arm was visible beside his hip.

'I can open doors for myself, thank you,' he announced to the uniformed officer behind him.

Slonský began to salute, but the Director motioned him to stop. This was a good thing, because Slonský had never been a sharp saluter. What he lacked in grace was matched by a lack of vigour, so his salutes looked like a schoolboy asking tentatively if he might leave the room who decided to scratch an eyebrow instead.

'This is an unexpected pleasure, sir,' he stammered.

'I bet it isn't,' the Director replied. 'Kuchař!'

'Sir?' the officer replied.

'Make yourself scarce.'

'Is there anything you want me to do, sir?'

'No. Just do nothing as usual. Maybe you can find someone who needs a door opening for them. Whatever you do, do it somewhere else for a few minutes.'

Kuchař closed the door behind him.

'Where do they find them?' sighed the Director. 'That, Slonský, was the gold medal cadet last year.'

Slonský was surprised and said so. 'He came above Navrátil?'

'Yes.'

'Good God, Navrátil must be thicker than I thought. He always seems so competent to me, but maybe it's just a long run of beginner's luck.'

'Or maybe the academy has no idea what the police service really needs these days. Of course, Kuchař's dad is a member of parliament.'

'It's just as well nepotism died out with the old regime, sir.'

'It certainly is. Sometimes I think I ought to take a Captain's job myself. You don't have this sort of rubbish to deal with. Well, I dare say you're wondering why I'm here.'

'Boredom? You lost a bet?'

'Close. I've been to see Lukas in hospital. The doctors tell me he's putting on a brave face but this has knocked him sideways. He's a good man but too conscientious for his own welfare. It seems that he has been ill for some time, but concealed it. The result is that he needed some fairly extensive surgery and he will be off for longer than we thought. In fact, he may not be back before he reaches retirement age.'

Slonský did not like the way this conversation was heading. 'Still, it would be a shame to leave him feeling discarded now, sir, after so much devoted service.'

'I'm not discarding him, Slonský, just facing facts. I have to be prepared for any contingency. If Lukas returns all well and good, and I can't advertise his job while he is still in post. But we need to make proper arrangements to replace him, either temporarily or permanently. I've been looking at some personnel files for the department.'

'Ah.'

'Ah indeed. Yours is a thick one. Quite a few disciplinary notes in it, I see.'

'In my defence, sir, a lot of those were earned under the old regime.'

'And quite a few weren't. However, there's nothing in there that prevents your being promoted if you choose to apply. The big thing is that none of the disciplinary hearings involve money or sex.'

'I have no use for either, sir.'

The Director looked at his briefcase as if it might bear a script for his next utterance.

'I trust you to keep this to yourself. I am not unambitious, Slonský. I am aware that the National Director of the Police Service is retiring next July. That is a little over seven months away. I hope that I don't come across as conceited if I say that I hope I would be a strong candidate.'

'I'm sure you would, sir. I'd vote for you.'

'Thank you. But if I go, and Lukas still hasn't returned, there'll be a risk that there will be nobody around who appreciates your qualities. Put simply, if you aren't a captain by July, you may never make it.'

'I appreciate your frankness, sir, but I'm completely unambitious. I don't mind staying a lieutenant until I retire.'

The Director leaned forward. It was quite intimidating.

'That's fine, but do you mind having Dvorník or Doležal as your boss? Or a complete stranger brought in from outside?'

Slonský felt a pang to his heart. That was a low blow. However much he told himself that he had no interest in promotion, he certainly did not want to have to call Doležal 'sir'. Time for some honesty, he thought.

'I certainly do, sir,' he said. 'I would rather swallow rat-poison.'

The Director stood.

'Then get your application ready or pray that Lukas recovers quickly. He's a good man, Slonský. When I visited him he told me his concern was that you would not be willing to carry on his good work, so I said I would have a word with you. I've done that, and it's now for you to decide what to do. Personally, looking at this folder and its enclosures, I think you may owe Lukas one. Actually, you probably owe him about eleven.'

'At least.'

The Director offered his hand, which Slonský took.

'Of course, if you foul up your current case you could be checking passports at the airport six months from now. But I don't think that's likely. A positive result would help your prospects, though.'

'I'll see if I can find a likely suspect and frame him, sir.'

The Director smiled. 'You're the officer least likely to do that, Slonský. Kuchař!'

The door opened and the young lieutenant stood to attention in the doorway.

'Were you eavesdropping, Kuchař?'

'No, sir.'

'Did you accidentally hear anything?'

'No, sir.'

'If you did, forget it at once, or your father will be receiving some of your most interesting parts through the post.'

'Yes, sir.'

'My car, Kuchař.'

'Yes, sir.'

Navrátil had paid a visit to Technician First Class Spehar who had been fascinated by the question he had to ask, but had referred him to Hynek for an answer.

Hynek was a person to whom normal dress codes did not apply. On this particular morning he was wearing a black t-shirt bearing an image of a clenched fist and the slogan 'Anarchy Rules OK' in English, together with checked Bermuda shorts. His long wavy hair erupted from his cap like a punctured horsehair sofa, and over it all he wore a navy blue anorak. Although he was indoors he had the hood up.

He offered a large, pudgy hand. 'Lemme see,' he said.

Navrátil held out the helmet and watched as Hynek deftly extracted the earpiece. 'Primitive stuff,' he said. 'Wonder which idiot gave him this crap?'

Spehar examined it, rolling it over as it nestled in Hynek's bear-paw hand. 'It's a model we've used, but not lately. The problem is that you can't encrypt this one on the fly.' Seeing that the importance of this was not clear to Navrátil, he expanded this view. 'The microphone collects a signal and sends it to the earpiece. That's straightforward. But anybody passing by with a radio scanner might intercept it and hear it too. And if you record the signal it's not much use in court because the defence will say that the signal could have come from anywhere so you can't prove that it is linked to the person you say is being recorded. So we use a model where the microphone encodes the sound electronically and the receiver unencodes it. You can't tell as the listener because it happens instantaneously, but it can't be done with this little chap.'

'Old crap,' agreed Hynek.

'The question for me,' Navrátil explained, 'is whether we can find the microphone that this is tuned to. It's presumably concealed somewhere and we need to know where.'

Hynek laughed. 'Is that all?'

'Yes. Can it be done?'

'Child's play.'

Hynek went to a steel cupboard and yanked the doors open. It looked like a teenager's wardrobe inside. One shelf was far from being level and there was a guitar inside, together with an assortment of cardboard boxes, an ice-hockey stick, a basketball and a large number of cables with assorted coloured terminals on them. Hynek rummaged inside, dropped the basketball on the floor and finally found what he was looking for. He had a black plastic box with a rotating switch on the face. He clicked a rocker switch on the side. 'Needs new batteries.'

A further excavation produced a small box of batteries from which he extracted two and inserted them in the gadget. This time when he flicked the switch the display panel lit up and a needle twitched across it.

'We're ready to rock and roll,' he declared in English.

Spehar gave Navrátil a look that demonstrated confidence in Hynek's abilities, if not in his use of language.

'Now,' Hynek continued, 'put the earpiece in your ear. When you hear the tone, give me a thumbs up sign.'

He rotated the dial. Navrátil listened intently. At first he could hear only white noise or silence, but after a few moments the crackling gave way to a low hum and finally to a clear tone. He raised his thumb, and Hynek wrote down a number.

'Same again, just to check. We'll start from the other end of the spectrum.'

Again Navrátil lifted a thumb when he heard the tone.

'Bang on,' said Hynek. 'We've got the wavelength. It's going to be low power, so you'll have to go to the murder scene and triangulate from there.'

'Couldn't you come?' Navrátil asked innocently. Hynek reacted as if this were the maddest suggestion he had ever heard.

'Me? Out there?'

Spehar intervened. 'Hynek is too valuable here. I could come if you wanted.'

'Yes, please,' said Navrátil.

Mollified, Hynek searched the cupboard for another instrument. This one was almost circular and consisted mainly of a dial with a needle at the centre.

'It looks like a compass,' said Navrátil brightly.

'It doesn't *look* like a compass, it *is* a compass,' Hynek told him. 'We use it to determine directions.'

Despite a brief period of reflection, Navrátil could think of no alternative use, so he nodded, which allowed Hynek to move on to the next item of inventory.

'Directional scanner.'

He handed this one to Spehar, as if it was far too valuable to give to anyone with Navrátil's limited technical skills.

'I've programmed it to the wavelength,' he explained.

Spehar plucked an earpiece from one of the cardboard boxes and tucked it in his pocket.

'We don't want to be seen using this,' he said, 'especially in view of what happened to Hrdlička.'

A thought occurred to Navrátil. 'If Hrdlička didn't get his listening kit from you, where did it come from?'

Spehar and Hynek looked at each other and shrugged.

'Not from us,' said Spehar. 'Can't think where else he'd get it.'

Slonský rested his elbows on the desk and dropped his chin onto his cupped hands. 'Which one?' he asked.

Peiperová pointed to the face at the end of the top line.

'That's Brukić,' said Slonský. 'Navrátil knows something about him. He's an associate of Savović.'

'What does associate mean exactly?'

'Well, someone who associates with someone else, Peiperová. It's not difficult. And we'd heard he might be in Prague. So this is the man who brought the girls in. Have you got a date?'

'Fifteen weeks and two days ago, sir.'

'That isn't a date, my girl, that's a calculation. What actual date?'

They walked to the calendar on Lukas' wall and counted back fifteen weeks and two days.

'Get Navrátil to check with his mate in the Bosnian police about that date. They ought to know we've got an eye-witness who can place Brukić on that bus with her. Will she give a statement?'

'I don't know, sir. She's very scared. She says Brukić can be frightening.'

'So can I, Officer Peiperová, and don't forget it.'

'No, sir,' Peiperová promised, though she did not believe him. 'But if she is right, then Brukić and the mysterious Czech man drove a girl to kill herself.'

'Yes,' mused Slonský. 'But illegal burial of a corpse isn't going to put them away for long, if at all. Sex trafficking is a better bet for getting them behind bars. Can you find her again?'

'They don't let her have a phone, sir. I've given her my mobile phone number so she can call me from a callbox.'

'Not on anything that says "Police", I hope?'

'Back of a card from a florist, sir.'

'Good girl. Innocent enough if someone rifles her handbag.' Slonský looked at his in-tray. It was depressing. 'You're an ambitious girl, aren't you?'

'Well, yes, I suppose,' Peiperová conceded. 'I want to see how far I can go. But I've got a lot to learn yet,' she added hurriedly.

'Of course you have. But I bet one day you'd like to be a captain, wouldn't you?'

'Yes, sir.'

'Go on, give it a try. Sit down, see what it feels like.'

'I couldn't, sir. That's Captain Lukas' place.'

'He's not here. It's my seat now. Go on, you may not get the chance again. See if you like it.'

Peiperová felt torn. It was only a bit of fun, though, so she gave Slonský a conspiratorial grin, ran round the desk and sat down.

Slonský stood behind her and bent to speak into her ear. His tone was almost seductive. 'Feels good, doesn't it? I bet that feels … right, eh? You could make yourself at home there.'

'Yes, sir.'

'Good!' barked Slonský. 'You're Acting Acting Captain. I've got to get out and do some detecting. Those papers in the tray need dealing with. Check there are receipts pinned to all the forms and leave them on the left side of the desk for me to sign them off. They go upstairs to that woman with the mad-looking hair with the white streak. Anyone who wants leave can't have it. We're far too busy. Mark it "Refused" unless you think I should make an exception. Any requisitions that

427

come in need an explanation, so collect the facts and I'll give you a verbal answer. Any questions, Acting Acting Captain Peiperová?'

'Just one, sir. Is there such a rank as Acting Acting Captain?'

'There is now, lass,' said Slonský, jamming his hat on his head and making for the door.

Chapter 6

Navrátil felt redundant. He perched on the low wall watching Spehar stroll up and down the road, occasionally sneaking a peek at the box in his hand.

'Well?' he asked after the fifth traverse.

'You're out of luck,' Spehar replied. 'I've tried walking on the other side in case it's very low power, but I'm getting nothing. You're sure Hrdlička was here?'

Navrátil stepped a few paces to his left, glanced up at the buildings opposite to check his bearings, and pointed at his feet. 'This is where he was when he was killed.'

Spehar took one last look at the gadget he was holding. 'Then we have to conclude that the microphone isn't transmitting any longer.'

'Flat battery?'

'More likely it was found and destroyed.'

Navrátil had not expected this setback, but was determined to squeeze the maximum information from the exercise despite this turn of events. 'Let's work backwards. Presumably Hrdlička didn't know that the microphone had been discovered, because he would have known he'd been rumbled and might be in danger.'

'If he can't eavesdrop, there's no reason to stay, is there?' Spehar agreed.

'So we deduce that it was still transmitting when he was killed. Now, can the person being listened to work out where the hearer is?'

'No. Think of ripples in a pond when you lob a stone in. From any pair of places the pattern of ripples might tell you where the stone must be, but being where the stone is can't tell you who is watching and where they are.'

Navrátil stood up and walked to the south a few steps. 'But you can work out where the hearer can't be, surely. If someone has one of those boxes you've got, he can wander around outside mapping where the signal can be detected. And if it's as low powered as you think, that wouldn't take him too far away.'

Spehar thought for a moment before answering. 'We can't be sure because we don't know what the power was. But I'm guessing that one of these old things wouldn't stretch across the river, so he'd know the listener must be on this bank. I suppose he could see who was here for a while and deduce that they must be the listener.'

'But they couldn't be sure. Anyway, Hrdlička had the helmet on, but he didn't have the earpiece in his ear when he was killed.'

Spehar put his arm round Navrátil's shoulder and led him away. 'I don't feel comfortable standing where someone was killed. It seems unnecessarily risky to me. Let's get a coffee at the end of the bridge.'

They sat down with their coffees, and Spehar glanced around in case they were being overheard. 'How cunning do you think these killers are?' he asked.

'We don't know. But I thought they were just thugs and racketeers. I didn't expect anything subtle from them.'

'I can think of one thing they could do,' Spehar continued, stirring his coffee as if it might aid his thoughts. 'If they found the transmitter, they might discover the wavelength on which it was transmitting. It's the same exercise as we did earlier, just in reverse — you put an earpiece in and scan till the transmitter can be heard. Then you line up a second transmitter set to the same wavelength, and you send a blast of noise over it. Perhaps an unpleasant squeal, or just a big bang. And you watch to see who jumps when they hear it.'

'That would work,' Navrátil agreed. 'And the natural thing to do would do to yank the earpiece out of your ear before it deafened you.'

'And the man who pulls the earpiece out is the one you kill. You'd need a few watchers in various places, but if you guess that the man who is listening is also watching, there are only so many places he can be.'

'And since we know what he was watching, we know where people could be watching him from. It doesn't help us much, though, does it? I'd hoped we'd find out where he put the microphone, and we're no further forward.'

Valentin stared morosely into his beer. Somehow this grumpy persona seemed appropriate to his new role as the recently dismissed host of a late night radio phone-in programme.

During an earlier investigation, it had suited Slonský to feed a tame journalist some juicy snippets that would provoke a reaction, and Valentin, as an old friend in need of a scoop, had come to mind. This breathtaking story had elevated Valentin from hack to investigative journalist, as a result of which he had been offered some radio work. Admittedly it was at a time of day that ensured that those phoning in were either cranks or insomniacs, but after a few months even those had given up on him and the listening figures dropped so sharply that the show was cancelled. This had been a considerable blow to Valentin's ego, which he had attempted to salve in the way he had always dealt with life's sideswipes, by the application of alcohol. Unfortunately the loss of his radio programme carried with it a reduction in disposable income, which was why he was delighted to see Slonský, who could usually be relied upon to stand a drink or two.

'You look like somebody peed in your pocket,' said Slonský.

'It feels that way,' Valentin replied.

A waiter was hovering, having correctly divined that this could be a lucrative night for him if he cultivated this pair. Slonský dropped his hat on the bench beside him, unbuttoned his coat and let loose a long, slow sigh.

'What will you have, sir?'

'A coronary most likely,' Slonský answered. 'But until that happens, let's have a couple of large glasses of our finest national export.'

The waiter listed the options, none of which appealed greatly. He even offered them one of those new beers flavoured with fruit juice, which made Valentin flinch. Suspecting that violence was imminent, Slonský gripped Valentin's arm and told the waiter two of the first one he mentioned would be fine.

'Fine?' hissed Valentin. 'How can you drink that stuff?'

'I'm paying.'

'Then it would be churlish of me to refuse your hospitality. But I worry for your palate.'

'You're becoming a grumpy old sod.'

'Becoming? It's my proudest boast. I complain a lot because there is a lot to complain about. Anyway, what was all that about a coronary?'

'Lukas is in hospital.'

'Lukas? What happened?'

'Something inside him was on the verge of going pop so they've whipped it out. He's putting a brave face on it but the Director says he may never return to work.'

'Will anyone notice?'

'I'll notice, thank you,' Slonský commented indignantly. 'I'm Acting Captain until it all becomes clear. And if he doesn't return I'm under pressure to apply to become Captain officially. I don't fancy sitting at a desk shuffling paper all day.'

'Then don't apply. When they ask you, use that phrase I taught you.'

'If I don't apply, they'll give it to Dvorník or Doležal.'

'Dvorník? He hasn't got time to fit it in between causing pregnancies. Which one is Doležal?'

'Long streak of misery. Thinning hair and a hangdog look.'

'Got him. Surely he isn't the vibrant face of a modern constabulary?'

'Doležal? His only function is to make everyone else look good. And he does that incredibly well.'

'I assume this means you're going to have to take the job or you'll finish up working for a halfwit and turn into a bitter, twisted old man.'

'It doesn't seem to have done you any harm.'

'I am one of a kind. It wouldn't suit you. So how have you escaped? Shouldn't you be filling in timesheets or something?'

'I've left Peiperová in charge. She's a good lass. Nothing will get past her.'

'Maybe, but she's only just left school. She doesn't have your experience.'

'Few have. That's the problem. I'm getting old, Valentin. I'm decaying.'

'Alcohol is a preservative,' the journalist mused. 'I learned that in biology all those years ago.'

'Is that a hint?'

'Well, this one seems to have evaporated while we were talking. Shall we have another?'

'Silly question.'

Peiperová adjusted her position so her head nestled on Navrátil's chest.

'You're what?' said Navrátil.

A woman in the row in front turned to glare at them. Navrátil raised a hand in apology and acknowledgement.

'You're what?' he whispered.

'Acting Acting Captain.'

'Is there such a rank?'

'There must be. Apparently I am one.'

'Well, of course I'm very pleased for you, but it's a bit of a shock. I hesitate to raise the matter of seniority, but I'm an Academy graduate.'

'Yes, but I've been an officer longer. I joined a few months before you.'

'Is there any extra money?'

'Of course not.'

'Just extra work.'

'Different work. By the way, I signed off your expenses.'

'That's very good of you. I'm entitled.'

Peiperová sat up and regarded Navrátil keenly. 'Are you put out?'

'Me? What gives you that idea?'

'The way you're biting my head off.'

'Ssh! I'm trying to watch a film here,' complained the old woman in front.

'Sorry,' said Peiperová. 'My boyfriend is being a spoilt brat.'

'Aren't they all, dear? You'll learn.'

Valentin had ceased to be good company. More accurately, Valentin had ceased to be conscious, and was snoring while propped against the wall in the corner. There was no point in trying to get him a taxi, because no driver would accept him as a passenger. On the other hand, Slonský could hardly frogmarch him all the way home, even if he had been disposed to let him sleep on his floor. He could not think of anywhere else to take him. Finally, inspiration struck, and he made a phone call.

The squad car was commendably quick, and Valentin was taken away for a night in the cells. He would be highly upset when he woke up, but Slonský had told them not to charge him so he would be free to go when sober.

The car pulled away, and Slonský stood on the pavement looking at the navy blue sky with its twinkling silver stars, so readily visible in the clearness of a sharp November night. Lukas was sick, Valentin was miserable, he was miserable, the simple cog-driven world he inhabited was coming apart. His life was going to change, whether Lukas recovered or not. This captaincy question was not going to go away. Well, if there's going to be change I'd better be in the driving seat for it, he thought. I must take control of my own destiny. He glanced at his watch. Too late to telephone tonight, but there was a call he must make in the morning. First thing. No, maybe not first thing. But sometime. Definitely sometime.

Chapter 7

The door to Lukas' office was open. Peiperová was sitting at the desk, her head bowed as she tapped numbers into a calculator and made pencilled ticks on the expenses forms in front of her. Navrátil hesitated for a moment, but finally gritted his teeth and entered.

'Yes?' she said.

'I just wanted to say I've been thinking about last night, and I realise I behaved badly.'

'Yes, you did,' said Peiperová, without looking up from her work.

Navrátil had not planned to say any more, but there was an awkward silence during which it was clear that absolution was going to be harder to obtain from Peiperová than it ever was from Father Antonin.

'And I want to say I'm sorry,' he blurted out.

Peiperová worked on. He willed her to tell him that it was all forgotten and it did not matter, but she just tapped at her calculator and ticked away.

'I'm very pleased for you and I should have said so. You've worked hard for it. I hope that we'll always be proud of each other's achievements.'

She finally looked up. 'You won't act like a spoilt child again if I get promoted and you don't?'

'I promise.'

'And you know if you make a promise and don't keep it you'll go straight to hell?'

'Yes. But I didn't think you were a believer.'

'It's not what I believe that matters. It's what you believe. And if you believe that telling a lie means an eternity of getting your backside roasted, then you won't tell me a lie and I don't have to worry that you're fibbing just to get back into my good books.'

'I wouldn't do that.'

Peiperová laid down her pencil. 'Shut the door,' she ordered.

'Why?'

'Because I'm not going to kiss you with the whole world watching. We Acting Acting Captains can't be seen snogging on duty.' She threw her arms around his neck and planted a kiss on his mouth.

'Do I have to call you Sir?' he asked.

She pulled him tight against her. 'You of all people should know I'm not a sir,' she said.

Mucha turned the key in the lock and nudged the door open with his foot, since his hands were occupied in bearing a tray. 'Room service!' he announced, causing a bleary-eyed Valentin to turn his face to the wall and groan anew.

'What time is it?' he asked.

'08.20. We've let you have a lie-in. But checkout time is nine o'clock because we have to get the room ready for the next occupant.'

Valentin levered himself to something closer to a vertical position. 'Dear God, how much did I have last night?'

'I've no idea,' said Mucha, 'but you've got a visitor who might.'

Slonský was standing in the doorway with a broad smile and an irritating chirpiness. 'Too much,' he said. 'Actually about two times too much and then some. You haven't been mugged. You spent all you had on you, and you've got a slate to clear next time you're in there. Not too much — perhaps four thousand crowns.'

'Four thousand crowns?' whimpered Valentin. 'Four *thousand*? What could I have spent four thousand on?'

Slonský shrugged. 'It's a combination of things really. Buying a round for everyone in the place didn't help. Then there was the bottle of genuine French champagne. I've never seen anyone dunk bread in it before.'

'Why didn't you stop me?' whined Valentin.

'Because when I got there you were so damn miserable and by the time we left you were happy.'

'Well, I'm not happy now.'

'Hardly surprising. You must have a head like a woodpecker's.'

'Yes. So please moderate your volume. And why didn't you take me home instead of banging me up in here?'

'Two reasons. First, I can't remember where you live, and second, no taxi-driver would take you incase you chucked up in his vehicle. To tell the truth, you nearly spoiled my cunning plan by picking a fight with Sergeant Vyhnal.'

'Yes, he told me about that,' said Mucha. 'He wasn't happy.'

'I'm not surprised,' said Slonský. 'I hear Valentin was a bit noisy.'

'I don't think it was the noise,' Mucha replied, 'so much as the bad language. And the reference to Vyhnal's parentage, which was unfortunate, because Mr Valentin wasn't to know that Sergeant Vyhnal actually *is* a bastard.'

Valentin held his face in his hands. 'I'd better apologise.'

'He's gone off duty,' said Mucha, 'but I'll see that someone tells him when he comes in tonight. Unless, of course, he's so upset that he tops himself.'

Valentin picked up his cap, scarf and coat and managed to drape them over himself in roughly the right configuration. 'I'm going home,' he announced. 'I may have a quiet night in tonight.'

'A quiet night in?' echoed Slonský. 'Should we send for the police doctor?'

'Ha-de-ha. I'm splitting my sides. Just leave me alone. Shouldn't you be out finding a murderer or two?'

'I suppose so.' He clapped Valentin on the back. 'Safe journey home, my friend. Take your roll. You'll want it when you feel like eating.'

'It'll be stale by then.'

'It's stale now,' said Mucha, 'but it's the thought that counts.'

Slonský bounded up the stairs but found his way blocked by Lieutenant Doležal, who seemed unusually animated.

'I understand that you're Acting Captain, and that's understandable, given that you're the senior lieutenant,' he began, 'but what do you mean by putting that girl in charge?'

'She's not in charge,' said Slonský. 'She's doing some of the administrative stuff to save me some time. On top of which, she'll do it better than me. She's a very organised girl, and I'm not.'

'She's sitting in the captain's office,' Doležal pointed out.

'What do you want me to do, pull her desk out into the corridor? She's doing part of the captain's work. People expect to hand their paperwork in at the captain's office. Some of it is confidential, so she can't do it in the room she shares with me and Navrátil.'

'It's not right to leave a young girl like that in charge of experienced officers. She handed out the duty rosters. You can't have a junior officer preparing those.'

'And what exactly is wrong with them?'

'Nothing. They're fine. It's the principle of the thing. It's not how things are done here,' Doležal argued, stabbing the air with his finger to emphasise the conclusive nature of his final point.

'Quite right,' said Slonský. 'We don't normally have this level of efficiency and it's going to take some getting used to. But we're all going to have to try. Now, if you'll excuse me, I must go and see if Peiperová has any work for me to do.'

Slonský pushed past and stomped along the corridor to his office. Navrátil was sitting in his usual place with his back to the window, and looked up as Slonský barged in, banging the door against the wall so that it rebounded but failed to close.

'Do you have anything to say to me?' Slonský demanded.

'About what?'

'Peiperová's new job.'

'I don't understand why you picked her and not me. I've been here longer and I thought I was your assistant.'

'Jesus Maria! Have you been talking to Doležal? It's not permanent, it's not important, it's just sparing my time so I can get on with fighting crime.' Slonský's face was turning from tomato towards beetroot. 'It's precisely because I want you beside me on this case that I detailed Peiperová to do the office work. She's good at it. She can count up to twenty without taking her shoes off.'

'So can I.'

'So can I too. But I'm playing this all by ear, Navrátil. I've got to keep the department going and solve crimes at the same time. I definitely do not need a bunch of prima donnas running to me to moan about favouritism or their hurt feelings.'

Navrátil held up his hands in surrender. 'I asked a question, sir. I got an answer. I'm happy.'

Slonský breathed deeply and flopped in his chair. 'Fair enough,' he said. 'Sorry, nothing personal.'

In the quiet that followed they suddenly became aware that there were three people breathing. Peiperová was standing in the doorway.

'Sir,' she asked, 'when can I go out and carry on my investigation?'

Slonský and Navrátil sat in silence.

'Not hungry, sir?'

'Not really. I thought pastry would help, but it hasn't. Roll on the end of the day when I can get stuck in to some alcohol.'

'We could try chasing some criminals.'

'We are, lad. I'm not sitting here for the good of my health. I've got an eye fixed on that nightclub.'

'I guessed that's why we'd come here, sir.'

'I want to see the doorman we met the other day. If Peiperová's contact is right, Brukić must have been there. I want to see if there's any evidence to back up Suzana's story.'

'Why would she lie, sir?'

'No reason at all, but that's a very different question to asking whether we can prove that she's telling the truth.'

A familiar figure in a black windcheater turned the corner and walked jauntily along the road. Slonský sprang from his seat and grabbed his hat.

'Remember the plan, son.'

Navrátil sprinted across the road and took up his position in the alley. The doorman tensed as he recognised the young detective and stopped walking, only to feel Slonský's hand on his shoulder.

'You do well to avoid him,' he said. 'He's not happy with you.'

'Why? I've done nothing.'

'You didn't tell us everything you knew. I gave you my number and you didn't ring me.'

'Oh yeah? What didn't I tell you then?'

Slonský whistled and Navrátil started to walk towards them, one hand swinging freely and the other jammed in his jacket pocket.

'What's he got in his hand? I told you everything I know. I swear I did.'

'I don't think you did,' said Slonský, 'but I'm prepared to tell Navrátil to hang on a minute or two before he teaches you a lesson.'

The hoodlum tried to make a run for it, but Slonský grabbed his collar and hooked his legs away with a sweep of his foot, leaving him sprawling on the ground.

'That's no good,' said Navrátil. 'I can't make them drop down his trouser leg if he's lying on the ground.'

They dragged the doorman to a low wall and sat him down there.

'They'll be missing you soon, so you'd better talk fast,' said Slonský.

'Don't let them see me talking to you,' hissed the doorman. 'If they see me it won't matter that I've said nothing. That Bosnian pig will have me gutted.'

'That would be the Bosnian pig your mate said hadn't been in the club?'

'I don't know about that.'

Slonský unfolded the fax once again.

'I asked him about this one. Now I'm asking you about that one.'

'They've both been there.'

'They bring the girls in, don't they?'

The thug nodded.

'Good. Now we're getting somewhere. Do you know when they're coming?'

'No. They're not going to tell the likes of us.'

'Fine. If you hear anything, you've got my number. Calling me would be a very good idea.'

The bouncer made as if to get up, but Slonský pushed him back down.

'You didn't tell us about the girl who killed herself.'

The look on the thug's face was easy to interpret. It was naked fear.

'I had nothing to do with that.'

'That's not what I heard. Did she squeal when you raped her?'

'I didn't do anything of the sort! I never laid hands on her while she was alive.'

'While she was alive. So you did when she wasn't alive any more?'

'They made us carry her out to the truck.'

'Where was this?'

'The girls live in an old student hostel. They have a dormitory there. It's good because it was built to keep the men students out so there's a concierge's kiosk by the front door. Nobody can get out without being seen.'

'Address?'

'I don't know the address. I could take you. Or I could draw a map,' he added desperately.

'A map would be fine. We don't want you taking time off work, do we?'

Slonský released his grip on the man's shoulder and motioned him to go. He looked at Navrátil for reassurance that he was not about to be stabbed in the back. Navrátil just scowled at him.

'You're enjoying that part far too much,' said Slonský. 'Ought I to be worried?'

'Just obeying your orders, sir. You said to act hard, so I did.'

'There's a side to you that would surprise Peiperová, lad.'

Peiperová had come to the Padlock Club earlier, which was how Slonský knew that the doorman had not started his shift. She had loitered around the district but had not been able to find Suzana again. She had, however, spotted another likely dancer and had followed her as she bought a few vegetables and a small piece of chicken. As the shopper waited to cross the road, Peiperová cautiously stepped alongside her.

'You should close your bag,' she said. 'There are a lot of sneak thieves around this area.'

The girl nodded her thanks and tried to close her bag, which was rather full.

'Allow me,' said Peiperová, who did not wait for agreement before pulling the zip shut.

'Thank you,' said the girl in heavily accented Czech.

'Ah, you're a foreigner! Where are you from?'

'I am from Bosnia.'

'Bosnia? You're a long way from home. Do you work here?'

'I'm sorry, I am in a hurry. I have no time to talk.'

'That's a pity. I have lots of time. I also have this.' Peiperová showed her police badge. The girl looked very agitated. 'I should ask to see your visa.'

'I don't have with me. I can bring to you.'

'No, you can't. You don't have one, do you?'

The girl's eyes filled with tears as she mutely shook her head.

'Don't worry, I won't arrest you. But we need to talk. When are you due at work?'

'At eight o'clock.'

'Then we have time. Let's go and have coffee together and you can answer my questions. Or we can go to the police station.'

'Coffee is better.'

'Coffee it is, then.'

Slonský rotated his notebook and squinted at the street sign. 'He's not Picasso, is he? This isn't much of a map he's drawn. But I think that's the road we want.'

'Should we call for backup, sir?'

'Is that your favourite phrase, lad? You always want to call for backup. If you were in charge the entire police force would be following each other around. We might as well hold hands.'

'I just thought he may have called ahead and they'll be waiting in ambush for us.'

'Navrátil, if he called ahead he'll have told them to watch for your deft work with the penknife and they'll all be cowering in corners cupping their groins.'

'Or waiting to shoot me as soon as I step inside the door.'

'Don't be a pessimist. I haven't got you shot yet, have I?'

There's always a first time, thought Navrátil.

Slonský looked up at the facades of the buildings, and instantly spotted the old student hostel because it had a sign saying Student Hostel over the door. He climbed the steps and paused at the top. 'This could be dangerous, lad, so make sure you stand to one side when you open the door.'

Navrátil tried turning the large brass knob which filled his hand. Surely small ladies' hands would never be able to grasp it, he thought. The door creaked open and they stepped inside. A little kiosk stood against the wall to the right. The appearance of visitors came as a surprise to the man sitting there, who bounded to his feet and quickly put a black peaked cap on his head.

'This is private property, gentlemen.'

'We're not planning to steal it. It won't fit in our pockets,' said Slonský. He waved his badge and put it away before the doorman had any chance to look at it. 'Slonský, Acting Captain, and Officer Navrátil. You're in luck — till the other day I was a lowly lieutenant, but you get the privilege of being raided by a proper officer. I want to speak to the girls you have here.'

'Girls?'

'Yes, girls. Men with lumps. You must have seen them around the place.'

'I'll have to ask the boss.'

The doorman picked up the telephone receiver to dial but Slonský quickly slammed his hand down on the rest and held it there. 'Phone calls are expensive. Why don't you make it later? When we're gone, for example.'

'The boss wouldn't like that.'

'The boss doesn't get to choose,' Slonský replied, keeping firm hold of the doorman's wrist.

'What do you want to see them for?'

'We'd just like to check their visas. I'm sure they're all in order, aren't they?'

'I really think I ought to call the boss.'

'No, you really ought to call the girls. If we do you for shoplifting, we don't let you ring a mate to put the stuff back on the shelf. Navrátil, send for a big wagon. A number of young ladies will be spending the evening with us.'

'They're due at work in a couple of hours,' the doorman protested. 'How can you have a strip club with no strippers?'

'Better get practising,' Slonský called over his shoulder as he bounded up the staircase. 'It looks like you may have to fill in.'

Slonský told Navrátil to stand at the top of the stairs as he walked along the hallway banging on each door in turn and yelling 'Out! Police!' When he reached the far end he turned round and opened each door. Women in various stages of undress tumbled into the corridor, and he shepherded them towards Navrátil.

'It's as well you didn't go in there, lad. Could have been too educational for a young man with a delicate upbringing. Now, ladies, let's see your papers please.'

Amid the general consternation a brunette was pushed to the fore.

'Please, we don't have,' she said.

'No papers? Tut, tut. Then we may have to send you home.'

The brunette translated. It appeared that this declaration met with general approval, and several girls ran to pack bags.

'Our passports are taken by bad men,' the brunette explained. 'They keep them so we cannot go.'

'Are you all Bosnian?' Slonský asked. There was some shaking of heads that illustrated that a couple of Croat girls were there, and at least one Montenegrin. The doorman appeared behind them.

'Your van's here. Can I come too?'

'Why? Are your papers out of order?'

'No, but if I come I won't have to explain why I let you in and didn't call the boss.'

Slonský lifted his hat and scratched his head in perplexity. 'I suppose I'm becoming an old softie, but just this once. Get the girls in the van and hop in yourself.'

The girls quickly packed and ran to the van, throwing their bags in and climbing aboard amidst happy laughter, followed by the old doorman. A couple of the girls reached down to help him up, then Slonský closed the doors and patted the side to indicate that it could go.

'I don't know, Navrátil, there's something wrong about people being happy to get locked up. The world's changing, you know.'

'Won't their boss be straight round to spring them?'

'Not if he doesn't have papers. But in any case they're not going to our station. I've told the driver to take them to Kladno. That should make it that little bit harder for their boss to get them out. And I'm sure Peiperová will be delighted to join us for questioning if it means she can drop in on her folks for a coffee and cake. Her mother does a very nice poppy seed cake, as I recall.'

The girl could hardly stop her hands shaking as she sipped her coffee. At first she declined a pastry, but Peiperová ordered a selection for them and was watching as her new acquaintance made short work of the plateful.

'I'm Kristýna,' said Peiperová, extending a hand. The Bosnian girl hurriedly wiped her sticky fingers on a napkin and shook it.

'Daniela.'

'Pleased to meet you, Daniela. I'm trying to get in touch with girls who work at the Padlock Club. Do you work there?'

Daniela shook her head vigorously. 'No, I work at the Purple Apple.'

'I don't know that one,' Peiperová confessed, though her knowledge of Prague's club scene was hardly encyclopaedic.

Daniela cast her eyes down and chased a crumb round her plate reflectively. 'It is … unusual place. It is club for women only.'

'I see. Gay women?'

Daniela nodded. 'But I am not such!' she quickly added. 'I don't like to work there. But it is better than other job they give me.'

'Other job?'

'When I come to Prague they tell me there is no job as musician in orchestra. I play flute. Also piccolo.'

'You're a musician? But surely there are jobs in bands here?'

'I don't have papers. They don't give them back when we cross border. And they took my flute. It is expensive to get another one. They tell me I have to be with men, or I can dance, so I dance for women.' She gave a bitter half-laugh. 'At least you don't get a baby with women.'

'Did someone you knew fall pregnant?'

Daniela nodded mutely.

'A Bosnian girl?'

'Yes.'

Peiperová believed she could guess the answer to the next question, but she asked it anyway. 'What happened to her?'

Daniela's eyes glistened with tears, and she wrapped a paper napkin around her hand as she pushed her knuckles into her mouth to stifle her crying.

'She cut herself dead.'

'She cut her wrists?'

'Please — wrists?'

Peiperová mimed cutting her wrists with her knife, realising a little too late that the waitress was watching. She came running and grabbed the knife.

'We don't want that sort of thing in here,' she said. 'If you're going to make a scene I shall call the police.'

Peiperová displayed her badge. 'I am the police,' she said.

'Then you should know better,' the waitress announced before flouncing off.

Slonský leaned back and opened the rear nearside door.

'Hop in, lass. Got the coffee and pastries?'

'There you are, sir.'

'Spot of good fortune your being in a café when Navrátil called. Now, what did you find out?'

'The girl Daniela doesn't work at the Padlock Club. She works at the Purple Apple. She knew the girl who killed herself, sir. She says that although they work in different places, the Bosnian girls sometimes meet in the markets. She overheard the other girl — she's called Milena, by the way — when they were out shopping and they spoke to each other. She met her again a couple of weeks later and said Milena looked awful. She had a bruise on her cheek and a cut on her hairline, and she looked like she hadn't slept for days. She said two men had raped her and now she was pregnant. That was the last time Daniela saw her. She heard a couple of days later than Milena had cut her wrists.'

'Did she know anything else that might help?'

'She said Milena lived in a hostel somewhere.'

'We know that, girl. That's where we've just been.'

'A women's hostel? Without a woman officer?'

'You can't be in two places at once, lass. And Navrátil escaped unmolested, though it was a damn near-run thing. I blame those dimples when he smiles. You must have noticed them.'

Peiperová fired a glare at Navrátil as if he had been bestowing his affections on the whole of Czech womanhood. Since he was studiously inspecting the wing mirror, he failed to notice, which only annoyed her more.

'Did she know who brought her here, Peiperová?'

'She knew both Savović and Brukić, sir. She says Brukić came with the minibus and Savović was waiting here when they arrived. She says somewhere in Hungary they got out of the bus and were put into a truck full of tins of peaches. After a while they were allowed out to stretch their legs and go to the toilet by the roadside, then they had to get back in for the rest of the journey.'

'By the roadside?' said Navrátil. 'Couldn't they make a run for it?'

'The men watched them,' Peiperová snapped.

'That's disgusting,' replied Navrátil. 'How embarrassing for them.'

'In the overall scheme of things, Navrátil, being watched while you have a pee probably comes a fair way down the list of nasty things that can happen to you compared with being beaten up and raped.'

'Yes, sir,' Navrátil agreed, 'but it's still wrong.'

Slonský eyed his assistant carefully. 'Your obstinacy does you credit, lad. There's such a thing as right and wrong and I was guilty of relativism. I should know, it was a regular complaint against me when the Communists were in charge. I kept arguing that maybe there was less theft in the Communist bloc than the West not because we were model citizens but because there was damn all to steal, and I got accused of inexact relativism. Plus cultural deviation, though I never quite knew what that was. And that's despite a week in Brno at re-indoctrination camp.'

'Re-indoctrination camp?' parroted Peiperová.

'Like Pioneer Camp but for bad boys. People like me who had forgotten that we were living in an earthly paradise. We had lessons on Marxist theory. There was a poster of Marx on one side of the blackboard, and a picture of Engels on the other side. I asked why we never got any lessons on Engelsian theory.'

'And what was the answer, sir?'

'I got taken outside and kicked a few times. And they took my soup off me at dinner time, but that was a blessing. Then I had a stroke of good fortune. The Central Committee of the Communist Party sent some bigwig down to see how the camp functioned, and he decided to speak to me. I said I was disappointed that we'd had no lectures on the important work of Engels. He asked if that was true, and the instructor was sacked when he heard that it was. I was sent back to duty as an exemplary student who had correctly identified the ideological deficiencies of a revisionist clique.'

'What important work did Engels do then, sir?' asked Navrátil.

'I have no idea, and neither did the bigwig. But he thought he should have known, so he couldn't ignore the fact that we hadn't had it. There's nobody as self-righteous as someone who doesn't know what he's talking about.'

They pulled off the highway and drove into Kladno. Peiperová had worked here before she moved to Prague and gave directions to the police station. Her old boss Sergeant Tomáš was standing by the front desk looking harassed.

'Am I glad to see you!' he declared. 'That crew of cats has been yabbering away downstairs since they arrived. I have no idea what they're going on about. Anyway, they're all yours.'

'Thanks for taking them in,' said Slonský. 'We wanted to get them somewhere where their pimps couldn't reach them.'

'I thought you said they were dancers?'

'They are. But some of them are horizontal dancers, so to speak.'

Peiperová smiled broadly as Sergeant Tomáš welcomed her back.

'How is Prague?'

'Interesting, sir.'

'Yes,' said Slonský. 'Your protégée has already made it to the heights of Acting Acting Captain.'

'Really?' said Tomáš. He motioned to them to go down to the cells, letting the young couple go first, then grabbed Slonský's arm to hold him back as they followed. 'Is there such a rank?' he asked.

'There must be,' said Slonský. 'She is one.'

Despite his insistence that this was a Prague operation, Tomáš readily joined in the processing of the girls and managed to find another female officer to help. Within a couple of hours they had collected names and addresses and taken something approaching a statement from each of them. Slonský and Navrátil had finished and rejoined Tomáš and Peiperová.

'What happens now?' asked Tomáš. 'The cells aren't big enough for fourteen of them. The doorman's all right — he gets a cell to himself — but the women can't all sleep in the other cell.'

'Have you got a hotel in town?'

'Yes.'

'Let's give them a call to see if they have a few rooms free. I'm sure we can beat them down on price at this time of night.'

'Isn't that going to be expensive, sir?' whispered Navrátil. 'Captain Lukas wouldn't sign it off.'

'No, but Acting Acting Captain Peiperová will. Especially if it means she can spend a night with her parents. Do they have a sofa?'

'Yes, sir.'

'Then why don't you pop off too and see the future in-laws? Take the car and come back for me in the morning.'

'Right, sir,' beamed Navrátil.

Slonský had given the girls their instructions. 'Dinner, then you go to your rooms and stay there. If anyone leaves their room they get taken back to the bad men in Prague. Understand?'

There was a lot of nodding and vociferous agreement with this plan.

'Then at 07:30 tomorrow we all have breakfast. I'm sorry you didn't have time to pack spare clothes...'

'Yes, we pack,' the brunette replied. 'We have bags in the big van.'

A poor young waiter was sent out to help the doorman unpack the bags and return them to their owners. By the time this was done Slonský had decided he just had time for a beer with Tomáš before he turned in for the night too.

'If you need some clean clothes I could raid the uniform store at the station,' Tomáš offered.

'No, thanks. I doubt you have anything that fits me. Prague never did.'

The waiter slid a large glass in front of each of them. Practised drinkers both, they caressed it with their eyes before taking a long slurp in appreciative silence.

'That was worth waiting for,' said Tomáš.

'It's a decent drop of beer,' Slonský conceded. 'Don't you get told off for drinking in uniform?'

'The district captain doesn't like it, but she's so uptight you couldn't floss her bum.'

'Maybe Peiperová will turn out like that.'

'Nah, she's a good girl. Knocks spots off anyone else I've had here. Doing well, is she?'

'Very well. Don't tell her I said so, though. She and Navrátil have hit it off.'

'Hit it off or had it off?'

'I doubt the latter. Navrátil doesn't hold with sex before marriage. I'm not too sure he's in favour of it after marriage, for that matter. Very straight-laced is young Navrátil. Another good cop, though. I'm bringing them on nicely. One day they'll be running the Czech police, you mark my words. And they'll do a damn sight better job than our generation did.'

They drank some more, then Slonský had a random thought. 'Didn't you ever want to go higher?'

'I did.'

'Why didn't you, then?'

'No, I mean, I was higher. I was a captain under the old regime.'

'What happened?'

'I arrested the mayor's brother in the town where I was. When democracy came, he got his own back. I came out of the police station to find people fishing a carrier bag full of crowns out of the glove compartment of my car. No idea how it got there. I never took a bribe. Mind you, plenty were offered. Internal Affairs were called in, and we had a little chat.'

'But you weren't dismissed.'

'No. They hadn't checked a key detail. I wasn't the last person to use the car. I'd lent it to the regional director of police the night before. They'd been so busy packing the glove compartment with used notes they hadn't realised I'd walked to work. I pointed this out, and they tried to tell me it didn't matter. He was obviously beyond reproach, so I must have put the money there. I mentioned the phrase "Beyond reasonable doubt" and the prosecutor agreed with me. Anyway, I knew if they didn't get me then they would later, so I negotiated a transfer. They cut my salary but they got me a police house rent-free so it made little difference.'

'And are you happy here?'

'Very. Due to retire next year or the year after. They leave me alone, more or less. The local captain knows I was a captain myself once and doesn't cross me too often. All in all, life is good. Until some big-shot Prague detective billets a busload of floozies on me.'

Chapter 8

Slonský was contemplating a very large plate of ham and cheese when his phone rang.

'Hello, Sergeant Mucha. How are you this bright morning?'

'I'm well, thank you. And how are you? More to the point, where are you?'

Slonský explained the events of the previous afternoon and evening.

'I know all that,' said Mucha. 'A couple of large Bosnian gentlemen came round last night and threatened the night sergeant with a fence post if he didn't give their girls back.'

'Which end?'

'What do you mean, which end?'

'Which end of the fence post did they threaten him with?'

'Does it matter?'

'I bet it would to him.'

'I think they planned to club him with the blunt end. Anyway, he took them on a tour of the cells to prove they weren't here.'

'If he'd had his wits about him he could have unlocked a cell and pushed them in.'

'I'll tell him that when he's stopped shaking. That'll make him feel heaps better. Anyway, the purpose of this call…'

'Oh, so there is a purpose to it, then?'

'The purpose of this call,' Mucha repeated, 'is to suggest that they may be on the lookout for you, since they knew to come here, so they may well think that wherever you are, the girls will be.'

'Very bright of them. As you can probably hear in the background, the girls are indeed with me.'

'You're not taking this seriously,' Mucha complained. 'You may get the pointy end of the fence post. Don't say you weren't warned.'

'Fair enough. But they don't know where to look for me, do they? Unless they're tapping this call.'

'Just in case, don't answer your mobile to any number you don't recognise. Is Navrátil with you?'

'Umm … he's nearby.'

'Then I'll call his number if I want to talk to you. What are you going to do with those girls?'

'We need to get them to a safer place. Eventually they'll go home, but we need a couple as witnesses. There are another couple that Peiperová found who need rounding up and keeping safe. I only know them as Suzana and Daniela, but when we're back in Prague we'll go looking for them.'

'You'd better not bring the girls back to Prague. Not unless you can put them in prison.'

'That's not a bad idea. And I bet that's where the Bosnians think the girls will be taken. How about sending a couple of our brightest to swing by the gates of Pankrác to look out for a welcoming party?'

'I might ask Dvorník to take a look. A pair of hulking Bosnians won't worry him.'

'Just make sure there's no bystanders. He'll be itching for them to produce a weapon so he can perforate them with some personal artillery of his own and some innocents might get hit.'

'You always tell me nobody is innocent. Everyone is guilty of something.'

'If you're going to quote my own wisdom against me I'm going to hang up and tackle my breakfast.'

'Bon appétit,' said Mucha.

Since Navrátil had no idea what time the Peiper household would wake up, he slept fitfully, but contentedly. Shortly after six o'clock Mr Peiper came down and boiled a kettle for his shave. He offered a blade to Navrátil, who shaved in the kitchen sink. The family had a hearty breakfast, leading Navrátil to wonder how Peiperová retained her figure if she put away this amount every day of her life until the last six months, and then Peiperová gathered up the plates and lobbed a tea-towel into his lap.

'I'll wash, you dry.'

Mr Peiper looked on with a measure of concern. 'You're not gay, are you?' he asked.

'No,' replied Navrátil. 'Just happy to earn my keep.'

'Dad,' protested Peiperová, 'lots of men help in the kitchen these days. You could give mum a hand now and again.'

'Best not,' said her mother. 'I've only got five plates.'

The two policemen who had driven the van to Kladno had been a little surprised to be put on the train back to Prague immediately after arrival, but Slonský needed the van to transport the girls and he did not want the men to know where he was taking them. Peiperová was detailed to follow in the car while Slonský and Navrátil delivered the women to their new place of safety.

If they were surprised to see where they had been taken, that was almost as much of a surprise to Lieutenant-Colonel Táborský, duty officer at the Boletice Military Reservation Office.

'So, Captain Slonský, these are our new guests?'

'Yes, sir. I'm very grateful to you for your co-operation.'

'I'm not quite sure what we'll do to keep them amused. There's a sauna, of course, and a games room, but it probably isn't a good idea if they use the sauna when the squaddies are there.'

'No, sir. Some unarmed combat training wouldn't come amiss, though. Some nasty types are after them.'

'I'm sure we can arrange that. I'll get the ranking woman officer to have a word with them about security. Don't want them popping into town for a hairdo.'

'Isn't it twelve kilometres, sir?'

'Yes, but they're young, fit women.'

'They are, sir, but just look at the heels they're wearing.'

Slonský had decided to do a bit of driving for a change. Having learned to drive behind the controls of a Czech army tank, his approach to lane discipline was lax to say the least, but the van handled in much the same way, and it was fun to watch Peiperová trying to anticipate his moves as she followed him along the road.

'So, Navrátil, let's recap. We know that Brukić was rounding up girls in Bosnia and that Nejedlý was shipping them to Prague where Savović found them work in the clubs and bars.'

'Or on the streets.'

'Perhaps. No hard proof of that yet. We also know that at least one girl killed herself after she discovered she was pregnant by one of the men who molested her. That death wasn't registered so there is a body somewhere that we could do with finding.'

'Sir, shouldn't we start with Hrdlička? We're assuming that because these guys are trafficking women that means they were also the ones who killed Hrdlička, and that doesn't necessarily follow. I was talking to Spehar and he explained to me how you could send electrically generated noise into Hrdlička's earpiece so you could see who was listening in, then they could kill him, but that all sounds a bit sophisticated for a bunch of Bosnians.'

'What's sophisticated about an alarm clock?' said Slonský.

'An alarm clock? What alarm clock?'

'See, these technical types have to overcomplicate things. It could have happened as Spehar said, but all you have to do is put an alarm clock by the microphone, set it to go off in ten minutes, and slip outside to see what happens. One of those old-fashioned ones with a really loud bell would do nicely. You don't need all this electronic jiggery-pokery. A cheap Chinese alarm clock does the job nicely. You know what a shock it is when one of those goes off by your bedside in the morning. Imagine having one inside your helmet. "The bells! The bells! They made me deaf, you know."'

'Sir?'

'Do you know nothing? Charles Laughton? Quasimodo?'

'Oh — the Hunchback of Notre Dame.'

'That's it. Went deaf because the bells were so loud. I bet that happened to Hrdlička. It's a low-powered microphone so he'd have the volume turned up full. Even talking into the microphone close up could be uncomfortable. Imagine what an alarm clock at half a metre would sound like. He'd be so deaf he wouldn't hear anyone sneaking up on him. I'm surprised it didn't burst his ear-drum. In fact, give Novák a ring and ask if Hrdlička's ears were damaged.'

Lukas must be one of the few people I know who would put on a tie when he was on sick leave, thought Slonský.

Mrs Lukasová brought a tray of coffee and placed it on the table between them.

'Shall I pour, dear?' she asked.

'Yes, please,' Lukas replied. 'Bending forward is still a mite tender,' he explained to Slonský.

'I should think it is, sir. That's quite a scar you were showing me.'

Mrs Lukasová lost her poise momentarily at the thought that her husband may have been exhibiting himself in public, however small the degree, but recovered and went off to make some other part of her house perfect.

'She's been wonderful,' said Lukas admiringly. 'I don't know how I'd have coped without her. And you, of course,' he added hurriedly.

'I'm delighted to have been of assistance, however small,' Slonský responded.

'I hear Peiperová has helped you considerably,' Lukas continued, with just a hint of an upward inflection in the remark as if a response were required.

Slonský took a draught of coffee while he debated which of the possible responses he ought to give. 'She is a bright girl, sir. She has introduced a number of efficiencies — though, of course, I'm sure you would have done so too.'

'Nonsense,' responded Lukas. 'It's all I can do to keep the top of the desk clear. How have you managed to cope with the workload and do your day job as well?'

A sudden rush of honesty overcame Slonský. 'I don't do anything the first time they ask. A lot of them don't ask again, so it can't have been important. I've delegated much of the work to Peiperová, and the others don't waste her time like they do yours because they know she can't bend the rules like a real captain can, so she isn't troubled with whingers and malingerers all day long.'

'That's not a very flattering description of your colleagues.'

'It's a very accurate one of Doležal who, no doubt, has had a grumble to you every visiting time.'

It was Lukas' turn to buy some time with a mouthful of coffee. 'He may have mentioned one or two things.'

'I bet he has. It would boost the morale of the department no end if you would let me post him to the Railway Police.'

'He's an experienced and diligent officer.'

'And a miserable git.'

'The two are not incompatible. And if all the miserable officers in the force were removed, we'd be very short of desk sergeants.'

That's true, thought Slonský. Even Mucha has his off-days.

Mrs Lukasová appeared again, bearing a small saucer in which a collection of tablets rolled around.

'You mustn't forget these,' she said, watching over her husband as he swallowed them obediently. Her duty done, she glided off to the kitchen once more, tracked by her husband's admiring eyes.

'A good wife is a great support to a man at times like these,' Lukas said. 'I'm sorry, that was tactless of me.'

'No problem, sir. If I were married to your wife I'd feel the same way,' Slonský replied gallantly.

Navrátil and Peiperová had gone out looking for Suzana or Daniela. After half an hour or so they saw Daniela looking in the window of a shoe-shop. Peiperová marched boldly up to her and planted a kiss on her cheek in greeting. The dancer stepped back in shock and nervously looked round. 'Someone may see you,' she whispered.

'We're just two girls meeting by chance,' Peiperová replied. 'This is my boyfriend, Jan.'

Navrátil shook hands formally. 'You must be Daniela. Kristýna told me about you.'

There was a further glance betraying alarm.

'He works with me,' Peiperová explains. 'Have you got time for a coffee?'

Daniela nodded hesitantly.

They found a café and took seats inside.

'We're pleased to see you're safe,' said Peiperová. 'We took a lot of girls to a place of safety this morning and I could take you there too if you wanted.'

Daniela bit her lip. 'Where is this place?'

'It's best if you don't know, then your friends will stay safe.'

Daniela understood. 'I heard something last night. Bosnian men came to our club late at night to tell the bad man you showed me picture of that they had lost lots of girls. I thought perhaps they ran away. I didn't know they were with you.'

'Best if you don't say anything. They know the police have them, but they're hidden. They tried to get them back last night.'

'I hear the man tell them to do this. He says they have to find girls or he will make the men into women.'

'What a charming man,' commented Navrátil.

'Charming?'

'He means not a nice man,' Peiperová explained, scowling at Navrátil, who resolved to eat his cake and keep quiet. 'If you want to go to the safe place, you need to pack your things and meet us.'

'Where? When?'

'How long will it take? An hour?'

'I can be ready quickly. I don't have many things to take. I find a bag.'

'Across from the Purple Apple club there is a little road. We'll wait at the end there with our car.'

'Not police car?'

'No, not a police car. It's blue and Jan will be driving. When you get there I'll be in the back and I'll open the door for you.'

Daniela became animated and left her coffee as she dashed off to prepare. Navrátil strolled to the door to watch over her as she ran to pack.

'I wish I'd been able to get ahead of her. There was just a chance someone would be waiting for her,' he said.

'But there wasn't,' said Peiperová. 'You worry too much. How long shall we give her?'

'We don't want to arrive too early and have to sit there in plain view. Let's stay here twenty minutes and then drive round. Just time to eat your cake. I don't want you reduced to skin and bones.'

Even Slonský needed clean clothes sometimes. He decided this was a good time to collect his washing and leave it at the laundry where one of a selection of globular women was accustomed to wash and iron it for him. It was an extravagance in some ways, but it reduced the number of clothes he ruined when he did his own laundry, besides saving him a task he loathed. He dragged himself up the stairs to his flat — described by the letting agent as 'bijou' and by everyone else as 'cramped' — and paused on the half-landing to gather his breath before resuming his assault on the summit. He was more than a little surprised to see that someone had preceded him.

'What are you doing here?' he asked.

'You said you would call, but you haven't,' his wife replied. 'I thought you might have lost the number.'

'I didn't give you the address. I don't give anyone my address.'

Věra had sufficient grace to appear slightly sheepish. 'Ah. I didn't deliberately deceive them.'

'Deceive whom?'

'The young officers at the desk. They asked me to produce some identification and they jumped to the conclusion that I must be your sister.'

'Sister? Why sister?'

'Because my name is Slonská and you've told everyone you haven't got a wife.'

'And they gave you my address.'

'No, they didn't know it. But they rang someone in personnel who dug it out. Please don't be cross with them, Josef.'

'Cross? Cross? I won't be cross. I'll be furious.'

'Is it such a big deal?'

'You could have been a terrorist. Or a gangster's moll out for revenge.'

Věra indicated her outfit, beginning with sensible shoes and topped with a plain headscarf. 'Do I look like a gangster's moll?'

'You could be in disguise.'

'It's a poor gangster who couldn't get someone better-looking than me, Josef. Are we going to stand out on the landing all afternoon?'

'I don't know what *you're* going to do. *I'm* going to go into my flat and bundle up my laundry.'

'I could do that.'

'No, thank you. I've done it myself since you ran off with your poet, and I don't plan to stop now.'

Věra's eyes glistened with tears. 'I'm trying to be civilised. I don't want anything from you, and I've conceded that I behaved badly and you've every right to be annoyed. Maybe you don't want to speak to me again, but I wanted to hear that from your own lips. I wouldn't forgive myself if you'd lost the number and I didn't make one more attempt to get in touch.'

Slonský sighed. 'Come in. I don't want the neighbours to hear any more than they already have.'

He opened the door and ushered Věra inside. She managed to stifle a gasp as she surveyed his living quarters. Under the window there was a single bed, at the foot of which stood a plywood wardrobe. A small table and two chairs formed the dining area. The room seemed to consist of a clutch of alcoves with no doors, except for one which led to a shower and toilet. A television and armchair occupied the corner to her right, whilst directly in front of her was a tiny kitchen area. The general impression was of being inside a 1970's time capsule.

'Good heavens,' she remarked. 'The people you put away live in better conditions than this.'

'Have you come to offer lifestyle advice or have a chat?' Slonský growled.

'I'm sorry. I just never thought...' Her voice tailed off. She reached into her sleeve and dabbed her nose with a small handkerchief. It was a gesture Slonský suddenly recalled having seen many times before. When she faced him her eyes were laden with tears. 'I feel so guilty,' she said, before dissolving into sobs.

She had not asked for it, and it felt awkward and a little silly, but Slonský found himself putting his hands loosely on her shoulders and patting her clumsily.

Navrátil checked his watch.

'She'll come, I know she will,' said Peiperová. 'It's only been ten minutes.'

'I'm not doubting she'll be here. I'm just wondering how long we can stay here in sight of the club.'

'It had to be somewhere she would go anyway. If she was followed, they'd think she was going to work until the very last minute.'

Navrátil nodded. If only he'd thought to ask which direction she would be coming from.

Suddenly there was a thud on the car windscreen. Navrátil jumped in surprise, seeing a blue holdall lying there. 'Get out!' he yelled. 'It may be a bomb.'

Peiperová tugged at the door handle, but it would not open. Like many police cars, the back doors could not be opened from the inside. Navrátil had crouched on the pavement but now returned to open the door and pull Peiperová out. Cautiously they approached the bag. The zip was slightly open, so Navrátil gently eased it a little further. He could see that it was full of clothes. The uppermost garment was a bloodstained blouse, and on top of that lay Daniela's passport.

Slonský felt disgusted with himself. It was a moment of weakness brought on by Lukas' fulsome tribute to his wife. He had managed for thirty years without a woman and he did not need one now, but somehow he had found himself pushed into the armchair while Věra removed her coat and boiled several kettles of hot water in succession.

'I like it like this,' he claimed. 'I know where everything is.'

'And it'll still be there, but it'll be clean. Put your feet up and let me get on,' came the reply.

A few swipes of her arm across the window led him to realise that Prague was not always foggy, as he had supposed, and before he knew what was happening the room was filled with light as she unhooked the curtains and bore them to the kitchen.

'I'll wash these,' she announced, 'but I think you'll need new. There are museums who would welcome them.'

'They're only there to stop nosy people looking in. Now I'll be plagued by peeping toms.'

'You're two floors up and, frankly, who would bother?'

'You've got a sharp tongue, woman.'

'I've needed one. It hasn't been easy for me either.'

'You chose…' Slonský began, before being interrupted by the ringing of his mobile phone. He listened intently. 'Calm down, girl! Where are you? Why are you there?' His eyes flashed with anger. 'You must have been careless. How did they discover what she was up to?' The answer cannot have satisfied him, because he slapped his hand hard on the table. 'Then how the hell did they know where your car would be? They must either have overheard you, or they got it out of the girl. You're damn lucky they didn't riddle you both with bullets. Now, get away from the car and I'll send help. When you hear it, come out of your hiding place, but not before.' He disconnected and grabbed his coat. 'I've got to go out.'

'I'm in the middle of this. I'll let myself out when it's done. Has something happened?'

'Navrátil and Peiperová went to pick up a couple of witnesses. It looks like one of them has been beaten up — or worse. Bloody idiots!'

'Then don't stand there fuming,' said his wife. 'Go and help them.'

Slonský stepped from the car and slammed the door. Flashing lights surrounded him as he looked around for his assistants, who separated themselves from a knot of uniformed officers to speak to him.

'I take full responsibility…' began Navratil.

'Shut up. I'll decide who takes responsibility, not you.'

In other circumstances Peiperová would have been concerned about Slonský's blood pressure. His face had passed from tomato to beetroot again and she had the strong impression that anything she said was going to make things worse, so she resolved not to say anything.

'Cat got your tongue, miss? Aren't you going to defend your useless lump of a boyfriend?'

'Yes, sir. It was my plan.'

'Who told you to bring her in?'

'No-one, sir. I just thought with the others in protective custody she might be at risk. If we could get the two women there too they'd be safer.'

'You were right about her being at risk, weren't you? But you were wrong about her being safer in your care. Jesus Maria, what a damn mess!'

'I'm sorry, sir,' Peiperová said. 'I'll resign my post here if you want.'

'Don't make a bloody shambles worse,' Slonský thundered. 'How is Daniela helped one bit by your resignation? And do you think I'm so shallow and vindictive that I'd get shot of you for one mistake?'

'If it's as big as this one, sir.'

Slonský ran his hand through his hair. 'Let's get her back.' He took a deep breath. 'Which car were you using?'

Navrátil pointed at the car which still had the holdall resting against its windscreen.

'Scenes of crime here?'

'On their way, sir.'

'How come you didn't see anyone throw the bag on the car?'

'I don't know, sir. I think I may have turned to talk to Peiperová.'

'You were in the back?' Slonský asked incredulously.

'Yes, sir.'

'In the back of a car whose doors can't be opened from the inside?'

'So I discovered, sir.'

'You could have been trapped in there, completely defenceless. Don't do it again.'

'I won't, sir. I've learned my lesson.'

Slonský walked a few steps away. 'Navrátil, get a description of the girl to the City Police. Any idea where she lived?'

'She didn't tell me, sir,' Peiperová replied.

'Navrátil, get on to the Army Camp. Tell them what happened and ask the officer on duty to ask the girls if any of them has any idea where Daniela lived. If she knew the one who killed herself there's a chance they know her too. Peiperová, I want you to go through that bag first chance you get to look for any clues that might help.' Slonský pointed at a clutch of uniformed police. 'You, you, you, you and you, come with me. We're going to take the Purple Apple to pieces.'

'What are we looking for, sir?' asked one of their number.

'How the hell do I know? Mainly, I want to cause them as much aggravation as they're causing me. Now, stop rabbiting and let's cause some mayhem.'

If the owners of the club had been in any doubt that Slonský was annoyed, they were disabused as he swept through the premises like an avenging angel. He had the customers marched outside and corralled into a holding area where Peiperová was detailed to take names and addresses. The staff were made to sit on the stage until Navrátil and Slonský had interrogated them for any information that might help them find Daniela. The small office was ripped apart by the uniformed men who were looking for anything with the name Daniela on it. They had been there for a little over an hour when Navrátil's phone rang and he scribbled a note in response to the call before running to acquaint Slonský with the details he had gleaned.

'Sir, one of the women at the camp says Daniela lived in a guest house in the same street as Mrs Pimenová's bakery, but she doesn't know where that is.'

'Maybe *she* doesn't, but there isn't a bakery in Prague I don't know, lad. Get the uniformed boys to round this lot up and get them to the station. You and I are going to sample the worst rye bread rolls in the city.'

Mrs Pimenová glanced up as the little bell over her door rang and two men walked in. The larger one was strangely familiar, but she could not quite remember why until he showed his badge.

'Mr Slonský! How nice to see you again. What can I tempt you with?'

'Everything in the shop,' Slonský lied. 'Are those curd cheese buns I can see there?'

'Fresh today,' boasted Mrs Pimenová.

'Then we'll have four of those,' Slonský replied, offering a substantial banknote. 'That ought to cover it — don't want to weigh my pockets down with small change. Now, I don't suppose you would ever serve Bosnian girls, especially … describe her, Navrátil.'

'Tall, dark hair with a tinge of crimson in it, slim, long fingers…'

'Daniela? Yes, she often wanted my poppy seed rolls. She said they reminded her of home.'

'Do you know where she lived?'

'Yes, in what used to be the old school on the corner. They've converted it into a sort of young people's hostel.'

Slonský thanked her profusely and promised to return soon. Once they were outside he told Navrátil to stop and think a moment. 'There's only two of us and we don't know who's there, so let's not rush in. Eat your bun while we think.'

Each took a bite and chewed slowly.

'Shall I give the rest to the birds, sir?'

'You can't make birds eat these, Navrátil. The poor little beggars will never get airborne again. Hang on, I've got an idea.'

Slonský marched across the road to the old school and banged on the door. When it was opened he showed his badge and waved the paper bag aggressively.

'Who bought these?'

'I don't know,' stammered the young man who had opened the door.

'And you are?'

'Filip. Milan Filip.'

'Make a note, Navrátil. The suspect Filip said…'

'Suspect? Why am I a suspect? I haven't done anything.'

'Were you here earlier this evening, around five o'clock?'

'Yes.'

'So you were part of the vicious assault of a young woman that took place here?'

'What assault? I didn't hear anything.'

'Take us to Daniela's room, right now.'

The young man collected a key and led them up the stairs. On the upper floor he knocked at one of the rooms, then, receiving no answer, he opened the door and revealed a very nicely furnished sitting room. He then used another key to open the connecting door to the bedroom. There was no mistaking that a woman lived here.

Slonský examined it closely. Although the bedclothes were disturbed, there was no sign of blood or violence.

'When did you last see her?'

'Earlier today. After lunch she went out.'

'Can she come and go as she pleases?'

'More or less. She's supposed to say where she's going. And the boss leaves a man sitting in the outer room to keep an eye on the girls.'

'So you knew they were illegal immigrants?'

'No,' protested Filip. 'I made it my business not to know anything. It only causes trouble if you do.'

Navrátil was bursting to ask a question. 'She had a bag of clothes, so she must have come back here around five o'clock to collect those. Did you see her?'

'No. And I was here at that time. She didn't come back.'

'Look in the closet, Navrátil. Her clothes are still here. You've jumped to a conclusion because her passport was there. She may never have got here.' Slonský turned to go downstairs, when a thought occurred to him. 'You said girls. Does she share this room?'

'Yes, with a Croat girl. Barbara, I think her name is.'

'And where is she now?'

'Probably at work. They work at a place called the Purple Apple. It's a g…'

'We know what it is. Come along, Navrátil.'

'Good evening, sir. This is an unexpected pleasure,' said Slonský, who recognised the number displayed on his mobile phone.

'It's not Sir, it's Mrs Sir,' said Mrs Lukasová.

'Captain Lukas is all right, I hope?' said Slonský, and Mrs Lukasová was pleased to note genuine concern in his voice.

'Yes, he's dithering about ringing you, so we've taken matters in hand. He's heard a rumour that you've lost a witness and he was hoping that you had matters under control.'

'Perhaps if I could speak to the Captain directly, I could set his mind at rest,' Slonský oozed, so Mrs Lukasová handed the phone to her husband.

'Good evening, Slonský.'

'Good evening, sir. I'll tell you the truth, then you can hand the phone back and say everything is fine. Navrátil and Peiperová conceived a plan to take the witness to a place of safety. It seems their supposition that she was in danger was right, because she has disappeared, and someone wants us to believe she has been maltreated, but the clothes we have don't appear to be hers.'

'Could you explain that last bit again?' asked Lukas, aware that he dare not say anything alarming but unable to follow the discussion so far.

'A bag of clothes including a bloodstained blouse and a passport were delivered to the two officers in place of the witness. Don't ask, it beggars belief, and I've already had words with them. We've traced the witness to a room and her clothes are there, and there's no sign of any violence, but we've got to go looking for her now. We didn't lose a witness because we never had her. It's a standard missing persons inquiry now, sir.'

Lukas sighed with relief. 'Ah, that's different. My information seems to have been unduly prejudicial.'

'You mean Doležal screwed with the facts when he rang you?'

'I don't think I said anything about that.'

'No, you didn't, but the long streak of misery is the only person likely to try to stitch me up. He may not be here when you get back, sir. I've got my eye open for a suitable posting in the mountains. What a shame that, unlike the Austrians, we don't have sewer police.'

Lukas permitted himself a small smile. 'Carry on, Slonský.'

'I shall, sir. Hope you feel better soon. My regards to all the ladies.'

'I just want you to know, Navrátil, that if anything has happened to Daniela you'll be personally supplying the meatballs at the next police barbecue.'

'Yes, sir.'

'And you can stop sighing with relief, Peiperová. I'm sure we can find some equivalent for you.'

'Yes, sir.'

'Now, think, the pair of you. How did they know that you'd arranged to meet Daniela?'

'We said nothing to anyone, sir,' said Peiperová. 'And I checked I wasn't being followed.'

Slonský scratched his head before replacing his hat. Somehow the action helped to invigorate the brain sometimes, and this was one such.

'It's you,' he said to Navrátil.

'Me, sir? I haven't done anything.'

'If they'd been following Peiperová they'd have snatched the girl before now. But you meet her, and within the hour she's been kidnapped. So the likeliest answer is that someone was watching you.'

'I didn't notice anyone, sir.'

'Of course you didn't, lad. They'd be pretty poor at their job if you did. They must have been waiting when we returned the van earlier. I went off to see Lukas, and you and Peiperová went to find Daniela — which you might have mentioned to me, by the way. Either we were both followed, or they hoped that you'd gone to fetch a female officer because you were going to lead them to the girls.'

'You're sure it's the Bosnians, sir?'

'If it wasn't them it's a hell of a coincidence. Now, the likelihood is that the men who did the snatching won't have done the questioning, so they'll take her to wherever Savović and Brukić hang out. And that won't be a hostel or a club because we'd be watching there. So I wonder where Savović lives? Navrátil, get your rat-catcher's credentials ready. We're going to see a man about some pests.'

The doorkeeper was not going to be taken in again.

'You're those policemen. I remember you. Got the murderer yet?'

'Not yet,' said Slonský. 'But we're working on it. When we were here before you told my assistant that the Bosnian gentleman had his wild parties at his flat.'

'I don't know anything about wild parties. He wouldn't invite the likes of me. I keep myself to myself, I do.'

'I wasn't asking what went on there. Where's his flat?'

'Come again?'

'His flat. Where is it? Where does he live?'

'I can't go disclosing personal information about tenants without a warrant! I'll get sacked.'

'Navrátil, we haven't got time to waste. Knock a few of his teeth out.'

Navrátil hesitated, trying to determine whether Slonský could possibly be serious. This hesitation was construed by the doorman as a premonitory display of menace, and he quickly sought a compromise.

'But if I was to leave my notebook open on the desk and one of you gents was to sneak a peek, that's not my fault, is it?' he hurriedly suggested.

'Of course not,' agreed Slonský. 'A man's notebook is his private property. He's entitled to keep his innermost secrets in it. Well, don't stand there gawping, lad — copy the address out and let's get down there.'

Navrátil and Slonský climbed back into their car and drove off across town to the address they had been given, which was on the city's southern fringes. It was dark by the time they arrived.

Having anticipated some kind of gated compound, Slonský was pleasantly surprised to find it was merely a villa with a low wall to the front, outside which a pair of large men stood smoking.

'Looks like the place. Keep driving, Navrátil. We don't want them to know our business. Turn right at the end of the road.'

It turned out to be a dead end, so Navrátil executed a U-turn and awaited instructions.

'Keep the engine running, lad. We're going to be retracing our route for about a hundred metres, then we'll take a sharp left once we're past the villa. Got that?'

'Yes, sir. Aren't you going to get in?'

'Not just at the moment. I just want to try a little trick I learned at the All-Moravia Artisan Sausage-Making Championship.'

Slonský walked over to the hedge and struck a match. Holding it to a small pile of dead leaves, he kindled a fire, and encouraged it by striking another match and holding it to the hedge itself, before climbing back into the car.

'Now we wait for it to take hold.'

After a few moments the fire, though not large, was exciting enough for Slonský to suggest a measured retreat. They pulled back into the traffic and were pleased to see the two men walking briskly along the pavement to investigate the blaze. A sharp left turn later, Navrátil and Slonský slipped over the side wall and reached the side of the villa without being detected.

Slonský signalled his assistant to maintain silence, a completely unnecessary gesture since Navrátil's own well-developed sense of self-preservation had suggested that course of action as soon as they left the car, and together they inched around the building looking for a quiet corner where they might peek through the windows.

The corner room at the back was well-lit, so they ducked down below the sill and made for the next window, where Slonský cautiously raised himself. He could see Savović and Brukić, who were engaged in a game of chess. There was no sign of the girl.

Slonský tapped Navratil on the shoulder and indicated that he wanted to move further away from the building into the garden at the rear. He pointed to a couple of bushes separated by about a metre, and gave Navrátil a gentle push, by which the young detective deduced that he was to go first, and scuttled across the lawn, being followed shortly after by Slonský.

In their hiding place, Slonský felt able to risk a whisper.

'They're too relaxed. They know they've got the girl. I'll bet she's upstairs. Watch the windows.'

'It could be hours, sir. And if she's tied up, she won't come to the window.'

'Got any better ideas?'

Navrátil peered into the darkness. After a moment or two he saw what he wanted, and ran back across the lawn towards the house. Although originally a single-storey building, it had been enhanced at some point by the inclusion of a room in the roof. Navrátil was slightly built, and although not blessed with great athletic prowess, he was a good cross-country runner, so he must have been quite fit, but Slonský was unprepared for the exhibition he was about to witness. Pausing only to give a sharp tug on the downpipe to test its soundness, Navrátil shinned up the drainpipe to the low roof, hoisted himself aloft, and gently crept along the rooftop to the dormer window, where he cautiously looked in.

He was about to return when the two men appeared at the side of the house brandishing flashlights. Slonský tucked himself behind one of the bushes, but was unable to warn Navrátil before he descended nor, from his hiding place, could he see what happened next.

However, he saw the beams of light sweeping round the garden and made himself as small as possible, which in Slonský's case was not easy to do, but fortunately the darkness of the bushes swallowed him up. Suddenly the men started shouting. In the emotion of the moment, they were yelling in their own language, which seemed particularly pointless to Slonský, though it was easy to detect that they were shouting some kind of warning. Confident that they were looking at the roof, he risked a peek, and watched open-mouthed as Navrátil ran up the roof, rolled over the ridge, and disappeared out of sight. The guards had finally removed their guns from the holsters under their jackets and were waving them ineffectually before retracing their steps to run round to the front. In the confusion Slonský slipped out over the side wall. If he could get to the car he could drive round to the front and scoop Navrátil up. Except, of course, that he would have to perform a U-turn in a tight side road. It was at this point that Slonský remembered that the car keys were in Navrátil's pocket.

Damn! At least he had heard no gunshots so far, and he was fairly confident that if Navrátil had made it to ground level with a head start, he may have been able to gain the street, but whether he would be able to return to the car was doubtful. Slonský briefly considered calling Navrátil on his mobile, but that might have been a bit of a giveaway if the young detective were hiding in the shrubbery somewhere nearby.

Hiding behind the car, he had an idea. He telephoned HQ, explained who he was, and issued his orders. 'All the cars you can, fast as you can. Lights blazing, sirens on full. And patch me through to the first officer to arrive.'

The response was gratifyingly quick. A couple of cars came bouncing round the corner and came to a halt with their lights illuminating the street and the two guards who quickly tucked their guns into the backs of their waistbands.

An officer in the first car opened the door and shouted an instruction. 'Put your hands up and lie face down in the road.'

To the astonishment of the guards, Navrátil appeared from a thicket across the road and lay face down as instructed. He had decided that the police had been summoned by someone who had taken him for a burglar; and even if that were not the case, people in the custody of the police are unlikely to be shot, so it seemed much the safest option.

It was at this point that Slonský managed to speak to the first officer on scene via the radio. If his instructions were a little surprising, Slonský was well enough known for them to be accepted without question. The officers picked Navrátil up and put handcuffs on him. He tried to speak but they instructed him to keep quiet. Slonský walked towards them, nodding a nonchalant greeting to the two Bosnians.

'Where was he? On the roof again?'

'Yes,' said the younger of the two. 'He was climbing on the roof. He wants to burgle us.'

'Ah, no,' said Slonský. 'That's not his style. He'll have been looking for a young woman. What does she look like?'

He gave Navrátil an encouraging nod.

'Tall, slim, dark hair with a bit of red in it.'

'And you followed her here?'

'Yes.'

The two guards looked at each other with undisguised concern.

'Perhaps I can come in and see the young lady,' Slonský said.

'There is no such girl,' the older man snapped.

'I think maybe this man saw our cleaner. But she does not live here.'

'It's not likely he'd be hanging around your roof for no reason. He's one of our best-known stalkers. Trust me, he'll have seen her. I'd best check. Take this villain down to the station and book him. And I don't want him marked, however disgusting he is.'

Slonský took a couple of the officers with him and insisted on searching the house, though he had misgivings when Savović raised no objection to his doing so. There was no sign of Daniela, nor any sign that she had been there.

Chapter 9

Peiperová had come in that Sunday morning and Slonský had barely spoken to her. Navrátil was in the same position, apparently suddenly invisible. The only relief they had experienced was when someone chanced to mention a critical mark Doležal had made about the progress of the investigation. Slonský had prowled the building like an enraged bear until he was satisfied that Doležal was not in, when he contented himself with an extremely abusive note stuck to the latter's desk with sticky tape, which he later thought better of and removed. And put back again, and removed once more.

Navrátil returned to the office he shared with his boss, who was busy scribbling notes in the margin of a folder. The atmosphere was as icy inside as it was in the street below.

'Sir, may I ask you something?'

'If you must.'

'Why did you tell the police I was a stalker?'

Slonský laid his pen down. That was a good sign, because when he was annoyed he would throw it on the desk.

'I told them that publicly, but I had already told the first carful that you were working undercover and I had to give a reason for you being on the roof that wouldn't blow that cover. And better for the thugs to think you just happened to follow the girl than that they think you're a police officer trying to *find* the girl, don't you think?'

'But if it's my fault that Daniela was snatched, as you said earlier, presumably they already know I'm police.'

'Maybe somebody does. But maybe they think you're a reporter, or a pimp, or a photographer for a girlie magazine, or one of those pests who keep offering women in the street money to do things he can video and put on the internet. All those would be better for your long-term health than letting them know you're a police officer.'

'I suppose so, sir.'

'See how kindly Uncle Josef looks after you?'

Navrátil chewed his lip in uncertainty.

'Out with it, lad.'

'I don't suppose you'd explain that to Kristýna, sir. I mean, Officer Peiperová. She thinks you know something about my private life that made the stalker story plausible.'

Slonský frowned. 'Well, you were quick enough up that drainpipe and onto the roof. Anyone would think you'd done it before.'

'I've climbed drainpipes, sir. But not for that reason.'

Slonský walked to the door and took a deep breath. 'Peiperová!' he bellowed.

The officer thus summoned opened her door and looked out as if unsure whose voice that could be. Since Slonský was the only person in the corridor, she could hardly pretend to any uncertainty about the source of the cry.

'In my office, lass.'

Peiperová obediently trotted along the corridor and took the seat in front of the desk as Slonský indicated. Navratil was to her right, perched on the front of his desk, which was at right angles to Slonský's.

'You are an intelligent young woman,' Slonský began. 'Look at him. Go on, drink him in. Scan him from head to foot. You will never see a pervert who looks like that. He's clean and tidy, and he polishes his shoes. He goes to Mass every week, and he has a season ticket for the confessional. He is good to his mother. According to the betting in the staff canteen he isn't even trying to get up *your* skirt, let alone anyone else's…'

'Sir!' protested Navrátil, while Peiperová blushed fetchingly.

'…so why on earth you would think that he would ever be a stalker is beyond me,' Slonský continued unabashed.

'Yes, sir. I mean no, sir.'

'You sound unconvinced.'

'I didn't want to believe it, but the officers who came to arrest him spun me a tale about how he was found.'

'Indeed?'

'They said he was incompletely dressed.'

'Navrátil? Incompletely dressed? Good God, woman, he won't even take his tie off in mid-summer. If there's one thing we don't have much problem with in Prague in November it's indecent exposure. I was there, and I can assure you that Navrátil behaved entirely properly. He even laid down tidily in the road with his hands up as directed. Now, I am going to go down to the desk, ask the duty sergeant to check the log for last night, and then I'm going to radio the cars involved to tell them the joke stops now. In the meantime, I'm ordering the two of you to kiss and make up, then we'll go and get some lunch. I feel in need of a sausage.'

Slonský marched from the room, closing the door behind him.

Peiperová ordered a plate of pasta with sliced chicken. Navrátil opted for a bowl of soup with dumplings. Slonský decided he would have a pair of sausages to start, with some fried onions and sauerkraut. He also announced that he suspected his brainpower was diminishing because it had been deprived of beer for nearly two days, and he intended to remedy this deficiency with half a litre of Plzeň's best. Since they were all working on what was technically a day off, he saw no reason why they shouldn't join him. Peiperová nominated a white wine spritzer as her drink of choice.

'Why would you want someone to water your wine down?' enquired Slonský, but ordered it through gritted teeth. Navrátil was torn between wanting to have a beer to bond with his boss and the fear that incipient alcoholism would be added to voyeurism on his fiancée's charge sheet if he did so.

'Is that two wine spritzers then?' Slonský asked. 'Or do you want them to top your beer up with mineral water?'

'Actually, I'm a bit cold,' Navrátil replied. 'I think I'll just have a coffee.'

'Better make it decaffeinated,' Slonský told the waiter. 'We don't want to excite his urges again.'

Peiperová's attention was caught by something behind Slonský. 'Isn't that your journalist friend, sir?'

Slonský turned to observe Valentin surrounded by a pile of crumpled newspapers.

'Yes.'

'Shall I invite him over?'

'No. He's working. We'll eat first and then speak to him. We don't want to spoil our meal by sitting with a miserable old codger.'

Just then the door opened, and Captain Grigar walked in, looked around and stomped over to join them. 'Thought I might find you here,' he began. 'We badly need to talk. So far as I can see, we're on each other's turf. I'm busting a gut trying to find out who murdered my man while you're swanning off rounding up trafficked girls. Where have you taken them?'

'I'm not telling you.'

'May I remind you I'm a senior officer in the Organised Crime Squad and you're not?'

'And may I remind you that the Organised Crime Squad is the most corrupt unit in the entire Prague police and leaks information like a sieve? Present company excepted, of course.'

The waiter arrived with the drinks, which brought about a hiatus in the conversation.

'Drink, sir?' the waiter asked Grigar.

'Like a fish,' Slonský interposed. 'Just bring a keg and a length of rubber hosepipe.'

'I'll have what he's having,' said Grigar.

'Another white wine spritzer then,' announced Slonský, seizing the one on the tray and knocking it back in one. 'In fact, we'd better have two so the young lady can have one, and I'll have her beer instead.'

'Actually, I'll have a beer too,' Grigar said.

The waiter slipped away before the order was changed again.

'I don't want to be difficult,' Grigar began, 'but I want to know how you're doing in finding young Hrdlička's killers.'

'You've seen Novák's pathology report?'

'Yes. Special forces' work, he thought.'

'We've established that Savović has been rounding up girls in the Balkans, spinning them a yarn about hotel work in Prague, and then putting them on buses escorted by Brukić. At some point the girls are concealed in lorries owned by Nejedlý, who also shares that building, and somehow they place them in the clubs. At least a couple of those clubs seem to be owned by the Bosnians. We've upset them a bit by taking some of their dancers to a place of safety.'

'What about Hrdlička?'

Navrátil interrupted. 'Where did he get his earpiece, sir?' he asked Grigar.

'Earpiece? What earpiece?'

'He was wearing an earpiece inside his helmet, but the technical department says it's not one of ours, so far as they know. We're assuming that the killer found the radio microphone and worked out who was listening in on them by setting off a loud alarm clock next to it.'

'Well I never!' exclaimed Slonský. 'Who would have thought it? How ingenious.'

Navrátil believed he was colouring, but continued gamely. 'Hrdlička wouldn't hear the killer approaching because he would be deafened by the alarm clock.'

'So why did he still have his helmet on when he was killed? Wouldn't he yank it off to stop the noise?'

'Good point,' said Slonský. 'How does this imaginative alarm clock theory of yours deal with that, Navrátil?'

Navrátil's mouth opened a couple of times, but no suggestion came forth.

'Perhaps that's what he was doing when he was killed, sir?' offered Peiperová. 'Nobody actually saw him praying just beforehand. Maybe he ducked his head to pull the helmet off and that exposed his neck.'

Grigar seemed to accept that. 'So the accomplice sees who reacts and then kills him from behind,' he concluded.

'There's no need for an accomplice,' Slonský muttered.

'No?'

'No. It's an alarm clock. They ring at a predetermined time. All he has to do is set it for, say, four o'clock and then make it his business to be on the river bank at that time. He can see as easily from there as he can from a window. There may be two of them,' Slonský added, 'but there doesn't need to be. One would do, too.'

Grigar rubbed his chin and took a reflective pull on his beer. 'I didn't authorise an earpiece. Mind, I would have done if I'd been asked. But where would Hrdlička get one? Why didn't he just ask for one from the technicians?'

That's another good question, thought Slonský. 'Isn't there anything in his notes on the case?' he voiced aloud.

'Very little. Hrdlička seems to have kept very sketchy notes, but then he didn't come into the office much while he was doing surveillance duties. It may be that there's a notebook somewhere we haven't found.'

'Was he married, sir?' asked Peiperová.

'Yes, with a little boy of eighteen months.'

'And he didn't say anything to his wife?'

'Well, she didn't know of any notes he'd made.'

'Would it help if I had a talk to her, woman to woman?'

Slonský grinned with delight. 'If anyone's going to speak to her woman to woman, you're the best qualified, lass. Unless Captain Grigar objects, I think that would be worth a try.'

'No, I don't object,' said Grigar. 'I'll give you her address.'

Their food arrived, at which point Grigar decided to take his leave. He tore a leaf from his notebook bearing Hrdlička's address, and arranged to meet the following afternoon for a more formal exchange of information.

Slonský fell upon his sausages with a keen display of appetite.

'Good, sir?' Peiperová asked.

'Don't know. I just wanted to stop the conversation so he'd go quicker. I can think of only one reason why Hrdlička would be using an unapproved earpiece. He didn't want his boss to know he had it. Which means he didn't trust his boss, which means neither should we.'

Valentin pulled up a chair. 'Was that Grigar?' he asked.

Slonský jumped theatrically. 'I thought you were the Golem for a moment. Don't creep up on people like that.'

'Have you been avoiding me?'

'No, I've been busy. Working. You know, doing my job.'

'I thought now you had these two those days were behind you.'

'You're talking to an Acting Captain, I'll have you know. I have other responsibilities now. The management of the department is in my hands.'

'As good a reason to think of emigrating as any I've heard in a long while.'

'I suppose despite your cheek you want a drink.'

'I won't insult you by refusing your offer. Shall I order some for you too?'

'Peiperová's already on her second. I'll have another beer, and Navrátil will dither for a few minutes before deciding he daren't have a beer in front of his work colleague.'

'He can have a beer if he wants,' Peiperová responded.

'Oh, then I will,' Navrátil declared boldly, before adding, 'Better make it a small one, though.'

'Is this just a way of passing Sunday afternoon or did you have something to tell me?' Slonský enquired.

'Well, originally I was going to check my sources about a story I'd heard that a young detective with your department had been caught exposing himself to young women, but I can see there isn't anything in that.'

Navrátil sprayed coffee into his soup. 'Where did you hear that?' he spluttered.

'I have a friend who has — no, may have — a radio scanner that occasionally accidentally picks up police frequencies, and who may have overheard Officer Pelc making a report to his dispatcher last evening. And obviously got completely the wrong end of the stick.' Valentin could detect a marked frostiness emanating from Peiperová, and decided to drop the subject sharply. 'Pleased to hear there's nothing in it, and I shall make a point of telling people so if I hear it said. However, the same friend may have overheard something else earlier that could be of interest to you. I mention it because he was struck — might possibly have been struck — by the odd coincidence of name.'

Slonský sighed. 'I am not going to go after your friend for listening in on police transmissions, so long as he isn't using them for illicit purposes.'

'No, he's just a boring nerd with no life.'

'I can empathise. So I'm interested in what he heard.'

'He says that when he heard Officer Pelc mention Navrátil, he thought that was interesting, because a few hours before he'd heard another officer mention Navrátil. This one said he was making arrangements to meet a girl later. And he was told to keep watching Navrátil and follow him to see where the girl was taken.'

'Did this friend of yours overhear any names?'

'As it happens, he did. The follower was told that the order to watch Navrátil came from Captain Grigar.'

'This puts a different complexion on things,' declared Slonský.

'Doesn't it just?' agreed Valentin. 'Is Grigar worried that he doesn't know what's going on, or is it more sinister than that?'

'You mean more newsworthy.'

'Well, that too. Though of course I couldn't publish anything that wasn't fully verified.'

'When exactly did this new policy of yours come in?' Slonský asked, arching an eyebrow to indicate that no possible answer was credible.

'I'm only trying to make an honest living and be a model citizen at the same time,' sulked Valentin. 'I don't know why I bother.'

Slonský cradled his beer for a moment and fell silent, usually a sign that he was bored, but in this case betokening urgent cogitation. 'Old friend,' he announced, 'there is the opportunity for some serious mutual back-scratching here. Navrátil, got any plans for this afternoon?'

'Well, I … shoes and laundry … maybe the movies…'

'Peiperová, could you give up the afternoon to visit Hrdlička's wife? Then Loverboy here will feel happier about driving Mr Valentin to a secret location he won't want to know about so even lighted matches under his fingernails can't get it out of him.'

'Who would put lighted matches under my fingernails? And if they're serious, I'd rather like to have something to tell them, otherwise they won't stop.'

'I think you'd like to have an exclusive set of interviews with women who have been trafficked to the Czech Republic for immoral purposes. The quid pro quo is that you mislead the Bosnians about where they are.'

'Deliberately mislead my readers? How unprofessional. I couldn't countenance such a thing.'

'Bottle of brandy for your trouble?'

'On the other hand,' Valentin mused, 'it's every reporter's job to assist the police in the detection of crime.'

'Is this wise, sir?' ventured Navrátil.

'It's for the girls' safety. Once they've been named and photographed in the papers, and the clubs they work in are made public, there's no point in the villains trying to get them back, is there? And with a bit of luck there'll be spontaneous picketing by feminists and church leaders outside the clubs — Navrátil, put together a list of people to leak it to, there's a good lad — so we get two benefits from it all.'

'Will the girls agree to be named?' asked Valentin.

'Not all, but some will. And we can give the impression that their virtue was protected by the prompt action of the Czech police who, once more, charged to the rescue of damsels in distress. So although the purposes were immoral, the girls are still pure. Well, as pure as they were when they arrived anyway.'

Peiperová immediately liked Mrs Hrdličková. She was no great beauty, but there was a warmth about her despite her loss. Hrdlička had been a good-looking man who must have had plenty of options when it came to a wife, so it was clear that he had seen something admirable in this short, rather squat woman with the untidy hair who was simply too strong to cry.

'How did you meet?' Peiperová asked.

'What a surprising question! The other officers haven't wanted to know that.'

'I'm sorry. I don't mean to pry. I just want to think about your husband as a person rather than only as a police officer.'

'It's not prying. I'm happy to talk about it. In fact, I think talking may help. You can't imagine how it feels when you kiss someone goodbye in the morning and that's the last time you see them.'

'My boyfriend is a police officer too.'

'Then you know the fear. Of course, you worry that it may happen, but you can't live your life that way, so you tell yourself that it won't. And when it does, you have nothing to fall back on. Just a big, dark emptiness.'

'You're being very brave.'

'I have to be, for our son's sake. One day I'll have to explain why Daddy didn't come home. It's hard enough now when he looks at the door and asks for Daddy. I can't imagine what it will be like when he's old enough to understand.'

'Mrs Hrdličková, I…'

'Helena, please.'

'Helena, had you been married long?'

'Nearly three years. But we'd known each other a long time. We were at school together, then Erik went off to university. He read psychology, but when he graduated he couldn't get a job, and someone suggested that he would be good as a policeman. He liked the idea, and he got accepted. He used to act and he was clever with disguises, you see. He could fit in. He had six months pretending to be a rock musician with a drug habit. I think he enjoyed that, because the police bought him a new guitar and they didn't make him give it back afterwards.'

'You must have waited patiently for him if you've only been married three years.'

'He wouldn't marry until he earned as much as me. I had a job at the hospital as a radiographer. I still do some shifts when Mum takes Petr for me. I may have to go back full-time to pay the rent here now.'

It was a nice flat, not grand, but clean and well equipped. Peiperová would have been very happy to have one like it. Little Petr had decided that she was sufficiently important to be shown his wooden racing car with two occupants. He picked each out in turn and handed it to her, reciting 'Mama … Papa…" as he did so. She had to turn away for a moment and dab an eye with her cuff.

'Did he tell you anything about the job he was on at the moment?'

'Absolutely nothing. He never did.'

'Did he have a desk or notebook where he may have left a clue?'

'Surely the police know what he was doing? Captain Grigar asked too, but I thought he would have known.'

'What exactly did Captain Grigar ask?'

'He wanted to know if there were any notes showing where Erik had got to in his investigation. I thought he would have known that. Erik used to do his reports when he came home and then drop them in at the station before he put his costume on.'

That is odd, thought Peiperová. Did Grigar suspect there was something that had not found its way into the reports?

'Could I see where he worked? It might help, you never know.'

'Of course. He used a corner of the bedroom. I'm afraid you'll have to excuse the mess.'

Peiperová looked around her. What mess? It looked immaculate. Assuming that Grigar and his colleagues had gone through the drawers of the little table thoroughly, she concentrated on the bookshelves. Although she was not a great reader herself, she thought you could find out a lot about people by the books they had. In this case, it was confusing because the couple had shared the shelves, so there were books about cookery mixed in with psychology textbooks, a couple of books about the Second World War and a volume of walks in and around Prague. There were a few folded maps as well, which she glanced through.

'Did you both come from Prague?'

'Yes, born and bred. Not this part, of course, but out to the eastern side.'

'What's the connection with Opava?' Peiperová asked, waving one of the maps.

Helena looked puzzled. 'There isn't one,' she said. 'I've never been there and I don't think Erik had either.'

Peiperová unfolded the map. It took a while to spot it, but there was a small red cross in one corner, in what appeared to be countryside, and a dotted line marked out an irregular area around the cross.

'May I borrow this?' she asked.

Helena nodded. 'If it helps.'

'I don't know. But it might be an idea not to tell anyone else I've got it.'

Four things were exercising Slonský's brain simultaneously. There was the problem of what to do with the women currently loitering in an army camp. This was fairly urgent, because putting young women in a closed camp full of young soldiers was just looking for trouble, though Slonský thought the soldiers would have to learn to look after themselves. They were armed, after all.

Then there was the vexed question of why Captain Grigar would have had Navrátil followed. He had known Grigar for around fifteen years, and although they were not close friends, he had always thought that Grigar was a good policeman and unlikely to do anything underhand. He would have liked to have thought that if Grigar wanted to know something, he would just have come and asked, which is what Slonský would have done had their positions been reversed.

His inclination was to confront Grigar about it, but if Grigar happened to be up to something, that might be the worst thing to do. Perhaps he should watch and wait rather than charging in with all guns blazing.

Next there was the need to do something about that creep Doležal. As Acting Captain he ought not to do anything drastic while Lukas was on sick leave, but on the other hand this was an opportunity not to be squandered to get the slimy streak of misery posted to a log cabin in the back of beyond — the kind of place where everyone played accordions all the time and the locals had sheep for girlfriends — if he could only think of a pretext. Perhaps it was even worth putting Doležal up for promotion if it meant he got a station of his own far from electricity and connected sewerage.

But the biggest issue that needed handling was the fact that his wife Věra was currently in his kitchen rustling up dinner for two. He hoped that the deficiencies in his domestic arrangements would put her off repeating the experiment, since she must be getting fed up with the disappointments inherent in his having only one saucepan and very limited utensils. Indeed, he had borrowed a couple of sets of cutlery from the staff canteen to ensure that they both had knives, but the happy humming from the vicinity of the hob suggested that his wife was prepared to regard the shortages as a justification for her act of charity in feeding him.

When they arrived home things had started badly.

'Sit down and take your shoes off,' she said. 'Surely you don't wear those around the house?'

In over thirty years it had not occurred to Slonský that other people removed their shoes indoors. He tried to recall the condition of his socks, which were likely to be in a state of dereliction, but he had not paid much attention when he put them on that morning. The only sure thing was that they would be black, because all his socks were. It made finding a pair so much easier.

Věra misinterpreted his hesitation as a desire to adopt husband and wife roles.

'Come on,' she said, kneeling in front of him and pulling on his laces. 'I'll do it.'

'No...' stammered Slonský, but in no time his feet were exposed to the cooling air.

Věra inspected the socks thus revealed. 'If you're ever found dead in the street at least Dr Novák won't have to take your socks off to put a label on your toe. I'll darn those for you when they've been washed.'

'It's not worth darning socks,' Slonský protested. 'They're cheap enough. I'll just buy a new pair.'

'Such extravagance,' tutted Věra, before she noticed that the pink heel was due to the thinness of the wool rather than a raffish design highlight.

She busied herself emptying the shopping bag in the kitchen area, and then produced a masterstroke of such elegance and cunning that Slonský was momentarily rendered speechless.

'There you are,' she said. 'Kristýna told me this was the beer you usually chose.'

Kristýna? When had she managed to talk to Peiperová? He suspected Navrátil had a hand in this somewhere, because he knew his assistant had Věra's telephone number, and it was in his romantic nature to play matchmaker given half a chance. Anyway, he could think about that later. For the moment, he must devote his whole attention to the important subject of beer. And wondering what Věra was cooking that smelled not bad at all.

Chapter 10

Slonský lobbed his coat in the general direction of the coat-stand and glided to the desk where he unfolded the morning paper. Valentin had worked at speed; the front page of his paper carried a banner headline proclaiming the wickedness of the Bosnians who tricked these innocent girls and the Czechs who exploited them. There was also a promise of further revelations in the following days.

Navrátil arrived and nodded a greeting.

'Valentin wasted no time,' Slonský announced, indicating the headline.

'We were there till late. He wants to go back again for some more material if you can spare me.'

'Of course. Anything I ought to know?'

'I got stopped by the traffic police and breathalysed.'

'You? Didn't you show them your badge?'

'Yes. That just increased the snideness. They said the car smelled like a brewery.'

'Well, of course it did. You had Valentin with you.'

'That didn't help.'

Realisation struck Slonský. 'You'd had a beer. They didn't fine you, did they?'

'By great good fortune, if you recall, although you offered me a beer you didn't actually get round to ordering it. I'd only had a coffee.'

'Another triumph of foresight. There — I saved you from yourself. You know the traffic cops love flinging the book at the rest of us.'

'How have you escaped for so long? Any alcohol at all should mean you get hauled in.'

'I just give them the evil eye. They can fine me, but I can bring them in and subject them to seventy-two hours of sarcasm without charging them.'

'Anyway, sir, I haven't said anything about the traffic police to … anyone else, so I'd appreciate some discretion.'

'And you shall have it,' Slonský beamed. 'Discretion is my middle name.'

Navrátil involuntarily glanced at the heavens in case a lightning bolt was on its way down to the room, but it seemed God was turning a blind eye to that one.

'What are the plans for today, sir?'

'I think you can arrange another day out for Valentin, while I put the wind up Grigar. But first, we must prepare ourselves properly. And that means a hearty breakfast, my boy. Is Officer Peiperová around?'

'I haven't seen her.'

'Then we will detour past the Acting Acting Captain's office, since she is invariably punctual, and sweep her away to the café on the corner to ply her with a tasty sausage or three.'

Peiperová was leaning over her desk with the map of Opava unfolded and another, more detailed one alongside.

'What have you got there?' Slonský demanded.

'Hrdlička had this map in his room. His wife says they don't have any links with Opava so she doesn't know why he had it. That made me think I ought to look into it a bit further. If you look over here, sir, you'll see a red cross and an area around it. I was trying to see if I could match that to something on this one.'

'And?'

'I don't know. It looks like a park or something similar. Lots of greenery, and maybe the cross marks this building here. A farmhouse, maybe?'

'Good work, young lady. I think while Navrátil drives west with Valentin, you and I might drive east to have a look around.'

Peiperová's eyes were bright with the excitement of the chase. 'We'd better get going, sir. It's three hundred and seventy kilometres to Opava. It'll take about five hours.'

Slonský reflected on this. 'Five hours there, five hours back, a couple of hours snooping around, that makes twelve hours. There's time for a good breakfast before we go.'

'Are you sure, sir?'

'Oh, yes. There's always time for a good breakfast.'

The drive to Opava was quite enjoyable. The best car they could get was a liveried one, which suited Slonský anyway since it reduced the chance that the traffic police would make him stop. However, he did stop a couple of times to answer a call of nature and stock up with pastries. Peiperová declined any, which only meant that he had the whole lot to himself, and was still chewing contentedly when they arrived at the end of the main road, the last clear marker on the map.

'Now, take the road to Šumperk. Then there'll be a right turn towards Opava and we follow the road through Bruntál and out towards Velké Heraltice. Somewhere on the left there's a lane into the forest. Once we're there we'll have to scale off the map and just see if we can work out what the cross shows.'

Peiperová continued to drive, but rather slower, glancing to each side in turn as if she did not trust Slonský's powers of observation.

'It's just kilometres and kilometres of damn trees,' Slonský complained.

'That's what forests are, sir.'

'Is it something buried in the woods then?'

'Sir, should we stop and ask somebody?'

'Actually, that may be a good idea. Let's go into Opava and find the police station. Maybe they'll know.'

The criminal police office at Hrnčířská 22 did not take much finding, and after introducing themselves at the desk they were taken to the office of Captain Herfort. They laid out their map and invited him to offer a suggestion. The Captain looked at it for some time, rubbing his chin reflectively, and then sent for the desk sergeant.

'Any ideas, Sergeant?'

'Isn't that the old baron's house, sir?'

'The old baron's house?' Slonský echoed.

'Well, it's not easy to be exact. But the estate had a big house and a lodge. The big house has fallen into disrepair and nowadays the owners live in the lodge, but that's nearer to the road than the cross here.'

'There's your answer,' said Herfort. 'I should have realised that was what you were asking about, what with the trouble this spring.'

'Trouble? What trouble?'

Herfort looked bemused. 'I thought that was what you'd finally come about. There was an arson attack on the lodge this spring. Fortunately it's well built and the arsonists were inept, but we reported it to Prague and nothing happened.'

'Why did you report it?'

'The attackers were overheard speaking. They were foreigners. The old couple weren't sure what language they spoke, but they understood a few words so it must have been a Slav language, I suppose. Anyway, since it was down to foreigners we thought we'd better tell Prague. Then a month or so later someone mischievously dammed the stream so it diverted into the grounds and flooded the lawn. I reported that too. We didn't have any evidence that it was the same men but it was pretty suspicious, I thought.'

'I'd have thought it too,' mused Slonský. 'So why didn't Prague?'

He was still pondering the question as they left.

'What now, sir?' asked Peiperová.

'When in doubt, eat. Let's find somewhere for lunch. We can think at the same time. But not here. Let's get nearer to the site of interest.'

They drove back the way they had come and stopped at the nearest village to the forest turning. Peiperová parked in the main street and they surveyed the options.

'Aha!' Slonský cried. 'Exactly what we need — a couple of old codgers.' He marched over and introduced himself. 'We're investigating the nuisances up at the old baron's house. Know the one I mean?'

'Yes,' said one of the old men, who gave his name as Jan. 'I worked there when I was a boy, on the estate.'

'Oh, yes?' said Slonský, squeezing onto the bench alongside them and motioning Peiperová to sit down without indicating where that would be possible given the lack of seats.

'That was before the war, of course, when the baron was still there. He was a gent. Of course, the estate was much bigger then. A lot more going on, what with the farm and the shooting.'

'It's all forest,' said Slonský. 'What sort of farming could you do there?'

'It wasn't so overgrown then,' the second old man, who introduced himself as Jakub, explained. 'It was surrounded by forest, but there were clearings and paddocks, and a few pens. They farmed pigs and deer mainly. But the big money came from the shoots. They ran boar hunts every year, wild in summer and driven in autumn. Us boys used to earn some pocket money driving the boar.'

'Wasn't that dangerous?'

'Life was dangerous then,' Jakub said. 'We didn't think about it. If there were a few of you in a row, and you kept your wits about you, the boar would retreat rather than take you on. Unless a sow had young there, of course. And you had to be careful at this time of year, because the boars have bad eyesight, and if they thought you were after their sows in rutting season they'd have you. But we'd get twenty of us and we'd drive the boars back with the men. It was good money. The baron paid a fair wage, but if they had a good day's shooting you could get a fortune in tips.'

Jan agreed. 'I once took home more silver from a day than my dad got for a week.' He chuckled in a mad old man sort of way, then continued. 'One of the hunters was pretty useless. I think he was a city boy out to impress the baron's daughter, but he had no sense about where the boar would be and he could barely get a shot off. I'd spotted a big old tusker limping because he'd got his legs tangled in some fence wire, so I told the young gentleman to drift off to his left and watch at the fringe of the wood, and I'd drive the tusker his way. Which I did, and somehow he went down. I don't know whether the young man shot him or he just died of old age waiting. Anyhow, the young feller slipped me a handful of silver for that one, about as much as I got in a month in the fields.'

'Ah, they were good days,' agreed Jakub.

Slonský wanted them to keep talking but his stomach was providing a bass continuo to the discussion. 'Where's the best place to get a beer and a sausage here?'

Jakub jerked a thumb over his shoulder. 'Over there. But they won't serve your daughter. Men only, that place. You could try the café with the green door on that side of the street.'

'That would be good. Would you care to join us, and we can chat a bit more about the old baron?'

479

The old men were quite happy to toddle over and, gently pressed by Slonský, conceded that a sausage and some potatoes would go down very nicely. And perhaps a few fried onions and some red cabbage, with a slab of fresh bread and a large beer.

When they were all supplied with a glass and some cutlery, Slonský resumed the questioning. 'So what happened to the baron?'

'The war,' said Jakub. 'He was German, you see. Well, over three-quarters of the people were. They all spoke German, the street signs were in German. They called Opava "Troppau" then. Us Czechs were a minority, and didn't we know it? They even wanted us taught in German in school. As far as they were concerned, this should never have been Czechoslovakia, so when Hitler came along they got the swastika flags out and welcomed him. In no time at all they'd burned the synagogue down. Mind, I don't hold with Christ-murderers, but it was a fine building.'

'The bit that got me,' Jan chipped in, 'was that some of them doing the burning were Jews themselves, rightfully speaking, but they saw which way the wind was blowing. Anyway, the baron went off to fight for Germany on the Russian front and never came back.'

'Any heirs?'

'He had an older brother in Austria somewhere, and his daughter. She would be about twenty when the war ended. Then all the Germans were kicked out of this country when the war ended and their property was confiscated.'

'The Beneš decrees,' murmured Slonský.

'That's right. The plan was to sell it all off, although who could afford to buy an estate like that I don't know, seeing as nobody I knew had a copper to scratch their … had two coppers to rub together, I mean, miss.'

Jakub was nodding vigorously. 'It was a crying shame. The communists came along and that put paid to selling it off, but they didn't know what to do with it. In the end they carved some bits off to make smallholdings and rented out the lodge. I can't remember who got it first, but the folks who are there now came in the seventies. They'd been farmers in Slovakia, near the Polish border, so they knew a bit about boars and stags. They stopped the rot, but they've never had the cash to get it back on its feet like it should be.'

'And now some evil devil goes and tries to burn them out,' Jan growled.

'I've heard there were some foreigners in the district around then,' said Slonský.

'I heard that too,' agreed Jakub. 'But there always are.'

'These might have been Bosnians,' Slonský hinted.

'If they stayed somewhere here wouldn't you lot know from the pensions and guest houses?' asked Jan. 'I thought they had to report foreign guests to you.'

'I doubt they stayed anywhere nearby. I think they just came for the day and then left. Any idea what happened to the baron's daughter?'

The old men stared into their glasses, which were almost empty. Slonský called the waiter over and ordered refills for them.

'That's very civil of you, thanks,' Jan said with a toothless smile. 'Well, now, I don't know for sure, but I heard that she'd married a soldier. Not her own class, of course, because there weren't any of them left, but at least she was safe from being molested. A lot of the women were, you know. It was shameful. And Czech hands weren't exactly clean in all that.'

'The Slovaks were worse,' protested Jakub.

'Goes without saying,' Jan agreed. 'They always are.'

Slonský unfolded his map. 'So if this cross is the old baron's house, what's that dotted line?'

The old men pored over it.

'See, Jakub, this little bit that sticks out, that'll be the old mill at the bend of the stream.'

'Yes, then this line here must follow the ridge or the path. And that's the big barn.'

They traced the line a bit further, than Jakub sat back in his seat.

'I reckon that's the old boundary, before they started selling bits off. That's what it was before the war.'

Navrátil's call was brief and to the point. The women in the camp did not recognise the old baron's house and denied stopping anywhere near a forest, except for a brief toilet stop.

'So where does that leave us, sir?' asked Peiperová. 'I don't get why Hrdlička would have a map of Opava showing a pre-war estate and not tell anyone about it. Maybe it has nothing to do with the case.'

'Maybe. But his wife hasn't got a clue either, and that argues for police work. Men talk about their hobbies to their wives, even if the women aren't interested, but it's hammered into us not to talk about cases.'

'But he didn't tell his bosses either.'

'We don't know that. We're deducing it because they've said nothing about it. If the notes we saw are all that exist, he didn't mention it, but they could be holding something back.'

'Would they do that to us, sir?'

'I don't see why not. I would. And now that I know that Grigar was having Navrátil followed, they'll have to pull my teeth out to get anything out of me.'

'You don't think they'd follow Navrátil to the camp, sir?'

'No, for three reasons. Navrátil's driving would make them give up through boredom. He's too bright not to spot he's being followed and if he did, he's good enough to shake them off. And even if they get to the camp gates, the army won't let them in without my say-so. Soldiers may not be too clever but they can follow a nice simple order.'

'Why do you say they're not clever?'

'If they were clever they wouldn't join an organisation that exists to get them shot at. Let's find out what happened to the report from Opava about the arson attack.'

'I got a photocopy of their file copy, sir.'

'Good girl. We can get Sergeant Mucha onto that. He's a wizard with filing systems and bureaucracy.'

'The sergeant at Opava told me they had a phone call from someone in Prague thanking them for the report and telling them it was being followed up, but he didn't see how it could have been when nobody went out there to have a look around.'

'Well, that stands to reason. If nobody said anything, Opava might think it hadn't arrived and get back in touch. If you want to kill it, you tell them it's here and being dealt with. Then you do nothing about it and with luck they'll forget they ever sent it.'

'Will that work, sir?'

'It always has for me. But that just makes this more of a puzzle. If Hrdlička doesn't want his bosses to know about Opava, why is that? Let's assume it's connected with the person he's listening in on. Grigar doesn't seem to know who that is, judging by the efforts he's going to to find out. But if it was Bosnians who burned the lodge — and I grant we don't know that for sure, before you butt in — then it's logical that he'd be listening in to Savović.'

'And if he isn't using a police-issue earpiece, that suggests that he thought someone would stop him doing it if they found out.'

'But why not just call him off? Why leave him watching the place but not give him the tools to do a proper job? It makes no sense.'

'Maybe he was acting on his own initiative, sir.'

'Come on, girl, use your brain. I'm as generous and understanding a boss as you could wish to have, but if you swan off all day every day I'm going to want to know where you are.'

'But you don't watch us that closely, sir.'

'I know you went to the ladies' three times on Friday.'

Peiperová's mouth dropped open. 'How can you possibly know that, sir?'

'I know everything. And what I don't know I make up convincingly, as I just demonstrated. You see, if you'd known you'd gone twice, or four times, you'd have known I was bluffing, but in the absence of any information, you swallowed my story. There's a lesson there, my girl.'

He then clammed up without elucidating what exactly the lesson was, and remained silent all the way back to Prague, except to remind Peiperová that she could put the flashing lights on and drive at a hundred and forty if she felt like it, given that they were in a car with POLICIE displayed prominently on each side.

Chapter 11

Valentin's paper had gone to town in its Monday edition. The story of the Balkan women was spread over six pages and was liberally illustrated. Slonský could not help noticing that the women were all dressed either in white or in embroidered peasant blouses.

'Whose idea was that?' he asked Navrátil.

'Mr Valentin's, sir. He said it emphasised their innocence. He made a couple of them take out nose studs and cover tattoos too, to increase public sympathy for their plight.'

'A typical journalist's disregard for the truth,' scowled Slonský, 'and I'm only jealous because it's a good idea. It's a bit rich of that brunette to claim that she fought tooth and nail to preserve her honour when you saw the eyes she was making at the lieutenant when they arrived.'

'Sir!' protested Peiperová. 'An invitation to be friendly doesn't mean that more is on offer.'

'I wouldn't know,' sighed Slonský. 'I haven't even had an invitation to be friendly for years.'

'I think this may help us, sir,' Navrátil said. 'I wondered what made Hrdlička turn his attention to Opava, because if the report from the station there was intercepted, I don't see how he could have seen it. Now, the copy that Peiperová brought back says the arson attack took place in early May. I went through Hrdlička's credit card and bank statements to see if he spent any money in that area, but he didn't. However, on Wednesday, 7th June, Hrdlička used his bank card in a book shop here in Prague. I went over there and they went through their till records, and that's when he bought the map.'

'7th June? Good work, Navrátil. Very enterprising. Remind me again, how does this help?'

'Well, I'm not sure. But something must have happened just before then to spur him to buy the map. And he didn't just requisition a police map, so he was already suspicious about a colleague then. Isn't the logical reason that he knew the Opava report had been suppressed?'

'Yes, but how did he discover that?'

'Maybe he overheard something.'

'He wasn't eavesdropping then. Remember the goddess said he'd only been there for a month or so.'

'She also said his name was Pavel and that turned out to be wrong.'

'Yes, but he could have told her that was his name to make himself hard to trace. She would know for herself how long he'd been standing beside her. Don't look so crestfallen, lad. I'm sure you're right, but I can't prove it, and we'll need proof if it goes to court. And it would certainly help the investigation if we could find out what put him on to Opava.'

'Sir,' Peiperová interrupted, 'can we find out what he was doing when he picked this up? It must have linked in his mind to an existing enquiry, and he can't have been tracking the Bosnians because none of us knew about them until a few days ago.'

'Error there, Peiperová. We didn't know these particular Bosnians, but that doesn't preclude someone else looking for a bunch of Bosnians who just happened to be the same as ours. If they are the same, which we don't know. But maybe you're on to something. Let's see if we can find out what Hrdlička was investigating in early June. We're going to have to ask Grigar. If we're not going to give the game away it'll require extreme tact and sensitivity. You two had better leave the talking to me.'

Grigar's office was empty, but the other desk there was occupied by a sandy-haired lieutenant. He was probably in his early thirties, though his hair had receded markedly at the temples which made him appear a little older. He must have been touchy about the matter, because he had combed his hair forward and across to conceal as much of the bare temple as possible. He introduced himself as Lieutenant Erben, and offered to help in any way he could.

'I'm investigating the murder of Officer Hrdlička.'

'Yes, sir. A shocking incident. Are you making progress?'

'Steadily, Erben. We believe that the attack may not be linked to this case, but to an earlier one. Can you give us details of the work Hrdlička has been doing over the past twelve months?'

Erben looked puzzled. 'I suppose so. It'll take a day or two. But I thought he'd been on the current case for over six months.'

'But what is the current case exactly? Tell us from the beginning.'

'We've been trying to shut down a protection and vice racket.'

'Protection and vice? Together? Isn't that a bit unsporting of them?'

'The suggestion was that someone was bringing girls in for the clubs. That's gone on for a long time. What was making this different was that they were threatening clubs that didn't take their girls.'

'It's coming to something when criminals come running to us for protection.'

'They didn't — not in so many words anyway. The thing with vice is that it's different.'

'How do you mean? Not like volleyball, not like ice cream…?'

485

'I mean that there's always going to be vice, so the best we can do is to keep it orderly. Someone coming in and upsetting the status quo usually leads to an increase in crime, so we try to avoid that. Better the devil you know, you see.'

'So you heard these people were rocking the boat and decided to track them down?'

'Yes, sir. But it's all done through intermediaries and we weren't getting anywhere. We trailed a couple of them to that building on the riverside but we weren't sure how that fitted in, so Hrdlička came up with a plan to watch the building and see just who came and went.'

'And what did he see?'

Erben looked uncomfortable. 'We don't really know. He made very few reports and the ones we got were very sketchy. He mentioned a property tycoon but when we looked into it that came to nothing.'

'Rudolf Smejkal?'

'You already know this?' stuttered Erben.

'I know lots of things,' Slonský said, fixing Erben with a gimlet eye. 'Lots and lots of things, some of which would make your hair curl.'

Erben appeared bewildered, but said nothing.

'Very good,' said Slonský. 'You've been very helpful, Lieutenant Erben. Please give my regards to Captain Grigar. He and I go back a long way together. Unless he's been up to something, of course, in which event we've never met. Come along, children.'

Slonský strode purposefully along the corridor, causing Peiperová to trot and Navrátil to jog to keep up.

'Did that get us anywhere, sir?' Peiperová enquired.

'Oh, yes. I begin to see light at the end of the tunnel. Or, at least, I can see where the tunnel is.'

'Where are we going now, sir?'

'To the hub of human existence, Peiperová. A place of happiness and plenty, called the staff canteen. My stomach thinks my throat's been cut. I've left my wallet in my coat — either of you got any money?'

Mucha was an indoor sort of policeman. He had done his time on the beat, but now he expected to see out the rest of his career as a desk sergeant, which meant he would be inside in the warm, with plenty of coffee on hand and, as senior sergeant and therefore compiler of the staff rota, regular hours. Except, of course, when his wife's sister came to stay, when he frequently discovered an urgent need to work overtime.

When he ventured outside, it was usually to go to another police building, because Mucha was a walking compendium of administrative lore. There was very little he did not know about filing, police procedures and the stuff that used to go on that nobody wanted to talk about. Archives that allegedly did not exist were open to him, because it was self-evident to their custodians that if he knew of the archives, he must have access to them. Over thirty-five years he had accumulated a lot of contacts which he was prepared to use shamelessly, and his own blameless police career meant that he was immune from reprisals if he felt like a little honest blackmailing of a colleague who might know something useful to him.

The task with which Slonský had entrusted him was an intriguing one. Trying to track the path of a police report was never quite as straightforward as it should have been, particularly if someone had attempted to conceal the traces. However, just as Dr Novák could trace a fibre carried from a room, so Mucha knew where the less obvious evidence of a document's path might be.

He began with the fax machine to which the arson report had been sent. Like all police machines, it had a built-in journal. This was printed out when it was full, and filed "just in case", like everything else in the police was filed "just in case", and Mucha knew where it would be. Having verified receipt, he discovered from the log where it had been routed, and duly photocopied the relevant page. He debated whether to head there next, but decided that Slonský might not want him to alert the officer concerned, so instead he used his initiative to look for any sign that the damming of the stream had been reported. It appeared about three weeks later in the log, and had been routed to another officer, but the name was crossed out and another written in. The obvious conclusion was that Officer A had suggested that it should go to Officer B who had received the original arson report, since it was likely to be perpetrated by the same villains. That in turn led to the conclusion that it was common knowledge that Officer B was dealing with the arson report, which was quite likely because Officers A and B worked in the same department.

Mucha buttoned up his greatcoat, carefully replaced his cap, and stepped out into the street. There is no doubt that a bit of inspiration works wonders sometimes, and a little voice was telling him that he ought to pay a visit to Gazdík.

Before there was Technician Spehar, there was Gazdík. The difference between them was that while Spehar was organised, technologically highly literate, and recognised his limitations, so that he employed others who, whatever their other characteristics, knew their stuff when it came to gadgetry, Gazdík refused to acknowledge any restrictions on his knowledge and surrounded himself with people who knew less than he did so as not to look bad. This probably went some way towards explaining why he had taken early retirement. He now ran a small repair shop where you could take a poorly performing radio to have it comprehensively ruined.

The little bell over the door announced Mucha's arrival, and Gazdík was pathetically pleased to see an old colleague. He insisted on making them both a coffee with a little something extra to keep out the cold, though since he was surrounded by two-bar electric fires and his soldering iron was in use, hypothermia seemed an unlikely prospect.

'It's always good to see someone from the old days,' Gazdík enthused. They reminisced together for a few minutes, while Mucha waited for his coffee to go cold so he could legitimately throw it away.

'I need a bit of technical help with a case,' Mucha explained, 'and I immediately thought of you.'

'That's nice,' said Gazdík. 'Not that Spehar isn't a good man.'

'Of course not, but this is a bit unusual. The fact is, an undercover policeman has been killed, and we can't go through normal channels for reasons I'm not at liberty to explain.'

'Oh, no, I completely understand,' Gazdík agreed. 'Mum's the word in cases like that.'

'Exactly. I knew you'd appreciate the subtleties. Well, it seems the officer in question had a listening device that he didn't get from us — for a perfectly good reason that I can't share with you.'

'Understood. Lips sealed.'

'Good man. Now, I got to thinking where a police officer would go to get one of those that wasn't official, but run by someone of proven discretion and probity. And that brought me to you.'

'Me?'

'Of course. Who else understands better that the police need to do these things now and again and that if official channels have to be ruled out…'

'For perfectly good reasons that we can't discuss…'

'Precisely, then of course a young police officer would come to you for advice. And, who knows, you might be able to find him something suitable that was no longer needed elsewhere.'

'Past its useful life, you mean?'

'That's right.'

'Of no value, so nobody would be too worried about getting it back?'

'Got it in one.'

'Well, of course old colleagues come from time to time. Do you have any extra information you can share?'

'He wanted a short range microphone and a radio earpiece. It looks like a little bean.'

Gazdík hopped off his stool and rummaged in a couple of boxes. 'Like this?' he asked.

Mucha had not actually seen the earpiece found in Hrdlička's helmet, but it looked like the description he had. 'Very like that. It would have been in the last month or so.'

'Then I think I may be able to assist. A young officer came to ask me for some help.'

'His name?'

'I didn't ask. I remembered him from my time, but he was very new then. These youngsters, there are so many that their names don't stick, you know?'

Mucha nodded, even though he disagreed. He could remember almost everyone's name. 'Did he explain why he couldn't use a police microphone?'

'No, and I knew better than to ask. I assumed he must have been in the traffic police, because he had silver paint behind his ear like he'd been hanging around a paint spray workshop, but he explained he needed a radio that would transmit perhaps sixty metres, and a small microphone he could conceal in an office. So that's what I gave him.'

Mucha pulled his cap on once more. 'You've been a great help,' he said. 'Perhaps some time when you're passing you can drop in to formally identify the earpiece. But ring first to make sure I'm there. I don't want other people knowing our business.'

'Certainly,' grinned Gazdík. 'Not a sound from me.'

Slonský knew Mucha had discovered something important when he saw the sergeant coming to his office still wearing his hat and coat. Mucha ignored the invitation to speak in the corridor and grabbed Slonský's arm, propelling him into the office and closing the door behind them.

Navrátil glanced up and saw the tension in Mucha's face. 'Do you want me to go, sir?' he asked.

Slonský raised a quizzical eyebrow but Mucha gave a discrete shake of his head. 'No need. But I didn't want everyone here to overhear this. I know where Hrdlička got his earpiece. He went to see Gazdík who set him up with one.'

'Gazdík?' said Slonský. 'Who in their right mind gets anything technical from Gazdík? He must have been desperate.'

'Or gone to the only person he thought a senior officer couldn't have nobbled. And I also know where the reports from Opava went to.' He unfolded the photocopies of the two pages and indicated the relevant lines. Navrátil was too distant to read them, but he could see the effect they had on Slonský, whose blood pressure rose sharply, causing his cheeks to redden and his nostrils to flare. Navrátil just had time to note the resemblance to an enraged bull before Slonský seized the pages savagely and threw the door open.

'Someone has some explaining to do,' he growled, stomping along the corridor and flinging another door so fiercely that its hinges squealed in protest.

The occupant was sitting at his desk in his shirtsleeves reading a report while chomping on a sandwich. He froze in mid-chew when he saw that Slonský appeared displeased about something.

'What?' said Dvorník.

'Of all the half-witted, cheese-brained nincompoops who have ever worked here,' began Slonský, 'you stand in a league of your own.'

'Why?' asked Dvorník reasonably, having taken the view that more than one word might be construed as provocative.

'Explain this to me,' Slonský snapped, and waved the pages in front of Dvorník.

'I don't know a thing about the arson report,' Dvorník protested, 'but when the stream incident came down the line and the station in Opava said they'd already reported the arson, I thought the same officer should deal with both enquiries. It seemed logical at the time.'

'So how did you find out which officer that was?'

'I asked the fax office who they'd given the arson report to.'

'And they said?'

'They said Lieutenant Doležal. So I went to see him and handed the stream one over.'

Slonský was not mollified. 'And it never crossed your mind to ask him why he'd done nothing in three weeks about the arson?'

'Of course it did. Well, not in so many words. I asked how it was going, and he said that Organised Crime had rung to take it off him because it was connected with an enquiry they were running, so he'd passed it on.'

Slonský straightened up and took a step back. 'I'll come back for you later.'

Doležal was more inclined to be combative. He agreed that he had received the arson report, and that Organised Crime had asked him to turn the report over to them.

'And you didn't think to tell Opava that?'

'If Organised Crime were already liaising with them about a case, they'd mention it, wouldn't they?'

'And if someone in Organised Crime was covering up a case he wouldn't, would he? And you would just have made that a damn sight easier for him. And you didn't ask Organised Crime to keep us informed?'

'It's their case. You can't ask them to report to us.'

'You can if it's ordinary crime. What evidence did they give you that organised crime was involved in this in any way?'

'Their word,' responded Doležal indignantly. 'If you can't trust a fellow policeman, what's the world coming to?'

Slonský seized Navratil by the collar, dragged him forward and pointed at him accusingly. 'Navrátil here is as simple and trusting as they come, and even he doesn't trust Organised Crime to tell us the truth. They spend their whole lives around hardened criminals. Some of it's bound to rub off. Now, think, man: who asked for the file?'

Doležal shrugged. 'I don't know. It was just a phone call.'

'And you didn't wonder how they knew about a case that had only just been faxed to us here?'

Doležal shuffled uncomfortably. 'No. Perhaps they'd discovered it by other means. They have their own informers, you know.'

'Thank you for reminding me,' Slonský hissed icily. 'Let me help you remember something in exchange. I am only Acting Captain at present, but I hear Captain Lukas may not be fit to return. If so, I shall apply for his job, and I expect to get it. And when I do you will be spending the rest of your career in a one-man police station in one of those villages where everyone is everyone else's uncle and half of them look like sheep. Do I make myself clear?'

'I think you're being unfair,' Doležal protested.

'I haven't started yet,' yelled Slonský. 'I can get a damn sight more vindictive than this, believe me. I have given forty years of my life to this police force. Through good and bad times, I believed it was the best hope we had, and that it housed some good people who one day, God willing, would see justice restored and corruption ended. Yes, there have been some useless idiots, some clueless bosses and some outright dishonest ones, but I've sweated blood for this force. And a good officer has been killed because he couldn't trust someone above him. You made that possible, Doležal. You didn't ask some obvious questions, and Hrdlička is dead as a result. It's just as well for you you're only terminally stupid, because if I thought you were corrupt as well you'd be dangling over the stairwell hoping your shirt collar is well attached. And the only thing that would stop me dropping you is that I'd be worried some poor innocent would be minding his own business in the basement when you landed on him.'

Doležal straightened his jacket and attempted to retain whatever dignity he had left. 'You're overwrought,' he said. 'Despite that, if anything occurs to me, I'll make an immediate report.'

Peiperová was on edge. She knew that what she was doing could go very badly wrong and, if it did, she would only have herself to blame. It would probably mean the end of her career in Prague even if she survived it, which was by no means certain; but she could think of nothing more constructive than to retrace Daniela's steps trying to work out where she had been kidnapped.

It had been barely thirty minutes between saying goodbye to Daniela and seeing the holdall thrown at their car. That was scarcely long enough for anyone to go anywhere with Daniela. She had not gone home, but her passport would not be there, so the assumption must be that the Bosnians had just picked up a bag of clothes, dropped the passport in, and actually had it with them while they were watching. But whose bag would be packed?

Milena, the girl who killed herself. Her things would have been put in a bag. They kept the bag and now they had disposed of it in such a way as to make us think it was Daniela's. The plan only failed because we were able to find where Daniela lived and discovered her clothes were still there.

Peiperová rang Spehar and informed him of her suspicions. If they ever found Milena's body, there might be DNA on something in the bag that would help to identify it.

'I've already set that horse running,' Spehar replied. 'They're checking the hairbrush and nail files first, but eventually they'll do the lot. I can tell you one thing — if your description of Daniela is accurate, it's not her hairbrush. The hairs are blonde.'

'Thanks. I'll keep looking for her.'

'It's not my business,' Spehar began, 'and I'm no detective, but how do you plan to do that?'

'I'm going to guess her route and look for places where she could be snatched without anyone noticing. After all, it was Saturday afternoon. There were plenty of people around. Even the Prague public would tell us if they saw a girl being forced into a car. Then the car must have parked up somewhere until they found us and dropped off the holdall.'

'Must they? Let's say it takes two men to grab a girl and push her into a car. I'll grant that one could hardly do it, unless he knocked her unconscious first. But once they've got her into the car, one can drive off, and the other hops out with the holdall.'

'But if she isn't unconscious, she can get out of the car if the other one is driving.'

'Then she was unconscious, or there were three of them, or she was too scared to get out because, for example, he had a gun.'

'She'd have to be stupid to walk down an alleyway,' Peiperová murmured.

'No, she wouldn't,' Spehar argued. 'She just needs to know her way around. If you're familiar with it, you don't think of the threat. I'm forever telling my daughters not to go down one of our local streets at night, but they say they've walked it all their lives. I'll bet she followed her normal way home. If she didn't, how could they lie in wait for her?'

Peiperová thanked Spehar for the suggestion and consulted her map. There was a walk of perhaps two hundred metres along the street from the café to a cross alley. The right branch could lead her home, but if she turned left she would come out almost at the side of the Purple Apple. She and Navrátil had gone a different way because they always had a car, but for a pedestrian the alley was much the shortest route.

Standing at its entry Peiperová could see how dark it was, the buildings on each side being three or four storeys tall, but you could never get a car along it with all these waste bins in the way. Peiperová contemplated telephoning Navrátil to tell him where she was, just in case of any untoward event, but decided not to do so because he would almost certainly tell her not to be so reckless, so she picked her way through the discarded cabbage leaves and newspapers, looking for a place where a car could be waiting. She walked all the way to the end, where the alley opened onto a broad, busy street, without finding a parking space, and took her bearings. If Daniela made it this far, she was almost home. She would turn left, walk along the street to the crossing, and then she would follow a residential street towards Mrs Pimenová's bakery and thence to the hostel. It was a longer journey by car, but quite a short walk; no wonder she said she wouldn't need an hour to walk both ways and pack a bag. But however you looked at it, logic said she disappeared in the alley. It was the only private place.

Peiperová retraced her steps, looking for a gate behind which a car could have been parked. She had walked about two-thirds of the alleyway when she saw a wooden gate, not in the best of condition, beside which there was a small notice on the wall.

It read 'Double Arrow Import Export Agency.'

Slonský was pleased to have something useful to do. Being in an unusually prudent turn of mind, he looked around for some marksmen to give him armed protection, but there were none around. He did, however, spot a familiar silhouette making its way towards the front door.

'Dvorník!' he bellowed. 'Not so fast.'

Dvorník's aversion to overtime was soon subdued by the prospect of being allowed to shoot someone, so he rushed to collect some extra ammunition and gave his pistol a cursory check before pronouncing himself satisfied.

'Just to get this straight,' he asked, 'who am I shooting again?'

'You're not shooting anyone,' said Slonský, 'unless it becomes absolutely necessary.'

'I see,' said Dvorník. 'And what might make it necessary?'

'Well,' Slonský answered, 'a detective might run amok if he's asked any more stupid questions. We're going to search a warehouse, and there may be some people there who object to having it searched.'

'I see. And what are we looking for?'

'A Bosnian girl. And don't ask me what she looks like. If we find any women tied up there, whatever they look like, we'll assume they're what we're looking for, all right?'

'Crystal clear,' agreed Dvorník. After a brief pause he continued. 'Shooting to bring down or to kill?'

Slonský bit his tongue. 'Use your initiative. If they're unarmed and no threat, it's probably best if you don't kill them.'

Navrátil drove them across town to the alleyway, where Peiperová was waiting at the end nearer the café. With the car parked, the three detectives joined her to walk to the old gate.

'Navrátil, I think you and Peiperová should go round to the other side of the building. There may be another entrance.'

'I've already looked, sir,' replied Peiperová. 'There's a roller door where trucks can back up but it's not wide enough to let them reverse inside.'

'Good work. But we still need to cover it in case there are people inside who try to escape. Dvorník, I'd feel happier if you went first.'

'You're leading the investigation,' Dvorník answered. 'Shouldn't you go first?'

'If you think I'm letting you walk behind me with a loaded gun, you've got another thing coming,' responded Slonský. 'Get in front where I can keep an eye on you. And let's all keep as quiet as we can, shall we?'

Peiperová and Navrátil walked off, and after giving them three minutes to get into position Slonský pushed the gate open. There was a crash as a metal bin toppled over.

'Damn!'

'No sign of a response,' Dvorník noted. 'Nobody came to look out. We may have it to ourselves.'

There were steps leading up to a door one floor up. When the buildings were erected they were probably flats, and this would have been the way to the middle floor. The door opened outwards, but it was locked.

'Shall I smash the glass?' Dvorník whispered.

'No need,' Slonský replied. 'Just watch for inquisitive bystanders. We're a bit visible here.' He produced a set of skeleton keys from a pocket of his coat and jiggled them in the lock. 'Bless them,' he said. 'Preserving a nice simple nineteenth-century lock like this. There we are.' He nudged the door further open with his shoulder.

'Is that strictly legal?' asked Dvorník.

'No, but we don't have a warrant,' Slonský replied, 'so it doesn't much matter how we get in, does it?'

'Just asking,' Dvorník shrugged. 'No skin off my nose.'

'Hush and keep walking. Let's see what there is to find here.'

They sidled along the corridor in the gloom. It was easy to see why a wider exit to the warehouse was needed, because it would be very difficult to bring anything substantial in this way. After about twenty paces there was a semi-glazed door, though the glass was so dirty it might as well have been frosted. Cobwebs laced the frame and Slonský could picture Věra feeling the need to give the place a good scrub before going any further.

He motioned Dvorník to keep quiet and they listened at the door. There were no sounds of movement, so Slonský lifted it slightly to prevent it scraping along the floor and eased it open.

The room was large, spanning the whole width of the building, and there was a pulley fixed to a beam which presumably allowed items to be lowered to the floor below. A sling dangled from the pulley, and a guard rail at the far side of the hatch prevented anyone falling from one side. Except that it could not be a rail, because a guard on only one side of a hole made no sense, and someone was slumped against it.

Slonský ran forward while Dvorník crouched with his gun ready, his senses sharpened by the threat he felt. The slumped person was a naked woman, dirty, kneeling at the edge of the hatch with her feet over the drop and her arms fixed to the cross-beam with cable ties which had bitten into her flesh. Her face was bruised, purple, swollen, and her mouth was bloodied where some teeth had been knocked out. She was still breathing, but not strongly.

'Get an ambulance,' Slonský barked.

Dvorník dialled the number and made the call, keeping his back to the wall and his gun raised throughout. 'What's that beside her knee?' he asked.

'Her left ear,' said Slonský. 'God knows where the other one is.'

Chapter 12

Peiperová could hardly grasp the cup. Her hands shook, and she did not know whether it was fear or rage, or a bit of both. 'How could they do that?' she hissed. 'What had Daniela done to them?'

Slonský bit into his *párek*. 'Because they're criminals. Criminals do that sort of thing. And she threatened them. If she just walked away without suffering for it, why would any of the girls stay? They can't lock them up, and they could just walk out of the club, so how do they keep them penned up? They keep their passports, tell them they'll be arrested by the likes of us, and beat up the odd girl to keep the others in check.'

'It's barbaric.'

'It's life. Get used to it. People do things like that. Or worse.'

Navrátil stared into his cup. 'Did the surgeon say…?'

'He can't reattach the ears, but he's taken a mould off each and he says the cosmetic surgeon can build her new ones from cartilage and skin and you'd never know. It'll take a few months, though.'

Peiperová stifled a sob by pushing her handkerchief into her mouth.

'Let it out, girl. But the most useful thing you can do for her is to punish the people who did it.'

'Savović and Brukić.'

Slonský swilled beer round his mouth to dislodge adhesive pieces of sausage. 'A bit of evidence would be nice before jumping to conclusions.'

'Who else?' asked Peiperová.

'Unfortunately, lass, the courts don't take kindly to "Who else?" as a prosecution argument.'

Navrátil pushed his plate away untasted.

'Eat up, lad,' ordered Slonský. 'You'll need that this evening.'

'I'm not really hungry, sir.'

Slonský patted the grease from his lips with a napkin. 'Let me explain why you should eat. It's late afternoon, and shortly we're going to go to the red brick building to arrest Nejedlý. Let's hope he's in, because this is carefully timed for maximum impact. We'll make a lot of noise about it so it'll get back to his associates. Then we'll bring him to the station and start questioning him. We only have to feed him after he has been with us for six hours, so he won't get anything to eat or drink until around eleven tonight, whereas you and I will be nicely fed and watered, provided we eat all our tea now. That gives us an advantage, Navrátil, and I want to keep it that way, so don't let me down. Get stuck in.'

'Can I help, sir?' Peiperová chipped in.

'We can only have two doing the questioning, but you can come on the arrest if you like. If he has a secretary you can tell her in lurid detail what we suspect her boss has been doing. She may have some interesting details of her own to add.'

The doorman half rose when they entered, but when he saw who they were he resumed his seat and decided to keep out of it. Slonský bounded up the stairs and pushed open the door of Nejedlý's outer office.

'Do you have an appointment?' the secretary screeched.

'No, but I've got one of these,' Slonský responded, waving his badge and nodding to Peiperová to stay in the outer office with the secretary.

Nejedlý was riffling through the files in a cabinet when they entered. 'And you are…?' he asked.

'Your worst nightmare,' came the answer.

'I'm not saying anything till my lawyer gets here,' Nejedlý repeated yet again.

'Who's asking you to say anything?' Slonský replied. 'Have I asked you a single question yet?'

'No,' conceded Nejedlý, 'but why am I here if not to answer questions?'

'Identity parade.'

'Identity parade? At this time of day?'

Slonský shrugged. 'If the crime was committed at night…' he began.

'What crime?'

'The crime you're accused of.'

'Which is?'

'I'm not telling you till your lawyer gets here. Two can play at that game.'

Nejedlý fidgeted a bit, folding and unfolding his arms. The silence continued for a while as Slonský read the newspaper and Navrátil stared into space.

'I suppose we're waiting for the others to get here,' Nejedlý offered.

'The others?'

'For the identity parade.'

'No, you're the only one.'

'How can you have an identity parade with only one person?'

'The law just requires that I have a sufficient number of others. And since I know you're guilty zero seems like a sufficient number to me.'

'Guilty? Of what?'

'I told you,' said Slonský. 'I'm not answering questions until your lawyer is present.'

'I'm entitled to know what I'm being accused of.'

Slonský pondered for a few moments. 'I suppose you're right,' he conceded. 'Let's start with trafficking women for immoral purposes. That should put you away for a generation or so. Sentences average out at twelve years but you've done a few runs and since your associates are nasty people a bit of their sentences will probably rub off on you. I'll be disappointed if you don't get a twenty year stretch. Don't you agree, Navrátil?'

'Yes, sir.'

Nejedlý puffed out his chest. 'Let's see what evidence you've got for this trafficking guff, then.'

Slonský raised the thick folder in front of him. 'Sworn statements from the trafficked girls, video footage of your vehicles crossing borders, sale of motorway toll coupons, and of course photographs of one of your warehouses with a half-dead naked woman tied to a beam while your friends cut her ears off.'

Nejedlý was shaken. He tried to regain his composure but it was obvious that he had not known about Daniela's injuries.

'You didn't know about the ears, eh? So what did you think they wanted to borrow your warehouse for? Playing doctors and nurses?' Slonský bellowed.

'I'm not saying…' Nejedlý began, cowering under the verbal attack.

'…any more till your lawyer gets here. We heard. We hear it all the time. But people do. You see, you can't afford to wait until your lawyer gets here. I wouldn't mind betting that your associates know you're here by now. They attacked Daniela so she couldn't speak to us, and she had nothing very useful to say. Imagine what they'll do to you once I let you go. There's probably a big black car on its way now. Waiting for your lawyer pretty well guarantees that they'll get here in time to practise their carving skills. Even better, your lawyer may insist on your being released until your trial. So all in all, we're happy to sit tight and wait.' Slonský inspected his watch. 'Oh, it's our coffee break. We'll leave you to think for a minute or two.' Slonský ushered the uniformed officer into the room and carefully closed the door. 'Sergeant Salzer is a good man. He has one great quality — he barely speaks. I like that in a policeman.'

He peered through the observation port. Salzer had emphasised his unwillingness to engage in conversation by pulling his chair away from the table a metre or two and was staring out Nejedlý in the manner of a heavyweight boxer at a weigh-in. Slonský had ensured that Salzer knew exactly what Nejedlý was being accused of, and Salzer, who had a daughter of Daniela's age, was going to do nothing except transmitting contempt through the air. Twenty years ago Salzer might have given Nejedlý a little tap with a clenched fist just to emphasise his feelings, but in the modern, democratic Czech Republic where there was a rule of law, he would content himself with throwing the little worm into his cell with undue force a bit later. Of course, there was the added pleasure of not offering the accused a sip of water for five hours and fifty-nine minutes, so Salzer had set the alarm on his watch to ensure he did not inadvertently offer it earlier.

'Well, that went well,' Slonský pronounced.

'Did it, sir?'

'Oh, yes.'

'What was in the folder, sir?'

'Eh? Oh, it's Doležal's personnel file. Can't think what that was doing on my desk. Now on to phase two. Klinger is waiting upstairs for his turn to question the suspect, so perhaps you'd like to go and fetch him, Navrátil. An hour or so cloistered with Klinger and Nejedlý will know what true terror is.'

Klinger was impressive, conceded Slonský. He had never sat in on a financial crime interview before and was quite fascinated, not to say baffled. Klinger rattled off the questions briskly with no change of tone, so it was impossible to tell whether the answers were satisfactory or not, and he kept up a sharp pace, hitting with a question precisely as the last answer tailed away.

Before long Slonský was fairly convinced it all hinged on Nejedlý's answer to question 101a on form 54 — or perhaps it was question 54 on form 101a — and why it did not tally with the answer he had given to question 27 on some other form. This must have been important because Klinger had highlighted it in orange on his photocopy, and if you knew Klinger's method you knew orange was always bad. So was green, but a different kind of bad. And you *never* wanted to see pink on one of your forms.

With a jolt Slonský realised that he must have nodded off briefly because Klinger was now going through the import regulations as they related to Serbian fruit, jotting down numbers on a pad of squared paper and clicking on a calculator before adding figures to a column. In the end the hour with Klinger ran to two hours, eighteen minutes.

'Satisfactory?' asked Slonský as they left the room.

'Yes, thank you,' Klinger answered. 'I think we can demonstrate a very large unpaid tax and duty liability there.'

'How large is "very large"?'

'All his worldly goods and then some. The vehicles are leased, and some of the buildings are rented, so he doesn't actually have a great deal. Or, more accurately, not a great deal that we can't confiscate as ill-gotten proceeds.'

'Couldn't happen to a nicer man. He didn't want to wait for his lawyer, then?'

'I don't recall it being mentioned. Anyway, I'll just write this up, then I'll come down and charge him, then you can hold him until his first hearing, and fraud hearings are notoriously slow in coming up.'

Slonský beamed. 'I do enjoy co-operating with other branches of the police service. We're all here to serve the public, after all. Well, must let you get on. And as soon as Navrátil gets here we'd better ask a bit about the abduction and trafficking.'

'Yes, where is young Navrátil?'

'Gone to get us a couple of hot bacon rolls and some coffee. The rules say the prisoner can be kept without food for six hours but it doesn't say that the same is true for detectives. I thought if we eat them in front of him it may help him work up an appetite.'

Peiperová was employing more subtle questioning skills. Nejedlý's secretary had been struck dumb by the story Peiperová had unfolded for her, so the young officer had suggested a brandy might be just the thing to steady her nerves. One brandy had become three, while Peiperová sipped a glass of mineral water.

The secretary's name was Petra. She was a matronly lady of about fifty who had been with Mr Nejedlý for about four years, having previously worked as an administrator for a theatre company that lost its funding. If she hadn't been desperate she would never have taken the job with Nejedlý who, she said, struck her all along as a wrong 'un, though she could not really say why.

'There were his friends, of course. A man is known by the company he keeps,' she explained.

'My mother used to say that,' Peiperová agreed.

'Mine too. They were rough types. Uncultured. I was surprised, because Mr Nejedlý was a theatre-goer, you know. Comedies, mostly. But not the sort to mix with hooligans like that.'

'Did you see any evidence of girls being trafficked?'

Petra shook her head emphatically. 'No. never. Well, when I say never, I mean hardly ever. He came in one day with a pink handbag he said had been left in one of the lorries. I asked why there would be a handbag in one of our lorries, and he said the driver must have invited a woman into his cab. Well, that was strictly against the rules, but the driver wasn't disciplined for it, so you have to wonder, don't you?'

'But you didn't mention this to anyone?'

'There's no-one to mention it to, dear. There's me and there's Mr Nejedlý. The drivers and warehousemen rarely come in.'

'There's no Mrs Nejedlý?'

'Well, there is and there isn't. I've never met her, but she used to ring in if her monthly payment didn't turn up, so I think they must be divorced. That wasn't happening so much lately, but there was a time when it was going on most months.'

'So things were getting better?'

'I didn't see how. There wasn't much more business. Of course, from what you've said I can see how it might be. Mr Nejedlý was running out of space to keep all these plums he was importing. He gave me a load of tins and he donated some to a homeless shelter, but he kept bringing them in, even though they weren't selling. At least, not as fast as they were arriving. But I suppose you can't ship girls in empty trucks, can you? They need something to hide behind. I blame those foreigners downstairs. I bet they got him into this.'

'So can you give us a statement describing what you saw?'

'I didn't really see anything. I can't help you.'

Peiperová dipped in her bag and produced a photograph. She passed it wordlessly to Petra, who gasped and clasped her hand over her mouth.

'Jesus Maria! Is that the girl found in the warehouse?'

'Yes. Her name is Daniela,' Peiperová added, having remembered the lecture that told her that people empathise more with others when they know their names. 'I knew her. I'd like to catch the people who did this, and I need your help.'

Slonský was going home. It was nearly midnight and Navrátil was just typing up a report.

'Come in an hour or two late in the morning, lad.'

'Thank you, sir.'

'Just leave that on my desk when you're done. Goodnight.'

Slonský clapped his hat on his head and strode downstairs.

The office door creaked open, and Peiperová reversed in with a mug in each hand.

'Are you still here?' said Navratil.

'Obviously. Unless you're dreaming, of course. I've been writing up Nejedlý's secretary's statement.'

'Did you get anywhere?'

'She's got a good memory for dates. She also has an office diary she'll bring in, along with Nejedlý's address book.'

'Good. I'm almost finished here. I thought you'd have gone home by now,' Navrátil added, accepting the proffered mug of coffee.

'I'm waiting for a strong man to walk me through the streets. If I go on my own I might get molested.'

'You won't get molested if I'm with you.'

'No,' she said. *Shame*, she thought.

Chapter 13

Nejedlý's statement was a curious mixture, thought Slonský as he read it through for the third time. He had been prepared to give full details of many things, but there were a couple where he claimed to know nothing, or, more accurately, nothing useful in one case and nothing at all in the other.

When Navrátil and Peiperová arrived Slonský recounted these as he paraphrased the statement.

'According to his account — and bear in mind he's a criminal and therefore probably a liar too — Nejedlý's business was entirely legitimate and very prosperous through the nineties. His downfall began with women — there's a lesson there, lad — and in particular the staff of a couple of clubs where he was wont to go to unwind after a busy day humping his plums onto lorries. He became a bit too friendly with one of them, and his wife caught him *in flagrante delicto* in his office. I think that's Latin for squeezing the fruit.'

'I know what it means, sir.'

'Jolly good. So his wife walked out and divorced him, and collared a good chunk of his net worth plus a monthly payment. This coincided with a downturn in the import-export trade and soon he was having trouble keeping going, to the point where he tried to get out of a contract to import tinned fruit from Serbia. His contacts there put an alternative proposition to him. Now, he claims that they threatened him, but if they did that why would they pay him handsomely too?'

'They wanted him to smuggle girls into the country.'

'Not necessarily to the Czech Republic, but here if possible because they could earn more here. And as a customer of the clubs in Prague he knew a few people who might take them. Before long the Bosnians bought some of the clubs — Klinger tells me this is called downstream vertical integration — and the profits became quite healthy. Nejedlý sent his lorries to Serbia, Brukić brought the girls from Bosnia, and then Nejedlý brought them home.'

'Why didn't Brukić just drive them all the way, sir?' Peiperová wanted to know.

'He had a very close shave with the Hungarians and he was convinced they were on his trail. Plus he could only bring six or eight in a minibus, what with the guards and luggage space he needed. This way he kept his hands cleaner — if the girls told their story, he could claim he only took them to Serbia and had no idea what happened to them after that.'

'Would anyone be taken in, though?'

'The likes of Brukić don't care what people think. They're only interested in what can be proved, and you couldn't possibly have proved that he was lying. Nejedlý claims that when Daniela was snatched he was just told they needed a safe building for a few days, so he handed over the keys to a warehouse he no longer uses. He knew nothing about her abduction or anything that happened to her.'

'Do you believe him, sir?' asked Navrátil.

Slonský sighed. 'I think I do, because I think he was keen not to know, so even if he didn't know particulars, he knew something criminal was going on. Anyway, what I find interesting are the things he says he doesn't know. He doesn't know who killed Hrdlička and says he has an alibi, though we know that's a lie because his hot kettle gave him away. But he says he hadn't heard any mention of the knight before the day of the killing, and then he only heard about it immediately after.'

'So why did he leave before the questioning?' Peiperová enquired.

'He says he had incriminating documents in his office and decided he had better hide them when he saw us heading for the building, so he took off down the fire escape.'

'But we weren't in uniform,' Navrátil objected.

'Maybe not, but we were talking to uniformed police and waving our badges around, and it seems he overheard one of your rat-catching visits. Then the other thing he claims not to know about is Opava. According to him he hasn't been in or through Opava and he has no idea why Hrdlička was so interested in it. Anyway, let's get down to business. We've got enough here to bring in Brukić and Savović but I doubt they'll come quietly, so we need to plan our campaign carefully.'

There was a prolonged silence as they waited to hear what the plan was.

'But before we do that,' said Slonský, 'let's get some coffee and pastries.'

The summons from the Director of Criminal Police came halfway through Slonský's second pastry, so he was obliged to put half the tartlet in his mouth in one go as he departed. The Director did not rise to greet Slonský or offer him his hand as he entered, which Slonský interpreted as bad signs.

'Good morning, Slonský.'

'Good morning, sir.'

'I thought I asked you to keep me informed of the progress of your enquiries?'

'I think that too, sir.'

'But you haven't.'

'Not entirely, sir.'

'Not at all, Slonský.'

'No, sir. I've been too busy detecting crime, sir.'

'Then there's no time like the present, seeing as you were detecting crime in the canteen.'

Slonský looked nonplussed.

'You've got a smear of blueberry juice on your chin, man.'

'Ah. Well, where to start, sir?'

'How about explaining why there's an army camp full of impressionable young cadets and a busload of prostitutes?'

'Place of safety, sir. I had to improvise somewhere to keep the girls out of the reach of intimidators.'

'That's worked, then, though whether the cadets will ever be the same again is a moot point. Then there's the girl who went missing?'

'Found in a warehouse in a bad way, sir. The owner of the warehouse is in custody and denies involvement in that. He's one of the people in the building Hrdlička was watching.'

'And what progress on trapping the killer of Hrdlička?'

'There's some oddities there, sir. Hrdlička was using a non-authorised radio microphone and earpiece obtained from an ex-policeman.'

'Don't tell me — Gazdík.'

'Yes, sir. Gazdík seems to have been asked to provide this because Hrdlička didn't want to go through normal channels. That implies that he didn't trust someone in his department.'

'Go on.'

'Peiperová visited his wife and found a map of Opava among his effects. He doesn't mention this in any of his reports, but his enquiries seem to centre on a derelict manor house. This is where we come to a delicate bit, sir.'

'You think you know who the officer is that Hrdlička was keeping it from.'

'Yes, sir. Captain Grigar asked Mrs Hrdličková what her husband had been doing at the time of his death and wanted any papers he had, but she says Hrdlička had already sent them all in. So presumably he was sending them to someone other than Grigar. Then there's the curious incident on the night Navrátil got arrested.'

'Yes, I heard about that. I trust there was some mistake?'

'I can't think of anyone less likely to expose himself than Navrátil, sir. It was a cover story I improvised on the spur of the moment to explain why he was on the roof of a villa looking into a woman's bedroom.'

'In the course of duty, I hope?'

'Yes, sir. Technically he was working overtime. Anyway, a source was listening to the police frequencies that afternoon when Navrátil and Peiperová went to meet the girl who was found in the warehouse, and the source says he heard Captain Grigar order that Navrátil should be followed.'

The Director put his pen down and stood up. Slonský tried to do the same but a gesture from the Director told him to resume his seat.

'I think better when I walk,' the Director explained. 'This is serious. Grigar is a senior officer with an excellent record. It's hard to imagine any kind of bad practice where he is concerned.'

'We can all be tempted. A nice nest-egg to take into retirement, a foreign holiday, who knows what it would take? And he's been pestering me for details of the progress of my enquiries.'

'I hope he hasn't got anywhere.'

'No, sir.'

'Good. I'd be put out if I thought he knew more about what was going on than I did. Have you spoken to Grigar about these suggestions?'

'No, sir.'

'Reported them to Internal Affairs?'

'No, sir. I didn't think I had enough proof.'

'It's their job to look for proof, not yours. I'll speak to Major Rajka and get his team onto it.'

'Thank you, sir.'

'So what next? These Bosnians are still out and about.'

'I plan to bring them in, sir, but I don't expect it to be easy. We may need armed backup.'

'I hope that doesn't mean Dvorník and his personal collection.'

'No, sir. But it's hard to think how best to do this.'

The Director looked at the map of Prague on his wall. 'Do you know where they are?'

Slonský walked over to join him. 'Savović's office is here. They share a villa here. Their clubs are here and here. The clubs are the place they're most likely to be but that means arresting them at night.'

'Let's try the office first. You interviewed him there so that's a possibility. If he isn't there we'll leave a man watching and we'll raid the club tonight. I'll organise some armed support for you.'

Slonský felt just a smidgen of concern at the use of the word "you". He had hoped his presence at the arrest might not be needed but managed to stammer his thanks. The Director examined his watch.

'Shall we say 14:30 for the roundup?'

'Yes, sir.'

'Good. Now to the other reason I asked you here. Captain Lukas was here yesterday to discuss returning to work.'

'Excellent news, sir. Shall I clear his room?'

'Not yet, Slonský. I hear you aren't in it anyway. I receive regular reports on the arrangements you've made.'

'Bloody Doležal.'

The Director smiled. 'You know a policeman never reveals his sources. Don't worry, I told you to organise it however you thought best and that's what you've done. I'm not going to criticise you for that. In fact, the department has never run so efficiently. I can't recall a time when so many reports arrived punctually.'

'I can't claim the credit, sir.'

'And you weren't going to get it. Officer Peiperová possesses a rare administrative talent. So much so that when Captain Lukas returns, I'd like her to come here to act as my personal assistant.'

Slonský was taken aback. 'I don't have to have Kuchař, do I, sir?'

'No, Slonský. Nobody should have to have a Kuchař, not even among my enemies. When his year is up I'm sending him to Interpol. With luck he won't come back. But I thought I've had enough of Academy graduates. It would be good to have someone who has come up through the ranks the long way round.'

'She's undoubtedly qualified, sir. And she's ambitious, and there's no doubt that being personal assistant to the Director of Criminal Police would look good on any job application.'

The Director coughed gently. 'It may be personal assistant to someone at a higher level by then.'

'We live in hope, sir,' said Slonský quickly. 'I'm just unsure what effect this will have on Navrátil.'

'Of course, there's no special relationship between workmates under your supervision, is there?'

'Not during work time, sir.'

'Not quite what the regulations say, Slonský. Perhaps separating them now would be a good thing in the long run.'

'Perhaps, sir.'

'Well, it's an offer, Slonský, not a posting. She's free to make her own mind up. Will you raise it with her?'

'Yes, sir. Maybe after the excitement this afternoon, sir, rather than before.'

'Good idea. But you haven't asked me when Captain Lukas will be returning.'

'No, sir. You'll tell me if you want me to know.'

'He may appear for a day or two before Christmas, but we're going to phase him back into work slowly in the new year. However, Captain Lukas has intimated that he plans to retire next July. I propose to appoint his replacement in May so Lukas can be around to offer support and guidance. Start thinking, Slonský. Do you want the job?'

The sausage tasted like sawdust in his mouth. For some reason he did not really understand Slonský decided he should pay a quick visit to Lukas to share the discussion he had just had with the Director.

'Come in, Slonský! Darling, Slonský's here! Would you like some lunch?'

'Thank you, but I've just had a sausage.'

'Ah, sausages! A thing of the past for me, I'm afraid. My stomach won't take it.'

'No sausages? Ever?'

'No. Too much fat, you see.'

Slonský needed to sit down. 'No sausages — for life. I can't imagine that, sir.'

'A sacrifice I'm happy to make if it means the pain doesn't come back.'

'But what kind of life is it without sausages?' Slonský whispered.

'I'm sure you didn't come to discuss the existential importance of sausages, Slonský.'

'No, sir. I've been to see the Director this morning who gave me the good news that you'll be back soon.'

'Part-time,' called Mrs Lukasová from the kitchen.

'Part-time,' agreed Lukas. 'For now.'

'Nevertheless, very welcome, sir. Less welcome was the Director's plan to get his hands on Officer Peiperová and make her his personal assistant.'

'Yes, he shared that with me. She'll be very pleased. She's an ambitious and competent young lady.'

'From the selfish point of view, I'd rather hoped to keep her. Competence isn't in great supply in the police force.'

'You've got Navrátil. You mustn't be greedy.'

'Will he be the same if she moves on like this?'

'Isn't he up for his lieutenant's grading next year?'

'He could be. Perhaps I should make sure he gets the paperwork in. That's one thing that shouldn't go into Peiperová's in-tray.'

'Very wise. Bring it to me and I'll sign it.'

Slonský was just getting into the car when Major Rajka phoned. Rajka was one of the good guys in Slonský's view, a relatively young officer who headed up the division that investigated the behaviour of police personnel. It was so refreshing to have someone running that team who was not the biggest crook in the police force, Slonský reflected.

Rajka asked a few pertinent questions, then said that he thought they should give Grigar some rope.

'If you mean round his neck, I'm all for that,' Slonský commented.

'If he's guilty, I'll agree with you, but what I actually meant was that we shouldn't let him know we're onto him just yet. I may just send a man to do some quiet digging and a bit of surveillance. Disclosure time, Slonský — I know Grigar, and I'd be very surprised if he'd done anything amiss. But I've been doing this work long enough to know that my instincts are by no means infallible.'

'I'd normally agree with you, sir. I just can't think why he would be watching Navrátil. Or, for that matter, why Hrdlička withheld his full reports. It can only be because he discovered something that made him distrust his superior.'

Navrátil started the engine as Slonský hung up, but before they had gone many metres the phone rang again.

'Novák here.'

'Ah, the prodigal returns. Where have you been when I needed you?'

'Speaking at a conference in Brussels.'

'What organisation was so desperate that they wanted you to speak to them?'

'The European Forensic Biometrics Group. You may not realise it, Slonský, but I am an acknowledged expert on footprints and foot recognition technology.'

'I don't need technology to recognise feet, Novák. They're the odd shaped bits that stick out at the ends of your legs.'

'Ha, ha. Give me a week or two to stop laughing. I'm ringing about Hrdlička's ears.'

'I thought you specialised in feet?'

'Do you want to know or not? I think your suspicion was right. He was subjected to a very loud noise that damaged an eardrum. It wouldn't be conclusive in court, but it's a fair bet.'

'Thank you, Dr Novák.'

'That's not all.'

'No?'

'You'll be very glad you had me to hand when I tell you the next bit. It occurred to me that the use of a short-bladed knife implied that the killer was right behind Hrdlička. And we know where Hrdlička was because we found him there and his knees were firmly in the snow. There's a footprint between Hrdlička's legs that attracted my attention. It's a left foot, which is consistent with a right-handed attacker leaning forward to push the blade home.'

'Anything distinctive about the shoe?'

'Oh, yes.'

Novák explained what he believed he could see.

'267 millimetres?' said Slonský. 'What's that, then?'

'Size 43. But the tread is characteristic. Of course, I can't swear to the identification of the boot without a tread cast, but if you find the man and he's wearing the boot, we've got him.'

Slonský fell silent during the journey to the red brick building, and remained immobile when they arrived.

'Are we getting out, sir?'

'Hm? Oh, yes, I suppose. I'm just thinking a moment.'

'I assumed we'd come to arrest the two Bosnians.'

'We have, but they'll be well away from here. Anyway, let's go through the motions. Did you bring a gun?'

'No, sir. I didn't know I needed one.'

'Good. You can go behind me, then.'

There was no sign of either Savović or Brukić in the office. But, by the same token, there was no sign that they had hurriedly emptied it of anything of interest, so Slonský and Navrátil settled down to read the files.

'Should we call the armed backup off, sir?'

'Why? If those two come back it would be good to have some people with guns in our corner. I shouldn't think they'll be too pleased when they discover that we've been through their papers.'

'Will they know, sir?'

'Certainly they will, because whether we find anything or not I'm going to take a few sheets and leave them an official evidence receipt. Let them fret about what I've found, even if I haven't.'

'It's just as well they've only been here three months, sir. Not too much to go through.'

'And they're not the sort of people to do a lot of corresponding. Record keeping isn't their strong point. Mucha would be appalled.'

They continued to rummage for about twenty minutes, until Navrátil came across a single sheet of paper.

'It looks like a fax, sir.'

'So it does. But why fax a map to a bunch of thugs in Bosnia?'

'How do you know it wasn't here, sir?'

'The date on the fax, Navrátil. It's dated April. But there are two features of this that interest me. I've seen this map before. And this fax was sent from a hotel in Opava.'

Chapter 14

'The hotel doesn't have a record of who sent it, sir.'

'But they know who stayed there, presumably?' Slonský asked Navrátil.

'Yes, sir, but none of the names I mentioned are listed in the register. They're going to fax us copies of the relevant pages just in case.'

'That's something, I suppose.'

'Shall we stand the armed squad down, sir?'

'I suppose so. I didn't expect them to be at the club anyway. They'll be lying low, but they can't do it for long without risking their empire being dismantled. As soon as word gets round the underworld that they're in trouble, the sharks will move in and they'll come back to find their staff have all left and their clubs have closed down.'

'What happens now, sir?'

'A beer and something to eat, I think.'

'I meant with the investigation.'

'That is connected with the investigation. I need to think hard, and beer helps.'

'Sarajevo say they'll send a couple of officers to escort the women back to Bosnia, sir.'

'Just the twelve, lad. We need to keep two of them for court appearances. What's Peiperová doing?'

'She's gone to meet the train with Daniela's parents on it, sir. It was due in around five o'clock, then she was going to drive them to the hospital.'

'That's a tough assignment. I'm glad she's doing it. She's good at that sort of stuff.'

Well, anyone's better at it than you, thought Navrátil, but decided to keep the thought to himself.

Slonský was very quiet as they ate. At one point he took out a tattered notebook and scribbled a couple of reminders to himself, but mainly he drank beer. Navrátil knew better than to try to match his consumption, and stopped after two small glasses. Slonský was then halfway down his fourth half-litre.

'Early night needed, lad. Tomorrow is going to be a long day. But I think it's going to be a really fruitful one.'

'How were the parents?' Slonský enquired the next morning.

'Very low,' replied Peiperová, 'as you would expect, sir. I had a chat with them after the hospital visit and they felt a bit better knowing that at least Daniela was still alive, and the surgeon showed them some pictures of the ears he's done in the past, so they felt a bit better by the time they got to the hotel.'

'Are we footing the bill for that?'

Peiperová coughed gently and looked a little embarrassed. 'I think you may have approved the expense, sir.'

'Did I?'

'In your absence, sir.'

'Is there anything else I may have done in my absence, young lady?'

'I don't think so, sir.'

'Nothing like signing anyone's transfer to the remotest police station in Bohemia?'

'I hope not, sir.'

'Well, it's not a big issue. Is Daniela being guarded in the hospital?'

'Round the clock, sir.'

'Good. Next to the bill for that a few days in a hotel will look like chickenfeed.'

Peiperová had that tickle in her throat again. 'I may have promised them a fortnight, sir.'

Slonský said nothing for a few seconds, causing Peiperová to feel her palms moisten as she waited for the explosion. 'It's not worth their coming for less, I suppose,' was all he said. 'Now, I've got a job for you. I want you to ring the police in Opava to ask them a very simple question.'

There was no need for a senior officer to go to Boletice to supervise the collection of twelve girls and the transporting of the other two to Prague but Slonský thought he ought to go to express his thanks to the Commanding Officer for agreeing to the plan so quickly. Since Slonský did not want to drive he decided to sit in the Bosnian minibus while Návratil and Peiperová drove in the car. The woman officer from Bosnia obviously fancied some female company, because she clung to Peiperová and finished up in the car too.

Mucha and Slonský watched the car drive off.

'Isn't it amazing?' said Mucha. 'They don't speak each other's language but they've chatted non-stop.'

'I pity Návratil. He's got hours of that ahead of him.'

'I might ring him on his mobile just to give him a bit of moral support.'

'That would be kind of you.'

'Would it? I'd better not then. Don't want people thinking I've gone soft in my old age.'

'Don't forget the little job I gave you.'

'I won't. By the time you get back I should have an answer for you, provided the details you have are accurate.'

'Excellent. Well, my chariot awaits. Thank goodness it's not insured for me to drive.'

Just then Slonský had an enormous stroke of good fortune. A taxi pulled up outside and Captain Lukas alighted. He still looked rather delicate, but he was obviously delighted to walk through the doors of headquarters for the first time in weeks.

'Do you have any plans for today, sir?' said Slonský.

'No, I just came to see old colleagues. Part of my recuperation, you know. Mustn't overexert myself.'

'That's quite right, sir. How would you fancy a nice drive into the country?'

Lukas spoke tolerable Russian, which Slonský had never really been able to get the hang of at school. If it had been a bit less like Czech he might have done better, but he would get the two languages mixed. After a shaky start Lukas and the Bosnian officer were engaged in sporadic conversation, so Slonský could sit back and think. At intervals Lukas would explain what had just been said, and Slonský now understood much more about Bosnian gangs and the challenges of policing in a country which had experienced a recent war. Thank goodness most Czech criminals didn't have rocket launchers and mobile artillery, he thought.

Once they had left the city they were able to catch Navrátil up and the two vehicles proceeded in convoy to the camp. After elaborate security checks the party was taken to the command office where Slonský expressed his thanks to the officer of the day and together they loaded the girls onto the minibus.

'These are all mine?' Slonský asked. 'I'd hate to think any of yours were trying to sneak out in disguise.'

'If their disguise is as good as this, I wouldn't mind,' smiled the officer. 'It's been … interesting having them around. It certainly smartened the lads up. They've never taken such an interest in physical training. And the evenings haven't been boring.'

Slonský felt himself judder. 'No hanky-panky, I hope?'

'No, none of that. Just music, chatter, and a lot of table tennis.' They shook hands, and as the officer walked away a thought occurred to him. 'And I bet there isn't an army unit anywhere in the country that knows more about hair extensions and pedicures.'

Dumpy Anna was looking frazzled. Wisps of grey hair escaped from her white hat and her skin was glowing and red.

'That was an experience,' she said.

'You wouldn't think a dozen slim young things like that could eat so much,' Slonský agreed. 'Of course, I never had daughters, so I know next to nothing about young women.' He surveyed the counter. 'Is there anything left?'

Anna wiped her hands on the towel slung from her belt.

'Fancy some liver sausage? I've got a bit out the back. I could do you a sandwich.'

Slonský was almost emotional. 'You'd make a smashing wife for someone, Anna.'

'I already have,' she said. 'Twice. The buggers both died on me.'

Navrátil and Peiperová had headed off to the cinema for a night out. There was a new film out involving some American actors whose names were obviously expected to spark interest in Slonský, but of whom he had never heard. He settled down in his office with the notes Peiperová had left him, the faxes from the hotel in Opava, and the photocopies Mucha had made after his search through the records.

Finally, it all made sense. He just needed a couple of additional snippets of information. The most important was where the suspects were, because he had no idea where to start looking, but there was little point in building a strong case if he had nobody standing in the dock.

Wherever the chief suspect had disappeared to, there was one place he was sure to come back to — eventually.

Unusually, Navrátil and Peiperová were watching the film. It included a scene in which a young woman was abducted, which started Navrátil's mind running through the circumstances of Milena's death. If she died at the hostel, there was nowhere to load her into a van except in the street outside. He and Slonský had been obliged to do the same when they arrested all the other girls. That meant the criminals had taken quite a chance, because they could have been spotted at any time taking a dead woman to a van. Perhaps they had been seen, but if so by whom? Presumably they did not understand what they were seeing and thought she was just ill.

But then Navrátil reflected that there was a bigger puzzle. He had been working in Prague for nine months and living in the area for a long time, but if he had been asked to bury a body by moonlight he would be pushed to think of anywhere. There were plenty of places if you drove out of the city, although even then disturbed ground would probably be noticed.

As they left the cinema, Navrátil was eager to test his hypothesis.

'They won't be there,' said Peiperová. 'The clubs are shut, remember?'

'They still need guarding. And they probably opened to serve drinks even if there were few girls. Come on.'

A Metro ride later they emerged near the Padlock club and approached the door. When the doorman saw Navrátil approaching he attempted to slip inside, but Navrátil ordered him to stand still.

'No rough stuff, just a question,' he said.

'I told you all I know,' said the doorman. 'More than was good for me, likely as not.'

'No, you didn't,' replied the young detective, 'because we didn't ask you one thing. When they buried Milena, they needed a local guide. You said you didn't go, but there must have been a Czech there. Who was it?'

The doorman lowered his eyes.

'Come on, answer the question,' said Peiperová, 'or we'll get it out of you a less friendly way.'

'I don't know his name,' he said. 'It was that older guy who brings the girls in.'

Nejedlý was having an uncomfortable time in the cells. Slonský had reacted to Navrátil's disclosure by going to the gym and borrowing an exercise bicycle. It was now installed in cell 7, to which Nejedlý had been conducted after he denied any involvement in the burial.

'It's not healthy for you being cooped up in that cell,' said Slonský. 'High time you had some exercise.'

'I'm not one for exercise,' Nejedlý responded. 'Besides which, that bike doesn't have a saddle.'

'No, you're wrong there,' said Slonský. 'It has a saddle, but it's sitting on my desk. You won't need it. We're going to help you get on and then you're going to sit nicely and pedal.'

'That's police brutality,' Nejedlý complained.

'How old are you?' asked Slonský. 'If you can think back twenty years this is soft stuff compared with what we did when I was trained. Believe me, I have a lot more tricks up my sleeve, and I'm prepared to use them one after the other until you tell me where Milena's body is and who buried her with you.'

'I didn't play any part in the burying!' Nejedlý pointed out. 'I just directed them to a place. Two of the Bosnian goons did the burying.'

'Descriptions would be nice. And directions to the spot where she lies, please.'

'What's in it for me?' Nejedlý was foolish enough to ask.

Slonský stood over Nejedlý and leaned in until their faces were almost touching.

'Shall I go and get some coffees?' offered Navrátil.

'No need,' said Slonský. 'You can stay while I explain to Mr Nejedlý that if he is uncooperative I will personally see to it that when Savović and Brukić are captured they get to share a cell with him, and then I will explain to the Bosnian gentlemen how helpful Mr Nejedlý was in furnishing the evidence that will convict them. I may embellish it a bit so that they fully understand that it wouldn't have happened without him.'

'They'll kill me,' Nejedlý wailed.

'I do hope so,' said Slonský. 'It would save us the time and trouble of a trial. And it would give us something extra to charge them with. A happy result all around, I'd say — but I can see why you might feel differently about it. Of course, they won't have anything quick and clean to finish you off with like a knife, so it'll probably mean strangling you with a knotted sheet or holding your head down the toilet till you drown. But I never doubt a hoodlum's capacity for revenge. In my experience, once they're riled they forget completely about the consequences, just so long as they can make someone pay for what they've done to them. It's short-sighted of them, I know, but they don't think about that.'

Nejedlý shrank back in the chair and murmured something.

'I didn't hear that,' said Slonský.

'I said I can take you there. So long as it's understood that I didn't do the burying.'

'Nothing is understood,' Slonský responded, 'until it's proved. But we can go for a little drive and see what we find. Navrátil, see what time Sergeant Salzer is on duty. I think he would be particularly keen to come with us, and we'll need an officer in the back of the car with Mr Nejedlý.'

'He's a nasty piece of work,' Nejedlý protested. 'He doesn't like me.'

'I'm sorry,' Slonský said, 'but if we have to wait until we find an officer who likes suspects before we drive them around, we'll never get anywhere. I'm sure Sergeant Salzer will be completely professional in his duties. Besides, if anyone is going to give you a slap, I outrank him, so I should get the first go.'

Navrátil conducted Nejedlý to the car by way of the toilets so that there was no risk of a puddle on the back seat, which seemed to concern Slonský considerably. Suitably handcuffed, Nejedlý found himself sitting next to Sergeant Salzer who, although not officially on duty until one o'clock, had been very willing to come in early when he heard the reason. Navrátil was driving, while Slonský sat in the front, but spent most of the journey turned round so that he could glare at Nejedlý.

'Head south,' said Nejedlý. 'We've got to take the Brno road.'

They drove in silence, punctuated only by the occasional direction from Nejedlý. Just past Újezd they turned off and drove along until they came to a wooded area.

'Park here,' Nejedlý ordered. 'We have to walk a little way now.'

Nejedlý led them down a track about thirty metres, and pointed to a small bank on their left. 'We cut into the side there. The tree roots made it too hard to go downwards from the top of the slope.'

'Very good. Sergeant Salzer will get the spade from the car, and then he'll hold your jacket while you dig.'

'Me?'

'Naturally. You can't expect us to do it.'

'Why should I do it? I'm voluntarily co-operating with your enquiries. I'm not a prisoner.'

'Good point. If you were a prisoner we wouldn't be allowed to make you do it, but since you're a volunteer we'll say thank you for agreeing to do it. And Sergeant Salzer will be so grateful he might not hit you with the spade.'

'He wouldn't dare,' Nejedlý protested.

Slonský could have told him that was a silly thing to say to Salzer, who hit Nejedlý across the knee with the flat of the shovel blade.

'Sorry, it slipped out of my hand,' said Salzer.

'Never mind,' said Slonský, 'these things happen. You'd better give the spade to me in case it happens again.'

Nejedlý sat on the bank and rubbed his knee. 'You could have done me a serious injury,' he moaned.

'And if we have to do it again, I'll make sure we do,' Slonský told him. 'Now, are you going to start digging voluntarily, or do we have to ask again?'

Nejedlý accepted the offered tool and began spooning earth away. It took only a few minutes to clear enough soil to reveal a bedsheet.

'Thank you very much, Mr Nejedlý. That's a crime scene now so we'll get the experts to finish the job. Would you like to sit in the car or are you enjoying the fresh air?'

'I'm not sitting in the car with him,' Nejedlý pouted, so when Dr Novák and his technicians arrived they were surprised to find him attached to a tree as a result of his wrists being cuffed on the far side of the trunk.

'That can't be comfortable,' Novák observed.

'You'd think not,' agreed Slonský, 'but of the options available to him, that was the one he chose.'

The technicians worked quietly and methodically for a couple of hours, and finally Milena was revealed when the cloth around her was unwrapped. Nejedlý turned his head away, but Salzer and Slonský turned it back for him so he could see better.

'What do you think?' Slonský asked Novák. 'Could this be a pregnant Bosnian woman who cut her wrists?'

'Well,' Novák replied, 'it's a woman, and she seems to have cuts to her wrists. Whether she's pregnant or Bosnian remains to be seen. And, of course, someone may have cut her wrists for her.'

'You think so? Did you hear that, Nejedlý? I suppose a judge might wonder why you would bury a body secretly if she committed suicide. It's much more likely that those who buried her killed her, don't you think?'

'They told me she killed herself,' Nejedlý protested. 'I wouldn't have had anything to do with it if I thought they'd murdered her.'

'Don't give me that garbage,' Slonský snarled. 'You'd do as you're told. I can't see you telling a pair of Bosnian gangsters where they get off. So, tell us who asked you to move the body.'

'It was Brukić. He'd got a couple of men to wrap the body in a sheet then they stayed behind to tidy up the room. A couple of Bosnians drove the van but Brukić told me to take them somewhere they could leave the body where it wouldn't be found for a long time. We thought of putting it in a sack and heaving it in the river, but there isn't anywhere you can go where you might not be seen.'

'By "It" you mean "Her", I take it? She's a human being, not a parcel,' Slonský interrupted.

'Yes. Her. Milena.'

'And it never crossed your mind that if she'd killed herself there was no good reason to deny her a proper burial?'

'She had no papers. We'd have had a lot of explaining to do.'

'She did have papers. Brukić took them off her, so Brukić could have given them back. And you've got a lot of explaining to do now. Concealing a death is a very serious offence. Unauthorised burial is another one. And, of course, so is murder.'

'Murder? She wasn't murdered.'

'You don't know that. By your own account they sent for you after she was dead. You can't know whether or not they killed her.'

'They told me she cut her own wrists.'

Slonský marched over to the tree, grabbed the handcuffs and gave them a sharp yank, pulling Nejedlý against the trunk of the tree.

'Shall I let you into a secret? Murderers lie. You can't believe anything they tell you. If you cut a girl's wrists with a razor, fibbing that you didn't do it seems like a relatively small bit of added naughtiness.'

Nejedlý's head drooped. He had the look of a defeated man, which seemed to Slonský like the perfect time to rub it in a bit.

'I wouldn't be at all surprised if they tried to blame you for the whole thing. After all, you personally accompanied the body to ensure that it was disposed of securely. Why would you do that if you had nothing to do with the murder? Those two will give each other an alibi and you'll be hung out to dry. Unless you get your side of the story in first, that is.'

Nejedlý slumped against the tree. 'Take me back somewhere warm and I'll tell you all I know,' he said.

'All he knew' turned out not to be much more than Slonský already knew, and in some respects it was rather less. Having returned Nejedlý to the cells, Slonský and Navrátil decamped to the canteen to await the arrival of Peiperová, who had been taking supplementary statements from the two girls who remained with them and who were now tucked away in a police barracks while the administration slowly ground towards finding them a police safe house.

Slonský had just collected a coffee when Mucha appeared with a brown envelope.

'Where have you been all afternoon?' he grumbled. 'You tell me this is important then you skive off and I can't find you.'

'We were digging up a body,' Slonský explained. 'That seemed more important at the time.'

'I don't think so,' said Mucha. 'Take a peek at that.' He pushed the envelope across the table. It included a couple of sheets of paper which Slonský inspected carefully.

'Good work, my old and trusted friend,' he announced. 'Have I ever told you that you're my very favourite desk sergeant?'

'Yes, whenever you wanted something.'

'Well, it's true. This is exactly what we needed. Now we just need to visit Nejedlý and if we're lucky Technician First Class Spehar will lead us to the pot of gold at the end of the rainbow.'

He shoved the papers back in the envelope and thrust them in his pocket without offering Navrátil a glimpse.

'There remains one loose end, though. And for that, I suspect we need to spend an hour in the Human Resources department.'

'Knowing their efficiency, you'll need an hour to get them to admit who they are,' said Mucha.

'True,' agreed Slonský. 'So we'd better fill ourselves with calories to guard against feeling faint while we wait. Navrátil, pass me the plate of pastries, and you'd better have one yourself.'

Nejedlý was slumped on his cot when Slonský breezed in.

'I thought you were finished with me,' he said.

'Almost,' replied Slonský cheerily. 'But it occurs to me that you may be able to assist us further with our enquiries. I want a mobile phone number, and I'm hoping you may have it.'

When he announced whose number he was after the look of surprise on Nejedlý's face told him quite a lot about the complex arrangements of life in the red brick building. Nejedlý said he did not know the number by heart, but it was probably in the diary in his desk. If not, the doorkeeper would have it.

'It's not in your diary,' responded Slonský, 'because I've already liberated that to my own desk. I'll give the doorkeeper a ring, if you have his number.'

Nejedlý knew that one, and in a few minutes Slonský had the phone number he wanted and was ready to visit Spehar. He knew from past experience that Spehar's team could find a mobile phone's whereabouts because Ricka had done that for him before.

'Ricka is on leave,' said Spehar, 'but it isn't difficult. If the phone is switched on I can find it for you.'

Slonský gave him the number and Spehar typed it into his laptop. A lot of lights flashed and a screen like a radar screen appeared, but despite several sweeps no little blip appeared.

'It's switched off,' said Spehar.

'Can we try again later?' Slonský asked.

'I'll set it to try every half-hour overnight, then we'll see how things look in the morning,' Spehar answered. 'Would it help if I found out when and where it was last used?'

'It might,' Slonský conceded.

'There's a bit of paperwork to fill out first,' Spehar informed him.

'This is Prague,' said Slonský. 'There always is.'

Valentin was putting himself outside a large brandy when Slonský dropped in for a quick beer or six after work.

'French brandy? Times must be good.'

'Times are most definitely not good,' said the journalist. 'That exposé you gave me has caused some ructions.'

'Oh, yes?'

'Yes! Our man in Belgrade had a couple of phone calls wanting the series of articles stopped, then last night his car was sprayed with gunfire.'

'Was he all right?'

'Yes, fortunately they missed.'

'Valentin, old friend, have another brandy and I'll explain it to you. There was no "fortunately" about it. If they missed it's because they meant to miss. It's not that hard to hit a car driver — after all, you know where he's sitting in the car. But much more importantly, it tells me where the people we're looking for have run to. They couldn't go back to Sarajevo so they had to find somewhere else to hide, and now we know where. I'll just ring headquarters and they'll speak nicely to the Serbian police, and with luck they'll arrest the bad men and your colleague will be able to drive around Belgrade in safety.'

'I'll let him know. He's quite shaken up.'

'Nonsense. There's nothing stirs up the blood quite so much as being shot at. It makes you feel glad to be alive. So long as you are, of course. Who wants a boring desk job anyway?'

'I do. That's why I can't understand those nutcases who want to be war correspondents. It's dangerous, the food is lousy and you don't get to sleep in a proper bed. Who wants that?'

'My sentiments exactly.'

'So you're after these Bosnians? What have they done?'

'Something really serious. They've annoyed me.'

Peiperová had returned just in time to be given the job of speaking to the Human Resources Department. Slonský had suggested going in person rather than telephoning because, he said, they can't put a personal caller on hold, though they seemed to be making a pretty good fist of it to her. After waiting at the enquiry desk for ten minutes, the clerk who dealt with her had pointedly looked at the clock which showed thirteen minutes to the end of the working day.

'Peiperová?' he said. 'Are you the one we've had all the enquiries about concerning this peculiar Acting Acting Captain rank?'

'Enquiries?'

'Yes, a number of people have asked about it.'

'Well, that's me. What did you tell them?'

'Oh, I didn't tell them anything. I referred it to my line manager for a ruling.'

'And what did he say?'

'She.'

'Very well then. What did she say?'

'She said that it needed to be approached from first principles. An Acting Captain undoubtedly exists, and has all the delegated authority of an actual bona fide Captain. Thus, she said, it follows that an Acting Captain must have the authority to delegate to an Acting Acting Captain. It's all highly irregular, of course.'

'Much of what Lieutenant Slonský does is irregular. But I'm pleased to hear that on this occasion he knew what he was doing. However, that isn't what I've come for.'

'It isn't?' said the clerk, sneaking another peek at the clock.

'It shouldn't take long,' Peiperová declared encouragingly. 'We just need a copy of a policeman's service record.'

'A current policeman?'

'Yes. These are his details.'

She passed a piece of paper across the desk.

'This isn't the approved form,' said the clerk.

'I'm happy to fill one in,' said Peiperová, 'but I wouldn't want to keep you after hours while I do it.'

The clerk thought for a moment, then handed her a blank form.

'I'll go and dig this out while you put his name here and your signature here. We can fill the rest in later.' He gave a strange gurgling giggle. 'Make sure you put your rank as Acting Acting Captain or I'll have to get it countersigned.'

Slonský was amused by the photocopy of the request form attached to the folder that Peiperová had just given him.

'Acting Acting Captain?'

'Yes, sir. He told me there is such a rank, and you knew what you were doing despite the sceptical enquiries.'

'Well I never. Still, that's one in the eye for Doležal. I bet he rang them at least twice. Now, let's see what we have here. Have you read this, Peiperová?'

'It's personal to you, sir.'

'Avoiding a direct answer, I see. Sit yourself down, lass. I've got something important to say to you.'

Peiperová did as instructed.

'Are you happy here, Peiperová?'

'Very happy, sir.'

'Good. So am I.'

'I'm pleased to hear that, sir.'

'The point is that the Director of Criminal Police wants me to offer you a job as his Personal Assistant. It's only for a year, but it means you wouldn't be a detective. On the other hand, it would look good on your record. Anyway, he wanted me to put it to you, and I have. Go away and think about it.'

'Thank you, sir. When does he want an answer?'

'I don't know, but the job starts in mid-summer. Personally I would be sorry to lose you but I mustn't allow my own thoughts to come in the way of your advancement, or do anything that might influence your decision. If you want to waste a year of your life sat behind a desk making coffee for a bigwig, that's your choice.'

The thought crossed Peiperová's mind that she had spent quite lot of the last six months making coffee when she wasn't being abducted or shouted at. It would undoubtedly look good on her CV, but then she could imagine Navrátil's reaction. It had been bad enough when she was made Acting Acting Captain, so what he would say about her being Personal Assistant to the Director of Criminal Police she could hardly imagine. But then she had to think about how proud her parents would be, which might get her mother off her back about the dangers of living in Prague, because it was a firm belief of Mrs Peiperová that every woman there was molested regularly. Like many maternal beliefs, it was unsupported by any evidence and unshakeable in the face of facts to the contrary.

'I said this puts the lid on the enquiry, lass.'

'Sorry, sir. I was far away. So we know who killed Hrdlička, sir?'

'Of course. That's been obvious for a while. And no doubt you've worked out why. But I couldn't see why Grigar was having Navrátil followed, and now I know. All we need is for Spehar to come up with the whereabouts of that mobile phone, and we spring into action.'

Peiperová was nonplussed. The identity of the killer might be clear to Slonský, but it certainly was not to her. And she had no idea of a motive other than the obvious one of avoiding detection, nor could she see how Grigar came into it. But when she asked for further details Slonský just told her to wait and see, wait and see.

Chapter 15

Spehar's call was brief and to the point.

'He put the phone on this morning and we've got a fix.'

'So where is he?'

'Opava.'

'I know that. But where in Opava? How close can you get?'

'Probably to within a block. Looking at the street map, I think he's in a hotel there.'

'Let me get a pencil and you can give me the address. Then I'll go for a drive.'

Navrátil had lost the toss of a coin and was sitting in the back seat while Peiperová drove. Spehar was under instructions to watch for any sign of the phone moving and to ring them at once if it did. Slonský had tipped his hat over his eyes and was having forty winks in the front passenger seat.

'It's three hundred and seventy kilometres, sir. I doubt we'll be there before bedtime.'

'Then we'll wake him up, lad. We're entitled to wake criminals up to get arrested. It says so in the law somewhere.'

'Yes, sir.'

'Besides, arresting people after bedtime is a lot easier. You know where they are. In the good old days we used to arrest people in the early hours. It wasn't to increase the terror. It just meant they weren't likely to be out when you called, because there's nothing more irritating than kicking someone's door in and finding they've gone out for a night at the pub.'

'Couldn't you just knock, sir?' asked Peiperova.

'You could, I suppose,' Slonský conceded, 'but any criminal with half a brain would turn the lights off and pretend to be out, so then you've lost the element of surprise. Much better to kick his door down and let yourself in to surprise him. Some of the best arrests involved getting the door patched up and waiting inside for him to come home. You should have seen the look on their faces when they turned the lights on and found a room full of police sitting patiently in the dark. Of course,' he said pointedly, 'to be able to arrest people in the early hours, you had to get some kip during the day.'

Given the lack of urgency that Slonský was exhibiting, it came as no surprise to Navrátil and Peiperová when he suggested stopping for something to eat, with the result that it was nearly eleven o'clock when they arrived in Opava. Slonský consulted his notebook and suggested a hotel he wanted to check out.

'I'm afraid we only have one room free,' said the receptionist.

'That's all right,' said Slonský, waving his badge perfunctorily. 'In a few minutes you'll have two. I just need to inspect your register.'

'We don't have a register. We're computerised.'

'Well then,' said Slonský, 'a list of who is staying here would be good, and I don't care whether it's bound, printed, illuminated by monks or tattooed on your arse.'

The receptionist looked as if she had been given a lemon to suck.

'I'd better send for the duty manager.'

'You do that, but give us the list first, or he'll have to come to the station to bail you out.'

She printed a list and handed it to him.

'Are these the room numbers?'

'Yes.'

'Good. And do you have a spare key to room 10?'

'I don't know if I can just give you a key like that.'

'If you don't, I'll kick the door in and you'll have a carpenter's bill, whereas if you give me a key, I can let myself in without causing any damage to the hotel. Wouldn't that be better?'

The receptionist handed over the key.

'Very good. Navrátil, just sneak upstairs and see whether there's any sign of him in the room. If there is, stay there and make sure he doesn't sneak out before the local lads get here. Peiperová, you tiptoe up behind him and bring back the message. And no nipping into any nooks and crannies on the way, you two. You're working.'

Captain Herfort and a couple of other uniformed policemen entered the foyer. 'Nice to see you again,' he declared. 'It will be good to get to the bottom of the monkey business at the old lodge.'

'Have you been watching for the suspect?' Slonský demanded.

'Yes, a plain-clothes man has been around since you called. We changed them at intervals so he wouldn't get suspicious. But so far as we know he's been in his room since mid-afternoon.'

'Very good. I'd like you to sit in on the questioning if you don't mind in case we need any local knowledge. Are you a local man?'

'Born and bred. I've never really wanted to work anywhere else.'

'Excellent. And I hope your colleagues are tooled up for the occasion.'

'Loaded up and ready to go. Are you expecting violence?'

'I don't know. But bear in mind he's killed a man with a flick-knife and he's trained in lethal unarmed combat. I doubt if he has a gun but he's still dangerous.'

Peiperová returned. 'There's a light under the door, sir, and we can hear a television or radio.'

'Good. Come on, then. I've got the key, Herfort. I'll fling it open then your two lads can charge in with their guns out just in case any rough stuff starts. Meanwhile you and I will let the dust settle before making our entrance. Peiperová, you and Navrátil make sure no passers-by get in the way. I don't want him grabbing a hostage.'

They mounted the stairs quietly and paused by the door to room 10. Slonský carefully lined up the key, then pushed and twisted in one move. The first man was through the door within a second, and within five seconds they were all in the room, looking at the puzzled face of Mr Brown, who was sitting up in bed.

'What in hell is going on here?' he yelled.

'You're being arrested,' said Slonský. 'You are not obliged to say anything, but anything you do say will be taken down and given in evidence.'

Captain Herfort checked Brown's clothing item by item before they let him dress, then he was handcuffed to one of the local officers and marched downstairs.

Slonský detoured to speak to the receptionist again.

'Your key, miss. Has the gentleman prepaid?'

'We've got an open credit card for him.'

'Jolly good. I expect we'll send someone over to take away his luggage tomorrow. No point in running up a big bill on his behalf.'

Brown was belligerent, which was a trait not calculated to bring out the best in Slonský. Before long suspect and detective were bellowing at each other like elks disputing possession of a crag.

'You've got no reason to arrest me.'

'If I hadn't, I wouldn't have done it. And as a matter of fact, Captain Herfort here arrested you. I just cautioned you, because I like doing that bit.'

'I have a right to know what charges you're going to bring.'

'And I have twenty-four hours to think about that. Apart from the murder charge, of course.'

'Murder? What murder?'

'The one you're charged with.'

Brown tried sarcasm. 'And just who am I supposed to have murdered?'

'The victim.'

'And his name?'

'You know it's a man then?'

'It's a fifty-fifty shot. I guessed.'

'Good. Then you can guess the name of the victim.'

Brown slapped the table in frustration. 'It's late. I want some sleep. If I have to sleep here that's fine, but just leave me in peace.'

'I can't do that. You said yourself I've only got a limited period of time before I have to charge you, besides which if I leave you by yourself you might think up all sorts of lies to cover your tracks.'

'Then get on with this charade. But be warned, my lawyer will be very active when he gets here.'

Slonský produced two of the pieces of paper that Mucha had found from his inside pocket. 'Recognise this? What about the other one?'

Brown read each in turn. 'So?'

'So you see that I know your motive. Herfort, it all begins for me with a little chat with Jan and Jakub.'

'The old pair? The ones who sit on the bench all day?'

'That's them. They said they used to work on the old baronial estate here when they were boys. That was when the manor house was occupied by Baron Gerhard von Troppau-Freudenthal. Gerhard had a wife and a daughter, and the old boys remembered getting a fistful of silver after they helped some city gentleman shoot a boar on the estate. That was presumably the rich man that Gerhard had earmarked for his daughter's future husband. Anyway, when the war came along Gerhard went off to do his bit for the Führer on the Eastern Front, and didn't come back. I imagine a similar fate befell his intended son-in-law, which is not surprising if he needed a boar's legs tied together with wire before he could shoot it.'

'I don't see the relevance of this…' began Brown.

'I'm coming to that. Fast forward to 1945, and the First and Fourth Ukrainian Divisions are sitting on Moravia's borders, all set to pour in and liberate us, not to mention almost everything that moved. It soon became clear that this was no place for a woman, because women of all ages were being raped and some were being killed. No doubt the Freifrau and her daughter the Freiin had the wit to try to get to the west, where the Americans were advancing. If you're going to get captured by either, the Americans are much the better choice. And eventually they made it, because there is paperwork showing that the Freifrau and Freiin were in a camp near Strakonice. But as Germans and the widow and daughter of a German army officer, I expect they didn't have too comfortable a time there. Most of the ethnic Germans were shipped to Germany and dumped in camps there. What saved the Freiin was that an American soldier fell for her. I don't have a photo, but I guess a twenty-year-old Aryan girl would have interested any bachelor who had been away from home for a couple of years. What made her doubly interesting was that the American soldier was ethnic German himself. So much so that in 1941 he changed his name. He used to be Braun and he became Brown, didn't he, Mr Brown? He was your father, and the Freiin was your mother.'

Brown nodded, but said no more.

'I assume that the title passed to your uncle in Austria, but that didn't really matter. It was the old family estate in Opava that interested you. Your mother never wanted to return, but you grew up obsessed with recovering it. Of course, you're a patriotic American — your mother was always grateful that the United States took her in and gave her a good life, so she must have been so proud when you joined the army and joined a Special Forces unit. Your service record is a good one, I'm told. The FBI understand these things better than I do, but I'm happy to take their word for it.'

'My service record will stand up against anyone's, but what does that have to do with anything?'

'We'll come to that. For the moment I just want to stress the Special Forces connection. Anyway, as we all know the Beneš decrees confiscated a lot of German property, but when the Wall fell there was a good deal of speculation that property would be returned or compensation paid. You even learned Czech so you could argue your case. Sergeant Mucha found a copy of your parents' wedding certificate showing they married near Strakonice in 1946, but he also found your affidavit relating to the old baronial lands that you lodged in 1992. The problem was that the new law only gives restitution if the lands were seized by the Communists, whereas yours had been seized before the Communists came to power, so the courts turned your application down. It's a common problem in Moravia, where the seizures were made by the provisional government. So, if you were going to get the land back, you had to buy it, which meant persuading the present owners to sell it. And that's where Captain Herfort comes in, because earlier this year you paid some Bosnians to frighten the existing owners into selling by burning down the lodge and flooding the parkland. Fortunately they were inept at both.'

'You have proof for this absurd assertion?'

'I have the man who says he put you in touch with the Bosnians. I also have a faxed sketch map you drew for them and sent from the hotel you were in today to the office of a notorious gangster in Sarajevo.'

'And did I sign that map? And was I staying in the hotel on that date? I don't think so.'

'Not under the name Brown, no; but there's an entry in the register under your mother's maiden name, which is the name you use whenever you're in Opava. You registered this time under the name von Troppau-Freudenthal. You even have a credit card in that name.'

'And is that some kind of legal offence over here?'

'Not at all. You're free to call yourself Mickey Mouse if you want, so long as it isn't done with intent to deceive others. But let's keep to the point, if we can. You hired some Bosnians to come to Opava and frighten the old folks out of their home. Your hope was that with a bit of damage, the owners would drop the price until you could afford it. This is where things get a bit murky but I'm sure you'll be able to clarify them for us.'

Slonský took a long draught from his coffee cup and continued. 'The incidents here in Opava were reported to Prague, where the Organised Crime Unit took an interest because they were already investigating the same Bosnians in connection with trafficking girls to the Czech Republic. One officer, a young man named Hrdlička, noticed that the reports weren't being acted upon. Somebody in the Organised Crime Unit wasn't fighting organised crime; he was working for them. And, Hrdlička being a bright lad, it occurred to him that if that was happening to these lesser incidents it was very likely that reports on his enquiries were being shared with the very people he was trying to investigate, so he stopped sending reports in. He adopted an undercover role known to comparatively few people so he could keep up the surveillance, and he worked outside the police structure to maintain as much secrecy as he could about his work. For example, he obtained a radio microphone from another source. Sadly, it was cheap rubbish, but he wasn't to know that.'

'Interesting as this is, it has no bearing on my…'

'I'm coming to that. Hrdlička was watching your building. He was actually watching the Bosnians on the floor below, but you weren't to know that. In fact, he was only interested in you as a means of keeping track of the Bosnians, if at all. You had been tipped off that he knew about the incidents in Opava and concluded that he was on your trail, and when he showed no signs of giving up, you decided he had to be removed. The sad thing is that he had no idea you were involved. I got off on the wrong track here. I thought Hrdlička's microphone must be in your office, but actually it was in Savović's. You just arranged with Savović to make a loud noise while you cruised the river bank looking for someone who reacted to the squeal in their ear. When Hrdlička did, you stepped behind him and used a spring-loaded knife to stab him in the neck. A knife very like the one we found in your jacket earlier.'

'"Very like" isn't "the same as".'

'I'll leave Dr Novák to tell me how alike it is. The point is that we have a lethal weapon in the hands of someone we know has been trained to use it, and who has a motive to kill the person who ended up dead. Your lawyer is going to have a wasted journey, because we're going to take you back to Prague as soon as a suitable transport arrives. I hope he doesn't bill you for the two-way trip, because ten hours of a lawyer's time can be very expensive.'

A nap in the police station staff room was not particularly comfortable, but Slonský saw no point in paying for a hotel given that it was 4 a.m. before they gave up questioning Brown. After a few hours' sleep and a healthy breakfast the detectives

528

returned to Prague. Slonský was much more inclined to talk on the way back than he had been on the outward journey, but he still refused to discuss Captain Grigar's role, arguing that he should put everything to Grigar in person.

'Sir, wasn't there a lot of guesswork in the story you put to Brown? What hard evidence have we got?' Navrátil enquired.

'We've got the wedding certificate and we've got Brown's service record, which gives the details of his parents, by the way. The coincidence of his mother's maiden name being von Troppau-Freudenthal was interesting enough, but the Americans helpfully noted that his father was himself an army veteran, so I asked for his record too, from which I pieced together their movements in 1945-6.'

'So how long have you known this, sir?'

'Not that long. Don't worry, I wasn't keeping it all from you. Mucha only retrieved the marriage certificate in the last couple of days. It was you who put me onto it all.'

'Me, sir?'

'You plural, not you singular. It was that kind and thoughtful gift of yours.'

'The sausage championship?'

'Yes. Remember that the criminals distracted our attention from one crime by staging a second one. I didn't think that was the motive in Brown's case, but I got to thinking that maybe we were seeing a connection that wasn't quite as we imagined it. And since the only reason I could think of for Hrdlička to do what he did was that he'd jumped to the conclusion that the Opava incidents and the trafficking of girls were connected. So they were, but only in the sense that the same people were hired. Nejedlý had met up with Savović and Brukić on one of his plum-buying missions and was working with them. When Brown needed some heavies Nejedlý told him where he could find them. And when Savović and Brukić needed a bolthole when they were kicked out of Bosnia, Nejedlý found them a place in the same office building. Nejedlý sat in the middle. It's hard to imagine a less competent criminal than Nejedlý, but he made it all possible.'

'What about Milena and Daniela, sir?' asked Peiperová.

'I think Milena really did kill herself. We might have a try at getting a murder conviction, but it won't be easy. There's no real evidence that the Bosnians were involved in anything more than disposing of her body. The wounding of Daniela is a different thing. Once she has recovered I expect she'll be able to give us a good identification of the people involved. She has already fingered Brukić as one of those who took part in it. The only concern is that she wants to go back to Bosnia and we need to be sure she'll return to Prague to give evidence. She'll get protection in Sarajevo but it's not impossible that Savović's friends will threaten her.'

'Sir, it's a bit underhand, but if we were to guarantee the cost of her operations she'd have a reason for coming back here,' Peiperová remarked.

'It's a good thought. And having been wounded on Czech soil she's entitled to compensation here. We'll pick up a tidy sum when we get Savović's business assets seized, which would more than cover the healthcare. Make her the offer, lass, and I'll get it organised with the Director. In any event, I want you to keep in touch with her.'

'She has nothing to keep her here,' Navrátil chipped in. 'She certainly wouldn't want to go back to dancing in clubs.'

'Ah, I'm glad you mentioned that,' Slonský beamed. 'Our respected leader had an answer to that.'

'The Director, sir?'

'No, Navrátil; Captain Lukas. Remember that Daniela plays the flute and piccolo. One of Lukas' daughters is studying music at the Conservatoire. I can never remember which one.'

'Eliška, sir,' Peiperová inserted, causing Slonský to marvel once more at how people can ever remember all these trivia like names and places.

'Yes, that one. She's managed to get the loan of some instruments and Daniela can practise there for a while. Eliška reckons there's probably some work going for a good flute player.'

'Ah, the wanderer returns,' said Mucha. He picked up a small folded note and held it out on his open hands like an altar boy holding a copy of the Gospels.

'For me? How kind,' said Slonský. 'What does it say?'

'It says that the Director of Criminal Police presents his compliments and wishes you to get your backside over to see him immediately. He wants to see you.'

'That's good, because I want to see him.' He pointed his thumb over his shoulder. 'Can you babysit this pair? It's a shame we don't have a crèche.'

'A small ball pool in the foyer would be an option. But I'll see they get a hot drink and a biscuit.'

'Very good. Don't let Navrátil have anything with bright food colouring in it or he won't sleep after lunch.'

Slonský ascended the stairs and straightened the nondescript piece of maroon cloth that passed for his tie before pushing the swing doors open and approaching the Director's office. Kuchař was sitting outside and jumped to his feet when Slonský approached.

'Good morning, Acting Captain Slonský.'

'Good morning, Kuchař. I have been summoned.'

'Yes, sir. I'll just let the Director know you're here.'

'If I just walk in, he'll know that for himself.'

Kuchař considered this briefly, but the confusion on his face demonstrated that he thought it inadvisable.

'He may be with someone, sir.'

'If he were, you would know about it, wouldn't you? Or do people drop down from the roof in the window-cleaners' cradle and enter via the window?'

'I've never heard of it, sir.'

'Never mind, Kuchař. Just poke your head in and let the Director know I have obeyed his command.'

The Director offered his hand, invited Slonský to sit, and listened to a summary of the cases.

'The confiscated money doesn't come to us, but I'll make some calls. I don't doubt that we'll find a way of doing it for the young woman. Now, Slonský, the reason I wanted to speak to you has nothing to do with this case, welcome though your report is.'

'I feared as much, sir.'

'Captain Lukas is returning part-time next week, and will — if all goes well — return to us full-time in the New Year. However, it is still his intention to retire next year. That may change, because he need not make a final decision until three months before he leaves. Either way, it's time you put in for your permanent captaincy.'

'Yes, sir.'

'Yes? You mean yes without an argument?'

'Yes, sir. If I've learned anything in the last few weeks it's that I don't want to have to answer to Dvorník or Doležal.'

'Who would? Doležal is an excellent officer but it's probably time that he went off and excelled somewhere else.'

'My sentiments exactly, sir.'

'Good. So all I need from you is the completed form, which by a happy coincidence I happen to have here.'

He passed it to Slonský, who was struck by an unusual feature of the form.

'This form I have to complete is completed, sir.'

'Yes. I thought it would save you time. More importantly, if it never leaves this office it won't get mislaid, will it? Just be a good chap and sign your name at the bottom.'

Grigar was tense. Even a poor student of body language could see that he was deeply uneasy, but Slonský had asked for the meeting and Grigar could hardly refuse given that he had asked to be kept informed of progress.

'You know Officers Navrátil and Peiperová, I think?' said Slonský.

Grigar nodded a curt greeting to each.

'Do you think we could ask Lieutenant Erben to take some notes for us?' Slonský asked.

'Is that necessary? If notes are needed, let your people take them.'

'If that's how you want it, all well and good. The first thing to tell you is that we have Mr Brown in custody for the murder of Officer Hrdlička.'

'That's good. Has he confessed?'

'No, but I'm working on it. He's been trained to withstand interrogation but I enjoy a challenge. In any event, we've got his boots.'

'His boots?'

'Novák identified some features of his boots that left distinctive footmarks in the snow. Something to do with American toes being bigger than ours, and a split in the sole tread that he can match, I think. Anyway, he was fairly convinced that it was an American make of boot, size 43, which didn't necessarily mean an American suspect, of course, but now that we have retrieved the boots, we can probably get a conviction based on the forensic evidence. We've got a knife that matches the murder weapon too.'

'You're the murder expert. If you think it would stick, I'm happy with that.'

'Whereas you're the expert on organised crime. When you get my report, you'll see there's a couple of interesting points on the running of this department. Hrdlička plainly didn't trust someone here.'

'That's obvious. He stopped sending in full reports and wouldn't tell me why.'

'No, because he didn't know who was leaking information to the very people you were trying to catch. And, so far as we know, he died without ever finding out. I, on the other hand, know who the naughty policeman is.'

Grigar's uneasiness level rose to critical. He leaned forward and looked Slonský directly in the eye. 'Tell me.'

'All in good time. Somebody intercepted the messages from Opava and saw that no action was taken, while also ensuring that Opava didn't take any because it was all in hand here. There are a limited number of people who could achieve that. And then there's the intercepted radio message telling one of your men to follow Navrátil.'

'When was that?' stammered Grigar.

'On the day that the holdall was lobbed on an unmarked police car and Navrátil was unjustly arrested as a peeping tom; which we don't talk about, by the way, because it was a completely unfounded but highly convenient allegation.'

'Why would anyone follow Navrátil?'

'To find out what he knows, I suppose, although he's such a helpful and transparent soul that he'd probably tell you if you just asked. But the other reason is that the officer was told you wanted him to do it.'

'Me?'

'Yes, and I know you didn't. But only one person could give the impression that you did.'

'Lieutenant Erben.'

'Got it in one. He panicked that Navrátil would discover his involvement somehow, so he had him followed and told the officer in question that you had ordered it. And Erben intercepted the faxes about the vandalism at Opava. Shall we invite him to come in?'

Grigar strode to the door and flung it open, but Erben was not to be found.

'He's gone.'

'I thought he might. After all, he has ears, and we didn't keep our voices down. But then you don't need to speak very loud when someone has their ear pressed against the door. I could see his feet blocking the light from the corridor under your door.'

Grigar grabbed his coat. 'He can't have got far. Come on!'

They all followed him down the stairs and towards the front door.

'If you're looking for Lieutenant Erben,' said Mucha, 'he's sitting in cell six. He unaccountably fell as he crossed the foyer. About five times, I think. Sergeant Salzer attempted to pick him up but he fell out of Salzer's hands a couple of times. That accounts for the shiner and the bruise on his cheek.'

'You knew?' said Grigar.

'I didn't have perfect proof,' said Slonský, 'but giving him a chance to run seemed to me to be one way of sealing the deal. I couldn't immediately see why they'd decided to bribe Erben, so I sent for his service record. His mother's maiden name was Nejedlá. Nejedlý is his uncle. That's why the Bosnians kept on an incompetent like Nejedlý as the middle man. He had the link to the police, and if they had upset him, he could have shopped them all. He'd have ended up nailed to a wall, of course, but he could have done it. And the prospect of retribution means that if he had any sense he'd shop them without giving them any warning that he was going to do it. It was interesting that when he was arrested Nejedlý said nothing about any family connection with the police, but Erben turned up at the desk wanting to see him. Fortunately the duty officers refused, because Sergeant Mucha had made it very clear that Nejedlý was not at home to visitors.'

Grigar removed his hat and rapped his knuckles on the counter top as he collected himself.

'I think we'd better go and speak to soon-to-be ex-lieutenant Erben. You might want to come too, Slonský, in case he slips out of my grasp and repeatedly bangs his face on the floor.'

'You think that's likely?'

'I think it's a racing certainty.'

Erben did not enjoy the next half-hour. If there is one thing an honest policeman truly detests it is a dishonest one, especially one who provides information that gets a colleague killed. Slonský formally charged him with being an accessory to murder and he did indeed fall over several times while being questioned by Grigar. Anyone wishing to increase their vocabulary of colloquial Czech could have learned quite a bit by listening to the interview.

Peiperová buttoned her coat and sat on the corner of Slonský's desk. 'Ready to go home?'

'Should we wait for Lieutenant Slonský to tell us to go, do you think?'

'He may be a while. I was going to suggest a hot wine somewhere but this office is more private.'

'Not here, Kristýna. He may walk in at any moment.'

'I meant for a chat. We need to talk.'

Navrátil hated that expression. It usually meant that trouble was on its way, especially when women used it. Was she about to break off their relationship?

'The thing is, I've been offered a job.'

'A job? Don't you like the police?'

'It's with the police, Jan. The Director of Criminal Police wants a personal assistant and he's asked for me. We need to talk about whether I take it. I like working here, but it would look really good on my CV and it's only for a year.'

'I see,' murmured Navrátil. 'Have you made your mind up?'

'Of course I haven't, otherwise I wouldn't be asking you what you think.'

'I don't know what I think. At least it's still in the same building.'

'And it's regular hours. Mum and Dad would be pleased to know I'm not going to get killed or kidnapped again.'

'So would I,' Navrátil agreed, 'but on the other hand we're a good team. And if Lukas doesn't come back Slonský might get promoted and then we'll get assigned to someone else, which probably means we'd be separated anyway.'

'Is that an argument for or against?'

'It's not one or the other, just a statement of fact. I don't know what I think, but based on Lieutenant Slonský's theory that beer helps the brain, let's go to the bar down the road and talk about it there.'

Slonský sat at his desk with the lights off and watched the snow gently falling. It had been an eventful year, with a new assistant, a second new assistant and an acting captaincy. And if Lukas was retiring then 2007 was set fair to be eventful too. It crossed Slonský's mind that he had not dealt terribly well with the Věra issue, because she was still coming round to feed him, do some sewing for him and generally ignoring the fact that they had been separated for nearly forty years. He was determined to avoid complications, but somehow his resolution was lacking when it came to ending the whole sorry mess. Besides which, she still had some of his curtains.

He collected his hat and scarf and wearily trudged downstairs. Discovering a corrupt policeman always depressed him like this, but never to the point of considering retirement. It was hard to think of any circumstances that would promote so drastic a move.

He nudged the door open and found himself in the foyer. Sergeant Mucha glanced up and nodded cheerily. Good old Mucha! Slonský had an unaccountable feeling that all was well with the world so long as Mucha was at the front desk.

'You're not thinking of retiring, are you?' he asked.

'All the time,' said Mucha. 'Then I remember that my wife's sister is staying with us and somehow the feeling wears off.'

'The world is changing, old friend. It's the end of an era.'

'What is?'

'Lukas is retiring in the summer, but it's highly confidential so keep it to yourself.'

'Confidential like don't tell me about it, or just ordinary confidential?'

'Confidential like you didn't hear it from me.'

'Are you going for his job?'

Slonský looked miserable.

'It's me, Dvorník or Doležal.'

'The answer is yes, then. You'd be a fool not to. We don't want a department run by a homicidal gun fiend or a teetotal stamp collector.'

'You've heard that rumour too?'

'Heard it? I started it.'

Slonský managed a smile. 'Beer when you finish?'

'Why not? Just the one though, because I'll get into trouble if I'm late home to eat.'

'I'm not really hungry,' said Slonský. 'I may just be able to force down a sausage.'

'It's what you live for,' said Mucha. 'Solving crime and the odd sausage.'

'Is there anything else in life?' asked Slonský, and walked out into the snow.

A NOTE TO THE READER

Dear Reader,

Thank you! You have generously given your time to read about Josef Slonský and his colleagues. How much time depends, of course, upon your reading speed, but whatever it was I hope you feel it was time well spent.

The first story is set in 2006 because it was then that my wife and I first went to Prague. I had an idea in my head, but it was only when we went to an ice-hockey game that we walked the route that Bear walks on the first page, and the action became set in Prague. I sat down to write one Saturday morning, and on the cinema screen in my brain where I see the scenes a battered old car pulled up and Slonský climbed out. All I had to do was describe him.

Slonský lived the first half of his life under Communism and he recalls what he was told to do then. He knows his hands are dirty, and he assumes that is true for all people of his age. That explains the difficulty he has in showing respect. He is coming towards the end of his career and dreads retirement, so his boss has a small hold over him. If he wants to stay on – and he does – he has to accept a trainee. Navrátil, young, intelligent, moral, earnest and devout, equally sprang fully-formed onto the page.

Other characters then began showing up and doing whatever they thought fit, and I had to try to keep up with them. They have their quirks, whether it's Klinger's obsession with order or Mucha's avoidance of his sister-in-law's visits by judicious arrangement of the duty roster that he has never admitted to his wife he prepares. Plainly these are fictional people and they do not represent or reflect on the police in Prague. Maybe that's a shame, because if I were murdered in Prague I'd be comforted to know Slonský was on the case.

He is slovenly, cynical, humorous and cunning. He likes beer, sausages and pastries. He is good company. He can tell a story. Above all, he is Czech, and proud of it, and I hope my portraits of him demonstrate my affection for Slonský and his people.

The second story came about when I read an account of a trial of a man who was alleged to have been a concentration camp guard. The witnesses were, perforce, very elderly, and it seemed to me that there was a dilemma here; they were entitled to justice for their suffering, but increasing age and the passage of time meant that the chances of a successful conviction were declining. It seemed to me that, to a greater or lesser extent, this must be true of all cold cases. There will come a point at which a conviction just is not possible.

This led to the idea of a crime committed under the old regime being investigated many years later. The previous book was set in 2006, so that established a time for this one; going back thirty years would make all the witnesses sufficiently elderly.

As for Edvard Holoubek, he came into my mind when I was watching a documentary about Erich Honecker, the former leader of East Germany. Their shared initials are either coincidental or some deep subconscious thing I cannot explain. In my mind's eye, Holoubek had the look of a Honecker in his old age.

In reality, the dividing line between the police and the army in Communist Czechoslovakia was not as clear as I describe here. They formed a state internal security service and people could move between them. However, many of the staff saw themselves as either police or army and spoke about them in that way. I will also admit to having simplified the system of ranks of police officers.

The final story in this collection was fuelled by a juxtaposition of two news items. One concerned the Bosnian police and their difficulties in dealing with organised crime given that the gangs had some very serious weaponry, and the other was a report of an elderly couple who had failed to recover their former home because the law on this did not cover cases where they had been displaced before the Communists came to power. However, it was Poland that supplied one of the key elements because it was in Kraków that we saw some wonderful living statues, including one dressed as a knight. You don't need to be Slonský to detect how I melded those together in this story.

If you have enjoyed this novel I'd be really grateful if you would leave a review on **Amazon** and **Goodreads**. I love to hear from readers, so please keep in touch through **Facebook** or **Twitter**, or leave a message on my **website**.

Všechno nejlepší!

Graham Brack

Sapere Books is an exciting new publisher of brilliant fiction and popular history.

To find out more about our latest releases and our monthly bargain books visit our website:
saperebooks.com

Printed in Great Britain
by Amazon

42434147R00319